THE FAMILY IDIOT

Volume One

Translated by Carol Cosman

Jean-Paul Sartre

THE FAMILY IDIOT

Gustave Flaubert

1821–1857

The University of Chicago Press • Chicago and London

Originally published in Paris as part one of
L'Idiot de la famille: Gustave Flaubert de 1821 à 1857,
© Editions Gallimard, 1971

The University of Chicago Press, Chicago 60637
The University of Chicago Press, Ltd., London

© 1981 by The University of Chicago
All rights reserved. Published 1981
Printed in the United States of America

85 84 83 82 81   5 4 3 2 1

Library of Congress Cataloging in Publication Data

Sartre, Jean Paul, 1905–80
   The family idiot.

   Translation of: L'Idiot de la famille.
   1. Flaubert, Gustave, 1821–1880. 2. Novelists,
French—19th century—Biography. I. Title.
PQ2247.S313   843'.8 [B]   81–1694
ISBN 0–226–73509–5   AACR2

CONTENTS

2/82

L'Idiot de la famille, or *The Family Idiot* as I have called it, is Sartre's last major work and a kind of summa of everything in the way of his philosophic, social, and literary thought that had gone before. It is, as Sartre says, an exercise in methodology—a case in point illustrating the procedure formulated in *Search for a Method.* But of course Sartre uses this "exercise" to lead us on an exhaustive search for Flaubert, whose person and persona provide opportunity for the empathetic, imaginative reconstruction of a psyche, for social analysis, for investigations of epistemological and ontological issues, for literary and linguistic speculation.

And the sweep of Sartre's varied approach to his subject includes as well the entire spectrum of language used in his previous work, from the colloquial verve of *The Words,* his delightful autobiography, to the highly abstract, even Germanic weight of *Being and Nothingness.* Such diversity determines the constant shift from short, punchy sentences and phrases that invite a kind of direct intimacy to the rather lengthy, sometimes convoluted attempts to negotiate the nuances of a particularly difficult idea; and the fact is that the work was written in a race against time—and encroaching blindness—and barely edited at all. These features have constituted its primary challenge to me as a translator.

Rather than find a uniform style in which to render the diverse styles Sartre employs, rather than smooth out the abrupt shifts and startling interjections of everyday language in the midst of philosophic discourse, I have chosen to try to approximate in English the texture of Sartre's original with all its idiosyncrasies; this because I feel that part of the interest and excitement of his work is conveyed by this journey over a rough but also remarkably engaging road through uncharted territory. That, at least, is what I have hoped to achieve while presenting a text that is at the same time readable and as clear as possible.

There are a number of people whose help in this project has been extremely valuable to me. I would like, first of all, to thank Christian Phillipon, whose interest in language and keen intelligence have been an invaluable resource; I would also like to thank Françoise Meltzer for her encouragement; and finally my husband Robert Alter, whose patience and occasional participation have been greatly sustaining.

CAROL COSMAN

Berkeley
October 1980

viii

The Family Idiot is the sequel to *Search for a Method*. Its subject: what, at this point in time, can we know about a man? It seemed to me that this question could only be answered by studying a specific case. What do we know, for example, about Gustave Flaubert? Such knowledge would amount to *summing up* all the data on him at our disposal. We have no assurance at the outset that such a summation is possible and that the truth of a person is not multiple. The fragments of information we have are very different *in kind*: Flaubert was born in December 1821, in Rouen—that is one kind of information; he writes, much later, to his mistress: "Art terrifies me"—that is another. The first is an objective, social fact, confirmed by official documents; the second, objective too, when one sets some store by what is said, refers in its meaning to a feeling that issues from experience, and we can draw no conclusions about the sense and import of this feeling until we have first established whether Gustave is sincere in general, and in this instance in particular. Do we not then risk ending up with layers of heterogeneous and irreducible meanings? This book attempts to prove that irreducibility is only apparent, and that each piece of data set in its place becomes a portion of the whole, which is constantly being created, and by the same token reveals its profound homogeneity with all the other parts that make up the whole.

For a man is never an individual; it would be more fitting to call him a *universal singular*. Summed up and for this reason universalized by his epoch, he in turn resumes it by reproducing himself in it as singularity. Universal by the singular universality of human history, singular by the universalizing singularity of his projects, he requires simultaneous examination from both ends. We must find an appropriate method. I set out the principles of this method in 1958 and will not repeat what I said; I prefer to demonstrate whenever necessary how this method *is created* through the very work itself in obedience to the requirements of its object.

A last word. Why Flaubert? For three reasons. The first, very personal, long ago ceased to be as salient as it once was in the origin of this choice. In 1943, rereading his correspondence in the bad edition by Charpentier, I felt I had a score to settle with Flaubert and ought therefore to get to know him better. Since then, my initial antipathy has changed to *empathy*, the one attitude necessary for understanding. Next, he is objectified in his books. Anyone will tell you, "Gustave Flaubert—he's the author of *Madame Bovary*." What then is the relationship of the man to the work? I have never discussed this until now, nor, to my knowledge, has anyone else. We shall see that this is a double relationship: *Madame Bovary* is defeat and triumph; the man depicted in the defeat is not the same man summoned in its triumph. We must try to understand what this means. Finally, Flaubert's early works and his correspondence (thirteen published volumes) appear, as we shall see, to consist of the strangest, the most easily deciphered revelations. We might imagine we were hearing a neurotic "free associating" on the psychoanalyst's couch. I thought it permissible, for this difficult test case, to choose a compliant subject who yields himself easily and unconsciously. I would add that Flaubert, creator of the "modern" novel, stands at the crossroads of all our literary problems today.

Now we must begin. How, and by what means? It doesn't much matter: a corpse is open to all comers. The essential thing is to set out with a problem. The one I have chosen is hardly ever discussed. Let us read this passage from a letter to Mlle Leroyer de Chantepie: "It is by the sheer force of work that I am able to silence my innate melancholy. But the old nature often reappears, the old nature that no one knows, the deep, always hidden wound."[1] What is the meaning of this? Can a wound be innate? In any event, Flaubert refers us to his prehistory. What we must try to understand is the origin of the wound that is "always hidden" and dates back to his earliest childhood. That will not, I think, be a bad start.

1. Croisset, 6 October 1864.

PART ONE

Constitution

ONE

A Problem

READING

When, bewildered and still "brutish," little Gustave Flaubert emerges
from infancy, skills await him. And roles. Training begins, and apparently not without success—no one tells us, for example, that he
had trouble walking. On the other hand, we know that this future
writer stumbled when it came to the prime test, his apprenticeship
in words. Later we shall try to discover whether, from the very beginning, he had difficulty speaking. What is certain is that he made
a poor showing in the other linguistic test—that chief initiation and
rite of passage—learning the alphabet. A witness reports that the little
boy learned his letters very late and that his family took him for a
backward child. Caroline Commanville gives the following account:

> My grandmother had taught her elder son to read. She wanted
> to do as much for the second and set to work. Little Caroline at
> Gustave's side learned rapidly; he could not keep up, and after
> straining to understand these signs that meant nothing to him,
> he would begin to sob. He was, however, avid for knowledge
> and his brain was always working. . . . [Since later Papa Mignot
> read to him,] whenever there were scenes over his difficulty with
> reading, Gustave's final argument—to his mind irrefutable—was:
> "What's the use of learning when Papa Mignot reads to me?"
> But school age was upon him, he had to know at any cost . . .
> Gustave applied himself resolutely and in a few months caught
> up with the children his own age.

We shall see that this poor relationship with words was decisive
for his career. Why, it will be asked, should we question the testimony

of Flaubert's niece? After all, she lived intimately with her uncle and her grandmother, from whom she received her information. We are prevented, however, from trusting her completely because of the false playfulness of the narrative. Caroline prunes, expurgates, softens; on the other hand, if the incident related does not seem compromising, she polishes it, violating rigor at the expense of truth. One reading is enough to discover the key to these double and contradictory distortions: she aims to please without abandoning the tone of good breeding.

Let us return to the passage just cited. We shall have no trouble glimpsing the truth of Gustave's unhappy childhood. We are told that the child cried bitterly, that he was avid for knowledge, and that his impotence made him miserable. Then, a little further on, we are shown a blustering dunce, stubborn in his refusal to learn—why should I? Papa Mignot reads to me. Is this the same Gustave? Yes, but the first attitude is provoked by an observation he makes himself: the contrariness of things, his own incapacity. The *Other* is there of course: the witness, the harsh surroundings, necessity. But this is not the source of the child's sorrow, the relation spontaneously established between the lifeless imperatives of the alphabet and his own potential: "I must but I can't." The second attitude implies a *combative relationship* between the child and his parents. Caroline Commanville tells us, in passing, that there were scenes—this is enough. These scenes did not occur immediately. There was time for patience, then for distress, finally for reproach. At first the family blamed nature, later they accused the child of ill will. He answered belligerently that he didn't need to learn how to read. But he was already defeated, already falsified: by pretending to explain his refusal, he confessed to it. The parents asked no more, and all their impatience was justified.

The defenseless humility, the proud resentment that makes the victim claim as his own the ill will of which he is falsely accused—these two reactions are separated by many years. There was a certain uneasiness in the Flaubert family when Gustave, confronted with his first human tasks, distinguished himself by his failure to perform them. This uneasiness grew from day to day, persisted, rankled. Violence was done to the child. This violence, scarcely evoked but legible, suffices to flaw the benign narrative. An odd confusion of Mme Commanville's increases our discomfort: she informs us that Gustave and Caroline Flaubert learned to read together. But Gustave was four years older than his younger sister. Supposing that Mme Flaubert had begun to teach him at around five years old, the youngest, age twelve or thirteen months, was attending the lessons from her cradle. Of course Achille-Cléophas's three children each in turn received private lessons from Mme Flaubert, the second nine years after the eldest had learned to read, the third four years after the second child had made his first attempt. Nevertheless, here is Mme Commanville, undaunted by these wide intervals, summoning in the same paragraph her two uncles and her mother. Why, when they did not study together? Observe: Mme Flaubert became the teacher of the brilliant Achille; her first success convinced her of her pedagogic gifts—Achille must have been a child prodigy—so she renewed the experiment with Gustave. And Caroline, the last born, mother of the narrator, learned at play. Gustave is squeezed between these two marvels—inferior to both, he doesn't look good.

It is as if Mme Commanville had launched into this comparison—which could have been omitted—in order to remind the public that the inadequacies of the future writer were largely compensated for by the excellence of the two other children. The uncle was already of age when the niece was born; when *Madame Bovary* appeared, she was eleven years old. Never mind; even to Caroline, who saw only what followed, Gustave's first years seem disturbing. There was the slowness, and then the "nervous attack," which she surely must have heard about early on. Nothing further was needed—she would take advantage of his fame but would never be dazzled by it. Mme Commanville, née Hamard, was a Flaubert on her mother's side; even in the funeral oration for her uncle she made a point of recalling her membership in the most illustrious scientific family of Normandy. To save the Flaubert family honor she flanked a genius bordering on idiocy with two good sorts, two brains, true progeny of the man of science. If this lady herself, half a century after the events, could not resist comparing the three children, it is not difficult to divine what Gustave must have heard between 1827 and 1830. But we shall have occasion to return at length to these comparisons. Our present task is to show that Gustave, by his deficiency, finds himself at the center of a domestic tension that will only increase until he has caught up with "children his own age."

Yet can we be sure that the child did not know his letters before the age of nine? Inclined to believe this, how can we allow that Gustave had learned to write only very recently when he addressed to Ernest Chevalier, on 31 December 1830—at the age of nine years—the astonishing letter to which we shall return many times in the following pages? On rereading, its solidity is impressive: concise, sturdy, and accurate sentences; the spelling is somewhat fanciful, but still within the realm of acceptability. No doubt about it, the author has a mastery of his graphic movements. He proposes, moreover, to his friend Ernest that he will "send him his dramas." The passage is not very clear: are these plays that he has already written or plays that he intends to write when Ernest "writes his dreams"? In any case the word *writing* already has for him that double meaning which makes it altogether ambiguous. It designates both the common act of tracing words on a sheet of paper and the singular enterprise of composing "writings." We thought to find a former idiot scarcely come out of the fog—and we discover a man of letters. Impossible. True, a change of surroundings, the intelligence of an educator, the advice of a doctor can all help backward children; it is enough to give them a chance. And for many stragglers, entrance into the world of reading comes as a true religious conversion, long and unconsciously cultivated, suddenly achieved. But these abrupt leaps forward compensate the backward child for perhaps one year, or two, to stretch things, but not more. Gustave, if his niece is to be believed, had four or five years to make up.

No, illiterate at nine years old, the child would be too seriously afflicted for his final sprint even to be conceivable. Gustave knew how to read in 1828 or '29, that is, between seven and eight. Earlier, his slowness would not have been so disturbing; later, he would never have caught up.

What remains true is that the Flauberts were concerned. For a long while Gustave could not grasp the elementary connections that make letters into a syllable, syllables into a word. These difficulties led to others—how can one count without knowing how to read? How can one retain the most basic elements of history and geography if the instruction remains oral? We don't worry about this today; methods are more solid, predictable; and, above all, we take the student *as he is*. At that period there was an order to follow and the child had to bend to it. So Gustave was behind, every step of the way.

NAÏVETÉ

Not completely, however. Papa Mignot read to him, the little boy was already broadly cultured, already literary. Novels exercised his imagination, provided new schemata; and he learned the use of the symbol. If a child transforms himself early enough into Don Quixote, he unwittingly incorporates the general principle of all transformations: he knows how to see himself, to find himself, in the life of another, to live his own life as another. Nothing of all this, unfortunately, was visible. The real achievements—new transparencies, the soul's clearings, reflections—were of a kind that only increased the number of his stupors, or at least did not reduce them. Mme Flaubert knew nothing about these exercises. And doubt was born: is Gustave an idiot? We find this alarm again in Mme Commanville's sprightly narrative:

> The child had a calm, meditative nature and a naïveté, traces of which he preserved all his life. My grandmother told me that he would sit for hours, one finger in his mouth, absorbed, looking almost stupid. When he was six, a servant called Pierre, amusing himself with Gustave's innocence, told the boy when he pestered him: "Run to the kitchen . . . and see if I'm there." And the child went off to question the cook, "Pierre told me to come see if he's here." He didn't understand that they wanted to fool him, and in the face of their laughter he remained a dreamer, glimpsing a mystery.

A curious and deceitful text. Beneath the surface of Caroline's good humor the truth breaks through: Gustave was a simple soul, improbably, pathologically credulous; he frequently fell into long stupors—his parents searched his features and feared he was an idiot. It might be thought that these confidences were made lightly, out of a sense of triumphant relief. That would be to misunderstand Gustave's mother; she never believed in her son's genius or even in his talent. In the first place, these words had no meaning for her; as the widow of a brain, brains alone were worthy of her respect. As a practical person, she recognized talent only in *capable* men who were valued as such, since their capability allowed them to sell their services for a higher price. On this account she must have prized the elder of her sons more than the younger. This is probably what she did, without loving him much. Her heart inclined toward the other, younger son, and then she had difficulties with her daughter-in-law. But she imagined that she remained at Croisset out of duty—Gustave was an invalid, he would die or go mad without maternal care. So we find this strange ménage: a pair of wounded recluses, each burying himself far from the world in the house at the water's edge and pretending to stay there only to care for the other. But Mme Flaubert's chilling solicitude demonstrates how little respect she had for her son.

7

First there was his idiocy, the father's alarm, calmed for a time, then all at once revived when Gustave was seventeen; the sterile years in Paris; and, to finish up, the attack at Pont-l'Evêque, serious illness, finally voluntary isolation and indolence: all of these misfortunes seem to be connected by a hidden thread. Something in the child's brain was defective, perhaps from birth: epilepsy—this was the name they gave to Flaubert's "disease," in short, chronic idiocy. He spoke, thank God he reasoned, but he was nonetheless incapable of practicing a profession—exactly what they had foreseen from his sixth year. He wrote, of course, but very little. What was he doing up there in his room? He was dreaming, he would throw himself onto his couch, prostrated by a new attack, or else he would fall into one of his old stupors. He was working, he said, on a new monster he called "la Bovary"; the mother, with a presentiment that he was courting failure, hoped he would never finish his work. Never was there a wiser mother's prayer, as she discovered when she learned that those ob-scene scribblings were going to dishonor the family and bring their author to the dock of infamy. Little Caroline Hamard was going on twelve years old; the details she reports to us were imparted to her by her grandmother in the years following the scandal. It is clear that the widow felt she was confiding a painful secret, apprehensions unhappily confirmed: "Even as a small boy your uncle gave us plenty of worry." Mme Flaubert was an abusive mother because she was an abused widow. She aggravated her younger son's "irritability" by accepting out of piety all the judgments of her adored spouse. Car-oline was her confidante. Gustave was taking a vengeful pleasure in educating his niece: I, the slave of the alphabet, taught by my suf-fering, I am teaching this child all there is to know without costing her one tear. But the grandmother had prejudiced the niece against him, and the girl remained prejudiced whatever he did; incapable of appreciating her uncle, she knew better how to take advantage of him than to love him.

In order to give the passage cited above its whole meaning, we must view it as a transcription, in an edifying style, of the spiteful babbling of two gossips, one an aging and garrulous woman, the other a petty bourgeois and not very nice girl of twelve or fifteen. They tear the old lady's lodger to pieces, the old woman out of distress and easily wounded vulnerability, the girl out of the malicious con-formism of youth. And it must have been the grandmother who said, "a naïveté, traces of which he preserved." Caroline is incapable of making so apt a reflection; besides, she would have had to observe the little boy's innocence for herself in order to recover it from beneath the various masks of the adult Gustave. Coming from Mme Flaubert, supported by the accompanying anecdote, the intention is clear: the novelist who claims to see into the hearts of others is but a fool, a ninny, who has preserved in maturity the exceptional credulity of his childhood. Furthermore, there is something strange about Gustave's encounter with the servant Pierre. At six years old even "normal" children have difficulty orienting themselves in space and time—they are hesitant about questions of being, of the self; their young minds are perplexed. But it is unlikely they would believe that this old fellow whom they see and touch, who talks to them *here* and *now*, is at the same time at the other end of the apartment. Not at six, nor at five, nor even at four. If they should "go look in the kitchen," it is surely because they lack a complete grasp of words and have only half understood or rushed off without listening properly, for the sheer pleasure of running and getting out of breath. The fact is that the oneness of bodies and their spatial perceptions are simple and obvious qualities; it takes mental effort to *recognize* them, but what will the child do if not internalize the passive synthesis of the outside world? Doubling, on the other hand, or the ubiquity of an individual being, is an abstraction contradicted by everyday experience and something that no mental image can support. In fact these ideas are characterized by their very complexity, and they can be drawn only from the disintegration of the identity; in order to conceptualize this twinning of the identical, one must be an adult and a Theosophist. A backward child may long preserve a confused picture of localized individuality, but the confusion will only take him further from these dichotomies; for just to dream that an individual is doubled requires a knowledge of individualization. Could Gustave be an exception? This would be serious, especially since he goes so far as to question the cook and, even after his disappointment, does not perceive that he has been duped. Happily, the rule is strict, as I have just demonstrated, and does not even tolerate the famous exception that proves it. In other words, the story is an invention, pure and simple.

Explanation through Trust

This instance of naïveté is only a symbol. Caroline found it to be reassuring nonsense and gave it the necessary little push. A symbol of what? Of a multitude of little family happenings, too "private," she thought, to be told. The little boy would have believed the servant, we can be sure, without such mental distortion. For the sake of a joke they could simply have given him false but realistic information: that his playmates had not yet come—when they were waiting behind the door; or that his father had gone "to make his rounds" without taking the boy with him—when the medical director was standing behind him, ready to grab him and whisk him off in the carriage. All parents are jokers; fooled since childhood themselves, they take pleasure in fooling their own youngsters, out of kindness. It never occurs to them that they might be driving their children crazy. The little victims must make do with the false feelings attributed to them, which they internalize, and with the false information that will be denied a moment later or soon afterward. These triflings are not always criminal; the child grows up, frees himself through questioning and refusal, coldly observes grownups fooling children. Yet Gustave remains marked. Mme Flaubert attaches enough importance to his demonstrations of naïveté to pass them on to her granddaughter. The mother would have it that this "innocence" has never entirely disappeared. Is Caroline right when she tells us that love is at its source? Certainly the little boy cannot imagine that adults would deceive through caprice. After all, Descartes finds no other guarantee of human knowledge: God is good, therefore he has no desire to deceive us. A valid reason. For Gustave it is more than a reason, it is a basic right. Trust always involves a calculating generosity: I give it to you, you must deserve it. And the little boy feels, in the transport of his enthusiasm: since you say it, it must be true; you haven't brought me into the world to mock me. But what is the source of this implicit faith? Carried to an extreme, is it not itself a defense? Doesn't it serve, at least, to replace something that has been lost or wanting, to fill a gap? We must advance cautiously when we are dealing with prehistory and when the witnesses are few and fraudulent. We shall attempt, through a description followed by a regressive analysis, to establish *what was lacking*. And if we succeed, we shall try, through a progressive synthesis, to discover the *why* of this absence. This will not be a waste of time. Since the stubborn naïveté of the future writer is the expression of a poor initial relationship with language, our description will at first aim only to articulate that relationship precisely.

Yes, the naïveté is originally just a relationship with speech, for it is through speech that these fabrications are conveyed. Further, since they do not correspond to any reality, one would have to view them only as lexemes. Little Gustave's misfortune is that something inside prevents him from grasping words as simple signs. Of course, even in a "normal" child a long learning period is necessary before he can distinguish the material weight of the vocable, its associations, the intimidating pressure it bears on the "object of locution," in short the magical power of its pure signifying value. But Gustave's naïveté, because it persists, indicates that he could not fully perform this task; he learns to decode the message, of course, but not to question its contents. A false thought is transmitted to him by the spoken word; soon even he—the little boy—is struck by its absurdity, but he doesn't question it. The meaning becomes substance—it acquires inertia, not by its obviousness but by its density. The idea has thickened, crushing the mind that contains it; it is a stone that can be neither lifted nor thrown off. Still, this enormous mass has remained *meaning* all the way through. Signification—that transcendence which exists only through the project that pursues it—and passivity—pure *En-soi*, material weight of the sign—merge together, a pair of contraries that interpenetrate instead of opposing each other. The most serious consequence is that the child derives no profit from the repeated deceptions. He is told a lie, he is made to believe that his father is gone, the father soon appears amidst laughter. But, for the child, this instantly revealed fraud never has the value of an *experiment*.

It will be understood that I am exposing appearances. To arrive at the truth, the terms must be reversed. It is Gustave's mind that is paralyzed before the spoken word—something is said to him and everything jams, everything comes to a halt. Meaning is not important, it is the verbal materiality that fascinates him. Yet this "paralysis" must be considered only a symbol; the mind is never paralyzed. The symbol can be understood in only one way: from his earliest years, the child is touched by human relationships through the *word*. Credulity comes to the children of men from those who affect them through language, that is, through the conductive medium of all articulated communications. It surrounds them from the beginning, they are born into it, shaped—for good or ill—to adapt themselves to it. When the sensory-motor apparatus has developed "normally," yet the child's response to the message is "abnormal," this double self originates at the difficult level where all discourse is man, where all of man is discourse; it implies a bad fit in the linguistic universe, that is in the social order, *in the family*.

To explore this strange credulity further, we should recall certain basic, general facts. First, the language of the speaker generally dissolves at once in the mind of the listener; what remains is a schema, both conceptual and verbal, that controls *reconstitution* and compre-

11

hension. Comprehension will be deeper, the more imprecise the word-for-word reconstitution. Now comprehension is a personal act. If the listener repeats what he has heard, he is merely lending his voice to a transcendent object that is realized through his voice and then flies off toward new tongues. If he *comprehends*, he reshapes the well-worn path *for himself*. In the end, the act is completely his own, although the comprehended reality can be a universal notion. Naturally, this is not a matter of thought without words; but intellection— or comprehension—when cqmplete, defines a virtually unlimited series of verbal expressions and creates an a priori *rule* for choosing among those expressions the one most appropriate in each situation and for each speaker. Thought, then, is neither one nor another part of the series—as if a particular expression ought to be privileged a priori; nor is it a capricious and transcendent option— how can we *choose* the spoken word unless it is *the* word itself? Rather, thought is at once the totality of the series—the differential relations that link together various expressions—and a distinct form based on the totalized series of those expressions that seems best adapted to the present situation. An idea that is comprehended is me, and it is all that is not-me—it is *my* subjectivity, exploding and collapsing, leaving my essence to be absorbed by the object. But am I ever freer and more unconditionally myself than in this "perpetual combustion" that continually expands until it embraces everything? In the same way, language is *me* and *I* am language. An idea, from this point of view, is inside me: the column—sun-drenched capital, pedestal in shadow— of sentences that express it and that define me *in time* as the reason (hidden to myself) for the words chosen, and *at this moment* by the sovereign choice of *one* expression in the infinite tangle of all possible expressions, defining me consequently by my appreciation of men and situations. And in the spiral garland of words must be seen, too, *myself in the Other*; language expresses human relationship, but it is the relationship of those who seek out the words—to support them, to censure them, to reject them—in each individual. The Other in me makes my language, which is my way of being in the Other. Thus, when man is language and language is human, each word tossed off in passing surpasses us with all its hidden connections to those who are speaking; when we, then, surpass each word in order to grasp the idea it embodies, that is, the infinite series of its possible substitutes, the permeability of consciousness is such that naïveté is no longer conceivable.

12

To be sure, we lie, we mystify, we deceive everyone all the time. But this is another matter. The mystification of adults reflects alienation—when they invent their lies, they are only concerned with sticking closer to truth. The cleverest liars invent their lies out of small, scarcely perceptible leeches, which they stick onto the skin of a known truth. In other words, language is the means of deception— and of course certain persons are taken in, others not—but language in itself is not deceitful. Certainly there are labyrinths, traps for the unwary, often in the end the word harbors a mirage. Yet quite simply language cannot be separated from the world, from others, and from ourselves. It is not an alien enclave that can outwit me or subvert my purpose; it is me, so that I am nearer to being myself when I am farther away—with others and among things; it is the indissoluble reciprocity of men and their struggles together embodied by the internal relations of this linguistic whole that has neither door nor window, where we can neither *go in* nor *come out, where we are*. The homogeneity of the word with all the objective and subjective determinations of man insures that it cannot come to us as an alien power. For how could this be? Language is within us because we understand it; distant as its source, unforeseen as it may be, it was awaited in the depths of our heart. In sum, it is comprehended only by itself, that is, it is obliterated, invisible; the thing itself remains, sign of the word which is abolished.

NAÏVETÉ AND LANGUAGE

I have described, of course, the abstract condition of adults without memory. Through memory, childhood corrupts us from its first words: we believe we have chosen them for their light and airy meanings, when they are actually imposed on us by some obscure sense. But these problems, essential for the analyst, do not yet concern us. The question here is to understand credulity, and after the preceding discussion we can only explain it by an "impact" of the word on consciousness. For little Gustave, everything happens as though the word were at once a meaning comprehended—that is, a determination of his subjectivity—and an objective power. The sentence does not dissolve within him, it is not obliterated in the face of the *thing spoken* or the speaker who says it. The child understands without the power to integrate. As if the verbal process were only half completed. As if the meaning—seen correctly—instead of becoming a conceptual and practical schema, instead of entering into a relationship with other schemata of the same kind, remained bound to the sign. As if the sign itself, instead of merging with its interior image, retained for the child's consciousness its resonant materiality. As if—in the sense that we talk of stones singing and fountains weeping—language were still, for the child, only noise speaking.

Is this attitude conceivable? It is, if comprehension is arrested before its completion. The idea remains captive of its expression, as much as of the sounds that bear it; for lack of control over the gamut of sentences that *might* restore it, the content of the signifier remains on the assertoric level—neither possible nor impossible, quite simply it is. The encounter with the signifier—real fact: the child has heard sounds—is not distinguished from this other fact: the real existence of the signified. And more generally, meaning—that strange amalgam of a resonant plenitude and a transcendence aimed at nothing—remains without the determination of modalities. In order to join meaning to hypothetical or apodictical modes, one must detach it from the "mouthful of sound"; but if being is its mode, this pure artifice, for want of definition in relation to the necessary, the possible, remains itself undetermined. It is not surprising, however, that under certain conditions the development of language is arrested, and that, as long as it is incomplete, verbal processes will seem meaningless. We have encountered such imprisoned thought, guaranteed but at the same time crushed by the actual presence of its sign, in magical formulas, in riddles, and in the *carmina sacra*; we find it each night in our dreams.

If Gustave, aged six, confuses sign and meaning to the extent that the material presence of the sign is the evidence that guarantees the truth of the meaning, he must have had a poor initial relationship with the Other. In effect, he believes everything he is told, out of awe before the verbal object, out of devoted love for the adults. But he does not *really* relate speech to those who have spoken. At first he perceives commands rather than statements; these impose themselves and then *he must believe them*, since they are a gracious gift made to him by his parents. Besides, lacking the reciprocity—however ephemeral—that establishes complete comprehension with all its forms, the speech of the Other seems to him a word that has been *given*, in every sense of the term. Speaking is not *expressing*; the sentence, ample presence, is a material gift—he is offered a music box, imagine, a musical trivet. If the music has meaning, so much the better; the gift is taken, kept, it is a souvenir. What is lacking, we see, is *intention*. The child adores the object bestowed upon him as evidence of paternal favor, but it is the same generosity that Gustave detects in his father's slightest caress. Speaking to the child or ruffling his hair amounts to the same thing. It might be said that between parents and children the gestures of tenderness—silent, effective, as "brutish" among humans as among the beasts—are the only *communication* possible. This child, wild and—if we are to believe his first writings—close to the animal state, can love others and believe himself loved only on the level of common subhumanity.

The most striking aspect, indeed, of his niece's narrative is that in the same paragraph she singles out Gustave's trances and his credulity. As though the trances were only repeated attempts to escape his credulity, as though the little boy tried to evade language by allowing himself to drift in silence. He is calm, doesn't breathe a word, lets himself be absorbed by the surroundings, the plants, the pebbles in the small garden, the sky at Yonville, the sea. One could say that he seeks to merge with unnamable nature, fleeing the weight of nomination in the unnamed texture of things, in the irregular, indefinable movements of the foliage, of the waves. I see surprising affinities between these first unconscious ventures beyond the self and the final vow of Saint Antoine—"to be matter." It is too soon, however, to elaborate. Let us limit ourselves to description.

Even when we look at things quite simply, as they are presented, it is striking that the silence of Gustave's trances is quite the opposite of the bronze tones, dull and implacable, that vibrate within him, those of *others* and his own, suffered, never completely understood. He would sit for hours, a finger in his mouth, looking almost stupid; this calm child who reacts badly when spoken to, feels less than others the need to speak—words, as we say, do not come to him, nor the desire to use them. This means, of course, that he does not communicate willingly. His affections are not in themselves directed toward others, they are not destined for others and do not seek *to be expressed*. Let us not then conclude that they are intentionally "egocentric"—there is no ego without an alter, without an alter ego; unexpressed to *others*, his affections remain for Gustave himself inexpressible. They are lived fully and vaguely with no one there to live them, no doubt because their substance is, as Lacan would say, "inarticulable." But is not the real cause an early difficulty with articulation, reinforced by a secret preference for the inarticulate? The evident connection between Gustave's inadequacies—as "object of speech" and as "speaker"—is persuasive: in the child, language is a poor conductive medium; through it not only is the relationship with the Other falsified, but also the relationship with the self. The little boy is badly anchored in the universe of discourse. The word is never *his*; the trance soon absorbs the word, and by and by the word, fallen from the sky, oppresses him. Finally, in the very depths of his interiority, the word remains external. That is, when it enters the child's ear, the object is not submitted to the classical operations: reception, apprehension, reclassification in a verbal series with respect to the permanent possibility of the subject. These operations occur automatically if the child is already language; or, if you will, to be language is to repeat these operations continually within oneself. Let a word present itself, it is language that receives language. But if the spoken word is alternately absent or deafening, as it is for Gustave, this is because his own disposition, the thread of his "ideas" and affections, is *not sufficiently verbalized*. At the age when everyone speaks, he is still imitating speakers; and if the sound that rings suddenly in him leaves an impression, it provokes him precisely through this sense of "estrangement."[1] And *estrangement* has only one explanation: there is no common ground or mediation between Gustave's subjective existence and the universe of meanings; they are two perfectly heterogeneous realities which occasionally meet.

A child of six ordinarily finds himself defined down to his very innermost being by others and by himself, for to live is to produce meanings,[2] to suffer is to speak. The child is receptive to external meanings because he is himself filled with meaning and producer of meanings (I am here translating the German word *sinngebend* taken in its phenomenological sense). Gustave does not produce meaning; within himself he is not defined by anything, neither by a proper name nor by the general name of what he feels. He lives, however, he savors his life, he projects himself beyond the boundaries of the self toward the world around him; but life and words are incommensurable. Actually, I am exaggerating. The verbalization of his existence has begun, for lengthy as his silences may be, he speaks, he acquires a vocabulary, he listens and comprehends what is said to him. Very simply, words never really define for him what he experiences, what he feels. Nor, doubtless, his true transcendent relation to the world. The objects that surround him are the things of others. His parents at times oblige him to define himself through signs that they have chosen: say hello to the lady, tell her your name;

---

1. This is Lacan's translation of the Freudian term *Unheimlichkeit*. [Usual English translation: "the uncanny."—Trans.]

2. It is not *only that*—it is first to work. But work as objectification is also a signifier.

where does it hurt? here or here? But, in telling the truth, he realizes that truth is alien to him. This is why he is the most credulous child; since he does not possess truth, since it is a relationship of the others with things and between themselves, since each *true* utterance, by revealing the shifting ground between existence and the word, is made manifest to him by the discomfort it provokes and never by something obvious, he relies upon the principle of authority.

Let us say he views words *from the outside* as things, even when they are inside him. Later this turn of mind will be the source of the *Dictionnaire des idées reçues*. At first, vocables are perceptible realities; then, their connections are effected from the outside—through accident, custom, institution; third comes meaning, the strict result of the first two but in itself *arbitrary*. Emma and Léon talk about Nature because the situation demands—through social habit—that it be discussed; not that there is any logical reason for it; it is simply that nature is evoked at a certain stage of sexual relations. At the same moment, thousands of couples say the same things in the same terms. The main thing is for all of these still platonic lovers to feel, through these banalities, a "communion of souls" with their future mistresses. In short, the connections of words are physical, they are the modulations of a song. The established words of lovers are meant to substitute for the caresses that are impossible at this stage, to lay the groundwork for them and, by the exchange of breaths before the kiss, to awaken a feeling of reciprocity. The meaning is there in the vocables, prefabricated; it is not needed *for itself*, but so that future lovers by sharing a preference create the equivalent of shared desire. In this conception of language—which we shall later discuss at length—we retrieve the child's previous refusals. As an adult, Gustave preserves "traces of his naïveté"; he also preserves, as an essential element of his character, his stubbornness in never entirely entering into the universe of discourse. Outside and inside, he views words inside out; in their sensual strangeness he takes commonplaces for imperatives engraved in the verbal matter that each individual is bound to reproduce by the inflections of his voice; he persists in thinking that the spoken word corrodes and can never completely define. In his case, the difficulty with learning to read comes from a general and earlier trouble, the difficulty with speaking.

Caroline's narrative at least allows us to ascertain all this; it does not give us the tools to examine thoroughly these first impressions. What, precisely, is this radical heterogeneity of Gustave's mental life and language? Merely to demonstrate an apparent incompatibility is

17

not enough; it must be defined with precision. Indeed, no human animal—I will even say no mammal—whether it speaks or not, can live without entering into the dialectical movement of the signifier and the signified. For the simple reason that meaning is born of the project. Therefore Gustave, badly adjusted as he is in the universe of *expression*, is sign, signified, signifier, signification to the extent that his most basic impulses are made manifest through projects. And he knows it. As he runs, smiling, to throw himself into his father's open arms, he is consciously determined by a sign that embodies a signified relationship between lord and vassal. Better, it is a *sign* rather than a caress. Why does he crave it if not because it *signifies* paternal love? Where, then, do the troubles begin, the aversions and the impossibilities? With spoken language? Why?

It is too soon to try to answer these questions. *Above all* it is important to support this description with other testimony. Let us not forget its fragility: two dubious paragraphs of Mme Commanville's decorous gossip that report, in a sweetened version, the confidences of Mme Flaubert. These confidences, furthermore, concern facts buried in the distant past—a quarter of a century *at least* separates Gustave's resistance to the alphabet from the moment when Achille-Cléophas's widow confides in her granddaughter. Might not this woman, prematurely aged by successive bereavements, have distorted or simply exaggerated her memories? After all, Gustave reads and writes fluently, well enough, in any case, to have written a masterpiece. His childhood aberrations were either not as marked as his mother pretends, or else they had no serious consequences. Certainly things did not go very well for Flaubert; he hated school life, student life, and as the victim of a "nervous illness"—which his biographer takes care to pass over in silence—he sought isolation at Croisset. But to reconcile this reputedly backward childhood with the troubles of adolescence and maturity, to explain one by the other or simply to use the later difficulties to confirm the statements of Caroline Commanville would be like pulling a rabbit out of a hat if we were not provided with an abundant, detailed testimony that comes only five years after the events in question—the testimony of Gustave himself.

Indeed, his first works deal continually with his childhood. Of course, all of us are constantly discussing the child we were, and are, but at certain periods we are less conscious of it than at others and describe this time past, and impassable, without knowing it. Adolescence in particular is often a point of rupture—we think of the present, of the future, describing what we believe we are today, wanting to know what we will be. In many of his early stories, the fifteen-year-old Gustave speaks knowingly of his early childhood, in particular of his stupors and torments when confronted with the primer. For himself, he has not ceased, nor will he ever cease, being that murdered child. We shall learn the reasons for this fidelity, but not right away. We must allow this life to develop before our eyes and for the moment ask nothing of Flaubert's memoirs but the invalidation or confirmation of Caroline's story.

Let us reread *Quidquid volueris*.[3] It is clear that Djalioh, the ape-man, represents Flaubert himself. At what age? This character is sixteen, a year older than his creator. But he is the product of a monstrous union. A scientist, Monsieur Paul, has in the interests of science had a female slave raped by an orangutan. In the anthropoid issue of this breeding, the simian heritage has arrested the human development. That is, Djalioh is *arrested in childhood*, just beyond the point at which man and animal are—according to Gustave—still indistinguishable. Does this mean that the young schoolboy wants to define himself as he is now, at his desk? Yes, and no. Gustave is not a "brilliant fellow," we shall see, but he is rather a good student; he reads, he writes, goes around with boys his own age, is elated by discussions of metaphysics with Alfred. He can allude to himself through Djalioh only if he holds his childhood to be the *consummate truth* of his fifteen years. It is this childhood—unforgettable, unforgotten—that made him what he has become; it remains within him, always in the *present*. But it is not so much the lived reality of his present as a universal axis of reference, an immediate explanation of everything he does, of everything he feels. The child is not the adolescent; he is the calamity that produced the other and limits his horizons. In this way, childhood is permanent, he touches it; if he thinks of himself, he

3. Any of Gustave's tales written at this period would reveal, upon inspection, the same theme. Marguerite, Garcia, the bibliomane, and Mazza are as much incarnations of Gustave as Djalioh. I have chosen *Quidquid volueris* because here the author's effort to describe his childhood aberration is more explicit. We shall later explore the strange "object relations" that can be glimpsed through these fantasms. It is to the point, nevertheless, to stress that the monkey and the slave represent not only Flaubert's parents. This is the period when Gustave, who was in love with Mme Schlésinger, delighted in sado-masochistic fantasies of Schlésinger's sexual relations with his wife. Gustave imagines the woman he loves in grotesque and obscene postures; she is the debased slave of her supposed husband. He too, then, is surely symbolized by the orangutan. Achille-Cléophas, by contrast, is—as we shall see—doubled: he is at once Monsieur Paul, who presides at the monstrous breeding out of a love of science, and the simian beast who impregnates a woman.

always refers eight years back to that time between two times when his troubles began.

We will not admit Gustave's testimony uncritically. At fifteen the young boy has passed—we shall see why—from flexible defense to counterattack. He begins by accepting the judgment of other people, by pushing it to an extreme: I was backward, worse still, an anthropoid. But he does this only to effect a sudden reversal of values and hurl the accusation back on his accusers. Ape-man—why not? Be animals if you can, strictly subhuman, anything rather than human beings. We are advised that Djalioh is somewhat unsuited to making logical connections; relations escape him. This is attributed to the peculiarity of his cerebral lobes, and the studious author describes the monster's cranial box: "As for his head, it was narrow and compressed in front, but at the back it showed prodigious development." Atrophy of the frontal lobes, hence of the intelligence; hypertrophy of the occipital lobes, hence of the sensibility. Did the young phrenologist read Gall? I rather imagine he took this foolishness from his father. It doesn't matter; what counts is that Djalioh, as the author will tell us when his creature has already gained our sympathy, is illiterate:

> "And so what does he do? . . . Does he like cigars?"
> "Not at all, my dear fellow, he can't stand them."
> "Does he hunt?"
> "Hardly, the shots frighten him."
> "Surely he works, he reads; he writes all day?"
> "To do that he would have to know how to read and write."

These questions are posed by some foolish libertines and the answers provided by the infamous Monsieur Paul. The author reports the dialogue without any commentary, but he is convinced that we will accept it at face value. Briefly, the question at hand is to *situate* Djalioh in society. These gentlemen inquire if he is one of them. No— no women, no cigars, no horses, no guns. Then he is suspect, he is probably an intellectual. Monsieur Paul has anticipated such a surmise. Intellectual? Not even that—he is unlettered. The scientist reveals the origin of the monster to the astounded guests. Unlettered, so be it. But why? Was his education neglected? Flaubert doesn't say. But he repeatedly stresses the scientists' interest in the most exciting experiment of the century, and in its happy result. Are we to believe that not even one enthusiastic biologist could be found to teach Djalioh his letters? Science demanded that he be put to the test, so we must assume an attempt was made. In vain. If Djalioh knows nothing, only his constitutional inaptitude is to blame. He cannot make connections between syllables. Nor, a fortiori, between concepts. Here is confirmation of Mme Flaubert's disclosures—*Quidquid volueris* testifies to a bitter and powerful memory resting on childhood failure. To be a Flaubert, to be seven years old and not know how to read, was what Gustave could not tolerate eight years earlier. At fifteen, this failure remains an intolerable reminder; it is misery and disaster, the origin of what he is, the humiliation for which he compensates by perpetual scrutiny—it is himself.

But Gustave goes further, and behind Djalioh's inability to comprehend the written language we are given a glimpse of his poor relationship with the spoken language. The author does not say expressly that Djalioh cannot speak, although he finds people who condemn his muteness. Let us say that in general Djalioh keeps quiet, and if he tries to speak, the words do not get past his lips and are, in any case, never heard. On one occasion his lips move but nothing comes out. Another time, "Djalioh . . . wanted to say something but it was so low, so timorous, that it was taken for a sigh." We remark that he catches his breath *in fear*. Yet the anthropoid, apparently docile and calm, does not seem to be particularly fearful of men; it is language itself that disturbs him. Caught halfway between the simian imitation of human speech and the conscious production of signs, poor Djalioh dares not make a sound, ignorant of what he is about, in terror of making a mistake. The same deeper cause constrains him to muteness and prevents him from learning his letters. A defect of intelligence? No doubt, but not only this; he has nothing *to say* to all these men who are not his own kind. The young storyteller, however, does not deny his character a vague need for expression. But, as Mme de Staël said of one of the lovers who were too young for her, "Speech is not his language." On one occasion, the ape-man comes upon a violin. He turns it over in his hands without really knowing what to do with it, he barely escapes breaking the bow; then, imitating musicians who have just parted from their pupils, "he draws [the instrument] to his chin." At first he plays "a false, strange, incoherent music . . . sounds soft and slow." Then he amuses himself: the bow "skips on the strings." The music "is lurching, filled with shrill notes, with rending cries . . . and then there are bold arpeggios . . . notes that run together and soar like a gothic spire . . . all without tempo, without song, without rhythm, no melody, vague and swift thoughts . . . dreams that pass by and escape, pushed by others in a restless whirlwind."

21

Yet it must be remarked that this improvisation is not intended to represent poetic ecstasy but rather the earthly passions of the poet. It is clearly stated, besides, that the anthropoid does not dream of attempting to communicate with his audience: "He looked with wonder at all these men, all these women [who at first laugh at the improvisation] . . . ; he did not understand all this laughter.[4] He continued." He does not play *for others*—he plays and the others are there. However, let us remember this attempt; Djalioh is transformed through the music, he expresses himself through music but he will not agree to define himself through spoken language.

Here is the monster, the idiot child: "fantastic according to some, melancholy according to others, stupid, mad and mute, added the wisest observers. . . . " The wisest observers, to be sure, are Madame and Doctor Flaubert, whose blind intelligence cannot distinguish between Djalioh's sighs and his efforts—rare, it is true—to pronounce a word: "Whether it was a word or a sigh," Gustave remarks, "was of little consequence, but inside him there was a complete soul." A complete soul: that is, the backward child was easily superior to the members of our species with regard to the depth of his tender feelings. The motif of the stupors, then, provides a counterpoint to the motif of language. Djalioh's life is cut in two by a catastrophe: Monsieur Paul takes him to France, there the ape-man meets Adèle, his master's fiancée, and conceives a violent passion for her; he is tortured to death by jealousy. But what concerns Gustave is that *before*, before his keepers took it upon themselves to teach him to read, Djalioh experienced a golden age: "Often in the presence of forests, of high mountains, of the ocean, his soul expanded. . . . He trembled all over with the weight of an inner voluptuousness and, with his head between his hands, he would fall into a lethargic melancholy. . . ." The author is careful to stress that the passions are not yet unleashed. Even at this age, however, if we are to believe him, the stupor seems to be a familiar outlet: "Nature possessed him in all its forms, the soul's delights, violent passions;[5] gluttonous appetites. . . . His heart . . . was vast like the sea, immense and empty like his solitude."

4. Comparing this passage with Caroline Commanville's text—"in the face of their laughter he remained a dreamer, glimpsing a mystery"—we can see that it involves an actual memory.
5. These passions, violent as they are, do not involve the harsh fury of human passions. Such passions, Gustave notes, contain no jealousy or even possessiveness; they address themselves to the whole of creation.

The symbol is precise: the ape-man, monstrous product of nature and man, must be both the pure object of man and natural subject par excellence. His most intimate relations are with nature and not with men—nature is *within him*, it is his pure existence; *outside him*, it is his own potential. His only potential; he can surpass himself only in the direction of nature, making himself so much more nature—that is, spontaneity without a subject—that he loses himself in the un-named, uncultivated virgin vastness of the ocean or forest. Nature is the meaning and end of his basic project elaborated in a thousand particular appetites; he *comes back to himself* from the horizons, he is a being from the *natural* distances. Between immanence and tran-scendence there is, in Djalioh, reciprocity; therefore, the author ins-ists, it could be said, according to the circumstances, either that he is diluted in nature or that the whole of nature enters him. Although this seems to be a matter of inverse modes, *they are actually the same* with a different emphasis—sometimes the soul appears as an infinite gap and the world is swallowed up in it, and sometimes it is a finite mode of substance; thus imprisoned within the limits of its deter-mination, it annihilates itself so that it can flow beyond its borders and *realize* its participation in the indivisible All, in the very movement that dissolves its particularity. Most important, the basic intention never varies—the goal in both cases is summation. Reciprocal sum-mation of the microcosm by the macrocosm, and vice versa. When this double simultaneous belonging of the soul to the world, the world to the soul, is the object of a concrete and lived experience, Flaubert calls it quite simply poetry. When it is actualized by gathering together all of being and all of man in an intentional synthesis that proceeds from the negation of any analytic determination, it might equally be called *metaphysical attitude*. Indeed, before ecstasy there is little Gus-tave, the waves of the sea, the dark sand where the waves subside, the clear dry sand they cannot reach, the remains of a boat stranded on the beach, a cabana, etc.; as soon as the metaphysical attitude is imposed, these objects are annihilated in favor of general determi-nations: place, time, the infinite, etc.

The reader will have observed that this attitude, while intentional and spontaneous, is *suffered* by the anthropoid and the child; they do not determine it themselves, *they are determined by it*. Poetry befalls the subman, as is sufficiently indicated by the word "lethargy" that Gustave uses to designate a certain phase of Djalioh's ecstasy—and even more by the irrepressible shudderings that accompany it most of the time. Poetry is *suffered*; we must add that it is *inborn*. What is given to the son of ape and woman cannot be given to the son of man, for intelligence and logic kill pantheistic intuition. The young boy is proud of his trances because he sees his animality continually revived in them. He knows very well that others think he looks stupid* at these times. He writes about it unmistakably and at length in *Quidquid volueris*. Mad with jealousy, the monster scratches Adèle with his nails. She escapes, he remains alone: "He was as pale as a wedding dress, his thick lips cracked by fever and covered with blisters moved quickly like someone speaking very fast, his eyelids blinked and his eyeball rolled slowly in its socket, like an idiot."

This last, terribly violent passage strikes us by a double inaccuracy, or rather by the same one repeated twice: "like someone speaking very fast," "like an idiot." We must pause a moment. Flaubert intentionally revives one of the stupors of his childhood; he shows his behavior *from the outside*, as it appeared to others, and he does not hesitate to qualify it by the words that were applied to him then—"like an idiot." Yes! I looked like an idiot, I mumbled, I rolled my distracted eyes, I was as pale as death! Why these smug admissions? In order to denounce the criminal thoughtlessness of his former judges who interpreted his dazed gestures only as signs of external weakness and did not understand that they screened the most violent storms. Imagine the passions that rage in Djalioh's soul: love and jealousy, remorse and savagery, gales, gushings, cyclones—a single one would suffice to shatter everything. But they are unleashed all together, with equal force and opposite meaning—they collide, ravaging the soul but mutually contained. The fragile simian body that anchors them, immobile and overwhelmed, is destroyed without a sign. Flaubert triumphs: here is what took place inside me! To put it differently, the adults viewed the stupors as *negative* behavior—absences, lacks, gaps in attention, a failure of adaptation. Actually, they were signs of "brutishness" in all its plenitude.

All his life, Flaubert attached a particular value to the adjective "brutish." "The best of me," he was to write years later to Louise, "is poetry, is the brute." Beginning with *Quidquid volueris*, he clearly contrasts Djalioh, "that monstrous freak of nature, [to] Monsieur Paul, that other monster, or rather that marvel of civilization bearing all its symbols, breadth of mind, a withered heart." Language, analysis, commonplaces—this is man. From the moment the human animal

---

* *Bête* in the original; as a noun, bête means "beast," as an adjective, "stupid." —Trans.

begins to speak, even before he can read, he abdicates his native poetry, he passes from nature to culture. We will note the consistency of the Flaubertian vocabulary, how many times Gustave repeats in his correspondence: animals, idiots, fools, children come to me because they know that *"I am one of them."* Not from any deficiency, but from a dark, rich telluric power that he preserved, thanks to the bad beginning that prevented him from ever becoming fully integrated into the world of culture. The adult speaks in the present: I *am* one of them. At thirty he believes that his childhood—frustrated, silent, sedentary, and mad—is still with him; the company of other adults, the claims of his mistress pull him momentarily away, out of it, but he falls back as soon as he finds himself alone again. This very rumination on the past reveals in Gustave the recriminator who progresses backward. But in the early years recrimination did not yet exist. I only want to indicate that Gustave always valued in himself *above all else* not the speaking animal, but the nonspeaking animal. By advertising their inability to understand the poet, Monsieur Paul and his friends merely bring the judgment down on their own heads—on the one hand this creature of silence, folded in on himself, and on the other the men of letters, the men of science who use language to go from one table to another repeating the same commonplaces issued from the same paltry wisdom; the literate man is the one disqualified by this comparison. Anyone who has studied Flaubert for some time will have no difficulty reading between the lines Gustave's venomous revenge on Achille: "Yes, at seven I did not know my letters and you, from the age of four, you read fluently. Afterward? I was a brute, meaning a poet, and you, you were a little doctor, meaning a robot, and you remained one."

In the period these early stories were written, Flaubert is categorical: poetry is a silent adventure of the soul, a lived event that has nothing in common with language; more precisely, poetry *takes place* against language. If this position is still only implicit in *Quidquid volueris*, it is fully developed a year later in *Mémoires d'un fou*. This time we are dealing with an autobiographical sketch. The author says *I*. Suddenly the symbol has changed: the *monster* is a *madman*. And the madman's first transports—the very same kind that Djalioh experienced in his golden age—are expressly linked to Gustave's early childhood: "As a child, I loved what I could see . . . I dreamed of love . . . I looked at the vastness, space, the infinite, and my soul fell away before this unlimited horizon." Here, there is no more virgin forest, but "the ocean" recurs a number of times in the first pages. From the time of his first vacations, the child felt bound to the sea. There is an inner relationship between the little boy and this vastness rolling back on itself which, in his eyes, always represents nature without men. In the passage quoted—to which we shall return—this ecstatic relationship is clearly translated into passivity: the soul *falls away*; this collapse—like an attempt to conquer the plenitude of nature by abandoning oneself to it—is Gustave's childhood stupor, here represented as a voluntary act performed for the purpose of possessing the perceptible infinite. Yet for the first time Gustave clearly poses the question of how to bind the undifferentiated intuitions of the poet to the language that must convey them: "I had an infinity more vast, if that is possible, than God's . . . and then I had to descend from these sublime regions toward words. . . . How to render through speech the harmony that arises in the heart of the poet? . . . to what extent can poetry humble itself without shattering?" It is a question, of course, of *poetic writing*, and this problem concerns the adolescent himself. The future writer in him dreams of glory, he tells us about his professional preoccupations; the contradiction that makes any transcription of his ecstasies impossible worries him, here; how will he make himself known as the brilliant poet that he is? But these worries are only the echo of older and deeper preoccupations. There was the undifferentiated plenitude, the child lived in it joyfully, and then all at once the descent again into the fire, the *summoning*, the forcible return to the words of others: "Gustave, where are you? Take your finger out of your mouth, you look stupid." It can be felt still more a little further on in the same *Mémoires* when Gustave declares that by this necessary descent toward verbal expression, the poet humbles himself, *humbles poetry*. He does not give his theoretical reasons—Flaubert never gives his reasons—but it is not difficult to give them in his place. Since the poetic act is produced outside of language and without it, since it is not necessarily *in itself* bound to the word, therefore its transcription is not *of itself* poetic—it can neither capture nor communicate the all-embracing experience. Contrary to what Joe Busquet will say later, one can translate "nothing from silence." Later, when the source of the poetic ecstasies has dried up, this total insufficiency of words to what ought to be their primary object will be a powerful reason for Flaubert to consider language as a separate order of things, which is self-sufficient and its own object. For the moment, let us see in it nothing more than the supremacy of silence reaffirmed. And the condemnation of the word: for the word, a product of culture, pretends to render the natural, intimate movement of the soul and yet

26

expresses only cultural, that is external, determinations. To analyze—
and language for Flaubert is analysis—is to kill. Words de-compose.
If the poet speaks, what more does he give us than the articulation
of the words themselves? A practical joker borrows a watch, takes it
all apart; at least he returns the actual mechanism, and if nothing is
missing it can be put together again. The fugitive poet who coins his
experiences is worse; he takes the watch and gives in return *separate
words*, which designate the parts of the object. The *word* mechanism
and the *word* ecstasy—what are they? *Things* distinct in their very
substance from the objects they pretend to designate. Cumbersome
things that occupy the center stage and obstruct the view, juxtaposed
solitary objects *more adjoined than articulated*, in short, molecules of
language. Whether reality is syncretism or synthesis, existence lived
from day to day or the sudden apprehension of the self and the world
in a mystic appropriation, it is situated on one or the other side of
verbal analysis. In any event, it is life in the present; syncretism,
"multiplicity of interpenetration," synthesis—reality is the animality
that cannot be decomposed, it keeps its silence.

This is what Gustave *thinks* at fifteen years old. With a surprising
strength of conviction. And of course it is all false. No doubt the
sentence is analysis, but it is synthesis as well. The Ideologues had
eyes only for the analytic function; they themselves had cut clauses
into words and words into syllables in order to apply, first, their
principles and methods to their own tools. Thus we see only molecules in the articulated discourse, to such a degree that this individ-
ualistic dissociation was at the basis of bourgeois ideology. It could
be that the fifteen-year-old Gustave's fables are a distant echo of these
"ideas"—through his father he knew Cabanis and Destutt de Tracy.
Half a century later the questions became more complicated; with the
dialectic, the problem of synthesis again becomes the first priority.
No one doubts today that a sentence occurs against a background
which is nothing more than *all* of language; no one doubts that the
whole of language is needed *in it* for the sentence to define its own
being and its meaning, which is nothing but *differentiation*. No one
doubts that *anything* can and must be given a name and is even named
by all the rest of language, uncovering and defining it, by *all* other
terms, as a certain vacuum which is already, negatively, a name. As
for *totalities* (ecstasies or long, somnolent vistas of passion), they are
never *designated*, meaning that they always involve new experiences
which escape previous nomination and do not necessarily—or even
very often—produce the word or sentence that best suits them. But

if we know that we are at once natural culture and cultivated nature, if we remember that lived reality rolls its words along, loses one, takes it up again, that the actual, in short, is already verbal—but simply incomplete—we will understand that the role of the word is not to translate the silence of nature into an articulated language. For everyone, speaking is an immediate and spontaneously lived experience, to the extent that speech is a behavior; inversely, what is fully lived is never untouched by words and often revives dated designations which allude to it without really being altogether appropriate. Thus the verbal act can *in no instance* be defined as the passage from one order of things to another. How could this be possible, since the reality of man living and speaking is created from moment to moment by the mingling of these two orders? Speaking is nothing more than adapting and enriching a behavior which is already verbal, that is, already expressive in itself. And this means to rework and correct our spontaneous babblings by living more deeply the passions that produce them; to live the original passion with fewer constraints and more radically through the liberating effort that clarifies it by naming it; and sometimes too, through a double error, to pervert the nomination by falsifying the passional movement, to disorder impulse by an error of nomination. The word is not given, it is. There are no words for what I feel, sentences are needed; and these disparate remarks represent simply my attitude toward myself. The word if I am content with myself, is always given; the word love, old as it is, can suffice for a long while, its lightning bolts still dazzling lovers who were formerly ignorant of each other. And if we want to refine it, there are infinite subdivisions: passionate love, respectful love, and the like, all these cases can be anticipated provided we accept—and who doesn't?—being predictable. And then, if the occasion demands, it will have to be recognized that the love which is lived cannot be named without being reinvented. One will be changed by the other, discourse and lived experience. Or rather, the claims of feeling and of expression are mutually heightened; there is nothing surprising about this since both issue from the same source and interpenetrate from the beginning. It may be that I am irritated today because the word "love" or any other does not do justice to such a feeling. But what does this mean? First, my *affection* declares that it *is not* a passive silence but a silent expectation, even an invention; otherwise what is the source of its claims, the urgency to find it a proper qualification? Briefly, on the level that I accept it along with its requirements, it is named and given a false name, and being provoked by this it requires not so much the studied redress of language as the deepening, clarifying, of its *reality*. The deepening, moreover, is required to perform a creative function, grasping my affection in its synthetic unity and, merely by doing so, *inventing* the verbal designation of this unity. Meaning that nothing exists that does not require a name, that cannot be given one and cannot even be negatively named by the bankruptcy of language. And at the same time, that *nomination* from its very origin is *an art*—nothing is given if not this claim. "We are guaranteed nothing," says Alain. Not even that we will find adequate phrases. Feeling speaks: it says that it exists, that it has been named falsely, that it has developed badly and askew, that it requires another sign or, lacking this, a symbol that might be incorporated and will correct its internal deviation. One must search; language says only that everything can be invented in it, that expression is always possible, even if indirect, because the verbal totality, instead of reducing itself, as one might think, to the finite number of words to be found in the dictionary, is composed of infinite distinctions—between them, in each of them—which alone make them actual. This means that invention characterizes speech—we will invent if the conditions are favorable; if not, we will have badly named experiences and live them badly. No, nothing is guaranteed; but it can be said in any event that there can be no a priori radical disjunction of language from referent for the simple reason that feeling is discourse and discourse is feeling.

At fifteen, Gustave declared the contrary. The influences of the father and the century do not sufficiently account for this stubborn ill-humor. From this period on he was a writer—with great power and ingenuity, a graceful style. Words obeyed him, they crowded under his pen; his eloquence suffered none of the difficulties that would create the grandeur and austerity of *Madame Bovary*, it flowed naturally. And yet, what purpose does it serve? To write that one mustn't write, that speech is a degraded silence. In his surliness, which the success at hand renders unjustifiable, we shall thus see a survival. It survives, and will survive, in and through an unforgettable childhood that conditions Flaubert's entire subsequent development. Later we shall see the complex reasons why the adolescent has turned himself into a man of letters. He is one, in any event, as we already perceive; at the age of nine Gustave decided to write because at seven he didn't know how to read.

We have proof: Flaubert's adolescent writings entirely corroborate his mother's memories, they allow us to catch a glimpse of the early experience such as it was lived from within. His writings hint that this experience—enriched and magnified through pride and resentment—was often repeated afterward and that the adolescent, like the child before him, never stopped suffering from a linguistic malaise or compensating for it by inexpressible ecstasies. Gustave, with a profound sense of his true problems—which should not be confused with lucidity—immediately puts his finger on the fundamental event in his prehistory; everything began with this poor insertion into the universe of language which is then translated into a dialectical exchange of silence and scrutiny. If we strip it of its hyperbole, *Quidquid volueris* confirms our hypothesis: the child keenly felt the incompatibility of affective syntheses with their conventional signs. The word was for him, first of all, the tool and product of the analytic operations that the adults, from outside, thrust upon him. Through words they communicated conclusions to him which he did not recognize. Not that he had other words with which to counter theirs—he seemed to escape from language through nature. Culture, for him, is theft: it reduces the vague and vast natural consciousness to its being-other, to what it is for others. The word is thing; introduced into a soul, it reabsorbs the soul in its own generality—a veritable metamorphosis. Analysis replaces internal links with purely external bonds. It severs, isolates, replaces interpenetration with continuity; universality does away with subjective singularity for the sake of collective objectivity. The soul, that cosmic and particular fever, becomes a commonplace.

We have shown that this doctrine is false. The abrupt split in Flaubert of the subjective life and language, of the intuitive and the discursive, of nature and culture, cannot be explained by the disjunction, in each of these pairs, of the first term from the second. It must be viewed not as a precocious grasp of the truth, but rather as the singular adventure of a child; various elements, external and internal, are interposed in order to attack what will slowly become his bête noire as well as the material of his art, the word. The doctrine he articulates in *Quidquid volueris* must be read solely as an effort to justify himself and to overcompensate for humiliations he could not forget. If we reject the falsifications, we shall be able to approach his first silences. And *first* we shall understand that they were not *truly* silences. Let us consider, for example, Djalioh's pantheistic ecstasies or those of the madman who writes his *Mémoires*—do we accept the notion that these ecstasies lack all verbal content? Impossible, since the floodtide of experience continually tosses up words and carries them along, pell-mell, sometimes on the surface and sometimes engulfing them so as to transport them invisibly underwater. Impossible above all because silence is itself a verbal act, a hole dug in language and which, as such, can be maintained only as a virtual nomination whose sense is defined by the totality of the word. At fifteen, Gustave wants *not to see* the words that haunt his poetry. Proof of this is that each time he comes to speak about his intuitions, he employs a rather impoverished and stereotyped vocabulary, always the same terms in the same order. Sometimes, of course, he evokes a simple infinite and sometimes an infinite "vaster than God's"; but these slight variations serve only to accentuate the invariability of the verbal theme. These devices will be found again and again until around 1857; traces of them remain in his correspondence until his death. Fluid, always novel, inexpressible, the ecstasies could be made the referent of allusions more nebulous, more capricious. Instead, everything is devised to last, to repeat itself without flagging. And then, take a look at the terms: world, creation, infinite. All these suggest an endless movement of the mind, a passage to the limit by surpassing all that is given. But Gustave did not discover these terms after the fact in order to designate a process that would have happened without them during the ecstasy; as the process remained virtual, this germ of recurrence had to be sustained and consolidated in each case by a word which was more or less submerged—one or another of the three we have cited—and which, in its materiality as a signpost, substitutes for the impossibility of putting his experience into words. The word infinite, for example, is at the heart of Gustave's poetic project. He never had poetic flights without utterance—whether spoken or seen is of little consequence. But known. And we must admit that the "original" silence is intentionally obtained not by abolishing language but by *passing it by in silence*. These observations do not probe the nature of his first stupors; at five, he did not know, I imagine, the word infinite, certainly not its meaning. No matter; at fifteen, through his drama of silence, he intends to reconstruct his childhood as pride alone has exalted and transformed it. The connections are preserved, big words have penetrated the adolescent's revery; but in the childish ecstasies a cruder language was disguised beneath a vaguer poetry that he refined in secret. By casting a veil everywhere over the works of man, the child produced within himself a nature without human beings. He refused to slip into the mold of sentences, protecting within his own deepest nature an incommunicable essence whose texture is the fabric of the world and which will always escape the adults. This is not at all the suppression of language but making use of it for another purpose. Gustave does not use words to speak; he employs certain of them in solitude without appearing to draw on their suggestive power.

What we must understand here is that Gustave *makes use* of words, yet doesn't speak. Speaking is, in one way or another, an act; the sense occurs to the speaker, linguistic structures are imposed but he can adapt them to his advantage, affirming, denying, presuming to communicate this and suppress that. During his ecstasies, Gustave—who is haunted by speech—does not appropriate the "holophrastic" names and phrases that present themselves. It is not that he refuses to use them—this would still be an act; let us say rather that he abandons himself to the forces of inertia. Note how he speaks about his poetic intuitions after the fact: he *receives* them, he tells us. The "sublime"—in the strictly Kantian sense of the term—attacks him; and what can Gustave do in the face of that aggression? He swoons. A passage from *Mémoires d'un fou* tells us he is "swallowed up." I will cite twenty others further on. These ecstasies, it seems, consist of two moments. First, the moment of *ravishment*. The soul of the young Ganymede is swept up by an eagle, it feels itself borne up to the *sublime height* from which the world—everything—can be seen. But "ravishment" implies "abduction"; Gustave ignores the ascent, he plays only with unforeseen assumptions. For someone perched on a summit who claims to see, at last, the undifferentiated unity of the multiple, this universal substance without detail and without aspect is also nothingness, the passage from being into nonbeing and its equivalent. In this moment, if the soul of the little boy feels bound by an internal connection to this utter abolition of the cosmos, it is insofar as the soul *wants* nothing, *feels* nothing, *desires* nothing. Pushed to the limit, it would have to lose consciousness of itself. After the ravishment, the possession. In *Quidquid volueris* Gustave clearly marks these two moments of ecstasy. In the presence of the sublime (ocean, forest, etc.), "Djalioh's soul expanded . . . he trembled under the weight of an inner voluptuousness . . . and fell into a lethargic melancholy." The second moment is more important; one might say that the first occurs only in preparation for the second, and that the little boy is looking for a way to take his leave, to slip away unnoticed, sheepishly, down the drain. Briefly, the aim is not even quietism, it is stupefaction, the presence of the soul in the body, which is so muddled that it could well be called absence. Still, this surrender—is it out of pride?—can be produced only on the heights. At least this is what he says. Is this altogether true?

The ravishment—"child, I loved what I could see"—is provoked by the *visible* world; his gaze must have run to the horizon; the amplitude and recurrence of the *thing seen* must have evoked place and time for this child so compromised by his family. He invests his gaze with the power to make his escape for him; in fact, the object is not seen for itself, or rather it is apprehended only for the immensity of which it becomes the plastic symbol. And in the beginning, this is only the movement of the gaze touching the sea, astonished to lose itself so easily, encountering no obstacles. Caught unawares by the low resistance of things, Gustave lets himself go in some kind of release of pressure; the slippery evasion that is *suffered*, that happens passively, transforms perceptible qualities into abstract supports for the flight toward the horizon; across the visible world he pursues the most universal structures of experience. Dilation, relaxation, expansion—but suddenly, impoverishment through dispersal. Perception becomes the systematic negation of all real substance in order to attain the void, a category resembling being and nothingness, internal absenteeism and external lack of differentiation. It is this first moment of ecstasy that the adolescent will christen "elevation" or a "ravishment"; that is, he gently falsifies its meaning. Gustave's original feeling—witness *Quidquid volueris*—was that his being expanded its limits horizontally, losing in precision and clarity what it gained in amplitude; other factors, which we shall mention later, intervene and change the horizontal movement into a *vertical translation*. In order to see things as a whole, mustn't they be considered from *above*? This new interpretation is only a substitution of *image*. A crucial substitution, certainly—since it introduces the theme of height and depth, assumption and fall, so important in Gustave's writings—but which does not modify the primary structure of the stupors. If we insist on it, this substitution prevents us from grasping the true nature of the release of pressure and the profound homogeneity of the two moments of ecstasy. Indeed, the assumption and the swoon are in opposition, rising up in order to drop down; later, Gustave will derive a whole mythology from this. But to be expanded and diluted are two processes so close to each other that the second seems to be a consequence of the first and perhaps its aim. A captive, incapable of rebellion, mimics an escape on the spot, and his rancor effaces all the determinations of his being, abolishing in the same gesture all his soul's wounds. The rush toward the infinite, in short, works, as in a dream, an infinite destruction for which the child is careful to thrust responsibility upon the external world; it is the world that has dilated or ravished him and destroys itself under his vacant eyes. Thus the swoon begins at the very first moments of the ecstasy, the dilation is a path toward lethargy, better still the lethargy itself finding a pretext for existing in time. We see that the abduction is only an embellishment. The little boy is not simple. One might say that he unites within him the permanent temptation to disappear and the pride, serious ambition, and jealousy of the Flauberts. The refuge in the infinite, in pantheistic ecstasy, the poetry of silence, the superb vindication of his animality—all this we now understand was added later on, I would imagine from the age of seven. More precisely, from the time the young boy became conscious of his inadequacy, from the time he internalized this *objective* humiliation in order to make it a permanent structure of his subjectivity. He fools himself, and since the stupor is his temptation he valorizes it, he transforms it under the guise of poetry into a noble annihilation, which might be called, to parody Marx's term, the "becoming-world" of Gustave Flaubert.

Is he fooling himself completely? No: this cheap finery rather poorly screens some sort of weariness with living, an immediate and permanent temptation to abandon life. Gustave is convinced that in an extreme instance—under the influence of an unbearable vexation, for example—the swoon might occur without ecstasy or ravishment, in all its naked negativity. Proof of this is that he himself says it, at the age of fifteen, in *La Peste à Florence*: the jealous Garcia witnesses the triumph of François, his older brother; he experiences such chagrin that he falls unconscious in the ballroom and has to be swept out early in the morning like garbage. If someone protests to me that this is a fable and that the author is free to invent what he likes, I shall ask, why this invention rather than another? I recall, indeed, the virulent madness of Garcia's passions—hatred and rage, the scorching coals of envy. Everything seems about to explode and, furthermore, everything does explode—Garcia ends by killing his brother. But the murder is scarcely convincing, and it is Garcia's self-punishing character that interests us most (we shall return to this overdetermined act). In any event, adolescent authors are rare who would not end the ball at the Medicis' palace and the suffering of the young Garcia with some burst of drama. What could he do? He could rip a gown, bloody a beautiful neck with his nails, *as he dreams of doing*. Or else he could insult a general and provoke him to a duel. Not that these acts of violence would flow directly from his passion; quite to the contrary, they would spring full blown from the pen because they are required by the most banal convention, and most authors, young or old, dare not cast aside the conventional. It seems natural that such volcanic feelings be externalized, that hatred be manifest as internal suffering, external aggression. In other terms, the *active* emotions—especially in the case of male characters—are abundantly described in our literature; there is scarcely any place, on the other hand, for passive sorrows, for blue funks, for white rage. They exist, nevertheless, hobbling legs, paralyzing tongues, releasing bowels; pushed to the limit, a person loses his head, falling like a log at the feet of the sworn enemy he would have liked to murder. When Gustave gives his victim Garcia a passive anger that results in the swoon and false death, he avoids convention without even thinking about it, simply because he invents his own truth. At this pitch of hatred, everything must be smashed or burst—he bursts. This manner of leavetaking is one of the two solutions intended to release his inner tension. Why choose this solution and not the other? Because he is defined by it in the very depths of his body and his memory. We are bound to recall Garcia's fainting fit when we see Gustave at twenty do a nosedive in the carriage and collapse under the eyes of his brother Achille in the course of the famous crisis that finally turns him into Gustave Flaubert. Quite often the younger son of the philosopher-physician boasts that he has powers of prophecy, and for good reason as we shall discover. It is impossible not to see that in the inanimate body of Garcia he prefigures the terrible passive violence to which he will subject his own body. Moreover, he will declare that in this crisis he discerns a strict culmination of his past life. That is, we must recognize in this crisis the effect of the offenses he suffered and the behavior which in itself resumes, radicalizes, and makes absolute all previous reactions. By his "nervous attack" Gustave takes a decisive step, finding a refuge in helplessness; but at the same time he establishes the continuity of his life, illuminates the past by the present, *recognizes himself* in Garcia's white rage, in his swoon, in the earliest stupors of the younger Flaubert.

Inertia, laziness, inner torments, lethargies—we encounter these features from one end of his existence to the other. Taken together they define a strategy that we shall meet again later under the name of passive activity, a kind of nervous weakness in the depths of his physical organism that makes surrender *easier*. In the beginning, the stupor is a combination of seemingly disparate conditions: frayed nervous pathways in the body, a vocation for apathy always seeking surrender, malaise, a bitter weariness with living and, in certain instances, the intentional use of these facilities to provoke the absence of the soul, the flight into living death. This surrender in itself implies a weariness that dates back to his first years. Living is *too exhausting* for him; he forces himself to pass from one moment to the next, but behind his desires, his pleasures, there is a permanent vertigo. Imagine a wounded soldier being pursued. He marches beside his comrades, they encourage him—if he hurries, they will escape from the enemy. He does what they tell him to do but he suffers, and above all fatigue, less tolerable hour by hour, extinguishes the desires he shares with his comrades. To join up with the regiment, to outwit fierce pursuers, to be nursed, healed—he wanted all that, but little by little he loses interest; if these incitements are reawakened, it is in the manner of imperatives and through the mediation of others. Cunning, then violent, finally irresistible, desire rises in him to give up, to leave his comrades, to let himself fall, and to lie passively awaiting disaster and death. He will succumb unless he is carried. But in the delicate moment when weariness and the desire for death poison his humble project of survival, when each step he takes, far from marshaling subsequent efforts, *is made to live in him*—"I can't hang on much longer"—as one of the last, this soldier resembles Gustave, *marching* the way the young boy *lives*, with the same repugnance and the same determination, out of obedience rather than the instinct for self-preservation.

One difference, however. If the wounded soldier lies down, if his comrades abandon him, he will die for good, he will reenter the great silence of inanimate matter. Gustave, like insects that become paralyzed when they are threatened, seeks a "false death." One might say that he scents danger or that he feels his wounds and tries to die while living in order to survive his own death, to make it an event that is lived and surpassed in the midst of his own life, and which is absorbed in his memory along with the danger that provoked it. We shall never again lose sight of this "false death"; at all crossroads, on all great occasions, Gustave will repeat this attempt at flight, which is always spontaneous but increasingly costly—he will be ruined by it. We shall observe how the process, without ever achieving lucidity, *gathers meaning* as it goes and becomes the basis for a defensive strategy. But it must be added that the "false death" itself, the momentary loss of the senses, is intended but never entirely achieved. As creator, the adolescent Flaubert allows Garcia to revel in it for several hours. But the character only makes manifest the unsatisfied desires of the author he incarnates. The young boy loses consciousness *within him* for lack of the capacity *in itself* to suspend even for an instant the faculties of the soul. The stupors never achieve the loss of consciousness which is their end and, as such, their justification; proof is that Gustave at fifteen can present them as *poetic* ecstasies. As for the false death at Pont-l'Evêque and the attacks that followed, he often repeated that these were marked by a paralysis of his body which rendered him unable to speak or move—and by the incredible visions of his overcharged consciousness. We shall return at length to the content of the ecstasies and the "attacks."

What is noteworthy for the moment is that from the first, the child—even before his exile from the golden age—bears life like a burden. We do not yet have the means to shed light on the source of his malaise. But it is to this, without doubt, that he is alluding when he writes to Mlle Leroyer de Chantepie: "It is by the sheer force of work that I am able to silence my innate melancholy. But the old nature often reappears, the old nature that no one knows, the deep, always hidden wound." A curious text whose apparent contradiction issues—as always with Gustave—from its richness. Indeed, one would be tempted to oppose the "innate melancholy," an inborn or constitutional aspect of character, to the "deep wound," an injury or trauma which by definition must be an event of his prehistory. But we must take a closer look; one might in fact say that the wound is an injury suffered, hence an accident of his temporality, and at the same time that it has a share a priori in his nontemporal being. And this is just what he means—it is our job to sort things out in order to understand. We shall try our hand at this later. Let us observe for the moment that this "nature"—which is perhaps only a first disguise—turns out to be his malady and at the same time the means, if not to cure it, at least to avoid it by brief, continually repeated escapes. For the deep wound that *they* have inflicted—this vertigo, this disgust with life, this impossibility of undertaking anything, this difficulty denying and affirming which bars his way into the universe of discourse—must be called, I believe, his *passive constitution*. It is this, in fact, that he denounces when he concludes that Djalioh "was the epitome of great moral and physical weakness with the full range of emotional vehemence." He does not even hide the extreme fragility of his fits of violence: it is the lightning, he says, "that burns palaces and is extinguished in a puddle of water." And we must try to find out whether his constitution has not in fact been *given* to him. But when he suffers from it, when he sees his fundamental indisposition as the consequence of a wound inflicted by others, he can momentarily set a limit to his misfortune by *improving upon his passivity*. Such is the origin of the stupors: each of them is an attempt to live to the fullest this ordinance *decreed* by inert materiality. And let us not view these attempts as full-scale undertakings—Gustave the child is not *made* to act; rather, he makes dizzying surrenders to that established nature which he feels in himself as the product *of Others*. Dizzying and spiteful: I escape from you by becoming, to spite you, what you wanted me to be. At five years old, of course, nothing is said, for the child would need to have a self-conscious lucidity that does not belong to this age. And above all, he does not *say* anything, even *to himself*, since he does not speak. Must we therefore conclude that these surrenders are not *experienced*? Certainly not, nor should we conclude that they have no intentional structure. But this will be our task when we approach the progressive synthesis, to establish the nature of a "passive activity." Let it suffice at this point to note that from early childhood Gustave can neither surface comfortably in the medium of human praxis nor let himself sink completely into the unconsciousness of the inanimate world. His domain is *pathos*, the emotions insofar as they are suffered without being assumed, and which ravage him, then vanish, having neither denied or affirmed anything, lacking the power to assert themselves.

Such is the reason—on the level of pure phenomenological description—for his difficulties in speaking and reading. Ordinarily from the time he cracks that ultimate nut, the sound track, a child emerges into the world of discourse. The synthesis of signs, already begun, accomplishes by itself the analysis of the signified. Syllables approach each other, stick together, the child's first faltering efforts produce a totality; from the vague background of the external world a form detaches itself, dispensing the elements that compose it. Since speech can be mute and muteness babbling, since nature and culture are not distinguishable and encounter each other again in the unity of the signifier, the signified, and signification, insofar as we have our origins in our prehistories it is clear that nothing precedes language and that we have passed effortlessly, through our simple, practical affirmation of ourselves, from the spoken soul to the speaking soul.

Gustave's passive constitution long detains him at the stage of the spoken soul; meanings come to him, like tastes and smells, he understands them—but not completely, since he cannot make them his own; what he grasps of them, in any event, is given to him by others. Unable to accomplish the act that is intellection—definite evidence on which to base our certainties—he is reduced to belief. The sentences of others are affirmed *in him* but not *by him*. This is what they call his credulity; indeed, he believes everything, and this is to believe nothing, it is only to believe. His credulity is merged with what he will later call his ''belief in nothing.'' He pronounces sentences, nevertheless, he repeats words or puts them together like flowers in a bouquet—he *is affected* by their vague, lingering sense. As long as no one thinks of giving him a primer, no one perceives that he doesn't speak, rather, that he *is spoken*. But from the moment he must learn to read, language transforms itself before his eyes—he has to decompose, recompose according to the rules, affirm, deny, communicate; what he must be taught is not only the alphabet but the *praxis* for which *nothing* has prepared him. The pathic child approaches *practice* and discovers he is not suited for it. Or, rather, he does not understand what is required of him. Previously, of course, he was docile and obedient. But this was bending himself to the will of the adults— *perinde ac cadaver*. Now he is commanded to act. But the act, even under orders, is sovereignty, that is, it bears in itself an implicit negation of obedience. For Gustave, reading will not only be an operation that the others demand of him without giving him the proper tools; it will be, above all, an exile. Faced with the primer, he feels he will be routed from the gentle, servile world of childhood.

He will learn his letters, certainly—we shall see at what price. Passivity is his lot, but he is a child of man, not an idiot, not even a wild child; like all men, he is a surpassing, a project; he *can* act. Only he has more difficulties than others, and more disgust. And then, he does not recognize himself when his docility forces him to become an *agent*; he loses himself, goes astray in an undertaking that provokes within him the creation of an *I* that is himself and yet is not at all his ego—the ego solicited by the adults but which, by its very function, escapes them. Action is the unknown, it is anguish; everything vanishes beneath him because he *surpasses everything* toward a goal that has been set for him. He will read, he will write, but language will always remain in his eyes a double, suspect creature that talks to itself all alone inside him, filling him with incommunicable impressions, a creature that *makes itself speak*, requiring that Gustave communicate with others when he has literally nothing to communicate. Or, rather, when the very notion and the need for communication are certainly present in him from his prehistory, but are strangers to the extent that the words inside him belong to *others* and cannot designate his own experience. We shall see that starting with this, we can establish the particular meaning of *style* in Flaubert, that is, his future practice in relation to the word. For the moment we have only managed to locate the trouble: the child discovers that he is *passive* in the *active* universe of discourse. Our description stops there; our present task is to review the course of this history and seek in the depths of the first years the reasons for his passivity.

Is his body responsible for it? To tell the truth, it escapes us. We recognize at the outset that we cannot know the vicissitudes of his intrauterine life. If, at least, the medical opinions on the adult Flaubert had come down to us, if some recorded "check-up" could provide us with information on the condition of the fifty-year-old, we might then enlist the aid of contemporary specialists in tracing our way back in time, step by step, to the original propensities of the *soma*. This would be merely conjecture, of course. It would be useful, however, to learn that Gustave at fifty had low blood pressure, that he was found to show traces of very early decalcification, etc. There is nothing of this kind; medical knowledge in 1875 remained rather crude in spite of the enormous progress that had been made. Even if such diagnoses had been preserved, there would be no hope of extracting anything that would be of help to us. His parents took him for weak in the head and said more than enough about that; but the organism? The weariness with living is there, it would never leave him. He will disguise it with much clamor and commotion, but not convincingly; until the end, his contemporaries would remark upon his crushing torpors, the drowsiness that overtook him at midday. No doubt there was a hidden correspondence between the apathy of this great strapping fellow—who appears to dismiss his organic constitution—and his lethargies, which entail intentional structures. But what proves that these biological dispositions, supposing they exist, are primary? These questions, when they are posed as generalities, still have no answers. What will happen if we particularize them? If we examine *one* among the dead—and not the most loquacious—as to the origins of these primary psychosomatic structures?

TRANSITION TO PROGRESSIVE SYNTHESIS

Our difficulty here warns us that regressive analysis has taken us as far as it could, to the phenomenological description of an infantile sensibility. Now the movement must be reversed. Let us proceed backward to the beginnings of this life, to Gustave's birth, and see if we are equipped with sufficient information concerning this prehistory to lure it to the surface; let us proceed, then, with the progressive synthesis that will retrace the genesis of this sensibility. Step by step, from the degree zero of this individual accident until the sixth year.

We are going to encounter on the way, one after the other, the various structures we have just made explicit. This is as it should be, since they will serve us as controlling indicators; if the movement of the synthesis is not derailed, we ought to succeed in reconstructing as the products of a history the stupors, the passivity, the weariness with living that we have discovered and demonstrated to be the structures of a certain life lived at a certain moment in time. But let us not be afraid of repetition—the material is the same, the insights are new; the child's qualities are going to shift from the *structural* to the *historical*.

We must try to understand this scandalous occurrence: an idiot who becomes a genius. We must, if we don't want to brazen it out with nonsense and turn these first stupors into a mark of election. We must do it for another reason as well, which is that we don't *know* anyone we love among the dead of former times. Gide, yes—but that was yesterday. The day before yesterday, there is nothing. The nursing, the digestive and excretory functions of the infant, the earliest efforts at toilet training, the relationship with the mother—about these fundamental givens, nothing. Whoever the great man may be, he declines as an adult, like Gérard de Nerval, to venture beyond a marvelous and tragic childhood, and we do not have a single detail. The mothers accomplished their tasks sleepwalking, diligent, often loving, more from habit than from awareness. They have said nothing. When one tries to reconstruct a life of the last century, one is often tempted to make its fundamental determinants correspond to the first conspicuous facts mentioned by witnesses. I know this only too well, since I committed this error some years ago when I first came in contact with Flaubert. I tried to *comprehend* his "passive activity" in terms of the seamless unity of his family group. And I was not altogether wrong—we shall see how the little boy, inessential mode of the Flaubert substance, is acquiescent in the depths of his being, and that this acquiescence embodies the arrogant self-approbation of the family through the mediation of each individual member. But this explanation comes much too late in his development; the child has already been penetrated by the proud, dour ambition that the medical director communicated earlier to his elder son. Gustave too did his apprenticeship in the family structures; his inertia comes from his acceptance of the Flaubert hierarchy and at the same time his inability to tolerate being on the lowest rung. Envy is already

41

born, resentment can become a paralyzing conflict; as an individual he has no value, while as an embodiment of the social unit, he shares with his neighbors an absolute but common value. This modest observation (which we shall soon explore more fully) suffices for the moment to demonstrate that at this point Gustave's intelligence is in the process of full development. In other words, we are at the end of a long evolution; he is nine or perhaps ten years old, and new factors must be introduced for the process of maturation to continue. So highly developed an affective nature will already be passive or will reject passivity.

Such was my mistake. But I exaggerate it purposely; if things were so clear-cut, the explanation of inertia by acquiescence would be superfluous. We shall see that it is not. For this reason precisely, passivity *does not simply exist*; it must continually create itself or little by little lose its force. The role of new experience is to maintain or destroy it. During all of the early years, passivity is constituted on that deep level where what is *experienced*, the signifier, and the signified are indistinguishable. In the course of the following years, this basic character of the sensibility no doubt curbed the child's general development, though it could not altogether arrest it since it was an integral part of the whole. The consequence is a hiatus, a disparity; the affective inertia rooted in Gustave's memory, as second nature and first habit, is out of phase, falls behind the general development. The child is taught practical behavior, he is—perhaps in spite of himself—active in a hundred different ways, running, playing, talking, listening, and watching all the other six-year-old boys; and this infantile passivity, a habit carried from the cradle, paralyzes his feelings. He *experiences* as pathic what would better be given over, perhaps, to a more masterful emotional state. Once experienced, everything takes on inside him some sort of profound, vaguely inappropriate obscurity; the paralysis indicates his inadequacy. At this more conscious and rational stage of development, paralysis is a poor designation for his *being-in-the-world*, which is not simply an "openness of being"—this would correspond to the passive feelings—but also, for some time now, a certain *practical* way of plunging into things, of conscious self-assertion through the reach of his aspirations. This is not a question of what is acquired but of what is made explicit. No matter; the little boy experiences his history with feelings formed in his prehistory. The displacement prompts him to make a modification—either smash everything or restore it. But this obligation is projected onto a shackled sensibility and can be felt only in terms of fate; the child finds himself at an intersection of fatalities. One might imagine that such interactions, the influence of an educator, of the family circle, of tasks so forcibly imposed that what is experienced, crossed by a current of expressive generosity, would partially destroy the introverted avarice that characterizes the child—who would discover that the fullness of "feeling" demands communication. In a certain way this is everyone's history. But not Gustave's. His family is a well, he is at the bottom; age and education slowly hoist him up—the bucket is raised, but how could the inner surface surrounding it be altered? Intelligence is established, behavior learned, there is always more abundant exploration, ample means for discovering the reality of the family situation but not for modifying it. Moreover, he finds that the family does not modify itself; the social unit is too integrated—a last, gratuitous turn of the screw. The result is that Gustave's "awakening to the world" is only an awakening to the omnipresent and omnivorous family; he will do nothing else in growing up but live out, at different stages, *the same* family constellation. New factors are former influences illuminated, reconsidered, effective through the mediation of an understanding which elaborates and amplifies them. In certain cases one might imagine that the act of making things explicit in this way might provoke a radical transformation of attitudes—this would be the case in a misunderstanding. No misunderstanding among the Flauberts; new determinations are only the old ones consolidated and aggravated, adapted to the ever richer relations being formed between the maturing child and the world around him. Thus *apathy* is first of all the family as it is experienced by a *protected* organism on the most elementary psychosomatic level—the level of breathing, suction, the digestive functions, the sphincter muscles. After the transformations that we shall try to glimpse, Gustave assumes this apathy in order to make it a more developed behavior and to assign it a new function— passive action becomes a tactical, flexible defense against a danger better understood, pure blind *sentience* becomes resentment. We will soon see this, but what is important here is to reject idealism—fundamental attitudes are not *adopted* unless they first exist. What is taken is what is at hand, limiting means; poles can be fashioned into spears, nothing more. Those pointed weapons, whatever one does with them, will remain pieces of wood, and their linear materiality does not depend on their new function but on the distant operations which produced that function and are preserved within it. So with emotional inertia. We have seen that it calls forth a stricter integration of the system as it evolves, but this isn't all; by the simple fact of *being there*, as pure receptivity, the inertia becomes visible, it is transformed into a *means* and suggests to the child how it can be used to advantage. Finally, when the inertia is entirely absorbed by the resulting praxis and is recomposed as the union of endured feeling and passive action, it will still preserve its archaic sense, just as the spear preserves the substance of the pole it once was. Preserved, surpassed, scored with new and complex meanings, this original sense cannot help being modified. But its modification *must be inclusive*, indeed it involves reproducing a new whole out of the internal contradictions of a previous totality and the project that was born of them.

To repeat briefly: I had previously interpreted Gustave's passivity as a product of his internal relationship with the family, and the interpretation is not invalid; between five and nine years old, that is how things happened. But without the reconstruction of the archaic substructure of his sensibility, that interpretation remains a wild, unsupported guess, its limits set from the outside; the very sense of the determination is concealed in the description. I have said that in the earliest years the organic and the voluntary are confused; thus, sense is material substance and material substance is sense. In a way, if every person in the singular contains in himself the structure of the sign, and if the totaled whole of his possibilities and his projects is assigned to him as its meaning, the hard, dark core of this meaning is early childhood. The apathy received, lived, consolidated in the first two years of life sustains the child's *inner* passive activity and all the corresponding outlets for feeling; apathy is at once the substance of the sign, the opacity of the signified (a mysterious bypassing of clarity in the direction of more obscure meanings) and the interior delimitation of the signifier. Restrictive truth and plenitude condensed from memory, the prehistoric past returns to the child like fate; it is the source of permanent impossibilities which subsequent determinations—and, for example, the little boy's sense of being-in-the-family at nine years old—would be inadequate to explain. And the past is also, through an original syncretism, the matrix of the most singular inventions, the inextricable confusion which these illuminate and which makes them better understood. Either we shall find the asphalt core around which meaning is formed in its singularity, or we shall find the underlying origins of Gustave Flaubert, and as a consequence the course of his idiosyncrasy will forever escape us. Without early childhood, it is obvious that the biographer is building on sand—he is constructing his edifice on mist, out of fog. The dialectical understanding can certainly build closer and closer to the last moments of a life; but it begins arbitrarily with the first date mentioned in the records, that is, it is based on the incomprehensible. And that obscurity, surpassed but preserved, remains its permanent limit and internal negation. If the dialectical movement does not find its true point of departure, it will never reach its goal. I can certainly invent highly ingenious conjunctions, no doubt I can anticipate the past that was the future of my great man, yet I understand that I do not understand and, consequently, that I do not understand what I understand.

This ignorance is fairly serious. There are men who have been created more by their histories than by their prehistories, mercilessly crushing within them the child they once were. They are no longer altogether singular, either—we find them at the intersection of the individual and the universal. But Gustave! From the time he begins to write, we have direct experience of the singular. In him at all times, whatever he does, *sense* becomes evident; it is the unity of the non-sense that defers or becomes a rational and practical signification. And hence childhood. Gustave, we know, is haunted by it; childhood is within him, he sees it, touches it continuously, the least of his gestures expresses it. It is therefore present for us as well, we discover it through the movements of his pen; but basically it escapes us, it is a chasm, and we can see only the edges of it. When we open at random a volume of his correspondence, his childhood leaps from the page but we do not *see* it.

The whole question is contained in these few words: Gustave never left childhood behind him. He says it, we know it; the adult is possessed by the miserable monster he was. On the other hand, when we try to amass testimony on his first years, we run up against a conspiracy of silence. First, no one took it into his head to observe youngsters and their mothers; and then, the backward little child didn't do credit to his parents; his entrance into life has thus remained hidden—a family secret. Under these conditions, a choice must be made: to abandon the search or to glean clues from everything, examine documents from another perspective, see them in another light and wrest from them another kind of data. Of the two alternatives, I choose the second. I know the harvest will be meager. If, however, we may learn some of the details or discover the importance of certain facts that we have neglected, we should attempt the progressive synthesis, make conjectures about these six missing years, in short, forge a comprehensive hypothesis which by a continuous movement relates the new facts to the difficulties of the sixth year.

The truth of this reconstruction cannot be proved; its likelihood is not measurable. To be sure, with a bit of luck we shall account for all that we know; but this "all" is so little—almost nothing. Must we take such trouble to achieve, in the final analysis, only this hypothesis riddled with uncertainties and ignorance, without definite probability?

We must. Without a moment's hesitation. I will give my reasons at once, at the risk of coming back to the same thing in conclusion. A life—a life is a childhood with all the stops pulled out, as we know. Therefore our conjectural understanding will be required by all of Flaubert's subsequent conduct; we shall have to introduce the hypothetical reconstruction of the earliest years into all the manifestations of his idiosyncrasies, fill up the voids we have described with those vanished and re-created years, be prepared to restore to this sensibility that shadowy core where the lived body and consciousness merge, that lack of differentiation *felt* as the carnal stuff of passions. Briefly, we shall be required to do this not once but at every step of the way—comprehensive synthesis stops only at death. If our reconstruction is not rigorous, you can be sure it will be instantly ridiculed. Let us go further; required on all sides, given, submitted to the strongest pressures, it must disintegrate or contain some truth. Indeed, let us not forget that from his thirteenth year the cards were on the table; Gustave wrote books and letters, he had permanent witnesses. It is impossible to take liberties with facts so well known, usually reported by several witnesses at a time or with the interpretations of Flaubert himself; on even slight acquaintance, the reality of this life and work imposes itself. Its density and sharpness are continual proof of its *truth*. Attempting to illuminate the life as it was lived by the black light of the first years, however, we shall see whether the gradual experience of the adolescent, of the young man, and of the adult is allergic to our hypothesis, tolerates it, or incorporates it and is thereby changed. Flaubert's adventure, then, as it draws near its end, will be the test of that rediscovered childhood and will determine in retrospect its resemblance to reality. This hope is enough for me—I shall give it a try.

We have established and described the distinctive features of the six-year-old child. These can be reduced to two basic determinations: one is the pathic character of his sensibility, the other is a certain "difficulty with being" which translates as a psychosomatic unease. If these tendencies were formed in the course of his prehistory, they must indicate a problem in the original relationship that binds the

46

child, flesh in the process of blossoming, to the progenitrix, woman making herself flesh in order to nourish, nurture, and caress the flesh of her flesh. Therefore we must trace back along the course of this life to the first moment when a woman makes herself flesh so that flesh can be made man.

I shall review here the generalities. When a mother nurses or cleans an infant, she expresses, like everyone, her integrity of *self*, which naturally sums up her entire life from birth; at the same time she achieves a relationship that is variable according to circumstances and individuals—of which she is the *subject* and which can be called maternal love. I say that it is a relationship and not a feeling; indeed affection, properly speaking, translates itself into actions and is measured by them. But at the same time, by this love and through it, through the very person of the mother—skillful or clumsy, brutal or tender, such as her history has made her—the child is made manifest to himself. That is, he does not discover himself only through his own self-exploration and through his "double-sensations," but he learns his flesh through the pressures, the foreign contacts, the grazings, the bruisings that jostle him, or through a skillful gentleness. He will know his bodily parts, violent, gentle, beaten, constrained, or free through the violence or gentleness of the hands that awaken them. Through his flesh he also knows another flesh, but a bit later. To begin with, he internalizes the maternal rhythms and labors as qualities lived with his own body. What is this exactly? The handled body discovering itself in its passivity through a strange discovery; if, for example, he is abruptly turned on his back, on his stomach, taken too soon from the breast, how will he discover himself? Brutal or brutalized? Will the dissonance, the shocks become the bruised rhythm of his life or quite simply a constant irritability of the flesh, the promise of great future furies, a violent fatality? Nothing is fixed in advance; it is the total situation that is decisive since it is *the whole mother* who is projected in the flesh of her flesh. Her violence is perhaps only clumsiness, perhaps while her hands bruise him she sings continually to the child who cannot yet speak, and perhaps when he can see, he learns his own corporal unity from his mother's smiles; or perhaps, on the contrary, she does what is necessary, neither more nor less, without unclenching her teeth, too absorbed in an unpleasant job. The consequences will be very different in the two cases. But in either, the infant, wrought each day by the care bestowed upon him, is penetrated by his passive "being-there," that is, he internalizes the maternal activity as the passivity which conditions all the drives and inner appetite-rhythms, promptings, and accumulated storms, schemes revealing at once organic constants and inexpressible desires—briefly, his own mother, absorbed into his body's innermost depths, becomes the pathic structure of his affective nature.

That doesn't tell the whole story, however. Margaret Mead has demonstrated how in certain societies the adult's aggressiveness depends upon the way he was fed in the cradle. That can be governed by custom—in one place they gorge, in another they feed grudgingly after letting the child cry. In our bourgeois society feeding is no longer regulated by mores but rationalized by medical prescriptions; in any case it depends upon family groups and individuals. At the age when hunger cannot be distinguished from sexual desire, feeding and hygiene condition the first aggressive modes of behavior, which means that need draws the infant to passive violence and pathic swoons; the child's first negation and first project, aggression represents transcendence in its most basic aspect, the primary relationship with the other and the primitive form of action. Thus we can understand that according to his nature and his intensity—that is, according to maternal behavior—the child subsequently becomes more or less passive with respect to his essential activities, more or less active with respect to the simple unleashing of his passions. Beyond properly organic functions, it is the mother who will dispose the baby to hot or cold fury, to fears that are fleeting or that attack or paralyze; in short, to the predominance of the *pathic* (emotion suffered, internal) or the *practical* (externalized violence, inner turmoil surpassed through an act of aggression).

The role of the body as given, preexisting, is itself variable; the organism under the influence of purely physiological factors can "be open," or "open itself" to passive emotionality; the pathways of nervous input—in combination with the "temperament"—can facilitate or even elicit the passive feelings and states of transport. This rightful priority (without need of sanction) will perhaps allow passivity to impose itself more often in ambiguous cases, when maternal actions are not in themselves of a kind that deprive the child of aggressiveness. Inversely, if the somatic givens are not favorable, the mother could excite *pathic* violence in the child only by specific and radical actions; this means that there are thresholds to cross and doors to force. And occasionally the door resists, the threshold is impassable. Thus in certain cases *organic predispositions* might elicit from the baby an attitude that *maternal behavior*, muddled and contradictory, would have trouble etching into his body. And in other cases maternal behavior might be so severe, its meaning might imprint itself so easily in the flesh that the induced reactions would be—in form and nature—highly *dependent* (these reactions would reexternalize the internalized behavior), if not *in spite* of the physical makeup at least by means of corporal neutrality. There are infinite gradations from one extreme to the other. Ordinary behavior is like gossip; neither the mother nor nature has fixed anything, so a person is only *most frequently inclined* in one direction or, at times, in another; in each behavior one catches a glimpse of the blurred outlines that determine it before a spontaneous reorganization goes beyond them toward new objectives. And without any doubt the combining in a single child of certain somatic predispositions and definite incitements—the internalized behavior of the mother—can be attributed at the outset to chance. But when the human being is at issue, chance itself is a producer of meaning; that is, *in general* existence assumes an artificiality without managing to create it, and in each particular case each individual must seem like a *man of chance* (insignificant)[6] or the result of a *particular chance* (oversignifying). This is what Mallarmé explains to us in *Un coup de dès.* The toss of the dice will never do away with chance, for it is contained in its practical essence; and yet the player acts, he casts his dice in a certain way, he reacts in one fashion or another to the numbers that turn up and afterwards tries to parlay his good or bad fortune. This is to deny chance and, more profoundly, to integrate it into praxis as its indelible mark. Thus the work of art is accident and artifice combined, and the more carefully constructed the more fortuitous it is; Nicolas de Staël killed himself because, among other reasons, he understood this inevitable curse of the artist and could neither refuse nor accept contingency. One solution: to take the original contingency for the final goal of the constructive effort. Few creators are resolved to that.[7] In contrast, the dialectic of accident and necessity is freely manifest without discomfiting anyone in each person's pure existence (that is, in experience surpassing itself as praxis and in praxis as it bathes continually in the life-giving medium of experience). I apprehend myself as a man of chance and at the same time as the son of my works. And soon I make my acts, my possibilities, into my most

6. An insignificant man is as fully signified and signifier as his neighbor, even if his neighbor is the "original" product of an extravagant childhood. All the significations of the human world determine his insignificance, be it by deprivation. He is compelled by his psychosomatic reality to signify *insignificance* through his projects; inversely, others and the world make of him a *signified insignificant*.

7. Flaubert, we shall see, is one of these few. That is the greatness of his work.

immediate truth; soon the truth of my praxis appears to me in the obscurity of the accidents that make me what I must be to live. But in neither of these extreme attitudes are fortune and enterprise separated. We see this in lovers: for them, the object of their love is chance itself; they try to reduce it to their first chance encounter and at the same time claim that this product of an encounter was always theirs. What all of us, we too, seek here is the lucky child, the meeting of a certain body and a certain mother, an incomprehensible relationship since it involves two products united for no reason; and at the same time, this relationship is the primary comprehension, the comprehensible foundation of all comprehension. Indeed, these basic determinations, far from joining or affecting each other externally, are immediately etched into the synthetic field of a living totality; they are inseparable, presenting themselves from the moment they appear as parts of a whole: that is, each one is in the other, at least insofar as the part is an embodiment of the whole.

We have at last traced the course of Gustave's life to its beginning; we shall now examine the first chance event that was surpassed in that life, the fundamental feature of its fate. Yet, as we have seen, the inquiry leads us to the persona of the mother. What the child internalizes in the first two years of his life is the progenetrix as a whole; this does not mean that he will resemble her but that he will be fashioned in his irreducible singularity by what she is. In order to understand the passivity by which Gustave is affected, we now turn back to the personal history of Caroline Flaubert. And not only to that but to the relations she maintained with her husband, with her first son, with her later children who died. It follows, naturally, that we *first* examine the chief features of Achille-Cléophas, of big brother Achille and, since this family is a social unit that expresses in its manner and through its singular history the institutions of the society that produced it, at the same time establish the basic structures of this solidly integrated little group, beginning with the general history it reflects. For it is in this setting woven by the trinity of father–mother–older brother that Gustave is going to emerge, and it is the being-itself of the small group that he must internalize first *through the mother* and the care she gives him. An internalization that is confused, opaque, since Caroline too expresses in her way, through her prehistory, the familial determinations with which she is going to imbue him. In other words, our only possibility of understanding the primary relationship of the infant to the world and to himself is to reconstruct *objectively* the history and the structures of the Flaubert family unit. We are going to attempt a first progressive synthesis, and we shall pass, if possible, from the objective characteristics of this unit, namely its contradictions, to Gustave's original determination— he being nothing more at the start than the internalization of the familial environment in an objective situation that externally conditions *in advance* his conception as *singularity*.[8]

8. Without going into details—we shall come to these as we proceed—it goes without saying that Gustave, even before being conceived, could only be a *younger* child.

The Father

When Gustave came into the world in 1821, Louis XVIII had reigned for six years and the class of great landowners had been largely reconstituted. For the fifteen years of the Restoration it would keep industrial development in check; this, during the first half of the century, remained noticeably slower than that of England. Nevertheless, the bourgeoisie maintained and frequently improved its position. The rival classes achieved an apparent accord and found an entirely provisional equilibrium, thanks to the customhouse politics they were both eager to impose on the government, insuring that certain manufacturers (of iron, textiles, steel) and all agrarian interests would be protected against foreign competition. The rising bourgeoisie and the declining class of landowners could meet only on the ground of compromise, but this compromise was necessary to the bourgeoisie, which was handicapped by its numerical weakness and by the equally meager numbers of the proletariat. In the census of 1826, of a total of 32 million inhabitants we find about 22 million Frenchmen living directly or indirectly off the land.

The area of agreement, therefore, would be protectionism. Indeed, on the one hand the landowners were Malthusians: they wanted to sell their wheat at a high price, and gave no thought to enlarging the market; the old methods of cultivation (fallow land, etc.) were preserved or revived. It was not until 1822 that France saw its first threshing machine. Undoubtedly the former royalist exiles—who had money—made certain arrangements in their domains which could have resulted in increased productivity. But for all that, production did not increase; costs were simply lowered while prices were maintained. The manufacturers, on the other hand, did not complain much

53

about the cost of living; one of them went so far as to write that the worker would work better if bread were more expensive. Manufacturers did not dream any more than "Agrarians" of increasing production. Capitalism remained domestic and cautious; it was satisfied with the old markets, and no one took it into his head to create demand by supply. The use of the machine was to spread very slowly. The manufacturer sought to control his production and satisfy predictable and limited demands. In a sense, craftsmen and workers encouraged this practice; these highly skilled employees feared disqualification and unemployment—and resisted the machine whenever it was introduced. In 1825, in the Seine-Inférieure, cotton weaving was done entirely by hand. As a result, large concentrations of workers were rare. The rural exodus was effectively stemmed, and the petty bourgeoisie, composed of craftsmen, merchants, and shopkeepers, was numerically very important.

The ruling classes, however, agreed only on customhouse politics. On all other fronts a silent but violent struggle ranged the bourgeoisie against the landowners. The latter were champions of an authoritarian monarchy that would be dependent upon the nobility—that is, upon themselves—and would impose Catholicism as the state religion. Semiofficial organizations (the most famous was the Congrégation) became responsible for religious and political propaganda, for espionage and intimidation. The more powerful bourgeois, even if followers of Voltaire, offered no resistance. But of utmost importance to them was the economic freedom they had achieved through the Revolution. Things deteriorated under Charles X, when the ultras spoke of reestablishing the corporations. In that period, indeed, the industrial and commercial class had two well-defined goals: to prevent the intervention of the state and the workers' union, and to control the government insofar as politics chanced to influence the economy. On these basic principles, theorists established that ideology which, while dated, is still virulent today and which we call liberalism. Industrialists, businessmen, aristocratic landowners, the powerful were in accord on one point only: to keep power out of the hands of the other classes. For 10 million taxpayers and 32 million inhabitants, there were 96,000 voters and 18,561 eligible for election. The nation, entirely excluded from public life abroad, plunged in apparent somnolence, deeply scarred by defeat and occupation, seemed frozen in a kind of rural torpor; everywhere traditional attitudes were affirmed, in the face of life or death. While England doubled and tripled its birthrate, the birthrate in France was maintained at around 55 per 10,000 between 1801 and 1841; the rate of mortality was substantially lowered from 1789 (33 percent) to 1815 (26 percent), but it was maintained without much variation during the whole of the Restoration; in 1789 the urban population made up 20 percent of the total population; in 1850, 25 percent.

The so-called "middle" classes, however, deeply resented the defects of the regime; they suffered at once from the high cost of living, the electoral system that kept them out of public affairs, and the competition of big industry. From their ranks the most violent enemies of the legitimate regime were to be recruited, and later the republicans. Lawyers, doctors, generally all those who practiced a "liberal" profession—and were therefore called "les capacités"—could be ranked in the upper levels of the middle classes. Most of them, educated under the Empire, received a scientific and positivist training that set them against the ideology of the ruling class. They were marked by the current of de-christianization that issued from the monied bourgeoisie around 1789; they had nothing to gain from the compromise that masked the fundamental opposition between the upper classes, which were, moreover, in collusion precisely to deprive them of any access to power. In the beginning, however, they put up little resistance to the masters whose servants and accomplices they were. First of all, they lived off the income of the landowners and the profit of the bourgeoisie; furthermore—and even more important—the "middle class," whose numerical growth was so recent, was caught in its own internal contradictions. The example of Achille-Cléophas, Flaubert's father, is sufficiently convincing.

This "eminent" man was not really a member of the electorate and certainly not eligible for office; in other words, the chief surgeon of the Rouen Hospice was a passive citizen. He did not appear, however, deeply to resent the disproportion between his professional merits and his status in the public life of the nation. For he had spent his youth under an authoritarian regime, and he owed everything to Napoleon. To Napoleon, or rather to the war, to the needs of the revolutionary and imperial armies. Under the Empire it was not enough to mobilize those with special skills; the professions had to be upgraded. Achille-Cléophas's parents sweated blood to send him to Paris for his studies. There he performed so brilliantly that the first consul ordered him reimbursed for his expenses, allowing the young man to complete his medical degree.

If we read his *Dissertation on the Manner of Treating Patients Before and After Surgical Operations*, presented and defended at the medical faculty on 27 December 1810, we see that he boldly entered into the dispute that had raged between surgeons and doctors the entire length of the eighteenth century and still persisted. When the long-robed surgeons and the short-robed surgeons—the barbers—were associated in the same guild under the title "licensed master surgeons and barbers," claiming the right to hold both offices, to cut off their patients' legs and "fleece" them too, the physicians took advantage of this to forbid them defense of the thesis, the title of professor, and the use of Latin. The profession fell into profound discredit and was not entirely reinstated by the royal edict of 1743, which restored their rights. It took the wars of the Revolution and the Empire to stem the tide of prejudice. The rise of Achille-Cléophas was therefore twofold: not only did he pass from one class to another, he entered a profession in the full swing of development. If he took part in the dispute, it was with the intention of definitively concluding it; he could assume this freedom since he was both a physician and a surgeon. The introduction to his dissertation indicates well enough the strength of his ambition:

> The surgeon who demonstrates his greatness in the maneuvers of an operation, where he must have a precise knowledge of anatomy, manual dexterity, perceptual acuity and mental power, becomes truly great only when, along with these qualities, which unite those of the physiologist and the doctor, he considers the general disposition of his patient, the particular disposition of his organs, the influence of all things that can be related to his patient, when he looks for and applies, before as well as after the operation, all the means necessary to insure that the outcome is a happy one—only then will he merit the name of surgeon or operating doctor; he combines two areas of knowledge, medicine and surgery, which always go hand in hand and which weaken and falter when they are disunited. . . . His functions extend before, during, and after the operation: in the first instance, he is a physician, in the second a surgeon, in the third he becomes a physician again.

Banal ideas today, but in his time "too often neglected," as he himself says. He recognized that many of his colleagues were unconcerned with such problems: "Surgeons can be said to have unduly neglected the attentions owed to patients before and after an operation. In part, they are liable to the same criticism that was made of Brother Jacques of Beaulieu, who never prepared the individuals he had to cut up and who committed to God alone the responsibility for their recovery after the operation." In other words, not all physicians are surgeons, but all surgeons must be physicians, and when they are, they achieve "true greatness." They know anatomy and physiology, surgical and medical techniques, and to this knowledge they add manual dexterity, perceptual acuity, and mental power. This is the portrait of Achille-Cléophas, provost of anatomy at the Hospice d'Humanité (Hôtel-Dieu) of Rouen. As he was, as he wished to be, pleased to attain a higher rank in which the practice of his profession might allow him to perfect and advance his art.

Until 1815, Achille-Cléophas was deterred from politics and active liberalism by a certain loyalty to the regime that had given him his opportunities. He was not a Bonapartist, however, and the Restoration did not appreciably change his status. But his activities as a surgeon and a man of science had long before alienated him from religion. Had he adopted the materialistic atheism of the eighteenth century? We do not know. What is certain, in any case—as his allusion to Brother Jacques of Beaulieu and other passages in the dissertation indicate—is that he was anticlerical.[1] Under the Restoration he passed for liberal, kept company with republicans, and did not hesitate to

1. We find in this "Dissertation" many characteristic features of Dr. Flaubert:

A. This surgeon claims to be a humanist and supports what has become today a basic principle for all practitioners: "*Nunquam, nisi consentiente plane aegroto, amputationem suscipiat chirurgus.*" But this humanism thinly disguises an authoritarian paternalism: the best way to obtain the patient's consent, Achille-Cléophas advises, is to lie to him. We can savor the following paragraph:

"One often induces the patient to trust himself to the instrument by telling him that only one or two incisions are to be made in order to avoid the operation itself. . . . It is in just this way that I have seen M. Laumonier, in whom the most delicate sensibility is united with the sang-froid of the surgeon, many times convince his patients, promising them that he will cut only into the skin in order to spare them the hernia operation, or the like. Let us never forget to prepare our patients' minds well, and let us remember this precept of Callisen: '*Nunquam, nisi consentiente plane aegroto, amputationem suscipiat chirurgus.*'"

The beginning of this passage has the sole effect, indeed, of annulling Callisen's formula, which passes for its conclusion: it is a matter not of convincing the patient to trust himself fully to the physician but, quite the contrary, of tricking him by convincing him that there will be no operation.

B. The dissertation is strewn—as was the custom—with citations: La Fontaine, Grasset, Delille, etc. It should not be thought that Dr. Flaubert—who in a letter to his son similarly cites Montaigne—was lacking in culture. But these citations were so well known at the time that it is easy to believe the surgeon read very little and must have made do, all his life, with the slim literary baggage he had acquired at the time of his studies.

C. As a good materialist, he does not hesitate to recognize that sexuality is a need. "The seductive attraction of the pleasures of love is as imperious for a man in a state of health as that which incites him to satisfy the needs of hunger and thirst." Here we surely see one of the influences that will prompt Gustave to theorize on "the noble genital organ." It is as the *satisfaction of a need* that the sexual act is repugnant to the younger Flaubert.

criticize the new regime, since he appears to have been the object of an official inquiry; his ideas nevertheless seem not to have been very formidable—the inquiry was abandoned without any fuss. He had, in short, *opinions* but was not politically engaged. For this intellectual was in many ways deeply bound to the landowning class. His father was a rural veterinarian and a keen royalist; Dr. Flaubert had spent his youth among peasants; his brothers, incidentally, had remained veterinarians. He alone had been "distinguished" by his intelligence; or, rather, it was the State that had separated him from his comrades and his peers and raised him abruptly above them. The condition of veterinarian was and would remain to the end his future perfect, that *to be* which had come to him from the depths of the Old Regime and from the familial past, and from which a mutation of society had torn him. Achille-Cléophas, as a result, exercised his profession with dignity but with the firm intention of improving his position by getting rich. In order to do this very thing, he returned to the rural world he came from. In the somnolent France of that time, one invested in real estate; when Dr. Flaubert wanted to "place" his resources—pruned from his increased value as a doctor in the eyes of the bourgeoisie—he quite naturally bought land. So this surgeon with Voltairean sympathies found himself reconciled to the big landowners who ruled France. He had certain interests in common with them; he concerned himself with the revenue from his lands and he too was in the position of supporting a protectionist regime. To the extent that the government protected farm prices, Achille-Cléophas was not at all hostile to the monarchy. Indeed, why should he have been? His attitude toward the Revolution must have been at the very least ambivalent: after all, the revolutionaries had thrown his father into prison; once freed, he had died in 1814 from the effects of his incarceration. And then Achille-Cléophas, a "self-made peasant," had acquired through his marriage a touch of aristocracy. As a physician he had quite properly married the daughter of a physician; but he discovered that his wife's mother was a lady of nobility and that she had had some property near Trouville which her daughter inherited. It was his interest in expanding that property that determined the doctor's investments. Gustave and later Caroline Commanville were careful to draw attention to Mme Flaubert's origins.

It is not at all certain that Achille-Cléophas had planned this "return to the land" all along; indeed, we know that he wanted to establish his career in Paris. Dupuytren, jealous of his disciple, might have sent him off to the provinces "for his health." We know almost nothing of this obscure story, except that the medical director never stopped fuming about it and considered himself exiled to Rouen. It must be noted too that this new city dweller, the grandson of a farmer, had as his best friend a liberal industrialist, Le Poittevin. Be that as it may, whatever his earliest aspirations and his later resentments, this great man from the provinces returned to the land, and the provinces were decisive. He was himself the living contradiction between country and city, habit and progress: as a landholder he cultivated his fields according to the old methods; as a physician he never stopped absorbing—and passing on—new knowledge. Punctual, conscientious, authoritarian, he seems to have preserved the austerity of the peasant mores which were evident even in his dress—the people of Rouen long remembered the goatskin he wore in winter to make his rounds. Although in terms of wealth he was actually inferior to both ruling classes, he may be said to have embodied the latent conflict between the industrialists with whom he liked to keep company and the former royalist emigrés whose lands bordered on his own. Through his own irritability, this passive citizen lived out the major conflict between those two classes. Equally a traitor to both, he rejected the ideology of the landowners but certainly not their ways, and never even thought of investing in industry. Thus—pushing things to the limit— it might be said that the liberal Dr. Flaubert contributed, at least on the economic level, to keeping France in a state of lethargy.

Indeed, the life of Achille-Cléophas is explained by this shift in social position. A royalist veterinarian, more than three-quarters peasant, who views the king as his lord and the source of all *patria potestas*, sternly raises a precocious youngster who passes over to a new social station. The ambitious youth, whose childhood was rooted in rural custom, cares for people while his brothers care only for beasts; he goes from the fields to the big city and becomes, under the Empire, a petty bourgeois intellectual. His rise continues under the Restoration; his learning, the ideology of the eighteenth century, the opinions of the liberal bourgeoisie all converge to give him a "philosophy" which does not entirely reflect either his "means of livelihood" or his "style of life." In particular, his authoritarianism as medical director and father does not mesh with his liberalism.

The child of a patriarchal family and separated from it by his functions, by his new honors, a displaced person, he founds a new family on the model of his original one. It has been observed that as the child takes on increased importance, conjugal families become less prolific; when the father and mother regard the newborn as an irreplaceable person, he himself becomes a Malthusian factor. In this way the individualism of the bourgeois couple prepares each offspring for an individual destiny, a prenatal egotism. But the Flauberts preserved the mores of the Old Regime: they had six children, three of whom died at an early age. There remained Achille, born in 1812, Gustave in 1821, and Caroline in 1825. The paterfamilias—whose function is to treat the human body as an object—still preserves the peasant attitude toward birth and death: nature gives man his children and nature takes them away. Among his bourgeois friends and colleagues, contraceptive practices are beginning to spread; he knows this professionally but remains faithful to the doctrine of laissez-faire. Quite honestly, his attitude would be perfectly justifiable if he were a believer. As an atheist, a physician, a bourgeois, his position seems more traditionalist than rationalist. And then, this authoritarian progenitor seems to be more concerned with providing his own descendants than with creating singular individuals. The Flaubert children will feel themselves to be lawful subjects as *heirs* but inconsequential as individuals. Indeed, there is a patrimony to preserve, to augment, consisting not simply of acquired lands but also of the father's scientific knowledge, his technical merits, and his social function; as a physician himself, he intends to make his sons physicians. First because it seems natural to shape them in his image, and above all because he has considerable influence; if his two boys enter his profession, he will use his credit later to assure their careers. Achille's, in any event, is determined in advance; he will of course have only *his* share of the material inheritance, but from the outset the whole of the scientific and social patrimony is reserved for him; following his father's lead, it is intended that he should become medical director at the Hospice in Rouen.

At this period, therefore, when the liberal bourgeoisie was in complete revolt against reestablishment of the law of primogeniture, Achille-Cléophas, liberal and bourgeois, while entirely in sympathy with the indignations of his friend Le Poittevin, had no hesitation in favoring the elder of the Flaubert sons at the expense of the younger. Why should he have tormented himself? He was absolute master in the family, as his father was in his. Dr. Flaubert had, in fact, only recently become bourgeois. Among the wealthier and, especially, those with old money, the patriarchal family was disintegrating. The mother assumed a new importance: at the end of the eighteenth century, in a family of Grenoble magistrates, Henry Beyle adored his mother and detested Cherubin; for Hugo at the beginning of the nineteenth century, the maternal influence was decisive; later, the life of Baudelaire, Flaubert's contemporary, was ravaged by the bitter passion inspired by Mme Aupick. Achille-Cléophas might have discovered, had he been inclined to do so, a typical conjugal family quite close at hand: Mme Le Poittevin, ornament of the liberal salons, owed to her beauty a very real authority; her son Alfred adored her and, as we shall see, died of that love. But undoubtedly the medical director did not trouble himself with these anomalies; he contrived that his wife remained, while he lived, that "relative being" spoken of by Michelet. Did he reduce her to subservience or did she simply lack personality? In any case, she was party to his rule. She loved him, there is no doubt of that; she wanted to be near the children only as his representative and, as mother and mistress of the house, to exercise only such authority as he lent her. Things went well so long as she refused to intercede with him, even when her children begged her to do it. Intermediary, if you will, but in a unique sense. We shall recognize in these qualities the role of the wife in the patriarchal family so well described by Restif de La Bretonne.

However, the little group of the Flauberts was shot through with contradiction. Patriarchal families, while often seeking to increase their patrimony, are based on repetition: the return of the seasons, the return of tasks and ceremonies; each generation comes to replace the preceding one and begins its life anew. There is little movement from one class to another. Neither tenant farmers nor landowners try to alter their social condition generally; an increase of wealth—gradual and modest at that—makes no difference to them. Further, it can be said that these communities have no history. This is how the surgeon's brothers lived—veterinarians and sons of veterinarians. An accident—intelligence—had thrust Achille-Cléophas into history: he began an adventure instead of repeating the adventure of his predecessors. This abrupt mutation delivered him to the ascendant forces of society. Science did not repeat itself. Nor the bourgeoisie, that class which a continuously accelerated movement was going to carry to power. Man of science and bourgeois, Achille-Cléophas was conscious of an irreversible evolution; his family would fall to the lowest rung unless it made its way up deliberately to the summit of French society.

The paterfamilias was basically—that is, from childhood—a peasant of the Old Regime or, what amounts to the same thing, a member of that rural petty bourgeoisie, poor and few in numbers, related by blood to the farmers they live among, whose mores they preserve. As the slave of intelligence, however, he had solidly incorporated analytic reason and the ideology of liberalism, products which had been slowly elaborated in the cities. He did not have at his command the tools that would allow him to ponder his actual existence, but he was unconsciously torn between permanence and history—history continually erodes permanence, which continually reasserts itself. This contradiction—which he lived out unconsciously—revealed itself to his bourgeois patients and to the students who surrounded him as a feature of his character; they found him authoritarian but accepted his capriciousness and his violent temper for the sake of his competence. "He is like that!" they said. Indeed, what is called character is purely a structural distinction and presents itself as a slight gap between the person's modes of behavior and the objective behavior prescribed for him by his milieu. This gap in its turn does not express nature but history, in particular the complexity of origins and the actual degree of social integration. Achille-Cléophas was not "integrated"—he remained, despite his rapid ascent, what Thibaudet calls a "done-me-wrong"; this is evidenced by the fact that Dupuytren's misdeeds, examined aloud before his wife and children, became a family legend. They provoked those famous fits of anger that sometimes ended privately in tears. Dr. Flaubert's nervous instability and mental tension were the consequences of his maladaptation; despite his success as professor and physician, or rather because of it, he must have struggled endlessly to become integrated in liberal society, reflecting its ideas better than anyone but disconcerted by its mores. Amid firm, calm, comfortable bourgeois, this workhorse with the nerves of a woman seems to have inherited the revolutionary sensibility.

To get to know his thoughts, at least at the beginning of his career, we must go back to his dissertation of 1810.

He clearly shows himself to be a vitalist. Indeed, he often invokes the notion of the vital force which is in constant combat with biochemical forces and neutralizes their action on the living organism:

> [Before the operation] a diminution of the elements becomes useful if the man who must undergo the operation is in pain, if his condition needs a rather large quantity of the vital force so as not to suffer some subtle and fateful change. In this individual, a good deal of food would produce either the feared change in the injured part or the indisposition we would call indigestion. The first mishap would occur if the vital forces were summoned to the stomach to aid digestion, the second if the displacement of these vital properties did not take place. . . .

After the operation:

> Do not cut either the hair or the beard during the first few days. When they are combed or cut, they become the seat of a more active movement of composition or decomposition (Bichot, *Anatomie générale*, vol. 4) which is probably accomplished at the expense of such activity in all the bodily parts and particularly in that which has undergone surgery. . . . Although the hair maintains the warmth of the head, it is not its cooling off that I fear . . . but the displacement of the vital forces and their passage to the head.

As for the rest, he still adheres to the fibrillar theory, since he speaks of the "cellular tissue" (what we would call "conjunctive tissue") in the sense employed by Le Cat in 1765 and Haller in 1769—this has to do with a tissue in the fibers of which are found cells that are only the products of the fibers. Vital forces, fibers—this what was taught at the medical faculty. This body of thought, which was thoroughly peasant in nature, must have pleased Achille-Cléophas; science was not so far removed, then, from his rural childhood. His mentor, cited many times in the dissertation, was Bichot. Did the medical director change his views later on? And to what extent? We don't know. In any event, Gustave never mentions that his father used the microscope—nor was Bichot partial to it. What is certain is that vitalism, already outmoded in this form, did not tally with the *analytic* rationalism which he made—Gustave tells us—the basis of all scientific research and which was, besides, the origin of liberal ideology. Here again we might speak of a gap between a certain aspect of his practice, based on feudal and rural beliefs, and the thought of his new class, which he adopted when he entered it.

Analytic rationalism, a product of the seventeenth century and used as a critical weapon in the eighteenth century by the philosophes, became at the beginning of the Empire in the hands of the "Ideologues"—detested by Napoleon—the intellectual charter of the bourgeoisie. It is at once a principle of method and a metaphysical hypothesis: "Analysis is always necessary, it is theoretically possible in all cases." This means that any whole, in whatever realm of being, can be broken down into simpler elements, and these, in their turn, into other elements, until one hits bedrock, that is, the *indivisible* core elements protected against disintegration less by their unity than by their absolute simplicity. The decomposition of course must be followed by a countertest—the reconstitution of the object under consideration. But, as the chemical analyses of Lavoisier seem to have proved, recomposition is quite simply decomposition reversed; in other words, an experiment is considered to be a reversible series which yields the elements from the whole and restores the whole from the elements. Thus, in most cases the countertest is made in ignorance of the true moment of synthesis, namely its dialectical irreducibility into simple elements. This idea provided the postulates—called principles—of classical mechanism. The ensemble of movements lodges in the frame of a space and time which are homogeneous, therefore analyzable. The indivisible elements to which the displacement of a movable body is reduced are the successive positions taken by objects over time. The *point* corresponds to the moment. Nature can thus be reconstituted from "material points" endowed with a finite number of properties and subject to forces independent of them. Given all the positions and the initial momentum of a system of material points, we can predict its entire evolution. The laws of nature govern the body and systems outside it; they constitute a complete system, which means that they are finite in number and precisely determined. These laws, to be sure—in particular the law of gravity—owe their universality to their elementary simplicity.

It should be noted that this conception, often referred to as *mechanistic* and which has not survived, represented a very real step forward in the area of biochemical research. Metaphysical forces were replaced by calculations, the magic of the concept by the experiment;[2] determinism was introduced, which represented both the first postulation of the unity of knowledge and the first decisive refusal to reduce the links in the chain of being to the necessities of thought. By contrast, on the level of the human sciences the system lost its rigor and its inflexibility; it was imported and applied by analogy, just as today by an inverse anthropomorphism we attempt to apply dialectic, a law of human history, to the movement of nature and particularly to quantum mechanics. In fact, the bourgeois public of the eighteenth century demanded that its philosophers—whether Hume or Condillac—show us, revolving within our own heads, a reduced model of planetary systems conceived after those of Newton—material points or psychic molecules, indivisible elements interconnected by a system of finite laws that remain external to them. These thinkers lodged the constellations in the mind, in the heart. The atom was

2. Condillac was moved to observe that analysis reclaims creation from a system of signs.

sensation, for others the core impression.[3] It was defined from the outside, since one lacked the power to cut it into smaller pieces. The laws of attraction consisted of finding resemblance and contiguity. Contiguity especially was favored by good minds; it permitted subtle gravitational forces to account for the linking of psychic objects whose only common feature was that of bearing no relation to each other. In addition, people wanted to recognize in this Newton's law itself, adapted to the realm of the psyche. Two psychic unities, once present together in the mind, attract each other as a function of perfectly external qualities; if one manages to reappear, the other will attempt to return, and for those acquainted with the whole succession of events, this tendency will sooner or later be strictly measurable. Man was robbed of himself as nature had been; in compensation, it was predicted that the whirlwind of atoms that composed him, governed by a rigid system of laws, might be perfectly calculated in advance if one knew at the outset the positions and momentum involved.

A single troubling problem remained: how this false unity of galaxies, this blockhead conditioned by an absurd memory to reconstitute fortuitous concurrences in the form of cock-and-bull stories, how this *internalized exterior* could comprehend, invent, act? The response of the philosophers varied; in general they came, like Hume, to concede to nature what they refused to man: a certain constancy in the linkages, clean and dry series, fruitful contiguities; in short, they accorded the external world that leavening of interiority which they refused to the internal. As for the virtues, they were broken down; beneath their complexity, analysis discovered basic attitudes. These had to correspond on the primitive level of psychic atoms: the simple principle of pleasure and pain corresponded to sensation. The child—as well as the adult—seeks pleasure and avoids pain. For certain thinkers, we have seen, hedonism was not enough: Bentham proposed a rule to calculate behavior; others—again following Newton, by the law of association—combined these molecules of virtue to produce virtue in its diversity. Pleasure became interest; hedonism lost its aristocratic cynicism and grew stout with the utilitarianism of the bourgeoisie.

Indeed the triumphant bourgeoisie wanted to reduce the old totalitarian organisms of the absolute monarchy to ashes. Their economic liberalism too was based on atomization. But at first there was

3. "All the operations of the soul are one and the same sensation, which is transformed in various ways" (Condillac).

no question of theory; in practice, the bourgeoisie reduced the social body to a molecular state, as witness the way the English bourgeoisie got rid of the last vestiges of feudal charity and transformed the poor into the proletariat. The notion of competitive markets implies in itself, in fact, that collective realities are simply appearances and traditions merely habits. The group is only an abstract rubric under which the innumerable relationships that unite individuals are entered into. The monumental edifice of mechanism is here at its moment of realization: the pivotal point, the basic determination of space and time, the psychic atom, the ethical molecule—all lead us to the indivisible social unit which is none other than the individual. No sooner is he "isolated" by the economist, however, than we see him swept up with his peers into a new whirlwind, for the laws of economics must remain external to us, the rich must sustain their wealth for the poor to be persuaded to accept their poverty. All would be lost, as Marx and Lukács have so aptly put it, if these iron laws, whose perfect cruelty seems to be a fact of nature, were suddenly revealed to be man-made. There is no question about it: the mechanistic view was able to account for the dispersal of atoms and the order imposed on them. Armed with analytic rationalism, the bourgeoisie can do battle on two fronts: through critical analysis it dissolves the privileges and myths of the landed aristocracy; and it breaks down its own class and the working class into individuated atoms with no communication between them. Supply and demand, competitive practice, the laboriously established bending of the particular interest to the general, the principle of the labor market—all these elements would be found *integrated* once more toward the middle of the nineteenth century, when Marx would write that the processes of production form parts of a whole. For the moment, however, the economists' interpretations remain analytic: the buyer and seller come alone to the marketplace, no group exploits them, no prerogative protects them; supply and demand define each one *from without*, and it is also *from without* that the price will finally be settled. But it is therefore clear that I must curb my feelings: I must produce more at the lowest cost, thus contain or reduce salaries; it is in my interest and by all accounts in the interest of my workers; they will earn less but the labor force will be more numerous. And it is naturally in the interest of my country. Through the suppression of the social organs of mediation and through the conquest of *real* property, the bourgeois gentleman fulfills himself—he is a thing, a small solitary atom cut off from all communication. All he can do for others is to lose himself by losing them; to try to help them directly would be vain and blameworthy. The only worthy altruism is an enlightened egotism: I pursue my own interest in conformity with the general laws of the economy. And these external laws are entrusted with producing general well-being on the basis of my particular enrichment.

This was the system; the entire bourgeoisie inhaled and exuded it, they produced it and were suffused by it. The system, continually original and self-renewing, is what the medical director was obliged to internalize. Achille-Cléophas was convinced of the reciprocities of perspective that he took for proofs. In the depths of the human heart he found indivisible impulses, which seemed to him to reflect material points, and these referred him to the atomization of societies or of human intelligence. Let us not reproach him for it; these mirror games are as good as proof for most people. Today we have other systems of reference equally fragile and confirmed in our own eyes by the same swiveling of images. Nothing can be done about it, since ideologies are totalitarian, unless everything is thrown into question— and it was not Dr. Flaubert's business to do this. In a single area, physiology and medicine, at least at the beginning of his career, he refused to find the simple elements which are universally implied by the principle of analysis. Did he ever read *La Génération* by Oken, published in 1805, in which the cellular theory is precisely articulated: "All organisms are born from cells and are formed by cells or vesicles"? How can we know? What is certain is that around 1830–40, the theory of the cell, long suppressed in France under Bichot's influence, saw a new development, and he could not have ignored this in his middle age. Did he perceive that the Newtonian mechanistic view of Buffon, which he surely read in his youth, accorded better with the philosophy of liberalism than the theory of "vital forces"?[4] Certainly he had some ideas, for at the end of his life he dreamed of retiring, leaving his position to his elder son and expressing his experience and his thought in a great treatise on general philosophy.

In brief, he was won over to liberalism rather late—in Rouen, probably. His only error, if it was one, was to be so penetrated by these regulated correspondences that he believed he had discovered them, when they were in fact a product of the ideology alone. He had certainly reflected on our condition; during Gustave's childhood he may have thought about it again. In any event, he had established

---

4. For Buffon, the living organization is constituted by the action of "penetrating and efficacious forces," which are specifications of Newtonian attraction.

convictions which he did not hestiate to express; if not, would he have merited the title "philosopher-practitioner" that Flaubert was pleased to give him? In any case, he was committed to the unity of knowledge; analytic philosophy received lip service, perhaps nothing more.

Nothing illustrates the contradiction between the ideology of the Flaubert family and its semipatriarchal practice better than the morality of its paterfamilias. Portraying his father under the name of Larivière, Gustave informs us that he practiced virtue without believing in it. Some years earlier, speaking this time about his mother, Gustave wrote to Louise Colet that she was "virtuous without believing in virtue." This was evidently an attitude both parents shared. It bears a trademark, that of La Rochefoucauld, reinvented and popularized in the eighteenth century under the influence of English businessmen and the empiricists, their hired thinkers, of Cabanis, finally of Destutt de Tracy and all the "Ideologues" who resurrected the theory to serve the needs of the Empire. We shall return to this. The essential thing for the moment is to note the principle: whatever the act, the sole motive is interest. Depending on the milieu and the period, this gives rise to a kind of skeptical and playful hedonism or to the more lugubrious kind of utilitarianism. The Flauberts had chosen utilitarianism—a serious couple, they did not believe in noble sentiments. How was it, in this case, that they were pricked by virtue? The fact is that they preferred the common interest of the family to their particular interests. Each was devoted to his task. The father was concerned only with caring for the sick and making the fortune of his line; the mother, rigid, cold, raised the children and managed the household. Austere, frugal, and quite frankly miserly, the Flauberts, carried along by the sweep of history, practiced a veritable puritanism of utility. They conceived of their family as a private enterprise, its workers connected by blood; and their goal was to accede by stages, through merit and the accumulation of wealth, to the highest levels of Rouen society. The virtue they practiced and imposed on their children was the strict surrender of the individual to the family group. A collective instrument ruled by mutual constraints, virtue was identified, in reality, with the work of social climbing to the extent that this hard labor was performed by everyone without being made explicit.

In fact, such utilitarian Jansenism represents only one aspect of the Flaubert family—namely, its driving social ambition. Based on analytic reason, it is perfectly adapted to the truly bourgeois—that is, conjugal—families whose individualism it reflects. But when the physician affirms its principles in front of his wife and children, he does it only to set forth the social and psychological atomism of liberalism. Doubtless this allows him to justify his enterprise, but at the same time he exposes it to possible disintegration and transformation into a sum of solitary units, each of which will pursue its own interest. Indeed, the morphology of the small group lags behind its ideology; whatever the physician might think, it is not utilitarianism that grounds the morality of the individuals who compose it. Ambition plays its part, but family cohesion and the surrender of each person to the whole can be understood primarily in terms of the inherited traditions of a feudal and theocratic society in which the paterfamilias is absolute monarch by divine right. Thus the begetting hero imposes on his House his own contradiction. He justifies the self-sacrifice he demands and which can be explained only by faith, by the doctrine of interest. For his children, in fact, the surrender to the family is experienced as a feudal surrender to the father. They will practice virtue out of love, out of respect. Their fundamental goal is to fulfill the orders of the Almighty. This association of atheists therefore has in spite of itself religious underpinnings: it faithfully reflects the image of its founder. Highly structured, it preserves the hierarchy of former times: the men first, the women after them with no power other than what they are given; among the men, the progenitor rules, then comes the elder, who is formed in his image and will succeed him, then the younger son. This family is not "polished," its members seem crude, unmannerly, indifferent to their surroundings—as witness the hideousness of their furnishings. A negative self-respect forever torments them and is quite simply the work with which they exert themselves—taking their bearings, determining their position and the social level they have attained and must surpass. This examination is carried on relentlessly, grimly, day after day: they envy their superiors, share the paternal resentments, spew out recriminations over nothing, dissolve into tears. But at the same time, the entire family cannot help but *live* its slow and sure ascent. Dr. Flaubert bought a house at Yonville the year of Gustave's birth; he acquired lands in 1829, 1831, 1837, 1838, and 1839 which extended the property inherited by his wife. Naturally, the parents deliberated over these investments in front of the children; their life is directed, the little group is not just a sphere fixed in space; in spite of its moorings it seems to its members like a journey, like a vectoral determination in time. But it creates in them an inevitable sense of the collusion of wealth and merit; the social progress of the Flauberts is insured by the worth of their chief, the irreplaceable practitioner. Science pays, it is fair; as the benefactor of humanity, a great man is compensated by the money he is given. Therefore, money is an honor. These notions are not at all in accord with the paternal utilitarianism; no matter, they have their source in his children's admiration for him. Achille and Gustave are identified with their master, and as soon as they find themselves among their fellow students or visit the parents of their friends, they participate in his sacred aura; each of them, representing to the world the founding hero, is judged *as a Flaubert* superior to the most eminent citizens of Rouen. Briefly, the little community integrates the contradiction of Achille-Cléophas—it has entirely surrendered to its historic enterprise; as a permanent substance, it is possessed by the wholly aristocratic pride of being a House. Among the children, the contradiction is temporarily veiled: to conquer Normandy is to, be forced to recognize a merit that exists but is not yet imperative. The Flauberts are *awaited* at the summit of the social scale—any delay is an injustice. When they finally get to the top, they will have *become*, in spite of malicious persons and their intrigues, what they were all along.

In any event, this organic and quasi-religious relationship of the children with their idol was experienced, through the fault of the physician, as a common solitude. Authoritarian and dry, given to outbursts of sentimentality addressed only to himself, irritable, prone to ill humor as a result of his nervous temperament, he curbed the spirits of his sons, at times craving their admiration, at times quite capriciously annoyed by them. How did he view his offspring? Without indulgence, we can be sure. He loved them as heirs to his name and his discipline who would transmit the torch of the Flauberts to their sons. But he certainly judged them very inferior to their father, to the founder Achille-Cléophas. Rather than by physical features or traits of character, he distinguished them by their age, their functions, and their duties. If they should die while he was still vigorus, he would beget others. Since they lived, he had to do them honor: he loved them whenever he could be proud of them. A great man, he could not have been more demanding or more authoritarian; but if he sacrificed his sons to his name, at least he regarded them as his true heirs, surrendered like himself to the good of the family, and like him dispensable. The paterfamilias of the aristocracy does not judge himself today to be superior to the paterfamilias of tomorrow; from one generation to the other the passing on of title and duties creates through time a profound equality that allows, in severity itself, all forms of affection. But Achille-Cléophas, as a gentleman proud of his House, was conditioned besides by bourgeois individualism. His exceptional success, his determined leap from one class to another, the profound feeling that his high merits had not been recognized, all contributed to make him mad with pride. No doubt he thought: My sons will be less worthy than I. They would certainly uphold the family honor, but it would be two or three generations before another genius took the destiny of the family in hand and finally raised it to the heights. The mother surely shared his opinion. Each of the sons was bursting with pride at being a Flaubert, neither of them knew the dignity of being himself.

We shall understand nothing about Gustave if we do not first grasp the fundamental character of his "being-in-class": this semipatriarchal community—with all the contradictions that corrode it—is at once his original truth and the perpetual determination of his fate. Later, rage or despair will impel him to hurl imprecations that seem to presage Gide's famous words: Families, I hate you. But this completely external resemblance must not deceive us; Gide, born half a century later when the structures of the bourgeois family were fully developed, is at once a product and an agent of their dissolution. Flaubert lived within the domestic group and never left it. That belonging was the subsoil on which his whole existence was built. This does not mean that he felt love or even tenderness for his parents; but he was at one with them, and the prefabricated solidarity which was then lived out to the bitter end was the permanent infrastructure of his actual existence. In his early childhood, he was not made, any more than his brother, the object of an exclusive affection. When a child feels that his mother regards his birth as something incomparable, he bases the serene consciousness of his worth on what he takes for his objective reality. For Gustave and Achille, this was not the case: the two little males were loved harshly with a conscientious and austere love that was not particularized. From one end of his life to the other, the younger son regarded himself as an inessential accident; the essential thing for him would always be the family. In his hours of doubt and anguish, in 1857, during the trial, in 1870, in 1875, it was the family that he found in his secret self, like a rock; what sustained this unstable personality, always humble and ready to condemn himself in his role as a singular person, was family pride and his sense of absolute superiority as the son of Flaubert. For this reason, the "hermit of Croisset," this "original," this "loner," this "bear," would never be what Stendhal was from his earliest childhood—an individualist. Yet around the same period, in the schools and lycées of France, bourgeois boys were growing up who were going to become the acknowledged writers of the post-romantic generation; and they were, for the most part, the authentic products of liberal individualism. These were the contemporaries of Gustave Flaubert; he would keep company with them and develop bonds of friendship with many among them. But in the midst of these molecules who asserted the molecular law, the Flaubert son would never feel at ease: he was not one of them. It is as though he were born fifty years before his contemporaries. We shall soon see the importance of this hysteresis and how it conditioned his social fate and even his art. Because of it, Flaubert would be transformed into that strange celebrity, the greatest French novelist of the second half of the nineteenth century. Because of it he was to become, at forty-four, that neurotic whose neurosis, even then, somehow needed the society of the second Empire as the only "secure" milieu in which it could develop.

THREE

The Mother

Caroline Flaubert, daughter of Dr. Fleuriot and of Anne-Charlotte-Justine, née Cambremer de Croixmare, had the saddest of childhoods. Her parents were married on 27 November 1792; people said it was like a novel, some even said they eloped. In any event, they loved each other passionately. On 7 September 1793, the young wife died in childbirth. The infant girl had to be put out to nurse. It happens rather frequently that a widower harbors bitter feelings toward the child that killed his wife; the criminal offspring is quickly filled with guilt. We cannot swear that this was so for poor Caroline; in any event, the doctor did not love her enough to want to go on living himself. *He suffered his grief bodily*, as he was bound to do, lost his health, and died suddenly in 1803. His daughter was ten years old. She seems to have spent most of these years in a deserted house, at Pont-Audemer, in the company of a father who was inconsolable and, like all widowers, gloomy. Double frustration: motherless, she adored her father; inattentive, perhaps morose, at least he was there, he was living near her. When this erratic flame was snuffed out, the little girl was alone. She lost the love of Dr. Fleuriot—who was scarcely extravagant with it—and above all, the joy of loving.

Orphans somehow experience mourning as repudiation: the parents are disgusted, deny them, abandon them. Already convinced she was at fault, did Caroline see her father's precipitous departure as a condemnation? We don't know. We do know, however, that at that moment her future needs were written in her heart: she would marry only her father. Two ladies of Saint-Cyr who ran a boarding school at Honfleur promised to keep her until she was of age, but they, in their turn, died. A cousin and notary, M. Thouret, ventured to send the unhappy, unlovable girl to the home of Dr. Laumonier, chief surgeon at the Hospice de L'Humanité—Mme Laumonier was a Thouret by birth. Caroline was sixteen or seventeen years old. One of Caroline Commanville's reflections sheds light on her grandmother's character: it seems that people had a good time at the Laumoniers'; morals were light. The "eminently serious nature" of the young girl "preserved her from the dangers of such a milieu." This child belonged to no one; she was passed from hand to hand, people would rather die than keep her; the dominant force was guilt. And lack of self-confidence. A rather rich emotional range, capable of violence, but blocked. An unbridgeable distance separated her from others, indifferent or mercenary, quick to trespass. No future, outside of marriage: in the present, no home; in the past, no roots. She is floating, hence her reserve, her extreme timidity, and her coldness too. Caroline Fleuriot, unsettled from birth, has nothing to do with—as Commanville puts it—"light morals"; light, she is only too much so; let someone lighten her more and she would blow away. What she requires is *some ballast*; she tries to put an end to her indefinite sliding by taking on the heaviest freight, virtue. She will be *level-headed* and sometimes rigid; having no anchor to throw down, she will attempt to find an axis—this will be the absolute vertical. The young girl doesn't know much, the ladies of Saint-Cyr taught her nothing; she is hardly more feeling, her icy years have frozen her. Soon now, she will love, and utterly; for the moment, however, her heart doesn't breathe a word. Not that it is dead, on the contrary, but the early frustrations have so conditioned it, she has such rigorous emotional demands, that she will not allow herself to become aware of them until the man has appeared who can satisfy her. While waiting, virtue, good deeds, godly habits help her to get her bearings. And pride. It is born in the guilty, in the oppressed and humiliated, sniffs around itself, seeking by rhetorical triumphs to compensate for the degradation it escapes. Caroline was not degraded in her own eyes, but *empty*; pride was born, not so much to give value to an individual singularity, but rather to stop at any price the sliding of a vague existence between heaven and earth; she had to find an attachment. Caroline imagined that she was nobility on her mother's side and "Chouan"* on her father's. In fact, her father had died too soon to have taken part in the insurrections in the west, and the

* [An insurrectionary force in the Vendée consisting of rebellious peasants led by returned emigrés, suppressed by General Hoche.—Trans.]

Cambremer de Croixmares, men of letters and priests, had never carried the sword. Caroline Commanville nonetheless writes: "Through her mother, my mother was connected to the oldest families in Normandy." And in his correspondence, Gustave often alludes to his aristocratic origins. This was one of the principal Flaubert myths. Who could have introduced it into the family while reeling off her memories to her granddaughter if not Caroline Fleuriot herself? As nobility, she had—in the absence of roots—a *quality*: she participated from afar, through blood, in the stable and certain order of a House. In short, she yielded early on to this abstraction, which provided her with an illusory security; the guilty young girl, dry and empty, minting the sense of her original sin in a superficial swarm of scruples, found an ego for herself only in others, as another. Over there, with the Danyeau d'Annebaults, with the Fouet du Manoirs, her inner emptiness recovered its true being, became a transient determination of the collective plenitude. Timid, frightened, proud and severe, virtuous through *need*, dedicated to this metaphysical being, the nobility recruited from the legal professions, and, in spite of the game of compensations, lost—in herself and in the world. Such was this child of sixteen when she met, in the living room of the Laumoniers, a young lecturer in anatomy, Achille-Cléophas Flaubert. Small, thin, and delicate, she had suffered from hemoptysis some years earlier; all her life she remained nervous, impressionable, hiding her permanent anguish beneath anxieties that were almost maniacal.

The young man and woman had scarcely met when they became engaged. For Caroline it was love at first sight. The brilliant doctor, sent from Paris by the great Dupuytren, authoritarian, virtuous, and hardworking, was nine years her senior; above all, he was an adult—in her eyes at least—a strong, substantial man: her father revived. Thanks to him, the dim, gloomy years of the boarding school, of exile, were cast into oblivion; she renewed the thread broken by Dr. Fleuriot's untimely death and found herself alone again with her father in an empty house; in sum, she turned backward and took up her life again as it had been at the age of ten. Being among the Laumoniers had caused her to lose her way; not so much through moral license, which did not affect her, but through the obvious reciprocity of relationships—no one was in command. In a strict hierarchy she would have found her place, but equality seemed to her disorder in the extreme. Her unhappiness came to her from the miserable failure of a couple; a conjugal family was constituted, had made her, and then everything had aborted—she remained alone, an absurd orphan. Against the fragility of an egalitarian love, broken so swiftly by death, she dreamed of a strict, noble order in which she would find her goal and the meaning of her life. Chance, for once, was on her side—she could not have done better than Achille-Cléophas. Newly bourgeois, he had one principle—drawn, as we have seen, from his peasant origins and his imperious pride: the husband is the sole master of the house. From his future wife he demanded that she wholeheartedly assume obedience, a relative existence: a wife is an eternal minor, a daughter to her husband. She agreed. They were two accomplices, as the curious episode of their engagement indicates. He saw her, judged her; the austerity of this adolescent girl was enhanced by the levity of her surroundings. The fiancé at once appropriated the rights of the deceased father, taking it upon himself to send her back to boarding school and allowing her to leave only on the eve of their marriage. One suspects that the Laumoniers gave their tacit consent; moralistic virgin that she was, Caroline must have embarrassed them. For her, in any event, this act of force had made her feel physically possessed for the first time—she felt she had a master and experienced that intoxicating certainty as sexual knowledge. The transference was complete; in her almost monastic cell, she waited patiently and submissively for the hour to sound when at last she would sleep with her father. Later, aged and widowed, she would evoke this strict measure in a complacently foolish manner. When Caroline Commanville wrote, in this connection, that Achille-Cléophas was "more discerning than she could be," one can hear the voice of her grandmother: "My future husband, more discerning than I could be . . . " Meaning: there was more to it than meets the eye, relations I didn't suspect, a threatening scandal; in my naïveté I surmised nothing, but my fiancé saw it all; at first I protested at the decision he wanted to make, I sulked, and then I deliciously recognized my wrongs; as always, he was right.

They were married in February 1812, and moved to 8, rue du Petit-Salut; they must have stayed there seven years. Mme Commanville writes: "During my childhood, my grandmother often made me pass by [in front of the house] and, looking at the windows, she would say to me in a serious, almost religious voice: 'Look, there I spent the best years of my life.'"

For us, this testimony is of primary importance. Seven years of happiness. Afterward, the unhappiness did not begin right away; for a while things were suspended, but the situation was increasingly menaced; moreover, her heart was no longer in it. What are the events that marked the life of the couple between 1812 and 1819? Well, first, one year less one day after the wedding, Achille was born. There is no doubt that he was well fed and cared for. The young mother loved this token of love. And then, Achille-Cléophas, by giving the child his own first name, had signaled to his intimates that he held this firstborn—there would be others—to be his successor, the future head of the family: here is my son, namely myself, today my reflection, tomorrow my reincarnation. The mother was informed of that predilection and shared it; she loved in her child the tender, vulnerable childhood of her husband, a childhood long thought dead, at last revived. As the object of such doting attentions, Achille was a child made to order: healthy, docile, bright. The mother took pleasure, later, in teaching him to read. However, the progenitor got his wife pregnant twice more—she gave him two boys. Two made to no purpose—they died at an early age. And this is what astonishes me: a single infant death is in general enough to plunge parents into grief; the Flauberts experienced two such deaths, one after the other— enough to ravage them and make them remember their first home with horror. Yet the aged Mme Flaubert, thirty years later, delights in returning nostaligically to rue du Petit-Salut, stopping in front of her former house and constantly recalling the happiness she knew there. If we cut her domestic life in two, as she invites us to do, it is noteworthy that *before* moving to the Hôtel-Dieu she had three sons, one of whom lived; *after* the move the proportion is reversed, and of the three children she bore, only one died. However, she herself tells us that in spite of these painful failures she tasted true happiness in the seven years she lived in rue du Petit-Salut.

How can this be? One point seems to me indisputable: the dead could not make the first seven years abhorrent to her, nor could the living bind her to the years that followed; so it cannot have been her offspring that made the significant difference. Happiness and unhappiness for Caroline Flaubert depended on a single person, Achille-Cléophas. Gustave himself testified to this in a letter to Louise: "She loved my father as much as a woman could ever love a man, and not only when they were young but until the final day, after a union of thirty-five years." To put it in context, these glowing words appear no more gratuitous than was Gustave's wont, and he seems to be offering his mother as an example to Louise: you are jealous, my mother was not, she loved my father a thousand times more than you love me. Here you are, an example to follow—love me and keep quiet. And then, little as we might have encountered it, we will

recognize a certain frenzy intended especially to convince others—
the tone of voice rises, hyperbole takes over to compensate for the
affective weakness of the statement. Perhaps he exaggerates his
mother's feelings. But happily we have this other proof, for which
admittedly he is the source but which does not seem to be a lie: Mme
Flaubert, a deist, had kept her faith while married to the nonbelieving
physician. There had to be a heaven for the mother she had killed,
for J.-B. Fleuriot, dead prematurely, and for the little angels God had
sent down to earth and regularly recalled before their time, by His
will. And then, a little love too for soothing the anguish of the guilty,
for brightening the thankless virtues she upheld out of fear. She was
one of those women who say, "I have my own religion," or "I have
my Good Lord," and who limit themselves to a somewhat cannibal-
ized Catholicism, taking its comforts, its incense, its stained glass
windows, its organ, and leaving its doctrines. Caroline's deism, her
"super" superego, was a recourse to God against the father; and
surely too it was the poetry of a blighted sensibility: harmonies, meditations, contemplations, exaltations. Lamartine was pleasing because
he represented the fragmentary but beautiful thoughts that crossed
one's mind during the mass. The fact is that one went and received
the sacraments—were it only for the worthy clientele and through
fear of the Congrégation.

We can be sure that Dr. Flaubert made no attempt to enlighten his
wife; she would have quickly abandoned her opinions had he shown
the slightest desire for her to do so. She kept them through marital
tolerance but without making them explicit, everything remained
poetic and vague; in fact, after the complete success of the transference, she scarcely had need of her "super" superego. And I imagine,
rather uncomfortably, that she might have appealed to her God with
a sentence borrowed from Achille-Cléophas. Never mind, she disposed her children, Gustave in any case, to receive vague intuitions,
appeals from on high. The medical director let her do it: religion is
necessary in the nursery and in the gynoecium, it is the best way to
keep women infantile. He took his sons in hand around the age of
five or six and with one breath scattered to the wind the fine maternal
dust that had gathered on their frontal lobes.

Yet, after seeing her husband and her daughter die, one after the
other, Mme Flaubert abruptly lost faith—a faith that had not been
shaken by the death of three children, offspring given and taken quite
absurdly. No doubt it was a terrible shock—not sufficient, however,
for her to commit the sin of despair. It is on the occasion of bereave-

ment that the nonbeliever is most often converted: he needs consolation and the assurance that life is not simply an idiot's tale; most
important, he needs to feel again. The first time her father abandoned
her, Caroline was ten years old, and like everyone else she consolidated her religion. The second time, she was more than fifty: this
would have been the moment to fall into the hands of priests. Nothing
of the sort. The widow reacted in a very unusual way—she broke
with God. Shall we say that she was pushed to it chiefly by the loss
of her daughter? Certainly the two bereavements are inseparable. But
it is the first that illuminates the second with its black light. The chief
surgeon, when he died, had reached his sixties—today this would be
considered quite a good age; at the time, people regarded such long
lives as the exceptional favors of Providence. At first sight, God seems
beyond reproach. He extended his benevolence so far as not to take
the father before the eldest son was of age to replace him. Still, the
aging wife of an old husband did not resign herself; after thirty-five
years of life together, the disappearance of Achille-Cléophas was in
her eyes as intolerable a scandal as that of his young bride Cambremer
de Croixmare must have been for the young Dr. Fleuriot. Such a
revolting injustice puts the universe in question: evil is all-powerful,
God does not exist. Gustave is right, she loved as on the first day.
For this relative creature, the chief surgeon surely represented the
unique source of her happiness. But that is only part of the truth; he
justified her, relieved her of guilt, legitimized her existence, he gave
her a reason for being—he was goodness itself. If the good dies,
nothing is left in heaven or on earth; she recovered the wanderings
of her youth, but without hope. All her life came back to her in
memory along with all her bereavements; she angrily dismissed the
Almighty—a settling of accounts. And then, above all, she converted
to atheism the way others convert to revealed religions, out of loyalty
to the dead; to possess him wholly, to *be* him. She accepted never
seeing him again on the condition that she could carry him in her
belly like a new infant, by assuming as her own the hard, imperious
doctrines that had contributed so substantially to her husband's glory.
While living, Dr. Flaubert's atheism guaranteed Caroline's religiosity;
in some obscure way, she regarded this nondogmatic faith as a minor
magic, suited to her sex; her man was atheist for two. Once he was
dead, she represented Achille-Cléophas; she spit out the Lamartinian
bonbons and took up the healthy cause of despair. This is what strikes
me: God had to be kept, or the chance of once more finding the soul
of the dear departed would have to be permanently renounced; she

banished the Almighty imposter and at the same time wittingly killed her husband forever—no soul, only white bones in the corrosive earth. That is, she preferred fidelity to hope: the physician-philosopher, in the name of his own principles, had to crumble into dust. She knew the consequences of the doctrine and nevertheless adopted it; to find him once more in heaven, that was good, but to represent him on earth in her own heart and for herself alone—she no longer visited with anyone—was better. Can we call it identification, reincarnation? No, but we can call it steadfastness; she would slip toward death as Achille-Cléophas had done, knowing that the ultimate wreckage is total, wishing she could rejoin her husband with every beat of her heart and *in this life* rather than *in the next*. All this was done without much deliberation; rather, there was no argument at all. She did what she had to do, she became herself by increasingly resembling her husband, a little more each day. Desiccated, empty, troubled with an infinite sorrow recited day after day, she engaged in killing herself with the Falubert utilitarianism: the family has to be served, and as long as it still exists, one does not surrender to death.

That is what I call love; it is a different kind of love, there is none stronger. Everything is here—the father dominated and guided her; stability, virtue, and sex all found their due. She had everything: the good had taken her and put her in his bed, she had borne this crushing angel, she was overcome; during the day, the paternal severity of the doctor troubled her, promising new ecstasies; docile and malleable, her obedience seemed to be the voluptuous extension of her nighttime submission.

I have said that the Rouen branch of the Flauberts was constituted as a semipatriarchal family. Achille-Cléophas established the family unit himself, he formed it—as we have seen—*like himself*, as he had been formed and looked forward to being. But he was not the only one responsible: his wife had been chosen with discernment and suited him to perfection; she took all the household tasks under her direction. Not that she held with this or that structure of the "social unit" or rejected another—she was quite unconcerned with such things. What mattered to her was the couple. And it was an exceedingly incestuous one. She confirmed her husband in his powers as paterfamilias in order to feel in her heart and her body that her father was her only lover. Her whole existence from marriage until death was marked, directed, penetrated—to the core of this patriarchy—by conjugal love. She became the accomplice of the all-powerful progenitor in order to defend the unity of this couple against the whole world—the couple from which she derived her sensual pleasure, her happiness, her place in the world, and her being.

As for the children, of course she loved them; through them she loved the father. She loved *in them* the fecundity of the father. Something else too; no doubt the little orphaned girl had often dreamed, in the only way she could, of retrieving her lost family. She wished for marriage, to be a mother in her turn and to make her mother live again through her own experience of childbearing. It was a relationship only with the self—the children, provided they were healthy, had the sole function for her of putting her in possession of her maternal capacity. Even in her most concrete dreams, they had to remain indeterminate. The most brilliant images of her fantasies were those that showed her in her new role: nursing, caring for, and raising a bunch of children. Or rather, what I've just said must apply only to boys. She would have them as long as God gave them to her; girls were a different matter: she *wanted one*. A deprived childhood—it is now known, thanks to the analysts—repeats itself with another child. Caroline, giving birth to a girl, was her own childbearing mother. The love and care she thought to lavish on her daughter were what had been lost by Mme Fleuriot's precipitous death. In short, another Caroline was awaited; if the former orphan who had recovered an incestuous father could succeed in creating an ameliorated version of her own childhood with a child of her sex, if, anticipating all the desires of this flesh of her flesh, she could in retrospect efface this early disappointment, smooth the talons of still rending memories, Mme Flaubert would have come full circle. Enjoying an eternal childhood under the paternal authority of her husband, she would root out her own real childhood, tear it from her memory by making a happy childhood for another. As proof of this deep desire, she gave her own name to the daughter that the medical director finally gave her after thirteen years. Nor is it an accident that the daughter of this daughter, in her turn, received the same given name: the most important thing, in fact, was to preserve the memory of the young mother who died giving birth to her, as Mme Fleuriot had done at the end of the preceding century. No matter; what a strange dynasty of Carolines whose first and last members murdered their mothers. The progenitor had made the royal gesture to his firstborn: "That's *me*; what proves it is that I call him Achille." His wife's intentions, thirteen years later, were little different, and no doubt she was inspired by her master: "That's me, me redeeming my own childhood, attended by a mother who lives to love me." Because of this, Gustave's sister was surely the favorite; in a way she represented the sole personal relationship that the wife of the medical director maintained with herself, the sole subjective intimacy to which the incestuous father had no access. In the very act of nursing her daughter, however regulated by objective considerations, she unconsciously created a world that he could not even imagine: *she gave herself the breast* in order to obliterate from the present the indestructible frustrations of the past; she made love to herself so that she could at least *give* the tenderness that she had not received.

She waited thirteen years for the opportunity, which came too late. Thirteen years, in the course of which Achille-Cléophas gave her five boys. The first she welcomed with pleasure—they had to ensure the perpetuation of the name; besides, the wife's wishes come after the master's, and furthermore the eldest should not be of the weaker sex. But from her second pregnancy she began to wait. There were four disappointments—Gustave was the third. In my opinion this explains her strange indifference to the first two deaths. God gave her these sons, she accepted them out of love for her husband, out of duty— the family must increase and multiply. But when God took them away, the mother's eyes were dry: if He took them back it was because they had been delivered to the Flauberts by mistake; you had to begin again, that's all, and try to do better; she was allowed to hope that the next one would be a girl. All the same, I suppose she was affected. The infants were dying in her hands, in spite of her capable and vigilant care; it was her mission to make them live, to protect them, and she fulfilled her duties admirably, alert and conscientious, never sparing herself. Completely innocent as she was, the deceased became her personal failures; murderer of her mother, the relationship with death seems to have been her fundamental bond with the world and with the Other, the origin of her guilt. It is a safe bet that she regarded each of these precipitous disappearances as a repetition of her original sin and at the same time the effect of some maternal curse.

Dr. Flaubert, happily for her, was immune to such subtleties. Naturally he preferred males, and above all, whatever the sex, he wanted viable progeny; but for years his worries remained benign; the eldest was doing well—that was the main thing. As for the other children, they were equivalent: each one represented the family, none could be the privileged incarnation. In short, he had scarcely any attachment to the newborn children. Moreover, at the beginning of the last century, parents were advised not to love their infants too much, seeing that they died like flies. The first two deaths certainly seemed regrettable but not exceptional; they were to be expected. Achille-Cléophas saw in the child barely thrust into the world a calculated probability for survival. These unique, unfortunate ventures took a bad turn under his very eyes and fizzled out, yet he saw them as nothing more than physiological accidents. Many children are needed to perpetuate a family, he thought, and many dead to make one living; the conclusion is obvious: a physician, if he is a philosopher in the bargain, must expect infant mortality and bear it with a firm spirit when it ravages his own family. Again, the individual is the inessential and transient form, the domestic community is the substance that produces the forms and reabsorbs them into itself. No doubt this rather brusque wisdom was best for Caroline. He probably explained to her that she was bringing into the world what I will call, since I know no other word that has the same meaning, "morituri."[1]

Sorrow, indifference—two burials, and then Gustave, the third son. The mother was not out of mourning, or not long. But we know that she was in a somber mood, and why: she could accept only a mournful happiness. Black justified everything for her, even sensual pleasure; an orphan, the mother of dead children, then a widow, she wore black her whole life, or nearly. These observations explain for us how she could speak of the first seven years "in a serious, almost religious voice." Submission, respect, austerity, devotion to the head of the family, and through him to the future family, nightly pleasures, the play of love and death; she needed this, nothing more. A brilliant life, liberal and expansive, would have reminded her of the Laumoniers' salon; in anguish and frigidity she would have refused such a life. Her sons, whether they were on earth or below, would always remain strangers to her: the paternal authority slipped between the wife and her children. Boys belong to their father, this is the rule, from the time they are ready to leave the nursery. Achille, since he was his own father in swaddling clothes, charmed her. The father claimed him after a while; she continued to care for him, she was the one who taught him his letters, but the little prodigy, the medical director's chosen one, escaped her. For her, he was reduced to the masculine fate his father had arranged for him, and became a stranger. This is what explains the near break between mother and son after the death of the progenitor. She bore a grudge against her daughter-in-law, of course, and then Achille was scarcely agreeable; but these

---

1. Like Goethe, who, when told of his son's death, calmly declared: "I knew I had fathered a mortal."

factors would have counted for nothing had she experienced the violent and mutual love for her eldest son that Mme Le Poittevin felt for Alfred. Twenty years later, misunderstandings and poor conduct can certainly corrupt such deep feeling, infect it with bitterness, and occasionally change it to abhorrence, but it will have left its mark and will sometimes be revived by a memory in all its naïveté, all its archaic power. Mme Flaubert did not love the chief surgeon Achille—a fact that Gustave intentionally insinuates in his correspondence. But this subtle, blameworthy indifference without animosity would not even be conceivable if she had loved him in the beginning. When he was a baby, she loved his father in him; when he became Achille, he no longer interested her. For neither of her sons did she feel possessive or jealous affection. She recognized that her rights over them first had to be granted by the father. She took no initiative, nor did she give them any order in her own name. The sovereign will of the husband made her the bearer of the *patria potestas*, she was the recipient of power, her authority only borrowed. This is what the medical director demanded of his wife. But far from obeying him out of habit and education or simply following certain mores, she delighted in submission, all the more authoritarian with her children the more submissive she was to the master. She did not convey their complaints to him—to dispute an order or raise her sons' objections would have been signs of *her own disrespect*. A *no*, whatever its origin, could not be pronounced before the master; in any case, it was blasphemy. The rest is obvious: unlike so many other mothers, she never took the part of her children against her husband; she was never tempted to defend them, because she was convinced that he was always right. She loved him too much and too loyally to try to manipulate him; and I contend that her greatest virtue was in not "knowing how to prevail upon" her husband. But this is a *patriarchal* virtue, to achieve and preserve which she refused all ruses—more or less dubious, more or less successful—that unite son and mother in conjugal families. Pushing virtue to the extreme, namely to the point of vice, she never *interceded* for her children. Achille-Cléophas was more formidable but more flexible, more capricious but more adaptable when he exercised his authority himself, more rigid and bureaucratic when his wife served as intermediary; until his death, the authority of the paterfamilias was wielded with absolute sovereignty over the two boys without the mother's ever tempering it with tenderness. How could she have done otherwise? She loved them, there is no doubt, but not tenderly, keeping her heart for the new Caroline who would be her new beginning. And if someone asks, what is love without tenderness, I will say that it is absolute devotion and collective valorization—I have no doubt that she would have ruined her own health to save her ailing sons or given her life for the life of either of them; this, in any event, is what she firmly believed. She declared, however, that she did not know anything about sacrifice; duty, nothing more. We must believe her in order truly to understand her. What did she want? First, to condemn certain women friends whose shrill maternal generosity— always breathless, always tearful, supported by their "sense of duty"—had no other end than the achievement of their own rights, and when these were not recognized, they were consumed by resentment. She, Caroline, had never *taken anything on herself*; she acted out of pleasure or to defend the interests of the family. The only *worthy* actions have their source in spontaneity. It is a good thing for a child that his mother doesn't pretend to sacrifice herself for him when she cleans him up; the *positive* aspect here is the interest Mme Flaubert had in the routine and concrete business of mothering. At least she spared the two boys the painful feeling that she approached them only by overcoming her disgust. But we shall follow her no further. In this utilitarian age it is true she lacked the theory of virtue; but if despite this deficiency she, like her husband, was virtuous, it was not—contrary to what Gustave says—through disposition but through *need*. It was in the accomplishment of prescribed tasks that she found her equilibrium and her earthly weight; nursing, caring for, spending the nights watching over an infant, she *took her bearings*—no drift, position fixed at two hundred fathoms from the earth. Only we must see clearly that she loved these familiar tasks for themselves and the accoutrements—diapers, swaddling clothes, the cradle—rather than the child. For this anxious girl, from the time of her first confinement there was a complete reversal of means and ends: the newborn was only the *object* of her attentions, the indispensable means for becoming the best of mothers; *generally* cared for, his singularity went unperceived, he was only required to live. The accoutrements of motherhood absorbed the love and did not give it back.

This generality was retrieved in the act of valorization: she held a plump baby in her arms, admiring in him the life source that had fathered him—the sperm of the progenitor become flesh. But whatever the child, the seed was the same, and in the first months of life the babies seemed interchangeable. In each one she also respected the intimately meshed families of the Flauberts and the Cambremer de Croixmares—which, all told, was only a socialization of her difficulty. But during early infancy, none of the children could be a privileged incarnation. We must come back to this: she loved in her sons the eternal recurrence—that is, the cyclical time of virtue—the paternal power and the House of Flaubert. Not any singular quality. In bourgeois families today the most adoring mother loves her son, in part, against her husband; this will be her revenge. When the child is scarcely born, she is eager to adore the individual qualities of this future progenitor; an adventure begins for both of them, unique and unpredictable and, for this very reason, lovable. Caroline, in 1830, had no reproach to level against the physician-philosopher; not that he was beyond reproach, but she had decided even before her marriage to accept as good anything he might do. This wife lacked the shadow of revolt that would have made her a mother.

More a wife than a mother—does that epithet fit Mme Flaubert? Not without qualifications. If it means that she made love more willingly than she made children, it would be a mistaken view, since to take pleasure in love she had to feel, clearly, that it was the sole means of producing children. She enjoyed love through maternal virtue. It might more aptly be said that, more than a mother, she was an incestuous daughter. There was nothing between her and her sons; the bonds that seemed to unite them were of course borrowed, joining the little Flauberts to their father. Communications with the mother were broken. Actually she was the sister hidden from her sons; they were entrusted to her care, as an older sister she was responsible for them before the paterfamilias, she loved them in him as Christians love each other in God. But the only direct relationship the children had with Caroline was *living* with her, by which I mean not only coexistence in the same place but belonging to the same House.

This is why the conjugal happiness of Mme Flaubert did not truly suffer from the first bereavements. Yet we know that it diminished perceptibly when she moved from the house in rue du Petit-Salut. What happened? We don't know the details, but the general conditions are clear. One condition was primary and at the source of all others: Caroline was put together in such a way that neither joys nor sorrows could touch her that did not issue directly from Achille-Cléophas. In other words, it was in her incestuous feelings that she was hurt. Seven years is a long time; snakes change their skin, many men change women every seven years. I am not saying that Achille-Cléophas changed women or even that he cheated, but simply that love, in the rigorous life of the medical director, had only a secondary place. Caroline, on the contrary, *lived for* love, it was an immutable force, her support and her sustenance; still more, it was the sacred sphere of recurrence. The continual, obstinate work of breeding and childrearing, which she did with only mediocre success as we know, became through love a poetic, religious task. She desired nothing, not even an intensification of feeling—she would not have thought this possible or it would have alarmed her. Simply this: continuity, the recurrence of all things, each year recalling other years, repeating the same promises, guaranteeing that the future is only a future remembrance, that nothing changes. Altogether, this is the stuff of happiness: first, one must be a vassal, then the order of states of submission and seignorial generosity must be fixed once and for all; everyone is given a place and keeps to it. With reciprocity, happiness disappears—good riddance. I do not claim that Caroline was immediately sensitive to the least alteration of her master's mood or feeling. But we can be sure that when the young wife did perceive it, she suffered or was at least disturbed; little as Achille-Cléophas may have changed, she discovered in some obscure way that her man's personal law was always to go on and never to come back, that her conjugal happiness was fundamentally endangered by the very person who secured it. For the first seven years, premonitions of this sort were not lacking, but they crossed her life, her consciousness, like shooting stars and were quickly forgotten. The physician-philosopher, however, in no way resembled those somewhat worn workhorses who until death mount their wives because they are *their* property and ought to give them pleasure, people who are deceiving and reassuring at the same time, who hardly change but give nothing. An anecdote reported by Gustave shows his father in a singular light. He must have adored women and charmed them, courteous as a prince with a mug like a peasant, and never doing anything to spare his wife the pangs of jealousy:

> I remember that ten years ago we were in Le Havre. My father learned that a woman he had known in his youth, at seventeen, was living there with her son. He thought of going to see her again. This woman, a famous beauty in her part of the country, had formerly been his mistress. He did not do what many bourgeois gentlemen would have done: he did not dissemble, he was too superior for that. He simply went to pay her a visit. My mother and the three of us remained standing in the street, waiting for him. . . . Do you think my mother was jealous or felt the slightest vexation? Not in the least.

This story provokes several observations. First this: it could be that Mme Flaubert felt neither resentment nor jealousy, but she might have suffered a thousand deaths and her two sons and her daughter would never have suspected it. What Flaubert can attest to is that there was no scene in the street, that his mother did not display any visible displeasure either on this day or the following—that's all. This is not so surprising. Mme Flaubert was not very expansive, and had she been, she would have categorically refused to let her two sons know of their father's indignity. Besides, dutiful daughter that she was, in this circumstance as in any other she must have concentrated on bearing her lot.

But it is the father that interests me on this occasion. There is a great deal of loyalty and a certain delicacy in a man who, after thirty years, determines to revisit a woman he once loved; he is doing homage to his mistress, he is coming to tell her: I have never forgotten you. The same man, unfortunately, behaves like a boor with his wife. I agree that he should not have hidden his intentions from her; the meaning of such frankness should be clear: one refuses to lie to one's equal for the double reason that the equality is based on the truth and a lie gives the liar an abject, momentary superiority veiling a permanent inferiority—fine. But "too superior" to lie—who knows if he was not telling the truth *to preserve* that superiority? The paterfamilias considered his wishes to be commands, it was the family's duty to submit to them without exception. He had to see an old mistress again—a royal, therefore legitimate, whim; he informed his subjects so that they might aid his plans; as for his chief vassal, his wife, she had only to make suitable arrangements. After which he placed her on the sidewalk with the children and obliged her to cool her heels while he overwhelmed the other woman with his graciousness. This dirty trick is striking; that it should seem so spontaneous, that the younger son should find it so natural, indicates that it must have been routine practice; that Mme Flaubert should not have been vexed suggests that the child-wife must have been trained early in the constant exercise of docility.

Caroline Flaubert, née Fleuriot, deserved the happiness she enjoyed for seven years; she knew how to contain herself. Yet this difficult art is not learned in one lesson. Orphaned and deferential, she had, I recognize, a vocation for it, but that is not enough; from the beginning she must have practiced enduring disgust, choking back tears, soothing spite. Above all she was asked to approve of everything in advance and on principle, like that peasant girl in a folktale who repeats on every occasion: "Whatever the old man does is done well." The wife of the physician-philosopher ends by embodying unconditional acquiescence. This cannot happen without pitiless, wearying labor—in exhausted souls, some faculties are hypertrophied, others atrophied. Because of her urgent need *to ratify*, her emotional calluses, and her willed insensitivity in certain areas, Achille-Cléophas's wife owed the trust the master had placed in her to the number of hoops she had jumped through. But jump through as many hoops as you like, you can't do it with impunity. De-Stalinization has multiplied neurosis in Europe; we must conclude from this that grievances ignored, truncated lines of reasoning, feelings swept under the rug, facts passed over in silence have been repressed, buried under the soul's floor, but not suppressed. Some are dead and stinking; others, buried alive, returned to the scene after the end of Stalinism, embittered to the point of madness. Opening their eyes, the "de-Stalinized" find themselves rootless in a world without signposts, dreadful and naked. No more myths, only mortal and passing truths; they had a rough time of it, like the Russians, and for nothing.

After seven years of private Stalinism, the Flauberts were not in nearly such serious shape. The husband was not dead; he continued to reign. But the story reported above proves that he was capable of passionate impulses. If he were a nobody, you might say that he knew how to love; in any case he held onto romantic and lively memories, disturbing loyalties. In the act of giving a son to Mme Flaubert, *what* was he thinking about? *Whom?* She must very quickly have perceived that he had "lived," that he valued his past life; the medical director was "too superior" not to inflict on her the tale of his loves, and she accepted everything, proud to be privy to this abundant memory. But by revealing himself in this way, her husband, without ceasing to be the father, became a stranger: every episode in his life, every inclination, every taste—these were flights. She sensed he was elusive in his very carnal presence, he escaped her through resolution; another Achille-Cléophas turned a hidden face toward a past which he had lived alone and which was concealed from her. It might have been nothing. As far as a woman might push identification with or surrender to a man, in whatever rapture she might have set out to cut herself off from herself, to take refuge in the absolute being of the husband, he always betrayed her—if only by the simple exercise of his acknowledged sovereignty. He was the independent variable his wife desired to push the integration of the couple to the extreme. This independence, however, which all his life he would never cease

89

to affirm, became in him and through him the original sin, the option that favors one sex at the expense of the other, the source of all infidelities. What this amounts to is that in order for the couple to be a single self, it is necessary to be and remain two. A physician consumed by ambition, the prudent administrator of his small fortune, the father and imperious husband, Achille-Cléophas belonged to his wife. Through old ecstasies lodged in the depths of his memory, through what can be glimpsed of a caustic, gloomy, nervous, and at times tender sensibility, through the tears he spilled for himself, through a singular and rarely conscious relationship with himself he escaped her, all the more surely because she didn't think to hinder him. Weak and guilty, did she need that solitude and that vulnerability? Daughters want for the most part *to be made the object* of paternal love. What daughter wants her father, that absolute subject, to become the permanent object of her knowledge and her charity?

Only feelings, then, changed in the seven years. Without this curious perspective on Achille-Cléophas we might have believed he remained the same until his death, having no time to become anything different. An overworked physician and intense researcher, when would he have questioned his life? In fact, he underwent continuous transformation; this restless man had his dreams, and fidelity cost him something. The tribute paid to his former loves gives us a glimpse of what he was during his engagement and the early years of his marriage: he overwhelmed Caroline with his austere gallantry, with an imperious respect rent at times by bursts of passion. And the same anecdote reveals the evolution of his conjugal conduct; at the end, he still respects his wife, enough in any case to tell her the truth, not enough to spare her a long wait, right in the street, while he goes to rejoin his youth and shed a few tears for himself. We have here the two ends of the chain—the deterioration in marital relations is evident. Perhaps seven years was enough to bring things to such a pass; more probably, however, the death of Laumonier took the young household by surprise at some intermediate stage in this evolution. Achille-Cléophas worked harder every day, out of a taste for work even more than out of necessity, and then, more and more frequently he would lie down by himself in the evening. The wife acquiesced or kept quiet, she affirmed in her thoughts that nothing had changed. The permanence of the setting, the repetition of her tasks—she was a mother and a housewife—masked the imperceptible distance that expressed, finally, the death of love. Caroline always loved; Achille-Cléophas no longer loved, or, if you will, he loved differently. The signs of that change swarmed, infinitesimal, obvious to the young woman who saw them without perceiving them; having entered uninvited and then hidden, they gnawed at her gently, and she did not deign to feel their teeth.

The move—expected, dreaded—was a catastrophe: it put things in quite another light. The new lodgings, first of all, were gloomy. They have often been described, along with Gustave's odd familiarity, from the age of four, with cadavers. But no one has speculated, to my knowledge, on how the young wife tolerated their company. Marked four times by death, she found it again—stripped, familiar, her neighbor. In the basement were the corpses, in the amphitheater dissected limbs, in the rooms of the hospital the suffering. She was the daughter and wife of physicians, true; she could have told herself with pride, if she had been so moved, that her husband was fighting hand over fist to save human lives. She was not so moved; her rather impoverished imagination lacked the resources to transform the father into a knight errant. Moreover, this warrior conducted his battles far away from her, leaving her alone in an old structure which was unanimously declared by witnesses to be hideous. We know what they are like, those hospital apartments; were they charmingly furnished, which was not the case, one would still enter with nostrils twitching, expecting the odor of phenol and decomposition. Through all the windows every morning bright and early the hearse of the poor could be seen going by—and not empty; prisoners in uniform could be observed crossing the courtyard or gathering in the portals; pale convalescents, these sick people rendered small services and sometimes served at the director's table. Sickness produces its techniques, and techniques produce their men; the physician's interior world between the hospital walls is penetrated by the exterior; public suffering crushes private life. For several years, surrounded by disease that reflected her bereavements as particular cases of French mortality, Caroline must have felt haunted, solitary and anonymous. Her husband left her at daybreak; if he ate lunch at home, he scarcely lingered over it and departed at once, only to return late and retire early; his new duties brought with them a considerable increase in his responsibilities and his work. The evenings became shorter just when more effort and perseverance were needed to shore up conjugal intimacy. What becomes of a young housewife when her home is turned into a public thoroughfare? Mme Flaubert, long secretive, closed herself up completely. Always submissive, always loving and loyal, she never stopped revering her husband or practicing virtue; but resignation—

without daring to speak its name—made her retreat, gave her a kind of frozen depth. It is in the light of this infinitesimal distance that life appeared to her and made her reconsider; new habits, or quite simply the old ones resumed in a strange setting, showed her her own person *from the outside*. To give life, to nurse in the realm of death—was this perseverance or incongruity? She ended by deciding in favor of perseverance, but without being able to obliterate the absurdity of her endeavors. As for her husband, a familiar figure that at a fixed time emerged against an unknown, almost hostile background, he participated, in spite of her, in the estrangement surrounding them. This means, in sum, that she had lost a sense of immediacy; nothing happened naturally any more, not even love. We can imagine that in the course of this silent observation she discovered the true meaning of her last happy years, and that the process of deterioration had already begun; that Dr. Flaubert had been estranged from her well before Laumonier's death, that the love women dream of is immutable and a man's love is not at all. But for my part, I would be afraid to give her an excessively lucid consciousness. In the absence of evidence another conjecture is more plausible: she did not want to understand that her malaise had begun at rue du Petit-Salut, nor, above all, that she had felt it without admitting it to herself; the full responsibility for her husband's estrangement, her anxieties, her slight depersonalization she attributed to her new lodgings—everything dated from the move. At the same time she did not hesitate to enrich her meditations by reviewing the previous years: there had been awkwardnesses, silences, interludes when Laumonier was still alive which she had screened out and which reappeared; but although she bitterly *felt* them as prophecies that had been realized in the present, she abstained from dating and localizing them. Rather than seeing in them the marks of a strict progression, she nursed her stream of reproaches against the Hôtel-Dieu, cemetery of the living, which had taken her husband from her. Achille-Cléophas emerged from these internal disputes as he had entered: head high, innocent; his feelings had not changed, it was universal death and the suffering of men, transparent panes slipped between the two spouses, that separated them. This falsification saved the years of happiness but at the expense of the present; Caroline had projected everything—deception, anguish, resentment, a sense of being fed up with herself—onto the gloomy walls that imprisoned her; the walls reflected her unhappiness as a whole.

I prefer the second hypothesis, someone else may prefer the first; it makes no difference, they are equivalent in terms of our objectives. More or less lucidly, with more real unhappiness or more bewilderment, the young wife discovers that she is numb with cold: it is death approaching her husband, who takes a step backward. It is almost certain that she shared her anxieties with the chief surgeon. Scarcely were they settled into the Hôtel-Dieu than he bought a country house at Butot, where they spent vacations; from 1820 to 1844 he spent the summer at Yonville; in '44 he acquired the property at Croisset, where he planned to live. From the first year, then, the discomforts of his winter residence were alleviated by his summer lodgings. It is difficult to imagine that such a fanatical researcher would of his own accord be separated from the site of his research; his wife's mood and perhaps her health must have changed; he must have noticed this and questioned her. A pre-romantic man, nervous, passionate, utilitarian and reasonable, he must have seen the Hôtel-Dieu through Caroline's eyes. Only for a moment, but long enough for him to honor her request. It is now a half-century since their dismal lodgings were secularized. No one lives there anymore; we men, we have acquired the sensibilities of our grandmothers.

FOUR

The Elder Brother

Born in 1812, Achille was nine years older than his brother. Voltairean irony, empiricist intellectualism, philosophical mechanism and analysis, the dissection of souls and the stench of the amphitheater, the suffocating austerity of the family group and the rigors of a sometimes capricious discipline—he knew it all. For him, nine years earlier than for Gustave, Achille-Cléophas represented the absolute. To this were added his own difficulties: he had brothers, sisters, who were born in rapid succession and almost as rapidly disappeared. These births must have disturbed him, roused his jealousy; the deaths, if he had ever had the time to wish for them, may have given him moments of secret remorse. In any case, the family was plunged into mourning. Achille's first years were certainly gray, or—who knows?—even black. In spite of this, he immediately broke through the circle Gustave would never crack. A studious and brilliant schoolboy, a distinguished university student, he would complete his thesis at twenty-eight, just when his younger brother at nineteen was questioning the future in anguish; four years later, while Gustave was slowly recovering from his "nervous attack," Achille began his tenure in "the most attractive medical position in all Normandy." If he did not yet fulfill all his father's responsibilities, he had been promised them, it was a matter of a few years. Later, around the time Gustave was afraid he had made his mistress pregnant and threw himself into an angry panegyric on sterility, Achille as a good Flaubert ensured the perpetuation of the family group by making a carefully considered marriage. The rest was predictable: Dr. Achille Flaubert was a highly appreciated physician, the income from his land inspired the confidence of his clientele; an amiable talker, he received "society"—the very same people his father had cared for but had not associated with. In short, he was not entirely one of the wealthy but he was a leading citizen. And with a good deal of influence—a definite influence on the prefects and an effect on the staff of the ministry through the channel of the local administration. Ministers changed and governments as well, but Achille's influence remained as great as ever, which is evidence of his opportunism.[1] The father Flaubert passed for a wise man, meaning that he didn't dirty himself with politics; a terribly opinionated man, he was constrained to curb his liberalism by peasant prudence and a sharp sense of his own interests. Inhibited, repressed, still more philosophical than political, as a bourgeois of recent vintage he had a bourgeois passion for freedom: free thought, free inquiry, free suffrage, free competition, free enjoyment of acquisitions. But the elder son was contemptuous of public affairs. One grain of liberalism out of loyalty to the progenitor and then, of course, order must prevail. Apart from this, his flexibility was the effect of his indifference. To be sure, political indifference is always counterrevolutionary; the massive depoliticization of the intellectuals which characterizes the second half of the nineteenth century is certainly counterrevolutionary, but Achille scarcely felt any attraction to the right as such. This is what allowed him to accept gracefully, without capsizing, the dangerous tackings of his time.

With him, it seems, the Flaubert family reaches a new plateau. "The Achilles" are polished, they have manners, good breeding; less crude than his father, the new medical director finds time to "be cultivated"—he reads, keeps abreast of things, he is careful to acquire the kind of "mundane" knowledge that feeds salon conversation. Even in his work the son raises himself above his father, or rather he is raised, medical progress carries him along; he is a contemporary of Claude Bernard. In the life sciences, observation is transformed into experimentation; this change affects him from the outside, but it does so profoundly: as a professor, he has to assimilate the new methods. It is about him that Dumesnil must have written that he "controls analysis by synthesis," not about the unhappy younger brother who struggles in the snares of philosophical mechanism and makes his escape through dreaming—and through infinite totalities.

At the very moment when Gustave, accused of pornography, is "led to the dock of infamy," there is already a movement afoot in high

1. He was city councilman under the Second Empire and continued to hold this office after 4 September 1870.

places to decorate Dr. Achille Flaubert; it may be that the novelist's escapades delayed the ceremony. Not for long; in 1859 the decoration is given to reward "a great talent, favored by fortune, forty years of a hardworking, irreproachable existence." When Gustave wrote these words he was thinking of his father; after 1860 they could be applied equally to the elder son.

What exceptional success! Achille manages to escape the basic contradiction of the Flaubert enterprise—the bourgeois family with a semipatriarchal structure. He pulls himself out of servitude without falling into rebellion and walks off in complete freedom. He has been able to create for himself a more developed enterprise in better accord with his bourgeois milieu, in brief, a typically conjugal family. He has his roots in the bourgeoisie, after all, since the physician-philosopher—a self-made peasant—fathered him within his new class. Achille could see in his father's crushing authority only a feature of character, not the customary exercise of *patria potestas* that Achille-Cléophas thirty years earlier had recognized in the authority of the royalist and veterinarian grandfather. And the difference meant that the chief surgeon, as a child, found the same demands and the same arbitrary power among the fathers of his comrades, while young Achille knew more than one father but a single paterfamilias. In short, the elder of the Flaubert sons did not have to make an effort to adapt the new social unit to the new society—he had the good fortune to be born into an ascending class at the moment of its ascent; it supports him, pushes, pulls him along and modifies *him* in order to *be modified* by him. All Achille has to do is let himself go; he is lively, hardworking, and flexible, and a single and continuous movement governs his milieu and puts him in harmony with himself. We have to admire this perpetually unstable and perpetually regained equilibrium— through this extrovert the history of the sciences is made, along with the history of institutions. Order and progress—doesn't he deserve this bourgeois motto? Doesn't he produce inside and out a kind of progress that remains, as Auguste Compte wished, the development of order? This fortunate man seems to have obliterated all his complexes and surmounted the objective contradictions of the family situation; this worker asks for self-realization only in scientific and medical labor; the liberal father, the jovial host knows how to combine the useful and the agreeable; head of the troop, he leads all the "best people"; "ego syntonic" extrovert, he never loses his sense of reality. After all, he helps the people of Rouen, he cares for them, he advises them; he is certainly "paternal to the poor"; if he does not have his father's caustic toughness, so much the better for him. The physician-philosopher was clearly too aggressively ironic to have been completely free of his old shackles. Character is essential, of course, but not to the point of character disorder. For this reason, Achille must be congratulated for presenting a softened image of Achille-Cléophas—that is progress.

At this point, everything collapses. As an analyst would say, Achille is certainly an "adult," but not a *true* one since adults are by definition false. These optical illusions are manufactured in certain milieux at certain moments; their pleasant appearance flatters us. Dazzled, still barbaric, our species in following them has set out upon the road of no return toward self-domestication.

It will be observed, first of all, that this amiable man enjoys the esteem of Rouen and has never done anything to deserve it. Why? The responsibility for the Hôtel-Dieu became a hereditary office, the feelings of devotion toward the father were transferred to the son; it was enough for Achille not to forfeit these feelings. For this reason the transition from the first to the second Dr. Flaubert is accompanied if not by a loss, at least by a lowering of energy; Achille, a good professor and a good physician, never knew his father's violent passion, that almost sinister curiosity which would keep him shut in with his feverishly consulted cadavers. Achille never finds the time to do personal research. Even if he did, his investigations would be conducted in such a leisurely fashion that they would not be completed. At bottom, he is curious only about achieved knowledge: Achille-Cléophas wanted to *discover*, Achille wants to *keep abreast of things*. Social, sociable, he sees nothing but advantages in knowing the truth through others. The father's mad, somber curiosity was the individual's connection to the mechanistic universe: he learned very little other than what he gleaned through his own powers; the son, by informing himself, learns much more and, above all, socializes knowledge. The scandal is the raw idea; when it is adapted, it brings men into harmony with each other without changing them. Achille is endlessly preoccupied with updating his information by appropriating the findings of others; he wants to maintain his social position, his reputation as a professor and a practitioner, in a time when the rapid development of the medical disciplines forces physicians either to stagnate or to read everything. He rapidly accumulates new ideas, or rather they accumulate in him because, among other things, knowledge is accumulation. But in spite of all this his relations to the people of Rouen, to his students, to his colleagues remain permanent, and permanence is his sole objective. He wants to maintain himself—nothing more; to progress through the progress of others in order to preserve his position in the bosom of the rising class. If he changes, it is to stay the same; he will consolidate his personal status, which is to perpetuate the status his father achieved before 1830 and then conceded to him. These two observations—one regarding Achille's family relations, the other his ties with science—reveal the actual daily existence of the heir; despite his obvious malleability, perhaps because of it, his is not a life truly lived but the equivalent of a very old person dead in the midst of things. We shall see that the bitter curse which until the end of his life keeps the younger son in a state of childhood, to his misery and his glory, originates in the crushing benediction that makes the elder into an adult by breaking his back.

Achille-Cléophas had plans for his family. When fathers have plans, children have destinies. As a physician, the paterfamilias was married to medicine and only wanted to father other physicians.[2] The Flaubert

2. This, at least, is what we learn from Gustave's niece, Caroline Commanville. A suspect witness, I know—vain, boasting, and with a couple of sizable misdeeds to conceal. But when she lies, be it by omission, her interests are obvious, she gives herself away. Yet this concerns something that happened before she was born, even before her mother was born—why should she go to the trouble of distorting it? She would lose credibility without gaining anything, since Flaubert has intimates who survive and may want to establish the truth. As for erring in good faith, impossible. She spent her entire childhood between Gustave and Madame, the mother; what she could not observe, she learned from them. René Dumesnil, however, declares quite plainly that the physician-philosopher expected to hand on his duties to his elder son and make his younger a court magistrate. This may be; regrettably he keeps his sources to himself. For my part, both versions suit me since in each of them we see the paterfamilias invoking the law of primogeniture—everything for Achille and what's left for Gustave. From this point of view I would lean toward Dumesnil's thesis; the disparity here seems more substantial and the paternal premeditation takes on the quality of harassment. Achille-Cléophas had only one pride and one passion: science. Upon it and through it he had founded his House. Can we imagine this rationalist comfortably contemplating the body of legal thought, dragged halfway between custom and reason, which claims the universality of an idea and which in fact prescribes only according to the Code? The jargon of the magistrates must have shocked the Voltairean who loved the beautiful, lucid language of the philosophes, the man of science who searched for precise words to designate rigorous concepts. If he had decided a priori that Gustave would take a degree in law, that he would establish his professional merits on the knowledge of the Napoleonic Code and on the hollow eloquence of the courts, his son must indeed have inspired him with profound disgust. So from birth Gustave was committed to martyrdom.

I don't ask so much of him; intolerable as Gustave's sufferings might be, there is nothing of the whipping-boy in him. This is precisely what deters me from taking Dumesnil at his word. One knows of irritable fathers who loathe one of their children from birth; old Mirabeau was like that, and when he was asked the reason for his loathing he answered, in different words, like the mother who hated her fifteen-year-old daughter: "It's her skin." But he had never seen fit to walk his son in his baby

family would be scientific; a torch endlessly rekindled by generations of the young and which the death of predecessors could not extinguish. The progenitor recalled his own difficult childhood, the risks taken; without benevolent counseling, would he have finished his studies? He congratulated himself on his comfortable circumstances—his offspring would have equality of opportunity at the outset. This meant that they were assured of going as far as the residency and the thesis. "After that," he thought—a proponent of free competition—"let the best man win." Dr. Flaubert favored no one, he was a liberal tinged around the edges with republicanism.

Put simply, it would have been a shame, it would have been inadmissible to let go of his titles, his duties, his clientele, his influence. As for sharing these between his heirs, impossible: should each get half a chair? half an appointment? His power divided is degraded, someone must take it from him *whole* and replace him one day in all his functions—even and above all as *head of the House*. Achille-Cléophas's ambition was never to despoil one son for the profit of the other, but to transform his respectable and lucrative profession into a hereditary office. In order to bequeath from father to son what the state gave only on merit, it was necessary and sufficient that the Flauberts, from father to son, were eminently deserving. This son of a royalist did not forget his birth, he remembered those aristocrats of the eighteenth century who transmitted their titles without assuming that the bourgeois elite would sooner or later become a titled aristocracy. In sum, the latecomer saw his adopted class under the aspect of a future nobility. To him, men of science would soon be

carriage, which the physician-philosopher did many times. No, when the child appeared—the second success in nine years—we can be sure that Achille-Cléophas made him very welcome. By what abstract sadism was he impelled to discredit him without knowing him, to leave the knowledge and the art of healing to his brother, why—without giving him time to demonstrate his capabilities—did he confine him in advance to lower functions? And what if this younger son had been a young Newton, or better, a Dupuytren? He would die in ignorance—what a loss of income for a utilitarian family! And then, old Flaubert loved money; even science has to pay, his male heirs are obliged to increase the patrimony—it would be a crime to diminish it. But a court magistrate lives on his income and sometimes on his capital, the state paid very poorly at this period. Just so: in order to perform an act of class justice, he had only to possess funds. If he had it in the beginning, thinks the progenitor, so much the better, on the condition that his fortune is doubled upon retirement. As for retiring from a career poorer than when one entered into it, no—one would have had to work without remuneration.

I opt for Caroline's version, her moderation seems right to me. But someone else may certainly prefer the other; neither the formulations nor the result of the investigation will be altered.

dukes and peers. He demanded of society that it grant scientists an authority in proportion to their real importance. But as a peasant intellectual dominated by his childhood, he could not help conceiving of medicine as a patrimony to transmit to his descendants. Circumstances come strongly into play: he enjoyed such credit in Rouen that he would not have had great difficulty designating his successor. His absolute power at the Hôtel-Dieu, the respect his colleagues bore him, the trust of his clients—all these objective facts defined the future of a Flaubert son beyond his death. Which son? If he determined to choose the better, he would risk losing support; wiser to decide everything in advance and present the pretender at an early age to the good city of Rouen; his colleagues and honorable clientele would have time to get used to him. Therefore it would be the elder. Two children left limbo, saw their big brother, and plunged back again. Big brother Achille became, alone, the fragile hope of a family plagued by death. When Gustave arrived, the chips were already down, and the difference in age was so considerable, there was no basis for comparison. What common measure can be applied to a little boy of ten who is about to start school and a young man who has just finished school and is going on nineteen?

Besides, Achille-Cléophas did not intend to despoil the newcomer; the office was indivisible, thus he had reserved it for the firstborn. But the property would be shared with complete bourgeois equity. Little Gustave, having completed the same studies as his brother, would have the same knowledge and might even surpass him in scientific research; and the father was certain that the profit would be substantial for the younger son as well—it is not excessive to have two good doctors for the county seat of the Seine-Inférieure.

One wonders why Achille-Cléophas, so proud of his office, of his professorship and its attendant honors, didn't feel he was favoring Achille quite outrageously when he plotted to pass these things on to him. The answer offers the key to the Flaubert enterprise and shows Achille quite naked, in his full insignificance.

The old man counted on his progeny to elevate his family to the upper reaches of Rouen society. "They will know what I do not." Achille was worth more than Achille-Cléophas—as we have seen, this is how the bourgeoisie views progress. The second chief surgeon, by virtue of the changing times, would effortlessly outshine the first. And then the patrimony would continuously increase, divided by depositions of wills, reconstituted by profits. That is what he wanted, the paterfamilias: he wanted the Flauberts to increase and multiply.

101

But the old devil is mad with pride—whatever his progeny might accomplish only redounds to his credit. A sudden mutation took place one fine day in a rustic family; the mother believed she had given birth to a veterinarian—she had created a physician. In him, a new species of Flaubert was born; thus the bird was born from the snake—as scientists were soon to say. The first bird was Achille-Cléophas; he had the audacity to pull himself up from the ground by means of an extravagant leap and settle himself on a branch. After this, of course, his descendants until the end of time would be winged—for the new species from the time of his appearance consolidated his specific features. This plumage on the shoulderblades of the first chief surgeon was a first cause, an original burst soon followed by flight, a savage, *invented* freedom. Afterward, what do we see? New beginnings. The future birds would climb from branch to branch; that goes without saying; but are these hoppings and skippings to be admired? They are the strictly predictable consequences of an unpredictable leap.

In other words, the first bird is the one and only bird—one ancestral bird and the infinite succession of his images, always more splendid, less and less vital. That is how the Flaubert family appeared to its founder. It is to this infinite glory—himself reflected successively in a thousand other *selves*—that he is dedicated. For the physician-philosopher, it might be said, history is made through crises; one series dies out, overcome by its own weight, another surfaces, quite new; the initial term is the only one that counts—if that is known, all the others can be deduced. Achille can be *deduced*. His father is convinced of it; out of this horrifying certainty he creates and kills his son at the same time.

Dr. Flaubert gives his firstborn a destiny, and Achille's destiny will be not even the future but the very person of his father. He was produced in the small archaic world of repetition. Doctor, son of a doctor, future head of the Hôtel-Dieu, as his veterinarian uncles were sons of veterinarians. But the veterinarian-progenitor, whatever his self-conceit, did not regard himself in advance as *the best*; he passed on to his sons a profession that he had inherited. And so it was with the landowners; from father to son the duty is the same—to preserve, to augment; but for this very reason the permanence of the enterprise demands the equivalence of persons. Achille himself knows that through paternal generosity he will *receive* all the distinctions and all the responsibilities his father has won. Therefore, whereas he might intend to excel in his specialty, he accepts his inferiority to the progenitor on principle. When I say "he accepts," understand my meaning: he is a child; speaking quite literally, he neither accepts nor refuses anything. But admiration and holy terror have already begun the work of identification; and then what unbearable pressure, a choice that is not even favoritism. For nearly nine years the relationship between the docile son and the incomparable father is going to remain singular; Achille knows nothing about the bourgeois stature of the chosen heir, deliberately particularized by the Malthusian practices of the parents. Briefly, the structures of the Flaubert family forbid the eldest any recourse to individualism; no one—especially not his frigid mother who is entirely subservient to the master—cherishes him as an individual. Yet except for a few bubbles of life that immediately burst, nothing will occur during his early childhood to trouble the extended tête-à-tête between father and son. Worse than this, the successive bereavements cast a shadow over the family, and the progenitor, while he is determined to procreate, begins to mistrust his seed; he wonders whether he will ever be able to give younger siblings to the eldest of his sons. Achille experiences the discomforts of being an only child without the advantages; the father sees in him the survivor, not the chosen but the sole (for the time being provisional) means of perpetuating the family. The child feels crushed by the daily insistence, the searching looks; it is his duty to shine, family honor demands it. Dr. Flaubert's pressing solicitude certainly involves attachment—the father prizes dearly the fragile hope of the Flauberts; and we can be sure that this paternal attachment affects the young boy, it is the deepest stuff of his being. But to the extent that this feeling is the expression of a strict claim, it resonates in the son as responsibility. When the physician-philosopher pays visits to the Hôtel-Dieu with little Achille, when he says to him, "If you work hard, in thirty years you'll be the boss and I'll be dead," when he amuses himself in the evenings by making his philosophy comprehensible to a childish intelligence, he is opening, whether or not he wishes to do so, the floodgates of filial duty: do everything you can to become me when I am not around any more; save the Flauberts. At the same time, of course, the father gives the child all the means of fulfilling the obligations that weigh on him; produced by the sperm, molded by the paternal hands, reproduced, supported, fashioned by science and the work of the paterfamilias, Achille knows his destiny very early—he will be, as son, a link in the immortal chain that is called Achille-Cléophas. Soft, sensitive wax, he feels the proddings that imperceptibly transform him into this very god who, after having ceded to him one by one his awful powers, will disappear like the phoenix in order to be reborn *the father* in the son. Achille will be his father's creature, he has no choice, the only spontaneity he is allowed is the practice of passive virtues: humility before his progenitor, a spirit of sacrifice, docility, receptiveness. But the master has spoken well: submission will pay off, it allows the victim to acquire progressively the attributes of the god who made him gasp. It becomes a prophecy: when the child bows to the *present* will of the father, he begins to distinguish his own future image. And it is the father all over again.

This is what I will call the objective and inviolable framework of identification. Objective because it comes to the child through the father; inviolable because this paterfamilias is a divinity for all his children. Is there any escape? No; as a possibility, identification was necessary. Listen carefully: it was necessary in this period, in this movement that was stirring up society, in this semirural family. Today, for example, marital conflict—always present even in harmonious households—leaves the child a certain choice. And of course it is his history inside him that will choose: at least—even if he becomes neurotic—*the choice will be his*. The number of authoritarian fathers decreased in proportion to the emancipation of women, and even at the beginning of the Restoration this aspiration to create one person *the same as another* occurred less frequently. It was not, moreover, a real danger among the landed aristocracy; the father was a nonentity, the son too, nothing could be more wholesome. But when the intellectual bourgeoisie decided to imitate the big landowners, all was lost: the father implanted in the son's mind a prefabricated intelligence. Not even his own, a family prototype. This is the case with Achille-Cléophas.

But Achille-Cléophas, understandably, would not execute the imposed model without motives that were very much his own and that defined him in his particularity. For every project is also a flight; Achille fled from his abusive father, the unbearable present, toward this same paterfamilias, his future. Subjectivity is the abrupt conjunction of the external world with himself in the process of internalization. It is in Achille and in him alone that the father can be doubled. Nor does the child escape feeling the unbearable contradiction between the family religion with which he is inculcated, though it is not named, and the liberal philosophy that is explained to him. The household gods and philosophical mechanism—what an aberration! The younger son will seek out the issues and finding the paths of inquiry blocked, he will live out this contradiction to the point of

stupefaction. The elder finds a way out: he is lucky enough to rediscover mechanistic philosophy by pushing subjection to its limit. Devotion prompts him to want *to be* his father, as he has been enjoined
to do; beyond that, the revealed religion, its affectations, the alleged
aridity of the analytic method are of little consequence. In his father's
physiognomy Achille discovers the features of the eternal physician-
philosopher he will be and will father when he takes a wife; he is
swallowed up by Achille-Cléophas and through happy submission
becomes the man, skeptical and virtuous by nature, the scientist, the
mechanistic thinker. Better, he *is him* since he *will be him*, since in his
eyes the charming doctor has taken it upon himself to be eminent.
The chief surgeon's authority and his contradictions crush the child
who cannot escape them without *becoming his own father*; let us understand that he reinvents the usual operations of identification and
makes himself the simple intermediary—indispensable but secondary—between the two progenitors born of a mysterious doubling but
strictly identical, the mission of each one being to represent the other.
Because of this, living out his objective necessity as though it were
the most intimate passion, he avoids Gustave's fears and disgusts.
The younger brother will despise analysis—even while making use
of it—for having too often been made its object. Achille, in a symbiotic
relationship with his father, employs it from childhood.

Or rather the father employs it for him. As luck would have it,
Achille-Cléophas is delighted to dissect the deep feelings of others
but has neither the tools nor the inclination to know himself; by
identifying with him, the young boy became a perpetual subject,
perpetually unknown to himself. The world alone was the object of
his surgical scrutiny. A scientist, a practitioner—pure intelligence. The
dead held no fear for him. In any event, no more than his own
feelings, forgotten and atrophied—this was his heritage. When the
father leads his son through the hospital, through the stench of the
amphitheater, he seems to be saying, "this nation is yours." This
nation of the sick and the dead is his empire; it pays. He looks upon
suffering and sees honors, profit. Not without feelings, to be sure,
a proper compassion. An adult sentiment and one that comes from
his father; a child given up to childhood without a mentor would feel
only horror. He also learns from the paternal lips that "healing is the
finest profession." If he happens to be afraid, his fear lasts only for
a moment; he is already future, already the man in a white coat,
already bending over the festering wound that frightens him in the
present. "This is what you will become." Unnecessary; this is what

he has become already. From the age of nine or ten he tries to imitate the "debonair majesty" of the physician-philosopher. As for illusions, I doubt that Achille had many. For this prefabricated atheist, faith is nothing more than obscurantism. What would he do with it? Spurned by his father, Gustave will allow himself to be tempted by religious subjection. But Achille? He is an accepted vassal. He rushes toward the open arms of the medical director. Achille is protected against Christianity by a more ancient and more demanding cult: he is the most faithful initiate in the religion of the family. His brother's anxieties will probably remain alien to him. Achille, spurious only son, single future survivor of the Flauberts, possesses his father and is in possession of him, he is possessed by him; as if Achille-Cléophas created in his son his most intimate thoughts, as if the son recognized in the father the fruit of his most intimate spontaneity. As future father, he impresses the present father with ideas that have no content, which he will conceive of later when he has become the father. In this trinity, the father thinks inside the head of the son, the son looks forward to a definite time when he will think through the head of the father. The submission was sweet. Viewed from the outside, the master, impatient and nervous, could yell, give capricious orders; a legislator by impulse, he could certainly decree laws so strict that they could never be obeyed. That's nothing—they could be circumvented through excuses, promises, tears; everything happens *externally*, the chief thing is not to be commanded *internally* by another. In Gustave, the firmly rooted Other will make his decisions for him— this is intolerable. But for Achille, since he is always in harmony with his creator, it is himself who decides in the Other; first of all, he is *the heir*, his entire young person demands the honors, the profits and responsibilities of the father. Therefore he must prove himself worthy in due course, and the present medical director is the only person qualified to form his successor. Achille puts his trust in his father; they have a common goal, Achille-Cléophas knows how to get there. Thus the most extreme severity will be irksome, perhaps, but not suffocating, it is a means and the child knows its end; it is a matter of facilitating the difficult maneuver by which a father bequeaths to his son goods that do not belong to him. The incontestable generosity of the ends reflects back on the means: the father produced and reproduced life, he generously gave his own essence to the little boy; in the present they are a single person in two, and severity itself is generous since it prepares the youngest incarnation of Dr. Flaubert to deserve the other's privileges. And then, the paternal commands reveal to the child *his* future whims: later he will have the same objectives, the same generosity for his son, the same apparently necessary severity. In some sense the paternal commitment to the will is softened; since it would govern Achille's future relations to his own progeny, the little boy can also understand it in terms of a highly intimate relationship between his future reality and his present childhood. It is Achille himself, having become the residuary legatee, who gives orders to the young rascal he has been, while dreaming of giving them to the young rascal he will some day father. In brief, everything is perfectly clear, he knows where he is going and how to get there.

Nothing, in fact, was so clearly *felt*; all this was obvious without words from day to day, with no delicacy and certainly with no emotional outbursts: it was the family, the external internalized, it was tradition, ownership, it was heritage. Achille comfortably established himself in the paternal role and believed he knew man by having "dismembered" the affections through analysis. Suddenly, what persisted as the object in him was no longer truly himself; he had no essential reality other than his father's, namely the mysterious unity of paternal powers. This unity in action is intellection; insofar as it remains imminent it is the center of a sacred *aura*. Intermediate states can be imagined; at the end of an enterprise that begins at birth and finishes with maturity, the child will come into possession of his father's *mana*.

It would be wrong to think of identification as a drama; it is a role, to be sure, but to the extent that it requires the internalization of an objective system it is also hard work. In this particular case, identity with the father's attainments cannot be achieved without repeating his dazzling scholastic studies. The whole system is ruled by a doubled term that one attempts to embody in the present through attitudes, but which must be approached primarily through a succession of real endeavors (entrance competitions, examinations, theses) each of which is defined by objective programs and leads to a definite future, foreseen in detail in the programs of the following year. It will perhaps be judged that this actual process—secondary school, medical school, the thesis—forced Achille to build the tools to combine his means in view of a short-term goal (for example, the solution to a scholarly problem), to develop in himself through practice that freedom of understanding which is called intellection. It is undeniable that these mental operations sustain him—outside of class he dozes, in examinations he is dazzling. And one might well ask what would have happened if he had been a fool, or more specifically, if he had not excelled in the sciences, if, like Gustave, he had preferred literature and planned to write. We would return once more, despite all efforts, to social atomism, implying *natures* rather than human nature. Variously gifted. Chance could have bestowed upon the Flaubert sons the same talents it had given the father, the whole history of the family could be viewed as a consequence of this, a question of red blood cells and gray matter—the identity of capabilities would originate in the identity of certain physiological traits, and its effect would be the enterprise of identification. This is bad materialism, bourgeois and molecular materialism, the very same materialism which the physician-philosopher took for a philosophy. This is to turn events and causes upside down. Achille did not owe his father's continued confidence in him to his exceptional intelligence; rather he owed his rare qualities of mind to the irrevocable decision that, from the moment of his conception or perhaps before, made him the crown prince of science.

Good sense is the best thing shared—a more difficult and a truer contention has never been made. The idea is poorly understood in isolation. Everyone wants to establish his hierarchy, one rarely places oneself at the summit, rarely on the lowest rungs; good and even bad averages are particularly sought after. But these onanistic vanities disappear in human intercourse—everything is equalized; the biggest fool invents troubling arguments, and you, reputedly clever, don't know what to say. In actual fact, you will be clever and truthful only if he joins you on the "upper" level; otherwise you will fall to his—that is what usually happens. In truth the levels are variable, but persons define them together; it is a social and codified relationship, exceedingly complex since it reflects not only objective structures—milieux, generations, classes—and the particular affinities between groups, between people, but also the prejudices of each, that is, a normative judgment on the absolute value of intelligence. For instance, your friend will consider you a brain all the more easily if he thinks intellectuals ridiculous and values only unreasonable violence or sensibility—which he pronounces to be irrational. He is classified by this attitude. Does he classify you? Hardly; but if you are a Jew, for example, you know that he is going to delight in proclaiming that you are much cleverer than he could ever be, and this suspect modesty betrays his profound antisemitism. In short, levels: variable, complex, they come to everyone through the Other; when we come to speak about the famous "stupidity" that Gustave denounces on every occasion, we shall see in detail that it is oppression. A man can be put into a position of stupidity; once he is in it he remains there, barring any way out. Inversely, there are intellects that engender privilege. Kings had style—naturally. Very simply, they were convinced that the national tongue was *their property*. As a small child, Achille understood that intelligence was the property of the Flauberts. He scarcely knew how to read when he let himself be penetrated by his father's ideas; without noticing, he adopted the concepts that rule the paternal thought, the tangible articulations of ideas; from premises to conclusions, his reasoning embodied the rigor of the exact sciences. This he did in order to become in advance, in an instantaneous celebration, a physician—sole resident master of the Hôtel-Dieu—and a scientist. Shall we say that this intelligence *imitates* or that it *borrows*? As you like. In my opinion the point is that the intelligence is awakened. The little boy, we have seen, has no faith in his own feelings and not much more in his body, I imagine, never having been the object of an exclusive love. Moreover, the feelings are atrophied and the body does what it can to become the father's—as soon as he can he hides his chin under the paternal beard. But the less he is attached to his singularities, the more he relies upon and surrenders to the flood of fire which cuts across the Flaubert enterprise and which the father has so effectively exploited. In Achille, intelligence is his supreme privilege and the source of his future rights, it is merit and God's gift, wholly within him as he is wholly son of the father and future father, on the condition that he employ it only for the good of the family. He is deprived, in a time of individualism, of all individual value, but precisely because of this he finds his reason for living in that admirable intelligence whose inessential servant (as an isolated molecule) and proprietor (as the future incarnation of the paterfamilias) he is. And can we say that that is enough actually to make him a gifted child, the first in his class in everything, a distinguished student? Yes, it is enough. When thought—which is stubborn, original, active—becomes *creative*, it must be explained by other reasons sought in other instances. But Achille *does not produce anything*—he understands everything. He does not raise himself above that characteristic we all have in common, a mental aperture. By this I mean that prospective but empty unity which defines a synthetic field where objective relations enter into coexistence and quite directly *establish reciprocal contacts*. Its source is the tension of the field, the simple expression of our biological and practical unity which imposes neither categories nor specific relations, but which does not allow contacts, whatever they are, to be isolated. As Merleau-Ponty says, man is the only animal that does not have original equipment, thus the dimensions of his mental aperture are not defined a priori; the diameter varies according to physiological and social factors, the nature of the individual or communal praxis dilates or contracts it. Misery, beatings, or exhaustion reduce it to a mere point, only to the extent that men are degraded to the level of the subhuman. When people eat to assuage hunger, when they are suitably paid for moderate work, inhibitions, defenses, taboos limit the aperture and succeed in blurring the lens with blind spots, posing principles, concealing conclusions. Or else one escapes from unbearable contradictions by means of mental absence. Mistrust also inhibits. All these restrictions come to each person from his prehistory—he repeats them as much as he submits to them; let someone deliver him and his mind will dilate—no limitation is prescribed to anyone. Except through physical accidents.

Little Achille, however, is altogether trusting. Moreover, the eighteenth century bequeathed to the father Flaubert his inclination to view things from a cosmic perspective; Achille-Cléophas investigated *nature*. As a physician he observed one of its infinitesimal details—the fracture of bones; as a philosopher he posited that in principle, the infinite universe is entirely knowable through reason. A mature science now exists which has triumphed over superstition. Very early in life, the child hears about Newton, Lavoisier; what he learns about them confirms his father's proud assertions; he thinks that Achille-Cléophas is continuing the work of the pioneers and that his elder son will continue his work. Science is reason objectified, intelligence is the subjectivity of reason: the second creates the first, the first guarantees the second. The little boy's intelligence, guaranteed by the centuries, is the permanent union of the creature Achille with his all-powerful creator; it certainly has to contend with the unlimited breadth of his mind. Intelligent through docility, he abandons himself to the truth without any prejudice, trustingly, adhering from the outset to the father's teachings. He perceives connections, learns to predict them and then to deduce them: Achille's intelligence is the superb inventory of the Flaubert patrimony, his future legacy. His is a born proprietor: to learn is to validate; with all his knowledge—known already by the father that he will one day be—he will make himself worthy of the honors and responsibilities passed on to him. In sum, in order to learn—that is, in order to receive—we have only to surrender: what holds us back are resistances whose origin is to be sought in the archaic layers of our personal history. But Achille, future father, residuary legatee, *puts up no resistance*: there is almost nothing in him that his father has not put there. Driven by the fierce ambition of his creator—claimed, internalized until it has become his own spontaneity—trusting, docile, sharing the physician-philosopher's ends and leaving it to him to choose the means, this child has no intelligence other than his conviction of being intelligent by divine right; nothing more is needed.

The eldest, whatever he was, had a mandate to relive his father's life. Therefore we find him launched on a never-ending progression. Was he saved? No, lost. The stage of identification should have been transcended, the ritual murder of the father accomplished. The external terms did not allow it: to become the paterfamilias was to be enclosed forever in the father's image. In fact, from early childhood the pride of the father and the humility of the child left no room for doubt, the creature would never equal the Almighty who had raised him from the mud. Through his implacable effort, the little Achille-Cléophas produced ex nihilo the famous Dr. Flaubert, his public incarnation; on his death the son would take up the role, without altering it at all—everything essential had been done. A dazzled slave, Achille let himself be persuaded, and this rather reassured him; as scion of an almost patriarchal family he felt the need that Gustave would feel later to adore an invincible master. Everything would have collapsed in anguish if he had imagined that one day he might surpass him. When Achille-Cléophas made clear that he was the archetype and that after his death there would be nothing more than a chain of repetitions, the son was in collusion with the father. In collusion as well when the progenitor promised to bequeath to the child his essence, but in a reduced form. A perfect arrangement: the extravagant lord would return to dust without losing an inch of his stature; in his absence he would remain superior in every way to the replacement he had chosen for himself; his yes-man was delighted. What an arrogant, peaceful dream: to become a power in this world and his own master without ever leaving a state of servitude. It takes very little to emerge into the vapor, into the interstellar shadows of anguish, indeed it is enough not to bow down; Achille avoided this all too human anguish. A new Aeneas, he bowed his head and carried Anchisis on his back.

Did Achille-Cléophas love his son? What we can say is that in his last years he quietly prepared to make a new beginning; his son Achille was close to him, helped him in everyting. It was necessary to complete the young man's education and, at the same time, to secure the support in high places that would ensure him his father's

111

post and honors; after which Achille-Cléophas would withdraw. Little by little, Achille would take on the responsibilities one by one, the father *would lean on him*. Freed from therapeutic concerns, the old practitioner could at last realize his desire to become wholly a man of science. He had acquired and transmitted orally all the medical knowledge of his time; that was not enough—*scripta manent*; he could not die without gathering his learning—some of which came directly from his experience—into a treatise on general physiology that would perpetuate his name. The physician-philosopher revealed his project to anyone who would listen; he did not refrain from adding that this final happiness would not be possible *without Achille*. Achille, or the keystone. Worn out by drudgery well before old age, the old doctor found hope, a taste for living, the timid ambition to survive only through the blind trust he placed in his son. We can imagine this reciprocity: the father procured his own future joys by preparing his son for future duties, future honors. The son could not help discovering that he was both the father's supreme end and the means of his glory: so, without being deprived of the pleasures of submission, he was allowed to display his generosity toward the magnanimous tyrant who had overwhelmed him with gifts. Everything joined them, these two men—the past, the future; in the present, every new patient occasioned complicity, they discussed the case calmly and the clinical idea would come to the fore in one or the other head equally. Is this loving? Yes. Achille's death would have crushed his father; this was Achille-Cléophas's love: a *practical* affection that could not be distinguished from work in common and a costly trust which the son produced in the paternal heart through twenty years of effort. This came into being slowly, imperceptibly: in the beginning, the physician-philosopher merely favored the elder son on principle; later he came to prefer him and then, toward the end of his life, to cherish him for himself. Between the two men there was no demonstration of affection—intimacy, that's all. In the long run, I suppose, Dr. Flaubert became attached to Achille's features, to his voice, to that long body, "all legs." Truly, whatever his physique, the father would have adapted to it; he saw it only as the trademark.

On 10 November 1845, Achille-Cléophas falls ill. Who examines him? His son. Achille finds that his father has a tumor of the thigh, which is spreading quickly. The best friends of the dying man, two highly esteemed physicians, hasten to his bedside; surgical intervention is in order, and again it is his son that the old doctor charges with the operation. The colleagues seem a bit put out, Achille is perhaps too young. Resistance is in vain—the medical director insists on his son, the operation takes place, he dies.

The anecdote is well known, but I have not seen anyone accord it the significance it deserves. To be sure, the choice has been viewed as a rite of succession, the most rigorous transference of power: the operator operated upon. A surgeon threatened by death designates his successor by investing in him the obligation to carve him up: you save me or you replace me; and if you save me, you will have proved your worth, you will succeed me in a few years. Perhaps this choice, which was soon known to all of "society," will appear to be some kind of public relations maneuver, as though the dying man had wanted to ensure that his office would become hereditary by bringing ultimate pressure to bear on the people of Rouen: "I am of the profession; if this man is good enough for me, rest assured that he is also good enough for you; I shall prove it by trying him out before recommending him to you." Indeed, this nuance is present, it is a determination of the act and of its objective sense; this does not mean, however, that it can be made to correspond to some autonomous and definite mode of subjectivity.

In any case, what matters to *us* is to describe and determine the relationship between this father and this son, such as it was manifest through this ultimate paternal gift. For it was a gift. Thirty-two years earlier, Dr. Flaubert gave life to the eldest of his children; he never ceased *reproducing* that life, he nourished his future successor with his own substance to the point where the son was transformed into the father's alter ego. At the moment of death, he makes his son a gift of his worn-out body, of his own life; he offers big brother Achille the most flattering patient—the best specialist in the county, admired, feared, respected by his clients, his students, and his colleagues. Why? To make a grand gesture, perhaps; should this be the case, it would have to be seen as much more than an ingenious publicity stunt. But that is only a superficial detail; entering more deeply into the sick man's caprice, one cannot help being struck by it as an expression of family pride: only a Flaubert can treat a Flaubert. It is the honor of this medical House. The imperious old man, crushed by illness, took to his bed only at the last moment; he chose his doctor, kept a vigilant watch during the surgery, and then died peacefully three weeks later in the bosom of his family, without having lost consciousness. Rilke would have been ravished by this self-willed death—it is in the image of a willful life. Most likely he guided Achille's diagnosis and later his knife. Achille's docility, however,

113

required a thousand times in other situations, didn't interest the father at all on this day. First of all, he would have found the same thing anywhere; his age, his learning, and his reputation would have ensured that the chosen colleague, whoever he was, would have accepted advice and demonstrated his deference and submission. But quite the contrary, after half a century of practice, Achille-Cléophas was convinced that docility did not help surgeons, that it only stood in their way. He taught his students that the supreme surgical virtues were still those he had demonstrated throughout his career: independence, the spirit of initiative, energy, and that one had to decide alone, as he had always done, if need be against everyone. What he required from his son in these crucial hours was rigor and authority, Flaubert qualities par excellence, transmitted from one generation to the other by blood and by example, at least since that tough customer Nicolas, Achille's grandfather, who was imprisoned during the Terror for refusing either to alter his opinions or to keep quiet.

If Dr. Flaubert chose Achille, it was chiefly out of a wholehearted trust that came as compensation, a few days before death, for the unquenchable faith of his elder son. The father did, then, appreciate the son's own merits. This abusive father had fashioned his future replacement so well that he made him, as we have seen, into his .opposite: a relative being, inessential and timid, who never determines himself *from within* but always in terms of the external model he has been given and wants to imitate in everything. To take only the matter of authority, for example, the father destroyed it in Achille from childhood; Achille's misfortune is the heteronomy of his will—there is nothing in him that is not imposed from *without*, nothing that expresses his original spontaneity. That spontaneity, furthermore, which was slowly and surely strangled, is no more than a word. It is therefore perfectly impossible for him ever to display that sovereign authority which belongs to each and every human being. Maniacal meticulousness, obsessive behavior, hesitations, silences, intuitive diagnoses whose reasoning remains obscure—these are measures to combat an insidious anguish, signs which alert us to the importance of the internal deficit provoked by paternal tyranny. His clients respect Achille but do not find him very persuasive. He will be like this until his death; he is already like this by the end of 1845. On the other hand, identification with the father, even while devastating the subservient son, requires that he produce in himself and project the appearance of authority. Appearance, nothing more; what we can say is that the son believes in the father and, as long as the father lives,

114

Achille has some insurance. Dr. Flaubert asks nothing more of him, convinced that this poorly played role is Achille's truth; the father believes that he has not only been reproduced but *remade*. He will therefore operate on himself with his son's hand, not by overwhelming him with advice but by having given him since childhood his own character, his way of seeing things, his own inflexibility. Is this relation of father to son really love? If you like. But it is a rare passion that brings two lovers into so much harmony with each other. For both Flauberts, the *essential being* of the son is the *character* he plays, and for both of them this character is the father. By choosing the son, by foisting him on his colleagues, Achille-Cléophas chooses himself. Defeated by the tumor, he rallies; thanks to his incarnation, he keeps the initiative; mortal danger has driven him to his bed, reduced him to impotence—at the same time he sits up, rejuvenated, stands leaning over his aged body and is about to wrest it away from death. One in two—he remains his own master till the end. Even if the operation should not succeed, at least he will have had the last word. Someone will die, mortal remains will be buried—Dr. Flaubert will survive.

But there is still more to it than such reciprocal identification. Looking closely at the objective meaning of his choice, one finds the mark of a deeper intention, unformulated, carnal, and tender, which seems to take us back to the obscure world of *endured* feelings. This man offers his son his old, worn-out body; he has decided to suffer through his son. Minutely; passively he *will feel* the incision of the knife in his flesh. It is as though he wanted to pay a debt of blood and enjoyed giving himself up to the young man's hands, as though this real and voluntary impotence were the price and mirror image of another impotence, that of the newborn in the hands of his young father thirty-two years earlier. Old Flaubert, as we have seen, did not want to disappear by conferring royalty on one of his colleagues unless he was a Flaubert. But we might say, inversely, that it pleased him while dying to receive humbly from Achille the gift of suffering, to search his son's eyes, his voice, his gestures for the least sign of reassurance, as though he had assumed the relative being that illness confers so that the transfigured heir might be raised by the father's withdrawal to absolute being. The father makes himself an infant, the son will determine the needs of the old body just as the medical director had formerly settled everything that concerned his children. But above all it is a sacrifice. The surgical intervention seems belated, success is not certain, Achille-Cléophas knows this better than anyone; if he is condemned, let death come to him from his elder son. "I have made you,

you have made me—we are quits. Yet—not completely; my blood is spilled under your knife, this is the transfusion of powers: in dying by your hand, I feel in the pain that the *mana* is leaving me and entering your body."

What is striking is the voluntary passivity. Inflicted suffering and death accepted in advance. Reclaimed, endured dependence, an abrupt reversal of roles, as in a Saturnalia, the father becoming the infant son so that the son is metamorphosed into his own father—all this is not consciously desired or seen or known, but *felt*. Achille-Cléophas plunges into that heavy, deep inertia which envelops physical pain and all feeling. It is through his son and for him, but above all *in him* that he tries his lordly generosity—like a sickness, like a passion. But how can we conceive of this if not as a burning passion? We must surely acknowledge that the final relations between father and son were lived with passion. Achille-Cléophas gave everything to his elder son: life, material goods, his knowledge, his position, and finally his body. He never loved in his son a unique adventure, an incomparable "monster," a hazardous life whose price is risk and inevitable death, whatever its course. He cherished himself in his son *as other*, and in doing so he made Achille into another Achille-Cléophas.

The most unexpected result of this relationship is that the old man, by giving himself up to the knife, deprived his elder son of even the possibility of deliverance through the classic murder of the father; certainly Achille killed him, but he made himself the docile instrument of a sacred suicide.

After the death of the chief surgeon, the elder son completed his identification with his father. The same town, the same position, the same clients, the same residence—this was the legacy. But he restored it: the same manner, the same habits. When he climbed into his buggy in a nearby village, the older people thought they were seeing the old Dr. Flaubert risen from the dead. In winter apparently the resemblance became hallucinatory: Achille persisted in wearing the old goatskin that had belonged to the paterfamilias. This accoutrement, already "eccentric" under the Restoration, was a mark of the progenitor's coarseness; in 1860 it became aberrant. No matter; the tall, spindly man enjoyed enormous popularity, and if people smiled at his dress it was in a friendly way, respectfully. It must be noted, simply, that this peculiar fur coat is not *chosen* but *inherited*; this man, so supple when he had to adapt to inconsequential changes, became rigid when someone dared to propose that he modify, even slightly, the role of the father, *his* role. Polished, refined by his new friendships, he was urbane in the salons, a clod on his rounds; in both instances, actually, he *perpetuated* the paterfamilias. Without departing from his peasant ways, Achille-Cléophas, more than anything else, wanted his family to rub shoulders securely with the elite of Rouen; Achille preserved the contrast and suppressed the contradiction by effacing everything. The goatskin no longer reminded the clients of the Flauberts' rural origins but merely recalled the respected figure of the physician-philosopher.[3]

The role, moreover, was not a silent one, Achille knew his rejoinders by heart. Louis Levasseur wrote in 1872: "He keeps a store of opinions, theses, doctrines from the paternal heritage which are for him the law of the prophets; he stubbornly opposes them to certain novelties—*Pater dixit*, and in order to remain on good terms with him there is only one answer: amen. He is so blocked by this that he digs his heels in beforehand against anything that could challenge his position. He would firmly entrench himself if he were not afraid that he would be accused of being stuck in a rut.'"[4]

He "digs his heels in beforehand against anything that could challenge his position"—here Achille's profound contradiction can be clearly seen. He has to adapt himself, to accept the new or be stuck in a rut, that is, lose his clientele, destroy the patrimony Achille-Cléophas had entrusted to him. But if in doing so he must abandon an opinion that his father bequeathed to him, he loses his bearings, he feels he has betrayed his creator and annihilated his own person by replacing rules with generalized indecision. In areas the father did not explore, he does manage to collect information and keep himself "up to date"; wherever the physician-philosopher stuck his nose, however, Achille refuses to change anything. The dated axioms, the outmoded methods that he obstinately preserves, these are survivals; he clings to them in vain, their relative importance continuously decreasing as the influx of new information threatens to make them

---

3. Gustave was not mistaken here. He wrote in *Madame Bovary*: "[Dr. Larivière] belonged to the great school of surgeons formed by Bichot, to that now vanished generation of philosophic practitioners who, cherishing their art with a fanatic love, exercised it with exaltation and wisdom! In his hospital everyone trembled when he was angry, and his students worshiped him to such a degree that they forced themselves, when scarcely established, to imitate him as much as possible. So that throughout the surrounding villages one found them wearing his long woolen overcoat and his capacious black suit, with unbuttoned cuffs partly covering his fleshy hands, very fine hands, which were never gloved."

4. "Les Notables de Normande," cited by René Dumesnil, *Gustave Flaubert*, p. 81.

marginal. Yet for him, the callouses, the cysts are the essential things, the innermost mark of his being, the very place where the life of repetition merges with the inert permanence of death.

Beyond these lasting conflicts, we can make him out rather well. And Levasseur, who seems spiteful but shrewd, gives us another precious piece of information: "He is overcautious, a punctilious fault-finder in his examination of the subject, as much out of concern for his reputation as out of uncertainty over the patient." All told, nothing could be better—should he have been negligent? But it is no accident that the author uses, in immediate succession, two pejorative epithets: faultfinder, punctilious. Achille had to be excessive, endlessly questioning the patient and his relatives and friends; every time this important man left his shell to make contact with clinical reality, he had to take the time to resurrect the dead old man and put him in condition to confront the new situation. The hesitant incarnation began by protecting himself against anguish and solitude through punctiliousness; his finical questions and often useless precautions were supplications, he secured himself against the methods of the new medicine through obsessional manias. And then, he gained time; when he was at last reassured, shored up on all sides, the timid man once more became Dr. Flaubert (father and son), he gave free play to the spontaneous movements of his mind with the conviction that the old man, as in former times, was thinking within him. Indeed, he was recognized as having "an intuitive knowledge of his art. He knew how to determine and diagnose better than how to define or explain." What has become of the brilliant discursive intelligence that won him such success during his school and university years? Was it snuffed out along with Achille-Cléophas? No. But defining, explaining, is a matter of supporting the diagnosis with certain theoretical and practical conceptions; in particular it is necessary to have very precise views on what we call today symptomatology. In this area, I would imagine, the philosopher-physician excelled. The fact is, he was in step *with his time*—a bit ahead, a bit behind like everyone else, but sustained, nourished, carried along by the sweep of the epoch. His colleagues everywhere in France had directly or indirectly had the same mentors, thus Achille-Cléophas considered that he had the right to their approbation. For him, diagnosis was always legislation. This splendid physician supposed that the particular case always involved general ideas and principles; at the same time, since there were more maladies on earth, and some of them stranger, than he had dreamed of in his philosophy, when he encountered an unknown variety he had the feeling that his diagnosis was creating a precedent, as though he were head of a tribunal. And if someone asks me where I have found all this information about the old man, I recommend rereading the portrait of Dr. Larivière in which everything is spelled out; in particular, it is instructive to consider carefully the relations between the celebrated doctor and his unhappy colleague.

A prestigious profession superbly practiced; what is it then that hinders Achille from imitating his father? I will answer: Achille-Cléophas himself. To liberate his son, another abrupt mutation would have been necessary. Lacking this, he was so infused with the paternal knowledge when it was vital that he was marked by it forever. Axioms and principles, rules and laws—this was intelligence in action; his father discovered relationships and brought them back to first truths by a continuous movement of thought. Achille imitated, then understood, he refused to take the road alone with rigor and spontaneity. The obsolescence of medical ideas was very rapid, unfortunately, from Claude Bernard to Pasteur. In all the sciences positivism tended to replace mechanism, which the new men of science judged to be contaminated with metaphysics. In fact, it was a matter of gently castrating the mechanism: materialism was severed from it in order to avoid, they said, falling back into the philosophical rut. Causes disappeared as well—which was not a bad thing—only laws remained. Briefly, Achille's contemporaries had evolved, his colleagues were making another medicine. Or shall we say that it was "neither altogether the same nor altogether different." Achille knew their ideas and rejected them, for the simple reason that he was Dr. Falubert II. Nevertheless, it must be understood that the aged father, if he had survived for some years, would himself have experienced difficulty in adapting; he might have rejected all innovations out of hand. But we cannot be certain of this; he had a passion for knowledge, and something of the concerns and discoveries of the new generation would have touched him. To abandon *my* ideas, that costs me something; but I would let them go, *my* ideas, more easily than if the Other, whoever he were, had etched them into me. Achille-Cléophas could change his principles if absolutely necessary—they were his. Achille cannot—they are his patrimony. He exhibits both an intransigence and an uneasiness his father never had; he is wary, on the least pretext he bristles or becomes stubbornly oppositional. And all at once fear engenders violence: one has to keep quiet or have a falling out with him. The problem is that he feels the paternal doctrine as *himself*, so successfully did Achille-Cléophas transform him into Dr. Flaubert.

And at the same time, this doctrine is responsible for the slight gap that continues to separate him from medical reality. He no longer has the language to define, deduce, explain. The only language he accepts, his father's, is quite unsuitable; indeed, it is preferable not to make use of it, for once they are formulated these truths seem dated. As for the other language, if he uses it he is committing an act of betrayal; he is an apostate. His stance of opposition to anything new is above all a sacred obligation. There is no doubt that his reading has some influence on him; nevertheless, he firmly adheres to inherited principles. Incapable of justifying his diagnoses, he most often has recourse to naked intuition. Naked—that is what others say. In point of fact, the synthetic idea takes form in his head from new findings that have slipped in, in spite of himself; on the outside the idea becomes practical and therapeutic, a product of actions, prescriptions; at the same time by straining words a little, the devout son, without opening his mouth, attempts to express this idea for himself alone, silently, in the paternal tongue.

After the death of the father, Achille will not even be the head of the Flaubert family. The transference of powers, however, was done correctly. He will have scarcely any influence on the inhabitants of Croisset, for the father inhabits him, an inert weight, like the sum of his incapacities. Achille is not a man but rather a "vacancy always in the future," since he is constrained to be a plenitude always past, never surpassed, another's plenitude. For his elder son the father was, when alive, always *the same*. From 1846 on, Achille finds himself committed to the most demanding kind of death. He stops living and dies day by day. He wants to be his living father; instead, he is his dead father until the very end. Achille, that great mournful clown, wants nothing except *to be*. All his adolescent and youthful efforts had but one goal: the rapid internalization of his father's *being*, making it his internal substance and his constant conditioning for *being* ready, in case of misfortune, to replace him on the spot. He succeeded; and afterward? In order to preserve this role he must abandon the research, the philosophy, even the intelligence and authority of the paterfamilias, in sum everything that defined the living father in his free existence. Achille's existence is over. It is a broken watch that stopped at 1846.

Is this to say that Achille was unhappy? I don't think so. He possessed his creator through the unworthy image he modestly presented to everyone. What a *sheltered* life! Each day he began all over again, happily, the cycle of paternal acts: hospital, amphitheater, visits, buggy and goatskin. This empty carcass dreamed only of repetition. After all, it was in the family: the veterinarians, sons of veterinarians, repeated their fathers' actions; the abrupt mutation of Achille-Cléophas freed one generation. Only one; the following reestablished on a higher level the eternal recurrence and its sacred ceremonies. It would be this way for centuries, until the next mutation. The heir enjoyed the father's clientele, fame, and fortune without thinking of expanding them—maintaining them was enough. He was not unaware that the honors and money were directed through him to the vanished founder, but this was precisely the source of his deep satisfaction: the attentions, the respect of the people of Rouen gave him the subjective conviction of being the best possible incarnation of the eponymous hero. Therefore his truth was the father, that protecting "ego" which was at the same time *his* ego; and his perfect security came to him from this strange and very intimate tension: he was never himself except in discovering his inferiority to the self. He was satisfied, at least pacified; and slightly mournful because of the emptiness he had created in himself. Mechanistic analysis, the father's lessons and their logical rigor, then later the necessity of *being only Achille-Cléophas* had brutally repressed, crushed, all the deep feelings, all the irrational thoughts that each of us ponder and that constitute our richness. He remained nothing. In him the irresistible brilliance of Achille-Cléophas was moribund. If he raised himself up a bit, it was his milieu, his class, that carried him along; but if he allowed himself to be buoyed up in this fashion, he made himself as heavy as he could: he professed to love the progress of medical knowledge in imitation of the progenitor, but at the same time he hated the changes that estranged him from his god. Considering only him, the eldest, the inheritor, the head of the family, the fall of the House of Flaubert seemed imminent. We would have wished him sons who would assume the dead grandfather's ambitions. They would truly have lived; for Achille—this is his only quality but it is rather significant—was *not admirable enough*, he would not have discomfited his children. Alas! Fate decreed that he should have only a daughter and that the Rouen branch of the Flauberts should die with him.

FIVE

The Birth of a Younger Son

The Flauberts settled in 1819 at the Hôtel-Dieu. Gustave was conceived some eighteen months later, at the end of the first trimester of 1821. He was born on 12 December, another child soon followed, and then Caroline in 1824. This means—weaning was quite late at the time—that Gustave's mother was still nursing him when she began her next pregnancy and that he was only one and a half at the time of his younger brother's death. He was three years older than his sister; so Mme Flaubert must have found herself pregnant once more when he was two years and a few months old. Thus, from the future writer's birth until his third year, Mme Flaubert passed nearly without transition from pregnancy to confinement, from nursing to mourning, from mourning to pregnancy and a new confinement. In nine years, three children; three children in less than four—from nonchalance to frenzy. Next there is dead calm; yet the mother is still young, thirty-one years old. No matter, the family is complete, the progenitor will beget no more. Don't the Flauberts make love any more? Let us return to our comparison. Three children in nine years: these lovers are dawdling, children come to them because they sleep together; three in four years: the parents are in a hurry, they sleep together in order to have children. Afterward, weary and contented, they must have occasionally renewed these embraces, which no longer had any goal and gave little pleasure. Such, at least, was the doctor's view of things. I am not certain that his wife renounced the pleasures of the bed with such good grace. But what can we say? Gratuitous pleasures frightened her; she had justified such indulgence by the need to perpetuate the family. The couple had conformed quite strictly to a course of family planning; with the work of the flesh accomplished, children brought into the world, it would have been reprehensible to pursue carnal pleasure simply for its own sake.

And why did they stop after the birth of Caroline? Well, here the reason is obvious and I have already stated it: Mme Flaubert wanted a daughter. Once she had one, they closed the book. Are we to imagine that Mme Flaubert was already thinking of a daughter when her husband begat Gustave? I believe so. We have seen that her childhood disposed her to find herself, to cherish herself, in the person of a new Caroline. We should not be surprised to learn, in some rediscovered letter, that she had wanted to escape from herself in this fashion, flesh of her flesh, from the moment of her first pregnancy. But this desire—supposing it was already manifest—had not yet become an imperious demand. As for demands, the incestuous and submissive wife hadn't any; the eldest was the father's son and his successor, she set aside her preferences without hesitation and was delighted at her immediate entrance into the empire of the sun; there would always be time later to rejoin the states of the moon, her own empire. Then came two more boys who retired with apologies. During the nine months of each pregnancy, the mother had plenty of time to dream of the future infant: if it were a little girl, she would be adored, given everything. In this free play of the imagination Mme Flaubert understood, finally, the strength of her desire: I *want* a daughter. But the little males died before disappointing her—sex was of little account when it came to health. What heredity was responsible for these accidents? Achille-Cléophas's parents and grandparents seem to have been very healthy; Caroline, on the other hand, could recall the bereavements of her childhood, the death of the young wife and above all the death of that frail father, always ill, who survived her by ten years; Caroline could recall coughing up blood herself.[1] A sad balance sheet; the orphan's deep guilt fed on these memories. She must have savored fully what certain analysts call the curse of the mother. Mme Fleuriot was telling her: you killed me, I curse you, the fruit of your womb will rot because you are rotten inside.

Happily, Dr. Flaubert, God incarnate, reassured and calmed her; and then as I have remarked, at this period of their life the child justified love but love came first. With seven years of experience, Caroline drew some very simple conclusions. For the purpose of breeding, properly speaking, it could be managed, she was fertile with a large pelvis; but without being unhealthy or even fragile, there

---

1. Overworked, Achille-Cléophas had also had attacks of hemoptysis.

was a germ of delicacy in her flesh which she transmitted to her sons that predisposed them to die; finally, her temperament—or rather the almighty doctor's—inclined her in spite of her wishes to bear children of the male sex.

Then came the beginning of the bad years; the hated Hôtel-Dieu revealed to her the very slight reserve of an excessively preoccupied husband. For the second time Caroline was frustrated by a father, and she was unaware that this withdrawal revived the unhappiness of her solitary childhood, the silent condemnation of Dr. Fleuriot. For the first time she wanted some compensation, and this could take only one form. A single form, strictly defined by her unhappiness—a daughter. We will never know if she had the audacity to talk about it in the master's presence, but it is certain that she made herself understood. Achille-Cléophas appears to have agreed instantly; a daughter, very well, she would have one. Against the indiscreet little males who had got into the wrong womb, against the fragility she passed on to her own flesh, there was a single tactic: erase everything and begin again, as often as necessary, in order to give birth to a little girl who would live. Achille-Cléophas certainly hoped a son would be born in the course of this quest—his spermatic honor was at stake. But before anything else he wanted to do it quickly. The couple had five or six years, hardly more; if they didn't hurry, the youngest would be the children of old people. Thus Gustave was born, the first result of the new family planning; it was his misfortune to be the guinea pig.

After the move, the young mother did not become pregnant for more than a year. When it finally happened, she had had time to brood over her regrets; the Hôtel-Dieu, internalized, had darkened her sensibility forever. Forever? That depended, it was a toss-up.

Heads: if the expected child was of the female sex, Caroline would learn an unknown love, a deep feeling she had never experienced before. This dutiful woman would know generosity, she would find herself in renewal and would be renewed in order to find herself. The father's imperceptible reserve and the avid abandon of the daughter would balance each other out; the Hôtel-Dieu would lose its symbolic value. It *represented* unhappiness, and Caroline would be living a new happiness; without disappearing, the old prison of sufferings would recede into the background and lose its spellbinding power. There is no dungeon so black that it is not illuminated by passion.

Tails: if by some misfortune she was carrying a male for the fourth time, she would not give birth to him without a terrible disappointment. The intruder's birth would confirm Mme Fleuriot's curse—the guilty daughter condemned to bear only sons. It was merely a brief step from here to the conclusion that these sons—except the first—would die in infancy. Besides, the mother's relationship with the child would not be renewed—resuscitated, nothing more. With less intensity; she would care for her little man as she had done three times, with application and devotion, without too much enthusiasm, fearing at the slightest discomfort that a sudden fever would carry him off, and silently reproaching herself for not fearing enough. A single modification: the last of the "morituri" had led his short life in the happy ambience of rue du Petit-Salut; this one was to be born in the midst of public suffering, in the ineffaceable soot; his appearance would be a profound failure for the young mother, sanctioning all failures past, present, and future, the overwork of a slightly distracted husband, the neglect she didn't want to admit to herself, all the bereavements, the infant's own future death. This bearer of unhappiness would bring down upon his own head and upon his relatives all the malignant powers whirling around in the hospice—he would be a child of the Hôtel-Dieu.

Nine highly agitated months. She must have imagined everything, poor Caroline, she must have hoped and despaired, sometimes welcoming a future daughter as celestial manna, at other times spitting into the ashes to deny the imminent son. No doubt these agitations of the soul remained hidden. But she could not dissemble her ardent wish to have a girl, to recreate herself. After which the midwife delivered her of a boy. He was shown to her with cries and laughter, naked and, as we are at birth, magnificently sufficient. If my hypothesis is accurate, the young mother viewed him as an alien creature; she had too fervently hoped to reproduce herself—in the literal sense of the word—not to resent the fact that an interloper had been created without permission in the flesh of her flesh. An Other. Who was of the party of the others, of soot, of death, and who came to suffer, to die on this earth in order to carry out the sentence delivered by an unknown tribunal. This birth threw the mother back on her own feelings of neglect. Happy to have a second son, Dr. Flaubert must have neither shared nor perceived his wife's dismay.

Caroline was a dutiful woman, and we have seen what this implies. She never hated Gustave, the emblem of her failure; she admitted her disappointment, nothing more. Beyond that there was a newborn child who had to be fed, cleaned, protected. She did what was necessary. But even without speculating on the hidden recesses of this deceptively transparent soul, it is evident that the object of these meticulous attentions could have struck her in only one of two ways: either as *her* failure as a woman and a mother—that is, as a detestable and entirely negative singularity—or in his pure generality as an infant. She preferred to see only a greedy existence which *was not* the desired daughter and which, apart from this quite definite negation, remained purely undetermined. A life with a sex, nothing more. What had the other sons been anyway—leaving Achille aside—if not the *general* objects of her attentions? She loved them with a general love which, as we have seen, respected the sex of the father in them and the future glory of the Flauberts. But she certainly must have experienced each masculine birth as a repetition. Living side by side they would have created and sustained their differences, she would have been forced to recognize their individual characters which coexistence would have emphasized—in their quarrels one might have seemed more impetuous, the other more spiteful. But they were born and died in isolation, there was no way to compare them. Each one seemed to the mother .the repeat of the one before. A return of births comparable to the return of the seasons, of seasonal labors and an ancient curse. Gustave was a repeat of the two dead children who preceded him. For his mother, he was dead from birth; she guarded him against death while inflexibly awaiting its arrival. For many parents their infant seems to be the most disarming present, the most sumptuous future; Gustave, no, not for the Flaubert parents. They were afraid, they concealed their feelings from each other, the father confirmed in a calm, professional voice that his son would live; these efforts may have prevented the word "decease" from being pronounced or from resonating silently in one of the two minds, but they did not prevent the child from being deprived of a future. The parents spied on this organism minute by minute, and their surveillance so absorbed them that they could not think of the coming years. Yet even before they are lived, these years are what individualize, not *subjectively* in a father's mind, but *objectively* as a prefabrication. It is enough for the head of a family to have failed in his life or to have succeeded—the child's fate is sealed; he is observed, he is judged: will he be capable of confronting the future that has been prepared for him? Yesterday's demands are today's plans, the guiding ideas that will direct the father and mother; the parents will begin, often very early, by giving the little human beings a "character" which is nothing more, truthfully, than the sum of paternal expectations: "the little fellow has my endurance, your good sense and sweetness," etc. Meaning, he will take

127

up the profession we choose for him. What happens subsequently is of little importance. By later internalizing this prematurely invented individuality, the child risks severe complications, but in any case the difficulties will be less serious than if during his first years the parents have more or less silently awaited his death. Gustave understood nothing of this, to be sure, he was fooled—except that a child is taught to walk differently for sixty years' use than for two; even the care of the most adept mother is provisional. This little boy is living like an amateur since he is going to die; he is busy *waiting*, like the young ladies of Passy today who take courses at the Sorbonne while *waiting* to be married.

Gustave was born between two deaths; doctors and analysts all know that this is a bad beginning. Yet a boy was born after Gustave and died at six months, when his brother was eighteen months old. With the late weaning then prevalent, for some weeks Mme Flaubert could nurse the two sons at the same time. Did she love the son who died more than the one who survived? Perhaps, though it is hard to see any basis for this preference—the intruder also took the place of the daughter she wanted. One can scarcely say that he was less marked than Gustave, whose existence recapitulated Caroline's misfortunes, including her conjugal disappointments. As for the next son, the die was cast and the damage done. It might be that the parents saw only his innocence and regretted his loss. Hardly. But the blow was chiefly felt by Achille-Cléophas himself; this time the physician-philosopher surely must have wondered if his semen had not gone bad. For an accredited doctrine—flattering to husbands—held that the spermatozoa were miniature men; the father thrust his little images into the mother, who nourished them with her fats and her blood but did not influence their nature. If Dr. Flaubert was fathering dead children, wasn't it because he bore within him the fateful principle of these passings? He began to torment himself. Uneasy paternity! In fact, it was chiefly his pride that suffered: what could be more humiliating for a paterfamilias than to have defective testicles?

What the couple clearly knew, in any case, was that very soon Gustave too would be taken from them. It didn't matter that he had resisted for eighteen months; the death of the younger brother was black and glaring evidence, blinding them to any other possibility. They could say of Achille—who had survived more than ten years—that he was spared. But the other one, no. When would it be his turn? Gustave was subjected to the most contradictory treatment. The surgeon, committed to the notion of free will, and his Stalinist mate wanted to fight against fate every step of the way; they exercised that tyranny over the child that doctors today call overprotection. For a shiver, a coated tongue: bed. Medicines. Force-feeding perhaps—this was common. And of course enemas. But in the heat of the struggle, they scarcely believed in their cause; they would do what was necessary, they would carry on until the very end, and when the fatal outcome—long delayed but inexorable—would annihilate such efforts and their object, the parents would have nothing with which to reproach themselves. Overprotection disguised resignation. Rather, this solicitude was in itself a denial; the Flaubert parents believed they were denying death when in their hearts they had accepted it. It was Gustave they denied. Living, he paid for all those self-willed brats. Just as when a play is foundering, the actors are resentful of the few spectators who represent all those absent.

I suppose, then, that Mme Flaubert, wife by vocation, was a mother out of duty. An excellent mother but not a delightful one: punctual, assiduous, adept. Nothing more. The younger son was handled overcautiously, he was relieved, his linen was changed lickety-split; he couldn't cry as he was always fed promptly. Gustave's aggressiveness had no opportunity to develop. He was nevertheless frustrated well before weaning, but it was a frustration without tears or rebellion; want of tenderness is to the pangs of love like malnutrition to hunger. Later the unloved child would consume himself, but for the moment he does not really suffer; the need to be loved is present from birth, even before the child can recognize the Other,[2] but he does not yet express himself through specific desires. The frustration *does not affect*

---

2. Indeed, the Other is there, diffused, from the first day in that discovery I make of myself through my passive experience of otherness. That is, through the repeated handling of my body by forces which are alien, purposive, serving my needs. Even on this level, however basic, love is required. Or rather, the attentions the baby receives *are* love. It is fitting in these moments that the child, discovering himself by and for this diffuse otherness, should apprehend himself in an external and internal ambience of kindness. The needs come from him, but the first interest he attaches to his person is derived from the care whose object he is. If the mother loves him, in other words, he gradually discovers his self-object as his love object. A subjective object for himself through an increasingly manifest other, he becomes a *value* in his own eyes as the absolute end of habitual processes. The valorization of the infant through care will touch him more deeply the more this tenderness is manifest. If the mother speaks to him, he grasps the *intention* before the language; let her smile at him, he recognizes the expression even before the face. His little world is crossed by shooting stars which *signal* to him and whose importance is chiefly to *consecrate* maternal actions to him. This monster is an absolute monarch, always an end, never a means. Let a child once in his life—at three months, at six—taste this victory of pride, he is a man; never in all his life will he be able to revive the supreme voluptuousness of this sovereignty or to forget it. But he will preserve even in misfortune a kind of religious optimism based

him—or very little—it *forms* him. I mean that this objective negation penetrates him and becomes within him an impoverishment of his life—an organic misery and a kind of ingratitude at the core of experience. Not anguish, he has no reason to feel abandoned. Or alone. As soon as a wish is felt, it is instantly gratified; let a pin prick him and let him cry, a nimble hand allays the pain. But these precise operations are also parsimonious; they economize on everything at the Flauberts, even time, which is money. Washing, nursing, looking after things—these acts are performed without rushing but without useless affability. Above all the mother, timid and cold, doesn't smile, or rarely, doesn't babble—why make speeches to a baby who can't understand? Gustave has a good deal of difficulty grasping the sparse character of his objective world, otherness; when he becomes conscious of it, by the time he recognizes the faces that lean over his cradle, a first chance for love has already escaped him. He has not discovered himself through a caress as flesh and as a supreme end in himself. It is too late now for him to be in his own eyes the *destination* of maternal acts: he is their object, that is all. Why? He doesn't know; it will not be long before he feels in some obscure way that he is a means. For Mme Flaubert, in fact, this child is the means of fulfilling her duties as a mother; for the physician-philosopher to whom the young wife is entirely devoted, he is primarily someone to perpetuate the family. These discoveries will come later. For the moment, he has passed over the stage of valorization. He has never felt his needs as sovereign demands, the external world has never been his oyster, his larder; the environment is revealed to him little by little, as it is to others, but he has know it first only in the dreary and cold consistency which Heidegger has named *nur-Vorbeilagen*. The happy exigency of the loved child compensates for and exceeds his docility as a handled thing; there is in his desires something imperious that can seem like the rudimentary form of a project and consequently of action. Without *value*, Gustave feels need as a gap, as a discomfort or—at best and most frequently—as a prelude to an agreeable and imminent surfeit. But this discomfort does not break away from subjectivity to become a demand in the world of others, it remains inside him, an inert and noisy emotion; he suffers it, pleasant or unpleasant, and when the time comes he will suffer satiety. We know how it is, a need pushed

on the abstract and calm certainty of his own value. In misery he is still privileged. We shall say, in any case, that an adventure begun in this fashion has nothing in common with Flaubert's.

to its limit becomes aggressive, creates its own right; but a Flaubert child is never famished—the child, stuffed by a dry, diligent mother will not even have this opportunity to break the magic circle of passivity through revolt. An imperceptible abruptness in the way he is handled encloses him; he nurses to the last drop, of course, but if he persists in sucking a dry breast two irresistible hands will, without violence, firmly remove him. Everything comes to him from the outside, he will suffer the end and the beginning, he will assimilate the Other more through privations imposed than smiles bestowed. To the small extent that he himself is disposed to it, this child without love and without rights, without aggressiveness or anguish, without agony but without value, is abandoned to the diligent hands that knead him and to the subjective stirrings of a "pathic" sensibility. By this I mean that as early as his first year, circumstances lead him to withdraw into himself. He has neither the means nor the occasion to externalize his emotions through outbursts of any kind; he savors them, someone relieves him or else they pass, nothing more. With no sovereignty or rebellion, he has no experience of human relations; handled like a delicate instrument, he absorbs action as a sustained force and never returns it, not even with a cry—sensibility will be his domain. He is imprisoned in it; later he will be confirmed in it by dignity. Anyway, it will be the site of gloomy sluggishness, of hates and loves that imperceptibly destroy the feelings, of everything that falls back on itself and is crushed and blocked and broken. Not ideas, above all never ideas: "Alfred had them; as for me, I don't have any." The idea is the simplest and most obvious form of our transcendence—it is a project. For Gustave it will come last. The little boy has the experience of sluggishness *first*; *in the end* he will go beyond it, when the habit of being buried in the self is fixed. Still, it must be added that the sensibility can be or is a project in itself; it has only to be strengthened by a little *stubbornness*—it aims for the object, claims it, assimilates it. So-called "active" emotion is to a certain extent communication: peevishness has an impact; and even fear, that enterprise of fleeing at the wrong time, establishes connections between the danger, the enemies, and the one who flees. Little Gustave learns to communicate only very late and very badly; his mother's attentions gave him neither the desire nor the occasion to develop this capacity. There he is, then, enclosed in the realm of the pathic, meaning what is suffered without being expressed.

The essential thing is this: active emotion is public from the beginning, it emerges in a world where the Other already exists—even as

131

the diffuse character of objectivity; it declares itself, it is a threat, a plea (look what you are doing with me), and aims to sustain itself through a praxis, it is violence transforming itself into martyrdom—in order to coerce through spectacle. Passive emotion is private; one can certainly make use of it as a sign and Gustave did not refrain from doing so—for example at Pont-l'Evêque—but it is not in itself a language, quite the contrary, it is a paralysis of movement and of the organs of speech. These are paralyzed, at least, when they already exist and are usable. Muscular hypotonia mimics the relaxation of the cadaver; this does not signify anything, it is a regression outside the world of signifiers and signified, regression toward a state that never altogether exists but that the unloved, well-tended child has—almost—known in the first months of life. The state of passive emotion is not a refusal to communicate, to express, nor is it—at first, in any case—a general project to dissimulate, *to conceal from the other* the fluctuations of the sensibility. Quite simply, it is pure receptiveness *before* any desire and any means of communication, and it is dominant in infants whom maternal behavior has not *first* opened to the surrounding otherness. Perhaps this passivity is the restitution for troubles which are purely *endogenous* and have accompanied development; at any rate, if it were simply a matter of living with organic disturbances, this task is *already managed, already psychosomatic* in what it revives and above all in what it rejects. Maternal behavior absorbed by the newborn and reducing him to *suffering* without *expression*—this is the meaning of the trouble, rendering him deaf and dumb like a legless and armless cripple who can only be distressed. Here is the origin of Garcia/Flaubert's swoons.

This is a fabrication, I confess. I have no proof that it was so. And worse still, the absence of such proofs—which would necessarily be singular facts—leads us, even when we fabricate, to schematism, to generality; my story is appropriate to *infants*, not to Gustave in particular. Never mind. I wanted to follow it out for this reason alone: the *real* explanation, I can imagine without the least vexation, may be precisely the contrary of what I invent, but *in any case* it will have to follow the paths I have indicated and refute my explanation on the ground I have determined—the body and love. I have spoken of maternal love; that is what fixes for the newborn the objective category of otherness, it is what in the first weeks allows the child to sense as *other*— from the moment he knows how to recognize it—the silken flesh of the breast. Obviously it is maternal behavior which sets the limits and intensity of filial love—the oral phase of sexuality—going from birth to the encounter with the Other—and which determines the internal structure of such love. Gustave is immediately conditioned by the mother's indifference; he desires *alone*, his first sexual and alimentary impulses toward a nurturing flesh are not *mirrored* back to him by a caress. It does not happen, or rarely happens—at three, at four months, during the whole first year—that this existent shape known as the *mother*, a confused heap of kindnesses, elicits in her turn a caress, a smile from the child. He is asked to be a healthy digestive tube—nothing more. There is nothing more solitary than sexual drives when no response is forthcoming. Nothing more passive: the flesh is there, one touches it, one devours it and then falls asleep, weary lover, sated diner. It will be found again at the proper time. In short, sleep, expectation, enjoyment. But the expectation, an inert assurance, and the enjoyment, scarcely distinct from nutrition— to the same degree that the Other is simultaneously the given nourishment and the person out of reach—define by their particular relationship a *pathos* of sexuality. We will see later that it is the pathic which would thoroughly color Flaubert's sexual relations.

And what about the child's malaise? It will be easier to discuss now that we know the fundamental reason for it: *nonvalorization*. This is not a matter of conjecture: a child must have a *mandate to live*, the parents are the authorities who issue the mandate. A grant of love enjoins him to cross the barrier of the moment—the next moment is awaited, he is already adored there, everything is prepared for his joyful reception; the future appears to him as a vague and gilded cloud, as his mission: "Try to fulfill us so that we may fulfill you in turn!" But the mission will be easy; the parents' love has produced it and continually reproduces it, sustains it, carries it from one day to the next, demands and awaits it—in brief, love guarantees the success of the mission. Later, in actuality, the child can find other objectives, conflicts which were at first veiled can tear the family apart; the essential thing has been achieved: the child is marked forever in the movement of his daily temporality by a teleological urgency. If later on with a little luck he can say: "My life has a purpose, I have found purpose in my life," it is because the parents' love, their creation and expectation, creation for future delight, has revealed his existence to him as a movement toward an end; he is the conscious arrow that is awakened in mid-flight and discovers, simultaneously, the distant archer, the target, and the intoxication of flight. If he has truly received the fullness of early parental attentions consecrated by the scattered smiles of the world, if he has felt absolute sovereignty in the earliest part of his life, before weaning, things will go even farther. This supreme end will accept becoming the unique means of fulfilling those who adore him and for whom he is the reason for being; living will be the *passion*—in the religious sense—that will transform self-centeredness into a gift; experience will be felt as the *free exercise of generosity*.

This impression is neither true nor false. It is obvious that life, taken in its naked form, "natural," considered only as the pure flow of organic impressions, would not offer *human* meaning—which does not mean that an animal or a man could not experience it *in itself* as *sinngebend*, that is, a reality invested with meaning. But it is equally clear that pure life as it is lived, simple "being-there" embodied in succession, in brief, all the forms of our *savored* factitiousness are handy abstractions which we never encounter without being affected by them ourselves—by isolating certain elements of inner experience, by deliberately ignoring others. In actuality, sense and non-sense in a human life are human in principle and come to the child of man from man himself. Thus we must repeat these absurd formulas back to back: "life has a meaning," "it hasn't any," "it has what we give it," and understand that we will discover our ends, the non-sense or the sense of our lives, as realities anterior to that awakening of consciousness, anterior perhaps to our birth and prefabricated in the human universe. The meaning of a life comes to the living person through the human society that sustains him and through the parents who engender him, and it is for this reason that he always remains a non-sense *as well*. But inversely, the discovery of a life as non-sense (of superfluous children suffering from malnutrition, riddled with parasites and fever in an underdeveloped society) is quite as much the revelation of the real sense of that society, and through this reversal it is life—as an organic need—which in its pure animal insistence becomes *human meaning* and the society of men which becomes *pure human non-sense* through the penalty of unsatisfied need.

When the valorization of the infant through love is accomplished badly or too late or not at all, maternal inadequacy defines experience as non-sense; inner experience reveals to the child a slack succession of present moments that slip back into the past. But subjective existence has no *direction* since it is not defined as the movement that departs from past love (creative) and goes toward future love (expectation by the Other, mission, happiness, temporal ecstasies). Of course, the frustrated child some years later will discover on his own that time is three-dimensional through the unity of his projects. He will even be able to give a meaning to the existence that overwhelms him, engulfs him, sweeps him along, and is only himself. But precisely the weakness of these ends imposed subjectively is that they remain subjective—unless they are claimed and objectified by a social current—and that they contain a kind of gratuitousness. Value and purpose are here reciprocally conditioned; the surpassing of experience is chosen in order to consolidate a failing sense of self-worth, but the inadequacy or nonexistence of valorization will destroy the objectives proposed to establish it. The question will arise: Am I really the person chosen for this enterprise?—Kirkegaard's "Am I Abraham?" Either, is the mandate in itself worthwhile? Can I accept it without knowing the authorities who issued it? (Kafka said, I have a mandate but no one gave it to me.) Or, as the adult Gustave would often wonder, isn't my will to write just foolishness? Am I not simply a collector, like a numismatist or philatelist? Briefly, the love of the Other is the foundation and guarantee of the objectivity of the individual's value and his mission; this mission becomes a sovereign choice, permitted and evoked in the subjective person by the presence of self-worth.[3] If this is lacking, life presents itself as pure contingency. Experience seems to be an irrepressible spontaneity the child suffers and produces without being its source, and simultaneously a bottleneck of accidents filing past one by one, none of them auguring the one behind or explained by the one before. Certainly intelligence and practice allow the child to recognize temporal forms in the surrounding world—ordered series, cohesive wholes, totalities that are totaled, rigorous connections of means and ends. The human being is taught to look for and to find the necessary premises of facts that jump him like thieves or scamper off between his little legs, and to see in them—unexpected as they may be—consequences; he learns effortlessly that nothing is without reason. But his trouble is intensified when he withdraws inside himself, for then he rediscovers an existence without a reason for being—his own. At the basis of this vague exploration he will discover, perhaps much later, a truth belonging to reason. The

---

3. The option's sovereignty is manifest in this contradiction; it presents itself both as a free determination of freedom in itself—which by itself would provoke anguish—and as the reinternalization of an external decree—which by itself would produce the most radical alienation. And in fact we quite often see the person having such a mandate pass from anguish to the consciousness of his alienation and vice versa. These difficulties, however, are secondary; they are annoying, to be sure, they are consuming—it is never amusing to be human. But the true malaise begins on the threshold of the human, when unloved children—the great majority—are staggered by a senseless existence.

being of the hammer and the existence of a man have nothing in common; the hammer is there to hammer, but man is not "there," he is cast into the world, and as the source of all praxis his essential reality is objectification. This means that the justification of this "creature of distances" is always retrospective; it traces him from the depths of the future and from the horizons, traces back across the course of time going from the present to the past, *never* from the past to the present. But these ethical-ontological truths must be revealed slowly. First it is necessary to be deceived, to believe in one's mandate, to confound purpose and reason in the unity of maternal love, to live out a happy surrender; and then to have this false happiness gnaw away at itself, to allow alien infiltrations to be dissolved in the movement of negativity, of project and praxis, to substitute anguish for surrender. These steps are indispensable, they are what I have called elsewhere the need for freedom. Truth is intelligible only at the end of a long, vagabond delusion; if it is handled *before*, it is only a real delusion. We know that the unloved child who discovers himself exists and is the foundation of all legitimation; he takes himself for a being without any justification. Frustration reveals to him a portion of the truth, but it takes care to hide the rest; in fact, when he experiences himself as unjustifiable in his being, he is a hundred times farther from his real condition than the privileged child who is perceived as justified in advance. For both take upon themselves the being of things, but the first perceives in himself only a diffuse and purely subjective flow, and he is locked into the present moment, which is the farthest point of the past, whereas the other grasps the life within him as the enterprise of the future, as the fundamental structure of temporality. Gustave is the victim of a mystification; since nothing is expected of him as the singular subject of his history, he will therefore be its object. Without a particular mission he is deprived, *from the start*, of the cardinal categories of praxis. Not that the future entirely escapes his purview, but—we shall come back to this— he sees it as the ineluctable result of an alien will; it can be prophesied but not *shaped*, since it is already accomplished. This practitioner's son must indeed have been rigorously conditioned by family life from the earliest age to exhibit so soon such a profound disgust with action in whatever form; in truth, not only does he despise practical life, he *does not comprehend* it. It does not enter into the limited universe he has carved out for his use at the breast of objectivity; or rather, if he lets the practical in, it loses its efficacy. Everything is past, even the future—everything is immutable in advance; concerted human effort will never be more than a futile ripple on the surface of a dead world. He makes an exception, as we shall see, only for demolition jobs.

Before quietism becomes his governing thesis and one of the principal motifs of his work, he will endure many more misfortunes, many factors will be introduced which we have not yet discussed. But that is beside the point. The source of this quietism is the infant's neglect; love is demanding—no one asks anything of an unloved child, nothing pulls him out of immanence. Or rather, since he continually pulls himself out of it like everyone else, he does it blindly, in a clandestine half-light—it is not required and has no charter. This strange condition is not seen but felt; he tastes its illegitimacy in the insipidness of his self-provoked discharge; its pale savor reveals the interchangeability of all his feelings—no one anticipates them, not even himself, hence they are equivalent. From horror to lust, they seem to be cut from the same cloth. However, even unforeseen they never seem to be unexpected because nothing else is. They arise, inhabit him, vegetate, and disappear, and others come, divers modes of the same nauseous substance. The experience of universal monotony he will later call *ennui*—with good reason; but "pure boredom with life" is a pearl of culture. It seems clear that household animals are bored; they are homunculae, the dismal reflections of their masters. Culture has penetrated them, destroying nature in them without replacing it. Language is their major frustration: they have a crude understanding of its function but cannot use it; it is enough for them to be the *objects of speech*—they are spoken to, they are spoken about, they know it. This manifest verbal power which is denied to them cuts through them, settles within them as the limit of their powers, it is a disturbing privation which they forget in solitude and which deprecates *their very natures* when they are with men. I have seen fear and rage grow in a dog. We were talking about him, he knew it instantly because our faces were turned toward him as he lay dozing on the carpet and because the sounds struck him with full force as if we were addressing him. Nevertheless we were speaking to *each other*. He felt it; our words seemed to designate him as our interlocutor and yet reached him *blocked*. He did not quite understand either the act itself or this exchange of speech, which concerned him far more than the usual hum of our voices—that lively and meaningless noise with which men surround themselves—and far less than an order given by his master or a call supported by a look or gesture. Or rather—for the intelligence of these humanized beasts is always beyond itself, lost in the imbroglio of its presence and its impossibilities—he was bewildered at not understanding what he understood. He began by waking up, bounding toward us, but stopped short, then whined with an uncoordinated agitation and finished by barking angrily. This dog passed from discomfort to rage, feeling at his expense the strange reciprocal mystification which is the relationship between man and animal. But his rage contained no revolt—the dog had summoned it to simplify his problems. Once calmed, he went off to the next room and returned, much later, to frolic and lick our hands.

This example sufficiently demonstrates that for the animal, culture, at first a simple ambience, an ignored lacuna, becomes under the guise of training the pure negation *in itself* of animality. It is a *fission* that leads the beast both above and below his familiar level, raising him toward an impossible comprehension just when his misplaced intelligence is collapsing in a daze. Nothing is bestowed by culture, but something is taken away; without ever achieving a reflective schisiparity, the immediacy of what is experienced is cracked, questioned. By nothing—therefore no hope of mediation; a shadow of distance separates life from itself, renders nature less natural. As a consequence, peaceful immanence is changed into self-consciousness. The transformation is never complete, it is pure movement; but this renewed questioning, this injection of the human as a denied possibility is translated by a kind of pleasure—the dog *feels alive, he is bored*. His boredom is life tasted as the impossibility of becoming man and as the perpetual collapsing of the desire to transcend the self in the direction of the human. In short, the little monsters forged by the king of nature know privileged moments when needs, satisfied, cease to constrain them and to justify them; then, if life through this distancing, which is not even self-consciousness, is delighted by itself as the negative limit of animal powers and at the same time as a ruining insouciance beneath a vague, unhappily impossible enterprise, each moment lived is felt as a restitution—through an oversight provoked by incapacity—of pure contingency, that is, of existence devoid of an objective. And this contingency, instead of being the simple, permanent structure of experience delighted with itself as a meaning, is in itself alone the animal condition and the stale intuition of this condition as an aimless succession of interchangeable and always varying states. Without culture the animal would not be bored—he would live, that is all. Haunted by the sense of something missing, he lives out the impossibility of transcending himself by a forgetful relapsing into animality; nature is discovered through resignation. Boredom with life is a consequence of the oppression of animals by man; it is nature grasping itself as the absurd end of a limiting process instead of realizing itself as biological spontaneity.

If Gustave shares this nostalgia with the beasts it is because he too is domesticated. Love teaches; if he is wanting, his training is to blame. With the first learned behaviors, the basic habits of cleanliness, the child will see only constraints if the reason for the apprenticeship is not clear. He will not integrate or claim these habits as his own; at best he will consider them a chain of conditioned reflexes, at worst an alien enterprise *within him*—that is, the reverse of an organized behavior. He internalizes it in this last case as an activity which is endured; custom learned by force and an alien imperative are united to determine the domination of his spontaneity by others. We shall see that in Gustave, passive activity is nothing more than a masked reversal of the imposed act turned against those who impose it. In other words, he will never oppose *acts* to the acts of others; he zealously obeys his parents' orders, is open to the new determinations with which they want to influence him, but he quietly makes certain that the consequences are unequivocally disastrous. Thus it is easy to trace back from the ultimate catastrophes to the original intention, which will be condemned a posteriori by its effects. Yet these vegetative effects must be lived out; in the attendant sufferings, through the flow of experience, their radical noxiousness must be discerned. Therefore to obey, to push resignation to the point of being no more than inert matter means to deny all responsibility, to allow the Other's enterprise to be developed in the self without casting aside its otherness. Actually such docility is not undiluted—surreptitiously Gustave makes a back-breaking effort to derail the process; chiefly he refuses to correct by himself the deviations which are inevitably produced in a mechanical system. Passive action, then, consists essentially of a pretense of inertia. This inertia—let us understand that it must first be imposed—is realized in the subjective existence of the patient well before he dreams of faking it. In fact, Gustave *will not choose* passive action among other equally possible modes of praxis; rather the praxis itself is produced as the internal work of inertia when it is impossible for it not to exist—Gustave, like all men and beasts, is defined by projects—and at the same time to appear to the self as transcendence and enterprise. Praxis becomes the *efficacy of the passive* because the child's conditioning strips him of any means of affirming himself, even the positive act of negativity. We shall come back to this; I only want to indicate that the little boy's first acts are experienced as pure sustained flow, without any subjective meaning, and at the same time refer back to a transcendental activity—namely toilet training—whose purpose and sense escape a priori the object of the training. In this first moment, loveless acculturation reduces Gustave to the condition of a domestic animal. He too suffers from the obsession with something missing. Culture is given to him as an ignorance which in the world of otherness is on principle a kind of knowledge; it forms him and remains alien to him. Education tears him away from himself without giving him access to the world of others. He is continually brushed by *comprehensible* objects outside himself—enterprise, intention, decision, spontaneity, the synthetic unity of a subject and his praxis; but these are precisely the things that elude him when he seeks to grasp them. Not that they are themselves alien to the movements of his life; on the contrary, nothing can make him stop existing and stop fulfilling himself in all the dimensions of existence; therefore he can have a presentiment, such as the correspondence between internal and external, and he is always on the verge of being understood by others and of understanding them. But it is the mediation that is missing—love. Furthermore, objective meanings steal away and allow themselves to be deciphered by the incomprehensible otherness that shapes him, while the most immediate determinations of his spontaneity seem the most distant, the most obscure, and plunge into darkness just as he is about to grasp them. His alienation is more immediate to him than his subjective truth, he continually falls back to it after these vague, slippery, dreamlike intuitions. The child, like the beast of culture, does not understand what he is in the process of understanding, what he seems to have understood; resigned, forgetful, he turns back to his unjustified contingency, to the passive succession of his affective states, as the animal turns back to his muteness. The fugitive moments of clarity that pass through him seem to have no recognizable function, for the moment, except to present his *nature* to him as inadequate—culture makes him feel deprived. He is already the *object of speech*, like our lap dogs, but *too late*—he is *rarely spoken to*, distractedly and unsmilingly. In this sense he is beneath the dog, who at least internalizes the love that makes him its object.

Without even this love, the little boy discovers himself sadly insignificant and fragmented. Superior to the beast, on the other hand, in that this internal fissure is already self-consciousness, nevertheless we need not believe that the shattered but indissoluble unity of the reflecting and the reflected manifests a simple ontological fission; self-consciousness in everyone has the basic structure of praxis. Even on the level of non-thetic consciousness, intuition is conditioned by individual history; the spiral movement of twinning can include a refusal, an approval, a futile effort to crush the two terms in the unity of the *En-soi*. Gustave, even in that fundamental "Pour-soi," labors under frustration; his self-consciousness is the intuition of a *lesser being*—nature—in comparison to that indecipherable and superior being, culture. His consciousness is a perpetual falling back which begins with a realm above that withholds itself and discovers existence to be a priori *a realm below*. This is not a matter of an inferiority "complex" or even of the feeling of inferiority—in what way would he be inferior? to whom? to what? But the realm above by its very absence or, if you like, by *its presence above determines the existence of the realm below* as *misery*, in the sense that Pascal meant the "misery of man without God." And this misery does not inform existence because it is lacking this or that quality; in itself existence is lack, it is *that* singular lack which defines *this* existence and which is not a lack of anything in particular. This is easily understood as the lack of love; when it is present, the dough of the spirits rises, when absent, it sinks. The unloved child suffers from neglect, from nature present to the self as inadequacy—through his futile efforts to grasp inaccessible meanings—as passivity and as pure "being-there" with no purpose or reason. Yet these negative and general qualities do not emerge from any comparison. It is simply the lack of love felt by the living person himself, at the level of the synthetic unity of his existence, as an internal possibility which eludes him just as he seems—continually—about to realize it. The child remains on the level of pure subjectivity; he does not define the love which is denied him as external, rather he defines *himself* through the empty category of objectivity as a reality that is powerless and unconnected—love is unknown but its absence is made known as a defect of being by the rising of this unleavened dough, sunk in advance. Ennui is the pain of love ignorant of itself. Through the intuition of contingency and monotony, even in the unpredictable, he discovers his objective character as someone *unloved*—his fundamental relationship with the Other—to be the subjective truth of his existence. To be loved would be to internalize the affection of the Other and to be fulfilled in and through this strange synthesis; not to be loved is felt and realized as the impossibility of loving oneself. And once again, let us understand that it is not the child's frustrated effort to love (to take pleasure), to give love to the living flow, that makes him what he is; simply, he *is*

141

dissatisfied, he feels the absence of maternal love directly as a non-love of the self. This hostility to himself is only a secondary characteristic; it cannot be very strong since the hated *self* can never entirely be an object for the self that hates. Nevertheless, this hostility is constant and it is the quasi relationship that is found in the non-thetic fissure of immediate self-consciousness. Just as the hated *self* is found *within the self that hates* as the deepest self—implying a continual merry-go-round—likewise the abhorred reality is found within the abhorrence as its basic nature and being. In other words, the feeling of repugnance by virtue of subjective reality is touched by the same insufficiency (contingency, passivity, insignificance, etc.) as the repugnant feeling. And this roughly outlined dichotomy does not even achieve a reflective schisiparity; as the two modes continually pass into each other and each one takes on the other's function in this way, the result is a certain lessening of disgust. Or, more precisely, disgust is disgusted *with itself* for not being more intense, more condensed, more necessary; in short, for participating in the being it exposes and for being, as disgust, implicated by the abhorrence it translates. And as we shall observe, two negations—on this ground—*do not add up to an affirmation*, they embrace without suppressing each other; disgust is felt to be disgusting and is not, for all that, experienced as more disgusting; on the contrary, it suffers an inner devalorization. What is the source of its mandate? Who authorizes it to display such repugnance? for what purpose? Disgust more than any other feeling has no justification. If it arises from an event and a substance with the rigor of a consequence following from principle, it might be a solid contempt; when it is vague, it flits around from one thing to another and fills everything, everything fills it. This is *ennui*— *boredom with life*: a diminished hostility which is the universal texture of experience. Non-love is internalized as the impossibility of self-love, felt as abhorrence; this, at the moment of its appearance, is degraded and becomes an indissoluble unity in the dichotomy—an obscene insipidness of taste, an uneasy and resigned malevolence in the tasting.

It is everywhere—it is Gustave's life itself; later, speaking of his adolescence, he will call himself a "mushroom swollen with boredom." And the word *mushroom* is there to underline the *quasi-vegetative* character of his existence and of the feeling that pervades it. He sees himself as a plant; with the organs of locomotion missing, it suffers its spontaneity, gratuitously but unceasingly produces its jams, its butters, stores up reserves which will allow it to pursue its illegitimate existence. But all these swelling juices, all these inert plenitudes, are precisely what he calls ennui. Never did Gustave dream of holding the external world responsible; after all, he embodies himself in a mushroom. No eyes, ears, or hands. Had it pleased the gods that boredom should come from outside, his case would be less serious. In fact, all young people are bored, they would like to go to sea or chase women, beat themselves or beat records; they stay between four walls with father, mother, brothers, in the ceremonious universe of repetition—the same memories, the same pleasantries, the same games. The impossible action they seek reveals to them the vegetative contingency of parents, furniture, their usual activities—living is a drain, they are buried alive in the "House of Nauseating Recurrence." But this minor form of ennui—which is not without complacency— is only a provisional vexation. The impossibility of acting will not last forever; this we know because the young man denounces the absurdity of his present life in the name of the inflexible necessity of praxis. The structure of "abhorrence" has not altered; the unattainable end, taken as justification, reveals a terrible, irrational plenitude. But the validating act is known already, it is played out in advance through imagination; the adolescent nurses the hope of being reborn, or rather of dying in the familial limbo in order to be reborn to true, legitimate life, namely to his *mission*. Gustave is more deeply scarred. Action, meanings, love and its tender promises—he missed them all at the age when he suffered this absence without having the means to comprehend it. Therefore he lived it out as a definitive insufficiency and as the acrid, vegetative abundance of his own juices, of the self. Mushroom: elementary organism, passive, shackled, oozing with abject plenitude—the image is accurate, this is how he experienced himself from the first days of his life. A little later he will universalize this boredom, a predictable and necessary operation. But he only extrapolates: he begins with the self and denounces in other men, in beasts, the same insufficiency revealed to him in his own life.

Ennui—this is the malaise. It is the living out of nonvalorization. From this we shall easily understand that Gustave entered the world of language at an oblique angle. Love gives, awaits, receives—there is a reciprocity of designation. Without this fundamental bond, the child is a signified without being a signifier. Meanings pass through him and sometimes take hold, but they remain alien to him—through these alien meanings the Other penetrates him; as *others*, they recede toward the Other; simultaneously inert, half-closed, they exhibit the power of the invisible occupant. Reduced to the contemplation of his passivity, the child cannot know that he has the structure of a sign and that the living transcendence of experience is in him, as in everyone, the basis of meaning. Thus language comes to him from the outside; meaningful transcendence is the operation of the Other and is accomplished by a meaning which is determined from without. He will interpret it as he did his first habits: it is something passive, an *objective* result of alien acts at the heart of his subjectivity. Words are things conveyed by the flow of experience; he will have a great deal of difficulty fashioning them into the living instruments of his own transcendence toward the external, and he will never succeed completely because he has been *made passive* by maternal attentions, and because transcendence and the project—his permanent possibilities for acting—have been stifled from the beginning. To speak is to act; since he suffers it, names are imposed on him which he learns without recognizing himself in them, that is, without claiming them as his own. These are alien imprints, landmarks for the others; when he fathoms their use and is penetrated by a slow osmosis of their meanings, he is quite far from inferring the beginning of a reciprocity. Others name him, he does not know how to name himself. It will not be long, in spite of everything, before he discovers in these determinations which touch him superficially an actual hypothesis of his essential reality. From the moment a child can apply a name to an object in his environment, he in effect assimilates the process of naming to the discovery of being. Gustave does not escape this rule, although he has been somewhat tardy in submitting to it. The dog *is* a dog, and the mother *is* a mother; each thing in its mysterious core possesses a name; let a voice awaken, mouth and ear delight in the truth. The younger of the Flaubert sons did not experience the designation of surrounding objects as *his* enterprise; he must have invested it more with submission than with spontaneity. No matter. Hardly has he arrived at the stage of *verbal ontology* when, willingly or unwillingly, his various labels must coincide with the features of his singular substance. He *is* Gustave, he *is* Flaubert, he *is* child, little boy, etc. From day to day the description will be more precisely elaborated. It comes to him *from without*, and what can he do but accept it? This is one reason—and not the least significant—for his stupors. Not that his feelings are by nature inexpressible—the heterogeneity of discourse and feelings is only a fiction in general, as well as in each particular case. Simply, Gustave's passivity makes the process of naming unilateral: the verbal act wounds him. Withered, compressed, with no future, no justification, his feelings do not claim to designate themselves, either for himself or for others.

We know why. Deprived of maternal solicitude, he never felt that he awakened interest in others, and in a way he is confined to living his life day by day without being interested in it himself. The intention to designate—meaning to know and to make known—is naturally encountered in every moment of his experience, but it is dormant. Awakened, its muteness is so profound that the words "would not get across." And then there is ennui, that self-loathing —why would he want to communicate his being-less, his non-value? When learned words diffuse their meanings, when these meanings penetrate little by little into the deep reaches of his passivity, they seem to him his very substance and at the same time foreiqn agents. Insignificant, they signify him; they signify to him what he is. But the verbal intention remains numbed, it does not extend itself toward the proposed meaning in order to claim it and shoot it back like a bullet. He already has masters, but not yet interlocutors. The result is *estrangement*—he recognizes himself readily in the terms of the discourse and at the same time finds nothing of himself in it. Or else he imagines that he remains inadequate to words, that they serve rich, complete beings, and that he escapes them through his thankless poverty. He is, he feels what they say—nothing else, nothing more, much less. The stupor in this case is born of that elusive, indefinable *less* which his very inconsistency prevents him from seeing clearly and from opposing to the plenitude of spoken words, But it also happens that the word in itself seems strange to him. The proper name, the customary qualifications are the very being of the child; only for lack of spontaneous assent, this being which is unquestionably his remains beyond his reach; *it is him*, the signified contents relate to Gustave alone—there is proof, but it is a piece of evidence directed to the wrong person. It could be said that it is concocted in order to present the little boy to some other consciousness. In this verbal intuition, the stupor derives this time from *otherness*; or rather, the child loses his way in the confusion of self and Other. He is himself as an Other and for an Other. The lack of distinction between these categories will not surprise us; in order to distinguish between them, to oppose them and then unite them by synthetic bonds in a perpetual transformation would require the simplest dialectical movement, the movement of life itself, nothing more. And this movement certainly exists in Gustave since the little boy, even in slow motion, is *in the process of living*. But he is blocked, suppressed, diverted by constitutional passivity, in immanence, like a subterranean river meandering; when the river flows later in the open, the harm will have already been done, silt will continually threaten to choke it. In the first years, in any case, the categories mingle and interpenetrate; when passivity is the only conceivable form of action, one must endure one's very ipseity as a being-other.

Gustave is struck dumb by the self, that is, by the word "myself." This index finger is pointed at his subjective life, it designates the oneness which corresponds to the pure feeling of living—and the unity—passive and active synthesis, both together—of the life flow. Yet if it is true that the taste of a bit of food in his mouth or the cold of early morning offer *in themselves* singular sensations bound incontestably to a *here* and *now*, it is also true that the insignificance of a nonvalorized child and the absolute equivalence of random sensations give to a sequence of such sensations a certain kind of generality. Gustave does not have much in common with the *fin de siècle* individualists; he would not have tried to hide in his mother's skirts, crying like André Gide, "I am not like the others." Actually, it is not even possible at this period to call him an individual. Unique? Common? The child does not pose such questions. Quite simply, without words, without ideas, he is tossed about from one feeling to another. And on the other hand, he recognizes unity when it is passive; through the general flow an inert identity persists which he unquestionably feels; but the active synthesis of the manifold—in sum, the person—which he knows how to see in others, in his father, always at work, in his mother, efficient and distant, does not exist in himself, or at any rate he hasn't encountered it. Grown-ups nevertheless hold him responsible for his actions—he is punished, scolded, rewarded. This is their way, he accepts it. But he does not grasp its meaning when he is the one implicated; from the time he is old enough to defend himself, he will dispute it. No man believed more sincerely, more aggressively, more desperately in destiny, a passive synthesis behind the scenes, a future truth, inert materiality prefabricated by self-styled grown-ups. "I do not feel free," he repeats in his correspondence. And metaphysics has nothing to do with this confident resignation. He wants to emphasize, first of all, that he never has the feeling of being an *agent* but always of being *acted upon*. Moreover, in the clearest and best developed passages, he finds fault above all with Louise's commitment to the will. According to the Muse, wishing and persevering are self-defining; the unity of actions unifies the character, and conversely. Quite honestly, this is popular opinion, but it is not Gustave's; he maintains that the consistency of his singular "person" and the perpetual recurrence of his actions are two independent effects of a single cause, which is the permanence of his objective fatalities. These—inert arrangements of matter, ruts, rails, tunnels, slopes, ramps, sharp curves—await him, will determine his speed and direction moment by moment. Through this endured and directed movement, Gustave is *assembled*, he feels contained by a steel corset; propulsion, pulsion, brake action and radio control from a future tower—this is his unity. If for an instant someone forgot to maneuver him, his crumbling flesh would be cast off, he would melt, a pool of fat on a railway track, or would disperse, go up in smoke, in the excessive emptiness of the universe. Nothing to fear: the future is memory, this is what he feels when he writes to his mistress, this is what he has always felt. The child would say *me, myself*, and the words in his mouth, in his head, designated a standard product, common and specified by its serial number, which derived its provisional unity from the labor exerted by the workers on their material and which lost this unity bit by bit through wear and tear under the action of external forces.

Does this destiny *think*, then? Where would the words come from? The ideas? From the first years the apparatus is installed inside him, and in the course of his life he will need only to invent suitable language; this will be his work, which might be called a "Discourse on Fatality." But in the beginning he has only a confused feeling when the physician-philosopher first says *you* to him; the word in this imperious mouth takes on entirely another sense: you, the responsible one, you who must obey me and who consequently can. The child does not yet know the parade, he does not yet know how to dissolve the *you* along with the *me* in the "he" of destiny; he receives this designation passively. *You*, that is *me* for *him*. That is to say, he accepts *responsibility* out of submission to the father and makes it into a peripheral aspect of his passivity. At the same time, I have said, the *you* awakens in him vague reminiscences—the memory of what he has never been, of what he cannot be, in silence. These substanceless recollections crumble into oblivion. But the amazement begins: the label challenges itself and challenges the child in his being. No— challenge implies opposition, the synthetic bond of negative reciprocity. Rather, it is a slight disintegration of reality that flows from the word to the person and back again from the person to the word. Me, that's me—the child unquestionably recognizes himself; and then, *it is not* me—the word becomes hewn stone, Gustave runs up against it; flung back, he contemplates this impenetrable mass which encloses him in the self and exiles him outside his being. *From what position* does he contemplate it? Has he taken refuge in silence? No, everything is speech. Nevertheless, he is lacking the words that would designate him more precisely. They are lacking but their place is reserved: muteness, future speech, is the intersection from which the little boy contemplates speech in its plenitude and his own insufficiency. But neither his age nor his passivity will permit him to look for a new expression; muteness, then, is passive expectation. Furthermore, we should not make it into a separate region of the soul—the whole body of the little Saint Sebastian is pierced with words whose shafts still quiver. In fact, to the same extent that muteness is speech, speech is in its essence mute. This is the stupor—the inadequacy of the word in action denounced by the word in its potential; distant, opaque, the word fascinates and at the same time arises in the depth of the soul inaudible, absent. The verbal act would put everything in order, it would define the absence by the inadequacy of the present term, and conversely; in short, the two terms would engender each other by their difference. But Gustave's passivity does not allow him to accomplish the operation, and so he waits. What is inside him when he sits there in a daze, sucking his thumb for hours on end? Nothing and everything: a half-language, a nonreciprocal relationship, lively mists transfixed by the stone that names them and astonished not to be petrified, the feeling of being a self outside itself, the expectation—indeed timid, disappointed in advance—of a metamorphosis. Life will consume these blocks of opacity, it will free the life they have imprisoned—or else be absorbed by them bit by bit, and the little boy will end by merging with the obscure material being that lacks interiority. It is in relation to this "me," the first designation of his subjective reality, that we must understand the increased frequency of the stupors. Every qualification of the child—"good," "bad," "calm," "overexcited," "tired," etc.—pretends to be a determination of his ipseity; and it is *his* to the extent that the ego is affected by it. Thus, whether they designate his moods, his actions, or his "character traits," the signs will share the ambiguity of the generating notion and of the word that expresses it. These remarks allow us to determine conclusively that the early stupors are not the effects of a nature-culture conflict but the symptoms of an internal disorder of language. The nonvalorized child can express himself only in terms of value; in effect, denominations are applied to his subjective reality which necessarily refer to the autonomy of spontaneity, to the synthetic unity of experience, to all the structures of praxis, that is, to the basis of all legitimation. This would be perfect if at the right moment Gustave could have exercised the sovereignty that these denominations legitimize. Loved sons are princes, they reign as favorites from an early age; but a child received with indifference is wild grass. No mouth gave Gustave, that weed, the language of useless plants, the only language that would be his own. Later, much later, he will invent it by himself; while waiting, the weed will express itself in the royal language, namely in human words that betray him. Or rather, no—he will not express himself at all. We know Gustave's passions through those of his incarnation, Djalioh: extravagant, inconsistent, variable, they mend, unravel, merge with each other, and are *experienced* without attempting to manifest themselves. The words furnished by adults pursue in these tuneless laments some sort of creative and sovereign spontaneity that the child never encountered in himself. Soon afterward, the adults vainly reconstruct the exact succession of notes, but it is no longer *the same*—the whole, without visible revision, is organized and presents the unity of an enterprise; a slight tightening will make the first and final chords reflect a reciprocity, each sound referring to those preceding, announcing those that follow and standing out clearly— a singular form against the background of the musical totality. Briefly, human language would humanize these colors and these pleasures, painting them as they ought to be and not as they are. When Gustave sinks into himself, when he suffers his moods, he never raises himself to the point of a desire for communication; and when he is raised *by the Other* to the level of discourse, he responds to the inducing words with words induced, without even imagining that he could relate them to himself. Soon it is to expression in general and in all its forms that this pathological faltering is going to be communicated. He lives in society, thus he *is expressive*—any of his gestures is "held against him" or can be. But the cold, slow, painful feelings which are crushed or inflamed or evaporate in the depths, in the heart's core—these are experienced as an organic diminishment, as a lessening of being: vasoconstriction, the slowing of the pulse, hypotonia or muscular relaxation. And although a change of color or a stammering can disclose them, they are not expressed, they are suppressed. The expressive order and the emotional order will be separated so early in the child that one can say with confidence that he never feels what he expresses and never expresses what he feels. All right, someone will say, what is he going to *present* to others? I answer: nothing. He *represents*, he exists in *representation*. Or, if you like, gestures and actions are organized by

149

themselves without reference to existing realities; they reflect to others what others would like Gustave to be or what Gustave would like to be for them—two ends which are sometimes in opposition and sometimes intersect. We will see later that the younger son of the Flauberts never stopped playing roles. A strange contrast between the social man and the weed growing in his depths, wild and patient, which languidly, passively, tries to distill—like a juice—the language of naked life. All of Gustave is here, however: a charlatan when he is a man, honest when he remains a vegetable life. Let him speak about himself in his correspondence, we find a tidal wave of ink. Let him invent, let him tell stories while declaring they are fabrications, and we shall not for a moment depart from the truth. But it must be understood that vegetable truth is the product of a passive activity: it suffuses the sovereign words with a profound sense that no word can be restored. We shall see all this. In any event, this is his art, this is his solitude, whereas the *representation* is lived out on the level of human relations in a state of overexcitement—generally followed by prostration. The presence of his fellow men is enormously disturbing to him; they make demands which are unfamiliar to him, and these must be met under pain of revealing the imposture—that Gustave is not completely a man. His gestures and mimicry jostle each other; this is farce, this is the circus, this is the "Garçon"; and if the spectators are convinced, so much the better—Gustave will try to observe himself *through their eyes*. I wanted to come to this at last, namely to pithiatism, for this is certainly what is involved. In society Gustave loses his head, he looks at no one and sees nothing—he *is seen*. Whether someone is or is not informed of his presence, this total visibility is in fact an internal disposition; pierced by a thousand looks, watched on every side, he is convinced momentarily that he is on a stage—a kind of theater-in-the-round—and that he must play five acts without intermission. With a single effort he pulls himself out of his melancholy lethargy, jumps onto the upper stage—the realm of mimicry, gestures, expressions, meanings—and there, by means of a directed nervous attack, transforms himself into a jolly, blustering fellow. Witnesses report to us that he was not very convincing. He himself does not want to know about it. If he is among men, he is visible; if he is visible, he acts; if he acts, the victory is won *de jure*. In the end, victim of that self he protects and has never encountered, he hears the silent applause of invisible hands—that is enough. Deaf and blind to the true reactions of his audience, he allows himself to be convinced by the enthusiasm of others that the interpreter and his formidable part are not and have never been anything but one.

It is plain that we are dealing here not with a deliberate falsehood or an actual game but with a defense against men. And that this defense, a massive distillation of signs, attempts to be a diversion—the ears are split by cries, the eyes fatigued by colossal and precipitous movements. But these dances, intended to win the audience over, imply a serious wound. Gustave has never believed, by himself and through himself alone, in being what he seemed to be. He believes he has convinced others and is fascinated by the belief he thinks he has given them. The *impact* of others is *so strong* that they reflect his acting back to him under the guise of truth and oblige him to share their mistake when he is in the best position to denounce it. And *so weak*, at the same time, that he hasn't the slightest interest in questioning them; in this game of reflections, they represent only the vacant principle of otherness. We shall have to return to this when we study his "neurosis"; the pathology of belief corresponds to hysteria rather than to that epilepsy with which he has so long been afflicted. What interests us for the moment is to examine his prehistory: may not the explanation for this hysterical vocation of Flaubert's be found in the passive constitution he was given?

It is truth that is at stake. For him to recognize and affirm anything—were it only disguising an error or a lie—it is necessary and sufficient that it bear the mark of the Other. And of course he would hardly be mistaken if he envisaged truth as a communal enterprise and a demand for reciprocity: I will never *know* anything that the Other does not guarantee for me, but it must be added that the knowledge of others has only myself as its guarantee. Yet Gustave is unaware of reciprocity. We have seen, we shall see still more vividly, that this relationship escapes him; when it is absent, he cannot conceive of it, and when it is present, he neither understands nor sanctions it, nor can he be satisfied with it. So persistent is he in this attitude toward reciprocity that either it breaks apart or he transforms it into a feudal relationship. We already know why. If he were active, he would create the experience of antagonism or of mutual aid—this is the world of men; but he is passive, submissive, because he submits to foreign domination; activity becomes a party to other people's attributions and Gustave can be their object. Their subject, never. Yet truth is always an enterprise; therefore, Gustave is either unaware of it or submits to it. Let us say that *he is unaware of it*. He has never had active perceptions—a blend of intuition and declaration—about his

151

own existence which are *conclusive* as to what they *verify*. I have said that this hazardous and timid life was going to provide itself with a language, but it is less a matter of the life's defining itself than of investing words with a certain flavor. It tastes itself and passes, and the tasting is not knowledge—it is fixed, like a parasite, on a moment of existence which draws it into oblivion. What is missing? The basic act: affirmation. Let us say that *he submits*. If affirmation is the essence of truth, it will be up to the Other to assent. The judicial act seems to the child an alien praxis. This act puts an official seal on words, on gestures, and marked in this way they have a strange power— they slip through eyes and ears like a sovereign edict enabling the being, such as he is, to see, to believe. Gustave's "naïvetés" have no other source: if the Other makes decisions, the unique foundation of knowledge is the principle of authority. Therefore the child adjusts his credulousness to the familial or social importance, to the age, bearing, and sex of his interlocutor. The losses here are considerable. The true statement is given in a proposition—an active synthesis— articulated by the Other; this is lodged in the child, with its articulations, as an originally passive synthesis. In this reversal, *what is said* loses its function. The same phrase addresses itself to the same objects, unites them through the same links; nevertheless everything is changed. To hear the words is to construct a synthesis, to construct it *in advance*. A hint is enough, half a word, half a phrase. Thought appears simultaneously to both speakers as the object itself before them—this tree, this crack in the wall, this chair—and as the active and practical exfoliation of *that* object with respect to the totality of the environment. This disclosure—an operation of one or the other— involves a transcendental indication, the invitation *to escape from the self toward . . . ;* and if the offer is accepted it also includes an act, induced yet autonomous, which is a reiteration of the first surpassing of the self—two men present to each other through the actualization of their presence, which is common to the thing. Altogether truth has the character of work, it is a controlled transformation of the thing in itself which continues to modify human relations through and by the modification of this reality. To modify it, of course, is only to continue to make it appear against the totalizing background without extracting it from the milieu that produces and sustains it, to allow it to develop in the black light of our scrutiny as it is bound to do irresistibly, and in any case in the night of unknowing, which is to say, of everything. But through this single enterprise man objectifies himself in the object he discloses. This means that the object, by its appearance, by its clarity, by the limits of the exfoliation, of developments hypothetically foreseen, defines its man, or rather its group, the knowledge already acquired, the methods, techniques, and relations of work. In designating the thing, in disclosing it as immutable under the name of object, man objectifies himself; in becoming an object *by and for* human praxis, the thing without changing designates man to his fellow as a *human object*. Let us suppress the moment of praxis for one of the workers—the littlest one, Gustave, as soon as he learns to speak—and what happens? First of all, this: objects without a name are not officially recognized or, more precisely, do not exist independently; they live as the concubines of being, as the little Flaubert is of existence. Truth—and error, obviously—has no meaning for him when he is alone. Three- and four-year-olds make conjectures, promise themselves to report such conjectures to their parents, then forget about them; these resurface if the occasion presents itself with predictable surprise—this is an exploration of the actions of *veracity*. Flaubert does not play at this game; passive, he allows the emotions he feels and the things he sees to disappear together. That they must have names, these alien realities, he has no doubt—for he has parents! But he doesn't think about it—what does he care?—and then, these names do not belong to him, the ceremony of naming is a privilege of grown-ups. At the least he might ask his mother, as do so many boys at his age: what do you call that? why is it like this? etc. But no, questioning presupposes that the act of naming has been done in isolation and in vain. We know very well that Gustave did not act, either in this way or otherwise. If the adults teach him the name of a plant or an animal, it is out of caprice or duty; having asked nothing, he will receive the word as a sacred bond between the parents and the thing. They have dearly wished to initiate him into this rite, he will serve the cult, a choirboy of language; he will even be required in certain circumstances to borrow this or that word and pronounce it—as he might be charged with sounding a gong or ringing the bells. Anyway, it is only a loan; after using it, the vocable is restored to the grown-ups' dictionary, which is not yet a dictionary of accepted ideas. In other words, Gustave engages in naming when he submits to the social world of communication; he names at the command of others, through them, for them. Returning to his solitude, he retrieves the semisecrecy of things and of himself; truth hovers about his head, and he doesn't even think to raise his eyes to see it. Yet the nominative intuition is the solid grasping of the thing, since the act gives it a name. Gustave is unaware of this intuitive plenitude. Not that the thing is not there, not that he doesn't see or touch it; he enjoys it with all his senses. But he fails to discover it as *object* since he doesn't engage in the enterprise of attempting to classify it in the herbarium of knowledge. This apprehension of the external world through the senses and emotions of a secretive child certainly results in confusing the boundaries of self and non-self. The general structure of *objectivity* is vaguely present from birth; before he can speak, the child spontaneously distinguishes what belongs to him and what belongs to the environment. Put simply, objectivity, for him as for most children, should continually call forth particular objectifications—the objective world should be peopled with objects. It is not. The intuitions of his sensibility do not invalidate nominative evidence, but they do not confirm it either; they are passively suffered without any reference to truth. They ought nevertheless to support the designation; but no thunder, no lightning, no fiat cuts across them, even if the current of experience brings with it the flotsam of half-forgotten words. In sum, no surprise, no particular questioning; lacking the capacity to be articulated in detail, the entire system at some point reverses itself. The question then bears on *everything*, and this is the stupor: why do names exist? But what chiefly concerns us is that the social moment of objectification is never corrected, contested, or confirmed by the intuitive return "to things themselves." Yet knowledge is based— directly or indirectly—on immediate evidence which is at once a thorough inspection, enjoyment, and focused attention. Through direct perception the thing possesses me by yielding itself, but I am affirmed by welcoming it "without foreign additions." Knowledge is rigorously impersonal and then it is us, and then me. The understanding of some particularity of the thing, inflexibly true—this is *our* common property; but through the intuition which verifies it once more, here and now, it is *mine*: it fulfills me, engages me, and defines me. Through evidence I appeal from rigorous impersonality to the historical community, and from others to myself; I recover myself by losing myself. This exercise is therefore *ethical*; it is an act that establishes the person but can be accomplished only on the foundation of a previously recognized *value*. The resort to the self indeed creates the subject's absolute confidence in his own person, but first he must assume it. Gustave, nonvalorized as he is, can under no circumstances consider himself a solid link in a chain of collective operations. Nor regard the simultaneous course of things and his own life as the guarantee of a verbal proposition.

The result is doubly disastrous: even the reality of his self remains alien to him, he knows it only by hearsay. In point of fact, the basic and immediate structure of the ego is the spontaneous affirmation at the heart of concrete intuition. For Gustave it is not that this ego eludes him, that it is confused or blurred, or that the child is afraid of confronting it directly; it is rather that the ego is of a different order of things and does not exist outside the universe of significations, that is, outside of language, the magical power of grown-ups. Let the word come to mind again unexpectedly, the child is panic-stricken and the stupor recurs. But except for these unpleasant encounters, no true link between act and being suddenly makes the object emerge through the subject and the subject through the object. This would still be negligible if in the social world the child had not received a proper name, a self, qualifications. Alone in the garden he no longer has to deal with them; but scarcely has his mother or the maid called him and he finds them again. Let someone shout to him from a window, "What are you doing?" and he passes from contemplation to the world of enterprise. Besides, we must recognize that he is in this world more frequently than in vegetative solitude. Yet every probable meaning includes in itself a mortgage on our belief; the universe of signs is first that of faith: in every phrase heard, in every word that vibrates in my ear, I discover a sovereign affirmation which pursues me, which requires that I claim responsibility for it. Two moments can be distinguished in this process, although they are in general confused. The declaration *affects me*, I *believe* in it as it is momentarily the royal act of the Other, his metamorphosis *into man*, for mistrust is a sickness. You have to begin with credence or to deny man—you make a fool of yourself in the beginning, but so what? After all, if the Other wants to be subhuman, it's up to him to prove it, not me. This first passive moment—one man's confidence in another—is immediately passed over on the way to reciprocity: I sovereignly affirm what is sovereignly affirmed to me. However, I would continually be taken in by lies, fallacies, if I did not have genuine *reducing agents* at my command. Or rather, I have only one, though it varies constantly: evidence. This means that I reclaim the affirmation from the Other, according to its requirements but in the presence of the thing, through my intuition of it. Belief automatically disappears—it yields to the act. Now I *know*: by means of a yes, a no, a perhaps which I wrest from the thing—or a silence which allows all conjectures—I have transformed probability into truth. Such at least is the ideal operation. In most cases it isn't possible. Or not right away. I remain then in the world of signs, authority, beliefs. In a word, *spoken* language without the corrective of evidence is charac-

155

terized by this basic feature: credibility. And this comes to me from others through their words, like the power of the ruler over his subjects. Belief is not a fact of individual subjectivity, and we are not *disposed* to believe through some inherited tendency; it involves an intersubjective relationship, an incomplete moment in the development of knowledge; it is the presence within us of an alien will combining words in an assertoric synthesis which fascinates and disturbs us until we make it our own will.

From the moment he is in society, that is, in the family, Gustave is outwitted, overwhelmed, penetrated by signs and their imperious credibility. He believes. But unlike other children, he never goes beyond this first moment of knowledge. This happens both because he has been made passive and because he has no reducing agent at his command. Actually, these two reasons are really one; the passive child cannot even conceive the project of appropriating for himself the act of others by reaffirming the affirmation or denying it. He is the one, to be sure, who maintains the synthetic unity of the proposition solely because it encounters an ambience of astringence and totalization in his ipseity, but he imagines he limits himself to supporting passively the synthesis effected by the Other. The phrase remains inside him as a multiplicity vaguely *contained* by the natural contraction of experience, and at the same time as a seal fixed upon his vague feelings to prevent their dispersal. But the verbal project depends further on clear evidence—the *perception* of the object can in itself impel the speaker to take responsibility for the affirmative or negative formula of which he is the agent, or to call it into question; it may be, too, before any hope of evidence, that different factors incline him to take a particular stand, in which case he will not decide anything without having demanded the pure vision of the thing. Neither of these possibilities applies in the case of Flaubert, and once more it is passivity that prevents him from establishing his intuitions as *truthful* evidence, in other words, from giving simple enjoyment the structure of an act; no reducing agents, no control. Never that solitude—provisional but essential—out of which the decision is made: "I am alone, and that is enough."[4] Gustave suffers from a disease of the truth; he lacks the chief categories, having neither praxis

4. In point of fact it is never only a question of the reactivation of another thought; and *my* affirmation draws its infinite strength only from the successive affirmations that precede and sustain it. Never mind. Without this spark in each thought, without the fiat that kindles here when elsewhere it has just been extinguished, truth could only perish passing from one mind to the other; for each of us it would be *alien truth*.

nor vision. As for the ego, it remains on the level of significations. Shall we say that for him, truth does not exist? Yes and no. Certainly skepticism is his vocation; truth for him is the science which he will pursue to the end of his sarcasms, and which he seeks to unmask in *Bouvard et Pécuchet* so that it will collapse under the weight of its contradictions. Nothing is certain since the evidence is lost; if the appropriate ideas are not specified, how can they be recognized? Everything is equivalent. And Gustave would have us know that he "has no ideas," that conclusions must never be drawn, that all opinions must be respected as long as they are sincere. The heart—that is, pathic compliance—here replaces the absent "criteria"; let one cling to certain prejudices with all one's might, let one kill if these are touched—or die—that is enough, they will be *valid*.

The operation consists of replacing evidence with pathic enjoyment, without changing its fundamental passivity; we are here at the beginning of a century that will invent the "vital lie" only at the moment it gives way to ours. However, it is already there, this lie, engaged by necessity, it sprawls on every page of the correspondence. As for religion itself, we shall see that for Flaubert it most certainly involves a fundamental truth; this is so because, in his view, religion is *instinct*. Truth is only the need to believe.

But from another viewpoint this emotional skepticism has nothing in common with pyrrhonism, a reasonable effort to deny reason, for it translates bewilderment, resentment, a cunning effort to substitute the heart for the mind and the irrational for the intelligible. This is not a doctrine, still less an enterprise—quite simply it is a way of life. In opposition to such lived-out, declared irrationality is the social organization of meanings; Gustave is immersed in it like everyone else, as he understands when he leaves his solitude. Yet this universe is *true*; proof is that it contains the word truth and that this word applies to certain verbal propositions. Gustave will tell us later about accepted ideas with a humor all the more bitter because he accepted all of his. In particular the idea of truth. Therefore he believes in it—it is the Other's will in him. Skeptical, he takes care not to draw conclusions—truth does not exist, for this would be to form an idea, to affirm, to lay claim. Socialized, he is inhabited by the thought of others, he submits to their assertion as to a belief. Thus truth—the verbal determination of the *expressive world*—is the foundation of his beliefs. And belief—like the nonreciprocal social relationship—is the sign of truth. This commonplace, an inert thought that passes from mouth to mouth and from brain to brain, enters Gustave's ear, crushes his young mind with the weight of accumulated affirmations, and is engraved there forever. It dominates and fascinates at the same time. The domination is triumphant otherness imposing itself on passivity; the fascination is the aura of an inexpressible and continually forgotten desire. How could the little boy say—and say *to himself*—that he is tempted to take up the task and affirm in his turn when he is lacking the essential structures of assertion? The entreaty, which he endures without understanding it, is in the sign itself, in the way it is communicated to him. The authoritarian voice of the medical director awakens in him, whether reminiscence or desire, the uncertain consciousness of neglected powers; he wishes to rediscover them and succeeds only in imitating the imperious accents that have troubled him. Domination, fascination degraded by imitation—this is belief for Gustave; which one can summarize by saying that it is defined as a surrender not prompted by grown-ups. This is how he experiences it; let a statement cause his surrender to the entire family, he will not hesitate to call it truth. Yet truth rigorously excludes belief. Not that I couldn't *believe* in some absent object known by hearsay, which was, moreover, and for others, true, namely perceptible; it's just that when *I believe in it*, it is not true; if I approach it and observe it, I no longer *believe* in it. Belief is the Other in me; truth is the object in front of me, an appearance which is liberating because it never takes place except by and for the free affirmation of the self. For this reason truth is never *subjective*, like a difference of *opinion*; it is praxis itself, the double and complex relations among men through their work in the world, and between men and the world through the reciprocity (virtual or real) of human relations.

All these features are contained in Gustave's notion· of what is true—some are even familiar to him. But by hearsay: truth, his father told him, is like this. Why not? He believes it, thus he neither knows nor feels anything. Truth, the comprehensive foundation of all the truths that embody it, can also create the object out of a rigorous intuition; after recourse to basic evidence, errors and particular truths will be distinguished no better than before—that is, without specific intuition. But truth—absolute, *unordered* totalization—will never more be confused with error, the supreme principle of all hierarchical order. Two worlds, the first of which rigidly repels the second. For Gustave there is only one—the world of order. Order and truth are inseparable; both are guaranteed by his father. And if in certain circumstances a proposition held to be true by superior minds happens to appear without a few of the features or groups of features which constitute what is true, the child might note this absence but will see nothing more in it than a call for prudence; he will not adopt the idea too hastily. The *object*—in this case, the truth, which is always absent—*does not resist* him; he believes in it without seeing it, or rather he substitutes belief for it. Truth for him is faith, since he has faith in the truth; he sincerely believes in the credibility of all significations—it is enough to eliminate malpractices through the precaution of usage, everything else is on principle an article of faith. The most diverse forms of expression—from mimicry to the "language of flowers"—are related to meanings—verbal or nonverbal—which are *true*, that is, believable simply because they are expressed. Faith will be hierarchical; it is proportional to the importance of the speaker, to his affirmative power. Thus the child, replacing truth with ordered belief, from the beginning confuses error and truth, bondage and liberty.

Empty and pursuing absences, belief nonetheless involves a certain subjective power; the Other within Gustave does the affirming, and this beguiling domination can engender strong feelings. Here we recover the plenitude of the *pathic*; not that it is the guarantee of the sign (the sign, inasmuch as it comes from the Other, is its own guarantee), but the child confuses the outpouring of passion with adherence or refusal—it is the passive image of the act. When he furiously repeats a maxim, he does not succeed for all that in appropriating it to himself. But the unleashing of affective forces gives some power to the repetitive imitation; there is no *vision*, no spontaneous passing from one phrase to another toward its object, but this does not prevent the pseudo truth from being profoundly *felt, experienced*. In order to make myself clearly understood, I will employ a comparison. Theater involves many affirmations; the characters can make mistakes, affirm out of passion, falsify their evidence, whatever—they see and say what they see, and the entire proceeding is an act. Yet after numerous rehearsals, I have ascertained that most actors are incapable of *representing* assertive behavior on stage. The same actors off stage affirm or deny as frequently as their audience, that is to say every minute. The moment they play their parts, however, action gives way to passion. Listen to them: they suffer what they are saying; if they must convince us, they will leave no stone unturned—the heated tone, frenzy, the savage violence of desire or hatred—except for the certainty of judgment based on evidence. This, when expressed, is an appeal to reciprocity; it is free and addressed to the freedom of others; but the actor wants to persuade *by contagion*. No sooner has he said, "The time is out of joint," than we already know we are entering into a world of tears and gnashing of teeth; he *does not know* that the time is out of joint, that is just the way it seems to him, he feels some sort of sorrow in his bones that tears this phrase from him like a cry. And this strange behavior has only one explanation: every dramatic work is fantasmagoric; the player, deeply engaged as he is in his role, never completely loses consciousness of the unreality of his character. To be sure, after the performance he may say the play is true; perhaps he will even be right. But this truth is of another kind, it concerns the basic intention of the author and the reality he has pursued through these images. In sum, *Hamlet*, Shakespeare's play taken as a whole, reveals a truth; Hamlet the protagonist of the play is a phantasm. And whatever the actor's opinion of the deeper meaning of the drama, his duty is to reproduce word by word, gesture by gesture, the totality of the work; this means that he is thrust into an imaginary universe, true perhaps as a whole but in detail devoid of truth. It is there, however, the truth; the word is pronounced in the play: the error of one character is revealed to the public, another's lie. But isn't this *imitating* the stupidity of the one and the other's imposture? Inversely, affirmation, certainty, evidence never appear on the stage, we see only more or less successful imitations. In truth, they are *always unsuccessful*— only a degraded image of the fiat can be provided. The talent of the player is not in question, it is the material that is bad. Since praxis is rigorously banished from all representation, willed firmness is replaced by the transports of sensibility; in other words, it is depicted by its contrary. Let a prince say: I am the prince, it is an act; but if Kean declares that he is prince of Denmark, it is passion supporting a gesture. Dramatic discourse offers no handle to verbal acts; the cultivated speech flows without the power to create or receive such acts—Kean is not Hamlet, he knows it, he knows that we know it. What can he do? Demonstrate it? Impossible; even before it is furnished, proof is integrated as part of the imaginary whole. Hamlet can convince the gravediggers, if he likes, the soldiers encountered on the way, but he will never convince us. The only means of making the play exist *for us* is to infect us with it. Affective contagion: the actor lays siege to us, penetrates us, evokes our passions by his feigned passions, draws us into his character and rules our feelings by his own. The more we identify with him, the closer we are to sharing his belief—ours still remains imaginary, felt but neutralized. In any case, it is *believing*, nothing more. And the player will not attempt to abandon the pathic register—which is equally that of faith—for if he did, he would be nothing but a frozen curiosity. It is at this point that the experienced actor will avoid speaking the lines or tirades which have universal bearing, and consequently concern us directly, as though they were truths. Hamlet's monologues, dark meditation and inner pause, perplexed contemplation of obsessions, pondered indecision, flashes of perception, must be murmured to oneself—in a monotone, blank, without intonation. The point is that he *speaks* his passions; he has achieved reflective distance. And his concerns are ours: life, death, action, suicide. Everything is generalized: to be or not to be? Who asks the question? Anyone, if we judge it only by the words. Therefore *I* do, in my present reality. But if only for a moment the doubts and arguments are universalized, as a sermon directed to me or as a common reflection on the human condition, everything crumbles, just as in the movies when an actor suddenly turns toward the camera and seems to look at us. The *act*— the look is such an act—punctures the fiction; Hamlet dies—a man in a doublet is left bringing us a message from Shakespeare. For this reason every interpreter of the role is forced to *singularize* the monologue, his duty is to conceal the fact that these words could be addressed to us; he seeks to contain us in the character, to imprison us in the world of belief. No, no—there's not a bit of truth in any of this, or if there is, you will wait until the end of the play before you find it—torments, nothing else, and these hardly concern you—what do you have in common with this Danish prince seen through the eyes of an Englishman of the Elizabethan age? The lines you hear are not even subjective findings, the testimony of a courageous lucidity, they spurt spasmodically from *endured* griefs as blood spurts from a wound; quite honestly, they embody Hamlet's torments much more than they attempt to express them. So the monologue will be *played*— happily, if the prince does not roll around on the stage or if he spares us his sobs. When the actor knows his job, we are Hamlet's prisoners until the curtain falls. Prisoners of belief—this is what masks the universal character of the truths the author shoots at us like arrows. Believing is not acting, paralysis stops us from going to meet the ideas that are flying about; by submitting to them we cannot recognize the praxis they imply, which is a thought. As for the interpreter, he has no need to reflect, entering into belief at the first cue and leaving at the last, sometimes a bit after that; he doesn't think, he feels. Is thought—as has often been said—harmful to the actor? Worse—in the exercise of his profession, including rehearsals, it is impossible for him. And this is why the best speak affirmative lines so badly; nothing is known, everything is believed, everything is doubly surrendered—to the author who freely imposes the text, the beliefs, the passions, and to the public who can sustain their faith and carry it to extremes or suddenly abandon everything and wake up alone in front of horrified sleepwalkers.

Gustave is like this: the receptacle of phrases deposited by others, learned by heart, experienced as surrender and therefore believed, he finds himself in a world where truth is the Other. No doubt it would look different to those who impose it and probably create it—the child is quite frequently assured of this. But he prefers to ignore this hidden aspect of the truth. When he enters into relationship with adults—that is, a hundred times a day—he hears their voices, their inimitable tone of certainty, and can only play-act conviction. This in a sense is the actor's position reversed: on stage he passes from certainties to beliefs by the requirement of *representation*, by that denial of all willful construction which obliges him to abandon himself passively to the fatalities of his character. Gustave, paralyzed at first, must abandon himself to alien words; they inhabit him like a text known by heart, and the passive assent he gives to them—out of submission and out of indifference—does not in itself contain the means of going beyond faith. His lived reality is the slow, vegetative flow of years; in the world of first truths and commonplaces he is lost without landmarks, believing everything because he knows nothing; this is what compels him to *play a role*. Actually, he does not recognize himself at all, he is not attracted to anything, he does not discover his singularity or even his anchorage in the medium of objective meanings; without the ability to choose himself by choosing the expressions that suit him, without ever having felt the fundamental need to express himself, he plays the drama of choice. In guiding himself by the supposed preferences of his parents, he adopts significations without any reference to a signified that doesn't exist for him, and when these significations are inside him, alien intentions that define him, he makes himself *through gestures* into whatever he is designated by the adopted *expression*. A double drama: choice is imitated, the simple result of his malleability, and hence external forces have decided for him; the only honest attitude would have been indifference, and this, precisely, was impossible since he had to submit to the verbal preferences of others. The character is played out, then, the one that has been attributed to him. But—beyond the fact that it is rather vague—he *does not feel* it as his reality; his own ego inside him is only an object of belief, as are its qualities, of which, as we have seen, he has a poor understanding. Therefore he expresses himself before feeling, since he plays at feeling what he expresses. Does he now feel the role he is playing? No, he *believes* he is feeling it. The drama is born here from belief, and belief possesses him, without solid reducing agents and singularly without evidence. So the drama must not be understood as if Gustave were conscious of playing it. But neither is he unconscious. Unlike a professional actor, he can neither fall in with his role nor denounce it in the name of his subjective reality; specified feelings are born from their very specification, though actually these are gestures. Gustave fully feels the poverty of their plots, the voids, the overexcitement which finally replace *experience* and are only a flight in the face of inconsistency. But his deeper life is unexpressed, inexpressible, unexpressive at least according to *this* plan, with *these* words; it remains out of range, very far away, very far below. Therefore this deeper life does not challenge new meanings and the drama that ensues—no conflict, no collisions, no evidence. What is spoken is feigned, what is *lived* is not spoken.

To believe is to believe *in someone* (or in something that takes the place of someone—we do not believe our eyes). This means, as we know, that the spoken words Gustave receives are inside him as imperative meanings. This means that their force is borrowed. And that the *absence of intuition* becomes a "rule to guide the mind." In general, things do not go quite to such lengths; a realm of knowledge and a realm of faith exist, their borders blurred but their clear zones quite distinct. Belief is a provisional state; even if one is convinced that in numerous cases it can be definitive, this is by accident and not essence. It *takes the place* of knowledge. I attach myself to this or that man who has seen what I have not been able to see; lacking the evidence myself, I place confidence in another's perception. But for Gustave belief alone *is* knowledge, there is no other. This is to be understood as follows: the permanent absence of active intuition is the result of passivity; the need for evidence is never felt. Yet perceptual evidence is the relation of existence to being and to itself; in a certain way this is nothing other than *existing* as a free organism which continually *reaches beyond itself* and *touches the world around it.* Trapped under the crusts and froths of passivity, Flaubert's existence is deep, it carries words along, it is already "acculturated" but remains out of reach, it does not offer itself as a complete way of "being-in-the-world" and of living. In the universe of expressed meanings, the words truth and belief shall be confused, or rather the second is hidden behind the first, the more imposing, and devours its flesh— leaving a ruthlessly consumed skeleton. As long as true facts are

163

disposed of, the maxim of belief is not too troublesome, and we can agree that if we believe what we don't see, we can't believe what we do see (because we *know* it). But everything changes when this is made the principle of all truth. This means that absence is the mode of normal being. Transcendent being does not surrender itself, immanent being is out of reach, life is an exile at the heart of a reality which neither from the inside nor the outside can be delivered to view. Others are intercessors; for Gustave they possess certainties he is ignorant of but which pass into meaning itself at the moment of transmission. The maxim now becomes: I do not see anything nor can I; the test of truth is that it is affirmed by others and etched into me by them. If the designated being is characterized by its nonbeing (which can of course be a being-elsewhere), the drama is no longer the imitation of an absence, it is being itself and truth. In fact, *imitation* is a game of being and nonbeing; it inscribes in being the nonbeing of a being, or, if you like, it presents a being through its absence. In any case the thing *imitated* is sketched out by the game of two nonbeings, and this refers to two beings of which one *is not* (*or is not there*) and the other *is not visible* (masked by appearance), *is not what is caught in passing* as its actual presence. And this is exactly what being is in a world where belief is proffered as knowledge. People live, they are, but being escapes them. Such a person *doesn't know* if he loves his mother, his brother, or rather he *doesn't feel* it; this is normal, since the being of that love is gone; yet the being must be signified to others to please them and to oneself as often as possible in order to keep it fresh. This expression of tenderness without inner guarantee, these impassioned signs without passion, must be seen both as the awakening of an acquired meaning, therefore a designation of being through repeated behavior, and as the *minimal* embodiment of that being in its absence to the internal world and the external. In the child, expression is necessarily drama, but the drama does not speak its name; it believes, seeks to believe in itself, to make itself believe— it offers itself as the work of truth. What is left is the void which these gestures— phantom acts—do not succeed in masking; hence one must escape by believing extravagantly. For belief—unlike truth—can expand indefinitely; in other words, the child seeks to compensate for the inconsistency of being by the impassioned violence of his faith. It *is at this level* that he must possess the real; he does not feel his love at all, though he fully experiences his faith in it—for in this faith he encounters the reality of love. But this is to be placed in an ever tighter state of dependence on others; belief, as we know, is only an imported affirmation that remains in us without dissolving and without changing into *our* affirmation. For Gustave to be more and more *believing*, he has to persuade others a bit more each day. Not with arguments—this would be thinking. By the dramatized transport that signifies his passion. He counts on contagion to elicit assent. From the moment this is given, the little boy takes it and is penetrated by it; his love is now imperatively marked in him by the Other, therefore he exists, he is certified. To be sure, this contagious impulse, supposing it is produced, can add nothing to the certainties of others, nor can it provoke an assent which has not yet been given. It is merely—as in the theater—a matter of infecting the audience with passion. Gestures provoke gestures: the child runs toward his father and the father opens his arms. Briefly, Gustave might *at best* be able to inspire belief. But precisely this limitation is not evident to him since he continues to confuse knowledge and faith, belief and affirmation. If he has persuaded the Other, the Other will show his new faith by gestures, by signs that the child welcomes as imperative assertions. It is above all in this respect that Gustave comes to resemble the actor—he suggests that others impose on him the feelings he wants to feel; this being, "ungraspable in immanence," must flow back to him from the outside. Thus the actor needs the public in order *to be* this Hamlet he represents; yet he knows profoundly that *he is not him.* The child does not know that he is playing a role or that the ego expressed scarcely belongs to him. But this is because he knows nothing, not even what *knowledge* means. He believes what is said, what he is made to say, what is believed. When the player on good days feels supported by the audience, he is roused, this emotion aids him, he draws new strength from it, it gives a kind of reality to the imaginary feelings he expresses. In these privileged moments his general certainties, without disappearing, let themselves be relegated to the heart's deepest place; it is no longer a question of *being* Hamlet but of brilliantly portraying a son's anger against his mother. The player is roused, he believes he is angry—he believes it through others and through the undifferentiated emotion that lends his rages a kind of counterfeit authenticity. Gustave has put himself on this level: his roused passivity can be excited only by disorder, excitement supports the drama and communicates to him a fleeting reality; he plays his part, he persuades others to invent under his direction the character which he internalizes in the shape of an ego and which will forever remain alien to his life. In other words, the character is at the same time a persona, a mask thrown over a void, a group of imperious directives that concern his future actions, inner object to the subject, continually reproducing and consolidating; and in its other aspect, turned toward darkness, it is the emanation of a primal passion, of excitation, of the general and unspoken need to be loved—in a word, the reflection of an obscure, subterranean pool ceaselessly moving and sliding over itself, ipseity. It is through this double aspect of the ego, the dramatized I, a drama which alludes to a subjective relation to the self, that he will later be able *to be the Garçon*, that is, to be himself in the Garçon, to make *this character* into his own designation even while rejecting it in the world of the Other, and further to internalize as purely his own qualities (unleashed passions, Pantagruelism) those he acts for others without possessing them. In the social world of signifiers/signified, Flaubert's ego can easily jump outside him to animate outwardly an alien role to which he rightly or wrongly lends a character identical to his in radically different circumstances (but symbolizing his own history), and of which he then says: *this is myself*, the "Garçon" is myself, Madame Bovary is myself. We shall return to this strange union of the author with himself, for it characterizes a very specific relation of the writer to writing and a whole section of the letters. Let us simply note what he does *not* say: I am Madame Bovary; this judgment would be a clear affirmation, an advance toward the object; the reexternalization of interiority would be accomplished in the sense of rational activity, but through that very thing the phrase would warn us to expect a bad novelist.[5] Quite the contrary: the neuter, la Bovary, *this* penetrates him from the outside and is discovered to be himself in passivity; or, if you like, he is himself the great creature lying between the lines, a creature that only the act of another will awaken. And through a drama with an inverted sense but an analogous structure, he can also pull the act from outside thanks to the beliefs his game inspires in others. Without being altogether niggardly, we shall see that he was always a bit close-fisted; this did not prevent him, from adolescence until the end, from playing generosity, believing that others believed him prodigal and conse-

---

5. The "I am Heathcliff" from *Wuthering Heights* has a different meaning. A woman (Kate) says: *I am this man*. In this active character in whom passion is always a radical praxis, Emily Brontë can embody herself. But she cannot say, I *am* Heathcliff; she is too active to say, Heathcliff is myself. This intimate bond is created by someone interposed, as if she were letting it be understood: this girl who says, I am a man, at the moment she says it, she is myself. This involves an intervening relationship between passive discovery and willful creation.

quently believing it himself.[6] This quality came from others to his self-other and so was easily integrated—the general rubric and the particular determination were homogeneous. The two limits between which the ego continually oscillates are thus the projection of the self outside itself into the qualities of an imaginary personage, by virtue of the unity of a character and a life, and the ingestion of external qualities—accessibleonly to others—and their integration with the same self, transcending the heart of immanence. With this radical difference between the two extreme attitudes: Flaubert, when he says I, is never sincere, he is play-acting, he is posing, he is posed. His correspondence and his rare autobiographical attempts must be consulted with circumspection—if he is telling the truth, he doesn't know it; what is not said and what is *missing* are much more revealing than the public confession or private confidences. On the other hand, when he is speaking about a fictional character—of whom he will then say, that is myself—everything is acceptable; guaranteed by the law of the imaginary, truth is established, little by little it impregnates the creature, certainly not by the power of affirmative fiat but by a new osmosis which we will describe in the second part of this work. What is certain in any case is that the ego in him is always invisible, ungraspable, and creates the object with an "act" of faith.[7]

6. All the same, he replaced the wild spending of income (if he had not, the drama would have been more difficult) with the pseudo-squandering of his "vital energy." The drama, then, is already symbolic.

7. It will be said that the ego in everyone is a determination of the psyche and that it is entirely conditioned by others, full of alien determinations which we can grasp in their abstract significance but cannot *see* because they appear only *to others*. Others alone can *find* me spiritual or vulgar, intelligent or dull, open or closed, etc. I can *know* that they find me so, understand the sense of the words which designate me, but these qualities—which express the relation to others—essentially escape me. These two points are true, I admit. But with most of us, passivity and activity are equitably joined: the dialectic of the ego (me—I—ipseity, otherness—act and drama) is a complex movement; and quite often the self is only the horizon of the *reflective act*: in this instance it is vision and promise, but the drama doesn't enter into it. There is an objective reality of the self, but this psychic object is, in form at least, the pure correlative of the reflective ipseity; better, the ipseity produces it by making itself into synthetic activity. To the extent that certain determinations of this object can issue from the Other, I am led to leave the reflective terrain, to recall certain behaviors which inspired the Other to call me irascible or pusillanimous, to consider them with the Other's eyes, to judge them as if I were myself another, and then to come back to reflection, to ponder my past intentions, to reject or accept the stranger's judgment on intuitive evidence, finally to reshape the object-unity of my reflective experience, the ego, with or without the proposed determinations. If I accept them, it is true that they will remain in me as unrealizable significations. It is also true that I will be tempted to make myself an actor out of impatience and in order to realize them. But *accepting*, in this case, is also taking a vow. Character is promise, says Alain. Thus the different forms of activity ordinarily present in the constituting or the assembling of the ego allow us to consider the

These remarks are not intended to *explain* Gustave's option of hysteria. First of all, the reasons for that option are much more complex; life itself will incite it bit by bit. And then—what in a sense amounts to the same thing—this singular problem is unlikely to have developed in such a young child. In the first years transitory symptoms might be found, but he is not, for all that, to be viewed as a hysteric, and nothing proves that the future option is predetermined by such indispositions. Most analysts hold that this neurosis, a global response to the situation as a whole, does not manifest itself before adolescence. Between thirteen and fifteen years old a little boy has "made the rounds" of his problems; he feels them more than he knows them but he experiences their urgency; he can then—and only then—choose the type of receptivity and activity to which he will conform all his life. Stupid, credulous, backward, little Gustave at seven years old is not hysterical—he still lacks the means.

Yet it must be understood that when psychiatrists in this regard use the words *choice* and *option*, they do not claim to refer to a metaphysical freedom; they wish rather to indicate that a total metamorphosis of the subject is involved and cannot be explained by a localized condition, as one would explain a particular disease. The rigor remains, but the determinist interpretations are dispelled; the neurosis is an intentional adaptation of the whole person to his entire past, to his present, to the visible forms of his future. It can be said equally that it is a way, for the totality of experience and the palpable world (through a particular anchorage), of making oneself bearable. This will be the hysterical "style," or the impossibility of living. But whether one takes the circularity in one sense or the other, a dialectical thought is required to grasp its necessity. Precisely for this reason hysterical neurosis can be compared to a conversion. And no one is unaware that the convert's fireworks put an end to a slow and secret labor that is spread over years. In order to fall at the feet of Christ after twenty years of militant irreligion, the former unbeliever must have unknowingly allowed the maggots to nibble away at his atheism—he looks around one day and it is nothing but lace. And behind

reflective ecology as a sector of knowledge and truth (which of course also means a sector of nonknowledge, error, and bad faith). Actually the operation assumes a constant reciprocity—which is what, at this level at least, permits the struggle against alienation and mystification. For Gustave, on the contrary, the ego *comes to him through others*; he doesn't dream of ratifying it but only of playing it in the sense it is proposed to him and in the way that confirms the demands of others. His ego is not only a psychic object but an *external and other object* introduced into the subjectivity from without. Or if you like, Flaubert's self is "allogenous."

this tattered rag, through its thousand holes, he perceives powerful troops already in place and in marching order. Before being converted he must be prepared for conversion. This means that his relations to everything have progressively changed—none of the changes was disturbing in itself, hence they all passed unnoticed. Language, for example, on certain significant levels, has taken on other functions: meanings are penetrated by symbolism, the word and the thing are confused, etc. These linguistic transformations have not been for the purpose of giving faith to the unbeliever; they have been constituted, however, as an intentional response to the requirements of the situation. But this response—partial totality—results in lowering the unbeliever's threshold of faith—in the logical sense of the term, the material density of the sign, for example, will more often seem to him like the real presence of the signified. And this attachment to the meaning of the vocable, this weakening of controls, all these modifications of the word have somehow created the object out of an intention: in a desperate situation the goal was to weaken rational demands in order to restrain oneself at the least cost. God is at the end of the road, but as soon as one begins to take words for objects and to believe that the moon is made of green cheese, He is neither anticipated nor desired; so it is that this officer, perhaps to blind himself further to the disorder of his particular existence, to the distressing absurdity of military life, chose to orient himself differently—just barely—in the universe of language. No matter. He will find God because he has begun to invent him. For God—among a thousand other bonds between man and the world and other men—is also this: a thickening of language, meanings intercepted by their signs.

This example will explain the importance I attach to these first connections between the child and expression. It is not enough to see here the surest way of arriving at Flaubert's work and of understanding it; we shall go much farther in knowing the man—and consequently the work itself—if we recognize in this synthesis of muteness and drama, of belief and passivity, a path that clears the way for hysteria. The source is objective—the unloved child is curled up in his passivity, in his contingency; but if the same lack of love effectively deprives him of the practice of truth, the little cripple no sooner begins to adapt himself to his infirmity—meaning here to deny it—than he internalizes it. Belief—the only resource which is objectively conceded—becomes a function; he tries to increase its intensity, he uses it intentionally to represent himself to the self he would like to be. And no doubt we shall discover a circular movement—he would not be his own actor if he were not condemned to believe without knowledge; but inversely, the condemnation serves him, he adapts to it. Yet this is saying too little; rather, through condemnation he is chosen as an actor, he will play *himself* in order to curry the favor of others and fulfill his need for love. We can already catch a glimpse of pithiatism at the outer edges of this process. Soon we shall see too how he sets up the stupor as a defensive weapon for himself; how belief and drama born of passivity will become in their turn the source of passive actions; we shall see Gustave in extreme danger act upon others, without speaking to them or touching them, without even appearing to see them, and without changing anything in the external world, through the simple pressure he exerts internally on his own body.

Our first picture is finally complete: passivity, stupors, credulousness, poor relations to language and truth, dramas, intentionally erected beliefs, and, at the end of the road, the possibility—already a likelihood—of the ditch, the tumble into hysteria. It all forms an embryonic system governed by a double denial—love escapes, and its flight is internalized by the child as his own vegetative inertia; valorization by the mother has not taken place, and Gustave lives this deficiency of the Other as his own purposeless, causeless flow, as the stupefying contingency of an inferior being. His astonishment will be explained later in his works. The character in *La Dernière Heure*, for example—who is Gustave himself at fifteen—writes: "Often when looking at myself, I have wondered: why do you exist?" With these words he reconstructs for us the vague meaning of his dazes—there is no metaphysical question here. And the child never asked himself, "Why is there being rather than nothingness? Why is this being precisely myself?" but much more simply, "I was born unwanted, now who will tell me what the hell I'm doing here."

We are not at the end of our difficulties. Indeed, if it is true that the first two years, which are decisive for development, shaped Gustave for suffering, it is no less true that he knew happiness, beginning when he was three or four years old and for a period we shall have to determine later. And then, however they are understood, neglect, maternal aridity engendered the stupor and the malaise. But as I have said, the child needs love without having the specific desire to be loved; therefore he feels—in the sense that gaslight can be called poor—his poverty of being. Sometimes to the point of ennui. I grant that much, to the point of anguish, but not rage. Yet we shall see later that he never conquered his anger from the time he entered school—

and in all probability well before that—until his voyage to the Orient; other factors must have intervened and he must have been thoroughly worked over. In other words, after the earliest period we record a few happy years—but *how* could this suffering flesh suddenly expand and know joy?—then, abruptly, rage and anguish burst upon him and the whirlpools of ink flow unabated. But *what new conflict* unleashed the horror in this inert soul? It is possible, indeed, to explain these two successive transformations by the simple development of objective factors, which we have seen internalized. But looking at the dates, we quickly understand: Gustave—at first to his greater happiness and then to his greater pain—has been put into contact with the social world by a new personage clamorously introduced into his life, his father.

SIX

Father and Son

A. A RETURN TO REGRESSIVE ANALYSIS

It was his mother's pious and glacial zeal that *constituted* Gustave a passive agent; Mme Flaubert was the source of this "nature" and the malaise through which it was expressed. She was the one who welcomed him as an undesirable—that is, as the little importunate male who took the place of a daughter; she was the one who could not help seeing in him a future victim of infant mortality and who constrained him to internalize this maternal prejudice in the form of a death wish or, more precisely, an inability to live. And if the overprotection—which first made him the *object* of excessive attention—originated in Achille-Cléophas's anxieties, the fact is that the child was subjected to it in his earliest years through the attentions Caroline bestowed upon him with a lukewarm alacrity. However, in his first works, restless and raging, it is striking that he never accuses his mother. He was *made* monstrous, he tells us bitterly; and he never refrains from denouncing the passivity which is his "nature" and his disease. But when he mentions his "anomaly" he seems to find it more *complex* than simple constitutional inertia; doubtless the inertia contains the "anomaly," yet it might be said to go beyond it, a complex edifice of which passivity is only the foundation. In any event, the progenitrix is not directly referred to; if Caroline is sometimes embodied—in a secondary character—it is as a victim, and she can be reproached only for being an involuntary accomplice. To whom? This is precisely what we must establish. In order to understand the reasons obliging the young author to rage on, or at least to follow the thread of his anger from one tale to another, we must come back to

173

those first stories. No longer, as we did in the first chapter, to fish for confirmations of detail, but to consider each story as a whole, namely to examine them one after the other for their meaning.

We have remarked that every time Gustave writes in the first person he is insincere; we must therefore put aside for the moment the autobiographical cycle which begins with that first sketch, *Le Dernier jour à Novembre,* and includes *Agonies* and *Mémoires d'un fou.* Later, when we know him better and have the necessary keys to decipher them, these works will yield us precious information. For the time being, to take them literally would only mislead us. On the other hand, Gustave reveals himself the moment he invents. And from his first known work to the writings of his fifteenth year he can do nothing else. It is here, therefore, that he must be sought, here that he waits for us. He will not tell us the objective truth about his prehistory, but we shall learn from him that other irrefutable truth, the way he felt the movement of his young life. Yet if we are attempting a truly regressive analysis, it will not do merely to observe rigorously chronological order; his life will have to be followed *in reverse.* In every investigation concerning interiority, it is a methodological principle to begin the inquiry at the ultimate stage of the experience being studied, namely, when it is present to the subject himself in the fullness of its development—whatever may happen subsequently— that is, as a summation which, though perhaps not complete, may no longer be continued.[1] First of all there is this to be gained: the richer the meaning, the more it approaches an impossible fulfillment, the more *comprehensible* it is. And here is the other advantage: the oldest intuitions, worn and stunted growths, not only do not contain the indication of future developments—although the subject may experience them as presentiments—but for lack of being grasped through their future vicissitudes, they do not even provide information about the archaic sense which possesses them and which they obscure by condensing it. On the contrary, if we lay the path *in reverse* by retracing our steps from 1838 to 1835, this regressive study, which is a systematic interpretation of the present in the light of the achieved future, will permit us to discover in Flaubert the subjective evolution of experience, that is, the perception he has of his own life in its dialectical movement of summation. When the inquiry comes to a

1. Let us understand that it can be perpetuated as it is, reappear intermittently, and consequently be integrated into a cycle of repetition, or be abolished in the more or less long term. In any event, however, the only change that can affect it is sclerosis or stereotyping.

halt for lack of documents, it will be time to find out what the writer *intends us to understand*; from the first signals, difficult but profound, to the rationalized but more superficial constructions of the last tales, something turned on itself endlessly and snowballed, an experience that sought expression a hundred times. What Flaubert thinks of his life, what we must reconstitute, is the time-bound unity of these multiple significations and the meaning discovered in them.

But it must be added that this retrospective method imposes itself where Gustave is concerned more than in other cases. Because of that peculiar quality which belongs to him and which I shall call prophetic anteriority, in each of these first works one keeps finding the same symbols and the same themes—ennui, sorrow, resentment, misanthropy, old age, and death—but each time under these rubrics new experiences are expressed in such a way that the motif always seems adapted to the present situation and always *anterior to itself*, constituted from the depths of the future like the premonition of a deeper and richer future experience which is outlined through the present, and from the depths of the past like a habit entrenched through repetition, and like an obscure *conatus*, immemorial in origin, in order *to give a meaning* to what is experienced. In sum, everything we find in these first works simultaneously *foretells* future ills and is *foretold* by former griefs.

Let me offer an example. In 1875, when his nephew's bankruptcy brought him to the brink of ruin, one of the chief aspects of Gustave's despair by his own admission was a premature aging. He often returns in his correspondence to this precocious senility and finds happy formulas to establish its features: sentimentality, stupefaction, the incapacity to "gain the upper hand," the presentiment of approaching death, the silent reeling off of distant memories. All this is *true*, we should not doubt it; in fact, he will die of this decline five years later. But if we go back to 1870, to the capitulation of Sedan, to the proclamation of the Republic, we shall be surprised to see him describe his shame and his unhappiness in the same terms. Certainly we shall later have occasion to study his total reaction to the fall of the Empire and shall find it much richer than the theme of senescence seems to indicate. Never mind. It is there, sentimentality, a presentiment of death, a reeling off of memories—Flaubert doesn't spare us anything. One motif stands out against the background of all the others—that of survival. Gustave is a "fossil," there is no place for him in the new society; it is chiefly in this respect that he resembles the aged, who

175

in effect outlive their times. They once had a period of passionate adaptation to life; but this is our author's opinion, this Prudhomm-esque formula which teaches us that one cannot be and have been. Gustave, in 1870, considers himself a "has been" and consequently no longer being. Thus his reversal of fortune in '75 could, all things considered, only *realize* what was already present five years earlier. No doubt it will be said—and it is true—that the disaster of Sedan and the fall of the Empire launched a process of involution that Com-manville's bankruptcy only hastened. But what then should we make of numerous letters written *before* the war which *already* describe Gus-tave as a fossil, as a pensioner, and finally as an octogenarian? And if someone wants to maintain that these images—exaggerated as they may be—are not so inappropriate to a quadragenarian who feels him-self growing older each day, I answer that the theme of precocious senilty is to be found in nearly all the letters he wrote to Louise between '48 and '49, that is, between his twenty-seventh and his twenty-ninth year. From their first days together he reminds his mis-tress that he warned her before any involvement: "If you were bent on finding in me the bitterness of adolescent passions and their fren-zied ardor, you should have fled this man who told you he was old at the outset, and before asking to be loved revealed his leprosy. I have experienced a great deal, Louise, a great deal. Those who know me rather intimately are amazed to find me so mature, and I am even more so than they think."[2] He is even more precise three months later[3] at the time of their near break:

Under my covering of youth lies a singular old age. What is it then that made me so old from the cradle, and so disgusted with happiness before having even tasted it? Everything that belongs to life repels me. . . . I would like never to have been born or to die. I have inside me, in my depths, a radical irritation, intimate, incessant, which prevents me from savoring anything, which fills my soul to bursting. . . .[4] When I cried out to you from the first, with a naïveté which you scarcely appreciated, that . . . it was a

2. 21 October 1846. He was twenty-five.
3. 20 December 1846.
4. We see here, dialectically bound together, the themes of ennui and old age. As this connection appeared even in his first works, it is permissible to wonder where it came from. We shall try here to show its meaning and function. But since it entered a child's mind to consider himself suffering from ennui in his earliest years, and old *from birth*, the two *words* must first have been given to him together. And surely the idea "Old people are bored [*s'ennuient*]" can be said to belong to the anthology of

phantom and not a man you were addressing . . . , you should have believed me.

This lover has only two concerns: preventing his mistress at all costs from setting foot in Croisset, and finding new reasons each time for arranging their meetings in Paris or Mantes. In order to restrain her he avoids as much as possible declaring a love that she might want to put to the test at once. Sometimes, driven to the wall, the ardor of the adversary or his own fatigue draws from him tender admissions that tear his throat as he speaks. Instantly he continues without disavowals to disqualify these admissions, and if possible in the same sentence. This is what explains the frequency of the tirades on his old age; passionate in the past, destroyed by unhappiness, he has lost the faculty of feeling. After this he can declare to Louise that he loves her, provided that he adds: if the word preserves any meaning from the pen of an old man who is no longer capable of love. He can also reverse the terms: I am old, therefore I do not love, but be happy since you are the only one who might at times be able to

national wisdom. Simone de Beauvoir has shown, in *La Vieillesse* [*On Aging*] how much truth it contains. Still, someone—or some persons—must have formulated this thought well before Gustave. Who? We will never know. We may, however, be surprised to read the following passage from Achille-Cléophas's thesis (defended in 1819): "One encounters rarely in private homes but rather frequently in hospitals a disposition of the soul detrimental to surgery. The condition of which I wish to speak is boredom, a kind of need which is to work, occupation, what hunger is to solid food; and just as hunger is not always so pronounced that it can make a man feel it is food that he lacks, so boredom often does not know what it needs.

"Boredom, which is produced in many different ways, for instance by the lack of things to keep one occupied, by the absence of an object with which one is passionately in love, by the monotony of impressions, which has inspired the saying

L'ennui naquit un jour de l'uniformité

is the result, in hospitals, of nearly all these causes joined together. . . .

"Children, rarely susceptible to the influence of habit, are rarely subject to it, while adults and above all old people are more vulnerable. The aged in particular love to preserve their customary way of being.

Certain âge accompli
Le vase est imbibé, l'étoffe a pris son pli

La Fontaine.

"An imprenetrable refuge from the winds and the rain, a bed more suitable to his pain, the most well-meaning care often cannot replace his hut or attic, the litter he shared with his family, and the feeble help he received from them:

Soit instinct, soit reconnaissance
L'homme, par un penchant secret
Chérit le lieu de sa naissance
Et ne le quitte qu'a regret.

Gresset, *Ode sur l'amour de la patrie.*

"This condition will disappear the moment the patient becomes acquainted with his neighbors;

rekindle my ashes. "You came along and stirred all that up again with a touch of your fingertip. The old lees boiled up again, the lake of my heart throbbed. But tempests are made for the ocean. Ponds, when they are disturbed, exude only unhealthy odors. I must love you to tell you all this. Forget me. . . ."

This confession of a veteran, made twenty times over, has another function as well. Louise is facile, a conformist, a bit cheap—three reasons why she knows "the world" rather better than the young recluse who has gone almost without transition from the family home to his apprenticeship and from this, after a few months in Paris, into seclusion. The poetic wonders of the Muse concealed a good dose of what one is pleased to call "experience." Gustave is annoyed, he doesn't want to be treated like a little boy. Experience, you bet he has it. To spare. And it won't be this little seamstress who will show it to him. Hence certain mysterious allusions to his past.

"My deplorable mania for analysis exhausts me. I question everything, and even my questioning. You thought me young, and I am old. I have often talked with old people about the pleasures here on earth, and I have always been astonished by the enthusiasm that lights up their lifeless eyes; they couldn't get over their surprise at my way of life, and kept repeating: 'At your age! At your age! You! You!'"[5] And a few months later: "I understand very well how idiotic I must seem to you, how ill-natured at times, how mad, selfish, and

---

L'infortuné n'est pas difficile en amis.
                                                                    Delille.

he will spin a tale of his woes, will hear the story of their hopes, will conceive some himself, will get used to accepting the services of the hospital staff, will above all single out the care of the nuns, administered more out of inclination and humanity than out of duty, and will judge favorably the practitioner, whom he will find to be sensitive and always respected."

As we can see, the explanation of boredom is simplistic. Nor is it less so when Dr. Flaubert notes that children are rarely subject to it, "while old people . . ." etc. If he surprised his son, at about ten years old, standing around yawning, wouldn't he have said to him: "You are bored? At your age! Children are not bored, only very old people are bored." And the little boy, interpreting this lecture backwards, far from thinking, I am not old, therefore I don't know what boredom is, at once referred to his true state and said to himself—with his familiar aggressive docility—I am bored, therefore I am old. In accepting his condition as octogenarian and—bad faith or misunderstanding—in being affected by his father, Gustave makes it consonant with the paternal curse: his father made him born old, wanting to die, disgusted by things here below; therefore his father gave him the "radical irritation" which is only the internalization of old age. However we interpret it, it is striking that Dr. Flaubert, eleven years before the birth of the son who will radicalize "spleen" in his life and in literature, should feel obliged to devote a long passage of his short thesis to this "disposition of the soul."

5. 9 August 1846.

hard—but none of this is my fault. If you paid close attention to *Novembre* you probably devined a thousand inexpressible things which perhaps explain what I am. But that time is past, that work was the closing of my youth.''[6]

Precautions such as these are common; in the face of too experienced a mistress, what greenhorn doesn't play the know-it-all? Unsuccessfully besides. He is transparent. You are putting on grand airs, Louise answers, "You are posing." And then, Gustave's calculated precautions are craven, they reduce him to the level of his Rodolphe; he is conscious of it, the criminal, and amuses himself with it. Does he lie? Not at all, few men are less dishonest. The fact is that he is insincere. And insincerity, unlike the lie, abuses us by means of the truth.

Between 1846 and 1849, Gustave did not write one letter that did not at least allude to his precocious old age. His amorous politics of *containment*, whatever Louise's impetuosities, did not require such extreme precautions. So he held back. Of course this theme served the rhetorical flourishes in which our would-be attorney was not lacking. But in the first period of their relationship he tried to express himself clearly. They became lovers at the beginning of August 1846. On the ninth, returning to Rouen, he was in love and did not measure his mistress's demands. Yet this is what he wrote to her:

Before knowing you, I was calm, I had come to be. I was entering a vigorous period of moral health. My youth was past. The nervous illness that afflicted me for two years was the conclusion, its close, its logical result. To have had what I had, something rather tragic must have happened earlier inside my brain pan. Then everything was settled again; I had seen things clearly, and myself too, which is rarer. I was living with the rectitude of a particular system created for a special case.

The autobiography is completed on 27 August:

That is old, very old, nearly forgotten;[7] I scarcely have any memory of it; it even seems to me to have happened in another man's soul. What is alive now, and what is me, has only to contemplate the other, which is death. I have two quite distinct existences; external occurrences have been the symbol of the end of the first and the birth of the second; all this is mathematical. My active, passionate life, full of contrary jolts and multiple sensa-

6. 2 Decmeber 1846.
7. Flaubert is alluding to his former love affairs.

tions, ended at twenty-two. At this time I made great progress all of a sudden and something else happened.[8]

Comparing the two passages, this much becomes clear: until the age of twenty-two, Flaubert's life has all the features of a fatal illness, his existence is only the aggravation of an agony; he suffers the way he breathes, and every suffering makes him die a little more. When all these conditions are combined, the organism gives way; worn out, breathless, the young man sinks into false death. The words "logical," mathematical" must be taken in the strongest sense; they were not chosen simply to indicate that the crisis was unavoidable, but to imply that this existence felt its decay as an internal premise, *its* fundamental premise. The attack, long foreseen, is an effect, a symbol, and a rite of passage—death and transfiguration. But *who* will be raised from the dead?

His appraisals of his second life, to be honest, seem contradictory. Sometimes it is the funereal calm of a pond—let sleeping waters lie or they will stink. Sometimes it is the beginning of a "vigorous period of moral health," and sometimes a "radical irritation." He goes further, he writes this surprisingly penetrating sentence: "I was living with the rectitude of a particular system created for a special case." This is the very definition of neurosis: defense mechanisms have finely tuned a system which is itself the illness. The Flaubert son is organized basically to suffer as little as possible. There is a hidden finality in the "falling sickness" and in the voluntary isolation that followed. In this neurotic "planning," the meeting with Louise was not foreseen. Gustave is disturbed for a moment but returns like a robot to his inflexibly rectilinear course; he just finds a new tactic and shows off his insensitivity out of fear of being too sensitive.

Nevertheless, the affective exhaustion does exist; he knows how to exploit it as a lesser evil, yet he submits to it. Lazarus is an old man—an exact but cold memory, a murdered heart, a weary lucidity, with no passion but that of knowing: "The depth of my emptiness is equal only to the passion with which I contemplate it." He constantly repeats this: "You ask me what I have passed through to arrive where I am: you will not know, neither you nor the others, because it is inexpressible. . . . My soul . . . has passed through fire. What a marvel it isn't reheated by the sun! consider this to be my infirmity,

8. He says twenty-two. But the crisis (January 1844) took place when he had just turned twenty-three. This is enough to demonstrate that he was anticipating it *for at least a year*.

a shameful internal illness that I have contracted from frequenting unhealthy things, but don't torment yourself, for there is nothing to be done."

The fire—this is still too noble; right in the middle of the paragraph Gustave drops his metaphor. His soul scorched? Surely not! Syphilitic, at the most. Poor thing, he is a victim of contamination. I leave aside the "unhealthy things"; not out of mistrust—the words are not just thrown in for effect and Gustave said what he meant. But we are still lacking the keys, and Louise must have lacked them too. What interests me in each of these two metaphors is the role Flaubert assigns to time: the second opens it out, correcting the first, which had collapsed it. The fire is the instantaneous calamity, the trauma. On the contrary, the decay by contagion is the irreversible and slow osmosis which internalizes the external by externalizing the internal; it is the family structure explored, lived out, tested in the course of an individual life which ends in January 1844. Each of these images implies: "They made me insensitive." But the first evokes a brutal accident and the second insists on the continuous progression of the illness. It is the latter that is found most frequently in the letters to Louise. Flaubert writes to her, for example, that he regards his short life as a "long history." One day he insinuates that his misfortunes began at seven years old. Another passage—already cited—invites us to think that sarcasms made him conscious *then* of the differences there had "always been between [my] ways of seeing life and those of others," and that he felt from this time the need to hide, to find for lack of actual solitude a refuge in himself. The original self is declared monstrous; he can kill himself, let himself be killed, escape by living in a tomb. In all three cases he will have carried out the collective sentence which anticipates not so much death as that which is ordinarily the consequence of death—burial. Here, at least, is one of the ways in which Gustave at twenty-eight imagines men and his life among them.

At first glance this new interpretation, without dissipating the obscurities of the first, merely adds its own. Flaubert tells us that he masked his sensitivity. Very well: Is this a reason for it to wither away? Actually, we cannot draw any conclusions; in very special cases the dissimulation can lead to exhaustion, but there are others, much more frequent, where the hidden passion is intensified. Yet Gustave is explicit: "I cried out too much in my youth to be able to sing—my voice is hoarse." Or else: "At fifteen I certainly had more imagination than I have now." It is not the isolation that breaks his voice, it is the

181

unheeded violence of his recriminations. Masked as they were, he had passions in his adolescence. And the keenest. But negative always—grief, envy, shame, rage—which meant that he was always thwarted. Recall how he qualifies the ardors of his youth: by the word frenzy—obviously—but also, unexpectedly, by *bitterness*; he can measure the force of his emotions only by his power to endure them—frustration and rancor, grief, the access of fury. His troubles are not caused by "difference" alone, they must have been intentionally inflicted, perhaps to sanction that difference; these troubles are what put on the rack an over-sensitive heart, and ultimately consumed it.

But if we look at it carefully, this new account does not contradict the preceding ones: the Fall is precisely the discovery of the "difference" *through the judgment of others*. This is what Flaubert means to suggest. A monstrous child in spite of everything knows the golden age of early childhood, he has not yet learned his "nature" since no one demands anything of him; as long as he is left in childhood, he is alone, nourished, protected certainly, but never *compared*. And then one day when he is seven, a sovereign judge discovers his particularity and defines it for him—here is the *Other*. Other as man. Meaning, of course, below the species, arrested in the "process of hominization." A flop, in short; the young boy is qualified by the man, therefore objectively. A *practical* qualification: certain kinds of treatment are suitable to this sub-man, others are less appropriate. Now that this determination by the outside world has stamped him from head to foot, there is nothing left for him to do but internalize it. He will see in it the sign of his abjection or his torments, rarely the sign of his value; he oscillates all the same—as we shall see—between the positive and the negative. But he will not doubt its truth, as the letter cited above proves: I am not like the others, therefore I conceal myself—*the cry of negative pride*. We shall soon discover the havoc the parents wrought in the name of the good by instilling in this soul the passionate pride of the Flauberts and at the same time depriving him of its satisfaction. But we do not yet have the right to be specific, for Gustave is not specific. I will even add that when he writes to Louise, he knows perfectly well how to begin the confessions and stop them in the nick of time. She believes she is in his confidence since he tells her that after reading *Novembre* she will have devined "inexpressible things"; but his insincerity is contained in the word "inexpressible," which is highly ambiguous. Does it suggest perceptions so subtle or so profound that there are no words to describe them? Does it suggest a family secret that *must be hushed up*? Gustave purposely is not clear.

For he takes the word up again some time later and, while preserving its ambiguity, insists rather on the second meaning. Louise asks him what painful adventures, what perpetual misfortunes warrant this jaded disgust, this boasting of old age; the sense of the question—after the answer—is clear: what *happened* to you? As to the answer itself, it is explicit but much less simple; Gustave begins by declaring: you will never know, neither you nor anyone else. This negation should suffice; it means: *I don't want to tell you.* But in order to soften this plea against self-incrimination he adds, "because it is inexpressible." And this time the unequivocal precision of the question favors more precise meanings in the response. What happened to you? Painful stories, which I won't tell you because they compromise my family. Yet this is not said; not expressly; after all, biographers have read and reread this correspondence without finding the least allusion to the child-martyr that Gustave thought in all subjective certainty he had been. Which doesn't prevent us, the moment we set aside the letters to Louise, from recognizing that their author, suspicious strategist, pushed confidences as far as he could. He was so fussed over in his childhood—for the simple reason that he wasn't like the other members of his family, the other schoolboys, the other university students—that his nerves finally shattered. But if he remains allusive when he mentions these *inflicted* sufferings, he is more open about his defensive maneuvers. Breaking all relations is self-mutilation: his strategy—a special system, which is of value only in *his case*—is his neurosis. Or rather the neurosis is the whole, the *stress* Flaubert experienced: the internalized aggression and the strategy which seeks to take the enemy from behind and surround him. If for Gustave the crisis at Pont-l'Evêque is the logical, mathematical conclusion of his youth, if he assimilates it to his past life like a glaring piece of evidence rather than an accident, it is because he perceives it to be the result of a struggle: what others made of him and what he made himself out of what they did to him, each of these determinations trying to crowd out the other.[9] But it is a *tragic* struggle—chance doesn't enter into it, nor does probability, always certainty. And the result will be strictly determined by the two adversaries—the battle of Pont-

---

9. What he makes of himself becomes, for and through the Other, an objective character which confirms the external judgment. Escaping, he is apprehended again, he escapes once more and is delivered through his flight to new apprehendings. Inversely, any objective character, wherever it comes from, is internalized as *otherness*; all the subjective enzymes are set to work to digest it. We shall see this in the second part of the study.

l'Evêque *had to take place*; it was ordered down to the last detail. Victory or defeat? We shall let Gustave decide for himself. What is certain, in any case, is that the false death and the "survival" that follows are *intentional* factors in Gustave's own eyes; aging is a product of stress, it sends the young man back to childhood and to the actions of the Other as they provoke and combat his own, to his own actions as he tries to disarm the adversary. It is all the more necessary to note this veiled frankness because in our retrospective analysis we are going to see it disappear in order to reemerge—more sharply—in the creative virulence of adolescence. By taking the earliest testimony on trust, we are frankly learning what—as far as I know—has escaped the experts on Flaubert: Gustave is subjectively certain that he has lived the most atrocious and rigid life from the age of seven to twenty-three. Not, as it is sometimes said, for having felt more than others the evils of our condition, but for having been exiled, frustrated, and tortured from the age of seven by his family—in other words, by his father. In tracing back over the course of time, we shall be even more convinced: the son's relationship with the sovereign father dominates Gustave's entire existence, and he is perfectly conscious of it.

Nonetheless, Flaubert in 1848, as in '70 and '75 but for other reasons, presents himself as a *survivor*. And we cannot forget that he is ill, that his youth is concluded by a terrible crisis, and that the new Gustave, after the attack at Pont-l'Evêque, has renounced the active life, sequestered himself in the Hôtel-Dieu and then at Croisset. It is therefore true in a certain way that the period following January 1844 can be considered a survival, a fragile and cautious old age; to Gustave the nervous illness seemed to be the death of his passions.

If the symbol "senility" seems admissible *after* the night at Pont-l'Evêque, which had the effect of transforming Gustave's life, what are we going to make of it when we discover it quite explicitly in the works *that precede* the "nervous illness"? From the first pages of *Novembre*, completed in 1842—therefore fifteen months earlier—the theme is stated: "My whole life is laid out before me like a phantom." We have read correctly: "My whole life." At twenty-one years old. This is not a matter of relating, like Balzac, a "start in life" or writing, like Goethe, an *Erziehungsroman*, but of showing us retrospectively a completed existence. One? What am I saying? A thousand perhaps: "To count the years. . . . I was born not long ago, but I feel burdened by so many memories, like old men by the days of their lives. Sometimes it seems to me that I have endured centuries and that my being includes the debris of a thousand past lives." It may be said that he had a presentiment of the neurosis, and no doubt he truly experienced the crushing, troubling fatigues which he had a perfect right to symbolize by "exhaustion" or senility. But what is striking, then, so much so that we take the young author more seriously, is his mysterious gift of *prophecy*; beginning in effect with these obscure sensations, he predicts the crisis and the survival that will follow. In fact, not only is the young hero of *Novembre* already the survivor of his life, but once again he is going to die in thought, and we shall see a second narrator rise from his corpse who will speak of the first in the third person. We are not told that this second narrator is old (or that he is young); quite simply, he exists only to contemplate this dead life and bear witness to it; he is a memory, a pure retrospective observation that does not exist sufficiently to be vulnerable to unhappiness, to passion—nothing will ever happen to him. Isn't it curious that Flaubert might have prophesied, four years earlier, the feeling he described to Louise on 26 August 1846: "What is alive now, and what is me, has only to contemplate the other, which is death"? In other words, what *Novembre* tells us about in advance is the attack at Pont-l'Evêque and its consequences. Why not? No doubt in this preneurotic phase of his life Gustave rests his prediction on the beginnings of a pathological experience—he is all the more certain of the final downfall because the fall has already begun; and later, after the attack, Louise's young lover will be much less irked at claiming as his own these adolescent prophecies because their despair and anguish were realized in his own life, in difficulties truly *suffered*. *Novembre*: this is the story of a tragic life illuminated by the evident necessity of a near death, a death inflexibly woven into a fabric of "estrangement" by life itself; an already foreseen survivor, this phantom which is nothingness becomes a subject through the annihilation of subjectivity, nonbeing deliberately confounded with the lucid consciousness of no longer being; and all this is propelled toward the ultimate confusion, the crisis, in which the irreversible metamorphosis of one form of life into another seems in advance to indicate the abolition of the living.

From 1842 to 1848 we might therefore find ourselves confronted by the strict unity of an inflexible process in which anticipations and reminiscences, far from contradicting each other, would be mutually illuminated by a reciprocal play of reflections. Through a system in operation, we might everywhere discover an understanding of the event that was sometimes retrospective, always real; as if the temporalization of the process were resumed by itself from moment to moment, its single variant being the proportion of the actual and the virtual, the experiential and the mythic, prophecy and recollection.

But if we accept this explanation, two facts remain which cannot be integrated. In the first place, the same breakdown occurs, to our knowledge, three times. In '44, in '70, and '75, it is—to credit Flaubert's testimony—the same thunderbolt, stealing upon him unexpectedly—the "nervous attack," defeat, ruin—everything goes up in flames, he falls, and he revives to discover that he has survived, that he has, as they say, "done his time" and that the illness has aged him prematurely. But his declarations of 1875, taken literally, invalidate those of 1870. If after 4 September he was that octogenarian, that fossil he claimed to have become, what did he still have to lose in 1875? And if he was desolate after the Prussian victory, if it seemed to push him into senility, hadn't he enjoyed a robust maturity under the second Empire, in spite of his complaints? Where did he go then, the old man of 1844, broken by life, by an unforgettable, irremediable collapse? Was that the man who now secures the favors of Beatrix Person, who thunders at the Magny dinners, who plays the courtier at Saint-Gratien, at Compiègne, at the Tuileries? You might say that with each "attack of age" he loses the memory of the preceding one; yet that isn't possible—Gustave forgets nothing, he himself tells us as much. Later we shall clear up this little mystery. Let us note only that in *Novembre* he has already presented to us the picture of an old age continually repeating itself. On every page a young life withers without ripening to maturity, miserably; on every page the young narrator sinks toward senility, toward death, sometimes by one path, sometimes by another, and is rejuvenated only to age again on the following page. Sometimes it is ennui that wearies him and sometimes sorrow and sometimes the abuse of pleasures of the imagination. We know he was disappointed, jaded, disgusted with dreams and solitary pleasures; he asks, "To dream about what?" and all at once his imagination revives and with a bound; he flies off toward the same dreams he embraced at the beginning of the book and denounced near the middle. The fact is that senescence has more than one meaning for Gustave. Long established in the soul of the wretched boy, though imposed on him from without, for him there are *agings*, each of which has its history, its meanings, its function. Would he have done better to present all his motives at the same time and through the combined effect of all these factors make his hero age only once? Surely not, for these motives are not necessarily mutually compatible, and we divine that the "attack of age" theme so dear to Gustave is an attempt to express, sometimes without much success, the irrational riches of experience; we shall soon see, in other words, that it is polysemantic.

These remarks allow us to introduce the second fact which I have said escaped interpretation of the prophecies in *Novembre*. If indeed the premonition in '42 of the troubles of '44 is thus explained by the young author's preneurotic but already pathological experience and, all told, by an anxious anticipation of the future catastrophe, we shall not accept without strong resistance the possibility that the same imagery—which unfolds like a fan at the first sign of illness—might be found before the circumstances that caused it to unfold. And even less so because Gustave, in letters to the Muse,[10] is categorical on one point: until fifteen he had the most madly passionate youth. Certainly there was bitterness in his passions; rage and despair overwhelmed him more often than enthusiasm. But he *was living*, he tells us. Fully. To the extent that he will later announce his pride at having been young so completely. The crisis of Pont-l'Evêque and the senility which, according to him, followed it were the consequences of his violent life; impossible, then, for the apathy of old age to have preceded the beginning of his neurosis—by moderating his sufferings, it should have prevented the *collapse* those sufferings are supposed to have provoked. Yet the fact is there; going back over the course of time, from his fifteenth to his thirteenth year, we are going to encounter *in all his writings* the full-blown phantasmagoria, that is, the mythic trinity: passive despair, old age, and death. Is Flaubert already ill? What then could be the source of the shock he felt in writing *Novembre* which we shall try to reconstruct in the next chapter? Is he adopting a fashionable theme under the influence of Romanticism? Perhaps, but why that theme? Romanticism can certainly take the blame; it is a Prudhommesque commonplace that experience, even as it enriches us, kills us little by little. What a surprise to see the child Gustave pounce on this adult proverb and make it his own. Can we say that he is lying, that he gives himself airs to impress people? It is unlikely; his public at this period consists of Alfred, who knows him inside out. Still, he might not have revealed everything to Alfred—he dreads being read for fear of surrendering himself. This suggests that he is conscious—more or less vaguely—of being represented by his characters. He stretches it a bit, exaggerates, that's all; he tells us in *Novembre* that as an adolescent he fell into inflated "rigamarole." This said, we must allow that he is sincere in this near

10. And later in his letters to Mlle Leroyer de Chantepie.

modesty—the fiction permits him to say what he feels. Let us read his first works; the moment he is asked, "What do you think of your life?" we are sure he will answer: "You've timed it very well; it just finished, my life; this is an old man, a dead man who is answering you." Whoever the protagonist, short as his life may be, and even if he meets a violent end, we shall see that he experiences *every age* but maturity. There is never any question of this—one enters the ultimate stage of life from the moment one leaves the golden age. A young man is old—senility devours his childhood; as soon as it has digested it, senility is discovered and suppressed as it is recapitulated. For Gustave even at thirteen, old age, the living image of death, is the reckoning annihilation; inversely, a life is reckoned only by annihilation—therefore experience is exhaustive only the moment a man can envisage his life from *the perspective of death*. As we see, this doesn't involve the decay of worn-out organs but a psychosomatic transformation whose origin and permanent cause is found in life itself being . *disclosed* in its truth and *situated*, whole, in the totality of being or the universe. Macrocosm, microcosm—how often we shall find these words appropriate to the medieval thought of Flaubert—the second, as a summation of itself, becomes the reflection of the first, which is the sum of nothingness. Man, mirror of the world; a gap conscious of its nonbeing in the bosom of universal nothingness. Aging is the relation, always close and deep, of the microcosm to the macrocosm; in a word, it is death in slow motion or, if you like, death itself becoming actual through life. One does not die of old age; according to the young Flaubert, one ages from dying. As to the whole truth, that homologous correspondence between the universe and the individual, it is realized here, at the end of a process of involution, by annihilation.

Yes, at fifteen, at thirteen, much earlier perhaps, he knew the violence and bitterness of unhappy passions; he burned, he shed tears, he hated. And at the same time he survived these youthful transports, the despair that tore him apart, astonishing the oldest old men, the stragglers, by his disenchantment. At least in those first essays, it might be said, the future crisis is not pictured. But it is, precisely. We shall see that it enters into the wretched boy's experience as a presentiment. Flaubert is not lying. On death, on aging, and on the weariness of despair—on these subjects he never did change his mind. For the rest, just compare the texts: no identity but surprising correspondences, fires called forth by the night, igniting other fires, the child's nods to the young man and the young man's to the child. At fifteen, Gustave could not write his bitter accounts without having obscurely foreseen the catastrophe of his twenty-third year; he could not, at twenty-five, make this the *logical* conclusion of his life if the adolescent ten years earlier hadn't caught a glimpse of the triad of the father and his two sons in *La Peste à Florence*. In this strange existence, all is reciprocity despite continuance, and through it. The past has led to the present, which, even while shaping itself according to protohistorical designs, remodels, transforms, and confirms the past. We have only to observe these exchanges, we will be at the heart of the dialectical movement of his ipseity, at the heart of Gustave's real torments and of his subjective history. It is for this reason that retrospective regression becomes necessary in his case, for only through this method can we decipher the oracles of the young sooth-sayer, *beginning with the future that verified them.*

1837: *Passion et Vertu.* Gustave is going on sixteen. This is not the first time he embodies himself in a woman—we shall see presently that he "projects" himself into Marguerite, a plain Jane, before representing himself in the splendid heroine Mazza. Mazza hardly resembles the pale heroes of the semi-autobiographies Flaubert will write in the years following; her life is certainly not "a thought," like the life of the madman who is soon going to leave us his memoirs; nor is it reduced to a long ennui, like the life of the hero of *Novembre*, a senile apathy crossed by flashes of rage. Mazza is not born with the desire to die; we find in her, finally, the bitterness and violence of adolescent passions. Flaubert doesn't lie. If he doesn't feel those passions, he nonetheless dreams of feeling them. Mazza's heart, quite frankly, is touched, but her sex is a furnace. A seducer has awakened her to sensual pleasure; at first disappointed, she is suddenly inflamed and would like her pleasure to go on forever. Her ardor frightens the lover, who flees—finished the rosary of orgasms; at once the conflagration spreads everywhere: she must either be consumed or be freed and reunited with the shocked seducer; as that doesn't happen, she poisons her entire family, a good-hearted husband and two young children. Quite uselessly, since her beloved in the meantime has married and informed her of this from the far reaches of America where he has taken refuge. There she is, criminal and forsaken—crime doesn't pay. Mazza has no choice but to poison herself.

In this brief and very remarkable work, Gustave makes us see *a person*; universalized by the sudden appearance of her animal need, she is individuated by the uncommon intensity and rigorous specificity of this "instinct." As Baudelaire gallantly says of all women: "She is in heat and wants to be fucked." Every minute, okay. But by the same man—he alone can fuck her who knew how to make her lust for the first time. All her unhappiness and all her singularity stem from this absurd preference—for the seducer himself is abject. She has lived, she lives, something happened to her, she will die from it. This person is a history, an irreversible adventure which ends very badly. Mazza is nothing as long as nothing happens to her. A sluggard. And then, this is the crucial event: a man, slowly, by proven wiles, transforms her into a lewd woman and, when he succeeds, takes flight, terrorized by the conflagration he himself has ignited. By this accident Mazza is formed—burning and at the same time frustrated. The good wife, tender and frigid, was a mere ingénue, a fool. Without the encounter that threw her into the arms of a seducer, she would have remained virtuous. And a nonentity. Flaubert doesn't mention this, but her superiority over us comes from her sex, empty and *ravaged by infinite desire*. What is the source of this desire? Are these insatiable demands within the reach of everyone? Did the meeting take place under particular circumstances? The author doesn't say. In a curious passage, he suggests that the lover is at first fascinated by this violence and that he himself cannot be aroused—perhaps he is more afraid of himself than of his mistress; one feels, in any case, that he has to make an effort to turn away from her. We are to believe, then, that naked instinct is the same in everyone, but that most people are so afraid of it they stifle it. It is to Mazza's credit—though she is soon to be punished by misery—that she should abandon herself to it. And then, in other passages, it seems simply that she is too richly endowed. Never mind; whether this temperament is her own or whether it is universal and she has been able to develop it, she would never have known it if accident hadn't placed a seducer in her path. History and innate gifts combine to bring her griefs to a white heat. Fulfilled, she knew indescribable pleasures; forsaken, her sufferings are endless. The line of her life is too pure, too clear, for us to reduce it to a succession of accidents. In truth, everything is connected: the strength of her character necessarily turns against her, confuses her lover, pushes her to crime and from crime to despair. Here, then, is both a person who makes and submits to a duration without return, and a duration which irreversibly makes a person and breaks her. Ventures, their results: the perfect equivalent of a woman and her fate.

An entire existence, as we see, is involved. Short but full: this is what *Novembre* and the *Mémoires* pretend to be; we know that Gustave wants to say *everything* in a single book and that he will do it, furthermore, in *Madame Bovary*. On the other hand, in *Passion et Vertu* we shall find no trace of certain themes which will fill subsequent works—from *Les Funérailles* to the first *Education*. Obviously; let us imagine Mazza indifferent or apathetic—there would be no story. As for the disenchantment that the young author will manifest at seventeen, there isn't any question of it when he is fifteen. Mazza, disappointed for a time by physical love, soon enters into an enchantment she will never leave. Ernest's departure plunges her into unhappiness, but she doesn't suspect the reasons, and down to the last pitiful message of this Don Juan—as Gustave calls him—she never stops loving him or wanting to be reunited with him.

Two motifs, however, are familiar to us. One, which seems highly misplaced in this burning adventure, is old age. The other is passivity. The first is so gratuitous, so awkwardly introduced, that it at once reveals to us its obsessive and archaic character. It is as if Gustave could not help introducing it into a narrative where it had no function. Ernest has slipped away, Mazza runs after him; too late, she arrives at Le Havre to see a white sail "disappearing over the horizon." Here she is on the way back: "She was terrified by the slowness of time, she believed she had lived for centuries and had grown old, had white hair, so far can grief be overwhelming, can sorrow be consuming, for there are days that age you like years, thoughts that carve wrinkles."

In one night her hair had turned white; people mentioned this sort of thing in front of little Gustave. Many times, and he listened excitedly. What luck if after some intolerable humiliation he could join his family at breakfast with a snow-white head. They wouldn't notice it immediately, and then, suddenly, silence! He would read the horror and remorse in his parents' eyes; he would tell them with a feigned humility: "There are days that age you like years!" Wonderful testimony, something on his head *would signify* his torments but to no avail; the metamorphosis would have happened unbeknownst to him, in the night; perhaps he would only perceive it when confronted with the amazement of his family. Passive activity, the somatization of despair. But Mazza, great and savage soul, does not despair. She has quickly understood that in order to be reunited with Ernest she has simply to massacre her family; she proceeds to carry out her plan—with impeccable result, and one admires her firmness as much as her temperament. In *Novembre*, senility is linked to experience, to exhaustion, to anorexia; one sees the break that separates the last tales of the autobiographical cycle. Mazza is not at the end of her amorous experience—never has her passion been so alive or her sex so ardently inflamed; she has lost none of her capacity to suffer—quite the contrary, her afflictions are only beginning. Grief will never "overwhelm" this Medea. This is so true, Gustave himself is so conscious of it that he dares not whiten her hair for good. She *believes* her hair has turned white, which is hardly likely in a woman so unreflecting, so far from any sort of narcissism. This means simply that the author dreamed this metamorphosis, that it is one of the themes of his controlled dreaming, one of the hopes of his resentment. It is he, surely, who said to himself hopefully, following a rebuff: This time it has happened," and who ran to the mirror to examine himself, in vain. His pen runs on and tells us his dream of resentment—it crowns Mazza with snow that melts a moment later. What concerns us, in any case, is that the young boy at fifteen reveals to us a way of aging quite different from those he will enumerate in subsequent works: old age comes on all at once through a trauma followed by intense grief.

The other already familiar motif, passivity, gives us access to the deepest and oldest structures of his unhappy childhood. Actually, Mazza *submits* to her fate. She will kill; someone will say: Isn't this pure act? Haven't her infanticides, for which there is no atonement, been carefully planned? Granted—we shall come to this. But let us first observe that, properly speaking, Ernest has given birth to her. Before knowing him, she was asleep; her disembodied soul was waiting in a state of stupefied limbo for someone to give her birth. The sad Don Juan busies himself with the task. Note that this is no bolt from the blue; Ernest is a specialist, seduction is an art, there are formulas, one lays siege to the site according to the rules; a discerning eye is needed, and occasionally genius. The theme belongs to the nineteenth century, which inherited it from the eighteenth; Hérault de Séchelles articulated more generally the means of manipulating every representative—male or female—of our species. And Stendhal in his youth was not content to put into practice the "method" of his cousin Martial; he also sought the precise means of invoking laughter in an audience, independent of sex and age. The results were disappointing: Hérault de Séchelles cut his own throat; Stendhal did not finish writing his comedy; as to Martial's system conscientiously applied to the lovely Mélanie, its only effect was to delay the capturing of a citadel that would have surrendered instantly and without a fight.

In any case, it was a practical application—*Les Liaisons dangereuses* bears witness to this—of the mechanistic determinism which seemed at the time to be the last conquest of scientific philosophy. If the same cause at any time produces the same effect, in order to obtain this effect it will suffice to set up the cause at the right moment—a sure way of achieving or being assured the most flattering conquests. But what interests Gustave is not pulling strings—he despises seducers and is revolted by opportunism. He is filled with enthusiasm for the inflexibility of determinism, both because—as his father repeated a hundred times—it is the basis of knowledge, that which allows an understanding of men, and because he himself feels *manipulated*. Mazza's second birth, therefore, in his eyes is not a result of chance, it was premeditated, a man wanted it to happen, made it the object of a consciously concerted enterprise. It is striking that the young woman could have lived more than twenty years in an uneventful daze, very likely happy, until the abrupt change that fulfills her at first only to make her the more frustrated afterward. Doesn't this first period correspond to Djalioh's golden age, *before* jealousy? And in both cases isn't Flaubert alluding to *his own golden age*? At seven years old someone pulled him out of limbo, gave him joy, and disappointed him. This behavior was premeditated. Love had to be followed by frustration, since the Don Juan of *Passion et Vertu* of course never intended to be faithful to Mazza all his life; after all, he ends up in America where he has taken refuge, and weary of his easy conquests—they are *inevitably* easy because he uses the right method—this bachelor gets married. A fine marriage, slippers, an obedient companion to keep house for him—they all come to this, young men of good family, even if they have to break the heart of a loving mistress. At least this is what was being turned out at the time; bourgeois literature treats the subject a hundred times from the beginning of the century to the beginning of our own (*La Femme nue* by Bataille is only a variant). No doubt Mazza's violence constrained Ernest to break off the liaison sooner than he would have liked; in any event, he would have broken it off. In sum, without this providential—or infernal—lover, Mazza would have passed unconsciously from sleep to death. He awakens her and suddenly gives her a destiny; Mazza's *history*, that adventure which is made temporal in her until her suicide, is foreseen by Ernest, so that living it out, for Mazza, is a form of submission from beginning to end.

One thing Ernest did not foresee: he didn't dream before going into action that this young, all too chaste sleepwalker would change under his expert hands into a fury. This time it is as if the roles were reversed: she alarms him. Why? Does he believe his health is endangered? This doesn't seem to be the case; the young woman, we are told, would ask her lover to make excessively frequent but not intolerable efforts. As a housewife she owed her attentions to her husband and her children; so Ernest presumably had time to "recuperate." No, it is naked passion that terrifies him; this mediocre man—petty vanities, petty pleasures—has suddenly discovered the crater of an erupting volcano. There is no danger, but our Lovelace, fascinated for a moment manages to stay on the surface and to deny in himself as in others the "appalling depths" Gustave will tell us about in *Novembre*. In a word everything is *historical*, everything depends on the relationship established at the outset between the two lovers, which they live out, each as it is defined by the other: Ernest's fear and impotence is Mazza's telluric power experienced by this poor man as a fascinating and mortal danger. Furthermore, it is he who has unleashed her diabolical violence. More must be said. Mazza—as the title indicates—is Passion itself with a capital P. She certainly does not embarrass her Don Juan by some unforeseen act. Nor by anything else for which she could be held responsible; it is by the tempests that torment her flesh, by the crazed need to which she submits—as the mercenaries in the Hachado Pass will submit to their hunger, which is imposed on them by the enemy. Yes, Mazza is *famished*. Famished by Ernest, and this is what terrifies the seducer, who decides to leave her to her hunger. Was there a filial love of equal violence in the child Gustave? Did he frighten his father by his demonstrations of tenderness? We might say so; for it is at the moment of frustration that Mazza embodies him unambiguously. The mood of the abandoned young woman is embittered; she becomes mad with pride and malice; she reaches the pitch of rage, of hatred. Against whom will it be unleashed? Against her executioner? Never, he is free of blame. And similarly the husband, the children: they are in the way, they must be removed, that's all. Mazza reserves her contempt and her abomination for the people around her; their paltry happiness is built upon premeditated mutilations. Do they even have sexual organs? No one has pleasure; children are born, it is true, but they are bequeathed a stunted life, refusing pleasure for fear of grief. Mazza curses her "fellow creatures" without perceiving—but the author is quite conscious of it—that she detests in them the paltriness of her fugitive lover. Ernest's *calculated pettiness* is a general crime of the species; but it is crucial that Mazza discover it through her particular bad luck, through *her* history and her "lust," gently awakened, then brutally frustrated and at the same time unquenchable. This particular and *dated* frustration—one day I dared to take pleasure, I suffer in consequence—gives her the mad arrogance to believe she is an aristocrat of unhappiness; pleasure or torment, the infinite passes between her thighs. But this arrogance itself is born of a singular misfortune, for the infinite, Mazza firmly believes, is Ernest's member. He penetrates her and she feels the plenitude of being; he withholds himself and she discovers in her belly the void where in three years' time Smarh will "whirl around." The despair and arrogance of this woman are a measure, though she is quite unaware of it, of the unbelievable disproportion between infinite desire and its infinitesimal object. One of Gustave's cherished themes: what is magnificent in absolute love is that it isn't justifiable and is never deserved by the quality of the beloved. Arrogant and resentful, he tells us that the Flaubert parents were not worthy of such love or such suffering. In any event, Mazza's hatred and contempt for the human race are not without a component of fascination or jealousy; as an adultress, forsaken, soon a criminal, she is banished from the earth. Her fellow creatures do not know it yet, and she hastens to despise them for fear of envying them. At the source of her wickedness we shall find none of the universal causes the author will ascribe in subsequent works, but rather precise events, the decisions of a nonplussed Lovelace, a singular situation creating envy, rage, and shame. It is all there, however: infinite desire as the negation of being and the inevitability of dissatisfaction. But these allegories which will find their place in the autobiographical writings are suggested by the author, and we cannot decide whether they truly reveal the deep meaning of the plot or must be viewed as abstract "superstructures" which express in their fashion an individual adventure. Gustave is more sincere at fifteen than at twenty. Deeper too—we needn't worry, he will be again—for it is in the total life of a woman conditioned by others even before birth and down to her physical behavior, her needs, that he seeks the motives of actions and thoughts in their singularity. Through Mazza we discover Gustave's ego, that is—and he is conscious of it—his alter ego.

Had he said of this first Bovary what one assumes he declared of the other, "She is myself!" one might have understood what this adolescent cried out in silence: "I have my vulture, born with me, foreseen before my birth by a tight-fisted Jupiter; I am what they have made me, a younger son of good family; between a predistination that defined me in my essence well before I was conceived and the terrible fate I've been assigned, I go forward cautiously, tortured by my intimate passions, which are as real and material as sexual need or a violent toothache." Gustave is undergoing a crisis, he shrieks his suffering, listen to him: "Ernest was charmed [by Mexico, to which he had fled] in this embalmed atmosphere of learned academies, railroads, steamboats, sugar canes, and indigo. In what kind of atmosphere was Mazza living? The circle of her life was less extended, but it was a world apart which turned in tears and despair and was finally lost in the abyss of crime."

It is no accident that in the work and the correspondence we find numerous echoes of this last line: the image of the narrow circle is not a transient symbol in Flaubert's work; it is part of his mythology. In the first *Education*, written before and after the crisis of 1844, Jules, in the final pages, defines the passional life—his life *before* the fall— as a crowded merry-go-round turning endlessly. And fifteen years later, Flaubert writes in anger: "I have reserved for myself a very small circle, but once someone enters it I grow red with anger."[11]

In *Passion et Vertu* Gustave is not concerned—as in the autobiographical cycle—with universalizing his experience. He never says: "I am just a man, like all of you." As we shall see, what is part of a developing self-defense at fifteen is not yet focused. On the other hand, he recognizes the narrowness and particularity of his experience: "It was a world apart." Can we say further that this compressed but unfathomable universe is limited to his house? It will have been noticed that "this world apart"—which (like the most private intimacy) is contrasted to Ernest's pathetic public concerns—is characterized by repetition; it turns and the same afflictions return without end; this means that Gustave's unhappiness is structural and not at all fortuitous: a good definition of a life that will continually unfold within the framework of the family.

Mazza commits a crime, which once again singles her out. Not only by the magnitude of the transgression but by her victims, who are designated in advance. Designated—by the animator of this Galatea and by the destiny he gave her. She liquidates *her family*. The author will never go as far as his creature, but he brought her into the world expressly to accomplish the deed he dares not undertake: the objective text of his phantasms links them together and consequences follow of themselves; written down, these phantasms take on a consistency denied the dream, yet without becoming realities. In Mazza, Gustave

11. 4 September 1852.

196

makes visible an experiment: the extermination of the Flaubert family. This is what he has earlier attempted, as we shall see, in *La Peste à Florence* and what he will fully succeed in doing—on paper—at the end of *Madame Bovary*. He dreamed of it for a long time; and we shall come back to this. The insignificance of the too trusting husband, the tender age of his two children, must not divert us—it is a trick. The crucial thing is not said. Or rather it is only half said; these good people do not humiliate Mazza, they do not deliberately make her suffer, but they *thwart* her—suddenly there she is, rooted in spite of herself, and her fury, her grief-inspired rages come from her family, though indirectly. One has only to leaf through the correspondence to see how much Gustave suffers from his deep-rootedness—without admitting, however, that he craves it as much as he suffers it. This time he gives himself permission to tear himself out of the family soil. He satisfies his resentment in one fell swoop; these three innocent victims conceal three guilty parties who are destroyed with no other form of trial. Of course Gustave doesn't breathe a word of this. But let us read what he writes about the mother's feelings after the extermination; we shall be edified. No remorse, quite the contrary, joy, happiness in the crime: "She was going to leave France after being avenged for profaned love, for all that had been fatal and terrible in her destiny, after being mocked by God, by men, by life, and by the fatality which had toyed with her for a moment, after having amused herself in turn with life and death, with tears and regrets, and having returned crimes to heaven in exchange for her sufferings."

Avenged? On innocents. When Ernest alone is guilty. Granted, she knows nothing about that. But then, where is the offense? The purpose of these long-premeditated murders was, in the beginning, only to set her free; it might be understandable that she should rejoice, criminally, it must be admitted, but with a kind of innocence due to the monstrous egotism of her passion. These obstacles did not matter to her except as they prevented her from joining her lover; she dismissed them, she probably no longer thought of them, joyously preparing to fly to Ernest—this alone must have mattered. Or else, sure of herself and her right, she might have indulged in the luxury of shedding a tear on their graves: poor children, I had to kill you, you did not deserve this premature death, but heaven so willed it. But no, she congratulates herself *for her crime*, and what appears in the few lines cited above is satisfied hatred. To be sure, we are persuaded that the joy of finding Ernest again is crucial; the satisfaction of resentment is something the young author intends hereby to point out in passing. This ought to be only a secondary benefit. The story would really prefer it this way. But it becomes central the moment it appears—infinite frustration has made Mazza wicked (we shall see that this is a characteristic the young author gives to all his heroes, and we shall find it again in Emma Bovary). Infinitely wicked. We know now *against whom* she has so long pondered her vengeance, against him who drew her out of nothingness even before Ernest gave her new birth, against him to whom—in ignorance, where it is still truth—she attributes all her misfortunes and who has intentionally produced them through rigorous planning: she avenges herself against God the Father. This is made quite plain: "She was mocked by God . . . returned crimes to heaven in exchange for her sufferings." What could be better? This is not the "happiness in crime" that Barbey d'Aurevilly will speak of later, which is born of a very special unconscious; this is the *joy of crime*. It will be noted that in giving back evil for evil she is convinced that she is escaping her prearranged destiny. We are told she made light of fatality. It is she, now, who is "mocked" by fatality. Let us take note in passing of Gustave's conviction that, for everyone, the chips are down before birth; one cannot escape unless one chooses radical evil. This evil already exists since the creature is its victim, since the victim is condemned to suffer until death; it is thus not a question of inventing it or of introducing it into the world, but of assuming it. The victim escapes his executioners by opting in his turn for wickedness—which is only the conscious sufferance of the self—and by understanding that it is in his nature to be unjustly *afflicted*. Mazza places herself on the same level as her tormenters—or rather of the great and unique Tormenter—by refusing to play the game, that is, to remain virtuous and be tortured in direct proportion to her virtue. She turns herself into an executioner to forestall her fate; since evil reigns in the world, she escapes unhappiness by opting for evil and making herself equal to those who pull the strings. This will not happen, of course, without scandalizing the Creator, who, as a good disciple of de Sade, has decided that Mazza should be punished for her virtues and through them. But it is an added pleasure to scandalize His Wickedness-in-chief by denouncing His hypocrisy. Mazza is a Justine who is deliberately transformed into a Juliette to make comprehensible this universal law of creation: the good are punished and the wicked are rewarded. Her arrogance was first nourished only by her infinite suffering, now it is affirmed against the eternal Father: this is vice assumed, pride of self and no remorse. Radical evil, according to the young author, is suffering refusing to be endured any longer and turning itself into praxis. To read between the lines, Mazza has two fathers: one is the insignificant Ernest, a simple instrument of Providence who put hell into her vagina; the other is God, who has foreseen and prepared it all. The two faces, in sum, of Dr. Flaubert: first, the progenitor, the symbolic Father, more powerful than Freud's Moses since he doesn't limit himself to giving the Law but, before any Ten Commandments, before birth, even before conception, bestows upon his second son a prearranged destiny and condemns him to suffer until death; the other, Achille-Cléophas, is the executor of exalted works, the earthly representative of the first, who has roused the child's blind passion expressly to frustrate it afterward (at about the age of seven). Hence this mad rancor of the passive plaything, of the marionette, against the Other—symbolic Father and frustrating father—hence the dream of killing *the whole family*. This means, read correctly, the father and *both* brothers. For Mazza has borne two little males. Gustave, in his homicidal dream, *dares not* survive the public sacrifice. He will kill Achille-Cléophas and Achille, and kill himself on their graves.

This is what confirms the end of the story. Virtue is inexorably punished. But vice is as well. Murders and suicide are not sufficient— these three wretched creatures pass from life to extinction without even being accountable for it. This would be too good; between the parricide and the fratricide on the one hand and the suicide on the other a certain amount of time goes by to leave space for punishment. In other words, when the adolescent embraces this vengeance in his thoughts, the Other in him is indignant and lashes out; the lovely dream of massacre is realized in anguish. Gustave's superego is scandalized, it compels him to plunge Mazza into despair—the day after her triumph a letter from Ernest informs her that he has been married for six months and will never see her again: "What shall I do?" she cries. "What will become of me? I had one idea, one thing in my heart, and now it is gone; shall I go find you? But you will chase me away like a slave; if I throw myself among other women they will forsake me, laughing, they will point their fingers at me arrogantly because they have never loved anyone, those women, they do not know tears."

The poor woman can do nothing but die. For Gustave, dying is leaving her hide in the hands of others; a police commissioner forces open the door, and his look defiles the beautiful, unveiled body which death has rendered more than naked. Ernest, however, continues to live; God rewards neither virtue nor vice, he favors only mediocrity.

Here is the true evil: an obscene look at a forsaken dead woman, delight in paltriness; the *others* triumph every step of the way.

By poisoning her family, has Mazza ceased to submit, has she seriously gone into action? No, these murders were foreseen, and so was her suicide. She was led by the hand. It was foreseen that her violent passion would frighten Ernest and that he would clear out under some pretext; it was foreseen that Mazza would fool herself and take his pretext on faith. From that moment, inflexibly, she *had to* convince herself that he was waiting for her, that her family alone prevented her from being reunited with him, and, mad with grief and malice, she *had* to eliminate this obstacle. At that moment, free to dispose of herself, she *had* to discover that the sole reason for her long frustration was her lover's decision. Her mad passion had simultaneously driven Ernest away and poured the poison into the glasses of her husband and sons, her own hand guided by remote control. An act? No, a reactive behavior, quite predictable; the cunning Creator, by making her believe she might escape her fatalities through a crime, led her in fact to realize her destiny to the very end.

Does anyone ever escape his destiny? This is the question Gustave insistently poses during his adolescent years; it is the question that will be posed with growing urgency until January 1844. Does he then want to change his life? He does. And to change his being. Why? He has not yet clearly understood why himself. What appears in any case in this story is that if such an alteration were possible, it would require recourse to more impressive means. Death and transfiguration: that is the only road to follow. If Mazza fails, it is because she remains within the narrow circle of her passions, spinning endlessly around and around. Gustave is spinning there too. Hopelessly. He does not yet know that it is he who must be killed, and that the death of the passions alone can give him rebirth.

Two months earlier, in *Quidquid volueris*, he had developed the same themes with greater insistence and, in a way, greater clarity. The character of the anthropoid was perhaps better suited at the time to his deepest intentions; Djalioh's very existence exhibits, more clearly than Gustave may have realized, the young author's confused feelings about prefabrication and historicity. We will not return to Gustave's description of himself; this portrait of the artist as a child—muteness, illiteracy, poetry—has been described above. But in the same chapter we cited a passage from a letter to Mlle Leroyer de Chantepie in which Gustave spoke of his "innate (therefore constitutional or inherited) melancholy" and, in order to explain, referred to a "deep and always hidden wound" (certainly an event of his prehistory). We wondered then, without yet being able to find an answer, about the significance of this grip of the *constitutional* as a *constituted characteristic*. Mazza's *awakening* put us on the right track; nevertheless, her new birth as Sleeping Beauty is only a metaphor, for when she meets Ernest she is a wife and mother; he reveals to her the pleasures of her senses but he does not create her ex nihilo. At once the theme is enriched and muddied. In *Quidquid volueris*, on the contrary, Flaubert's happy embodiment in Djalioh yields the author's feelings without disguising them; the anthropoid, in effect, resembles Pascal's man after the Fall: he cannot make an idea his object since a historic adventure has made him descend to a lower level, and even while retaining certain characteristics that God gave him, he has lost others—innocence for example—as the result of a forbidden act, that is, an act which didn't enter into the plans of the Creator. And, no doubt, it was Adam alone who fell. But since we are born of him, through persons in between, he has transmitted to us his fault, his fall, and his exile, in short, his historicity. Adam is not in the least *definable*: he is at once what he has been made and what he has made out of what he has been made, thwarting and diverting the divine plans; it is history alone which allows us to understand the father of men and all men who are born of him. Also for Pascal, our *human reality* is at once constitutional and constituted. Before the Fall our species did not exist—it was Adam who made himself human through sin and by calling down upon himself that highly singular act, the divine curse. At fifteen, Gustave assigns to the birth of Djalioh the function Pascal assigns to the Fall: that of an absolute beginning. Neither angel nor beast, says Pascal; the angel and the beast correspond to ideas since neither of them has slipped. And Flaubert: neither beast nor man. By his origin, in effect, Djalioh, the son of a woman, escapes the *general essence* which characterizes orangutans; the son of an ape, he escapes what the young author believes to be *human* nature. We have seen, we shall see, Gustave in the autobiographical works appeal to frequentatives, to generalizations. Here, more sincere since he is presented in disguise, he refuses—as he will do for Mazza—to distinguish the hero of his adventure. For the hero is a monster, that is, a being who is singular by definition.

Our linking of Flaubert and Pascal is all the more justified as Gustave loves to repeat: "I believe in the curse of Adam." What does this mean if not that in man, existence precedes essence? There is nonetheless a crucial difference between the two conceptions. For Pascal, the curse comes after the fault: the Lord had created man in his image, he destined him to do good and to transform His glory; the fault comes from Adam himself, namely from that portion of darkness and nothingness which exists in every creature and over which the Almighty, the plenitude of being, is unable to exercise power. For Gustave, the curse of Adam is a leavening put into the very dough of which he is formed. He is born cursed, and he sins—as the Creator has foreseen—in order to justify the curse. Man's historicity is not born of his project, of the praxis which might be its issue; quite the contrary, the intended praxis is nothing more than man's realization, providentially guided, of the destiny which has been assigned to him by the Other. History is the Other; every man is born with his own history etched into his body like an incurable wound—he must only *realize* it. Miserable and evil, he must legitimize the sentence a posteriori and at the same time realize it quickly, whatever he does, but through his actions as he tries to meet the greatest sufferings half way. Guilty and punished, then; and nevertheless innocent, irresponsible since the Other made him commit the transgressions which will incur chastisement. We should not be surprised by such notions, which were fashionable at the time. Byron's Cain cursed God and reproached him for having foreseen everything, including the fratricide that damned him. Alfred Le Poittevin, who around the same time introduced Gustave to philosophy, did not shrink in his *Poèmes* from defying the Creator and blaspheming joyfully. These splendid bursts of anger were supported by the reasoning of the Encyclopedists, of Diderot, of Voltaire: either you created me *knowing* that I would kill my brother, that I would betray Christ, therefore you are criminal; or you did not know, therefore you are not the Almighty. But witticisms of this kind influenced Gustave only to the extent that they served the deep feeling within him. When the young boy soared with Alfred to metaphysical heights, he inveighed against God because he saw in him, confusedly, the image of his father.

Look at Djalioh: in a sense no one influences him; his impulses, his desires, his passions remain spontaneous until his death. This means that they express nothing other than *his being*. But his very being does not belong to him since he has been fabricated by another. Monsieur Paul, amateur biologist, wanted to perform an experiment—in order to implicate all scientists, the young author emphasizes that the Academy of Sciences had long been immensely interested in such a cross-breeding and had claimed that it might be attempted; until then, Gustave suggests, only the means were lacking. Let us note in passing that Achille-Cléophas was a man of science and that science is denounced here—between the lines, of course—for its inhumane cruelty. Briefly, Monsieur Paul had the express intention of crossing ape with man—impelled by curiosity and certainly by sadism. If he succeeded, the product of the cross-breeding would in a sense lead an *experimental life*. Through his constitution and his behavior he would recapitulate an important stage of evolution. Monsieur Paul attempts the deed, and—Flaubert is not without malice—the procedure is remarkable for its ignoble brutality: a black slavewoman is penned up with an enormous, mad beast who rapes and impregnates her. The product of this coupling, a child of madness and terror, of animal lust and suffering, surely cursed by his mother (this is not said but its very absence leaves a suspicious gap—is it believable that Gustave hasn't imagined this woman's feelings toward the beast she carried in her belly?)—this product is Djalioh, neither man nor beast but with a physical makeup and behavior that express both his quasi-human reality and his bestiality. Can we believe that these two sides of his character are harmoniously matched? Quite the contrary, this monster is continually torn apart by their irreducible contradiction. A desired contradiction, for he was created expressly to reproduce the impassable opposition of nature and culture. *Born to suffer*—this too was premeditated; he *must* suffer and be torn apart by his conflicts so that he can fully become the anthropoid that science wanted to place under observation; this means that someone sketched out in advance the narrow road that will lead him to crime and suicide. Monsieur Paul does not foresee this tragic end in detail, but it will not surprise him; he is not unaware that what characterizes this driven monster is the *impossibility of living*.

It is highly significant that Gustave should have given this amateur scientist the entire responsibility for the experiment and its result. *Quidquid volueris* is an act of accusation. If the author had simply tried to portray himself, if the image of the ape-man had attracted him solely because it accounted for his difficulties, for his deficiencies, and the poetic transports that compensated for them, if resentment were not the principal source of this invention, he would not have found it necessary to place Monsieur Paul at the origin of this unnatural mating. Indeed, the story would still hang together if the rape of the slave had been presented as a chance occurrence. An orangutan ravishes a young black woman, rapes and then releases her; Monsieur Paul, happening to come along, learns the story, adopts the little monster, and takes him to Europe to show him to the academicians. What would this alter? The ape-man's solitude among men, his inner conflicts, his sensitivity, his impaired intelligence, his jealousy, his rages, his criminal acts of violence, and his death would all be preserved. All except one thing: the guilt of the progenitor. In truth, if Gustave made his Djalioh a laboratory child, if he was pleased to present this life, spontaneously lived and suffered, as the unfolding of an "observational experiment," it was because it was not enough for him to claim—with shame and pride—the title of monster; he needed a malevolent will at the source of his being. Everything was so strictly settled in his head that in order to tighten the intrigue he wanted the child of a rape to perish committing a rape. Djalioh/Gustave forcibly takes and kills Adèle, the very young wife of Monsieur Paul, who is not otherwise affected; after which, mad with rage and grief, the anthropoid hits his head against the wall with such force that he beats himself to death. Mazza's death did not in any way save her from other people; the commissioner calmly enjoyed her nudity. The poor anthropoid, still more unfortunate, escapes neither Monsieur Paul nor science: he is stuffed and put in a museum, and any student can go and look at him. As for the sinister amateur biologist—an automaton who would be a demiurge—he of course remains, like Ernest, the only survivor.

We notice here, as in *Passion et Vertu*, a multiplication of paternities. The true father of Gustave/Djalioh is Paul. The enlightened author of family planning, it is he alone who has decided in full knowledge and conscience to create this laboratory child, this anthropoid—a younger brother—to meet the demands of an inhuman knowledge. But when it comes to carrying out the experiment, he is doubled and transformed into an orangutan—Dr. Jekyll and Mr. Hyde. Double subject of rancor. Imagine this mating from the point of view of the organizer: it is a cruel but rationally devised enterprise which has serious objectives, a pitiless act but one which is coldly and carefully thought out. Think of it as a singular event that took place on a certain night in 1821, probably in March, an act of obscene violence, absurd, suffered in horror, in grief no doubt, by the woman who is its victim, experienced as a strange fit of animal madness by the lusting male. As if a profound disgust, rooted in Gustave's prehistory, were at last expressed. Whatever the progenitor's merits, intelligence, and knowledge, even if an accurate calculation had proved to him that it was in his interest to increase the family, procreation—that necessary passing of cultural man back to the *natural* ground of his being—cannot be anything but shameful. Two human creatures—one of which is changed into a beast of prey—make the beast with two backs, roll together in blood and muck; the product of this monstrosity, resulting from willful murder, carries within himself, as his deepest nature, the night a venerable man of science, transformed into an ape, raped his slave. Madness and terror, bloody degradation, here is his *natural* contradiction: isn't he the fruit of an obscene act of violence and an abject acquiescence? Hasn't he necessarily internalized both? This is a fantasy, to be sure, but one that holds fast; several years earlier, in the scenarios for melodramas that we still have, Gustave is pleased to show us guilty mothers treated cruelly by seducers who rape or deceive them and in any case abandon them. We shall have to return, when we broach the subject of Flaubert's sexuality, to this primary imagery: the mother raped, fallen, punished. In him we find a mixture of sadism and compassion. It is man who is unforgivable. Curiously, one might say that the defect of this calculating being, even when lust transforms him into a beast of prey, is that he *does not feel enough pleasure*. For Gustave—we shall come back to this—it is the woman who feels sensual pleasure (on the condition, of course, that she is not raped), and we shall have occasion to examine this attitude, which he articulates two or three years later in his notebook, dreaming of being a woman in order to know carnal pleasure. But in his adolescence Flaubert does not reproach the fair sex; quite the contrary, he envies the passivity of the mistress who moans under the caresses of her lover and the passive ecstasy afterward, so close to his own stupors and raptures. A little later, however—after *Quidquid volueris*, before the note he jotted down in his copybook—convinced that the wife incites the husband to make love to her for her own pleasure, he describes copulation by reversing the terms in *Mémoires d'un fou*. The man in any event remains bestial, but it is not lust that first bestializes him, it is drink; the woman profits from his drunkenness to kindle his lust—he takes her, she has pleasure. This is her aim, no other. And the child, "tender measure of love," who is born nine months later, having been desired by neither of the spouses, is the fruit of chance, a superfluous intruder, reflecting in his frightful contingency the fortuitous accident that pulled him out of nothingness. We can well believe he will be an *unloved* child. In short, it is now the woman who is charged with the crime of having engendered him. No great surprise, for he has just related in the preceding pages his unhappy love for Mme Schlésinger. He so begrudges her her attachment to Maurice, that vile, vulgar, grotesque character, that he will decide once and for all that women have a marked preference for cads and fools. Under these conditions, why not exaggerate? Mme Schlésinger, in conformity with her sex, is perpetually in heat and makes Maurice drunk so she can slide under him and get fucked; it is his resentment against Elisa that blurs the evidence and masks his original horror for the mating that engendered him. Indeed, emphasizing the accident of procreation, he unwittingly screens out that other aspect which in his case, and for him, remains fundamental: premeditation. The interference of the two motifs in *Mémoires* is all the more manifest since *nothing* in the austere demeanor of Caroline Flaubert could betray the virtuous bacchant unleashed at night, behind closed doors, in the hands of the progenitor. Furthermore, at the Hôtel-Dieu family planning was openly declared: one created children, there was failure; when one of them died, one began again. Besides, Elisa figures in *Quidquid volueris*, written after the famous holidays at Trouville—she is Adèle, passionately loved by Djalioh, who *because she is a woman* has the stupidity to adore her husband the robot. Thus the theme of this short story is richer, more complete, more directly connected to the author's prehistory than the declarations of the *Mémoires*. Gustave's basic grievance against his parents does not have to do with the accident of his birth. Certainly he feels the accident—it is the factitiousness, the singular flavor of experience as it expresses in its irreducible but "indescribable" originality the uncontrolled violence of a copulation, the spouses abandoned to the filthy kitchens of nature. But it is not so much this brief folly that he despises; quite the contrary, it is the premeditation. No, the anthropoid is not the product of chance: he has been sought for a long time and sought *precisely as he is*. Achille-Cléophas had decided that he would engender Gustave, and it is indeed Gustave that he engendered. *Quidquid volueris* is a long, rich meditation on birth. A child of man wonders: "Why was I born?" And this reflection has nothing metaphysical about it; the adolescent wonders what it means to have a man for a father, a grown man with his habits, his prejudices, his ideology, his knowledge; what does it mean to be the younger son of Dr. Flaubert?

The answer is clear. I am not the product of a blind flick of the prick—or at least I am not only that. I am above all the child of an idea. My father *invented* me well before begetting me. He didn't conceive me for myself, for my happiness, to give me his love; I was, in his mind, not an end but a means of realizing his plans, an instrument of his familial ambition. To achieve his ends, it seemed to him that

I had to be an *inferior*; in other words, this rustic, this creator of a patriarchal family governed by the law of primogeniture, could not be unaware that he was creating a *younger son* nine years younger than his brother. I accuse him of having wanted me not in spite of this handicap but *because of it*, and of having knowingly created me, in consequence, for my unhappiness.

Thus, although the young boy is conscious of his passive temperament, his instability, his stupors, his poor relationship with language, his incapacity to act,[12] he is far from attributing the responsibility to Caroline Flaubert's earliest attentions; he skips over his birth and looks for the cause of his "anomaly" in his prehistory and, farther back still, in a fiat pronounced by the absolute Other. Above all, let us not view this act of accusation as the effect of a transient mood or some adolescent paradox. Gustave's rancor is so tenacious it leaves him *all his life* with a radical disgust for procreation, a declared preference for sterility. One example suffices as demonstration. In 1852 Louise announces to Flaubert that she believes she is pregnant by him. Some days pass and she "reassures" him—false alarm. Here is what he answers her on 11 December:

> I shall begin by devouring you with kisses, I am so carried away with joy. Your letter of this morning lifted a terrible weight from my heart. It was high time. Yesterday I could not work the entire day. . . . Every time I moved [this is in the text] my brain throbbed in my head, and I was obliged to go to bed at 11 o'clock. I was feverish and generally prostrate. For three weeks now I have been suffering from horrible apprehensions. . . . Oh yes, the thought tortured me; two or three times I saw lights before my eyes—Thursday among other days. . . . The idea of giving life to someone *horrifies me*. I would curse myself if I were to become a father. A son of mine! Oh! no, no, no! May all my flesh be lost and may I never pass on to anyone the vexation and shame of existence!

What agitation, what frenzy! I know, he did not want to be bound to Louise, already quite cumbersome in his view, by an additional tie or to give her the rights of a mother when he had refused her the

---

12. Even more than in *Passion et Vertu*, the final violence, murders, and suicide seem purely pathic. Djalioh doesn't want to rape or kill Adèle—he tears at her with his claws when he only wants to caress her; similarly, he has no notion of killing himself—the tempest in his body, an *endured* tempest, flings him headfirst against a wall. In short, he has *done* nothing; this destructive explosion is not even a refusal, it is the somatization of the impossibility of living.

rights of a mistress. And then, even if she were to be discreet, he was afraid of becoming bourgeois: "Paternity would have made me return to the ordinary conditions of life. My virginity in relation to the world would have been destroyed and I would have sunk into the pit of common miseries." But although these considerations might cause him anxiety in the strict sense, they were not sufficient to motivate his agonies. He had to harbor within him *the hatred of paternity*. And the reason for it had to be profound in a different way. "I would curse myself if I were a father"; this can be explained only by the innuendo: "Because I cursed my father." A little later he adds: "I feel calm and radiant. My entire youth has passed without a blemish or weakness." Begetting—is this a blemish? a weakness? Then Dr. Flaubert is guilty who "passed on [to Gustave] the vexation and shame of existence." Flaubert, victim of an abusive father, refuses to surrender by becoming *this* father in his turn; what horrifies him in the son with whom he is threatened is himself. One word is striking: virginity. This thirty-one-year-old man has had many affairs; never mind, if the mating is sterile his purity is not contaminated, it is only the transient contact of two skins. With procreation, man is soiled by the shameful chemistries he has released in his woman's belly; love, then, is related to defecation: Gustave would have *made excrement*—because his father did when he engendered him. At this moment the curse turns on itself: Gustave curses his father because his father cursed him.[13]

It must be noted that Djalioh—this is Gustave's artfulness—does not seem to hold a grudge against Paul for having brought him into the world. Moreover, the story makes a case for a golden age preceding the misery and death of the anthropoid, while Gustave denies the hero of *La Peste à Florence* a happy childhood. The fault—or the mistake—seems rather in having brought him to Europe and among

---

13. A passage that we have already cited leaves no doubt about the underlying identity of Monsieur Paul. He is, the narrator says, "[a] monster or rather that marvel of civilization, who bore all its symbols, breadth of mind, a cold heart." However, the parallel between the two monsters—"Here is nature's monster joined with that other monster"—even as it is imposed has a tendency to veer away from and mask the symbol. Gustave sets out defeated in advance, meaning that he will never dare to compare himself at length and explicitly to his creator. This is understandable. Between an authoritarian father and his son, relations are unilateral; to establish a comparison, some reciprocity must be at least theoretically possible. For this reason Gustave can

men; the initial malaise issues from this. And then the drama explodes when Paul, quite within his rights, marries Adèle, provoking his creature's impotent and savage jealousy. *Who* can complain? No one. It is obvious that the girl can marry only a *man*, that is, a member of her own species. The human race can tolerate if absolutely necessary the molesting of a black slavewoman by an ape—the victim is on the outer edge of humanity; but for a white woman, a bourgeois French-woman, such mismatches are forbidden. Furthermore, Adèle can only be horrified at the notion of abandoning herself to the embraces of Djalioh, this sub-man whose inferiority—in the eyes of the world—

curse his progenitor in secret, but he is not permitted to place himself on the same level; Achille-Cléophas, the perverse god, remains sacred even in his perverse de-mands. From the moment that Djalioh and Monsieur Paul are compared, Monsieur Paul changes personalities. In fact, most of the time he is a dandy, an idler, an alert and ill-natured imbecile, lacking any sensitivity. This scholar is only an amateur and is happy only in the salons, in the company of half-wits "in yellow and azure gloves with lorgnettes, swallowtail frockcoats, medieval ideas, and beards," who might be fops or industrialists from Rouen but are surely not academicians. In these passages Paul is only raw material for Ernest, the pitiful Lovelace of *Passion et Vertu*. Moreover, he has two quite different functions in the plot: he is the terrible demiurge, a marvel of civilization, who succeeds in a widely awaited experiment by creating in cold blood a suffering flesh whose undeniable destiny is to die of sorrow; and he is also an "up-to-date" landowner who keeps company with snobs, who parades mornings "in the Bois de Boulogne" and evenings "in the Italiens," above all he is the beloved and highly indifferent husband of Adèle, whom Djalioh so desperately covets. Between Paul I—who explores the world and serves science—and Paul II, amiable product of fashionable Paris, there is no obvious connection. But no incompatibility either: the *amateur* biologist might be both at the same time or in succession, that is obvious. If this were the case, however, he ought to frequent men of science, to observe his creature with them, in short, to take the experiment to its logical conclusion. But he does nothing of the kind. Or, if he does, we are not told. Gustave notes in passing the naturalists' lively interest in the monster. But Paul II, once the cross-breeding has succeeded, seems to be uninterested in the result; he trains the anthropoid in every-thing, indiscriminately, vaguely scornful, as a domestic who is completely devoted to him, as a curiosity who provokes laughter in society. Above all, his extreme "cold-heartedness" blinds him to the love and merits of the wife who lives only for him. Might not Paul II be Achille, the usurper, the cold benefactor of a paternal love that would have fulfilled Gustave had he been its object? Yes, there is no doubt that this is the case, and the comparison can be established between the two brothers, the elder of whom is so well attuned to logical connections and the younger to the movements of the heart. Taken in this way, Adèle is the father's supreme grace given to the first son, refused to the second. But let us not forget that the story was written after the meeting at Trouville; this means that the young woman serves another purpose, which is to represent Elisa. Flaubert's jealousy is divided into two stages: he is jealous of his brother and of Maurice Schlésinger; so that Monsieur Paul, to the extent that Adèle embodies the phantom of Trouville, must exhibit some of the features of Maurice, an unworthy and tepid lover, as Arnoux will do in the second *Education*.

is quite evident. Briefly, in all human justice this disgraced rival is eliminated in advance; or rather, his love isn't even noticed. No doubt Djalioh triumphs over his miserable superiors by the immensity of his love. But what scale of *human* value puts sensibility above intelligence? To whom could the monster appeal the judgment leveled against him? Heaven is empty, God doesn't exist. And then, if he did exist he would be a father, he would judge in favor of men. Thus the Other *has always* won out, well before Paul could have conceived of making his experiment; Djalioh has already lost the moment he begins to love. He suffers from frustration, true, but from a *legitimate* frustration and one he would consider as such if he knew how to reason. This is what the author wanted: to set everything against himself, reason, law, even love (it is *normal* for Adèle to love Monsieur Paul) this amounts to recognizing that he is a monster, a sub-man not comparable to his brother, and that as a direct consequence he doesn't deserve anything he desires. Following which, leaving Djalioh, distracted, to beat his head against this blinding evidence, Gustave turns quickly back to his father: yes, I am worthless, without merit or right, why did you make me like this? Indeed, it must be understood that the little boy Gustave, embodied by Djalioh, hasn't the means of feeling and expressing rancor any more than the ape man; both must live out wholeheartedly and innocently the condition another arranged for them. The final catastrophe—which is written into their fate—will be all the more staggering as they will have neither foreseen nor comprehended it. More profoundly, the younger son of Achille-Cléophas, by virtue of the passive character he was given, cannot revolt, nor does he wish to do so—we shall take this up again. In him spontaneity must be obedience and faith; thus, realizing through himself what the Other has prescribed, he abdicates all responsibility for the misfortunes which befall him according to the established plan—it is his Creator who has slipped into him to manipulate him. There is, then, only one guilty party: the all-powerful father. Guilty in whose eyes, since there is no judge? This is where Gustave lies in wait for us; by means of the narrative he is doubled, the storyteller is *someone other* than the possessed child. While he suffers in ignorance, incapable of bearing a grudge against anyone—in part because he was put together in such a way that he is lacking the capacity to make logical connections—the author is disengaged from him and is a witness; better, he turns his story into an act of accusation. Discreet, veiled, tortuous, this indictment is not any the less objective. Never, of course, does the author say: "I accuse"; the exposé of the facts

210

nonetheless is meant to be tendentious. Everything happens as though little Gustave, wholly occupied with living, were saying in good faith: "If I suffer, it is my own fault. I have only myself to blame and I am thankful to the grown-ups for their good offices—I know that they serve higher interests and I trust them with all my heart," while in the meantime an anonymous and reflective consciousness has transcended this ignorance and verified the horrible truth, the crime of Achille-Cléophas. From this, one can conclude in the first place that Gustave's attitude toward his family is fixed: no resistance or revolt, a deep and proclaimed faith but a controlled obedience which provokes the worst catastrophes by obliging the adults to recognize that they are the ones, through their cruel and stupid designs, who bear the entire responsibility. (I shall describe this tactic later under the name "gliding"; we shall see that it is a praxis of passivity.) In the second place, the attempt at doubling informs us of the literary comportment of the young writer—nothing in his narratives is gratuitous. Many authors, who in their maturity have spoken about themselves at length, are in their first works enchanted simply to tell pretty stories or to write conventional poems about death, love, broad emotions which they have not experienced. Gustave at fifteen years old—at thirteen too, we shall soon see—wrote *in order to be understood and to be avenged*. He endlessly ponders his situation, first from one angle, then from another, but for reasons which are not yet clear he can raise himself to reflection only by meditating on an imaginary character who might be considered, if you will, a possible Gustave—realized, perhaps, but in another time or another world. The essential thing is that the relations are the same and the material singularities different.

We shall have occasion to see a hundred times in the course of our study that this *reflection through imagining* is characteristic of Flaubert's bearing toward the self. We must not assume that he first seizes upon the truth—his true feeling, his true vision of his past, of his own history—and then disguises it out of prudence, like Pepys inventing a code for his journal out of fear it would fall into other hands. Gustave is certainly tormented by the urgent need to know himself, to unravel his tumultuous passions and find their cause. But he is put together in such a way that he can understand himself only through invention. Thus, from this period on, literature is his refuge; he never invents anything but himself, and by writing out his phantasms he manages confusedly to dominate the disorders of his emotions and, through unreality, to vault over his real situation. But if fiction succeeds in

211

pulling him away from what is immediate, if he takes a deep interest in his first works, the need to know himself never comes to him in the half-light of youth as anything but an irrepressible desire to create other characters.

Here, then, Monsieur Paul stands accused. On this level, there is no more need to look for a judge—who would be better qualified to deliver a verdict than his own creator? From this perspective, Gustave had the supreme pleasure of creating after the fact the man who created him and of endowing him in imagination with a radically malevolent will. Literary creation, or the creature's revenge.

These remarks allow us to enter more completely into the indictment implicit in *Quidquid volueris*. We have seen in fact that before his decline Djalioh knew a golden age. In order to judge Monsieur Paul equitably, someone will say, these first years must at least be taken into account. But are we truly to believe that Djalioh used to live in a cloudless paradise? Certainly, the son of the ape and the woman "received" ecstasies. But on closer inspection there is something suspect about them. I am not even referring to the lethargic fits of melancholy in which they are regularly dissolved, or to the attendant tremblings. I propose simply that we reread Gustave's portrait of Djalioh *before* the departure for Europe:

> His youth was fresh and pure, he was seventeen or rather sixty, one hundred and whole centuries, so that he was old and broken, worn and battered by all the gusts of the heart, by all the storms of the soul. Ask the ocean how many wrinkles it has on its forehead; count the waves of the tempest. He had lived for a long time, a very long time, not at all in thought but . . . in the soul, and in his heart he was already old. However, his affections were not directed toward anyone, for there was in him a chaos of the strangest feelings [*sic*]. . . . Nature in all its forms possessed him, the soul's delights, violent passions, gluttonous appetites. He was the epitome of great moral and physical weakness, with an emotional vehemence that was yet so fragile it shattered at any obstacle.

Flaubert will add later that before jealousy flung him into passionate desire, Djalioh loved Adèle "like the whole of nature, with a gentle and universal sympathy." Indeed his heart "was vast and infinite because it comprehended the world in its love." It is surely not surprising to see the motif of old age reemerge here; what does seem more curious is that it is applied to the child during his early history, in other words, during the golden age. For Mazza, paroxysms of unhappiness have almost turned her hair white. For the child Djalioh, it is the repeated ecstasies, passions without tears, that have transformed him into an old man. As though he were saying to us in the first instance: "upon leaving childhood, I was broken by unhappiness," and then, at two months' distance: as a child I was happy, happiness aged me." From one short story to the other the symbolism is reversed. There is only one way of explaining Gustave's obstinacy in constantly introducing the leitmotif of senescence and the contradictory use he makes of it: these surface meanings retrieve a deeper sense which the author tries to suggest, and if he fails it is that he both loses his way and lacks the appropriate tools. At the end of the chapter we shall try to clarify this polyvalent symbol. For the time being we must proceed cautiously.

Old—Gustave repeated it to Louise a hundred times, meaning apathetic, anorexic. In short, moribund or dead. This at least is the sense he gives the word in his twenty-fifth year. At fifteen it means something quite different, for Djalioh, the child-dotard, has lost none of his capacity for suffering. Or for desire. Let Adèle chance to appear and it is hell. What, then, is the meaning here of the words "battered, worn, broken"? Why does anyone want to make a centenarian out of this young man? It is all the more disconcerting as Gustave, embodied in his character, aims to present a summary of his first seven years. Yes, the little boy's happiness lasted seven years, and then unhappiness descended upon him—he knew the shame of being a monster and the savage jealousy. But the lightning struck an already hoary head. What can this mean? He can of course rationalize this strange fantasy: neither simple sorrow nor joy, he can declare, exhaust the body and the soul; it is their intensity. Positive or negative, passion ages us at every age in proportion to its violence. Are we not told of Djalioh that nature "in all its forms possessed him. The soul's delights, violent passions, gluttonous appetites"? From birth the heart of the ape man must have been pandemonium. But these few lines are surprising; they detonate just at the point where they seem superfluous. Indeed, when Gustave tries his hand at painting Djalioh's love for Adèle, he writes:

> Where intelligence left off, the heart began its reign, it was vast and infinite for it comprehended the world in its love. And he loved Adèle [before jealousy], but at first like the whole of nature, with a gentle and universal sympathy; then little by little this love grew to the extent that the tenderness for other beings

213

diminished. Indeed, we are all born with a certain amount of tenderness and love. . . . Throw casks of gold on the surface of the desert, the sand will soon engulf them, but gather them together again in a heap, and you will form pyramids. Well, he soon concetrated all his soul on a single thought and lived for this thought.

A remarkable description from a fifteen-year-old pen. And right. Not only in its generality but above all when it is applied to the author himself. The time is not far off when Gustave will say, "My life is a thought." But the very truth of this passage mitigates against the meaningless rigamarole of the lines concerning old age. Before "gathering together again in a heap" the casks of gold and love he possessed, Gustave scattered them in the desert and the sand engulfed them. No acts of violence. Or storms—this diffused soul gave the universe only a gentle affection. A double mishap is required to focus the soul; a finite object concentrates in the self the infinite power of loving (here Djalioh is joined with Mazza); at the same time another appropriates this object, and frustration exasperates desire. Under these conditions, how is it conceivable that the "gusts of passion" at a moment of innocence and cosmic sympathy could shake a heart to the breaking point? And what is the source of this "wear and tear"? The source of old age? The reader doesn't make any progress; Djalioh's inexhaustible and inspired receptivity evoke childhood and its infinite resources. Is it possible for a child to be degraded by poetic experience, even if his distressed quietism makes him experience fully the soul's agitations, ecstasies which are endless but anguished in their excess? In the same way, Djalioh *does not retain* his feelings. The young author has the malice to insist on this commonplace, that lability is a specific trait of the higher simians. Remember, at the end of the last century, the inexcusable Zamacoïs: "A butterfly has just passed between you and his anger." The anthropoid retains the inconstancy of the ape: he is seized by the most intense emotions, and suddenly they release him and disappear. "He was the epitome of great moral and physical weakness, with an emotional vehemence that was yet so fragile it shattered at any obstacle, like the senseless lightning that overturns palaces . . . and is extinguished in a puddle of water." These strange lines, their inaccuracy underscoring their profundity, must be seen as a studied avowal by the author—Gustave is visited by raptures and desires which occupy him for a moment and collapse at the slightest obstacle. He abandons himself to them rather than mastering them; before the unhappiness that concentrates all his power for suffering, he was the recipient of passions, but what he lacked was the minimum of synthetic activity which would have allowed him to prolong these passions for a moment and integrate them as part of his unity of self.

Can we imagine a similar disintegration of experience without destroying the very idea of a subject? Yes and no. The defect of the question is that it is posed in intellectualist and Kantian terms. If we remain on the affective level, as the author invites us to do, it is much less difficult to allow that blocks might be isolated in the flow of experience despite a deeper unification without which a human life would be impossible. Gustave insists so often that he has had *a number of* lives, we have to believe him; let us understand that his childhood is characterized for him by the sudden emergence of episodes unconnected to the actual train of his perceptions—waking dreams, stupors, or unclassifiable feelings which he endures without being able to identify them. These subjective determinations have two complementary, though apparently contrasting, features—repetition and novelty. Emanating from the depths of the same person, they are frequently reproduced in one disguise or another; but since they are labile by nature, since the passive psyche experiences them without being able to hold onto them, they always seem new and singular. It is to these ungathered or poorly gathered fragments of his experience that he alludes in *Quidquid volueris* and later, when he writes in *Novembre*: "I have lived many lives, a thousand lives." These repeated illuminations which dazzle him and are snuffed out without his knowing what they illuminate, where they come from, or whether there is a path to their source, impress him chiefly by their novelty. The subjective thread of experience—slow flowing of a "passive synthesis"—is too slack, his *persona* too indistinct, his sense of the real too vague for him to consider these states as slight, wholly anecdotal vacillations in the enterprise of living; they occupy him as much as those organized forms which *the others* call reality. For him their every appearance is another birth, and when they disappear they seem to die. This is how he can see in each of these episodes, without metaphor, a whole life—doesn't he feel himself becoming *another* person every time?

This is nevertheless what he calls *old age* in *Quidquid volueris*. He is unable to see it as an *accumulation* of unprecedented and singular experiences; rather it marks a perpetual disintegration, the consequence of his passivity. The image itself of the ocean, that multiple and "always replenished" unity, is meaningful, for it is poorly welded to the object it is supposed to symbolize, so poorly that it makes evident the uncertainty of the thought itself. The watery continent is old, Gustave tells us. "The winds wrinkle it." This is true, but its wrinkles never stop changing; in a dead calm they disappear. And must the churning of the sea in a typhoon be called wrinkling? Disjunct unity, multiplicity haunted by oneness, broken synthesis; swept each day by the same tempests, the ocean *never accumulates*; it will preserve its accessibility to the end. In spite of Neptune and his white beard, nothing could be less appropriate than the repeated attempt to impose on it an image of exhaustion. By contrast, the movement of the ocean, an unfurled falling back, rather well represents the ebb and flow of little Gustave's pseudo-pluralism. Later, out of humility as much as a taste for fitting metaphors, Flaubert will attempt a furtive reclassification of his images; to Louise, in a letter we have read, he describes himself as unhappiness and illness have made him—a calm and fetid pond with troubling dregs. Never to be stirred up. And he adds: "Tempests belong to the ocean." The sense is clear: I have— they made me—a small nature, my calm is deathly; if you stir me up I stink; great natures are made for great passions. The sea is inexhaustible, like youth.

In *Quidquid volueris*, however, he is conscious of his weakness; while he speaks hyperbolically about the storms that have broken his childhood, he recognizes the parasitic nature of his ecstasies. He would like to explain them plainly by the action of the external world: "His soul, catching at what is beautiful and sublime . . ., clung fast and died with it." Gustave is no longer anything by himself; to be specific, he is a vampire who needs the blood of others to live a few hours and who dies at the cock's crow. A new soul is a new object; when the object has disappeared from the perceptual field, this soul is annihilated. And what happens between the disappearance of one external stimulus and the appearance of another one? *Nothing*, Gustave seems to be telling us. Nothing, meaning the indefinite cover of native ennui or the return to the tomb of the vampire, annihilated until the following midnight. This time we can understand the real meaning he gives to the words "old age"—*in this story, at this age*; its function is to record his passivity, his "relative being," and his conscious inability to generate his own enthusiasms. When he spoke of himself as *worn, broken* by storms, he was lying—the tempests spared his golden age. But *it is true* that he remembers this childhood as a time both of wonder and of an anorexic apathy; he lived reluctantly, drowning in boredom, save when an external circumstance awakened

im. Old age has the function of reassuring him: it accounts both for
he inconsistent multiplication of disparate emotions and for the cold
acquiescence that sustains their existence without tying them together. But this metaphor is a confession—Gustave's golden age must
have been gloomy. A child alien to himself, he enfolds alien lives
within himself, intuitions that surprise him by their strangeness, that
are endured while he is in a stupor and disappear, leaving behind
only jumbled memories. They are chiefly striking in their quasi-pathological character. Rather than *make* experience even while submitting
to it, he abandons himself. His ipseity remains, but as a malaise, as
an impossible task.

Caroline Flaubert can be held responsible, in a way, for the *estrangement* that makes Gustave feel the unity of his experience as a
plurality in inert syntheses—didn't she *make him passive*? But Gustave
does not seem to comprehend the exact role his mother played in his
development; the adolescent at fifteen holds Achille-Cléophas alone
responsible for what he finds *already blighted* in his golden age. This
is not said; weakness and vehemence are simply Djalioh's lot, nothing
more. And as we have seen, as long as he is not torn away from his
native land, from the virgin forest, from the ocean, it is not such a
bad lot. At least, Gustave forces himself to show it in a positive light.
But all we need is to pay attention to the images he uses to perceive
beneath the child Djalioh's altogether Apollonian emotionality a fundamental and veiled violence. We have just quoted a sentence that
seemed to assimilate the anthropoid's dazes to the attacks of vam-
pirism. But we had it garbled; it is now proper to restore it in its
entirety, namely with the comparisons to which the young Gustave
is so partial. We shall see that the effect is rather grating: "His soul
caught at what is beautiful and sublime, as the ivy catches at debris,
flowers at spring, the tomb at the cadaver, unhappiness at man, clung
there and died with it." The soul catches at the sublime as the tomb
does at the cadaver, as unhappiness at man? These images will seem
incongruous, but Flaubert did not choose them at random. Was it
simply that he was under the influence of a certain Romanticism?
Pétrus Borel's images were even worse.) No doubt, but why this
Romanticism? "Hell and damnation!" It was the fashion. And afterward? The Goncourts would later reproach the adult and celebrated
Gustave for wanting to "shock the bourgeoisie," and we shall discuss
this again; but what bourgeoisie would this child, who wanted only

one reader, want to shock?[14] At this period his adolescent pen never stops; rather than slowing down to look for the appropriate expression or metaphor to express a particular thought, he prefers to jot down, with the unity of oratorical movement, diverse, sometimes contradictory approximations which approach the idea in question from different angles and correct each other through their opposition. The meaning is not given through a single image; in its complexity it appears beyond *all images* although each one pretends to deliver it in its entirety. This elaboration by successive corrections appears nowhere better than in these lines. The first image, spontaneous, immediate, springs out of the author's need to emphasize strongly the parasitic nature of the ecstasies. How could Gustave do better, to express the relative character of this soul and its necessity *for living* where it is by fastening itself onto the external world, than by comparing it to a parasitic plant? Is this even a comparison? Parasitism is the dominant structure of the idea that must be rendered, but it is also the genus of which ivy is a species. The choice of the plant has the unique function of giving a material existence to this concept; it becomes a vegetative force. But as often happens, the idea is found to be overwhelmed by its materialization, which does indeed carry a negative determination that Gustave at first considers displaced; the ivy is beautiful but the "debris" is not, so that the meaning is reversed: it is not a monster fastening itself to beauty; it is a likable plant (a flower of evil) drawing its sustenance from refuse, from offal. Might not the word "ruin" have been more suitable? Perhaps; this isn't certain, but in any case its negative charge is strong. Gustave, however, does not erase anything; it doesn't occur to him that true parasites live by consuming other lives; his first thought is to wind his climbing plant around something inorganic. No sooner has he tried this first approach than it troubles him, and in order to correct it he immediately goes to the opposite extreme, that is, to the conventional: "debris" is replaced by "spring," worthier, according to universal folklore, of representing the gentle power of renaissant beauty. But suddenly it is the first term of the comparison that is altered, transformed by the second and by the banality of the common meaning if the object is beautiful or sublime, the soul's relation to it must be positive, and this can be, says the anonymous stupidity of the great majority, only if the soul, like the beautiful or sublime object, is em-

14. Two, strictly speaking, when he was still friends with Ernest. He will be precise on this point a year later at the beginning of *Agonies*.

218

bodied in some *aesthetic* reality. The soul-flowers will harmonize with the spring—an Apollonian image: beds of roses bloom in the tender springtime warmth; it is the only image which isn't shocking for the simple reason that it is banal. It is also the most facile, the most careless: can one seriously say that flowers "catch at spring" and cling there, that they live in symbiosis with the sun? Not unless they are produced in certain external circumstances constituting a favorable atmosphere for the bud—then the nuance of passive activity is preserved. The *stimulus* comes from the outside, were it only to allow the actualization of what is potential; in return, the plant *clings* to the external factors which condition its existence, a mysterious and nearly inert energy allows it to absorb light and fashion it into the instrument of its belief. Is this the vampirization of the sun? Certainly not. The sun, to follow the popular metaphor to its conclusion, resembles the cause of the stoics, which acts and produces its effects without any loss or simple alteration of its substance; it is a gift, generosity. Through this Apollonian figure of speech the young Gustave seems to testify to an optimism that he is rather far from feeling. As if in a game of disconcerting seesaw, he could not act on one of the terms without as a consequence effecting a modification of the other, which causes his thought to veer off in another direction. In fact, the young boy's basic concept would be—if he could express it exactly—a radicalized Platonism. The love of beauty—child of penury—Gustave regards as an exacting vacancy, a shameful and desperate nonbeing conscious of its ugliness. This oscillation from "ivy/debris" to "flowers/spring," namely from one malaise to another, reveals to Gustave through its double inadequacy the obscure but fundamental intention which has twice tried to manifest itself and which the heaviness of written words has twice betrayed. What intention? Well, we shall find out at the same time as the author himself. To begin with, let us note that the third comparison rises up like a violent negation of the second. The optimism of the "flowers/spring" relation was inferred; scarcely written down, this poetic vulgarity repels him, it is not his own, he doesn't recognize himself in it, it is an anonymous product of the stupidity which has slipped into him. He reacts—new revision, new correction—by pushing everything into blackness: the "tomb/cadaver"pair corresponds to an active return to absolute pessimism; this time Flaubert does not spare the splendid or sublime object which fascinates Djalioh any more than he spares the soul of the poor anthropoid. The inessentiality of the soul is preserved—it is the cadaver that creates the tomb. But what a strange observation that would turn incorruptible beauty into a skeleton. It will be contaminated by it. Nevertheless the third comparison marks a progression from the preceding two. The negative emphasis is first put on the soul: it was ivy and a bed of roses, here it is malignant and incomplete. The tomb, of course, is properly speaking a dark cavity three-quarters empty. What does it contain? Rarefied and stale air that is never renewed, a corpse in a coffin. Yet the coffin is not always present; there are tombs that *await* their future inhabitant. Figuratively this place represents death, inflexible necessity, the ultimate term that life carries within it and nourishes as its ultimate internal event and its accomplishment—death, parasite of life, this is what suits Flaubert. Isn't he thinking, this younger son, of those family crypts where the children's place is marked from birth between the still living parents and the deceased grandparents? The soul, in any case, becomes deathly. It is death and it is dead; the ivy and the roses lead a relative, borrowed existence; at least they live by drawing from other lives. But in this new light the anthropoid's soul *within him* seems to be the consuming principle that dissolves him; viewed from the outside, it is the tomb of beauty. His expectation is no longer even lived passively, it is totally inert; it is a cavern, a material void. A work of man, the tomb awaits the dead man who will justify it, and when it has received him, it lets him decompose without deriving the least profit. No symbiosis for Djalioh; beauty, when he encounters it, works only to actualize this devitalized vessel by becoming uselessly tainted. In a word, beauty too is death; it is not without reason that Gustave compares it to a cadaver, and we shall see much later that this lame metaphor contains a prophetic intuition of the ideas that Flaubert as an adult will apply in his art without the power to make them clearly explicit. Thus the future artist's close bond to beauty as subjective *eidos* is explained. The connection from one to the other, we shall see, is the "absolute point of view" that Gustave will also call style and that we shall define as death's perspective on life. For the moment we shall examine this new image for other information about the young author. Indeed, it will show us that the soul of the child Djalioh *during the ecstasies* is *vacant*; avid and wretched, it awaits with an inert impatience the destruction of a life inside it—the life of its unhappiness—and through the flood of beauty the destruction of all lives. At once the fourth comparison, a new revision, fully reveals Gustave's meaning and his motivations, He has been unable to satisfy himself with the "tomb/cadaver" pair. The inertia of a sepulcher is not a happy symbol for passive activity and it is not admissible that it "clings" to the cadaver it contains. On the other hand, Gustave is still quite a long way from understanding the inspired prophecy which gives us a glimpse of his future aesthetic of death. He himself is scandalized; to the extent that like everyone, more than everyone, he is superficially prey to the commonplaces of his times, the adolescent feels that beauty, since it is the supreme value, must be represented on the "ontic" level by the supreme possession of the living, by life. Here, then, is the second term, man, raised from the dead—this Lazarus who already felt his wrappings being removed rises up and leaves the grave where he was to be buried. For once, Gustave the misanthrope gives credit to his fellow men: it is the "human being," living, musing, and suffering who will embody the aesthetic object and become the measure of all things. On the condition that he is a *man without hope*, in other words, born in hell. The comparison works this time; unhappiness thrusts itself onto the newborn, clings to him, and since this is a singular destiny it dies with its victim in order to rise again elsewhere, on the occasion of a new birth. Unhappiness—is *that* the soul? Precisely: in each of us the soul is the singular principle of suffering. Without the body it could not live; but this parasite fastens itself onto the organism and torments it to death. Then it is extinguished. What is it exactly? An endured, incurable injury, the "deep wound" Gustave mentioned in a letter to Mlle Leroyer de Chantepie? Or else a malignant will, an injurious animosity? Must it be seen as the internalization of evil that has been done to us, or as evil itself, that which we do, which we do to ourselves? For Gustave these go together. We internalize as injury the injustice of others, we externalize it again as malice. It is curious that he complains *in the same terms* at the beginning of *Mémoires d'un fou* and after more than thirty-five years, when, in 1870, the capitulation of Sedan is followed by the Prussian invasion and the reestablishment of the Republic: I, who was so tender, men have made me dry and malicious. Finally, the ecstasies themselves are represented differently; in that obscure and passive *anima* which awaits the encounter with beauty in order to be actualized, one senses something sinister in the very choice of symbols, the ambiguous and mingled presence of evil and unhappiness. Does this mean that the young author, after three abortive attempts to render his thought, finally managed it in the fourth, and that the last comparison was the only one of any value to him? Certainly not; if that were the case, wouldn't he have deleted the others? The "unhappiness/man" pair undoubtedly corresponds to a deepening of the idea—Gustave has a sense of his purposes. But he keeps all the imagery despite its imperfection; the other metaphors add indispensable nuances to the *meaning* he intends to express. Moreover, the soul might be defined by unhappiness. But this comparison by itself does not take into account the torpor and passivity suggested by the "tomb/cadaver" pair. Without this, the sufferings of Djalioh/Gustave could be imagined as the gadfly of legend, the lively and frenzied executioner of the unfortunate Io. The parasitism would be lost to a frustration which, from this very fact, would appear as an active and frenetic principle. Finally that gloomy tunnel of death, the discontinuity of the dazes, and perhaps the sufferings would be forgotten. And the flowers of spring also have their function: if the basis of the ecstasies is violence, "bitter" mournful desolation, they are nonetheless rapturous on the surface. The comparisons taken together tend to present the ecstasies as suspect joys which plunge the child into a terrified estrangement; he submits to them greedily, he hangs on to them, but at the same time he has the feeling that the cure is worse than the disease; furthermore, it is not uncommon for him to have fits of trembling and for everything to end in a terrible sadness and false death. When the sublime object has disappeared, Gustave/Djalioh *endures* death in the form of lethargy.

As I have said, the meaning lies beyond these contrasted metaphors, and we have accurately grasped through their juxtaposition the direction of the thought of this young author who wants to suggest the "inexpressible." This method, in sum, is only the literary exploitation of passion. An *active* writer would have hammered away at finding the exact, precise, unique formula that says all there is to say and nothing more. Flaubert, on the contrary, produces his comparisons in successive spurts, or rather they produce themselves in him; he submits to them and transcribes them without being able to master them through actions; each one is self-contained and immediately motivates an emotional reaction which will be a new approximation. There is no choice involved here; precisely because they have burst from his pen like blood from a severed artery, each one is validated in the child's eyes by its spontaneity. Besides, this hesitant effort that fails by its very passivity, these hesitations corrected by other approximations, these veerings that throw the author from one image to the other all combine to give us, behind the innocence and tractability of the "tranquil" child and in spite of the apparent discontinuity of his inner life, a glimpse of an unbroken violence that sets him against the Other, of a malign intention that condemns him as spiteful, the better to pass judgment on those responsible for his unhappiness.

Let us not forget that these descriptions and comparisons refer to the period of innocence which he will represent two months later, in *Passion et Vertu*, as a gentle, ahistorical somnolence in a universe of repetition. Is Gustave, then, unhappy and spiteful from the time of his golden age? That would be unlikely if he were referring only to the passive constitution he received from his mother. To be sure, this manifests itself by a poor insertion into the world of language, which is translated as a perpetual questioning—the unloved man, having never felt that his birth fulfilled an expectation, cannot understand what he is doing in the world. "We are superfluous, we laborers in art," he will exclaim in 1870. And this is certainly what he feels during every moment of his early history: a superfluous man, the leitmotif of an entire life. But at four years old he didn't formulate the question; let us say that his sensations were in themselves of an interrogative nature. The result was a malaise which was undoubtedly hard to bear at times, but until his seventh year the child had two compensations available to him: one was self-forgetting, the passage from daze to ecstasy; the other, which we have not yet discussed, was paternal favor. There is no doubt that in his first years Gustave was the object of Achille-Cléophas's love, and we shall come to this when we again follow the royal road of progressive synthesis. It is true that this love—solely by the fact that it was the father's—came too late in his early history, that is, after the child had gradually discovered himself and had been *fixed* under the expert hands that constituted him. Dr. Flaubert *loved the unloved child*. This was crucial, but it wasn't enough. It would have been, perhaps, if it weren't for Achille-Cléophas's capricious inconsistency (meaning, of course, what Gustave took for caprice), which hurled the little favorite from the height of his borrowed grandeur and replaced him, after his terrible disgrace, by an unworthy rival, the usurper Achille. No matter; despite its insufficiency the father's tenderness was experienced in the first years as a glorious happiness which might *almost* justify the inopportune birth of Gustave's younger brother; evidence of this, as we shall see, is that Gustave retained several dazzling memories of his early childhood. At this period the little boy could not yet foresee that the chief surgeon would be the main factor in his next frustration; consequently, he probably could not have *experienced* his ecstasies as he describes them to us in *Quidquid volueris*. Does this mean that he describes them at fifteen *otherwise* than he felt them at five? In the meantime other events had occurred; he had a deeper and more painful experience of himself within the family. Isn't he projecting retrospectively the frustration born of disgrace onto an age when he didn't suffer from it?

The truth is that from his earliest works, Gustave indicates clearly that he had a highly ambivalent memory of his earliest years. He describes them sometimes as a happy sleep (Mazza), sometimes as an incessant torment (Garcia), sometimes, as in *Quidquid volueris*, as an ambiguous period when terror and calm voluptuousness coexisted in the same state of ecstasy. What matters to us for the moment is that he attributes his unhappiness from birth *to his father* and not to Caroline—the author of his days prefabricated everything in advance. Even down to his melancholy passivity. Very specifically, he *gave him a soul*, that is, an inner rupture. Indeed Djalioh's soul, his deep wound, is only the contradiction in him of the animal postulation and the human; it is the profound distress of the beast haunted by the half of man that was put into him and by the whole men who surround and observe and test him; it is the ineluctable obligation, the desire, and the impossibility of raising himself to the level of humanity; it is the challenge to nature by culture and vice versa. For this reason it can at times be conceived as an utterly inert vacancy, a tomb, in the sense that its determination of animality—however challenged in its immediate reality—remains an impenetrable frontier, and what constitutes culture in it figures as a pure void that cannot be filled, an *elsewhere* at the heart of consciousness, in short, a gap in the soul whose pure "being-there," immobile, permanent, has all the features of inert materiality. And at times, if one takes into consideration the intrinsic reality of the animal nature that questions *itself* in the name of a beyond it cannot even imagine, one will conceive of the soul from the perspective of what Hegel calls (in the *Phenomenology of Consciousness*) unhappy consciousness—the only difference being that the contradiction of the universal and empirical singularity is a given— as a certain moment in the dialectical process (which means that it formulates *itself* for itself, is then manifest as something that can be surpassed and ultimately will be surpassed), whereas Djalioh's unhappiness cannot formulate itself for itself because of the absence of one of the terms of the contradiction, hence it is lived blindly and for the same reason cannot in any way be surpassed. Considered, however, from either perspective, the soul appears to be *suffered* by the body to which it clings and to be something that has *happened* to man and to itself, whether it is seen as a set and *suffered* prohibition—the inert, unbridgeable limit of experience—or whether it is envisaged as *pathos*, that is, as impotence *felt* through futile outbursts. In other words, Gustave—wrongly but explicitly—holds Dr. Flaubert responsible for his passive constitution. He has neither the means nor the desire to explain this passivity by maternal behavior. Monsieur Paul, however, *is* the source of Djalioh's passivity: by deliberately creating the anthropoid, he gives him *pathos* as his essence. This pathic animal will have the most exquisite sensibility—meaning that he pushes *receptivity* to its limits; he can be made to suffer more than another since his brutishness makes him react to premeditated aggression only with *passion*; but in so doing, and this is his original frustration, he shows himself to be beneath praxis, which is by definition human. In order to establish a strict relationship between an intended objective and the means at hand, one must possess the ability to make "logical connections" and a prospective constancy which allows one to focus on and stick to a project even when the reasons that determined it are momentarily eclipsed. In a word, aside from the power of affirmation, what Djalioh forever lacks is what the Americans call a capacity for *postponement*. Gustave *willed* it; Djalioh is passive because he is three-quarters ape; he suffers from this because he is one-quarter man, and this explosive mixture has been willed by his creator. We shall not call this his essence—which would presuppose that such a contradictory being can make a concept his object. But the impossible contradiction that has been deliberately produced in him by another to the extent that it is self-conscious makes suffering, properly speaking, his historical truth, his soul; and Gustave's soul was born before he was, as a project of Achille-Cléophas, who was not afraid to father that anthropoid—a younger brother. For Gustave is a younger brother irremediably, just as Djalioh, the product of man, is irremediably brutish. And the passivity of the child of man comes—he believes—from his fundamental powerlessness to modify a situation that horrifies him; were he to murder Achille (we shall see that he dreamed of doing it), he would never be anything more than a junior murderer. Flaubert comes back to this a hundred times in succession: the soul is instinct.. And instinct, as a passional challenge to the imposed finitude, is the fundamental religious impulse. If powerlessness, in effect, endeavors to wrench itself away from despair, what can it do but dream of the supreme and superhuman praxis, of the miracle, the gift of love, which has the additional advantage of instantly overturning the scientific laws that the Achille-Cléophases take such trouble to establish? But this postulation of the All-powerful by powerlessness must remain a futile appeal; the moment it takes shape, it is affectation. Here then is the strange instrument of supplication the father forged for the son: the soul, that fundamental evil, misfortune and malice inseparably bound together and determined by an insurmountable historical contradiction, the soul, conscious impotence, vain appeal to a miracle of benevolence which alone could give Djalioh rebirth as wholly a man or wholly an ape and, throwing Gustave's birth back to 1810, transform a younger son into the older brother of his older brother. He who wills has no soul—souls are only for the most unfortunate who bear the greatest guilt. The soul is born of exile, of a familial refusal, of a curse; it is made—suffering and cruelty—out of a negation of this first negation. But the negation of a negation, for him, is pure negation, the reason being that this passive agent would not know how to achieve that negation through an act—such as radical refusal or revolt. The soul must also be seen as a living death, old age endlessly begun anew, the simultaneous appeal to God and to nothingness—the soul is a *pathic* and *futile* negation endured in a convulsion of the entire body, never externalized through openly challenging conduct. Thus it can appear at the heart of the living substance as an inextricable entanglement of masochism and sadism; at the same time it is a gap, an evasion, and a pursuit that attempts to vampirize the things of this world, lacking fresh blood; indeed, everything invariably falls into this void, where Smarh is soon going to whirl around for all eternity. To those who would not like to see in *Quidquid volueris* an exposé of bitterness, and in this wholly feminine anima the internalization of the paternal curse, I extend an invitation to reread with me *Rêve d'enfer*, that "fantastic tale" which Flaubert finished on 21 March 1837, when he was fifteen years and three months old, and which I believe despite some Romantic rigamarole to be the most profound of his first stories.

Rêve d'enfer

Once again a duo: the duke Almaroës and Satan are sons of the same father. And the role of paterfamilias is played this time by God himself. The duke is an electronic machine "cast onto the earth as the last word of the creation." The eternal Father, discontented with his earlier creation, man, invented this prototype according to very careful plans. He decided to preserve—who knows why?—the human form, but sickened by that malformation the soul, he avoided giving one to the duke, preferring to conceive him as a kind of computer. The robot was not in on the secret; as he possesses the general features of our species, he assumes he is a superman until the unlucky day when he has to recognize that he is only an automaton, a piece of controlled matter. Here is how he relates his discovery and his deception:

> Little by little these dreams that I believed I would find again on earth disappeared like illusions; the heart shrank and nature seemed to be aborted, threadbare, aged like a deformed and humpbacked child with the wrinkles of an old man. I attempted to imitate men, to have their passions, their interest, to act like them; this was futile, like an eagle trying to hide in a woodpecker's nest. Then everything darkened in my sight, everything became just a long black veil, existence a long agony. . . . I tell myself: "Senseless is he who wants happiness and has no soul! senseless . . . he who believes that the body makes one happy and that matter gives happiness! This mind, true, was superior, this body was beautiful, this matter was sublime, but no soul! no belief! no hope!"

Appearing here *for the first time* is the theme of dissatisfaction and ennui; indeed, we shall see that the characters of the earlier works, frustrated and spiteful, are much too tormented to allow themselves the luxury of ennui. Even here, the other in the duo, Satan, will be the plaything of the most painful passions; a mingling of remorse and malice will take all his attention without respite—a total inaccessibility. This leitmotif will disappear in the later tales: Djalioh and Mazza, far from being blasé, strain against their frustration. And when this theme returns in the autobiographical cycle, the inadequacy of the external world will be offered as one of the reasons for the author's precocious aging. Here, curiously, it is nature that is struck by senility. Yet simultaneously nature is reproached for its puerility. It is "aged like a deformed . . . child with the wrinkles of an old man." In fact, this botched universe is eternal; eternity preserves in it the continued childhood of the work that issues from the hands of the Creator; it preserves its senility, too, its wrinkles, which have nothing to do with age and simply indicate that the Demiurge has botched the job.

But Gustave's first works are there to bear witness to the fact that the little deformed monster with his precocious wrinkles is none other than the author himself. It is he who sees his childhood as a *constituted* old age. Why is it nature here that he accuses of senility? It is because at first he doesn't really know where he wants to go with it. I have said that he wrote at this time in order to clear up the question of his estrangement indirectly by embodying it in a character who re-pre-sents it to him at a distance. The theme of dissatisfaction, entirely

227

new and entirely obscure, is at the origin of this new writing. But at the moment it makes its entrance into Flaubert's work, in which it is about to play a major role, it is not yet disengaged from a more archaic and undoubtedly more profound motif. The author hesitates and cannot at first make up his mind whether our sad sojourn on earth is not rather good for Almaroës the superman or whether, on the contrary—here the theme of guilt—a soul is necessary in order to desire the pleasures of this world. Or, if you will, the self-justification which is a response to a more profound self-accusation is wholly infused in this first moment with that guilt from which Gustave wants to be cured. Why, then, don't I feel anything? Reply number 1: because deep inside me I was born old. Reply number 2—the first product of self-defense: because the one who is constitutionally old is not me, it is the world. What then? Would Gustave, under the name of Almaroës, deny himself that exacerbated sensibility which he will give himself a few months later under the name of Djalioh? To this question I answer that we must wait; the young author doesn't know where he is going, he invents this hero, the unfeeling man. To see what will happen. And his uncertainty is such—at least in the first pages—that he goes so far as inadvertently to concede to his robot the anima he will deny him in the later pages. He writes: "[This] was a mind pure and intact, cold and perfect, infinite and regular as a marble statue that could think, act, contain a will, strength, *a soul in fact*,[15] but one whose blood could not beat warmly through his veins, who could comprehend without feeling, who could have an arm without a thought,[16] eyes without passion, a heart without love. Lacking too was any need for life . . .! All was for thought, for ecstasy, but for a vague and indefinite ecstasy that is steeped in clouds . . . and derives

15. My emphasis.
16. The young author's hesitation is such that he writes here "an arm without a thought," and two lines below "all for thought." There is no contradiction, however, except in *expression*. The meanings are compatible: the thought which is lacking in the secular arm is the great constructive dream with roots plunging down into the affective nature. It is also that pathic presentiment of life that Flaubert means to indicate in the autobiographical cycle when he writes, "My life is a thought." But when he defines Almaroës by these words, "all for thought," he *at first* opposes understanding—a rigorous system of scientific information—to the organic needs and to the passions. The ambivalence here is clear; later Gustave will be horrified by our all too human needs (and doubtless they are repugnant to him even now), but the absence of needs is presented in this text as inferiority, it is the chink in the armor. The apparent opposition between the two parts of the sentence stems in any case from the poverty of the vocabulary. Gustave's ever-flowing pen assigns to the same term two functions which are hardly compatible.

228

from instinct and constitution." Indeed, this description conjures up not so much naked matter as some perfect understanding. It is surely not *anima* but *animus*, his masculine side, mind, intelligence in action.

The words here clearly reveal certain influences: "the marble statue" very specifically recalls Condorcet and to a lesser degree La Mettrie; Gustave was evidently acquainted with these philosophers through his father. Man is an animal-machine since reason is doubly conditioned—from the inside by psychological determinism, from the outside by the rigid connections of objective sequences. But Gustave cannot refrain from transcending this automatism of precision by suddenly making thought synonymous with the "vague" ecstasy, or if you will, by presenting the ecstasy as the *terminus ad quem* of thought. How badly suited to the robot these ecstasies are, which a few months hence are to characterize Djalioh's anima. However, the adolescent hardly praises them. In *Quidquid volueris* he will insist on their cosmic aspect—the soul expands to the point of encompassing the infinite; the ecstasies are, at least on the surface, the monster's pride, and they are what give this miserable illiterate his grandeur. In *Rêve d'enfer*, however, it is the aspect of privation that is first made explicit; the infinite becomes the indefinite; the empty raptures are lost in vagueness, in the clouds; in this form they seem very close to the primitive dazes. But that is not the point. Even though he denounces the insufficiency of these mystic states, can we not see a supreme intelligence in them or, if you will, analytic understanding surpassing *the self* toward a syncretism that should, on the contrary—according to the norms of the time—precede the analysis and furnish it with its material? Gustave is convinced, furthermore, that mathematical precision cannot produce these nebulous determinations of experience. For he suddenly reintroduces "instinct" and (passive) "constitution" in order to make them the true source of these states. This is the reestablishment of the soul below and above reason as the foundation of all irrationality, and particularly of the intense desire to be *elsewhere* and to break the chains of finitude.

Yet this strange portrait is of Gustave himself, and we shall understand its contradictions if we reveal its primary intention. This much is clear, however: Flaubert meant to put into it *simultaneously* the primitive instincts, original desire, the dazes *and* the desiccation that his father's mechanistic philosophy provoked in him. The marvelous intelligence he gives his hero is not his own but the intelligence of Achille-Cléophas or, more precisely, the intelligence that Achille-Cléophas possesses and would like to give him. And when he denigrates his ecstasies he is speaking from his father's point of view. Inversely, the idea develops in him that this hyperrationalization of his being, if it had to be accomplished under the chief surgeon's control, could end only by tearing out his soul and replacing it with a rigorous system which would be consonant neither with the younger brother's basic "instinct" nor with his constitution.

Between these divergent features, the fruits of the adolescent's deep crisis, there is a single connection—*coldness*, the approximate *but not symbolic* designation of an intimate experience. Whether he gives himself over to operational calculation or is lost in the clouds, Almaroës feels he is, in himself and immediately, a being "whose blood could not beat warmly through his veins, who could comprehend without feeling . . . , who could have a heart without love." This means that the duke can reduce external objects or the feelings of others to their elements or lose himself in the pantheistic totalization of the cosmos, but he is incapable—unlike men—of desiring the things of this world one by one in their singularity. The superman has this in common with the subman Djalioh, that neither of them can share human aims. But Flaubert seems to have experimented just "to see what would happen." Being embodied, the beast is consumed by its soul; it has only too much feeling. The robot knows everything on our planet and on others; he has innate knowledge; God has made him this way. At certain times it seems that Almaroës draws his information from himself alone—all he has to do is to submit his innate ideas to a computer, the secret of which the Almighty has given him. But what will always prevent him from knowing the humble joys of men and their enormous sufferings is his lack of sensibility. Wholly knowledge and praxis, the *pathic* in him is atrophied.

In the pages that immediately follow this self-portrait, Flaubert still hesitates between pride and humility. The first explanation of this splendid anorexia is the arrogance that breathes it into him: he is too great for this world, he might flare up all of a sudden—and what a blaze! But nothing is worth the trouble. Almaroës

came among men without being a man like them . . . and with a superior nature, with a more elevated heart which asked only for passions to be nourished . . . [but] was withered, worn, offended by our customs and by our instincts . . . the hot embraces of a woman . . . would these have made him throb one morning, him who found at the bottom of his heart an infinite knowledge, an immense world? . . . Our poor pleasures . . . all the earth with its joys and its delights, what did all this matter to him who had something angelic about him. . . . All this nature, the sea, the woods, the sky, all this was small and miserable. He didn't have enough air for his lungs, enough light for his eyes and love for his heart.

This time we know what to think. Gustave would ask only to desire earthly pleasures; all his unhappiness comes from the fact that they are not desirable. We might be reading—already—a page from the *Mémoires* or from *Novembre*; the defensive tactic—to throw all responsibility onto the Other—tilts the passage toward the objective and purpose of universalization, in short toward the insincerity of the autobiographies. Indeed his explorations pass beyond themselves, from the particular to the universal, but they stop in midstream. He will come in *Novembre* to consider the most general and abstract character of all men and all things, their *being*, as a taint—existence as an imperfection of nothingness. But in *Rêve d'enfer* he does not rise to such a radical challenge; microcosm and macrocosm are connected, and both of them are quite particular. There is that abnormal creature the duke Almaroës, the product of a singular fiat, and then there is this small, shabby creation the earth, with its flora and fauna, definite species, enumerated, classified, always similar and reproducing themselves in a tedious cycle of repetition, each one imperfect in its monotony and, while perhaps the object of a special decree, borrowing in its factitiousness a nauseating appearance of accident. Badly baked earth, soft in some places, burned in others, surrounded by its mantle of water-vapor, the sky. This little world, the product of a malicious Demiurge, is presented by the author as a bad *signed* picture, a bad child, spoiled—a certain painter, a certain father failed.. A historical and dated error. The homogeneity of the microcosm—Almaroës taking Gustave's place—and the macrocosm—our planetary system—is established; these are two singular products of the same will, the first-created made to serve as prison for the second. In *Rêve d'enfer* Gustave seems infatuated with artificiality; he quite clearly refuses to be a product of that ignobly fecund nature he mistrusts. The materials come from her, but a supernatural intelligence and will were required to assemble and rework these materials. "He is," says Gustave of Almaroës, "the last word of the creation." In brief, he confronts this limited universe with a feeling of superiority; between the painful production of the earth, of the miserable organisms vegetating there, and the fabrication of Almaroës, the factory was modernized. Gustave dares finally to avenge himself on the others and with precisely the

231

anomaly they condemn; he takes their gibes and hurls them back again: "[I am] withered, worn, offended by your customs and your instincts! [My anomaly is normality itself, since I owe it to] a superior nature, a more elevated heart." And if I do not deign to interest myself in the progress of the world it is because I refuse to lower myself, as they do, in satisfying my needs. Sublime robot, I answer my accusers with a quick retort: you accuse me of lacking heart when I am consumed by the great Desire for All? It is you, your hearts atrophied, whose desires are little by little reduced and stereotyped. From the age of fifteen Gustave is on the brink of discovering one of the key values of his universe: the greatness of man is measured by his dissatisfaction. What temporarily diverts him is the particular character of the reproach that was leveled at him then. Flaubert's parents must have been troubled by his anorexia. "This boy," they would say, "has no taste for anything; nothing interests him." But this absence of feelings and desires is pure privation; by itself it involves no malaise, no suffering, either for Gustave or for the observers of his life—the child is not a fallen god who remembers heaven. They feel unhappy, this is not in doubt, but for other reasons—as we shall see in this same story. As to his indifference, it is the others who notice it and make him notice it. He doesn't love his grandmother, perhaps, or not enough, he isn't enthusiastic about his studies, he isn't attracted by the noisy, rough games of his age group; he is found at first to be difficult, he rarely feels affection for the friends of his family. And afterward? It didn't create suffering, it was literally *nothing*, and one cannot imagine he was grieved by it *unless* the sacred authorities denounced this nothing as a deficiency. It is to this denunciation that he responds by tearing it from himself and hurling it back at his accuser. Though it may strike some obscure chord in the depths of his being, this dissatisfaction is born *under Gustave's pen*—before it is felt and fully conscious—as self-justification and an argument *ad hominem*. Nothing makes him feel better than this accusation of senility abruptly cast against the world. Gustave thinks he hears a rumor: little old man, deformed, wrinkled soul? He stiffens and cries out to the universe: Old man yourself! Old man in childhood? Why not? We shall soon see that this peevish defense, still abstract and not exempt from verbosity, was oracular—as is the rule with Flaubert. It was not only his future attitude that he prophesied, it was also that of his century, or rather his half of the century which began in 1848 and extended after his death, marked by him in indelible ink.

The fact remains that in this story the ideas are not yet mature; moreover, Flaubert stops short. At Satan's first appearance, a change of point of view. Almaroës confesses to the Demon, who is highly skeptical, that having no soul he could not love. This abrupt change of symptom is striking—at the beginning of the narrative Almaroës seemed to possess a soul, now it has been withdrawn; out of a reflex of arrogance Gustave explained his emptiness, his ennui, his insensitivity *by excess*. Now we might say that he has suddenly decided to plead guilty; he explains his cold blood *by defect*. If the robot lacks warmth it is because he *is not adequate* for love. It seems that with a touch of inspiration the author could have discovered at this point the meaning of the story he had blindly begun and in which he found a new symbolism for rendering his hazy, profound idea. The proof: our duo from here on will be charged with opposing pure soul—embodied by the Demon—to pure matter, to which the superhuman duke is finally reduced. Almaroës, who has "something angelic" about him, is transformed all at once into a cold automaton; he is lent the perfect insensibility of something inorganic. The Devil develops his theme: "You desire nothing, Arthur, you love nothing, you live happily because you are like stone, you are like nothingness." These words will be taken up later in *Novembre*: "Those long stone statues lying on tombs—their calm is so profound that life here below offers nothing equivalent . . . one would say that they savored their death . . . , if it were still necessary [after death] to feel something, that this was its profound nothingness." One day, toward the end of his life, Flaubert will reveal to us the affirmation hidden by this negation—his last Antoine, in the last lines of the last *Tentation*, will whisper that prayer of all weariness: "To be matter."

Has Satan spoken the truth, and does the stripping away of the soul give the sublime automaton, if not happiness—where is that to be found?—at least perfect quietude? We might say so at times. On reading this passage, for example: "And so this man who seemed so demonic and so dreadful, who seemed to be a child of hell, the thought of a demon, the work of a damned alchemist, whose cracked lips seemed to swell only to touch fresh blood, whose white teeth exuded an odor of human flesh, so this demonic being, this deadly vampire was nothing but a mind pure and intact, cold and perfect." Coldness and perfection: here at least is what, without providing anything positive, removes any possibility of suffering. The machine desires nothing—no possible frustration. It is never disturbed; so it will never know the anguish of paralysis or of spinning in a void, or

233

the panic of feeling itself give false information in response to precise *stimuli*. But upon reflection we begin to doubt. Why has this mind, pure, intact, cold, been given such dismal features—does he have to appear to others as "the work of a damned alchemist?" Why do the teeth of this inorganic creature—who takes no nourishment since he has no needs—exude an odor of human flesh? Almaroës is not even misanthropic—why this cannibalistic aspect?

Let us note in the first place that the physical aspect of the robot is explicitly provided as a disguise. We are informed that "this strange and singular being came among men without being a man like them, took on their body *at will*, their forms, their speech, their look." Therefore he is responsible for his features, for his demeanor: "The leaden look, the cold smile, the icy hands, the pallor . . ."—*he takes these on himself* quite as much as he does the satin softness of his skin, which is "white like the moon," or his blue hair. In a word, he chose the body as symbolic of his subjective state. These words "at will" were not written inadvertently, and they are confirmed in a variety of ways. This first: "He passed quickly among the silent peasants . . . , was lost to sight, swift as a gazelle, subtle as a fantastic dream, as a shadow, and little by little the sound of his footsteps in the dust died away and no trace of his passage remained behind him unless it was fear and terror, like pale light after the storm." A little further on the author names these excursions "winged journeys." This robot leaves footprints only when he wants to—the most sublime form of matter is characterized by the freedom of dematerialization. Almaroës, we are told, has no soul; granted. But in the first pages he has no body either, unless this is understood to be that unbalanced phantom, the simple image of his frustration. When the duke and the Devil pay a brief visit to Julietta, they are seen "glued against the wall"; the head of the family takes down his rifle, cocks it, and fires. In vain; the bullets are lodged in the wall in the right place, and the "two phantoms disappear." That Satan should be a phantom, fine, he is only a soul. But the duke, that fragment of matter, lacks even Satan's impenetrability. To the extent, however, that the contrast between the two is admitted, Almaroës's materiality is insisted upon. After his meeting with Satan,. "Arthur opens his huge green wings, extends his snow-white body, and flies off toward the clouds." Wings, a bird's equipment—even better. Surely this is the best metaphor to make visible the state of ecstasy, and the words "taking wing" and "flight" will now continue to flow from Gustave's pen. But in context the terms must also be taken in the literal sense. Arthur lies on the air;

if he is raised to the clouds it is because the air supports him; this means of transport is no longer magical but physical. In the last squabble with the Demon, Almaroës finally receives strength and impenetrability: "The burning breath that was exhaled from his breast repelled Satan like the wild vibration of an alarm bell ringing out suddenly in a church, blasting, shaking the pillars, and shattering the vault." This Proteas, then, represents the infinite avatars of matter. Sometimes he seems made, like the gods of Epicurus, out of a stream of atoms so subtle they cannot be distinguished from an insubstantial phantom; and sometimes, speaking of his "lethargic body," the author does not hesitate to lend him the "haughty conceit of brute and stupid matter," without losing sight of the fact that a few lines earlier he endowed his creature with a terrible genius. Briefly, Almaroës is given the exterior that suits his inner disposition. If he flees from men, he runs without touching earth; if he seeks ecstasy, he is heavy as an angel, as an airplane taking off, retracting its landing gear. For daily use this perpetual and untiring movement has *chosen* a worn-out organism, a wrinkled face, hollow eyes, just as he has chosen to reside in a decaying chateau—to the point that one doesn't know which of the two is mimicking the other, the emaciated alchemist or the heap of stones barely held together by the ivy. Goethe's influence on this imagery cannot go unnoticed; that scholar "with the pale forehead . . . hollow and reddened eyes . . . with white, taut skin . . . thin and elongated hands" is Faust before his encounter with Mephistopheles, just as Julietta, the third protagonist, is directly inspired by Gretchen. It is the memory of Faust that sometimes sidetracks Flaubert's intentions and transforms the iron duke, for example, into a *seeker* who knows everything in advance. But the young man is impelled to give the robot the features of an old man for reasons that lie deep within himself. Listen to him describe his character's moral state: "Existence [was no more] than a long agony. . . . After having seen races of men and empires pass before me, I [no longer] felt anything throb in me. . . . All in my spirit was dead and paralyzed" And Flaubert says besides: "He loved the long, extended vaults where one hears only the night birds and the wind from the sea; he loved those heaps of debris supported by ivy,[17] those dark corridors, and all that aspect of

---

17. The theme of the ivy, present here six months before its use in *Quidquid volueris*, rather clearly reveals its negative elements. In *Rêve d'enfer*, then, the relations are reversed: the ivy is the *practicing* subject, it holds together the inert materials which would be dispersed without its synthetic effort. But of course the word "debris" does not here allude to the beautiful or the sublime; it simply designates the elements glued

death and ruin,[18] he who had fallen from such a height to descend so low, he loved what had fallen too; he who was disillusioned desired ruins, he who had found nothingness in eternity[19] desired destruction in time."

Almaroës is not unfeeling; this is the surprise. How can a machine suffer? He has no soul—Satan has told him clearly that this is his extraordinary luck. No soul, no suffering. Except for one thing that the Demon cannot know: pure understanding deprived of a soul suffers precisely from not having a soul. This is his chief frustration, confessed in shame and proclaimed in resentment: "No soul, no hope!" The most manifest if not the most profound reproach the adolescent addresses to his father is that the father made him lose faith: this apathy that you call senile, you gave it to me by infecting me with agnosticism. We find here once more the judge/penitent who voluntarily confesses his crimes in order to be able to denounce their true author, who guided his hand. The death of God is not a localized absence; in Gustave's eyes it is the radical metamorphosis of all into nothing; his indifference, then, represents only the internalization of nothingness. This is what explains those words "fallen from such a height . . . so low," which at first sight seem to evoke the Platonic reminiscence, the hallucinated and vague memory of a dwelling in

together by an involute experiment. The synthetic activity prolongs the agony of the ruins and, worse, degrades them. We contend once again that in Flaubert's work there are abiding motifs, operational schemes that pass from one work to the other and in a general, unchanging perspective can express the positive aspect of this experiment as well as its negative determinations. The close affinity "ivy/debris" is a line of force, it is a fold of the creative imagination; the word will determine the symbolized reality— whether the ivy *supports* or *clings* changes everything. Briefly, we might talk about a passive synthesis whose operative signification is determined each time on the level of practical intention. This does not mean that the conglomerate in itself and before any intervening determination might not have an indicative value. But it is not in itself *expression*; it is more deeply the indistinctness of the structure and its surpassing of itself. What it offers is never the *signification* but the sense—we will return to this soon.

18. This castle is without doubt a transposition of the Hôtel-Dieu; but here the symbolism is explicit.

19. To tell the truth, Gustave is not too clear on eternity. Sometimes he takes the word in the sense of *immortality*: "for he was condemned to live," and this endless life is conceived by definition as a temporal process. At other times it is clearly the negation of all duration—right here, for example. And it also happens that Almaroës imagines his own death: "He knew that a day would come when nothingness would obliterate this God, as this God would one day obliterate him." "Condemned to live" would in this case signify that he cannot kill himself with his own hands but that the Almighty has regulated him like a clock. In the end he will stop. In this same passage, a little further on—others in the same story contradict it—God himself is mortal, which, if the author had needed to do it, would demonstrate clearly that God represents the paterfamilias.

heaven. We know that the context prohibits such a Lamartinian interpretation. The robot, created by a labor performed systematically on
samples of cosmic matter, has surfaced *in the world*; it is the soul for
Lamartine and for Plato, the soul alone that can recall the *spiritual*
existence it knew *before* falling into the body. The body of Almaroës
as Gustave conceives it can have only a material memory which bears
solely on the materiality of the cosmos. Consequently, it seems at first
that he has not fallen from anywhere. But the context enlightens us:
it is "disillusionment" which is symbolized by the fall. Arthur believed
he had a soul—he was undeceived. He is suddenly blasé: God is dead
and the soul simultaneously abolished; what remains is a colorless
world which plies its drugs and its pleasures at a high interest but
which will never again be transcended toward the absolute. Because
for Almaroës the soul, if it existed, *would constitute* itself as trans-
ascendence, starting from dissatisfaction. But since he initially complains of not being able to desire the meager goods of this world, and
he attributes this anorexia to the deficiency of his anima, we understand what Flaubert wants to tell us: what is missing in Arthur is the
great desire that will consume Mazza, the power to claim the infinite
through the finite. A wholly Christian conception; in the final analysis,
the love we bear God's creatures—be it carnal—is addressed to God
Himself. And inversely, if we did not love God, even unwittingly, we
could not love anything, even a woman's body. Almaroës is not deprived of God for he is convinced of His existence; but it is the Creator
who, by depriving him of a soul, has made him incapable of loving
his all-bountifulness, his almightiness, and consequently of loving
what is. Two symbolic systems have been telescoped: God is at once
the paterfamilias anxious to beget a perfect son, a superman, strictly
according to the rules; but this same symbolic father, feared, admired,
cursed, has wanted to instruct his creature in agnosticism in order to
perfect his work. Behind the magnificent duke we glimpse poor Djalioh; Gustave addresses Achille-Cléophas softly and tells him: You
wanted to make me your disciple and your rival, an impassive, cold
scholar. A thousand thanks, but you see, I was not worthy of that
grandiose project; I was passion, I was instinct, my constitution compelled me to believe rather than to know, and for this reason I was
inclined to become a believer. You have repressed, restrained my
religious nature, and you wanted to substitute for my vague ecstasies
dry data that I did not understand, not possessing that affirming and
negating power which belongs to you and which has been the glory
of our family. Of all this, what remains? A complete system of *knowl-*

edge, each particle of which must engender the following, which I recite by heart without *knowing* it; and then a defective heart, riddled with prohibitions, its transports clearly broken from the start, and the feeling that everything is absurd, beginning with knowledge, in this barren world in which I drag my helplessness around.

This translation allows us to interpret certain contradictions already noticed in Almaroës. This pure and mathematical spirit knows vague raptures generally ignored by mathematicians; he is happy while he thinks he has a soul, he is in agony when he perceives that he hasn't. The young boy, although embodied in Almaroës, cannot be entirely identified with his character; Dr. Flaubert did not *suppress* the soul of his younger son, he simply repressed it, drove it down to the deepest part of his being. The child feels cut off from it by that instrument of torture, *animus,* the perceptions of others, that system in which from the outside they have implicated his spirit but in which he doesn't recognize himself. Hidden, bullied, the best and most intimate part of himself nonetheless continues to exist; it is this part that sends him indecipherable signals which, piercing through the steel wall of acquired learning, sometimes provoke him to sad ecstasies experienced furtively, shamefully. It is this part of himself, finally, which secretly despairs, without his even having the right to take up the despair and recognize it as his own.

But thoughts are pyramids. Well before the appearance of Satan, the duke knows his destiny: "Nothing for him henceforth! everything was empty and hollow; nothing but immense ennui, terrible solitude, and then centuries to live, to curse existence, he who yet had neither needs nor passions nor desires! But he had despair!" Usurped despair—where could it come from? Arthur is too great for this world, yet he must endure its most fundamental frustration, for he has been refused precisely the power of suffering. Yet if the soul is frustration, the frustration of a body is a soul. "Crude and stupid matter" in its compact impenetrability is pure being and the *lack of a lack.* This absence of the negative at the heart of complete affirmation becomes, when felt, a soul in reverse, the negation of an elusive negation. Despair at not loving, at not being able to desire. In any event, despair is a constitutional feature of the soul. Ennui is pure being in its universal equivalent; but in the long run ennui turns into despair. Briefly, there is in matter an obscure *conatus* toward nothingness, and this vacancy at the heart of the plenitude returns to the duke-robot all the negative feelings. Simply, they are of the second degree: he desires to desire, suffers from not suffering, and so on until we reach the

level of reflection. The soul will be an immediate, spontaneous unhappiness for Djalioh; for Arthur it is reflective. For this reason, despite the influences of a jerry-built Romanticism and an irritating
tendency to hyperbole, *Rêve d'enfer* is a rich and profound work which
owes its interest to these two characters, elsewhere always opposed,
here complementary; it is the dictation of a barely controlled dreamlike
state, which at first doesn't know where it is going, and Gustave's
first flush of reflective consciousness. It is the dream in fact—the
dream of hell—which, through its sinuous twists and turns and its
apparent inarticulation that nevertheless constitute some kind of
warning, poses to Gustave the questions he tries to answer not by
forging a new myth, but by attempting to reflect on this nightmare.
We should't understand this to mean that reflection awakens him—
reflection takes place while he is dreaming. On this level, which is
not ethical but ontological, the plenitude of being is haunted by the
impossible nothingness. The origin of this infrastructural signification
has already been divined: it is the impossibility of saying no, experienced by Gustave as the unbearable plenitude of an agent who is
constituted as passive. Almaroës, the king of praxis, in fact only obeys
the artisan who fabricated him—revolt against his condition is forbidden him. And this forbidden, hence *inconceivable, unspeakable* revolt, drowned in docility, indestructible nevertheless since it is
produced by being as its impossible desire for obliteration, is the soul
of the slave, the spirituality of matter.

Here we see what Arthur's physical aspect is meant to demonstrate:
not the eternal youth of matter and understanding, but the eternal
old age of a desolation which dares not speak its name and which is
none other than the soul. The text is clear: the duke suffers no earthly
privation since he has no desires. He curses his existence in its totality.
The removal of the spiritual organ has the same effects as the removal
of the prostate: the aging of all tissues. As for the terror this monster
from hell provokes, as for the odor of freshly drunk blood that escapes
his mouth, these effects are specifically intended, by Almaroës and
through him by the author, to show that this perfect mind knows all
the blacker excesses, even hatred. Showing the sea to the Demon,
"Here is what I love, he said, or rather what I hate least." What he
hates most: God. He "spent centuries cursing Him" and sometimes
dreams of annihilating the whole of creation. Wait a minute, isn't
hatred a passion? Yes, precisely, and for Almaroës it is only that.
Whereas in reality this complex feeling is consistent only in the vigilance that accompanies it and in the patient schemings that, arising

from it, willfully transform it into malice and give it the objective status of an enterprise. A hatred which doesn't surpass itself in an affirming act is only a dream of hatred. Let us say that it is the phantom content of the virtual soul which haunts matter; magnificent and puerile, the metaphysical vision of an unhappy child, Almaroës is the universe, that material passivity which God drew out of nothingness and sculpted for His glory and which *must submit* both to its Creator's inflexible laws and to the impotent hatred of Him which is the secret threat of its being. In Gustave this is a secret and ineffectual malice, engendered and masked by ennui, which we shall have to describe later under the term resentment.

Yet the spiritual principle, very archaic and long since abandoned, was the first creation of the Demiurge; before Almaroës He had made men, and before men angels, pure souls lacking bodies. One of them turned out badly, the Devil. Flaubert's intention is to set the soulless body and the disembodied soul against each other in a pitiless duel. Satan, the king of earthly souls, was cursed with the conviction that the iron duke is a man and that one of his subjects is hidden inside this computer; he wants to tear him out and lead him to hell. Satan persists in this despite polite denials, spares no efforts, kidnaps the prettiest girl in the world, makes her fall madly in love with Arthur, and throws her at the robot's feet—in order to tempt him, with no appreciable results as one can well imagine. Made desperate by his failure, Satan suffers a thousand deaths, gnashes his teeth, shouts, weeps, and finds his only consolation in damning the poor lovesick girl: "No, no, you have no soul, I was mistaken, but I will have this one." A little later, the brawl; the Devil loses his head and wants to jump into Arthur's feathers: "Those two incoherent principles battled each other face to face. . . . You should have seen them struggling, body and soul." The battle's outcome is not in doubt; the duke gets the better of Satan straight away and goes off to drag his spleen and his indifference elsewhere.

It is tempting to take this confrontation for a simple exercise in rhetoric: "You shall oppose the distress of the disembodied soul to the lethargic indifference of the soulless body; you shall end by insisting on the necessity of uniting them." But there is nothing in it. First of all because this union—the Creator's second attempt—gave birth to man who proved to be, as we know, highly inferior to what was expected of him. This second misfire is represented by the new woman, the pure Julietta, who passes as Mazza will do from a chaste slumber to the infernal anguish of love and ends as one of the damned. And then, when the two monsters do come to blows, Gustave distances himself a bit to leave them ample space and reflects: "How grand and sublime they were, these two beings who, if joined, would have made a God: the spirit of evil and the force of power." Hence the union is envisaged; but supposing it could take place, neither unhappiness nor malice would vanish. No doubt the two combatants are both frustrated, and we shall see Satan complain bitterly at his lack of a body. But as we shall become aware, it is not this frustration that makes him unhappy; if he had the opportunity to inhabit an organism, far from being soothed he would take bitter criminal delight in joining physical evil to spiritual evil. A god born of the union of brute force and malice? God protects us from such a god: he would have no other purpose than to destroy the world. Moreover, as we have seen, Almaroës is not deprived of a certain kind of soul. Inversely, Satan possesses physical powers more effective than he says. For this reason, Flaubert insists, these two principles are not complementary but *"incoherent."* It is thus appropriate, in order to understand the meaning of the conflict he has imagined, to examine Satan the anima as we have done Arthur the animus. Let us continue our reading.

> "What do you have that causes your glory and your pride,
> pride—that essence of superior minds? What do you have?
> [repeats the duke]; Answer!"
> "My soul," [says the Devil].
> "And in all eternity, how many minutes of happiness has this
> soul given you?"

In this dialogue Satan claims to be proud of *having* a soul. But he confesses elsewhere, "I have *only* a soul"; these very words are improper. Christian man, that composite being, can declare that he *has* a soul and equally that he *has* a body, for in each case he is speaking from the point of view of the unusual totality that he *is*. But Satan, he who "can neither take nor touch" for lack of physical organs, *is* only a soul, or rather, since it is a matter of a myth deliberately chosen for his own aggrandizement, he *is the soul* and nothing more (in spite of certain powers we shall soon discover). Can he, under these circumstances, claim that his soul "causes" his pride? No, but it *is* his pride. Or rather pride *is* his soul, its leavening. The theme of pride which we shall find in the autobiographical writings and in the notebooks makes its first explicit appearance here. Flaubert, more wicked or more profound than the Devil, has Almaroës say that pride is the *essence* of superior minds. We have read correctly; not "the property of superior minds" but their *essence*. This is indeed what produces their superiority, that is, their very being. We have encountered this idea—only more hidden—in *Passion et Vertu*. Mazza is mad with pride. But it must be noted that she was not always this way; it took her boundless misery at Ernest's desertion to provoke the haughty arrogance that makes her despise the world. Pride, the supreme value, appears when suffering is infinite; it is nothing more than the permanent, unflinching consciousness through experienced pain of one's implicit capacity for suffering. Unhappiness and pride are at the origin of the soul. The first creates the "wound," the second, refusing any remedies, explores its features, the sum of unhappiness it can bear. This is why Satan, after his arrogant declaration, doesn't stop groaning and immediately seems to contradict himself.

> I have only the soul, the soul with its burning and barren breath, which consumes itself and tears itself apart. The soul! but I can do nothing, I can barely brush a kiss, I can only sense, see, but I cannot touch, I cannot take. . . . If only I were a beast, an animal, a reptile . . . their desires are satisfied, their passions are assuaged. You want a soul, Arthur? A soul, but have you considered it carefully? Do you want to be like men? . . . to sicken with despair, to fall from illusions to reality? A soul! but do you want sobs of dumb despair, madness, *idiocy*?[20] You would fall into hope. A soul—then you want to be a man, a little more than a tree, a little less than a dog?

There is some incoherence in these lamentations. In the first part of his complaint, Satan denounces the misery of "having only a soul" and not being anchored by the material weight of the body; in the second part—"Do you want to be like men? . . . to sicken with despair, to fall from illusions to reality?"—he holds anima *in any case* to be the absolute principle of suffering. Addressing himself to Almaroës, who claims to be wholly body, the Devil tries to make him understand that however perfect the robot's material organization, he *would become man* (a little more than a tree, a little less than a dog) by the simple insertion of some bit of anima into his heavy mass. In a sense, the two frustrated beings do not have the same conception of this spiritual principle.

20. My italics.

For the duke it is simply what is lacking to his perfection—sensibility. For the Devil it is an evil, whatever the circumstances, for the moment it combines with a body it becomes exclusively an agent of torment; it is a pain that wants soothing; so the unhappy being, weary of suffering, *hopes*—and nothing is more degrading than to delude oneself to the extent of humbly placing trust in a universe where the worst is always certain. He will also know disillusionment. Hope is his sin. His debasement as well—a Byronic theme: he who does not curse God does not deserve to live. Despair, the answer of the cosmos—that crusher of hope—is man's return to this truth. But according to Gustave, man cannot rest here; he must die or hope again. Satan alone is radical evil because he is pure and undiluted anima devoid of material baggage and knowing it, conscious that he is forever deprived in this way and that the death he has so longed for is forbidden him. Deprived of the earthly weight that would anchor him, that would absorb some of his energy and damp the intensity of his internal movements, he is present to himself without the slightest opacity. Pure reflective consciousness of an infinite pain, he draws his pride from his despair. He is not one to dally with illusions; his knowledge of himself has long since convinced him that he is condemned for eternity.

Condemned to what? and at what price? One might say at first glance that Satan symbolizes infinite desire, always active and, lacking organs, always frustrated. Observe how he never stops craving a body: "Oh! if I were a man! If I had his broad chest and his strong thighs . . . so I envy him, I hate him, I am jealous of him: I can do nothing, I can barely brush a kiss, I can only sense, see, but I cannot touch, I cannot take: I have nothing, nothing, I have only the soul. Oh, how many times have I crawled over the still warm corpses of young girls! How many times have I turned away despairing and blaspheming!" The rhetorical meaning here is clear: the soulless body cannot know desire, but the disembodied soul is a desire without appeasement; to enjoy, one must possess; to possess, one must take. But when scrutinized, the symmetry seems forced. Without matter, is it only pleasure that is refused to desire? Isn't it, more radically, desire itself in conjunction with *reality*? The soul is not an inert gap, and neither is it a void hollowed out of nothingness. Nor does Flaubert conceive of it as a spiritual substance—which he could not do without conceding it some satisfaction; no, in his eyes it is a defect of being, a torment of materiality. For this reason he chooses as its symbol Satan, whose parasitic existence was denounced by the Church Fathers. The soul has no proper consistency; it is relative to the body as the image is relative to the real thing, as evil is to good. It is Mazza's insatiable desire, the absence of Ernest's sex *in her own*. This invisible fissure presupposes the unity of the cosmos; eliminate the matter it torments and a phantom is all that remains. More precisely, an imaginary desire. What does Satan tell us? That he cannot *take*? But taking is at once the act and its end, the coveting and the pleasure. It is with his broad chest, his powerful thighs, his arms, his hands, his sex that a man "takes" a woman; but these are the same organs that give desire its reality. When Satan crawls over the corpses of young girls, what can he want? To enter them or to possess the organ that will give him the desire inseparable from the possibility? Therefore the condemnation of anima has bearing on its essence, which is to devour itself and lose itself in contradictions. It is infinite desire, to be sure, but devitalized by a fundamental castration. Desire is identical with nonsatisfaction because it is in itself paralyzed by deficiency. Therefore the soul is an *imaginary construct*—unless it is attached to a body; it is *the desire to desire*, and, unable to give a particular body to its lust, it dreams of being the desire for everything. Doubtless Flaubert meant here to refer to that inexpressible" longing, of which he will say in *Novembre*: "Vaguely I coveted something splendid that I would not have known how to formulate by any word or make specific in my thoughts in any form." *"Incessant"* covetousness, he will add. Incessant rending, burning and barren, nameless, whose profound contradiction is to negate itself by affirming itself, whose suffering is only the subjective manifestation of its ontological inconsistency. In this case shall we say that this suffering itself is imaginary? Why not? This suffering at least has no more reality than desire. We shall soon see, however, that it conceals other kinds of suffering that are quite real.

And why is the fallen angel punished? For his revolt? He is quite incapable of rebellion. To tell the truth, as we shall soon discover at the end of this analysis, he is punished for no reason at all. But what can be demonstrated at this point is that the victim is also the executioner. To begin with, pride for Gustave is a *black feeling*. This is because it comes, as Genet says, *afterward*. It has nothing to do with the assurance that certain men owe to the experienced certainty of having been *awaited* before their birth, thus unconditionally *recognized* and then *constituted* by a mother's creating love. The tranquil ease that comes from a happy infancy is *white*. It is not even incompatible with modesty. For Flaubert as for Genet, quite to the contrary, pride is born on ruins; it is not even a compensation, it is an attitude that is born out of absence (for the thief, the unknown mother represents a deep and deeply felt emptiness) or indifference (Caroline's cold attentions gave Gustave no feeling of having come into the world in answer to a prayer, in response to an appeal). Far from filling this essential emptiness or drawing attention away from it, black pride is that emptiness itself, conscious of itself and affirming the radical superiority of the negative over the positive, of nothingness over being, of privation over satisfaction. It is the exile scorning from the height of his exile the miserable doings of those who are comfortably integrated, it is the unconsoled man preferring his radical frustration to the mediocre pleasures of his peers who are content with so little. In other words, black pride is born in the person who claims to *choose* the unhappiness that is imposed upon him. Hence Gustave's ambivalence with respect to his own pride; this leap quite effectively pulls him out of humiliations but at the same time constitutes his perpetual torment, since by refusing mediocre satisfactions he has chosen to anchor himself on the absence of everything, that is, literally, on *nothing*, on an essential and endured poverty. If you don't have *all that is desirable*, better to have nothing, to be nothing in nothing. The suffering demonstrates that the soul was vast enough to contain the world; sustained, continued, it proves that the soul has made an ethic of assumed frustration. But what a shame it is for those full of such pride when people who think they are clever boast to them of their meager advantages—the Devil's sons then have only their destitution to display. We shall come back to this. For the moment let us note that for Satan, pride—the choice of nonbeing, therefore of the wound—and the soul being one, this attitude seems at once to be the basis of an aristocratic morality and radical evil. Since *black* pride has chosen the evil it endures, the consequence of this is a reversal of values—the highest being the closest to absolute nonbeing—which amounts not to eliminating ethics but to basing them on a table of antivalues. No doubt evil is endured, it has been inflicted on Satan by the Other. But since pride is only the assumption of this inequity, the entire soul is darkened, as if the basis of its existence were the intelligible choice of radical evil.

Indeed, everything follows from this first choice—Satan's wickedness is only another aspect of assumed evil. First of all, there is envy; it arises from the comparison between the penury Satan claims for himself but from which he suffers, and the minor riches (small talents, small pleasures) he scorns in others, though he cannot help thinking that these are unjustly distributed. Cruelty follows; Satan is victim of the absolute evil whose true author is God; but while asserting his claim, in his rage he sees not only the evil to be endured but also the evil to perpetrate. Suffering, the soul creates suffering; the suffering and the cruelty of human souls is a balm to his anguish: "When I see," Satan says, "the souls of men suffer like mine, it is consolation for my grief, happiness for my despair." But let us not forget that the Demon's malice is ethical. The Great She-Devil—Satan is female around the edges, see how he "drags his breasts in the sand"—reigns over souls; over her subjects she has a sacred authority which she uses to lead them gradually to their doom, all of them, in order to take revenge for the misery that consumes her but also to make them share it. The Devil with his first act of choice decided implicitly to generalize evil, to make it the framework of the spiritual order he governs.

Here then is the adversary Gustave wants to set against his duke: nonbeing, arrogant impotence, suffering, the *imaginary* impulses of great desire, the voluptuousness of malice. All souls will burn. But not all men; there are some who have no soul, like Almaroës. No hell for Ernest. Nor for Monsieur Paul. The damned shall be Mazza, Djalioh, and poor Julietta, who committed no crime other than—under the Devil's influence—passionately loving a robot.

This grip of evil on the secret wound, this nothingness which lurks in the depths of organisms and whose unique virtue is to go beyond determinism, not by altering the course of things but by challenging it through suffering—the Devil cannot make practical use of it without the means. When the soul is a flaw of the body, it is acted upon through the body; and how can one modify a material system without being provided with at least an embryonic materiality? This is what God and Gustave have conceded to the Prince of Darkness. Let us note, to begin with, that the Great Doom-bringer who sullenly proclaims: "I have power only over souls," if he is deprived of touch and of prehensile organs—hands, hooks, pincers, whatever—recognizes nevertheless that he enjoys an excellent view. Does Gustave indeed hold sight to be the least material of intersubjective communications? Or should we not recall this disclosure of some years later: "As a child I loved what I could see"? Does the Devil resemble this dear, ungainly, somewhat awkward child, strained in his movements, who may have rejected physical contact as too compromising a proximity but whose gaze glanced off the waves and was lost in the infinite? His first connection with Almaroës, in fact, is *vision*. And how does one communicate with this material opacity except through the senses. God, no doubt, master calculator, can conceive of him and divine his actions by understanding alone; but if Satan were capable of this, if he knew how to execute the intellectual operations that the supreme Engineer *invented* to project his robot's actions into infinity, Satan would know that Almaroës has no soul and that to seek his damnation is wasted effort. In fact, anima/Satan situates himself in the realm of the mind opposite animus/Arthur and observes him *from without*, as a scholar would do, served and at the same time baffled by the compact impenetrability of this organism. That would be nothing, but the Devil has more than an amusing physical trick up his sleeve. If you shoot at him, he conjures away the bullet, carries it through the wall, and sends it back suddenly through a window, shattering the panes. Now he wants to damn little Julietta; where does this arm come from that allows him to "draw her away with a powerful hand"? Later he bears her through the air, as do all the Satans Gustave has conceived and will conceive down to the last *Tentation*. Diaphanous as the young girl is, she weighs something; therefore her ravisher must effect a miracle or, himself governed by the laws of gravity, be in possession of a pair of wings and the capacity to use them when necessary. The miracles themselves, moreover, would demonstrate that he was in direct touch with nature. And he does not refrain from employing them. Before coming to blows, the two monsters challenge each other—like Moses and the sorcerers of Egypt! "'Satan,' Arthur asks, 'can you stop a wave? Can you knead a stone between your hands?'" And the unhappy Prince answers "Yes," without further comment. So he could give himself hands stronger than a blacksmith's tongs to work a stone the way others might work clay, but couldn't find the equipment to grab a girl's waist? Could it be that Gustave deplores if not his impotence, at least his frigidity? In any case, here are "those superhuman beings" confronting each other. How? Can a soul practice judo? For the combat to take place, whatever the result, some contact is necessary, hence a certain homogeneity. And if the electronic duke prevails, it is certainly not because, as matter, he has matched himself against a spiritual power which in any case he could neither seize nor even conceptualize; it is because he has confronted a less well equipped adversary with the indestructible cohesion of his parts—the better man has won. Satan *sees*; he is *visible*; he grabs wayward girls with an iron hand, but an arm of steel can make him bite the dust. In sum, the anima possesses a materiality which, far from appearing as a primary attribute, is present as its product, like a provisional carapace which it keeps hidden in case of emergency in order to confront with manipulated inertia the passive resistance of external matter. Satan's body is a surpassing of nothingness in the direction of being to the same degree that Almaroës's *animula vagula* is the unpredictable surpassing of being toward nothingness.

We are concerned here not with two incoherent and separate principles but, in both cases, with Gustave himself reflecting on what seems to him to be his own incoherence. This doubling of himself is the equivalent of a simultaneous double interpretation of his intimate experience. *Rêve d'enfer* is the adolescent's surprising attempt to apply two different keys to his life. In each case he reveals himself in his totality, assuming only that one of his parts is more or less atrophied; and in conclusion, on the occasion of the long-awaited duel, he tried to reveal his truth in a global opposition of self to self.

By comparing the two monsters, in effect, we ascertain that they are not so very different: both have been deliberately produced. And by the same father. The absence of the mother is noteworthy; in the novellas we are studying, the sons are engendered but not born. A man awakens Mazza from a lethargic sleep. A man determines the cross-breeding that will produce Djalioh—the black slavewoman, an indispensable receptacle, disappears after the birth. In *La Peste à Florence* the family conflict sets old Cosme against his two sons, and not a word about the mother; undoubtedly the paterfamilias is a widower. *Rêve d'enfer*, by making its characters issue directly from the Creator, is relieved of resorting to the mediation of a female belly. Moreover, the two enemies are brothers, sons of man but not of woman; perhaps this is what explains their frustrations. Are these frustrations, distinct in nature, so different in effect? The Devil is unhappy; so is Almaroës.

Essentially, the fraternal enemies suffer from the same anorexia which makes them both inhuman, one through the superiority of his organization (but we know that it conceals a fundamental defect—thus the superman is secretly a subman), the other through the inferiority of his equipment (but we know that Satan, the subman, surpasses the most splendid representative of our species—that is, the most wretched—in his unequaled capacity for suffering; thus the relationship is reversed, and the subman gains the right to rule over souls, namely over the sufferings of men). What then is the source of their difference? Why does Satan's despair, instead of coloring his anorexia, become permanently realized as the *true* determination of this mythmaker? The reason is that his perpetual desolation is a fixed response to a very old catastrophe; the soul defines itself in its purity of *memory* as the inconsolable meditation on an original punishment—whether or not there was a crime—on the thundering judgment that determined its Fall. Almaroës/Gustave is not fallen—this is why his soul remains virtual and his hatred of God seems to be an objective and practical relationship with the Supreme Being. Gustave/Satan, at a moment in the beginning of history, is seen torn from paradise and hurled into the depths, and he never stops falling; this historical and Pascalian relation to an irreversible event is at the source of his subjectivity. This, I should say, is what makes a soul of him, this tie to an altogether vanished and virulent past. It is also the reason for his anorexia; how could this wounded soul—we might call it *Fall Remembered*, for it is only that—devoured by humiliation, by resentment, by remorse and regret, how could it amuse itself with the baubles of our world, where would it find the time to desire them? In actuality, the Great She-Devil, devoured by her historicity, is *inaccessible*. When she envies men who covet the body of a woman, it is their accessibility she envies, their permanent possibility of escaping history and of living in the present. This Pascalian devil is Djalioh's older brother.

Could we call Almaroës Monsieur Paul's older brother? This is more complex. The Duke, like Vaucanson's automaton, must represent the pure present, even if it is allowed that a superhuman intelligence presided at his making. This is particularly central, we have noted, as he hasn't spent any time in heaven—the Creator scooped up a portion of the earth's minerals and put him together by sovereign fiat. It is all the more believable that at his appearance he believed he possessed a soul and preserved—Gustave assures us—the horrible memory of his disillusionment. But then? The Devil has no reason to envy him! When he congratulated Almaroës for being pure matter, Satan said to the duke: "You want a soul? Do you want to fall from illusion to reality?" Bitter irony, the young author must have thought; if the soul is defined by the *Fall* (the word "to fall" is not accidental), then what is Almaroës, whose whole life is explained by an original fall, by a deception he doesn't perceive? But Gustave goes further; carried away by his pen or impelled to shuffle the cards, he goes in many passages so far as lending the duke the Platonic reminiscences that ought properly to belong to the fallen angel. Arthur confides to us that his birth was a letdown; before seeing the light of day he knew the delight of uncreated things: "Indeed, I remember, it was a moment when everything passed by me and evaporated like a dream. I came from a state of intoxication and happiness to life and

249

its ennui; little by little those dreams I believed I would recapture or earth disappeared like this revery; my heart contracted." It is Satan's place, certainly, to confide in us this way, first because he is an angel because the heavens were his home, and then because his punishment consists of nursing the memory of the celestial abode from which he is forever banished. Yet he doesn't breathe a word of this, not ever negatively; it is as though he were afraid to talk about it—why should this be? Why does Gustave, disguised as Almaroës, allow himsel allusions to the reveries of the golden age that he forbids himsel when he gets inside the skin of the Devil? The reason is simple and permits us to enter further into the author's intentions: Arthur is *guilty of nothing;* God conceived him, manufactured him, and failed Or, rather, He succeeded, alas! The error was in the very conception It is the Almighty who is accountable. The noble victim of the Creator sacrificed to an idiotic plan for perfecting His old, disastrous piece of work rather than scrapping it and beginning again, or, better still taking it back with him into nothingness forever, Almaroës rises up against his Lord. As equal to equal he judges Him, defies Him, and the fierce hatred he bears the Creator in no way differs in its objectivity from a legitimate condemnation pronounced by a constituted body The martyr suffers an aristocratic sorrow; this is his stoicism: having never erred—how could he, an automaton whose cogs and wheels have been put together by the Other in such a way that they can produce only predictable results?—he has nothing to hide. It is to him, therefore, that Gustave entrusts a recollection of the vague ec stasies of his protohistory; in the mouth of the robot, flawless and beyond reproach, the recollections ring like a condemnation of the father. Let us translate. The golden age was the age of raptures and faith; the little boy, under the influence of maternal religious senti ment, believed he had an immortal soul which would one day be united with his dead brothers in paradise. But in such families a little boy at a particular age belongs to his father. Achille-Cléophas inter venes, expounds mechanistic ideology, the bubbles burst—this is pos itivism. Of course, it is only a question of aberrant metaphysics, but Gustave manages to believe it; his former hopes continue to haun him, but he no longer sees them as anything but phantoms. It wil be observed that *Rêve d'enfer* does not contest the fact that the animal machine Arthur is perfect in his way. This suggests that Gustave though not *convinced* of it, does not contest the paternal ideology—i probably *is* the truth, it must be since Father says it, but this truth should not have been spoken. Gustave reacts like a cancer patien who cannot forgive those close to him for telling him of his condition. The young boy's soul was his ignorance; knowledge dissipates it, leaving that dangerous product the body, an aggregate of automatons surrounded by other aggregates. In the "autobiographies" this theme will evolve and become personal and abstract; Gustave will present his disenchantment as an effect of his own experience. But *Rêve d'enfer* is categorical: God the Father, a transparent symbol, is denounced— here is the responsible party.

The profound difference that separates Arthur from Satan resides, we have seen, neither in the essential nature of his frustration nor in its consequences. The Devil, of course, is very wicked; but it should not be thought that Arthur is so good. The former says: "When I see the souls of men suffer like mine . . . it is a consolation . . . for my despair." And of the latter, Flaubert writes: "He who was fallen from such a height . . . loved fallen things, he who was disillusioned yearned for ruins . . . , [he who] had found nothingness in eternity desired destruction in time." I recognize that this text is chiefly concerned with dilapidated castles and that it is less serious to enjoy the view of a fallen stone than to enjoy the sight of a "fallen woman." Still, this *considered* love of an *indestructible* being for "destruction in time" is disquieting. A man too is destroyed in time; who knows if one day, out of boredom, Almaroës won't make up his mind to take a representative of the species and speed up the process of decay? In any case, throughout the novella he preserves an indifference tinged with hostility toward those inferior beings whose physical aspect he has assumed. If Satan differs from Arthur, it is that the fallen angel is *guilty*. Almaroës has fallen from above—the fault is God's. If Satan was cast out of heaven, the fault was his own and everyone knows it. Not that he was being punished for his wickedness; that, as we have seen, came afterward—it is pride or assumed evil. Did he rebel then, as legend has it? Flaubert does not breathe a word on this subject, but it is hardly likely that he imagined an angelic insurrection; revolt was not his forte. No, the Devil is the Devil because he is punished, that is all. Guilt is his essence; obviously that is nothing to boast about. Furthermore, the poor Demon hardly boasts at all—no sooner has he affirmed his pride, urged on by the iron duke, than it is diffused in moans and groans. Clearly he nurses a powerful resentment against his Creator, and the fact is that God does not come out clean in this story; if He is omniscient, he knew of the fault and the punishment *before* pulling the bad angel out of nothingness. But where Almaroës challenges the Demiurge with his

251

insolence, Satan, the cunning, timid, respectful creature, harbors a furtive hatred of the Eternal Father; crushed by a grudging admiration, he even prays to the merciless Author in his troubles. Couldn't it be said that the accursed Demon suffers an incurable love for his executioner? The truth is that his guilt—whoever is responsible for it— makes him ashamed; his infinite hatred is powerless, or rather it is turned against himself, self-punishing, and makes him a masochist. After Almaroës has roundly defeated him, we see him humble, enjoying his defeat almost as a gift: "When he had spent a long time savoring the rattle that escaped from his chest, when he had counted the agonized sighs he could not suppress and that broke his heart, when at last, rallying from his cruel defeat, Satan raised his bowed head to his vanquisher, he saw once again the automaton's cold and impassive gaze which seemed to laugh in its disdain."

It is conceivable that under these conditions the Devil does not want to return to the past. He reflects endlessly on his years of happiness, he dwells on them; if they go unmentioned, it is because his disgrace tears him apart. Humiliation strangles him—he feels condemned for an inadequacy of being. Doesn't he say again and again: I have only the soul! I have only the soul! And certainly this means: I have no body. But also: intelligence made me defective; that is why I did not know how to give pleasure. Or perhaps it was my apathy? Couldn't the absence of a body also be a symbol of Gustave's passivity? No equipment, no tool: praxis is impossible. In short, he has *done* nothing—and for good reason—that might displease the good God; if he displeases, it is through the being that God gave him. A displeasing being, as it were—Satan is forced to recognize it; God being the point of view of the absolute, if He repulses Satan it is because he *is* absolutely repulsive. Furthermore, the argument— valid—that he turns against his creator (why did you make me so that I must deceive you?) is weakened by the fact that *being* is not only in relation to God but in relation to oneself in God. And since he *is* monstrous, his relation to himself is immediate disgust. Yes, for God's sake, when the offense is this deep it must be lived out, or, as we say so aptly these days, it must play itself out; the concrete, the immediate must be *realized and endured* in all its horror. After this *hallucinating* process, which is quite simply called experience, any attempt to thrust responsibility onto the Creator, however justified, can only be a discursive effort, abstract and secondary. Indeed, his *being-object* is what he complains of to God, but what he encounters in a continuous intuition is his very existence; when Flaubert says, much later: "As for me, I do not feel free!" he means that he suffers the being that an internalized Demiurge has given him. So be it. But the way it is suffered, this being (the most passive agent cannot escape it), is by seeing it emerge in the self as if—irrespective of the whole and of the creation ex nihilo—one were continually creating it down to its smallest detail, with the grace of God to sustain it and preserve its bitter or insipid taste. In short the Devil, that pure but scarcely *individuated* subject, "exists" in his self-loathing and, in order to preserve the boundaries of Gustave's Catholic concretism, defines his being-object (conceived as what he was made to be but also as what escapes him, as what is apparent only to the eyes of the Almighty) by what is available to him through his being-subject. Satan, transcended-transcendence, defines the origin of his troubles as his being-for-the-other, that is, his being-other, an ineffable objective guilt. The Prince of Darkness is hardly likely to forget that the God he seeks to condemn ("Why did you make me monstrous?") is the principle of all plenitude and all order, in brief that He is what is true, real, good! If the Demon was made to be condemned, to feel in the disorder of his soul a fathomless hatred, it is because this dissonance was needed for universal harmony. Raging but defeated in advance, he could be said to consider himself the victim of an unjust injustice. When he decides to protest against the evil done to him, he has *already* perceived that this evil is none other than the good and that he lacks the means to oppose the venerable decision that made him its beneficiary. This because the Supreme Being at the core of His luminous essence needs His night side, and this dark side, this absolute but localized evil, reduces both the criminal and the victim—namely him—to impotence.

What is there to do in this case but to desire pitilessly, arrogantly, and *for everything* nonbeing, disorder, vice, and unhappiness? If evil is his empire, the Devil has no other ambition than to extend it. *Condemn* the good? Impossible. But one can try to weaken and subvert it. This maniacal and lachrymose Devil has the ball in his corner—souls are his, abandoned by God. His power over them is absolute. Look at poor Julietta—scarcely has he made his appearance than she wants to run away; in vain: "She could not rise . . . ; she forced herself again but she could not make a move, her iron will was broken before the fascination of this man and his magical power." He knows how to inspire her with love. Unfortunately for the poor soul, the Demon uses his magnetic power only to turn her fascination onto Almaroës—who doesn't give a damn, as we well know. Briefly, the Lord of Darkness loves souls and could make them love him, but he doesn't care about them—he wants only to send them to perdition. Strange solitary passion: to repulse, to break, to destroy, to refuse communication, reciprocity. Highly orthodox, of course—evil is as rigorous as good; enlisted in its service, one desires it alone. Wickedness is as unconditional as goodness and has as its sole purpose the realization of the worst. *Therefore* desire and love are only the means; Satan snivels, but whether he likes it or not he is compelled by his pitiless enterprise. No one can tell us, then, that he finds the leisure to nurse other passions—no hobby for the Devil. In other words, all-powerful even when he is in his empire, when, if he couldn't love at least he could imagine loving and could make himself love for the sake of what is good, enjoying the vast adoration of souls, negativity triumphs. He desires evil as Arthur desires nothingness, and he has only one true wish: to universalize evil and sin. To ensure that his enterprise shall never be deflected, that he shall have no respite, that he shall seek unswervingly and with all his heart to do the greatest evil, to do himself the most harm, he must have the divine concurrence of his blessed Master; a blessing must sustain his impotence, he must in effect have a mandate. Indeed, he does, and he knows it. When he sets himself against providential order to bring about disorder, he is only following his nature, that is, conforming to the essence God gave him. In this sense he is not even the master of his own enterprise, on the contrary, it is the enterprise that possesses and pitilessly maneuvers him. When he "goes from bad to worse," he is bound to accomplish the mission that the Almightly in His goodness has assigned him; doer of low deeds, when he assumes his noxious nature and takes it even further, in this too he is conforming to the designs of the Almighty; by making evil his sole end, a deliberately sought objective, he relieves the Creator of His responsibilities.

Let us translate. Satan is also, above all, Gustave, the frustrated younger brother who at that time willingly called himself wicked. How are we to understand this? As follows: I can love only what is explicitly for the unhappiness of those I love. For Satan loves souls, his subjects; what wouldn't he give to take Almaroës's soul, believing that the robot has one? But he loves them in order to *send them to perdition* and derives his bitter happiness from their eternal misery. This is how I am: pride and envy make me wish a thousand deaths every minute on all the members of my family. I delight in macabre fantasies. True, I do no great evil. At least that is how it seems. For me, in fact, my mental exercises play the role of magical incantations; without hands, without arms, since action is forbidden me—the imaginary misfortunes I heap upon those closest to me have a direct and maleficent influence. This is not what he *says* in *Rêve d'enfer*, but it is what he means. A letter of 1853[21] confirms it:

> A man who has never been to a brothel must also be afraid of hospitals. They are poetries of the same order. He does not see the *moral density* that exists in certain kinds of ugliness. . . . These beautiful exhibits of human misery . . . contain something so raw that it gives the spirit a cannibal's appetites. It rushes to devour them, to assimilate them. With what reveries I have often remained in a whore's bed, looking at her threadbare couch. How I have constructed fierce dramas at the Morgue, which I used to have a passion for visiting, etc.! Furthermore, I believe that in that place I have a faculty of special perception; I am an expert on the unwholesome. You know what an influence I have upon madmen and the singular adventures that have befallen me. I would be curious to know if I have kept my power. . . . Madness and lust are two things I have probed so deeply that I will never (I hope) be either a madman or a de Sade. But it has taken its toll. For example, my nervous disorder was the foam from these little intellectual whims.

Deliberately cultivated inclination toward the "unwholesome, intellectual whims" systematically repeated, "cannibalism" of the mind awakened by the "moral density" of ugliness and misery, fantasies concerning prostitution, illness, and death—here is the *imagination of evil* conceived as an enterprise. We shall note the striking assimilation of lust to sadism: "I have probed lust so deeply" (*in imagination— intellectual whims and no doubt masturbation*) "that I do not risk becoming a de Sade." The adolescent's sexual fantasies are consistent with Satan's platonic loves: to love souls is to damn them; to enjoy a beautiful body is to make it suffer. And above all Gustave would have Louise understand that these exercises had a protective function: he was released through such malicious fantasies, they drained off his resentment. Deliberately toying with madness, he avoided falling into it *for real*. This perpetual exasperation, however, shattered his nerves. Briefly, he is obsessed with rage, he tries to assuage it through an imaginary wickedness which extends to the entire species and does evil to no one. This is the soul, this is the Devil: there is no hint of sexual desire, only the memory of an ancient frustration, reawakened humiliations feeding the desire to bite, to claw, to kill, a sadism sat-

21. To Louise Colet, 7–8 July 1853.

255

isfied by terrifying "rêves d'enfer," dreams of hell. The consciousness of his guilt, the original cause of his fall, no longer leaves Gustave and, on the contrary, heightens a masochism which runs through all his tales. This masochism, more radical than that of the Marquis, structures every plot in such a way that the awful criminal is just and *right*, while the innocent victim, more profoundly, is guilty and deserves to be punished by the vile torments that afflict him.

Nevertheless, we have seen that the other Gustave, the iron duke, can hold his head high and look his Father in the eye. It must be acknowledged, of course, that he too is a loser by accepting the dismaying philosophy he is administered. The Father is just when he punishes the Devil; when he disillusions Almaroës, he is truthful. Truthful? Not altogether, however; he wanted to deprive his creature of a soul and did not perceive that the soul is none other than this privation. Above all, Arthur is a flawless monster, and his good Lord cannot deny His responsibilities, although the immense plenitude of being that is cosmic materiality leaves room only for a phantom negativity, for a dream of frustration. How is it that these two incarnations of Flaubert should be, from this point of view, so different? How is it that he should have told his *entire* history from birth to the Fall twice in the same story, the first time claiming his innocence, the second pleading his guilt? On the one hand Gustave is a learned heap of "stupid" atoms; he was given material energy, the present moment, and eternity. If his actual existence goes a bit beyond the initial plan, if he possesses a phantom soul, if he has memories, if matter in his case is haunted by memory, it is certainly not his progenitor's fault. On the other hand, here he is, provided with a history by a moment of divine anger, irreversible, indelible, the Fall; through historicity he escapes abstraction, his soul is a memory wholly mobilized by meditating on a family incident and by the bitter consciousness of a fault for which he is pardonable without ever having committed it. Historicity, atemporality of the mechanistic moment: two poles, two "incoherent" interpretations of the same existence. It would seem, then, that Gustave must choose one or the other. Yet, he is so far from choosing that he *links them* in the same narrative and displays each interpretation in the features of one character in conflict with the other. So? Guilty or not guilty? What does he decide?

Nothing. This "fantastic tale" comes to no conclusion. Obviously Satan can do nothing against Almaroës, but what can Almaroës do against Satan? The fisher of souls will fish for the soul of Julietta under the mournful eye of his old adversary, after which he will resume his jeremiads; the automaton, however, will resume his alchemical labors and his solitary walks; apart from the death and damnation of a young girl, nothing has happened. Rather, nothing *could* happen. In the light of later stories, however, one can interpret this and look for a meaning in Gustave's indecision. It is certain, in fact, that Flaubert projected himself simultaneously into two characters because it did not seem possible to portray himself in only one. It even seems likely to me that Satan was introduced along the way, when Almaroës appeared incapable of embodying *all* of Gustave, especially his guilt and resentment. We are dealing here with a typical doublet: the author is wholly the original character and wholly the spun-off double as well. This *dual* structure of the narrative is characteristic of a profound alienation; the author, inhabited by the Other, tries to resist the internal division that threatens him by reestablishing in his writings a unifying bond between his ego and his alter ego. But in considering *Quidquid volueris* and *Passion et Vertu*, we perceive that the doublet is itself *doubled*. In other words, each half of the pairs "Djalioh/Monsieur Paul" and "Mazza/Ernest" involves two characters, only one of which represents the author.

Yet Monsieur Paul corresponds to Arthur as much as Djalioh does to Satan. Is he not a "marvel of civilization"? Unquestionably he has been deprived of a soul; when the anthropoid rapes and murders his wife almost before his very eyes, Monsieur Paul preserves the same calm that Almaroës displays when Satan thrusts his claw into Julietta's throat. On the other hand, Monsieur Paul is a scientist; he explores the world and, by means of an inspired experiment, reproduces this creature—so useful to science—who falls midway between the simian and the human. Knowledge and praxis, perfect insensitivity: these are the chief features of Almaroës. Yet Monsieur Paul—a hybrid composed of Achille-Cléophas, Achille, and the Parisian dandies who dine at Tortoni's—has nothing more in common with Gustave than the comical experiment that made Monsieur Paul Gustave's progenitor. Why does Gustave refuse to recognize himself in this pearl of culture? He doesn't say, but it is obvious: Monsieur Paul has no soul *but he does not suffer for it*. Quite to the contrary, its absence makes his life easier; far from stifling his desire for the things of this world, it allows him the joys of vanity. Djalioh's creator has a good head; logical connections are solidly anchored in him; when necessary, he knows how to act. Still, he is only a robot. In writing *Rêve d'enfer*, Gustave sustained a profound—but untruthful—conception of knowledge which could occur only to a lost, passive child considering science

257

from the outside. If being is only matter, if strict laws regulate the materiality of the cosmos such that everything has its sufficient cause outside itself in some maker himself conditioned externally, if being is no more than this for men, those singular accretions of materiality, if, for them, knowledge appears when psychological determinism is discovered by chance to reinforce logical necessity, and if this knowledge is nothing other than natural law itself such as the confluence of determinism and necessity allows man to represent for himself through the determination of a brain, then consciousness, like other facts of the universe, is strictly a product of the laws of nature, primarily those which, like Newtonian mechanics, regulate systems in movement from without. The homogeneity of consciousness and that which is known is such that the supposed procedures of the scientist are manipulated within him from without by the totality of natural sequences. In other words, science is no autonomous quest for truth; it must be seen as the entire universe transforming itself within a brain into a representation of itself. Scientific intelligence, far from being a quest, a desire, an appeal, fuses with the pure movement of matter; if the circumstances are such that all foreign admixture is prevented by the concatenation of psychic determinations, the scientist's thoughts—external to themselves—are nothing other than the universe itself being realized by "logical connections" through a microcosm rendered by external factors—by the systematic repression of pathos and instinct—as stupid and unyielding matter, the very matter of which it is made. Or, if you will, if mechanistic monism is real, knowledge in man is nothing more than the pure movement of materiality delivered to itself by the suppression of all dreams. It is this conception—assimilating the logical connections to the laws of nature and, at the core of a rigorous monism, making knowledge the equivalent of naked materiality—that allows Gustave, beginning with *Rêve d'enfer*, to assimilate Arthur's superhuman understanding to the "stupidity" of matter. Reading the paragraphs I have cited one could readily charge him with inconsistency, but nothing is farther from the truth. He is logically consistent with himself and with the father's mechanistic philosophy as well: if knowledge is not constituted through a synthetic and practical surpassing of the knowable, the subjectivity of the experimenter must be immediately eliminated in order to allow empirical associations and logical connections to be developed like a bit of matter ruled by its own external laws. Being and knowledge are identical. But taking this line he ends fatally by considering that pure intelligence—a material system determined by external causes—can be assimilated to the densest sort of stupidity. We shall see that this stupidity is, first of all, the invasion of the mind by the weight of the commonplace. But what is more ridiculous, to open oneself to proverbs and proverbial locutions, the tag ends of universal wisdom, or to abandon oneself to one's own weight and the mind to its pure materiality, to the physical forces that will mechanically and predictably produce in it knowledge, that is, universal matter representing itself? We shall understand later that Gustave considers Monsieur Homais an intelligent man—the only intelligent man in the novel, apart from the fleetingly glimpsed Dr. Larivière— and at the same time a perfect idiot, a worthy counterpart of the abbé Bournisien; the priest is abandoned to base material needs, but Homais has turned his brain into an adding machine. Can the dilemma be escaped, stultification by the body or by the intelligence? It cannot. Yet it can. By a single means: dissatisfaction. We know very well that this negative movement, this disconnection cannot find its source in the plenitude of being. Nor should we imagine that it could *act* on the materiality it challenges through its simple endurance—it would need *real* claws to change reality. *Nor does the negative principle bring deliverance*; since Achille-Cléophas has spoken the truth, salvation has no meaning. It gives us value. That is all. Almaroës is no more sympathetic than Satan (we shall see that *never*, save in two instances, do the characters who embody Gustave awaken our sympathy; that is his choice). But he *is as good* as the queen of souls; beyond the indestructible power and obtuse inertia of his thought, governed from without, pure block of materiality, a soul is born to him—a fragile despair. What is this despair? A humble, allusive denial; is there *another* truth? Difficult to believe. There would have to be another Demiurge, more powerful, who would make a fool of ours. Or perhaps an effect without a cause—the Flaubert effect. Matter would be fissured by an invisible fault, if only because the plenitude of material being cannot represent itself without a fundamental relation to some lack.

But nothing is explained in *Rêve d'enfer*; Flaubert says simply: this duke, fierce and eternal, is myself. In fact, it is not altogether him. At this period Gustave was certainly not distinguished by his excellence in the exact sciences. Arthur is actually what Gustave is afraid of becoming. There have been the conferences with the father, the patient articulation of a philosophy which depoeticizes the world by reducing it to what it is; the younger brother is crushed. Almaroës's rage at the discovery that he is in reality a material system serves only to translate the young author's just indignation. And then, no doubt he dreamed about his career, and his father must have vaunted the scientific profession. Gustave is horrified by that prospect, for to be a man of science is to compound his own materiality. It isn't enough to know that one is an accretion of molecules and conditioned down to the least options; one ought to have no interest in anything other than molecules and, divesting oneself of one's sensibility, apply oneself to being only a precision machine produced by the blind universe and conditioned by it to manufacture knowledge; better still, *to be* knowledge, that is, cosmic determinism representing itself in its universality at the expense of all singularity. As a doctor, would Gustave lose his soul? He was worried about it, and this is one of the meanings of *Rêve d'enfer*. Perhaps too these philosophical conversations made him feel—in spite of his resentment—some warmth for Achille-Cléophas, that rigorous and—in his son's eyes—omniscient surgeon whose positivism did not protect him against a deep moroseness, fits of anger, and even fits of weeping. In this case, Arthur should also be seen as an embellished portrait of the paterfamilias: he is only a collection of atoms, a machine for making knowledge, he knows it, he says it with pride and perhaps he weeps—could he have a soul? It is useful, moreover, to recall that around this period the positivist philosophy of the credulous Flaubert did not conflict with the cynicism of Alfred Le Poittevin. The doctor no doubt presented his mechanistic views without pathos; this is simply the way things are. He could draw only one conclusion: that morality is a fraud, which scarcely disturbed either his intimates or his clients since he was "virtuous by nature." But on Thursdays, Alfred amused himself by taking up the same ideas; they did not precisely correspond to his thoughts, as we shall see, but he entertained them for several hours, several months, practicing his nihilism. His young friend would leave these discussions appalled. In Alfred's mouth the colorless positivism of Achille-Cléophas became a horrible negation of everything; Alfred is the one who showed Gustave "nothingness in eternity." For this reason I am inclined to think that in creating the "Almaroës/Satan" pair, Gustave intended to air the slight reservations of an unhappy and disturbed adolescent with respect to the summary and universal executions Le Poittevin performed each week with such brilliance and alacrity. It is as if he were saying to Alfred: "You are free to strip me of my last reasons for living, you have the strength, you have the ideas, the logical connections. But as for me, I am only a frustrated child. Your reasons for despair are universal and joyous. Doubtless you curse God. But that's for having created the world. As for me, I am unhappy without knowing why, because of my intolerable singularity." This last conjecture would explain why Flaubert, who in the other stories— *Passion et Vertu* excepted—portrays himself in a rather pathetic light, adorns Almaroës who is his creature and his incarnation with such superhuman qualities: Almaroës is also the Alfred he loves, whom he would like *to be* but thinks he will never have the strength to follow to the end.

In sum, Almaroës appears to be the inorganic Gustave that the father's philosophy of mechanism and Alfred's nihilism[22] prompt him to conceive, awakening in this child, who has need of faith because his passivity disposes him to belief more than to knowledge, a disillusioned and permanent horror which is nothing other than his soul. It is the same Gustave, fascinated by the chief surgeon's glory, who tried one last time to follow his career and was terrorized by the pure *exteriority* that the man of science must embrace in order to allow the movement of the external to be developed in him; and it is still Gustave appearing to himself as in a dream with the terrible qualities he admires in Alfred, yet simultaneously struck by his own inferiority (Alfred "has ideas"; as for me, I can only feel), which he asserts with a surge of pride as what might be called his negative superiority. At the same time, the robot suffering from his automatism presents a dreamlike image of the father saved by his anxiety and the demonic power of the magnificent and disquieting friend, whose perfect suicidal nonchalance can also be symbolized by Arthur's anorexia. But it is also true that this fantastic character, in whom the author wanted to contain and telescope several possible variations on his being between these two extremes, the father and the friend, represents for Flaubert his own anorexia as well. It is Gustave who does not succeed in sharing human aims, who has no desire for the things of this world and for this reason feels in his malaise different from all the others, yet cannot confront them, in arrogance, with an ego that is *the same as the self*. It is Gustave in the character of Almaroës who tastes the insipidity and the false plenitude of being, it is Gustave who is overcome by ennui with no compensation but the increasingly rare, vague ecstasies his Creator had not foreseen. Finally, it is Gustave who imagines himself as an automaton, in other words a child of man conceived and brought into the world in order to accomplish, no

22. In the event these allusions to Le Poittevin should appear obscure and without justification, I refer the reader to the chapter that deals with the relationship between the two friends.

261

matter what he might do, a prefabricated destiny. Automaton today, anthropoid tomorrow: two different symbols alluding to the same deep wound.

These efforts to *construct* Almaroës prompted the author to associate him with Satan. The young author's malaise doesn't allow him to enter into his character completely; what will he do with his terror in the face of his friend's paradoxes, with the crushing afflictions that send him to his bed, sometimes inert, rigid with despair, and at other times bellowing, sobbing, battling his phantoms like one of the damned? With the envy, the dark jealous ambition that torments him? With the infinite, unsatisfied desire? Almaroës can adequately embody Gustave's stoicism and his anorexia. But he doesn't give expression to Gustave's vast, bulimic soul, which would like to devour the universe. Above all, Gustave conceives himself to be a singular adventure, a history; we know that on this point he is a committed Pascalian. Yet in spite of some allusions to Almaroës's supposed *past*—allusions that are completely inconsequential, as we have seen—it is impossible for him to introduce into the temporalization of a destiny the instantaneity of materiality as mechanistic ideology presents it to him. An oracular child, his anguish is historical to the extent that, for him, history is prophetic. Prophetic time—"the worst is to come, that's certain, it is on its way; each moment is more intolerable than the one before, which allows us to foresee the exquisite torture that will be achieved by annihilation"; this is what he needs, this is what the mechanical system named Arthur cannot give him. The automaton, if you like, is prefabricated, but destiny is missing, that is, a temporality based on a cumulative memory. For this reason, as we have seen, he can be known in the abstract like a clock.

The Devil, in a sense, has no more history now than the duke, since he is condemned for eternity to the same unhappiness. However, his history *has happened*: he enjoyed divine favor and then lost it. And the soul of Satan is nothing more than the perpetual pondering of this historic drama, which continually revives it; thereby this sacred mystery, the glory of the Fall, is always becoming temporal.[23] It is at once the archetypal event to which all the thoughts of the unhappy creature refer and, in the moment he is thrust into his past, a concrete repetition through remorse and resentment of the temporal movement that gave him a taste of the joys of heaven, only to deprive him of those joys for eternity. In other words, the remembrance of paradise

23. Satan renews it each time he claims a soul.

lost is itself in dynamic movement: Satan renews his fall by thinking about it; this means that grace and disgrace in their contradiction and their temporal unity are the permanent determinations of this soul. A fall that is unending—in the present case this means not continually accelerated downfall but the indefinite return of the same event; Satan's despair is not a fixed state but a continually renewed process (everything was so beautiful, I felt so happy, so proud! Second time: why was it necessary, etc., etc.). Not that the Devil passes without respite from hope to despair—although some of his remarks indicate that he is not immune (unlike Almaroës) to the temptation of hope; "God will allow himself to relent, one day I shall be pardoned," he thinks, even if he reproaches himself later for the "baseness" of having succumbed. But with every beat of his heart he must begin again the intolerable recollection of former joys (already poisoned by the knowledge of what followed) in order to proceed from this, in shame and rage, to the sudden consciousness of his damnation.

In a word, Satan is pure memory, inaccessible, closed around old griefs in contemplation of which he exhausts himself. He is also a question without an answer. I have said that remorse and resentment do battle within him, meaning that he forever wonders, bewildered, what crime he has committed. Not for a moment does Gustave/Satan plead innocence—the paterfamilias is never entirely condemned nor is his judgment ever attributed to caprice. In the same way, Gustave/Arthur never dreams of questioning the paternal philosophy. But just as he reproaches the chief surgeon for having told him the truth—a position of weakness, beaten from the start—so the Demon, without denying that he is at fault, bears a grievance against God for having punished him. The Eternal Father did not remember that He had once loved His angel; He did not think that in the name of that love, still so vivid, He could pardon the offender. Or else, granting that all sin must be punished, He struck the guilty party too harshly and withdrew, leaving him shame as his portion, shame and the terrible knowledge of his existential inadequacy. Satan symbolizes this questioning and rancorous guilt; the character imposed himself on the young author in order that he might articulate in an allusive fashion his dark musings on predestination. This memory, shut like an oyster, lives on in the present only in order to re-present the past. Deplorable victim of an atrocious and sacred justice, he has been punished, properly speaking, by the inequity of the bountiful God. In other words, recrimination strips him of the power to enjoy the present. However, as we have seen, Satan professes to be prey to infinite and insatiable

263

desires; only the lack of organs, he tells us, makes him deficient. He is boasting. In actuality, he affects imaginary desires because he desires to desire. And why should he want this? In order to wrench himself away from the ponderings that tear him apart, from the grip of the past, from that retrospective passion which makes him advance backward, his eyes fixed on a childhood lost forever. In order to deny his anomaly, "to be like the others," to savor present pleasures, to be in the world, to live in the present. Still more, to negate the deep, narrow circle in which his passions revolve, to set against the iron collar of his finitude—heavier for him than for anyone else since it is nothing but the corrosive memory of an archetypal event—the immense abyss of his unreal desire for everything, that is, for the infinite. These remarks will have to be kept in mind when we study the imaginary structures of experience in Flaubert. For the moment, let us confine ourselves to observing that this driven, morose, fierce, and wretched adolescent wants to take, and refuses to give himself, the freedom to desire, to love, in a word to live. The family besieges him and occupies him, he cannot see beyond it; he harps on his grievances, and when he wants some respite he can only *dream boldly* against the narrow destiny planned for him, which he already prophesies.

From *Rêve d'enfer* to *Quidquid volueris* Flaubert's spirit changes: he preserves his feeling of inferiority, but his remorse diminishes in direct proportion to the growth of his resentment. The progenitor loses the sacred aura he preserved even in his inequity—he was God, he becomes Monsieur Paul. This robot no longer has anything in common with Gustave. Djalioh himself is subhuman as a result of defective intelligence—this, Gustave thinks, is surely what would have disgusted my father. But he soon shifts aggressively to the counterattack. (1) The poor anthropoid is "really inferior" in the area of logic. But the guilt that tormented Satan has given way to the monster's feeling of innocence; Gustave says straight out to his father: "I am what you made me; you alone are responsible." (2) In the opposition between logic and sensibility, Flaubert clearly states his disgust for the former and his preference for the latter; he might hesitate for a moment, but now his choice is made: he will be a poet. I am not proposing that there may have been a conversion or even a sudden and definitive decision after much vacillation; let us simply say that his awareness of himself deepened, that he repressed his shame, that he stifled his heartfelt cries of guilt and consolidated his catalogue of antivalues, the soul and evil, beauty as the choice of unreality. And then, he sets in motion his drama of infinite desire; Satan becomes Djalioh, who in turn becomes Mazza. Mazza the damned, whose passions churn and who is also fixated on a magnificent past that will never return, but whose bitter regret, instead of being directed toward a lost childhood, is aimed daringly at the sensual pleasures she enjoyed with Ernest. In *Passion et Vertu* the soul has continued to be memory and frustration, but it has acquired what it was lacking in *Rêve d'enfer* by becoming insatiable desire. We have seen above by what sleight of hand Gustave was able to preserve vast regret for the infinite and represent it by that very nostalgia that devours a woman's sex; he is indeed convinced, in a highly Christian fashion, that through each of its parts, the creation is desired as a whole, and beyond it the Creator. Therefore he will be inclined to defend his anorexia by claiming that the tender love he bears the whole world is exclusive of any particular lust (thus Djalioh, before the onset of jealousy—which is his Fall—bears Adèle the luminous and calm affection that he has for everything in the cosmos), or to magnify his most singular desires by declaring that they are addressed to God—absent, hidden or nonexistent—through his creatures, and that those desires will remain as such forever unsatisfied. The accent, then, is on the subjective. Ernest, a pale copy of Monsieur Paul who is himself a degraded Almaroës, is not intrinsically worth a moment of regret, but the Great She-Devil Mazza loves in him nothing less than the cosmos that produced him; for her he is just a pretext. The fire in her belly which is her grandeur comes from herself alone.

At the time of writing *Rêve d'enfer*, Gustave was more sincere and more vulnerable. Between Almaroës the anorexic and Satan with his phony lust, he hesitates. If he created the second, it is because he was ashamed of an apathy for which he was undoubtedly reproached; if he made the first triumph, it is also because he was proud of that apathy. From this point of view the battle between the two monsters is of great interest. Obviously it is inspired by the first part of *Faust*. As is the central idea, the temptation, which appears here for the first time and which will become one of our author's chief themes. It should not be viewed, however, as a simple, unoriginal imitation. The two protagonists in *Rêve d'enfer* are both incarnations of Gustave, and he is conscious of this in a more or less muddled fashion;[24] thus the particular flavor of this fantastic tale comes from the fact that Gustave dramatizes his own temptation and fails, not by excess but by default. If we set aside the "damnation," which is here only a fashionable hyperbole—besides, Almaroës is already damned since his Creator made him the gift of eternal despair—what remains is that a certain younger brother, made spiteful by family troubles, sets out to arouse desire—in its most immediate and most profound form—in the jaded son of a surgeon with mechanistic views, and he does not succeed.

No conclusion, as I said. Now we know why. The Demon cannot tempt Almaroës—to arouse desires the tempter would have to be capable of feeling them himself. Yet this is impossible, he is too *mobilized*; were he more accessible, furthermore, he would lose his grief—Almaroës does not attribute enough importance to himself to take his desires seriously. What *Rêve d'enfer* is lacking is the theory of the great desire which Gustave will later formulate with the utmost insincerity. The consequence of this lack is the author's anxiety, the quasi-sincerity with which he states his problems without offering solutions. *I am two persons,* he thinks. And he says: it is impossible for me to be Satan and Almaroës at the same time, those two incoherent principles. In fact, as we have seen, the two monsters are not so different: both are in despair, therefore both have souls; both can act on matter, therefore both have bodies. The incoherence cannot be conceived as an *internal* irreducibility of their natures; rather it comes from without, it is the environment that produces at times one, at times the other: Gustave is Satan *in the family*, he is Almaroës *in society* and in relation to the things of this world. What indicates that he is actually the dialectic unity of each one is that in fact—and in spite of what the young

---

24. We shall have to examine later what *incarnation* means for the young Gustave. But the reader has understood by now that the adolescent, while continually tormented by the same problems and writing only to find solutions to them, *never* deliberately intended to portray himself; the characters he invents, the situations he puts them in are never simple disguises for the author. Or, if they are, the adolescent is not entirely aware of it and never *intended* it. He frequently believes that the story he invents has seduced him by its richness or its pathos. Everything depends upon the subject, the inspiration, the moment—at best a thin, half-translucent film separates him from his protagonists; in other cases, like Hegel's consciousness he is projected, objectified, alienated, and *does not recognize himself* in what is only his external re-presentation. The basic but implicit motif of each narrative, then, is the desire to see himself as Other— that is, as the others see him—for the simple reason that he takes his being-other for his truth. But in the very conception of this Other, a stranger, the fundamental intention is immediately altered and this stranger *represents* the self as an unfathomable opacity.

author believes—when he feels he is Almaroës, he does not for all that cease being Satan at heart. This is because his father's philosophy is only a secondary factor in his anorexia, the primary one being his very old disgrace. It is because they made him Satan that he became Almaroës.

The Creator, furthermore, has reunited these two principles at least once. Between his first production, the soul, and the last word of creation, the machine, he created that composite being, man. The systematic young author does not forget to introduce a representative of our species into his narrative. This example of God's work, we suspect, is not a success. As Satan says, Julietta is "a little more than a tree, a little less than a dog." Her function is to represent passion. In the beginning, of course, there is innocence, still waters. But from the moment Satan possesses her, Julietta begins to suffer. "Like one of the damned." Read for yourself:

> There was such passion in those cries, in those tears, in that chest heaving tumultuously, in that weak and ethereal being who dragged herself on her knees along the ground; all this was so far removed from a woman's cries over a piece of broken porcelain, from the bleating of sheep, from the bird's song, from the barking of dogs that Arthur stopped, looked at her for a moment, and then continued on his way.
>
> "Oh Arthur, have mercy and listen a moment! How I love you, I love you! Oh, come with me, we will go away and live together far from here, or look, we will kill ourselves together . . ."
>
> She fell on her knees at his feet, rolling onto her back as though she were going to die. She was dying, indeed, from exhaustion and fatigue, she writhed in despair and tried to tear her hair out, and then she sobbed with a forced laugh, tears choking her voice; her knees were lacerated and covered with blood, for she loved with a lacerating, total, Satanic love, this love forever consumed her, it was furious, surging, exalted.

Unlike Marguerite, Julietta will never know plenitude, she is obliged to love the one among all creatures who cannot love her. When I say she is obliged, I do not question the volition of Satan— for whom the poor girl is only a means of condemning Almaroës— but that of Flaubert himself, who will much later observe that two lovers never love each other *at the same time* and that one of the two always suffers for love. In any event, this savage passion will never pass beyond the state of *privation*. Seeing her writhing and sobbing on the ground, we recognize in Julietta a familiar figure: the child of sixteen seems to be a first draft of Mazza; she has her violence and splendid boldness. Alone on a cliff, she waits for Almaroës as her younger sister will soon wait for Ernest to return. He comes, she lies down on top of him: "She pressed herself against his chest, she covered him with her kisses and her caresses, he remained calm beneath the embraces, cold beneath the kisses. Here was a woman wasting with ardor, squandering all her passion, her love, her poetry, her intimate and consuming fire to awaken the lethargic body of Arthur, who remained insensible to her burning lips, to her convulsive arms."[25] In short, she persists in vain, he remains impotent beneath her caresses—out of indifference—and she remains a virgin to his forbidding body. As for the "intimate and consuming fire," Gustave will localize it more precisely in *Passion et Vertu*.

All conclusions are therefore prevented. Three creatures—two curse the Creator and the third prostrates herself stupidly before him without avoiding damnation in this world and the next. A trinity of incarnations: if you have only a body, you will know nothing of desire; if you have only a soul, you will be merely an eternal resentment; if you have both, you will suffer hell and your miseries will be strictly in proportion to the strength of your passions. A trinity of equally impossible attitudes: stoicism engenders ennui, revolt is crushed in shame, love leads to despair. In other words, there is no *tenable* attitude. What Gustave seeks to prove in this philosophical tale is the impossibility of existence for a conscious being. Existence, in effect, manifests itself as unbearable pain and by the same token is sooner or later suppressed.

Gustave exists, however; he *holds on*. If he thinks and feels what he writes, why doesn't he burst with rage and suffering? Let us come back to the character of Julietta. By what he reveals and above all by what he conceals, Gustave instructs us on the sensibility and duplicities of the adolescent. In Julietta—as in Mazza later on—passion is aroused. Still, we shall be given to understand that Ernest's mistress has a strong capacity for pleasure and that the seducer has only to awaken it. As for Arthur's timid lover, *did she have sensual feelings at all?* We shall never know, since the Demon's artifice is based on suggestion, hypnotism: "It was surely a love inspired by hell, with its

25. We note Almaroës's position: he is lying on his back, indifferent, inactive. It is the woman who is stretched out on top of him, who manipulates him, caresses him and with her hand or her mouth tries to spark his ardor. Gustave describes here, not without pleasure, the erotic posture that best suits his passivity and revives maternal manipulations. We shall discuss this later.

extravagant cries, the fire that lacerates the soul, *consumes the heart*; a satanic passion, utterly *convulsive and unnatural*, so strange it seemed bizarre, so powerful it ended in madness."[26] The emphasis here is on the parasitic nature of the feeling: far from producing it spontaneously, the soul is infected by it from without, the feeling feeds on the soul, which suffers it like a mortal illness. At the same time these quite vivid impressions are in some way suspect. Indeed, everything that comes from the Devil is inconsistent by nature: money, when he gives it away, is transformed into dead leaves. It could be said that these pangs of love are at once unbearable burnings and utter pretense—*they lack substance*. And the Other in Julietta embellishes this insufficiency by the extravagant cries she utters on command, by the convulsions into which she is thrown. This intolerable and phantom pain is felt by the bewitched girl only with its exaggeration—it is a game to some degree, but she cannot help playing it. She must continually *strain*, throw herself immoderately at another, shift from gesticulation to paralysis and from paralysis to gesticulation in order to conceal from herself the insufficiency of feeling. There is no doubt that Gustave is describing here his personal experience: he is the one who is complaining of suffering too much and at the same time not enough, he is the one who scrutinizes his sensations and who declares them to be "so strange they seem bizarre." At this last turn of phrase the reader is tempted to laugh. Wrongly. Like all the false naïvetés swarming in Flaubert's early works, it has a precise meaning. It is as if the author had written "*such strangers*," wishing to imply here the *otherness* of experience. The nature of diabolical sufferings is such that they are more created than suffered and that one *is constrained by oneself* to create them. But the *alter ego* which constrains is other than the panting ego exhausted by its sudden leaps. It is as if infernal love were a *forgery*, a hallucination of the sensibility, an exasperation of the emotional conduits. Is Flaubert trying to describe an instance of autosuggestion? We cannot decide for the moment. But in any event we do not doubt that the possessed suffer. To progress further we must continue our reading.

Repulsed, then, Julietta abandons herself to despair. Not for long: "Despair had given way to dejection, wild cries to tears; no more outbursts, deep sighs, but sounds spoken so low they lingered on the lips, for she feared that in crying out she would die. Her hair was white, for unhappiness had aged her; it is like time: short-lived, it

26. My italics.

weighs heavy and hits hard." What curious prudence in this desperate girl—she restrains herself from crying out for fear of dying. True, she has grown old. From unhappiness. As we have already seen, this is only one of time's contradictions: the more intense it is, the less it needs to be prolonged; infinite, it crushes its victim in a moment, the result being that if she still lives, she no longer suffers. The character of Julietta is of keen interest since Gustave is embodied in her as well. As Satan, as Almaroës, he speaks of his suffering and its causes; as Julietta he *describes* that suffering, he tries to give us the flavor of this *experience*. Yet the emphasis is *on the gesture*—tears, sighs, whispers. To cry out is to suffer, perhaps to die; stop crying out and you no longer feel; to restrain yourself from crying out is to be calmed *inside*. The dejection that follows despair suggests some kind of sinister ataraxia based on the anorexia of old people, a strange confusion of experience with its signs. At the outset, this unhealthy and unnatural passion manifested itself by shrieks and convulsions, as if Julietta sought to compensate for some kind of insufficiency of her pain by the exaggerated violence of the *physical* agonies that express it. One would swear that Flaubert, after some bitter vexation, took refuge in his room and in his solitude found himself constrained to mimic (but not without some secret witness—we shall see that he felt permanently *visible*) the emotion by which he believed he was affected. Everything begins, then, with a crisis of possession: he falls, struggles, starts, throws his arms and legs in every direction, shrieks, if he is sure of not being heard, and if not borrows Satan's panting or Julietta's sighs. The result is an immediate aging, by which we understand that he is worn out; once exhausted, he plays dead and has no more strength to feel; out of breath, he is even unable to cry out. And then? Well, he revives, dejected but calmed: the flood tide has ebbed, ennui flows on again, fragile and disheartening. Did he lie to himself, then? Did he play out the drama of suffering without one moment of real pain? I don't believe this is so. An objective and complex relationship of the child with his family constitutes the original situation; this situation is structured such that Gustave is simultaneously produced and rejected, or rather he is forever produced and reproduced as an outcast in his own eyes. It is, in a sense, an abstract structure of the "social unit"; and yet the child rediscovers it as the general meaning of his existence beneath every concrete disgrace, each attempted aversion. In a wounding remark by his irritated father Gustave recognizes his original unhappiness. He recognizes it but without much understanding; it is this, nevertheless, this "primal scene," that makes the paternal rebuff unbearable to him—the rebuff would slide right over him, leaving no trace, if it did not seem to him a symptom of his consuming pain, of the "obscure disaster" that made him what he is. Transfixed, all he can do is bring the catastrophe to mind, explore it and be penetrated by it, comprehend it in the past *and in the present* as the permanent meaning of experience. But out of a similar impulse, gripped by fear, dreading to discover once and for all that the primary determination of his being is none other than the paternal curse, he tries to escape it. To deny it? Impossible, his rancor is too strong, too vigilant; it is not even a question of concealing it from himself, since a short time before, in *La Peste à Florence*, he spoke about it openly. What is he to do then but immerse himself in the expression of his pain to the point of transforming it into a role? He plays at suffering so as not to suffer any more—cries and gesticulations divert him from the suffering they are supposed to signify; he exerts himself to the point of exhaustion. His aim? Since he cannot escape his disastrous destiny and since he takes pride in tearing himself apart—as his resentment also requires—he will act in such a way that his misery, pushed to its limit (meaning, in fact, energetically imitated) is transformed into gloomy indifference. The pseudo-internalization of the intolerable is in fact only an externalization pushed to the extreme, which in the first place diverts the young martyr and in the second tires his suffering, in the sense that we say a salad is tired. This is flight in advance. Strange behavior: a truly unhappy person suffers insincerely. We should not be astonished, however; one can die of sorrow, but no one suffers without faking.

Sometimes Gustave's gymnastics are inadequate. How could he admit to himself that he uses them to calm down, he who "does not want to be consoled"? He must establish that insensitivity is worse than pain. This is what is served by the myth of old age. Indefinitely repeated torments, Flaubert tells us, become less and less painful, but this progressive anesthesia is not a lesser evil—on the contrary, since it results from decrepitude. It is not a matter of habit; the tortures inflicted escape our clear consciousness in order to run through the organism and little by little dry up our sources of life. The summation of unhappiness is death by erosion, the radical abolition of the condemned; old age, that incapacity to feel, prefigures it. Thus poor Julietta has grown old at sixteen, before dying of love. Thus the unfortunate Gustave, when choked by rancor and rage, takes a little drop of old age to get out of trouble. But it isn't enough to play out the drama, one must be capable of taking it seriously. Gustave maintains that he is flayed alive and that nothing is worse than his fate. At the same time he is conscious that his sufferings—in part due to his own precautions—are not commensurate with his objective unhappiness. One of the functions of aging will be to fill the void that separates the two: the body comes to take the place of the soul, hence the adolescent can witness his torments to the exact extent he is spared from feeling them; still, he has to believe. Here we find the first occurrence of a major theme: autosuggestion. Senescence is only a verbal solution *unless* Gustave feels it in his bones, unless he endures it each time not as a passing fatigue but as a somatization of his psychic pain.

Rêve d'enfer is a systematic act of accusation. The accused is God; pseudonym: Achille-Cléophas. His first crime is that while he demands love and is lovable as well, he drives those who love him to despair. The unfortunate Julietta learns this by sad experience. This creature is naturally good; she worships her Creator; in the depths of despair she rejects the idea of suicide in order not to displease him:

> She believed in God and did not kill herself. It is true that she would often contemplate the sea and the cliff, a hundred feet high, and then would begin to smile to herself with a grimace that would have frightened children. Quite mad indeed, to stop before an idea, to believe in God, to respect him, to suffer for his pleasure, to weep for his delight. For you, Julietta, to believe in God is to be happy—you believe in God and you suffer! Oh you must be quite mad!

God in this text is at once an idea—which Achille-Cléophas has destroyed in his son—and a living being, a father one respects. This explains the curious line: "For you, to believe in God is to be happy— you believe in God and you suffer." When he truly thinks about God, Gustave might indeed write that faith brings happiness. But he would add that his father has contrived things so effectively that faith has disappeared forever: "I no longer believe in God and I suffer from it." On the other hand, if the Eternal Father is a stand-in for Achille-Cléophas, the term is correct, for it must be understood that to have a father, to respect him, to suffer for his pleasure, to weep for his delight is to be happy; I have a father and I suffer. This progenitor will be found suspect who delights in his children's tears, even if he makes them happy. But Gustave sees nothing reprehensible in this: he himself would cry with happiness and for the sole pleasure of Dr Flaubert, if only his father would take an interest in him. But he won't, that's the point—Gustave has a father *and* he is unhappy; the progenitor, he thinks, has turned away from him because he reproaches his creature with being what he deliberately made him.

For this is the Almighty's second crime. He is interested only in his own glory and just indulges in a hobby—the universe taken as a whole; he sacrifices his creatures to his plan out of a cruel and idiotic willfulness. Never does he have regard for these creatures taken for themselves as individuals—family planning is everything; each creature receives an essence, the original formula which defines it with respect to all the others and determines the objective it will attain at the price of its happiness and its life. This charming but stubborn Demiurge, malicious and blundering, succeeds only in making himself hated. And his third crime—for stupidity is criminal—is not to have understood that the creation, his hobby, was nothing but a huge wreck, to insist on trying to improve it when it should have been destroyed and, moreover, should never have been undertaken in the first place. Which provokes Satan's final supplication:

> There was a strange cacophony of tears and sobs in the air, it was like the death rattle of the world.
> And a voice rose from the earth and said:
> "Enough! Enough! I have sniveled and suffered too long, enough! Oh, have mercy! do not create another world!"
> And a gentle, pure, melodious voice like the voice of angels was cast upon the earth and said:
> "No! No! this is for eternity, there will be no other world."

Here again, in very explicit form, we find Gustave's horror of fecundity. Isn't it over with? You have ruined us all: Achille, that automaton, and the two others who are dead, and me, the ape man, and my younger brother dead at an early age, and this sister who I know is going to die.[27] Isn't that enough? No? Don't you see, then, that you have never created anything but unhappiness—corpses or fools? For you, each new experiment is merely a capricious, bastard invention, realized in a fit of animal lust; but for the creature you pull out of nothingness it is a cup of bitterness that must be drunk to the

---

27. Several months later he was to write *La Dernière Heure*, a curious work which represents the shift from fiction to autobiography. The hero says "I," as in the *Mémoires*, and before shooting himself he is supposed to review his entire life. So far as one can judge (the work remained unfinished), it is the life of the young Gustave. There is a single but considerable element of fiction: the hero has just lost his sister, whom he adored. Gustave's sister Caroline was in fact in delicate health; he must often have dreamed she would die. In *La Derniere Heure* he kills her, prophetically.

dregs, a capital punishment in which he is both executioner and victim.

To whom is he speaking? The chief surgeon, no doubt; but through him he is condemning life in all its forms. Wherever it comes from it is a mandate for suffering delivered by the cold or sadistic will of a Creator. In short, the reproach is generalized: through his father he is speaking to all fathers. Or, if you will, what inspires him with the most concrete horror is the necessity that man be the son of man, born with an already formulated past and a mortgaged future, appearing in the world as an assemblage of means arranged beforehand to achieve a certain end, which he internalizes and which belongs in him to the Other. This is the meaning of the answer, tinged with black humor, that God gives him: rest assured there will be only one world, this one, for *eternity*. Let us translate: this means a single Flaubert family, no other members but *these* for your entire existence.

The most obvious meaning of *Rêve d'enfer* could be summed up in a single sentence: "I curse the day I was born." Gustave curses that day because he is convinced that a curse is at the origin of his birth; he sees himself and sees his road of misery, he feels behind him the terrible Jehovah who pulled him out of the slime that there might be a man on earth to commit the original sin. Fated to commit an unforgivable error, he is therefore despised by the author of his days and punished in advance, chased out of paradise in advance; he is created for crime and unhappiness—therefore cursed. Gustave is a cursed child: he was made to witness his indigence and to be punished for it by pangs of pride and ambition. In *Rêve d'enfer* he turns the curse back against his Creator.

In November 1836, Gustave was not yet fifteen years old. He had just completed *Biblomanie*; here are the first lines:

> Giacomo the librarian . . . was thirty years old but he already seemed aged and worn; his body was tall but curved like an old man's; his hair was long but white; his hands were strong and nervous but dry and covered with wrinkles . . .; he had an awkward and constrained manner, his face was pale, sad, ugly and even insignificant. This man had never spoken to anyone . . .; he was taciturn and dreamy, sad and morose, he had only . . . one passion—books.

The moment he sees one, he is transformed:

"His eyes lit up . . . he could scarcely contain his joy, his anxieties, his anguish, his pain . . ."

This is not yet the insensible Almaroës—the fire is not out, Gustave burns with passion. The younger son twists and turns like a stick in the flame. . . . Nevertheless, how paltry the furnace seems, for the librarian has everything invested in one mania:

It was not knowledge he loved, it was its form and expression; he loved a book because it was a book, he loved its smell, its shape, its title. What he loved about a manuscript was its old, illegible date, the strange, bizarre gothic letters, the heavy gild-ing that encrusted its illustrations; he loved its pages covered with dust, inhaling their subtle and tender perfume with delight; he loved that charming word *finis* surrounded by two Cupids borne on a ribbon . . . or resting on a basket among roses. . . . He passed in Barcelona for a strange and demonic man, for a sage or a sorcerer.

He scarcely knew how to read.

Hold on! Here is the first specific allusion to the difficulties Flaubert experienced at around the age of seven learning his letters. For this reason, the simpleton's passion is mediocre only in appearance; it refers, I am sure, to a marvelous childhood memory, to the time when Papa Mignot read him *Don Quixote* and the child Gustave mused on the book's beauty. Who doesn't have similar memories? At that age I was reading the works of Jules Verne without much enthusiasm, but I was overwhelmed by the beauty of the red and gold binding, by the pictures, by the gilt-edged pages. We hesitate in the face of this marvelous object: is it only a means of communication? Perhaps, on the contrary, it is the end itself? Perhaps the story told is only a means necessary for producing such formal beauty? For Gustave this mag-nificence contained a mystery—an object of such perfection had *a meaning* as well, it was a message to be deciphered. First of all he encountered the form, which represented itself, and then when Mig-not began to read, he perceived the content, the idea. Not enough attention has been given to this novella, which reveals to us one of the factors of Flaubert's—altogether relative—formalism. For this pro-found but lost little boy who didn't know how to read even after his parents had decided to teach him the alphabet, and who defended himself against their reproof by saying: "Why should I read? Papa Mignot does it for me," the book's meaning first seemed to be a secret beauty that was supplementary to its form. The book was its own affirmation, it was a tangible object, a little piece of architecture that was nearly self-contained. After that, others could extract sentences, a story. *Bibliomanie* proves that he retained this impression. Later, much later, after disappointments, a hundred vicissitudes, this is the impression he will rediscover—except that the object of his craft will present itself as an architecture of words, of transcribed and harmonious sounds, dense and brilliant like a gilded page. We listen to the sounds for their beauty. And through them, unnoticed, we are penetrated by the meaning of the words, a singular and sacred mystery which—unlike any other information—is not separable from the verbal form which expresses it and is only the "afterworld" presented through *those words*. In all likelihood, the beauties "in-octavo" that Mignot leafed through scarcely troubled Gustave in his golden age; they became art objects or rather emanations of celestial beauty, even as they were instruments of entreaty when the little boy understood that he was expected to decipher them and when he felt the malign resistance of their splendid materiality. At that time he loved—painfully—those arrogant pages, facing him with their cruel muteness; it may have been that the unformulated, obscure intention took shape to write for an elite of *illiterate readers*; or rather, more precisely, to transform for a moment the members of this elite into awestruck illiterates by making the beauty of words, of phrases, and of their architecture equivalent to the resistance offered him by printed matter.

But at fourteen he has only sensed the sadism of beauty. What he wants to express simultaneously is his passion and his resentment. The young author's anomaly constitutes the very essence of Giacomo. It is in no way depicted as a state; it is a desire, a privation; it "absorbs him completely" to the point of suppressing—or nearly so—all organic needs, which horrified Gustave. "He scarcely ate, he no longer slept, but he dreamed whole days about his *idée fixe*, books." We note Flaubert's rancor toward knowledge and any form of culture. What Giacomo cherishes in books is the *artificial*. But let us not begin to imagine that he appreciates them as products of human labor, man's will to communicate by signs; Giacomo's perversion (Flaubert presents it as such but sees nothing reprehensible in it) consists of treating these products of human labor as if they were the fruits of the earth and singularly denying the human purpose for which they were made. This parasite of our species steals books even when he buys them honestly, since he diverts them from their true function and collects them like butterflies. A double negation: he prefers *anti-physis* and human creations to nature, on the condition that he can treat them like natural objects having no author and serving no purpose. This is to deny man in his product, to enslave knowledge and human relations to the single function of serving as an inessential pretext for the creation of beautiful but meaningless objects. Giacomo *refuses to be human*, that is, to share our ends; he has chosen one objective that disqualifies all the others and reflects his singularity. After this, it is not at all surprising that the good monk is reputed to be wicked. Certainly he hasn't done anyone any harm, but his passion is in essence malign. And this is not my extrapolation; read the following: "Giacomo had a treacherous and malicious manner." The fact is that he lives like a stranger in our world: "As he went through the streets he saw nothing of all that surrounded him, everything passed before him like some fantasmagoria whose enigma he did not understand, he heard neither the footsteps of passersby nor the noise of wheels on the pavement; he thought, he dreamed, he saw only one thing: books." This memorable description would seem to be a confession: Gustave recognizes here what his niece will call his "naiveté." She shows him tricked by adults and gripped by estrangement, "glimpsing a mystery." He paints himself as Giacomo with the same colors: distracted, the world seemed to him like a "fantasmagoria whose enigma he did not understand." Astonishingly vague but ever-present, this obsessive, unformulated question to which he does not want to find an answer. Fundamentally, we know, it is not the world that is astonishing but our presence in the world if our early childhood did not (falsely) justify it. Gustave is and will remain until his death bewildered, a state of mind rather suitable to that superfluous beast, man. But in this novella he attributes his bewilderment—which derives from the structures of the Flaubert family—to the single-mindedness of his passion. As for that, I would call it *homicide* if I had to give it a name, so inhuman or, more precisely, antihuman are Giacomo's thoughts—especially the most beautiful of them. In this passage he dreams he possessed the library of a king:

"How comfortably he would breathe, how proud and powerful he was when he looked down the immense galleries, his eyes lost in books! When he raised his head? Books! When he lowered it? Books! to the left and to the right as well."

There is a kind of dark power in this evocation. We imagine these "immense galleries" deserted—a columbarium; the books are its urns; a cataclysm must have engulfed humanity; infinitely alone, Gustave the king exercises his omnipotence on vaguely enchanted things. Furthermore, his passion is not limited to ridding the world of hu-

manity; it is violently opposed to those who share that passion. How
he hates them! How he would like to murder them! He has no human
relations, after all, except with mortal enemies.

And chiefly with *one* mortal enemy, Baptisto, who is richer than he
is and takes everything from him. The tale is built on the theme of
jealousy, like those that come before and those that follow; we will
not learn much about Baptisto except that he is put there expressly
to torment Giacomo. The important thing for Gustave is to particu
larize his pain and find someone he might make responsible for it
his rival, though he may have greater means, is quite precisely his
double, his brother. By acquiring the incunabula he covets under
Giacomo's very nose, Baptisto tortures him with frustration. And
certainly Satan, the disembodied soul, and Almaroës, the soulless
body, will be frustrated too. But the frustrator is the one who created
them, giving each one his particular anomaly. Here Gustave does no
bother to explain the monk's anomaly—he is simply made that way
he could even find fulfillment if he had wealth. Things being what
they are, it is an equal, a peer, who frustrates him; he is the one
Giacomo must hate. From *Bibliomanie* to *Rêve d'enfer*, we see how
much the theme has been enriched but also to what extent its primary
meaning has been obscured. In a sense, of course, Arthur and Satan
are rivals, peers, and the victory of the first constitutes the unhap
piness of the second. But in truth the Devil, who is evil and despair
would be unhappy even if he had not met Almaroës; it is the Eterna
Father who is really guilty, and suddenly each of the duo embodies
Gustave in his own way. The Eternal Father is not represented in
Bibliomanie; and Baptisto *is not* Gustave. He is no one at all, in fact
since the young author has neglected to describe him; let us say that
he is simply the *Other*. He resembles Giacomo in every respect (ever
in his mania as well as in his character and analogous features), save
that he challenges the monk in his material otherness, enters into
competition with him, and is always victorious. We shall find that
Gustave's twinning in *Rêve d'enfer* masks an earlier theme in which
the duo, far from embodying the author each in his own way, share
roles, one representing Gustave and the other his executioner.

Behold this Giacomo who, at thirty, appears "aged and worn."
What is consuming him? His mania? We are told on the contrary that
it rejuvenates him, he catches a glimpse of a rare book and he is ten
years younger. His troubles? At the beginning of the story these are
still only vexations. In fact, since all it takes is a book to make him
lose his senile air, his awkwardness, his moroseness, since he resume

his wrinkles and his usual bearing the moment he leaves his library, we must conclude that age does not depend here on years or hardships—it indicates *indifference*. This is just the way Flaubert will characterize his precocious senility in his letters to Louise—he survived his youth and no longer feels anything. The reason for that indifference, he says, is a long sequence of unspeakable troubles. There is nothing of this in 1835; what is involved is not acquired apathy but a constitutional lack of interest; Giacomo's soul, occupied by a single passion, harbors no other desire. Abandoned, nearly devoid of needs, the organism consumes itself in places and withers in others. In the same way, Arthur's old age is the result of his anorexia. Sometimes Gustave's confessions to the Muse invite our caution; does the author believe that the monk's indifference to everything is an innate feature of his character, as he tries to convince us it is? It is striking that this thirty-year-old man should have no family—when family relationships play such a role in Flaubert's novellas *before* the first autobiographical works. Is Giacomo born out of the air? It is Satan, conceived a little later, who gives us the answer: the Demon was created and defined by a long family history; he is nothing more than a memory and what this memory shuns—inner vacancy. Isn't this also true of Giacomo? But someone will say that Giacomo is burning up, consumed by bibliomania. What about Satan? Doesn't he collect souls? Here we see Gustave's familial adventure, wounding him, leaving him torn apart. But this wound, which in relation to the past is only the permanent expression of an ancient disgrace, must also be conceived as a strict determination of the future; the privation undoubtedly leads to inaccessibility and consequently to indifference, but suffered as a lack it defines itself in terms of a strict determination of the future as the *desire for a certain object*. Satan's curse, his wound, prescribes his future objectives: the generalization of evil and the damnation of souls—no pardon possible; in other words, the irreversibility of the past leads to despair. But this irreversibility, recognized and lived out in desperation, leads to the inextinguishable passion to do harm. In this specific case, the relation between frustration and the desire born of it is almost too obvious. But usually the relation between what has been refused to a soul and what it wants to appropriate is not a reciprocity of symbolic reflections; too many elements are involved in Giacomo's case for us to be able to recognize the original lack in the explicit mania. Let us observe, nevertheless, his desire to kill man in his work and to make knowledge a means of producing the inhuman beauty of those objects that do not in the least belong to nature, and his disinclination to recognize here the mark of human labor—can this desire appear gratuitously? Isn't it, in another form, birth itself, which in the cursed soul is born of his malediction? Giacomo's passion—its destructive aspect—compels us to seek its origins in an ancient resentment, like the misanthropy Gustave proclaims in the letters he wrote in that period; the monk loves books against men, therefore the hatred of men comes first. We are not told this in any way, it is made manifest to us chiefly through his indifference; neither philanthropist nor misanthropist, he has no rapport with the species. But the malignity, the perversity, the sadism of his mania remain. For Gustave the soul is double-faced: one side is exigency, and the reverse, injury. Accessibility, a perpetual present—this is youth; earthly appetites and nourishment have no history. Inversely, the man who has been wounded by too singular a childhood displays indifference to everything except the call of too rigorous and exclusive a vocation, which is nothing more than his childhood transformed into destiny; he is old in advance, and his life is so predictable it seems to have been already lived.

Giacomo, then, is quite mad, exceedingly malicious, and altogether inhuman; his tastes, at once infantile and senile, discourage our sympathy. Gustave emphasizes the monk's offenses as much as he can and clearly wants us to condemn him; the fact is that he often takes his readers for adults who are serious, calm, wise, philanthropists—in short, idiots. These are the people to whom he reveals—certain of shocking them—that the monk is almost illiterate and never gives alms. But no sooner have you judged his character than the young author will ask you what right you have to judge, and in the name of what. Indeed, by the end of the tale he speaks of the librarian as one of those rare, strange men who are "openly ridiculed by the multitude because it does not understand their passions and their manias." What gives these stories their very particular tone—and this story more than the others—is that everything happens as though Gustave meant to emphasize some kind of *positivity of the negative*. By this I do not mean that he poses the negation simply in order to deny it. No; bibliomania remains an absurd project, against nature and inhuman. Rather there is a *core* to the privation; the "lack"—whatever it is—contains some kind of sovereign affirmation of the creature's right over creation and consequently over the Creator. The objects of our passions are equal in value. *Intensity* alone counts: you have only to carry your wrong to its logical extreme to be, finally, right. Happy and torn apart, Giacomo becomes quite masterful when he steals

Baptisto's bible. Masterful and guilty; this self-destructive act brings swift punishment—death. The young Flaubert's heroes, those wicked creatures, succeed in annihilating themselves. It is as though the child *had to play at losing* because of some original and irremediable condemnation which he had neither the right nor the power nor the desire to challenge. Thus the defense can begin only after the defeat, when the enemy is long since in the field, occupying the strategic positions, and armed resistance is not even conceivable. What can Gustave, or those who embody him, do but *plead guilty*, reveal the facts to the prosecutor rather than to the defense and then, at the end of his tether, turn the argument around and show in this undeniable guilt, in this mental misery he proudly acknowledges, the mark of an infinite abyss, of a wound that a criminal progenitor gave him at birth, and of some kind of aspiration which, whatever it may be, constitutes his invisible greatness—the only greatness possible in this world?

In this sense the title of the novella is deceptive; instead of *Bibliomanie* it should read *Graphomanie*. The author attacks himself with furious humility; he writes because he does not like himself, but the consequence is that he does not like what he creates. He scribbles away; he will say some time later that he is like a numismatist, a philatelist. Naturally, he finds in his very unhappiness a dreadful salvation; a mediocre scribbler, he is eaten alive by this vulture—the desire to be a great writer. Genius becomes his basic privation. Or rather, if the soul is defined as a certain desire hollowed out by a certain history, his is a double privation. On its dark side, memory turned toward being, it is meditation on an irreversible catastrophe; on the other it is a calling, a vocation, but no one is there to call him. It is the future that issues the call, determined by frustration—which demands to be effaced. Gustave's fundamental possibility is nothing more than his wound claiming the only balm that might soothe it— glory, humiliation redeemed. But if we have understood the course of this negative thought, we perceive that the young author is convinced of being at bottom committed to despair—*he should have had* genius. Why of course! If desire, infinite but singular, is a memory returned as prophecy even as frustration defines in the future the sole plenitude that might have filled its emptiness, at the same time Gustave experiences this frustration with resentment, with sulking, like a martyr who must go to the extremes of destitution and suffering. This means that he imagines his fundamental possibility only in the form of a fundamental impossibility. *Impossible glory* is the future expression of the irreversible past disgrace. It is impossible *because it is necessary*. The unhappiness endured in the guilt is projected into the future as the failure of the single action Flaubert could and might want to undertake. The adolescent is damned; his only claim to greatness in the shabby wreckage that will destroy him is the immensity of the genius which haunts him and which he is denied. *Bibliomanie* dissembles the frustration but cannot hide the resentment; the meaning is clear, if not for Gustave at least for us, his readers: manipulated from birth, aged by a memorable fall, I was given only one desire—grating, bitter, insatiable; apart from that I don't give a damn.

On another point this crude and profound work turns out to be more explicit than the subsequent works will be: it stresses the repetitive character of Giacomo's troubles; they are entirely foreseen, each one being the copy of the one before, the monk *expects* them. Baptisto

> had for a time taken away from him . . . everything that seemed rare and old. . . . This man became a burden, it was always he who carried off the manuscripts; at public sales he would outbid and prevail. Oh, how many times did the poor monk in his dreams of pride and ambition see coming toward him the long hand of Baptisto, passing through the crowd as he did on auction days in order to rob him of a treasure he had so long dreamed of, had coveted with such love and egotism. How many times . . . was he tempted to commit a crime in order to achieve what neither money nor patience could have done; but he repressed this idea in his heart, tried to deafen himself to the hatred he bore toward this man, and slumbered on his books.

The poor librarian *expects* his misfortune for the good reason that it is endlessly repeated and strikes him every time in the same way. The ritual is permanently fixed: the sale begins, the rival appears, they open the bidding, hope and despair alternate, Giacomo discovers "with horror that his antagonist becomes fired as the price mounts," he begins to fear, and then he is no longer even afraid—he knows. He still fights. In vain—the chips are down. He retreats scarcely a moment from the enemy's triumph, from public humiliation and frustration: "The book is passed from hand to hand to Baptisto; the book passes in front of Giacomo, he smells its odor, sees it slip away before his eyes and stop at a man who takes it and opens it laughing." The torment of repetition. It is a "running joke," the eternal recurrence of the same sufferings. Scarcely begun, the scene is already present to him in all its details; nothing is left but to live it, or rather to relive it. Despairing in advance and even in moments of hope, the monk deludes himself willfully, even in his disillusionment, because the moment is set for him to fall into the trap. The strange taste of experience, necessary and perhaps absurd—since the evidence of its necessity does not spring from some internal logic but from its useless repetition. He feels a fastidious disgust with himself, but the strictness of the ritual is so inexorable that every particular impression is felt—an atrocious masochistic pleasure, the sensual delights of pain—as the identity of the recollection and the expectation.

It will have been observed that the monk is struck down "in his dreams of pride and ambition." The best way to put it would be to say that the author is in fact speaking to us about something entirely different from what he pretends to discuss. And of course collectors do have ambition, vanity too, the satisfaction of alone possessing the rarest item. But Gustave's *tone* warns us: his gravity, the complicity he proclaims between the librarian's pride and ambition adequately indicate that—to fool the eventual reader and especially to mock himself—he wanted to embody in an absurd mania his two essential passions. The "compensatory" character of each of these—as much as the ritual aspect and the eternal recurrence of the agonies inflicted upon him—gives us a precious indication of the nature of these unflaggingly repeated torments. I see here two orders of unhappiness confounded into one. The location of the ritual repetition can only be the family. The father is grand master of ceremonies, he established the procedure and is charged with seeing that it is respected; the mother assists him, and the children play the roles assigned them at birth: Achille is the eldest, Gustave is the younger brother; little Caroline plays the role of the beloved little sister. For the moment we can determine the content of these ordered, endlessly recurring events only formally and in a general way; there were celebrations certainly, birthdays, and then Achille's brilliant academic success had to be celebrated—not without some pomp. But there were also vacations, the Flaubert family's yearly departure for Yonville or Trouville, the fortnight they spent with Achille-Cléophas's mother; on a more daily basis there were the meals which at certain times reunited parents and children with all members present—fixed hours, an invariable ritual that the father imposed as a function of his professional obligations. There were evenings as well. The little girl and the younger brother stayed only a short time, they were sent to bed early; but when Achille was there, Dr. Flaubert must have detained him to have

283

a "man to man" talk with his eldest son. Yet all this must be seen as only a frame; the true repetitions—sanctified pleasantries, stories of old events retold a hundred times, anecdotes known by heart that had to be heard again when Achille-Cléophas was in a good mood, value judgments invariably pronounced, winter and summer, on the same actions and the same persons, etc.—were products of the familial memory. Through these, the Flaubert unit affirmed its identity, the perpetuity of its structures, and its hierarchy. And this, of course, was what little Gustave could not abide; through its repetitive circularity a witticism, a jest, the evocation of a memory made him rediscover the irreversibility of his fall and, simultaneously, an immovable order of which he was the victim. *Bibliomanie* tells us why Mazza's passion, fettered by her family, revolves in a narrow but deep circle. What Gustave is describing here is the cycle of familial repetition which, through the eternal recurrence of ceremonies, always provoked in him a profound realization of the archetypal event and the established structures of the Flaubert unit, experienced by the younger son as the impossibility of his own existence.

A merry-go-round, then, of predictable transgressions—this is the fundamental order of his unhappiness. Another, secondary order is superimposed, also cyclical: to every vexation he reacts *through writing*. He shuts himself in and tells his story in order to unburden himself and to take revenge upon his persecutors. This is always a failure; we surmise as much here, later we shall see clearly that Gustave is not happy with what he writes. His fulminations look like damp fireworks to him. The familial transgression is unbearable, but Flaubert's bitter exposé denouncing it is only mediocre in his opinion. The father's curse reaches into areas which on principle ought to have escaped it. This is a new circularity: Gustave suffers, but every time he wants to bear witness to his sufferings, he misses his shot. No one will know of his sufferings, which are "inexpressible," unless he has genius. Every story is a suit brought against his persecutors and lost— the Other is utterly triumphant.

How does Gustave/Giacomo react to these perpetual aggressions, to these perpetual "failures" of his defense? With Julietta's way of improving upon the manifestations of her unhappiness in order to feel it less? Not at all. Either the adolescent at fourteen has not yet ventured to resort to these practices, or quite simply he is less *contrived*, more sincere. Let us continue our reading. Giacomo covets a Bible in Latin with Greek commentaries; a rival robs him of it; frustrated, the librarian begins very romantically by tearing at his own chest. But he leaves the auction hall and soon his grief takes another turn:

His thought was no longer his own, it strayed like his body with no aim or intention; it was unsettled, irresolute, ponderous, and bizarre; his head felt as heavy as lead, his forehead was burning
. . .
Yes, he was drunk with feeling, he was weary of his days, he was sick of existence.

No sooner has the sharp emotion of the defeat touched a raw nerve than it evaporates. Too heavy, the feeling crushes him and is transformed into a state of extreme dejection. Thought itself, that bloodhound, is lost in a daze. It is an instantaneous exchange: the body absorbs suffering and gives back decrepitude. This description is the more convincing as it is least expected. Most frequently, suffering serves *to put things in order, to come to terms*; a catastrophe is internalized through the effort of reflection; the mind is minutely intent upon the least bearable memories and provokes them. This is the "monologue" that will soon become one of Gustave's familiar ploys. To Giacomo, that old librarian of fourteen, this obsessive self-consciousness is something totally alien. Mistreated by fate, he absents himself, no more person; traffic passes by, this vacant soul is an intersection of laughter, conversations, songs that remain alien to him: "But it seemed to him that it was always the same sound, the same voice, a vague, confused hubbub, a bizarre, clamorous music that droned in his brain and oppressed him." He wanders here and there, goes home "exhausted and ill," "lies down on the bench of his writing table and sleeps." Happy the suffering that leads to sleep through exhaustion. True, the monk awakens feverish—"A horrible nightmare had sapped his strength." He still had some strength, then? Two lines above we were told he no longer had any. A little earlier, furthermore, following a grave disappointment—a bookseller informs him that he just sold *Le Mystère de Saint Michel* for eight maravedis—Giacomo "drops in the dust like a man wearied by an obsessive apparition." Nothing could be clearer: when he is threatened, Giacomo takes refuge in old age. This defensive absenteeism is practiced by insects; it is called, improperly, the reflex of simulated death.

Where does all this come from? Why is ordering, here, replaced by an experienced disorder? Does he want to suffer? Of course not. But who does? Still, how can it be avoided? If he sometimes escapes exasperation, that nervous distraction, it is because his objective unhappiness allows it. The sole advantage of all too predictable evils is that one can, by faking, defend oneself against them. Little Gustave owes his passivity, his dazes, his crushing fatigues to maternal handling. He sets out to exploit them; from early childhood his thoughts run away with him, and he will make use of this, these absences will be arranged. We shouldn't think, however, that he makes them happen at will; such a will, conscious, decisive, could not display itself without the carefully constructed scaffolding collapsing. Gustave, moreover, who is the most obstinate of writers, lacks the means *to will*, to engage himself deliberately in an enterprise. Quite the contrary, in order to slip away quietly a *passive option* is necessary—meaning, as we shall explain later, the passive choice of passivity; one abandons oneself to the gaps in the soul, to the mists, and, for having obeyed unreservedly by declining all responsibility, one ends by gropingly directing one's own fatalities. Gustave faces the worst *expected* sufferings in advance with the limp bulk of his brutishness. Is it Achille's birthday? Perfect—the soul is off duty, it will be back tomorrow. There are exclamations, embraces, Achille-Cléophas's worthy successor is declared the honored heir before Gustave's very eyes. But nothing reaches the younger brother; aggressions are deadened in the padded interior, the stridence of raw nerves is transformed into thickened ripples, slowed by the unthinking substance with which his brain is filled. Between aggressions, Gustave monologues. We have seen what he *says to himself*: I will kill my rival. This is what everyone does in retaliation. But while he is attacked, he closes up shop—no one there; in the deserted house voices, noises are heard but they come from outside; in the deserted rooms no one can reproduce or comprehend them. Later, when the occupant reappears, the worst is already over. The body, however, has absorbed it all. It is exhausted, feverish, sunk in an unhealthy sleep, troubled by nightmares. Such defensive absenteeism accentuates the physiological involution. Repeated a hundred times, an act of aggression provokes nervous lesions. *Stress*—here the symbiosis of attack and defense—serves only to exacerbate those lesions. We have rediscovered the dialectical trinity: the internalization of evil, the soul's eclipse, the exhaustion of the body which plays its own role as well as that of the absent soul. This process is what Flaubert designates by that unique concept, aging. Alfred wants "to live without living"; as for Gustave he means to *suffer without suffering*: to believe in this process is to grow old.

Has he said it all? No. *Bibliomanie* clearly shows us that Flaubert's verbal and conceptual apparatus is related to an underlying intention. But what? What is this intention? What is the "deep wound?" Who is Baptisto, that forever victorious and deeply detested rival? In order to retrieve the material and concrete content of these obvious, somewhat abstract elements, we must continue our research, going back to the first works, which are more open and naïve. *La Peste à Florence* dates from September 1836. Flaubert was fourteen years and nine months old. *Un Parfum à sentir* is dated April—he was fourteen and three months. *Un Secret de Philippe le Prudent*, according to the Charpentier edition, was also composed in September 1836. But in the same edition it precedes *Un Parfum à sentir*. For my part I maintain it was composed in '35: Gustave's basic themes are present but not at all "brought out"; he submits to them without mastering them, which will allow us to distinguish radically two motifs that Flaubert's observations subsequently linked together (especially in *La Peste à Florence*). I shall therefore discuss this third story after the other two. This said, the regressions that threaten a writer at every turn, the traps that lead him astray in himself and temporarily rob him of the clarities that guided him, the effort which is demanded of us in everything simply in order to be intellectually faithful to our own thought— all this is known only too well. If *Philippe le Prudent* was written later than *Un Parfum*, there is a provisional involution of Flaubert and his problematic; yet for all persons involved in self-searching, these involutions are so frequent that I cannot see why the uncertainties of *Philippe le Prudent* constitute an absolute proof of its anteriority. In any case, the matter is unimportant.

La Peste à Florence begins with a prophecy. The two Médicis sons, François, the elder and Garcia, have gone to the seer. She is an old lady, of course, a grande dame in her youth, now decrepit, with a "magnificent head of white hair." To the first she says, "Your projects will soon be realized, but you will die through the betrayal of someone close to you," and to the second, "The cancer of envy and hatred will consume you . . . and in the blood of your victim you will find expiation for the humiliations of your life." The prediction is fulfilled point by point. We know that for Flaubert it is linked to strict determinations: the structures of the Médicis family can be lived out in the individual history of each member only in the form of repetition. The law of primogeniture, for example, is a permanent structure which refers to social institutions; this is manifest to Garcia, the younger son, by the daily recurrence of his humiliations. But this repetition has a certain direction: the individual adventure stretches from birth to death; the fixed return of the fatal constellation saps the strength, meaning that the crises have the same content but not the same intensity. Their meaning itself varies with respect to the temporal order; each one hastens the end of the process, but the first blindly prepare the final blast, senescence and exhaustion, while the following make us see, in all its singularity, the inevitable demise to which we are brought. Nowhere subsequently—except in *La Légende de Saint Julien l'hospitalier*, written when Flaubert was fifty-four—will he show us so clearly the strict connection between family life and this prophetic anguish. Old Béatricia is only a romantic accessory; actually it is Garcia himself who grasps the nontemporal necessity of the structure through his own temporalization. What is more, he recognizes this. Two days later, at the moment of murdering François, he reminds his brother of the oracle with wild jubilation: "You see, the prediction is right—do you see the places where my hair is missing? Do you see how my eyesight is diminished and weakened . . .? For I have spent the nights crying out in rage and despair." Everything is connected: family structure, history, prophetic power, and aging.

Could two days of weeping truly weaken the eyesight? Garcia is exaggerating. It is true that he has been sniveling for forty-eight hours; but the seer said nothing he did not know since childhood. Since childhood he had watched François sweep up the paternal favor, the honors; the patrimony will revert to the eldest, the heir, and *destined* by his birth to be Cosme's successor, *he is made the destiny* of the younger brother he despoils. Garcia's future is revealed to him every day through minor humiliations—this is their meaning, they realize the future in the present. A social institution, the permanent reason for his unhappiness, is embodied in François and manifests itself through the father's lavish displays of love for the future head of the family. Thus each ordeal is new—for François's good fortune is revealed through circumstances which continually vary and send him little by little toward that ultimate success, his father's death and the passing on of power—and each ordeal is at once familiar, foreseeable, and foreseen, yet must be lived out to the very end. Poor Garcia is not spared a single detail. Dramatic authors usually delete extraneous and tedious scenes which, as we say, "create useless repetition." But the creator of the Médicis and of the world is not concerned with such things; on the contrary, he delights in repetition, in scenes that "add nothing." François comes out the winner, we know this already, we demand some editing; the Almighty is obstinate, it is the *repetition* that interests him—the elder has to steal the show every time. For Garcia as for Giacomo, to foresee and to feel are one; promising indefinite reproductions, the younger son's feeling is exasperated at having been predicted, and at being predictable.

Gustave is not God. As an artist, he *suggests* the tedious and unnecessary repetitions that make up the thread of Garcia's life, but he presents us with a central event summing up all that has preceded it and everything that will follow—the triumph of the right of primogeniture. François has just been named cardinal, the pope has signed his nomination. The symbol is clear since Gustave hasn't bothered to transpose it, at most replacing the name of Flaubert with that of Médicis; but it is instantly apparent that he has preserved the essentials. First of all, old Cosme does not on this occasion make his eldest son an advance against his legacy—he does not *give him any of his possessions*. This refers to the fact that Achille-Cléophas—as Gustave is not unaware—must equitably divide his personal fortune among his heirs. On the other hand, the head of the Médicis house is involved in intrigues close to the pope to obtain a prestigious honor for the family's eldest son; this is what Dr. Flaubert will do when he makes arrangements for the public authorities to grant Achille the office that does not belong to him and is not hereditary. This is how the chief surgeon honors the right of primogeniture, and Gustave is exasperated by these virtuous maneuvers and by the preference they imply. He is so unconcerned with disguising his rancor that paradoxically he has given François a religious honor and made the younger son, Garcia, serve obscurely in the army with the rank of lieutenant, when everyone knows that under the Old Regime the sword and the military were the prerogative of the eldest and it was often the youngest who entered the priesthood. The reason is obvious; François, though a model of physical prowess, will be a *cleric*; this means that he will found his honor on *knowledge*, like Achille—whom an unjust father wants to make into a prince of science. Cosme makes poor Garcia a soldier in order to get rid of him; hence his lot is violence and action, and ignorance. All his life he will practice a profession he detests and for which he is not at all suited. This time Flaubert cites the reason for his resentment quite openly—or rather one of the two reasons for his grudge against his father. Abusively reviving the abolished right of primogeniture, Dr. Flaubert seeks to privilege his eldest son and offer him the most attractive medical career in all of Normandy. He invites him to walk in his footsteps, to share his glory and even enlarge it, he offers him a rich and elegant clientele, all the great names of Rouen; he loves this marvelous son enough to want to survive only in him.

Undoubtedly the novella was written in a fever—it may have taken the place of a collapse that would have crippled Gustave for some time. I conclude from this evidence that a particular event revived his fury, but we shall never know. Let us recall only that Achille was twenty-three years old at the time and was very close to finishing his studies. *La Peste* dates from September—did the future physician do brilliantly in some examination? Did family festivities take place at around this time, in July or August? All we can say is that Cosme de Médicis intends to give a magnificent celebration to fete François's nomination; Florence is in a festive mood; the younger son's presence is indispensable. This is the height of sadism; in *Bibliomanie*, the victim is forced to witness the triumph of his executioner, in *La Peste* he must go even further and applaud it. For Garcia this fatal blow is foreseen, inevitable, and unacceptable. Nothing new here, however, he has seen others; but what does happen is that a symbol does more harm than the object symbolized; the years are gathered together in one night, the invisible is suddenly seen, an abstract curse is incarnate and holds sway. By the light of the thousand torches of the procession and the ball, the cardinal's honor will dazzle the younger son.

> When Monseigneur's carriage will be seen in the streets of Florence rolling across the cobblestones, if some child . . . asks his mother: "Who are those men in red behind the cardinal?"—"His valets"—"And that other one who follows on horseback, dressed in black?"—"His brother" . . . Oh! pity and mockery! And to think that he must . . . call him Monseigneur and prostrate himself at his feet!

The conclusion is obvious; he writes: "I will not be present at these festivities!"

He is present, however, at the ceremony: "He contemplated all this with a sad and despondent air . . . like the dying man gazing at the sun from his wretched bed of agony." *Agony*—the word Gustave takes up again at the age of seventeen for the title of his first autobiography. As for the "dying man gazing at the sun from his wretched bed," this image will be found again, we shall see, in the last pages of *Novembre*. As it happens, unhappiness has aged Garcia all at once—as it will Giacomo—and this weakness prevents him from truly feeling his fury. All the same, his passions are too powerful. They are suddenly un-

leashed: "The sight of his brother irritates him to such a degree
. . . that he is tempted to scratch and tear at the woman whose dress
brushes against him in passing." Just as Djalioh, burning with jealousy, claws Adèle with his iron nails, and Giacomo, as we have seen,
bloodies his own chest. Is it purely a literary motif, or did Flaubert's
rage inspire this feminine mode of attack? In any case, the furious
impulse marks—in all the instances I have just cited—a paroxysm of
aggressiveness and the beginning of his crushing decline. François
perceives his brother's malaise, approaches and questions him with
a condescension that pushes the unhappy man to his limit. Is Garcia
going to draw his sword? Plunge his dagger into the cardinal's stomach? Not at all. François walks away; a little later: "A man had just
fainted on a bench; the first valet who passed by took him in his arms
and led him out of the room—it was Garcia."

In *La Peste*, Gustave invents nothing; this is clear. The genre, on
the contrary, would have demanded that Garcia draw his sword. But
he is too cowardly to draw against his brother. Too cowardly? So he
has to faint. The adolescent, unconscious of this flagrant contradiction,
has chosen to situate his own failings in an epoch of blood and violence; his hero must kill or die, you might say, and later of course he
does kill—François will perish by his brother's hand. Further on we
shall see how this assassination should be interpreted.

Let us return for a moment to the insane hatred that ends in collapse. Garcia loses consciousness; his false death is an escape. We
should add that it is also a wager: "I will not be present at these
festivities." And again—who knows?—a sentence that the guilty party
carries out himself. In any case, the younger Médicis son resembles
the hero of *Novembre* in the way that he absents himself through
thought—without lifting a finger. Less happy and less systematic, he
will achieve only a provisional demise. But after all, is the attack at
Pont-l'Evêque any different? What is striking here is that he could so
early have had an exact sense of his emotional constants. In adversity
the body of this adolescent surreptitiously entreated him to let go, to
abandon himself to gravity, to turn himself into a cadaver or an inanimate thing. The perpetual proposal of annihilation always remains
his most immediate temptation, as it will be later for Saint Antoine.
Indeed, Garcia's crude and brutal conduct gives us a better understanding of Giacomo's disorders. A first time the monk *falls* into a
faint; the second time, after the auction, wandering at random, nearly
unconscious, he *swoons standing up*. When we view *Bibliomanie* in the
light of *La Peste*, we can see that it is only a step from the swoon to

the daze, and from the daze to ecstasy. Torpors, fogs, apathies—recapitulated deaths. In effect, it isn't necessary to go to the very end; when you feel pulled backward or ready to fall on your nose, the brakes are put on and the fall is stopped. The important thing at each recurrence of unhappiness is that surrender to the void is possible. What is in question here is not consciousness—Gustave lets us know by repeating several times in the *formal* texts of his correspondence that he never loses consciousness—but, rather, the *degree of presence in the world*. The victim and manipulator of obscure forces, the young boy when danger threatens makes dizzying retreats. But since he keeps his senses intact and limits himself to "distancing" himself from reality, in what realm of being does this rather real child move, withdraw, approach the world, take his distance? I answer flatly: in the realm of nonbeing. We shall soon learn that Gustave is only half real; we shall study in detail the phases of the defensive movement which I call here, for lack of a better definition, his process of unrealization. But before we proceed further, we shall first go back to *Un Parfum à sentir*, and then to *La Peste à Florence*, in order to illuminate the episodes we still find obscure.

First, let us jump to the end of *Un Parfum*. Dreadfully ugly, ill, abandoned, almost mad, Marguerite is in the depths of abjection and despair. What is more, the crowd—Baudelaire's "vile multitude"—pursues her with its hatred and its insults. In such a situation, to think of suicide is hardly surprising. What is surprising is that the idea of suicide comes to her *suddenly*, like a flash of genius, and that it seems to her less a decision to be made than the discovery of a secret.

> "Madwoman! madwoman," cried the people running after Marguerite.
> She stopped and struck her forehead:
> "Deadwoman!" she said, laughing.
> And she hurried off toward the Seine.

Who is Gustave talking about? Archimedes? Eureka! She strikes her forehead and laughs; she will drown herself, certainly, but the text makes it quite clear that it is not the result of a voluntary fiat; the suicide appears to be a consequence that issues solely from her discovery. Indeed, she has just deciphered the absurd enigma of her life. The crowd—which to some extent represents the Greek chorus, and more radically the "world" in all senses of the term—rejects her unmercifully. It is not a matter of exclusion, of putting her in quarantine or exile; it is her life they begrudge her. She is condemned to death from birth for the sole reason that her ugliness is intolerable. This is her insight: ugliness, inasmuch as it is identified with the universal rejection it provokes, is her essence. Let us say, if you will, that it is her *essence-other*, inasmuch as it is linked to what she is for others and through them; never mind—beyond it, what else is there inside her? Nothing that is not the internalization of her physical defects and of the reaction she elicits in others. Nothing but a puff of air, "a perfume to be savored" (in the words of the title), which we shall not know much about since it will be lost in nature, no one having thought to sample it. Her essence, in contrast, is strictly defined as a prohibition; she is a woman who carries within her the radical negation of her being, which is prohibited from living. She will assume that essence through suicide and will be realized by doing away with herself.

Does Flaubert blame the crowd for focusing only on her appearance and ignoring this "perfume" that is Marguerite's soul? No. In the only line where he refers to that ineffable fragrance, he puts it *on the same level* as the "visible" beauty of her unfeeling and corrupt rival, Isabellada. Earlier in the tale, one of the characters attacks the unhappy woman sadistically, having cornered her in a window recess:

> She could no longer escape from him, he could spit all those insults in her face, he could tell her every last one of her miseries, tell her how ugly she was, show her what a difference there was between her and the [beautiful] dancer [her rival]. . . .
> "Oh Isambert! what have I done to you?"
> "Nothing, but you displease me. . . . Why do you cry all the time? Why do you look so gloomy, so unpleasant? Why do you have such a revolting face? . . . Oh no, you are too ugly!"

This man is quite malicious, certainly; yet at the age of twenty-one Gustave himself will deliberately adopt Isambert's malign aversion to ugliness. Let us read this passage from *Novembre*:

> Passionate for what is beautiful, ugliness repelled him like a crime; indeed, there is something atrocious about an ugly person; from afar, he is frightening, close up, he is disgusting; when he speaks, you suffer; if he cries, his tears irritate you . . . and when he is silent, his immobile face seems to be the seat of all vices and low instincts.

And Gustave adds: "Thus he never forgave a man who had displeased him on first impression." Ugliness is the fixed symbol of crime. This is what he states explicitly in 1842; but beginning in 1836, he is so convinced of it that he generously gives poor Garcia the blackest soul, the most awful miseries, and the most repulsive features. We have only to leaf through the *Mémoires* and *Novembre* to see that this disgust, timorous and tinged with sadism, is one of his most constant characteristics. At more than fifty years old (in January 1874) he writes to Carvalho:

> I left the theater feeling as if I had been hit over the head with a cane. That wasn't all! Outside, at the door, the wardrobe keeper stopped me and I was violently seized by the man's hideousness. For Vaudeville must make me experience all feelings, including "dread!"
>
> As this dread had chilled me (in God's name he is ugly! what teeth!), I arrived at the Censor with a completely new physiognomy and character. . . . The shadow of Flaubert . . . conceded everything out of weariness, disgust, flabbiness, and to have done with it.

Does he take exception elsewhere to Isambert's sadism? Not at all; he describes it without indulgence but without anger, and I maintain that Gustave's feelings toward this character are ambivalent; this is self-evident, since he is representing the animosity of others against the author and, at the same time, the malign dread he feels at the sight of ugliness. As for the ignoble populace, he does not reproach them for detesting what is ugly, but rather for debasing hatred as they do all the feelings they appropriate. The worst sadist, furthermore, is Gustave himself, who writes this novella only to torment his creature with intolerable tortures, who has invented Isambert expressly in order to address himself, through this character, directly to Marguerite and to tell her of all the horror she inspires in him. Whether he is conscious of it or not, the young author in his turn plays the role he attributes to the Eternal Father and to the paterfamilias: he has deliberately created a hideous creature and offers himself the luxury of cursing her for the defects he has given her. This is what gives the story all its ambiguity. For at the same time the unfortunate woman is charged with embodying her author. We are bound to find this surprising if we recall that Gustave was handsome—people told him so and he knew it. Yet this ravishing blond boy is the attacker of a homely woman; betrayed, beaten, chased away by the man she loves, mocked, half eaten by a lion, detested by the people and escaping lynching only by suicide—Marguerite owes all her misfortunes to her pathetic face. The author projects himself into her, but she resembles him so little that he passes easily from masochism to sadism. As though he were saying to her: "It isn't possible to be so ugly—you are doing it on purpose." This is true, but I see the reason for it in a stroke of genius on the part of the young boy; he has found a sure way of proving that he is merciless with himself, of recovering in the self the whole world's abhorrence of him, of understanding and sharing it, of making it the very source of the misfortunes he inflicts on Marguerite, of protecting himself from the slightest sympathy for his heroine, namely for himself. He projects in her his anomaly in the form of the vice—because for him it is one—he most detests; therefore he will be able to forget that his victim is none other than himself and to treat himself as others do, as a *scapegoat*. Any further doubts that Marguerite represents him will be dispelled if we remember (1) that the duos of *Quidquid volueris* and *Rêve d'enfer* are present in this novella as they were in *La Peste à Florence* and in outline in *Bibliomanie*, where Baptisto exists only to maintain the internal tension belonging to all these stories (a space structured by an opposition between two persons, the frustrator and the frustrated); (2) that here one man is being fought over by two women, one of whom, with very little sex appeal, possesses a soul, namely the infinite capacity for suffering shared by Satan, Djalioh, Mazza, Emma, all the avatars of Gustave Flaubert, while the other, pretty as a picture but dry, selfish, heartless, belongs to the line of robots—Arthur, Paul, Ernest; (3) that the man is effortlessly conquered by the vamp—who drops him just as quickly—and that poor Marguerite, the *lawful wife* of the disloyal man, is deprived by the usurper of a love that was *hers by right*; (4) that the homely woman's suffering is accompanied by a strange pride and—as Gustave purposely remarks—by malice. It is nevertheless true that in *Un Parfum* he has chosen to *make himself horrible*. Of course the theme is inspired by a commonplace of Romanticism; the authors of the time delighted in casting the sublime in repulsive bodies. Gustave treats the subject in his own way, *pitilessly*; Marguerite's soul, furthermore, is sublime only in its capacity for suffering; her love is never shown to us in anything but its negative aspect, its magnitude measured only by the magnitude of the despair that consumes the poor abandoned woman. Most important, the drama is played on two planes at once. On the higher, it allows Gustave to introduce the idea of *fatum*, newly acquired in its philosophical form, I imagine, but something that the little boy had long perceived as the *meaning* of experience and its purpose. On the lower plane, which is hidden by the higher, it is a settling of accounts. And

295

Marguerite's ugliness allows the story to be told on both planes at the same time. We shall understand this better by examining more closely the defect with which the handsome adolescent afflicts himself on paper. Indeed, if ugliness represents the leprosy from which he believes he is suffering, which others detest in him and which he detests with them even while detesting them, the chief aspects of the symbol will provide us with information about the object symbolized.

In the first place there is a received and constitutional determination. Let us understand that Gustave begins by pleading guilty, but only to clear himself soon afterward. He is born with a defect in his mental conformation, just as Marguerite is born with an unpleasant body. He immediately asks: "Who is at fault?" and answers, like Charles Bovary: "No one, it is fate." Marguerite is hideous—it is not her fault. And poor Isambert, if a bit sadistic around the edges, is not at fault either. Shall the populace be blamed? Well, no; men are simply made in such a way that they hate ugliness and misery. In sum, everyone is acquitted. Such indulgence in an unhappy child filled with rancor must be somewhat suspect. It is proclaimed, however, and Gustave believes in it; he will believe in it all his life. But it must be observed that those acquittals are not founded on mechanistic determinism—which his father tried to teach him—but on the Fate of antiquity. Flaubert means to leave no doubt on this point, and so from the first lines of the novella he gives destiny its Greek name, *Anangkē*. Moreover, *fatum* as he conceives it is precisely the contrary of determinism. If we adopted the principles of Dr. Flaubert, obviously we would acquit everyone, and from his point of view we would be right: the world is a whirlwind of atoms which are displaced, united, and separated according to inflexible laws; no one created it, no one governs it. Marguerite, the entirely fortuitous result of an encounter of causal series, is merely a fact—and a fact exterior to her, since everything in her including "herself" is exteriority. Isabellada's beauty, her venality, are facts as well; nothing can be said about her except that she exists. There is neither good nor evil. Simply what is false and what is true. Knowledge has practical applications which allow men partially to direct their lives since it teaches them how to reproduce such and such a cause in order to obtain such and such an effect.

Fatum for Gustave is the necessity for a life to be lived until a death which is defined in advance and awaits one at a stated hour and place, and for that life to take its course tediously by way of a series of episodes which has been outlined in detail before birth. In a sense, his father would not have contradicted this since he must have thought, like Laplace, that a superhuman intelligence knowing the laws of the universe and the present state of the particles composing it would be in a position to foresee the succession of its subsequent states until the end of the world. But it would have been a misunderstanding. For the chief surgeon, one can modify a situation by acting on the factors that determine it; not for Gustave, for whom the most considered, the best calculated actions one undertakes to modify destiny can do nothing but realize what was written." Hence our irreparable lives must all reflect alien intentions, and the exteriority of determinism is replaced in each of us by the interiority of *slave-will*, engaged despite itself in realizing the *alien-intention* that has decided its destiny. Suddenly we see the idea of culpability reborn. All innocent? And if we were all guilty, beginning with those others who manipulated us even before we were conceived?

We shall return to the question. For the moment we must try to understand Marguerite. After proclaiming her innocent, Gustave, by having recourse to *fatum*, makes her responsible for her ugliness. Of course he doesn't say so, but in every line we can read that it is an *offending* ugliness. As a mechanist he would note dispassionately the action of physio-anatomical structures on the comportment of those animals so rigorously conditioned morally and physically, human beings. But he is very far from this since *in the first instance* he maintains that disgrace of the body is unforgivable; he believes he has discovered some sort of malign purpose in it; one is ugly *in order to displease*—this is almost the language Isambert uses to Marguerite. Besides, Gustave resurrects here what passes as "folk wisdom"— don't people speak of aggressive ugliness? He knows it, and so resorts to the people; Marguerite *provokes* them to pass judgment: Isambert, Gustave, and the crowd condemn Marguerite to death for *the sin of ugliness*. A strange idea: on the one hand it makes ugliness a received determination subject to an external law and which, as the passive result of heredity, intrauterine accident, etc., is maintained through passivity; and on the other hand, more primitive, more profound, it holds responsible those who are afflicted. Strangely, however, this double and contradictory determination accounts rather effectively for our spontaneous reaction. In man, everything is wholly man; a face, for example, is both given and experienced—it is an inertia troubled by acts of communication, endlessly disturbed, pervaded, agitated by expressions which claim it as theirs and manifest themselves by it, through it, by composing its features. Not for a moment does the human face exist in the solitude of being: it is experienced, understood, it is a *physiognomy*; even repose—the calm of the vacant eyes of Greek statues—is intentional; it signifies the adaptation of the interior to the exterior and, paradoxically, the total mobilization of the body. All at once the material of the expression itself becomes expressive. Doubly so; a red nose conditions a smile, up to a certain point: the beauty of the smile can make one forget the redness of the nose, and above all the physiognomy—in sleep as in waking—becomes a permanent expression. Etched by meanings, this flesh gives to each his singularity, his irreducible materiality; it participates at once in the general intentionality and seems in its very structure the manifestation of a profound intent. One might say that physiognomy, matter determining form, the deeper smile glimpsed beneath the superficial smiles, is the inertia of being manifesting itself as choice. This impression is not entirely false, to the extent that it could be said of everyone that at the age of forty one is responsible for one's face. And then it is true that the sense of being ugly makes one uglier. But what is of concern to us is that a face—chained freedom, surpassed materiality—evidently justifies this first impulsive confusion between the aesthetic and the moral. Beautiful, it is reassuring; ugly, it seems to reveal the hideousness of a soul; worse, it seems to conceal misfortune. Witches nearly always have two or three of these traits; they are unhappy, strange (out of the ordinary or alien), and ugly. The ugliness is not necessary, but when it is present, the two other traits are part of it; a truly ugly woman is arresting, discordant in the midst of dull, run-of-the-mill human faces, and there is no doubt at all that she is unhappy. It is at this level that we must understand slave-will. The ugly woman is not contagious like a victim of cholera or the plague; such persons can transmit only the evil they suffer, and nothing prevents one from rationally imagining the contagion as *exteriority*, from the mechanist and determinist point of view. But the witch does not communicate *her* evil; thus the Neopolitan who meets a homely woman thinks his wife is going to die or, better, that he is about to break his leg. In this sense, he discovers in the sorceress an anonymous malignity which selects its own victims, assigning an unavoidable catastrophe to each one. This kind of spiritual power does not of course belong to the witch, who often is not even conscious of the evil she does; however, the malign power is manifest *through her* by means of the misfortune that struck her first and which she had to internalize, live out from day to day, which she supports in short by the sole fact of existing and being afflicted. This is the source of the

contamination for the popular mind. It is obvious that the evil principle which purposely created this unfortunate creature that she might
suffer and do harm goes quite beyond her; yet it can be said that she
lives the evil which has befallen her, that she has internalized it as the
permanent principle governing her perceptions, her feelings, and her
conduct—in sum, that she reappropriates it and takes responsibility
for it. Why? Simply because it extends itself in her as the sufficient
reason for her life and because she appropriates it as the very substance of experience, perceiving, feeling, choosing, deciding that she
is, knows how to be, and will remain the irremediably hideous woman
evil has made her in her very being; that this hideousness is not an
inertia but something she must surpass and consequently assume by
each of her choices (just as her immoderate taste for pastries, for
example, is a substitute through displacement for a sexual desire that
her body—she is well aware—prevents her from satisfying; as, too—
more than mirrors—the way others look at her and behave toward
her constantly reveal to her the affliction she would'like to forget, and
consequently this unmasked ugliness is the basis of the antagonistic
relationship she maintains with them). Free will? No, for she cannot
make it exist, and thus motivate all her actions. But slave-will certainly,
for as long as she doesn't kill herself she is implicated in the malign
decision that engendered her; better, she *is* this decision extending
itself in the freedom of its creature but remaining there as destiny in
order to push her, in spite of herself, always to the worst—to what
will give her most pain, to what will do others most harm. In effect,
a decision made at any given moment can seem innocent enough to
her and without any connection to the evil that devours her. But evil
is within her since it is her totality and her destiny; it deviates the
chosen action toward itself, that is, *in all cases* toward the worst; the
unfortunate woman is guilty of this too, since even when she pretends
to be unaware, she is profoundly conscious of it.

Obviously I have not attempted here a true phenomenology of
ugliness; I wanted to explain, by reasons that I shall not call objective
but intersubjective, the reaction it provokes in a great number of
people. Gustave as an adolescent was one of them. We know he was
superstitious and prophetic; if in *Madame Bovary* he was more than
generous with premonitory intimations, it was not with the childish
plan of giving an additional twist to the novel by conveying a presentiment of the end from the beginning; it was rather that he saw
his own life peopled with intimations—presages of the worst, in general. Ugliness was one of them. For a passive and cheerless child

convinced he was being led toward the most horrible end by an ineluctable destiny, to encounter a man physically disfavored was an actual trauma. It must be recalled that in periods verging on mental depression, the strength is lacking to master and go beyond the apparition of a hideous face, of a sinister and unnatural expression—it impresses itself on the mind and remains, the prophetic image of our own evil. Gustave is certainly not on the verge of depression in his early adolescence, but he shows some signs of it; words and things sink into him undigested, transformed into inert threats by his own inertia. For this reason it is true that ugliness offends him and frightens him—it is his inexorable destiny gathered up in a face and offered *whole* to his intuition. The more passive we are, indeed, the more the key to the world, praxis—that hand-to-hand struggle against destiny—has slipped out of our grasp, the more we *submit* to the hideousness of others, the more it seems to us insurmountable as the unbearable determination of experience in ourselves and in the other, whom we conceive in our image, the inert, painful support responsible for an atrocious destiny;[28] and the more it seems to be the intolerable truth of this world. This is what Gustave is like, this is how he will always be. For him, Marguerite is *guilty*; this victim has her slave-will, meaning that destiny, determinism against the grain, is in her as it is in Gustave. The *freedom to be unhappy*. She is left the choice of means, but whatever she chooses will result in the prescribed end which can only be an aggravation of her misfortunes. In some obscure way she knows this, and it is her greatest fault; she knows when she attempts a course of action that she is merely getting closer to the objective disaster that has been decreed on high. In other words, being is a choice; in each of us it is simply the choice of the Other. Hence there are two guilty parties: I, who assume and realize this bad, transcendent choice through my particular options, and the Other, the sadistic creator who created me for crime and misfortune. This is what Gustave was getting at—the judge/penitent accuses himself the better to condemn the Other. I agree, he is unpleasant, he is malicious, with every beat of his heart he brings forth this radical evil which is the identification of crime and misfortune, the subordination of a conscious and responsible self to an *alter ego* produced in him by the Other. Doubly foul, Marguerite, an image of the author, is condemned

---

28. The ugliness of an actively functioning person engaged in a collective enterprise scarcely intrudes—or intrudes not at all—on his motivations. Reciprocally, his comrades do not notice it, or they forget about it. This is because praxis has other criteria.

to be free—free for evil—that is, to internalize this inert determination of ugliness which is what provokes the external evil (malevolence, sadism, scandal, lynching) and, in reaction, the internal evil (suffering, shame, envy, wickedness). Between these two kinds of evil a dialectic relationship is established that will not end even with Marguerite's death (her corpse ends up on a dissection table). But the *Other*? The one who created Gustave? The one Gustave imitated—surely to understand him better—by creating Marguerite? Isn't he, under the name *Anangkē*, the primary criminal? Here we return to predestination. But this time the younger son is much more explicit. Let us recall that *Eureka* which is immediately followed by a definitive plunge. Marguerite has understood that she was *rejected* by the tribunal of her peers and that the harsh judgment served only to disclose an ontological defect which had deprived her from the first of the right to live. Consequently for Gustave, born guilty, namely an inferior Flaubert—something a scientific celebrity, justly proud of his eldest son, could not acknowledge—it is a defect of being, a defect of his being. Yet even as lacuna this nonbeing has an ontological status—he *is*, meaning inertia conditioned by exteriority but also by permanence. Of course the child has to internalize his hollow emptiness in the form of original sin. But the fissure in the plenitude of the real did not begin by itself—someone must have put it there. Who then, if not the God who made Satan and Marguerite, the father who made Achille in his image and Gustave in the image of an anthropoid or a despised ugly duckling, universally rejected? The original act is described: it was a *considered* defect (otherwise would he speak of *fatum*?) that produced a creature in order to taint it with nullity. Nullity having been the real aim of the creative project, the void that results, a parasite of being, is in itself an ontological disgrace as a *nonbeing that exists*. The disgrace will end if this presumptuous nothingness comes to terms with himself and recognizes by doing away with himself that he was created and put into the world only *to be no more* or, if you will, only that the Other might implant in him that final aim which is also the temporal development of his essence: self-suppression. A paradoxical situation: the author of his days rejects him by creating him, he creates him so as to reject him and so that the creature in good time shall take responsibility for this rejection and despise himself enough to end his life. Gustave, however, means to say precisely that neither father nor God is the cause of Marguerite's suffering. Only *fatum*. But as we have seen, it is the young author himself who has created the poor woman in hatred and so that the

whole world shall condemn her to death. He may well have suffered
and clenched his teeth when he let loose his fury on the unfortunate
woman and above all when he despised *himself* in her. This said, what
does he want us to think? That his father loved him and then rejected
him? No doubt. The frustration of love is at the center of the narrative.
And what else? That the same Achille-Cléophas in begetting him
wanted to reject him? That he deliberately gave him a defect unacceptable to the Flaubert family, which is the same thing as driving
him away with the very act that brought him in? Let us note that in
Un Parfum, Gustave the creator is his own father, but the acrobat
Marguerite loves and who abandons her for Isabellada is also Achille-
Cléophas. As if Gustave were saying to the chief surgeon: "You have
stopped loving me because I disappointed you. I don't hold it against
you, for I really am disappointing. But I do reproach you for having
made me like this." Such a grievance would be preposterous, in spite
of all the sophisms we have just quoted, if Gustave believed himself
the victim of a physical or mental deformation; even if he believed
that those who suffer from such things end by internalizing them, he
was not unaware that these are unforeseeable accidents and that the
head of a family has neither the intention nor the means of inflicting
them. What, then, is the existence at once natural and institutional
that in all good conscience he can reproach Achille-Cléophas for having wanted to give him? *Un Parfum à sentir* does not tell us; on the
other hand, it is revealed in an extraordinary text, *La Peste à Florence*,
to which we can now return.

> [Garcia] was weak and sickly, François was strong and robust;
> Garcia was ugly, awkward, he was sluggish and without much
> spirit; François was a handsome, dashing young man. . . . *He
> was therefore*[29] the elder son, the darling of the family—to him
> went all the honors, the glory, the titles, and the offices; to poor
> Garcia, obscurity and scorn.

We have read correctly: François is personable, capable, stalwart,
therefore he is the elder. Two ideas have come into conflict and interpenetrate. Both are quite reasonable: he is the elder son, to him
goes the inheritance; this fine gentleman is the pride of his whole
family. A piece of true foolishness arises from the entanglement of
these ideas: he has all the desirable qualities, therefore he is the elder
son. And Garcia? Oh well, he has none of them, therefore he is the

---

29. My italics.

younger son. For Gustave, the right of primogeniture—nature and culture bound together—determines a child's qualities, and the first-born will be the best. Why? Because he is the first. We might be tempted to say that Gustave is explaining himself poorly, that Cosme *recognizes* these qualities in François because he is the future head of the family, but he doesn't really possess them. No, no—the ideas are fixed, clearly expressed, repeated twenty times in the novella. It is *true* that Garcia is cowardly, malicious, weak, and ugly; as for his brother, I shall not go so far as to say that he is a paragon, but only because Gustave hates this sort of man—awesome, attractive, brilliant, with a capacity for instant and spontaneous adaptation to all situations that is necessarily accompanied by that cardinal vice, complacency. François is Henry as he appears at the end of the first *Education*. But as for beauty, intelligence, courage, and strength, yes, we can rest assured that he possesses them and that they form part of his birthright. As if these virtues flowed spontaneously from his right of inheritance, from his future as paterfamilias.

Is this foolishness? I would rather see it as a spark of genius born of suffering and hatred. It is certainly not true that elder sons have greater worth than younger sons; but the father's favor and, in feudal societies, the absolute certainty of one day being master of the house often give the first son a serene audacity, a happy submission, the consciousness of his duties and his capacities—in sum, of all his opportunities at the outset. After that, what he does with them is strictly his own business. The paterfamilias is at once his creator and his master, but also, since the firstborn must replace him, his most intimate possibility. In our conjugal families the love and confidence of the mother give her favorite child—who is not, far from it, always the eldest—what I earlier called sovereignty. When her favorite is the younger son, the result is compensation, a complex game of disequilibrium and (unbalancing and balancing again) an internalization by the children of the parents' antagonism; the chips are not down. Not always, of course. In "patriarchal" families the father reigns, and since the hierarchy of the sons is based upon the right of primogeniture, he produces his favorite by a mere act of sex, *in objectivity*. He will love him whatever his face, but not like mothers who prefer the flesh of their flesh to any other without demanding anything. That objective love, founded on a social convention which itself expresses the whole society and the collection of institutions that guarantee its order, is at the same time an unreasonable claim and a kind of generosity. Besides, the father does not address himself to the little accidental and fortuitous life just born but to the social being of his replacement; for the little favorite to internalize that love and to become conscious of that objective being, namely of his absolute and superior excellence, amounts to the same thing. Thus François's qualities are nothing more than the happy development of his opportunities. He is capable because he feels comfortable in his role as future master; he is a fine speaker because language, like everything else, is his; his benevolent nobility indicates that he is conscious of the extreme responsibilities he will assume upon the father's death. For the same reason Garcia, secondary by essence—that is, on the level of paternal fiat—is sorely lacking the love that would have allowed him to love himself. What good will it do him to exert himself, to learn, to make progress? We understand, he must keep in line—live in his place, never higher, this is primary. The two brothers are equally alienated; in each of them existence is subordinated to being, namely to the Other. But alienation serves François, while it does a disservice to Garcia. The date of his birth prescribes the limit of his ambitions. He's spineless, they say? It's his duty, for goodness' sake—let him not take it into his head to eclipse the future head of the family; and then, why knock himself out since in any case the honors and the money will go to the firstborn? François is *self-sufficient*: he depends only on his father, that is, in a sense, only on himself. It would be of no account to him if old Cosme, after begetting him, had made children by the dozen—his prerogatives would not be encroached upon. Garcia, that relative being, is conditioned down to his innermost thoughts, down to his character, to his bones, not only by his abstract condition as younger son but by him who makes that condition concrete and unbearable, by that brother who sees him, who talks to him, and whose shining virtues—which are privileges—have the direct effect of raising the shadows of vice in the younger brother's heart. Even vice itself is relative in Garcia; it is not born directly from his singular essence, it exists only in relation to François's virtues. Garcia's being is reduced to his being-other, it is a limit imposed a priori by the Other; it is a negation imposed by the father in the imperious form, "Go no further," and embodied by his older brother whose plenitude returns him endlessly to nonbeing. Hence the unique and futile passion of the younger brother to substitute himself for the future head of the family, by killing him if there is no other way.

And yet, although his passions are inscribed well before his birth in his status as younger son, they will not appear if he doesn't realize them; his murderous intentions cannot spring from his essence—even though they are included in it—as mathematical properties; they will exist as real and dated determinations *on condition that he is moved by them*. It is true that his cowardice—to cite only one example—is induced by his brother's courage, but it would be only virtual if he hadn't actually taken fright and fled the battlefield. It is here that we rediscover Marguerite's slave-will and finally understand the symbolic ugliness the author has given her. For when he takes flight, when he is consumed by jealous ambition, when he dreams of killing François, Garcia is made totally responsible for his subjective reality; it is he and he alone who is affected by these malign impulses and who makes them exist. Here he is, horribly guilty. But on the other side, albeit without excusing him, Gustave tells us clearly that in actualizing his vices or meditating on his sinister projects the younger son of the Médicis is only internalizing the status that has been imposed on him and defines him by privation. In other words, when Garcia dreams of assassinating François, he *realizes* his condition as younger son. He realizes it *spontaneously*. And quite as spontaneously when he falls unconscious during the ball. But spontaneity does not exclude heteronomy, quite the contrary. Alienated spontaneity, directed freedom—this is slave-will. Marguerite was guilty of internalizing her ugliness: indeed, she did it spontaneously, but she was made in such a way that she had to perform this internalization to the exclusion of any other. Similarly, Garcia has license to internalize his imposed essence so as to bear all the responsibility for it. In effect, he is himself executing, and at his own expense, the prenatal judgment that condemns him to mediocrity and envy; he is therefore guilty. His soul is black, he is tormented by an impotent and jealous ambition, he exudes malice—therefore he is the younger son. Here we are led back to root evil. The young man is punished from the time he is conceived for an offense it was decided he will commit. More precisely, the offense is only the inevitable internalization of the anticipated punishment; malicious because he is younger, younger because he is malicious—this double bind reveals to us Garcia's profound unhappiness, which is his haunted soul. Whatever he thinks, whatever he feels, whatever he undertakes, he actualizes his unsurmountable condition as younger son.

Is this what Marguerite's ugliness symbolizes, then? Is this the crime for which Gustave blames the paterfamilias? After *La Peste à Florence* we have no more doubts, this is it. Indeed, on that memorable night when he created Gustave, Achille-Cléophas might have feared that his future offspring would be infirm or ill, but he could not have foreseen it with any certainty; he was taking his chances, that's all, and for this his son could not strictly hold him accountable. On the other hand, nine years after the birth of Achille the chief surgeon had one assurance—formal but absolute: whatever might happen, his first son would be nine years older than the newcomer. Here it is, the worm in the apple, the fly in the ointment: *younger son*, the child would be born a younger son; the father of the Flaubert family knew it and this assurance did not restrain him. Better, since he wanted this second son, it was only *in order to have a younger son* that he fathered him. So what! someone will say, that wasn't doing him such a great wrong. Let us not deceive ourselves. The condition of a younger sibling is variable; everything depends upon the family unit and its structures. Of two brothers who are not twins, one must perforce be older than the other; this physical necessity does not in itself constitute a destiny unless it is coupled by a cultural determination. Even more so, if a universal institution is involved: the child submits more easily because "this is how it is." But when Gustave came into the world, the right of primogeniture was abolished. Yet among the Flauberts a form of it still existed. It was the progenitor's pleasure to maintain it. The family structure was such that this preferential system appeared as both an objective determination of social mores, which was in principle no longer valid or had passed in certain privileged circles from institutional rule to custom, and in a generally hostile milieu as a free decision, as a subjective fiat by the paterfamilias. In a society where the right of primogeniture, suppressed by law, existed in pockets here and there, a capricious and sovereign subjectivity reanimated it in a particular instance and affirmed it by creating a younger son so that he might be affected by an inferior status. In other words, the father had "his idea"; Gustave, in any event, is convinced of it. And what does it mean to be a younger son if not to feel one's being—that is, one's status—as *other*? Let us understand that it is at once desired by another and makes Gustave, a relative person, *other* than the Flauberts—who are all absolutes. Better still, to be a younger son is to differ from oneself; the spontaneity of experience tends to be supremely self-affirming—that's me, I'm living, I feel alive—but the status of youngest contains and denies this spontaneity; the moment the child affirms himself he feels secondary, he lives the contradiction of his *existence* and his being as Marguerite lives her love and her ugliness. As a younger son, Gustave is inferior and responsible for his inferiority. In the Flaubert family, you are not "inferior"—you must be worthy of the glorious governing father. If he has cursed you in the process of making you, thus deciding that you should be unworthy, there are only two solutions. Push your spiteful submission to the limit and *realize* yourself as nothingness by fainting or suicide; or push your furious revolt to the point of murder. Two solutions which for Gustave are only one. Two ways, to be sure, of making oneself relative. But above all, two ways of living out the contradiction to the end, that is, without neglecting either of the two terms. Chained freedom: the absolute has only one way of making itself absolutely relative and that is by abolishing itself; but at the same time, the other solution is a given, for if by suppressing himself as an individuated person the young man *realizes himself* as younger son, he will abolish himself as younger son if he decides to survive *in person* and suppress the elder. It's quite clear, in fact: a younger son who has gotten rid of his older brother with a dagger's thrust, unless the business is conducted in the greatest secrecy and nothing at all leaks out, runs a strong risk of being condemned in the eyes of his judges as a junior murderer, which is one way among others of showing himself to be relative and second and thus spontaneously to express his pure prefabricated essence and assume responsibility for it. Condemned to death, executed, he will have rejoined Marguerite, by way of a detour, in the nonbeing which is her lot. Without escaping, for all that, the eternal and prenatal verdict; once dead, Marguerite ceases to be ugly only to become carrion, and once executed, Garcia will remain *in saecula saeculorum* a younger son. Quite simply, of these two inseparable enterprises the first represents the practical movement of realization, and the second is only its imaginary reversal. Gustave of course never really attempted suicide. But he considered it, he saw it as his innermost possibility—hesitating before a real solution and finally setting it aside, or rather deferring it; in principle—even if he sometimes took pleasure in imagining his own death, his father's remorse, etc.—this deferred act, always ready at hand, seemed like an inward determination of the young man, virtual, if you will, but not imaginary. Kill Achille? This is one of the adolescent's fundamental desires, but it is an unreal desire that is manifest at moments when the author abandons himself and gives over his pen to a directed oneirism. If we look more closely at the last pages of *La Peste*, we shall see what real intentions hide behind this dreamed desire.

False death, fainting spells—the child never manages these, never goes further than the stupor and lethargic melancholy. In other words, he never loses consciousness; but the story of Marguerite proves that many of his stupors were the consequence of a preliminary illumination, which is always the same. The *idea bursts* upon Marguerite, and the poor homely thing is off to drown herself. We know what she has suddenly understood: the unbending rejection with which they confront me is written into my being in advance; *it is myself*, a conscious fault in the plenitude which in order to make itself whole requires my death; detestable and detested, I detest myself to the point of self-destruction. This is my essence, and my suicide will fulfill me as the supreme object of universal hatred (mine included); through the annihilation that is *my* categorical imperative, I will become what I am. The young author thinks and feels the same way, less dramatically but just as profoundly. Whatever the violence of the passions provoked by the eternal recurrence of familial ceremonies, each of which reinstates him as younger son, those passions cannot challenge his acceptance a priori of the paternal curse and the consciousness of his own guilt. This means that they are experienced from the perspective of self-destruction, which helps to account for their passive character; faced with Achille, rage can overwhelm him but it will be white rage; disarmed in advance by a fundamental acquiescence, it can only be turned against himself, against his unworthiness, and mimic death. I say *mimic* because when it is a question of suicide, the young author at fifteen doesn't find any solution satisfying. Marguerite *ends her own* life; the water of the river is the necessary instrument, but there's a problem: for her end to be pure, she should kill herself by her own hand at the moment when universal rejection, once internalized, is joined with the being-for-rejection that her creator gave her. The experienced and conscious unity of this double negation ought by itself to be death, without recourse to a material tool. It is for this reason that Gustave some months later allows Garcia's passive rage—which corresponds to the same sudden consciousness—to precipitate his false death, a fainting spell of the sort that the author came close to but never knew. Rejected by Cosme and by the Florentine aristocracy, the conclusion is self-evident in the poor lieutenant's parasitic existence—he loses consciousness. This false death represents a progression in Gustave's oneiric thought: it is so perfectly in agreement with the requirements of the situation, so spontaneous as well, so discreet that no one takes notice of it. The ball continues; in the early hours of the morning, when the last guests have left, they sweep out the hall; an unflappable servant throws him out with the garbage without any loss to the world's plenitude. However, Gustave is not satisfied with this perfection. The fainting spell is very good—he sees it as the radicalization of his stupors, their *meaning*; but precisely because these lethargic and conscious states are familiar to him, because the momentary abolishing of his consciousness seems to him in these moments of flight to be his temptation, he is not unaware that false death, if it could take place, would be followed by resurrection. He will go further in *Novembre*, we shall see. But at that point he has entered the preneurotic phase. For the moment, he dares not push things to the limit; losing consciousness is a rehearsal for death, not death itself. And then, for once, he would like under the cover of oneirism to settle his account with Achille. Thus Garcia recovers, and in the last chapter of the novella we see him slay François with his own hands.

This is the second solution: crime. It is shocking, we see it as a weakness, pure and simple, to resort to force. But it must be understood that this is the sole revenge that could satisfy Flaubert; if Garcia paid some officers to assassinate the cardinal, he would be resorting to the force of others. What the young author wants is to suppress his impotence as a *relative being* by coming to terms with the Other, with the absolute truth that has made him relative down to his very bones. It is not enough to suppress this odious absolute, he must above all be replaced; cowardly, passive, a poor duelist, Garcia must become the elder brother by destroying that strapping fellow accustomed to professional soldiering, whose younger brother he was made. Let us read over the last part of the story carefully; we shall see that it has all the characteristics of a dream. Gustave was sleeping with his eyes open when he wrote it, and his intentions are less hidden than in the subsequent stories.

Everyone has gone to the hunt on horseback. The cardinal is in riding dress and carries a sword. He "veers off to follow the deer's track"; Garcia, "dressed in black, somber and pensive," "*mechanically*" follows him. They go "deeper and deeper" into the wood. They dismount and sit on the grass. "Here you are, Cardinal," says Garcia, and draws his sword, which, given the position he was in, must have been accomplished with some difficulty. François, insulted, takes a while to understand. Finally he rises, while Garcia, still seated, breaks into sobs. "You are mad," he says. Garcia responds to these words with the words: "Mad? Oh yes, mad! assassin? perhaps. . . ." And then he suddenly stands up, at least I suppose he does. For the author doesn't say a word about it. But here is the text:

309

[Garcia] sobbed and it was as though the blood were leaving his veins.

"You are mad, Garcia," said the cardinal, getting up, alarmed.

"Mad? Oh yes, mad! assassin? perhaps. Listen, Monseigneur Cardinal François named by the pope, listen"—it was a terrible duel, to the death, but a desperate duel, the very tale sends shivers of horror down the spine—"you always had the advantage, society protected you, well and good. You've tortured me all my life, now I'm cutting your throat."

And he knocked him down with a furious arm and held his sword to his chest.

Why didn't François disarm his brother? Why didn't he at least prevent him from getting up? What is this "terrible duel"? Did the cardinal in his turn draw his sword? In this case, why does he let himself be "knocked down with a furious arm"? If there is a surprise attack, there can be no duel; if there is a duel, Garcia has to lose. Furthermore, Gustave seems at times to be telling us specifically about a combat (it was a duel . . . etc.) and at times about a murder (assassin perhaps . . ."). The strangest thing is the end:

"Oh! forgive me, forgive me, Garcia," said Fran̂ois in a trembling voice, "what have I done to you?"

"What have you done to me? There!" And he spat in his face.

"I give you injury for injury and scorn for scorn. You are a cardinal, I insult your dignity as cardinal; you are beautiful, strong, and powerful, I insult your strength, your beauty, and your power, for I am holding you under me, you quiver with fear beneath my knee. Ah! you are trembling! Tremble, then, and suffer as I trembled and suffered. You didn't know, you with your vaunted wisdom, how like a demon a man is when injustice has turned him into a wild beast. Ah! I suffer to see you live, there!"

. . . .

And a piercing cry escaped from beneath the foliage and sent a nest of owls flying off.

Garcia remounted his horse and was off at a gallop; there were drops of blood on his lace ruff.

It is said specifically that *weakness insults strength* by mastering it. This would be possible if Garcia had organized an ambush. Gustave doesn't even think of this; the quarrel must work itself out between the two brothers. And then, above all, he wants the impossible—for weakness to remain weakness even at the moment it subdues and mocks strength. So what! you will say, a weak person can always kill strong one, all he needs is a lucky hit. That's true. But this isn't the issue in our story. Nor does Garcia knife his brother in the back; this little shrimp plants himself in front of the big hulk of a man and with only one arm—the other is holding his sword—with his left arm, knocks him down. After which he puts his knee on his brother's chest; then the two men must have rolled on the ground together, and the little one, using some Greco-Roman thrusts, must have pushed the bigger man's shoulders to the ground. Where were their weapons at that moment? Did Garcia drop his? But we are told he "held" it to his victim's "chest." Then he must have picked it up and risen nimbly—that implement is not convenient for striking at close range. Unless he knocked his brother to the ground while he was standing. But it isn't the sword he is holding to François's chest: "I am holding you under me, you quiver with fear beneath my knee." Here is Garcia, then, standing and kneeling at the same time; he is cutting François's throat while pinning him down with a sword *in the heart*. In the last chapter we shall be presented with the cardinal's corpse; bruises are found on his knees. So the unfortunate man didn't fall on his back? Yet Garcia *knocked him down*. These contradictions prove that Gustave is not taking care to give us a visualizable scene. We are reading the discourse of an assassin, and it is through one of his own words that we learn the outcome: "There!" says Garcia. And this indicates that he has struck. But the act takes place between the lines; Gustave has replaced it by a line of dots, as was done in certain novels when lovers were sleeping together. Why this discretion worthy of classical tragedy? Well, first of all because the murder scene is not capable of realization, the slightest detail would underscore its improbability. And then we know Gustave's passivity, his contemplative quietism—he is comfortable when he is describing *exis* (objects, ceremonies, attitudes, habits), uncomfortable when he must relate *praxis*. But the fundamental reason is something else: to make us visualize the crime he would have to live it, and that is just what he is forbidden to do; living it would then be committing it. Without any doubt he wanted *to have* Achille *killed*, but not to kill him with his own hands.

See how the taste for detail returns to him right after the assassination. He is pleased to tell us that Garcia "had drops of blood on his lace ruff." What clumsiness! He smears himself with blood, leaves his victim lying there, and rejoins the retinue! Naturally the body is discovered and reported to the duke. This idiotic fratricide announces its author so quickly that Cosme cuts him down with a thrust of his sword. Obviously what is involved is what the analysts call a self-punishing act, intended to force the paterfamilias himself to kill his son. We see Flaubert's malevolence, which would be astonishing in the adolescent if it were thought to be calculated; but that is not so—it precisely expresses the original situation. Garcia says to his father since you counted me out when you gave me life, finish the job, with your own hands do away with this life you condemned to annihilation. The passage is striking in its rigor: "A man is like a demon when injustice has turned him into a wild beast." Garcia, the product of prenatal injustice, realizes himself as they made him and behaves like a wild beast by assassinating his brother. The wretched man, having become what he was, calls for the punishment that does away with him; and it is Cosme himself, responsible for his birth, who must assume the responsibility for his death. Admirable, just, and nevertheless guilty, the duke condemned the child well before creating him suddenly the meaning of that life is to compel the judge himself to execute the sentence he has passed—if I realize myself at last as you wanted me to be, you will be forced to kill me. It is understood that the crime is a *means* of finding death while avoiding suicide; it is not accomplished for itself but in order to unleash Cosme's vengeance. A strange reversal: injustice has made Garcia unjust; since he is unjust, to do away with him is just. Indeed, before striking his younger son, Cosme declares, "stamping his foot, 'Oh yes, let justice be done It is necessary, the blood of the just cries out for vengeance against us; well, then, vengeance!'" It all happens as though the progenitor were making reparations for his own initial fault. To give life to a younger son is to fate him to come up against his older brother and as a consequence, be compelled to liquidate himself. Gustave dreams of defying his father, but that defiance supposes an irreparable act which is repugnant to Flaubert's imagination. For a long time now in fact, he has been affected by passivity; for this reason the report of the fratricide is skipped over—reporting it is almost committing it Does he desire to kill Achille? No, he desires to desire it in order to become at last the monster they want to make him. The child denounces the father's offense by submissively fulfilling his intentions the father will have reason to punish his son, but in so doing he will demonstrate that he was wrong to create him. Gustave's offense disappears with him; a single guilty party remains—Achille-Cléophas Thus *La Peste à Florence* is an "experiment." Marguerite's suicide didn' satisfy Gustave; his rancor remains unassuaged; not yet having come to the point of "death by thought," he risks killing Achille and making a quick getaway, and is delighted to detail the consequences of his crime. Death by thought will be an *arrest of the feelings* through a consciousness of the impossibility of living; capital punishment is the same *arrest by death* in the dimension of otherness. Regardless, the emotional discharge is too strong; the child is overwhelmed at having dared fratricide, even in imagination. He will not try it again; in the subsequent narratives the victims will be killed by each other but they will not touch their executioners; Djalioh rapes and strangles only Adèle and her child; Mazza poisons only her weak husband, her children; Messieurs Ernest and Paul, the torturers, enjoying universal respect, will survive the massacres and die in their own beds.

In *La Peste à Florence* and in *Un Parfum* we have learned one of the grievances Gustave nurses against his father: that he made him a younger son and ostensibly preferred his elder son to Gustave. In this form, the wrongs of the Flaubert father are likely to remain somewhat abstract, and it seems remarkable that Gustave suffered from them so severely. It must be observed, however, that the little boy's unhappiness was doubled by the fact that he was conscious of his basic unworthiness. It is true that, according to him, the unworthiness flowed directly from his character as younger son. But doesn't this involve a construction, a rationalization of his primitive feelings? The advantage of the tale entitled *Un Secret de Philippe le Prudent* is that the theme of the elder brother and the enemy-father are dissociated. Philippe II, the father of Carlos, has suffered all his life from seeing his brother preferred to himself. It is this unjust preference, no doubt, that has made him unhappy and malicious. We must assume this is why he inflicts such torments on his son. This son, still quite young, is of course an old man; he is sequestered by his father, who spies on him, in the company of the Grand Inquisitor, through an invisible peephole he has had made in the wall. Carlos is not unaware of this— he feels he is *visible* and *seen* even in his solitude; not for a moment is the father's gaze turned away from him—he notes his son's gestures, reads his soul. Carlos knows himself to be inhabited by the stare of a malevolent father who alienates him by objectifying, or affecting with otherness, his most intimate subjectivity, which becomes *other* for itself because it is *other* for the absolute Other. Here is the result, which is the painter's first self-portrait:

[Don Carlos] had lovely black hair. . . . His limbs were well-proportioned, his waist was that of a twenty-year-old, but if you

313

could have seen his hollow cheeks, his blue eyes so sad and melancholy, his forehead full of wrinkles, you would have said he was an old man. There was such sadness and bitterness in his eyes, his pale forehead was furrowed with such premature wrinkles that it could be easily seen this man had suffered atrocious, outrageous, unheard-of troubles.

It seems, then (and for this reason I believe *Un Secret* was written before *La Peste* and *Un Parfum*), that Gustave's two grievances against Achille-Cléophas were first experienced separately. Especially since Charles V's preference for the handsome Juan of Austria, while mentioned, does not appear unjust; Gustave seems to *give him reason* to feel this way. It is this preference, nevertheless, that has formed Philippe's suspicious and jealous character; it is his *secret*—but at that time the young author was ensnared in his myths. Garcia is malicious because he has been mocked since birth, because his father wanted him as a younger son; thus he is found to be both guilty and innocent. Philippe, in contrast, while he may have suffered his father's unjust predilection, which may be the cause of his iniquitous conduct toward his own son, is not innocent for all that. It will further be observed that his destitution remains on the emotional level and is not accompanied by frustration with regard to his inheritance. Juan is a dead archduke. Philippe is an absolute monarch. By contrast, Gustave complains of being spied on by his father, whose surgical eye penetrates to the depths of his soul. It seems, then, that this grievance comes first and the other is a later addition; only subsequently are they merged in a skillful construction. Before he felt frustrated by his older brother, Gustave had the feeling that his father saw through him and read his soul like an open book.

This hypothesis is confirmed by a reading of *Matéo Falcone*, a novella written toward the middle of 1835, when Flaubert was thirteen and a half. The story of little Albano, of course, was not invented by Gustave; he borrowed it undigested from Mérimée. It is close to plagiarism, such as children will do at this age; but one wonders why, of all the works he read, the young author chose to plagiarize this one. The reason becomes clear when we read Gustave's work. In Mérimée, the hero is the father; the author seeks to reveal the substance of Corsican honor and to what extremities a man can be driven by it. If Gustave rewrote it, it was not because he found strength or beauty in the work of his predecessor; rather, he found himself in total disagreement with it. In his work the hero is most certainly Albano. He is not concerned with denying his fault—the little Corsican has betrayed an outlaw for the sake of a watch. Therefore he is a criminal. Yes, but he doesn't even understand what he has done and conceals so little that he takes the watch and, laying it on the ground, "watches it glitter in the rays of the sun." This, as we see, involves a self-destructive act, as in *La Peste à Florence*. Matéo returns, sees what has happened, takes his rifle, and kills the child. Gustave, vehement at that period when it came to condemning or absolving, doesn't offer a word of protest; in the eyes of the unwritten law, this child—who dishonors his family—is punishable. The idea of annihilation by the father, which in *La Peste* one year later is "brought out," is at this time a definite emotional theme born of rancor and regret which remains latent and still undeveloped. The child does not yet say, "Kill me, you who made me this way," but his morbid daydreams are fueled by a vague desire: fathers like Ugolino eat their children; eat me, since I shamed you, rather than executing me as you do. Furthermore, he does not conceal the fact that this excessively strict justice is punishable; Albano's mother dies of sorrow, and the rigid father, responsible for two deaths, remains alone. It will be noted that this is the first time Mme Flaubert appears in a story—only to die. Much later, in *Novembre*, she will reappear—the narrator will dream that she drowns herself. Toward the age of thirteen, trying to explain the unhappiness of an earlier childhood (this is not in doubt; he is at boarding school, and the formidable Achille-Cléophas can track him down only twice a week), he still preserves the idea of a mother who was more indulgent than Moses the terrible—she was cold, but sometimes she took him on her knee and spoke to him about God. First the paterfamilias stole him from her and from God in order to crown him with his favors, and then he withdrew his favors from him.[30] Gustave reproaches Dr. Flaubert *before anyone else* for this disgrace; but he is beaten since he is also conscious of having merited it.[31]

30. We have his projected melodramas, collected by Bruneau in his admirably documented work on Flaubert's *Oeuvres de jeunesse*. There the mother is constantly present. We shall examine them when we shall try to understand Flaubert's sexuality, or the "oedipus complex" in a semipatriarchal family. Most of these melodramas are contemporary with the novellas we have just analyzed.
31. I am leaving aside a very significant novella, *L'Anneau du prieur*. Bruneau has shown that it was directly inspired by a model essay published in a manual of the period. But this is not the reason we have set it aside, for Gustave himself recognizes that the meaning he gives the story is entirely personal and contrary to the one proposed by the model. Although it may still concern the relations of father to son and the excessively cruel punishment of a guilty party, the principal theme—the summation of experience—constrains us to examine it in another chapter, when we shall ask ourselves why all the works of Flaubert are exhaustive summations.

We shall end with the beginning; at thirteen, Gustave composed a literary journal[32] for himself alone. We have the "sixth evening" from it—the others are lost. In it, Gustave describes a *Journey in Hell*, and this is what we read: "And a man, a poor man in rags with white hair, a man burdened with misery, with infamy and opprobrium, one of those whose forehead wrinkled with cares reflects at twenty the misfortunes of a century, was seated at the foot of a column. And he seemed like the ant at the foot of the pyramid. And he watched men for a long time; everyone looked at him with disdain and pity, and he cursed them all; for this old man was Truth."

The first known work, the first appearance of the theme of senility. This time, someone will say, there is no question of self-projection; he develops a banal allegory in all objectivity. Can one be so sure? I note that this old man is *"one of those* . . . whose forehead reflects at twenty the misfortunes of a century." He has brothers, then, sisters too perhaps—these characters are soon going to make their appearance and will be named Carlos, Marguerite, Garcia, Giacomo, Djalioh, Julietta, etc.—the description fits them all. It fits the hero of *Novembre* still better: he complains of growing old from ennui, the mal du siècle. On the other hand, it hardly suits its object. Nontemporality, objectivity, impersonality—these qualities are so manifest that popular imagery takes them into account and conventional wisdom shows us truth as unknown, disguised but impassive, never laughing or crying. It is represented specifically as a young nude emerging from a well—youth being the equivalent of eternity; but no one except Gustave would think to present it in the guise of an old beggar. As for the curses, they are even less suitable, lending it passions, injustice—in short, assimilating truth to error. For this reason Flaubert's allegory is suspect; truth is confused with the one who possesses it and is burdened by it. The author shows us men who are implacable against one of their own. Thus—by a striking similarity—"the crowd" will pursue Marguerite with its threats and insults. And why this surliness, if not that he knows the secret that men want to conceal from themselves? He is a traitor, an intruder who is continually on the brink of revealing to them the final word on the human adventure. They shout to make him keep quiet. They hate his precocious senility itself, for it is a sign of the harm that conscious knowledge would do them.

32. Ernest sometimes collaborated on it.

This very young old man is Gustave himself. Crushed, rejected, the child already possesses a "complete presentiment of life." In this sense what is true is *in him*. But in another sense he is the truth of the Flauberts—as the colonized man is the truth of the colonizer, the slave of the master. A latecomer, unfortunate, tainted, he believes that what his parents hate in him, their product, is a realistic and not very flattering image of the family group; the child, to strike back, curses those his unhappiness accuses and who have the impudence to reproach him for it. Truth, like ugliness, is a vice; furthermore, Gustave makes no distinction between the two. What is involved is one and the same permanent and visible denunciation of the species in one of its members. And the reaction of the species with a death sentence. What appears clearly in this "journey in hell" is that an enraged youngster has already slipped into the skin of an allegory and has suddenly transformed it. Since when? There is no way of knowing. It is even impossible to decide to what degree Gustave is conscious of embodying himself. Not that the operation takes place without his knowledge, in the shadows, but *on the contrary* because the project is not adequately determined. Indeed, the role of symbol still remains highly ambiguous—one gets inside an idea only to find oneself inside a character, and vice versa. Yet this allows us to advance the proposition that the original intuition had only recently found its verbal expression. *Before the age of thirteen*, Gustave already considered himself an old man. He would grow older, but whatever the age of his arteries, the age of his heart would be fixed: from thirteen to fifty-eight he was once and for all a centenarian.

We shall need only a few words to indicate the meaning of the myth of senility at the moment of its first appearance: the man sitting at the foot of the column is old because he knows *the* truth. What truth? The same one that Flaubert makes Satan articulate in conclusion:

"Show me your realm," I said to Satan.
"Here it is."
"How is that?"
And Satan answered me:
"The world, that is Hell."

If the world is hell, we are damned at birth. This means first of all that creation is judgment: procreation is equivalent to condemnation. Such is the meaning of Adam's curse. But there is another consequence of this assimilation: since we are guilty, the Devil wills us in advance the worst torments. We all have a destiny, and with a little

317

courage and lucidity each of us could prophecy his own. Cursed, the man of truth knows that he lives in hell and that he *deserves* his unjust suffering. For this reason the rest of the damned reject him; they do not want to know about either their fault or their damnation and persist in explaining the inflexible movement of life by the encounter of causal series, instead of seeing in each of their misadventures the effect of a malign decision on the part of the Lord. But the prophetic intuition of the man of truth has no rational basis, it is his heart that feels it as subjective certainty on the occasion of each particular suffering. Let us understand that *true* pain is all-encompassing; it savors itself as a premeditated consequence, as a repetition—all told, as a promise of increased torments; in short, any *felt* unhappiness summarizes the whole of life, from original sin and the Fall to capital punishment. And of course annihilation can be replaced by simply fainting. But fainting is itself annihilation. Flaubert confirms this idea in a letter written in his prime at the age of thirty-one:[33] "I am sure I know what it is to die. I have often clearly felt my soul escaping from me, as you can feel the blood flowing out in bloodletting." Fainting is not an *image* of death, it is death itself; in the first place you lose consciousness, but *most importantly* it is a conclusion—a whole life exasperated by a singular unhappiness is swallowed up. To be sure, you survive; yet this is in no sense a revival but rather an aging. After several brief existences, you are a hundred years old.

From the age of thirteen Flaubert associated life and destiny, suffering and punishment, the father's exquisite sovereignty and diabolical paternal injustice. False death and survival. He summarizes all of these still rather roughly outlined themes in two motifs: the myth of the original damnation that makes this world a unique hell, and the myth of the hundred-year-old child. To die is to internalize objective truth, to carry out the prenatal judgment brought against each of us by our father; to grow old is to somatize moral suffering and to survive, bloodless, apathetic, the mind empty and the body exhausted, until the next "false death" and from this to the next until radical totalization, that is, annihilation. It is striking that our analytic regression should have allowed us to discover a motif that is profoundly buried in the autobiographies and in the works that precede them, hidden under its own embellishments—that of predestination, by which we understand the prenatal condemnation to unhappiness and death decided by the father before conception. If the world is

33. 27 December 1852.

hell—an idea that Gustave would cling to all his life—it is because I is an Other; *before the age of thirteen* and—as we shall prove—from his seventh year, Gustave discovers in himself a horrible otherness fixed long since by the admirable and sadistic intelligence of Achille-Cléophas, which causes the unhappiness and the shame he must nonetheless live out to the bitter end since he is nothing other than this, which is nonetheless other than himself. For this reason he projects himself into his novellas and makes himself into *another* without much comprehending his enterprise, at times in order to scrutinize this alter ego he cannot observe in himself as it is already part of the observation that is trying to discover it, at times because his otherness prevents him from knowing anything that is not himself as other. For the same reason he attempts to double himself in these writings in order to grasp himself as one and the other; he succeeds, however, in only one instance, in *Rêve d'enfer*, in which the theme "elder son–younger son" does not intrude to confuse and deflect his enterprise. He will come back to it, however, in his major works; we shall find the first and second narrator in *Novembre*; Henry and Jules in the first *Education*; Homais and Bournisien in *Madame Bovary*, Frédéric and Deslauriers in the second *Education*, and finally *Bouvard et Pécuchet*. At the source of all these doublets—which are sometimes two aspects of himself, sometimes himself and his opposite, sometimes two opposed principles—we must place a malaise that dates back to his prehistory and finds its first expression in *Un Parfum à sentir*.

Regressive analysis through the examination of the early works referred us to the objective structures of the Flaubert family. These parents were not tender but virtuous by nature, they did their duty; we know that the extraordinary idea Gustave secretly had of his father, without quite admitting it to himself, cannot correspond to reality. Achille-Cléophas was authoritarian, passionate, sometimes tearful, certainly overworked; events made it such that he understood his younger son less and less. It is regrettable for Gustave's happiness that this man of science should have adopted mechanistic philosophy (but could he have done otherwise? it was the bourgeois, *therefore* the progressive ideology of his time) and that he understood nothing about literature; we shall see too that he was close to considering his younger son a backward child, which humiliated his paternal pride, and that he made the mistake of letting Gustave know it. But he was not an ogre, his students loved him, his elder son and his wife adored him. For Gustave to have believed that Achille-Cléophas had cursed him in creating him, they both must have been victims of that awesome family the physician had begotten and the children were supposed to perpetuate. As far as our author is concerned, after this retrospective study—which demonstrates the profound sincerity of his desolation, his ennui, his pessimism, and his misanthropy, and their roots in a disconcertingly early period of his life—it seems a proven fact that to be born at this time, into this family, and to be born the younger son was to fall into a mortal trap. The task of the young victim was to internalize in displeasure the contradictions of this transitory and poorly balanced product, a semipatriarchal family group founded and dominated by a mutant who had had a peasant upbringing and who had leaped all at once to the upper reaches of the middle class with the title *capacité*, preserving in himself that explosive mixture of rural tradition and bourgeois ideology. In this sense the child we have encountered through his first works is nothing more than the family itself as experienced by one of its members, defined a priori by the place he occupies within it as the real substance of the communal subjectivity. But this member, a determination of intersubjectivity, grasps experience in himself as damnation pure and simple; *by living* he conducts an experiment in the impossibility of living. How can this be? How could the offspring of a happy and prosperous family come so early to hate humankind, beginning with himself, to see all men as victims and simultaneously as executioners? How could he have found so early "a complete presentiment of life," which indicates that he considered all human existence as fated and at the same time thought that the worst was always certain? In order to decide, we must follow the same path again in reverse. We shall take the child when he leaves the hands of Caroline Flaubert and we shall try, through reports, through the correspondence, the same works taken this time as unquestioned testimony, to recompose his life as it was lived from day to day. In this progressive synthesis we shall allow the experience to develop itself before our eyes as *stress*, which is the inseparable unity of aggressions and defense; in a word, we shall try to effect a comprehensive restoration of this existence considered as a totalization in progress.

B. Vassalage

During the first two years he was in his mother's hands, Gustave was a weed; he lived haphazardly, without knowing why, feeling somehow superfluous. From the time he was three or four years old, his father took an interest in him; the child promptly adored him. What does this mean? How did this cheerless and superfluous life respond to the first marks of love it was given?

The child, of course, has said nothing on the subject. But if we examine the adult writer on his earliest childhood—the period before the fall—we shall see that it is not the lost happiness he regrets, but rather what Gide calls fervor and what Gustave calls "simplicity."

Just what he means by this we are told in an unpublished passage from *Madame Bovary*: "Happy period of her youth when her heart was as pure as holy water and, like it, reflected only the arabesques of the stained glass windows with the tranquil elevation of celestial hopes." "A simple heart," "a pure heart" is not vexed or torn by the conflict between reason and faith—its natural movement bears it upward, it is raised in adoration. Of whom? God, a lord, a father, an employer—it doesn't matter, it is the elevation that counts, whatever its object. And this elevation is an immediate given of the affective nature. Jules Lemaître, that ingenious imbecile, has complained that Félicité was stupid. Where does he get such a notion? Flaubert never thought she was. For him, we know, the worst stupidity is intelligence. The "servant with the great heart" puts her genius into her life. She doesn't reason, but she *understands* because devotion is itself a kind of understanding. Didn't Flaubert repeat countless times that idiots, children, and madmen felt they could trust him "because they know I am one of them"? And of course it is not true, Flaubert is not simple, for he was raised in spite of himself to the level of contradiction. Nevertheless he preserves the nostalgia of unity, all the more powerfully because it is nourished by an obscure reminiscence comparable to the memory of another life. There is a state of innocence; certain people lose it for good, others retrieve it intermittently, still others preserve it from childhood until death. And this state is always characterized by adoration. When the subject considers himself inessential and his lord essential, then he becomes "infinite" and "profound." It is this vagary of the heart and mind united in a total act of love that whispers to Charles the unexpected words: "It is fate." This alone raises him above Homais and Larivière himself. The true cretin is Rodolphe, who finds the wronged husband "a bit low." A text cut from the definitive version spells it out: "For [Rodolphe] understood nothing of the empty passion of pride, of human deference or the consciousness that plunges whole into the beloved, hoards its feelings, kneads and molds them to the proportions of a pure idea by dint of breadth and impersonality." We are far removed

321

here from bourgeois individualism; on the contrary, the only feelings that find grace with this misanthrope are those that shatter the individual. On this level the "humble," the "imbecile" are "unlimited," and the universality of feeling gives their thought depth.

That which marks the infantile origin of this notion à la Rousseau of native innocence, of impersonality dissipated, lost in the social world of individuals—personalized by real property and the particularization of interests—but sometimes revived by a total devotion, is Flaubert's idea that the purest love is perfectly incapable of protecting the beloved. Charles, for example, did not save Emma from unhappiness and death; he succeeded only in making her despise him. Félicité once defended her mistress's children against an angry bull. But what can she do about the disasters that are about to strike the family? What can Justin do but decorate a grave? And little Roque? And Frédéric himself, what can he do for Mme Arnoux? This sublime but ineffectual love is that of a child who sees his parents suffer without daring to make a move and without the means to help them. To please them he gives himself entirely to the trifling tasks they entrust to him, but with no illusions. The bond Flaubert remembers, which he magnifies in *Un Coeur simple*, is the bond of vassalage. Under the Old Regime it defined the social conduct of the vassal—he had to lend his military force to the lord under certain circumstances; as for his feelings, they were his own affair. In the world of childhood, in which Flaubert all his life would dream of immersing himself once again, it was the reverse; a kind of quietism, that will be discussed later, made actions impossible. The elevation of the heart is all that remains. The image of the basin of holy water is quite distinct: one must have a soul that is naked, spacious, vacant, calm enough to reflect the master; this reflection of the infinite in the finite, of the sacred in the profane, gives the creature his full dignity. The finite and contingent substance, when it is pure, reflects lovingly and passively an infinite power which at the same time expands its limits and reinforces its unity. There will be something of this in Flaubert's pantheism, and it is in just this way that he will understand—emotionally more than intellectually—the relation of the finite world to the infinite attribute.

Do all sons feel the same adoration for their fathers? Certainly not. Especially in conjugal families in which love is opposed to aggression. And certainly Gustave, as we say, "has his oedipal problems"—which we shall discuss again when we study his sexuality. But the structure of this semipatriarchal family as well as Mme Flaubert's character was opposed to the classical trinitarian relationship which is found these days at the basis of our sensibilities. Indeed Caroline, lacking love or perhaps the ability to externalize her love, had left her younger son like a fish out of water, living without any reason to live—something he would later call, obscurely but not without justice, agony. All these determinations of his sensibility, and down to that ego which was born in him with weaning, were momentarily nullified when Achille-Cléophas took an interest in him; the child threw himself on this raison d'être, but already frustrated by love, he could no longer find his justification in the magnificent lord's feeling for him, which was benevolent yet lukewarm. He did, however, find justification in being allowed to love. The glorious surgeon *himself* had his full raison d'être—God, the king. And this sufficiency allowed the forlorn child to feel his existence finally as a right: he was born to adore his father, who had made him to reflect that glory which he radiated in his fashion, for which God, it seemed, created us.

A curious letter of Gustave's will confirm us, in these views: "Vigny's book rather shocked me. . . . I saw in it a systematic deprecation of blind devotion (the cult of the Emperor, for example), man's fanaticism for man. . . . What is beautiful in the Empire is the adoration of the Emperor, an exclusive, absurd love. Sublime, truly human."[34] He was twenty-five when he wrote those lines. How could he fail to see that his idea was destroyed by the very words used to state it and that nothing is less "human" than the extreme devotion of one man to another, which creates as the essence of our species a *being-other* and shows us our common condition as contemptible in ourselves, yet admirable in the stranger? I contend that he does in fact see it all, as witness the word "fanaticism," which was, we know, in disrepute. Flaubert uses it purposely in order to shock, with the intention, as we shall see later, of portraying the positive by its negative aspects. And let us not forget that for the same reason he presents the highest principle of his ethic as a maxim of esthetic disorder: this devotion is not *good*, it is *beautiful*. And we are not unaware of the fact that beauty can be terrible. No matter; he discovers himself in spite of it when this sentiment delights him to the degree that he calls it "truly human"; while the adverb is once again misleading, referring to that other norm, truth, the word "human" reveals everything. There is a Flaubertian humanism which is the human relation to vassalage and which he contrasted violently to the ideology of his

34. He is referring to *Servitude et grandeur militaires*.

class about the time it was organizing to overthrow Louis-Philippe. And the principal concern of this "humanism" is not only to puncture particular interest, it is also and perhaps chiefly to oppose the devotion of brotherhood. In brief, at this period the Flaubert son was doing battle on two fronts: one, bourgeois utilitarianism, the other, socialism. He despised the reciprocity of bonds at least as much as he despised atomism. What irritated him about the great social ideas fermenting around 1848 was that they denied the aristocratic *gift* in the name of the community of the species: man is never for me, nor is he *an other* since we are precisely the *same thing*. What I do for him I do for me, he does for me and for himself. This universalist vision does not make solidarity a merit but the necessary means to hasten the advent of the human. Flaubert understood mutual aid only in the form of a sacrifice: someone gives his life for someone in the absolute conviction that his own life doesn't count and that the other life is indispensable on earth. But the reason for this feudalism is clear: to the extent that being is a right, Caroline did not give her second son the right to exist; he would find that right when his father smiled at him, in the permission Dr. Flaubert gave him to reflect his father's venerable essence or to lose himself in it. If veneration is his raison d'être, it exists only as his *being-other* insofar as it was created to deny itself for the sake of another's profit.

It will be remarked that the letter cited above is hardly favorable to the Empire; nor is it more so to the person of the emperor. But Flaubert is twenty-five; the little vassal has long since fallen into disfavor and has scarcely any more illusions about his lord. What he regrets when he recalls his golden age is not the ungrateful object of his worship, but the wholly subjective attitude of vassalage. Thus, while admiring the "sublime devotion" of Napoleon's old guard, he destroys the meaning this devotion had for them—they believed they had found in Napoleon "merit worthy of reverence." For Flaubert, who belongs to the next generation, the object of sacrifice is dubious—in the sense he can write that devotion is *absurd*—but this hardly matters since the sacrifice alone, whatever its object, can elevate the human soul. The feudal edifice is cracked and, in a sense, overturned; the master is only the essential means one chooses in order to become a vassal. We now understand what is involved in the fanaticism that enchants Flaubert and the remote origins of his horror of egalitarianism. Two men who are equal are merely weeds; how can reciprocity alter their status? Equality is universal contingency. If he thinks this way it is because he feels deprived of a mandate. In order to make a man "truly human," that is, justified, it takes two men who are related hierarchically. Still, only one thing is certain: the inferior will be saved by his devotion; for the superior, everything remains undetermined. The vassal, furthermore, realizes his full humanity by destroying himself—in vain—by negating the self for the other's profit.

In sum, for the child Flaubert, vassalage is the means chosen by an inessential being of winning the right to be essential by trading on his inessentiality. His vassalage reassured him during his golden age by concealing his destitution and the emptiness of heaven—the world is full as long as the master remains absolute. From this point of view, he is the gift giver: he gives his person to admire, to serve; he has the extreme generosity to make explicit demands. But the most beautiful gift is the one the vassal will make by sacrificing his life if need be. It is true that this life is nothing; it is worthless and will be justified only by the sacrifice that will end it. Later we shall see Gustave, through a classic reversal, willingly become lord since he cannot remain in his condition as vassal. This is because fundamentally, for reasons that spring from his early history, bourgeois individualism, that solitude of egalitarian atoms, horrifies him. Hence passive pederasts, as they get older, become active and envy the submission of their young lovers. But if Flaubert was fixed in this feudal relationship, if all his life he nurtured this fantasy of devotion which could never be discharged or realized except through written words and histrionic scenes, if this petit-bourgeois intellectual, profoundly misanthropic and with very little liking for himself as well, used this dated ideology as an aggressive weapon against his own class, it was out of profound resentment against his father, the man who never let himself be totally adored; for the good lord set his vassal in the permanent pursuit of vassalage by a frustration that goes back to the first years.

One day, in a letter to Louise, Gustave waxes enthusiastic: what a beautiful book one could write by simply retracing the experience of modern man "from age seven to twenty." Taking the phrase as it is—which does not mean as it *is offered*—we may wonder why seven rather than ten, the age of entrance into school, or fifteen months, the age of weaning. And why not say quite simply, let us recount the whole life of our characters from birth to death? But when we are familiar with Flaubert, we know that his "axioms" have two simultaneous meanings: the immediate one that aims at objective universality, and the other deeper one that governs the first and relates directly to the author and his singular experiences. Actually, the first collapses under the slightest scrutiny because it has no real existence outside the other, which produces and supports it. The axiom is a way of speaking, and Gustave knows this very well; politeness or prudence makes it a duty to express as objective and abstract truth a certain subjective perception of himself and his life. Flaubert is actually saying: what a beautiful book I could do if I wrote about my life *from age* seven on! And this time we are spared any surprise; if Gustave writes "age seven," it is not that he thought there might be a general quality to the seventh year or that it marks the beginning of what we call today hominization. But *in his particular case, for reasons that concern him*, the golden age ended and the "sarcasms" began when he was seven years old. Or rather, the survivor of Pont-l'Evêque is convinced that his life is entirely played out. After which he must live it out, weaving anew this already accomplished life and destroying himself in the process. At the age of seven a particular unhappiness resulted from an unexpected blow, after which the unhappiness had to be made temporal, elaborated in an interminable process. Flaubert might have said, in brief: "we are constrained to *become*, without respite or return but repeatedly, what we *are*." Through this perception we are in a better position to understand the supercilious confession the young man makes to his mistress: "I have *always* seen life differently from others, and this has forced me *always* (but not sufficiently, alas!) to isolate myself in a solitary harshness, with no escape. I have so often been humiliated, I have caused such scandals, such indignation, that I *long ago* came to realize that in order to live peacefully, one must live alone."[35]

Indeed, Garcia was made malicious by the "sarcasms" his family aimed at him *from his birth*. However, must we take altogether seriously this "always"? For Garcia, yes, but not for Djalioh, or for Mazza, or even for Marguerite, who surely never knew happiness since she was *always* ugly, but whom we meet as she enters hell. Even Almaroës experienced some kind of illusory contentment as long as he believed he possessed a soul. I shall soon return to this apparent contradiction, one of the terms of which has unhappiness beginning at birth, the other at seven years old. Let us say for the moment that Gustave discovers *at the age of seven* the anomaly, the "difference" that has *always* separated him from others. The first "sarcasm" hits home and reveals to him all those he merited through his original defect but was spared—out of pity or perhaps because the executioner was wait-

35. I have italicized the three temporal determinations.

ing for the right moment—but which are summed up, a swarm of hornets, in a single unforgettable sting which at once defines the past and the future. When I say that there was only a single mockery, understand: there were many of them, on the contrary, but within a brief span of time, and they came neither from Achille, always away at school, nor from little Caroline, who was only three years old, nor from Mme Flaubert, for whom melodramas and gossip implied a certain indulgence; in *Mateo Falcone*, for example, incapable of opposing the barbaric decision that the Corsican code of honor imposes on her husband, incapable even of the gentlest reproach when her lord and master has killed her child, the mother confines herself, passive like Gustave, to dying discreetly without a word, without a negative thought. The master himself remains; what has he done? He has scornfully revealed to his son his true nature. Thus, as the stories of Almaroës and Djalioh demonstrate, it hardly matters that the shameful discovery of the self comes at a certain time; what is discovered is a congenital defect—the iron duke has come into the world *without a soul*, Djalioh is an anthropoid *from birth*. These defects, furthermore, cannot be altered. At seven Gustave knew about his *immutable* difference, which in spite of his extravagant pride he never once claimed as a source of superiority. The pink elephant can't see his own hide—as soon as it is pointed out to him, he looks for a hole to hide in, dying of shame. Not that this voluntary seclusion isn't accompanied by bloody self-mutilation. We shall come to this. For the moment, what matters is the age of the discovery. Two or three gray years—Mme Flaubert had produced him but had forgotten to give him his visa. Happiness came with the father and lasted from age three to seven. Before reconstructing the paternal curse, the obscure disaster that put a permanent end to that happiness, we must attempt to describe it.

During the first few years, the paterfamilias had neither the opportunity nor the desire to exercise his Voltairean irony at the expense of a child who could not have understood it; the surgical scrutiny remained sheathed. All told, during this period Achille-Cléophas acted like a good fellow, satisfied to have finally succeeded in his efforts; he failed in the subsequent endeavor, which must have made him a bit more attached to his younger son; when he made "his calls" in the outlying areas of Rouen, he enjoyed taking the little boy with him in his carriage. Vassalage not being contested, there wasn't at this time the slightest reason to invent that crazy issue, identification. The feudal bond—which is precisely the reverse—developed freely;

far from appropriating the existence of the lord by imitating his actions, the little boy had two ways of internalizing his objective vassalage: he made himself the pure mirror of the master's merits, not recognizing that he had any other right than the duty of reflecting those merits; or else, utterly submissive in those moments when he fell into an ecstatic daze, he lost himself in his good lord, his particularity diluted in the paternal essence. Not that he *became* his father he knew his limits only too well, and the infinite distance that separates a useless and gratuitous representative of the earthly fauna from a man with divine right. Annulled by this mystic homage, Gustave remained pure abstract difference, with nothing to differentiate himself from the encountered plenitude except the vacant consciousness of being nothingness and of vampirizing the plenitude of man, namely the infinite power of Achille-Cléophas. By inviting the child to keep him company on his rounds, the father engendered him anew, willed this little unchartered adoration; he permitted Gustave to be the mirror of his virtues, or else he enveloped him, absorbed him, reabsorbed him into himself without relieving him of the sense of his finitude. The child preserved just enough consciousness to profit from the villagers' triumphal welcome. We know this, for he has described it: a cloud of dust, the galloping horse, the cheers, the crowd pressing around the carriage, the women in tears, one of them taking the doctor's hand. This is medicine, this is glory: hope fulfilled, feverish and grateful glances, universal respect; in even the smallest village, the common people who are suffering repeat: with him, I am at peace, he will save me. The little vassal imagines glory as a universal vassalage; we shall encounter this sentiment again, turned around, in his future relations with his readers. Through the father, for the moment, glory belongs to the child. Not directly of course, but when the lord sometimes allows his creature *as other*—meaning as an insufficient parasite—to participate in his essence. The first dazes—which probably went unperceived—marked the child's ecstatic relation to the father. Relations to things are always, originally, human relations. The father not being often at home or, if he was there, having scarcely any time to spend with the child, the world—that mirror of the father and his divine power—the world in which the sick existed in order to be cured by science was, in the absence of the paterfamilias, the object of Gustave's dazes, which had their source, as we know, in his pithiatic "constitution" and, through poor use of speech, in his relations with his mother. Disconcerted, he fell into

328

ecstasy, into the golden age; he fled from his mother, a harsh and frigid love, toward his father or the infinite scene of his exploits.

Nevertheless the family belonged to him, and above all the House. He was the youngest and most submissive member of the Flaubert unit, but if he pledged himself to the lord and if he was accepted, he was integrated into the profound unity of the group which existed only through him. The place of inferior vassal that Gustave occupied at the bottom of the ladder was the expression of paternal will; to remain there out of submission was another way of living the feudal bond and the only way of meriting the outings in the carriage. Ultimately it comes to the same thing, whether you communicate with the supreme chief through the hierarchy by obeying him in everything, whether you have the privilege of losing yourself in him, or whether you reflect him through ecstasy with no intermediary. Gustave obviously noticed that the latecomer to the House of Flaubert was also the only one the paterfamilias took with him in his carriage. Mme Flaubert never accompanied her husband, she had enough to do to manage her household. Nor did Caroline, the younger sister, who was too little. Nor Achille, who was away at school. As to actual goods, it is the father who possesses them. But through his master, Gustave participates in the perpetual ceremony of approbation. The little boy discovers the objects which were there *before him*; for him, to discover is to appropriate, to see what an eminent eye well before his birth drew out of the primitive undifferentiated state, to touch what a strong and agile hand touched before him. The House contains and encloses him, but the proprietor devoured, digested, assimilated him to his own substance; in this sense the House becomes the fixed image of the father. The paternal power is manifest everywhere; from the cellar to the attic, nothing is found that he did not desire or at least tolerate. The space between the walls is criss-crossed with the paths he has trodden; Gustave walks in the shadow of a materialized, omnipresent will; this is what he loves in the house and what conceals from him its gloomy hideousness. His lord is there, under this roof, scattered over these furnishings, inert, mysteriously dormant; the father has made himself thing; without ceasing to surround, to protect his child, he gives himself, and the little boy possesses him in turn, on the inside. Between the vassal's homage and the master's gift there is reciprocity; one pledges *himself* to the other, body and soul, the other gives himself too, in a way, but in his material being—he entrusts to his faithful the properties that will always manifest *his presence*.

329

From the time of the Revolution, the bourgeoisie trained its children to make careful distinctions between human relations and "real" property, the direct, legal, unconditional bond between the acquirer and the thing acquired. But Gustave the vassal unconsciously rediscovers the structures of the Old Regime: the possession of material goods is a holding, it is based on the relations between people which are perpetuated in the form of continued gifts and immutable obligations. For the little Flaubert, love and property are not separable— one is the measure of the other. Moreover, since this little intruder derives his right to be born only from his relationship with the progenitor, he bases it equally on his possessive relationship with the material whole that represents him; feudal property, which is the bond of person to person through the thing given, becomes for Gustave in his golden age a fundamental structure of his right to live. The child doesn't know this, of course. He lacks the words, as can well be imagined. And the ideas. And the grasp of relationship—all the instruments of thought. But all he has to do is live—the synthesis is outside him; he will internalize the objective articulation of homage to the overlord and the family fiefdom for the simple reason that it exists and that these practical realities are not separable. Their connection, *experienced*, becomes a subjective structure within him. Not that it is ever felt or suffered; it is a matrix, an infinity of *practices*— actions, emotions, ideas—evoked by the most diverse situations and unwittingly, invisibly marked; without ever assuming its role, these practices reveal or reproduce the original connection in the objects they pursue. Thus the subjective moment is the moment of mediation; the first relation is internalized so as to be externalized once again in all other areas of objectivity. In this ultimate form the transmitted mark seems unrecognizable from one object to another; furthermore, everything conspires to transform it—occasion, place, purpose, structures, and the logical links in this new region of being. Nevertheless, these diverse markings come to look the same to us as soon as we recall the primary structure. This is a matter not of recovering a universal concept among particular examples but of recognizing the original precision of the articulation in the singularity of its subsequent projections. Precision is itself singular, it has the unity and the individuality of a "code," namely a singular method of decoding.

I shall offer only one example, the way in which the immutability of this first connection illuminates one of Gustave's strange obsessions. From one end of his correspondence to the other, a treatise of futile greed, he proclaims that he would like to be rich, fabulously rich, that he has a hunger for gold and precious stones, that he will die without them. Not once, however, does he imagine that a fortune might be *made*; the only admissible wealth is what is inherited. To be sure, this was a common notion in his era; the bourgeoisie had difficulty disengaging from old ideologies. The ownership of land had become bourgeois, but it still imposed its own values, and then, this was the period of domestic capitalism, when the factory was bequeathed like a domain. And Gustave, an heir himself, finds he has neither the inclination nor the means to become rich by profit and economy. But that doesn't matter; for Gustave's fortune to reflect exclusively this declining tendency, it had to be made precisely by the objective connection that sustains it. Besides, he pushes everything to a passionate extreme, having contempt for profit and all work related to it, dreaming of a rajah who will make him his heir; he is overcome with rage to hear that one of his friends has just come into an inheritance—he goes so far, indeed, that once again he finds himself alone. This pure consumer will live on the patrimony and out of contempt for profit will refuse to augment it. Is he forgetting that Dr. Flaubert got paid for his work? That the property at Trouville was acquired for the most part by means of clients' fees? On the contrary, he never stops thinking about it, but the origin of the patrimony— even if it is sweat and blood—is not important; gold is always ennobled through *transmission*. Earned wealth is an incomplete being, still hideous; once transmitted it is brightened, humanized, the gift transforms and completes it, it achieves spiritual plenitude in the hands of the heir. A deceased master showers gold on his servant, who gathers up this ringing and weighty inheritance; through it, he is commissioned not to incarnate the deceased but to be the repository of his power. The servant in turn will be transformed: a creature of chance, he was living without rhyme or reason when an admirable generosity singled him out, a dead man gave him the mandate to live by a rigid and last act of will which penetrates and justifies him—he is consecrated. It will be said that benefactors are not so generous; birth, promises, good and faithful services generally give the future legatee a right to the legacy. Gustave would agree with this on condition that the lord should not be bound by anything. In the final analysis he must bequeath as he wishes, for without complete freedom generosity does not exist. For the paternal fortune to revert to the son—even if he has merited it a hundredfold—as a preference and a gracious gift, it is necessary and sufficient that the father during his lifetime should always have had the right to disinherit him. If he could have and did not, the will is an act of seigneurial love; in the hands of the sanctified son the gold becomes the paterfamilias himself with his demands and his bounty.

We shall not waste time underscoring the fiercely reactionary character of Gustave's obsession, which is striking even for the time. It is more valuable to recall that it has its roots in Flaubert's early childhood, in his first years, which made him forever incapable of distinguishing property from gift. It has already been surmised that this incapacity will later inflame his *envy*; love and money, being inseparable, will fascinate him by their reciprocal symbolism—the absence of one betrays his frustration in the other, and vice versa. We shall see the close connections between jealousy and fealty. Let it suffice to note that this conception of wealth, which saves the child from his original contingency by the domestic tie that binds him, the inessential being, to the donor, in essence to the paterfamilias, contributes from the age of four to grounding Gustave's ontological dignity on this fundamental postulate: *being a landowner*.

The family belongs to him as well. Achille still exists, but he is not a source of irritation because he seems quite natural, like everything encountered by the child's awakening consciousness; beings are there, immemorial, more familiar than distinct, they are the *setting*, recognized well before being known, and they are what can also be called first nature since the child's being is reflected by his surroundings to the extent that his body is defined by what surrounds it. This is also *reality*, accepted in advance provided it is tolerable; the child, too absorbed in learning about it to contest it, makes it the measure of being, of truth, of good. The objects surrounding him, without leaving the plane of immediate life, receive a de jure existence, a status. The rights of the adults guarantee the newcomer the legitimacy of his birth. Therefore Gustave *recognizes* Achille as the big brother when he scarcely knows how to talk. The eldest by endowment, for to the little vassal's respectful conservatism the hierarchy of the Flauberts is order itself. The revered father, source of all power and all credit, has sovereignly decided that his wife should give him two sons nine years apart; in both sons the judicial act has engendered the fact; creatures of the same demiurge, Gustave must reject his own status or recognize Achille's. Better still, once recognized, the big brother gains the capacity to recognize. If he is approached by the child, if he smiles at him or speaks to him, he takes part *to his advantage* in the forever deceptive and forever repeated ceremony of welcome. He declares that Gustave, far from being a weed or an intruder, is the desired guest. This is the eternal recurrence of the archetypal act which nonetheless did not take place—the opening of doors. If the two boys were close in age, one or two years apart, their relations— without losing their judicial basis—would be very different. Passionate, certainly. Possibly amicable. But nine years—or nearly—is too great an interval. To be sure, at the time of Gustave's birth Achille is only a little boy. But scarcely has the younger brother started to talk than the elder is sent off to school; there he works zealously, invisible except on vacations. He is indeed part of another world, a miniature adult. The child only wants to obey him—they say his brother is a big boy, already "rational"; Gustave knows that reason is not a privilege, quite simply it is a question of age: the elder son has it and it is waiting for the younger. Achille's superiority being therefore only provisional, it can be calmly acknowledged. Gustave makes so little trouble that his submissiveness gives him an advantage; absorbed by his studies far away, Achille is exiled most of the time among the non-Flauberts, an inferior but innumerable and dangerous species. Promised the same exile, Gustave for the time being enjoys the comforts of childhood: he doesn't leave the family hearth; his mother is devoted to him; when she has looked after his needs she takes him on her knee and talks to him about God, the Father of all fathers; Dr. Flaubert takes him on his rounds; the Le Poittevins, close friends of his parents, are always ready to baby him—in short, he obeys everyone and they repay him with tenderness. A bit scant, the tenderness, sometimes even disheartening; but tepid as it is, he feels it, it is the ambience of his life. But what about Achille? Isn't he too a cherished son? Of course he is; Gustave is convinced that his older brother inspires his parents' deep attachment for the simple reason that good fathers must love their children. But the poor exile, absorbed in his studies, scarcely has the time to *experience* the physician's benevolence; in sum, he has the right to this love, but Gustave, more fortunate, also has the pleasure of it. He understood very early that this privilege came with childhood; so he wasn't at all jealous of Achille, who had the misfortune of having left it behind. Gustave knows that he will soon reach his brother's age and status, but he is not in a hurry to abandon his prerogatives; he will grow up, this is his duty and his right, but as late as possible. Indeed, he often noted afterward that an obscure resistance marked his early childhood, as if he repudiated the notion of leaving it. But what is of significance to us now is the establishment of the internal apparatus that is going to torture him. Since he believes he is better off than Achille, he forgets

333

to envy him; this would be an excellent start, if at the same time the younger son were not fooling himself—trustingly, he recognizes the judicial status of all the family members so that they may be empow ered to recognize his. This means that he acknowledges their rights— and once internalized, these become his duties. Achille is his superio in age; Gustave doesn't hold it against him, quite the contrary, he uses this fact as a means to bury himself in childhood. Furthermore he knows that the hierarchy is not definitive—the younger son wil only too soon attain the sorry privileges of the elder: reason, school exile. What he does not know is that among the Flauberts the statu of eldest son is an immutable distinction, not that minimal advantage that dims and disappears in bourgeois families when the brother. have both reached adulthood, but the granted right to replace the paterfamilias after his death. The unhappy boy is willing to respec Achille and obey him; he thinks this will be only temporary. In fac he is deceived—the gap persists until the father's death; after 1846 static and sacred, it will be perpetuated by the final will of the de ceased. What can the younger son do against it? He let himself be persuaded from early childhood that the quantitative difference ir age symbolized a qualitative but provisional difference in merit; he immediately became implicated in advance by the benefactor and the clauses of the will. He can protest in vain that this was against hi wishes; the enemy is in position, the frustrated adolescent offers a rearguard battle; but in order to reject the superiority of the firstborn he should never have recognized it. "I only accepted it for a while," he would answer. Yes, but this was enough; behind a condition o fact he has accepted the existence of a right. The essential maneuve is accomplished. Achille's judicial status is reproduced, experiencec by the child himself, and the father's sacred power need only maintair and consolidate it.

And what could be more imprudent for the younger son than to recognize the firstborn—the first-come—child's right to be loved? O course, the child is blind rather than generous—he affirms the righ because the fact escapes him. But he has fallen into the trap: even i love is displayed—I mean the father's love for the Other—this othe love will be judicially based. What does the little boy have to complair about? If he had read in his lord's eyes an unknown tenderness tha wasn't meant for him, could he condemn it, shout that he was being robbed, despoiled? That would be understandable if the surgeon hac preferred strangers to his own sons. But it is Achille we are talking about. This time the right is stated first, like a principle; reality seems

334

to answer to his demand and to be situated in him; the burning substance, love, fills the abstract form, the form contains the raw substance and justifies it. We can discuss it, certainly, we can judge this paternal love excessively passionate, but these are the least important questions. Indeed, if Gustave ever discovered that Dr. Flaubert bore a deep love for his elder son, he was stripped in advance of the means to protest. He was robbed. That's how it is. But it is a legitimate theft; in the name of the Flaubert Order, to which Gustave himself lays claim, the charge must be declared inadmissible, the plaintiff must be dismissed and forced to rejoice in the feeling that his father has pledged himself to the defendant. If the younger son gives in and rejoices, does this at least mean that he is resigned? No, it means that he loses his self-control; frustration torments him, all the more bitterly as he dares not call it by name.

In short, everything is settled. In the first period of Gustave's life, the first son disturbed the second so little that he calmly internalized the right of primogeniture and at the same time made it one of the permanent sources of his domestic duties. The motif of internalization has not been forgotten for itself, nor has some sort of access of virtue; it was necessary: the little Flaubert group was so rigorously integrated that each of its members was at once an incarnation of the totality and an expression of paternal power, that synthetic force which produced and united them. Therefore, the rights of each are reflections or complements of the rights of all the others: by recognizing Achille's status Gustave has affirmed his own. The sacred power of the father being judicial, none of his creatures achieves the prescribed plenitude without realizing—in himself through the others and in the others through himself—Flaubert-being as de jure existence. The result is that Gustave's feelings, united by organic impulses and judicial claims and exacerbated by their reciprocal conditioning, fully merit the Greek name pathos, which Hegel gave to the passions of classical tragedy.

In his brother, then, he first recognizes the family as subject to rights; he recognizes himself as well, *being*, like each of them, the whole family. He doesn't need to claim directly the right to be loved, since love is given; but when he claims it for his brother in following that sacred principle that good fathers must love good children, he speaks unwittingly in the name of the entire family, which derives its organization from Achille-Cléophas. Through these prescribed operations, through these positions assigned to each one with a view to *maximal* efficaciousness, the father inhabits the family; he is normative—it is an environment of being-as-duty; but the family group demands that his integration be love. Love is a duty for the creator—it cannot be dispensed to the creatures one by one, in detail, but the demiurge must love generally all of his creation. In this same love, united in the enterprise by the original affinity of all its members, each one sees the whole spectrum of communal duties, and quite as much his particular duties as they are completed by the duties of the others; the right to be loved becomes for each person his reabsorption into the whole and his immediate restitution in the form of a validated, anchored part. Thus there is only one Flaubert lover, the shifting relation of the whole to its parts. Gustave gives a judicial hearing to his father's affection for him by claiming it for his brother as well. This child, as we know, is not an individualist, he is ignorant of the incomparable passions unique creatures evoke; he posits Flaubert love, the actual unity of the mother and the children in the father's heart. He demands all of this love for each one, and consequently for himself. This indissoluble and true unity of the little group will later ensnare him and—as we shall see—strip him of the power to say no. Indeed, favoritism, if Achille-Cléophas really practices it, can be played out only within the sacred little world, and will somehow appear to be a consecrating power in the eyes of its victim; he can neither blame Achille-Cléophas for loving Achille too much—is he capable of deciding what is too much?—nor excuse him completely for not loving Gustave enough.

Here is the essence of the business: Flaubert love, as the little boy feels it, is in one sense a formal and judicial synthesis, an integration, in another a tender solicitude—a bit dry sometimes, a bit distracted, but not entirely lacking in warmth since it is addressed to a child. The malaise will begin the day Gustave believes that his brother too enjoys possession of the paternal heart. In brief, it is spontaneous feeling that will suddenly be thrown into question. Not for long; the unjust preference in love will quite soon dismiss the brother dispossessed by the clauses of the will. In other words, what the House of Flaubert—resembling most patriarchal families in this respect—called love was the father's devotion to the entire enterprise as well as all the dispositions he had made—and continued to make every day in order to preserve the unique object of his interest. After this, of course, it was not necessary for the paterfamilias to love—in the sense we use that word today—or to indicate with clear signals the emotion he experienced in the presence of a child of his House. Gustave, to the extent that he knew himself to be the object of a particular attention, had soon learned that this favor was not addressed to his person but very simply to his age—and that the father's tenderness would not survive the son's childhood. If he should discover that Dr. Flaubert felt the same weakness for the young man Achille, the little boy would be shocked. The golden age, then, is not exempt from contradictions. This is the first contradiction—established rather than lived. The second, on the other hand, is obscurely felt.

The individualism of the liberal bourgeoisie had the advantages of its discomforts. It found man isolated, an atom, and valuing him on the basis of this solitude it severed the last ties; suddenly each monad is unique, or rather the relations which are based on a comparison remain *external* to the substances compared. In particular, this bourgeois morality dissolves within it any *organic* relationship—one which, for example, would determine the being of the younger brother by that of the elder. In other words, raised by individualists Gustave would have suffered less or would not have suffered at all; inferior, yes, *on the surface*, but in truth unique. The Flaubert family reluctantly accepted the economic liberalism and social atomism of its new milieu from which it derived its utilitarianism, but it flatly rejected the ethic of conjugal families and birth control, that individualism which would have endangered its unity or its line.

Gustave is *a* son, *the* younger brother of Achille, *the* older brother of Caroline; he *is* the whole family, the whole family is in him. There isn't a thought or an emotion that isn't related to him—he is the axis of reference. His sufferings—as we shall see later—his rare moments of splendor, even the feelings he will later confess to Mme Schlésinger, are all connected to the House of Flaubert: he loves, hates, dreams, philosophizes, is enraged *for or against it*. This means that *he* is the *opposite* of an individual. Indeed, after his nervous illness when he achieves the *status* of individualist, Flaubert will feel constrained to enhance that status in disguised forms; he can accept being a monad only if he is chief monadic dignitary—an anchorite, a brahmin, or "the hermit of Croisset." Not being a familial or divine right, individuality can at least be reduced to one's concubinage to oneself, and this self-consciousness is lived like a marriage between sovereigns. As a child, an adolescent, Gustave knows and appreciates himself only in his familial reality, as an internal determination of the Flaubert family. Worst of all, he condemns himself in advance—he judges himself according to the norms the Flauberts have adopted. Even when he has invented others less deeply hostile to himself, the new set will be based on the old, the new being less an attempt to reverse the old than to forge, beyond it and in another, freer world, values that are at once purer and *less real*. Reality *is* the House of Flaubert; its values are practical; that is, they issue from performed functions and aim to codify functional acts. Utilitarianism is the Flaubert ethic which Gustave will never stop fighting in himself and thus accepting, the hydra whose heads grow back each time they are cut off. But it is not an abstract principle; on the contrary, it is the most rigorous of *specific* terms, indissolubly bound to the domestic economy. This organization distributes roles; persons will be determined, along with tools, as the means of continuing the enterprise—each is treated by the others and treats himself as a means, never as an end. As for a final purpose, there is none. Or, put differently, the purpose, once attained, becomes a means of attaining another end—*semper excelsior*.

This directed utilitarianism is nothing more than *ambition*. This term must not be understood primarily as a vague passion, coming out of the blue, quite by accident, rather, it is a continual process: a little group is determined for a time by its objective ascent and produces the means of perpetuating it. Dr. Flaubert was a *mutant* still ignorant of his mutation; nevertheless he had to internalize it. It became a *certainty* within him: the past secured the future in pursuit of a magnificent ascent, and suddenly that certainty was a pitiless rule—Achille-Cléophas had to be the means of its continued success. His family, kneaded by his hands, was end and means at the same time. It was through the family and for it that the social success of a veterinarian's son had to be pursued beyond one generation. Thus he put double leavening in the family dough: the unconditional promise of success and the absolute imperative to sacrifice everything to it. In other words, *ambition* is the very essence of this family, its raison d'être, the project, which is both dynamic and fixed, that shapes it out of its devotion to the father and through him to the century; ambition is what defines each new member through all the others and compresses the family's integration to an extreme. Furthermore, it is *experienced* by each of the family members, individually and collectively, as the real movement of the enterprise—income, economy, land acquisitions, the growing clientele, the increasing reputation of the medical director, all these things are felt in common, all contribute to giving the family's common life a vectoral determination, a meaning. Children and parents feel they are taking off; progress is not only the end and the means, it is the vital element, their setting; for each of them it is a subjective impression of speed, all the more clearly since this speed is variable and there are sudden halts. The ascendant force of the little group constitutes the common substance of each particular mode. For each of them it is duty—sooner or later it must be carried on by conscious effort—but even more, it is love; by embracing the movement, by letting yourself be carried away and preparing for the future exaltation, you enter into the father's vision, you identify with the revered creator, sing his praises, solicit and obtain his approbation. Each family member reflects for all the others the harsh will of the lord—they love each other in him as Christians love each other in God. This adoration conceals from the children the heteronomy of their will, for ambition and the father are one; their passion does not distinguish between the two. It isn't enough for them to be docile slaves, they will be zealots. In other words, a Flaubert son is ambitious from birth; he breathes ambition, he eats it, he hoards it, it is the movement of his life, the meaning of his fundamental love, the secret of his absolute importance and his inessentiality, it is the particularization of the common project by its free,[36] singular project. Without even knowing it, Gustave is the incarnation of family ambition; his fundamental project is to raise himself as high as possible in order to throw himself into the arms of the master, to identify with him, to contribute with his own hands to the elevation of the entire family. In his House there is a perpetual communion of saints, all merits are transferred from each member to all other members; distinguished from the earliest age by the father's distinctions, he will subsequently glorify the whole family by his own glory. The child's first impulse carries him toward the heights—that is his place; but he attaches only a relative importance to the admiration of the masses. Mankind's recognition of his value is only an indispensable condition for his true consecration; inessential and celebrated, he turns back toward his own people. If they tell him, you are certainly worthy of us, he can die contented. And of course ambition is only a dream of love. From the moment he thinks more specifically of his future, it shows its other face—raw greed; he must get rich, amass titles, honors, but we must understand that this bourgeois arrivism is nothing more than the arrivism of the paterfamilias.

I can imagine how many times, in the gloomy apartment at the Hôtel-Dieu—where the ugliness of the furnishings so clearly bespeaks a utilitarian stinginess, the sacrifice of everything for success—Gustave's mother must have told the little boy about the great man's childhood, the miraculous awakening of his genius, his path to glory,

---

36. When I say free, I mean that there is spontaneity, though springing from a prefabricated essence.

every record broken. This wife, married so young, had as much adoration for the master as she had "glacial" contempt for the non-Flauberts. She presented Achille-Cléophas, therefore, as the only example to follow. To begin with, it was a duty, since the son had to be like the father; later it would become a reward, since the child, through rigorous asceticism, would end by appropriating his virtues. As ambition was for the father, so the father is at once a model and a promise for the child; puritanical arrivism can thus give birth to optimism: in the end, good is rewarded. This vain childishness, transforming his enterprise into a fairy tale, made it accessible to Gustave. A whole life seemed to be already laid out, and all he had to do was travel through it at a gallop to the point of victory. The wild hope at the heart of the project hid its barrenness from him. The ramparts would be quickly breached, it was possible because someone else had already done it; I would wager, in fact, that Achille's first success, before it overshadowed him, only encouraged the younger son. It would be easy, very easy: what the first Flaubert had done the second had no difficulty doing again; and the third, when his career was in full swing, would easily break both their records.

Here we have the second contradiction, certainly more profound than the first because it continually structures the movement of experience. Gustave is Caroline's son as much as Achille-Cléophas's. There will never be any misunderstanding between this couple, since the wife claims only the right to obey her husband. Her younger son, however, internalizes a virtual contradiction which will never set his parents against each other. Gustave, in effect, is *first of all* Caroline's product, she is the one who nurtures him and first attends to him. Dr. Flaubert, who oversees the infant's early education from a distance, is fooled, everything seems to be in order. He praises the young woman's maternal alacrity, inviting her to overprotect the child; but he has no inkling that these first maternal actions translate into facts the unexpressed indignation of a wife disappointed by her new lodgings, by her husband's increasing coldness of late, by the appearance of a fourth boy when she wanted a daughter, and that these actions have the effect of constituting a superfluous brat, lovelessly stuffed, quite surprised at surviving the death that has carried off two of his brothers. Undesired, undesirable, with no raison d'être, at the first paternal smile he heads into the world of the father; in order to derive his judicial status from his lord's demands, he is integrated into the Flaubert enterprise, which, internally and externally, is at once an ascendant force, family unity, love, duty, and, above all, praxis.

Achille-Cléophas's pride, in effect, is not simply the inert memory of the mutation that turned a country boy into the greatest physician in Rouen—and the richest; it is this mutation continued by him and through him; it is his prodigious appetite for knowledge that compels him to dissect nonstop; it is his lust—still fully a peasant lust—for profit that makes him invest all he has in property; it is the admiration and silent demand of his students who contrain him year after year to renew and expand his courses; it is the favor of Rouen's high society, his clients, who are beginning to open their doors to him; it is his relentless contempt for the nonmutants, for the poor who don't get rich, for the rich who are born to opulence. In short, the pride of the gentleman has nothing to do with pathos, it is lived *in acts*.

Who, then, becomes conscious around 1835 of this furious activity as the secret cohesion of the family line and as the ascendant movement that sweeps him along and that he must internalize and then externalize again by practical actions that will demonstrate, in his person, the Flauberts' utter superiority to the human race? A young man who regards himself as an outcast, constituted without his consent by his mother's efficient austerity. Scarcely had he entered the father's world than love enabled him to understand, though he did not cease *to be superfluous,* that glory was his lot, that when he reached manhood he would have to go on horseback or by carriage into the villages and hamlets and ride among the prostrated peasants. This indeed is the paternal image Gustave carried with him, and he excluded from it neither utilitarianism nor even a hint of stinginess— the art of economizing, at least. Yet the maternal image, or rather the child's first experience, squarely contradicts it. Not that the maternal image is *in itself* truer or deeper, but it is the thread of his subjectivity; whereas the paternal Gustave is the internalization of his objective condition. Certainly he *feels* within him the force that transports him, he *works at feeling it* in order to escape the original stagnation, and he *also feels* that it is his duty to appropriate the ascendant force that he can only endure. But this duty is all the more imperative as the means are lacking to fulfill it. Here is a child incapable of affirming or denying, rediscovering his gratuitousness as soon as his father turns away from him and able to escape it only through his stupors—by what miracle could this quietist, oblivious of the self, turn into a sage, a subject of history? Little Gustave's arrivism is intact—impulse and obligation at the same time—but it collides with his passivity, constituted from the earliest months as a fundamental passivity to such a degree that the child is *spoken* rather than speaking, a flux of passive

341

syntheses, vehicles of intentionality that cannot be accomplished. What is he to do? He feels the Flaubert ascent in his bones, he has heard it described every day, represented by the father. Therefore it is inside him—he was made an arriviste. His pride becomes *ambition suffered*; indeed, it is still only the appropriation of paternal ambition through love, but what was praxis in Achille-Cléophas necessarily becomes pathos in Gustave, a phantom activity that he cannot even imagine, which haunts—like anxiety, remorse, a permanent and unrealizable beckoning—the inert flow of experience. Moreover, he doesn't have much difficulty feeling this pride, the internalization of the pride that unites all the members of the House and is in essence nothing more than the superb madness of the paterfamilias, when it reflects the eminent visage of Dr. Flaubert or when Gustave loses himself in paternal glory. But in these instances he forgets himself and enjoys an *alien* pride; as soon as he recovers himself, this intransigent audacity, the affirmation of the self against all, disappears, contradicted by the deep humility of the unloved child deprived of the instruments (arrogant demands, affirmative power, activity) that would allow it to exist.

Let us not confuse this *unrealizable* pride with the grim pride evidenced in his first works; that pride will come *after* the fall; based on rancor and frustration, compensation for an unjust yet only too just disgrace, it will be Gustave's pathos, the vulture that tears at his liver until it kills him. For the moment we are in the golden age—I am referring to the slight difficulties of paradise. Caroline and the other hagiographers of Achille-Cléophas are the joy of the little vassal who listens to them; yet, I see in their accounts one of the secondary sources of his "estrangement." He is forced to learn a practical language, *the* language of praxis, but its meanings, without escaping him entirely (they apply quite well to the actions of others), are never measured by his subjective certainty. They designate him nevertheless: he is a Flaubert son, he will imitate his father and save the sick, increase the patrimony; even better, the medical director and Achille offer such a familiar, everyday example to him, that he is thrust directly into the foreground, participating in the familial substance. But without his own approbation these words remain *dead letters inside him; he must believe* what he is told because he is incapable of realizing the meaning of the words by a mental thrust that goes beyond them. It is the future of the family that is made manifest, a future that envelops him as well; he wants it, he wants to contribute to creating it, but if he acts, his dreams are instantly dissipated by the troubled but certain consciousness of his impotence. The others made him ambitious, and so he is; he is infused with the arrivism of the Flauberts, but it will not be long before the collective ascent becomes a source of continual humiliation. As a passive agent he will feel pulled along by the family cord, a dead weight that doesn't participate in the common effort and may even slow it down. A *passive man with ambition*—what could be more wretched?

All of this is only roughly outlined, intuited, vaguely experienced—as anxiety, perhaps. But in the physician's carriage, Gustave is the king's son. Otherwise, if he is disturbed by a glimpse of the future, it is because the future is his as other; since it is understood that he will have to prove himself as a new Achille-Cléophas, he defends himself from the start through passive resistance, that is, by abandoning himself to what he is. This is one reason—and not the least important—for his stupors: Gustave is afraid of *what will be*. We shall see throughout this study that he will never stop being afraid of it. A little bit latter we shall see him play eternity against time, because he wants to halt his destiny. He will succeed, furthermore, at the price of a neurosis. For the moment, he is scarcely interested in eternity, and it is not certain he even knows the word itself; the stupor is primarily a refusal to grow up and confront the problems of knowledge, of practical life; when anxiety plagues him, he "dulls" himself and tries to return to his past—to a present without problems. This apparent regression is a surrender to the self: the pure present is identified with the past, and the flux of perceptions poses as a diluting diffusion of the soul in the palpable universe. this involves the simultaneous abolition of a superfluous ego and of the future.On this level, the stupor is an answer and the child already knows how to use it. Since the others want to force an experienced and previously structured whole into a *role* for which it is not suited, Gustave makes use of the mists that frequently invade his consciousness in order to forget and lose sight of that role.

At this period Gustave has another reason for clinging to childhood. He senses obscurely—and quite in spite of himself—that his father's love is addressed less to his person than to his age; by growing up, won't he turn into Achille? (He is not yet disturbed by his brother's privileges.) But of course he will turn into him, first he'll be Gustave the beloved, then Achille the brilliant student, finally the incarnation of Achille-Cléophas in all his power and glory. The little younger son eagerly—but in terror—desires one day to equal the greatest of the Flauberts. But he is in no hurry to be like the studious Achille, who

is not there, who leads a dreary life away at school, and who know
the revered severity of the paterfamilias rather than his tendernes
and his indulgence. Gustave for the moment is only Gustave; a good
natured lord makes him a gift of his person and his smiles withou
asking anything in return but an obedience the little vassal is onl
too happy to give. Why not anchor himself in early childhood? Gus
tave feels obscurely that this is the golden age, that he must stay her
and never grow up. Later on we shall see that Flaubert has an in
voluted conception of temporality, the rule being that everything goe
from bad to worse. Many things that do not appear until later dispose
him to take up this prejudice. The fall is one of them, of course. Bu
it is helpful here to note the primary option that will be found ove
and over again, particularly at the time of his "nervous attack" i
1844: the refusal to become an adult—in other words, the refusal t
define himself within the family through other relationships with eacl
of its members. Everything stands: Achille is the future image o
Gustave. But relations between the father and his elder son seem
quite dry, and Gustave senses that for him the period of praxis wil
be a time of failure and exile. The dazed condition, then, translate
both the conscious incapacity and the refusal.

Basically, the dazed condition is a result of the stupor itself. Thi
characteristic, which would be preserved throughout Gustave's life
would itself become a *function*—we all recall his amazement at th
"infinite stupidity of the bourgeois." We shall come back to this. Bu
for the moment the fundamental thing is his obscure consciousnes
of the contradiction between experience, endured rather than mas
tered, and the persona that is imposed on him by language, by be
havior, a persona that he must also live out, a rich and uncertai
succession of perceptions without ego, that ego stamped in him b
others, which seems to him to belong to someone else. Some childre
would react to this incomprehensible malaise with anger or with a
escapist hyperactivity (what mothers call "overexcitement"). Every
one only uses, and can only use, the means available to him. Bein
passive, Gustave breaks through this passivity—estrangement bring
him to the brink of fainting. He has said as much; in his stories h
made that estrangement, as we have seen, the extreme limit an
meaning of his dazes. And this is true. Except that he never actuall
loses consciousness. The ego disappears but thought, as if freed
proliferates. A queer kind of thought which, because it cannot b
verbalized, is not separated from feeling, and, never affirming itself
crosses in multicolored fragments a consciousness that is divide

between pleasure and fear. The description Mme Commanville has left us, which she had from her grandmother, is significant. During such moments, Gustave would look quite stupid and suck his thumb. These details suffice to characterize an attitude well known to pediatricians, which corresponds, according to them, to moments of "intense ideation"; he is busy with all his fantasies, and especially those concerning his identification with animals. On this point Gustave has given us precious information in his letters to Louise: he attracts animals because they "know I'm like them." This conviction is the source of one of the last scenes in the first *Education*, in which Jules cannot get rid of a dirty, wretched dog who is obviously himself, or rather his own life. This scene grows out of the rather widespread belief among children—and it is particularly strong with Gustave— that they are animals; spoiled and lovable like domestic pets and at the same time, like pets—when the parental constellation claims it— without a visa. Gustave adds: *they understand me*, they know I understand them. What is meaningful here is the profound assimilation of the idiot to the beast, a defensive assimilation since the idiot, a failed human being, is defective in being an idiot, in not developing all the potential of his species. The fox, of course, has all the reason in the world to be a fox and the wolf to be a wolf. It is as though Gustave were confiding to us: as a child, the grownups took me for an idiot, when actually I was a little animal. Rancor has complicated the theme in *Quidquid volueris*, written much later, since the ape Djalioh has been forcibly given a human character, to his great unhappiness. In its first form, from the years five to seven, the assimilation of the human child—by his passivity a stranger to culture—to an animal, fully expressing his species *from birth*, appears as an expression of Gustave's refusal to grow up and to confront culture, already embodied by the primer that is waiting for him. Rather than open it, that incomprehensible object which ought to transform him into a man, Gustave loses himself in nature or makes himself into nature, a product of the earth. The man he will describe in his first novellas is historical and Pascalian, but he is not a fallen angel, he is an acculturated beast; culture is the Fall, he senses it, and his eyes, like the eyes of the ape in Kafka, that other victim of an abusive father, will betray the "bewilderment of trained beasts." He will enjoy playing the idiot or the force of nature for the simple pleasure of symbolically destroying in himself and around himself things properly human. Tempests will ravish him, destroying human effort; nature clearly affirms its absolute superiority over the inventions of man and their applications, demonstrating that our species, so proud of its amphibology, is not the center of the world and can be wiped out by a cataclysm like some long extinct animal. In other words (although the child may have had no way of formulating this thought as we do), what repulses him in man is history, which makes him unthinkable and contradictory; if he wants to remain an animal it is because beasts have no history and because each individual beast is definable, even classifiable, by the completeness of a concept that wholly embraces it, leaving no place for *anomalies*; hence it is equivalent to all other examples of the species, and whatever it might do, it is limited to *realization*. Thus childhood is no longer an age but an animal category: there are monkeys, there are dogs, there are children. Perhaps, if carefully inspected, the child is merely a dog who is unaware of itself. This is the best way to ensure that one will never leave the early years, the golden age, and it is also a good procedure for escaping from that eternal babbling, speech, to the truth of beasts, which is silence. Naturally, the operation is accomplished through words. But the vocables "dog," "cat," "chick" serve only practical schemes; shrouded by experience, they invisibly guide mute fantasies. In any case, the meaning of these identifications is clear: culture being recognized as the preorgative of adulthood, the child radically rejects it by becoming nature once and for all. At the same time the child finds a myth to explain his first resistance to acculturation: he is a beast, beasts do not speak. Finally, by conceiving of himself as one of those domestic pets that provide a permanent opportunity for grownups to display their tenderness, he tells us of his hunger for physical affection. The future is denied: the lap dog is born; it will be a puppy, then an adult, then a tired old hound without ever leaving the hearth where it was born, without doing anything to deserve the love that will be lavished upon it. It will find happiness in repetition and of course in worshiping those gods who bend over it and speak gently to it without requiring it to understand what they say.

Here we have Gustave's golden age: need, love given, received, passive spontaneity, and boredom broken by notable absences in which the little boy, transforming himself into nature directly by pantheistic ecstasies, or indirectly by playing his role as pure animal, dreams of making the present eternal. Is it so marvelous, this paradise that precedes the Fall? Yes and no. First of all, he is living in the heart of death, represented by father and mother each in his own way. Caroline provides him with an image of private death: two little males died before his birth, a third will die soon afterward; surrounded by these singular little adventures that so quickly unfold from birth to annihilation, Gustave feels in his very bones an intimacy with their destinies—he too was born to die quickly and senses that Mme Flaubert treats him like a *moriturus*. That doesn't frighten him, and—much later—it will even be the basis of his art. "I was born," he says after the Fall, "with the desire to die." This is not quite accurate; the desire came, properly speaking, at the age of seven and depended upon what might be called "the being-to-die" of his passive nature. Thus the desire to preserve the eternity of childhood as it was during the golden age might simply have been confused, at that time, with the other eternity promised by the mother with which Gustave was not familiar, the eternity after death. Nothing ever prevented the unloved child, the unwelcome child, from vaguely considering—as Marguerite will do in bitterness and clarity—his probable approaching death as a return to order. And this vague presentiment gave experience, even in that early childhood, a kind of sinister savor. The daze, or the suppression of an uncertain ego to the advantage of the living animal, or the experienced infinite, was also the incomprehensible dream of his suppression by death. There was an enormous difference, however: with Gustave dead, dogs, cats, and tigers would not cease to exist, nor the ocean cease to perpetuate the image of the infinite.

Dr. Flaubert, who worked away in the basement dissecting cadavers, and every morning visited the dying who would expire in the afternoon, was public death. He represented society's right over the dead. This work of the revered lord did not disturb the little boy, however, any more than the huge green flies that escaped from the basement to drone in the garden where he played with Caroline; death was the raw material of the paternal genius, therefore fear had no place. What Gustave learned, on the other hand, and what he repeated over and over again in his works, is that the dead assume a supreme nakedness, a nakedness that lacks the means—by a gesture or an expression, by grace or beauty—to defend itself, and this means that death is a horrible survival which leaves the dead without recourse against the whims of the living. For this reason Flaubert pushes his sadism beyond Marguerite's suicide in order to deliver her to the scalpel of the two medical students, and has poor Djalioh stuffed and

347

the beautiful Adèle—loved madly by the anthropoid—disinterred as a skeleton.[37]

These two conceptions, maternal death and paternal death, take opposite sides in his mind. Vaguely at first, then with age more and more harshly. Indeed, for a monster the first kind of death is almost desirable: he is poorly constructed, he comes apart; being unloved, he rejoins the nothingness from which he was mistakenly pulled. The second kind of death is a perpetual condemnation; dead or alive, the monster is eternally superfluous, the wretched creature belongs to men and to the worms that do with him what they will; in short, suicide itself does not save superfluous children, it socializes them.

At the age of five, Gustave does not clearly formulate this contradiction for himself inasmuch as he is resigned to die and cannot even imagine killing himself. Let us say simply that he is troubled by this contrast: on the one hand those pure, luminous absences, the dead children of Mme Flaubert; on the other, those indiscreet and voluminous presences, the good doctor's dead. To which death is he promised? To pure annihilation—something that probably resembles his ecstasies—or to some stinking residue? Whatever it is, he carries death within him; the parents' overprotection and the family's bereavements have put it there, and it is both an interrogation of his near future and the meaning of his dazes, that loss of consciousness he never achieved. Later, it is not so much suicide that he desires, which may merely deliver him to men, as maternal death, annihilation, taken to an extreme, since he would like not only his body to be reabsorbed into nothingness but even to leave no trace in the memory of men. He is not yet there at five years old. But since he is passive, he feels closer than other children to that absolute passivity, annihilation; it is at this point that he feels old, dead in advance, and that he conceives of death (we shall soon see more clearly) as a still suffered passivity, the degree zero of life.

For these reasons I imagine that the golden age for Gustave was, in spite of everything, a period of rather gloomy estrangement. Passive and fortuitous through his mother, condemned through his father's love to hyperactivity, mad with pride through the internalization of the Flaubert ambition, yet in his superfluous contingency not finding the least reason for being, unskilled at speaking, at un-

37. In *Agonies* he reworks this scene and shows us, in a very improbable but typical fashion, a "great man" disinterred—unspeakable as it is—before the crowd, the same crowd that wanted to lynch Marguerite.

lerstanding the speech of others, replacing evidence with the principle of authority and primary certainties with beliefs, tormented by
he incessant question, why was I created? from which he drew only
he intermittent presence and rather lukewarm tenderness of an
overworked father (present enough to charm him for a moment, too
late to constitute him), this sensitive child was afraid of nothing, this
much is certain. The House, the mother's efficient attentions, the God
he sometimes spoke of, the magnificent father who made him a gift
of his tenderness, the justification of his contingency through vassalage, the harmonious return of the seasons and family celebrations,
and, at the heart of this repetition, the inflexible ascent of the Flaubert
line—everything was, as we say today, a source of "security." There
remained the "estranging" contrast between a vital flux without ego
and an absent ego which the others knew and named Gustave; and
on another level that premature familiarity with death which seemed
to him at times the fabric of his subjective life and at times the absolute
otherness that threw him into the hands of the others, like a thing
for which they would have the *jus utendi et abutendi* and which nevertheless would be him. Free-floating anxiety, vague and perpetual
questioning hidden beneath an eager submission. What remained
was the boredom common to all children but exacerbated in him by
his passivity. The only moments—still ambiguous, however—when
joy transported him onto a calm disquiet were those dazes that he
also called—though much later—ecstasies, when the alter ego disappeared and the world became the child.[38] He describes such moments powerfully in the first *Saint Antoine*, and we shall return to
them at length. For now it is enough to say that these ambiguous
states prefigure the crisis at Pont-l'Evêque, which is, in the final analysis, only their radicalization; they are therefore—if the word has any
meaning—at the very origin of Flaubert's genius, and one of the
objects of this book is to demonstrate the fact. Here is the other
singular feature of his golden age: when the child knows happiness,

38. It may be pointed out that there were Dr. Flaubert's "rounds" as well, a thrill
for the child, alone in the carriage beside his father. This is true. But I note that the
little boy's happiness was based in this case on the loss of himself. He was only the
reflection of paternal excellence, or else he was dissolved in the father's bounty. There
is no doubt that his joy was consumed by anxiety. When the child lost himself in the
world, the world asked nothing in return; as for Dr. Flaubert, the child could neither
reflect him in peace nor serenely be dissolved in him; he was the terrible Father, his
love was pitiless demands that the little boy did not entirely comprehend, for this
magnificent progenitor was basically active, and demanded acts. Gustave would later
forget the fear; at the time, however, it was actually stronger than the joy.

he is already fashioned for the unhappiness that follows; his happiness is congential unhappiness. He does not know it yet, but we shall see that, by the very way he manages the situation into which his parents have thrust him, he is preparing with his own hands the little hell that will be his lot after the Fall and forever.

C. Inadequacy

Mme Caroline Flaubert tried to teach Gustave his letters. Wasted effort. The murderer of her own mother immediately became defensive and rejected in advance any charge against her, as we see from Caroline Commanville's testimony, which sounds like an echo of her grandmother's protestations: "It's not my fault; I succeeded beautifully with Achille." Later she added—for her granddaughter's benefit: "With your mother, too!" If she isn't the problem, then it must be her son. The resistance can only be coming from the child.

The resistance does exist—now we know the reasons for it. When Gustave sits in front of an open primer, it is as if he were being shown two basically different objects presented as one. You may say that this is true for all children. Indeed; but the difference between reading and speaking, considerable as it is, is not usually an unbridgeable gap. For oral language, in most cases, is itself an *activity*.

In most cases but not in Gustave's. We know already that he is *spoken*—the words come from the adults, enter his ear, and designate him as a certain object incommensurable with the inert flow of experience. Of course, he can be spoken only if he speaks, and speaks *to himself*; in spite of everything the apprenticeship in speech surely must be a praxis, but the passivity the child has internalized does not give him the tools that allow him to *recognize* this praxis. For the same reason the activity is never followed through: retained, deciphered, memorized, the word remains *the speech of the Other*, and its sense is not distinguished from its sound, that is, from the speaking voice. On this level, oral language exists for Gustave as a syncretism—it is a mode of being within him that directs him without involving him and in which sense and substance are undifferentiated. It is presented by whole phrases still more than by words. Or rather, in this first stage, the phrase is word and the word is phrase.

He perceives written language as an object radically distinct from oral language. To this child accustomed to and fascinated by blocks of sound that haunt him without belonging to him, the adults offer a tool he will appropriate only after a process of systematic decomposition, followed by regulated recomposition. In other words, he is invited to forge himself an instrument through an actual activity, the first moment of which is, quite rightly, analysis. For all children, analysis presents the greatest difficulty. But particularly for Flaubert. Precisely because he never distinguished sense from sound itself, he feels repugnance for an operation aimed at breaking the word down into letters, that is, into nonsignifying elements. Language is the essential form of his alienation, which is what prevents him from grasping its "conventional" character. Speech is the mother, in him, and it is the father, both all-powerful; when Gustave uses speech himself, he experiences it as a regurgitation. In brief, the block of sound is indivisible since it is the Other; it has no universality—even potential—since it appears to be a projection of incomparable individuals; it is not an indefinite possibility since it is always *current* and *imperative*. What is proposed to him through the primer is another language in which matter and form—sense and non-sense—are rigorously distinct; beyond that it is a set of impersonal possibilities which exist for everyone but do not designate any particular master— the field of universality and reciprocity. In short, it is the opposite of what he is usually given, the opposite of the Flaubert language which belongs to the paterfamilias like a house, like each child, and which represents the acoustical setting of a particular sovereignty; it is the opposite of a power *lent* by the father to each member of the family and the opposite of the movement of vassalage. The child cannot understand it at all; the analytic idea disturbs his passivity as well as his feudal syncretism, and the conventional character of the letters does not accord with his sense of the phrase as an integral thing; the egalitarian universalism of common language shocks his thinking, which reflects a hierarchical and singular order. To learn how to read, he would have to shatter his inner conception of language, that is, radically to change his relation to the self and to others. And of course this can be done; but not without mediation. The adult is capable of such metamorphoses if the situation warrants it. With great effort the child will get there, *in time*. But the identification of the two languages will always remain imperfect; until the end of his life, Gustave will see written language as an inessential mode of the Word destined to lay the groundwork for the absolute verbal form, which is oral language. For this writer, writing will never achieve its full autonomy. Hence the difficulties the backward boy encounters all come from the fact that he does not understand the function of written language and is unaware of the correspondences of phoneme and morpheme. We

351

know the difficulty Djalioh experiences trying to grasp logical relationships and that this inaptitude is the cause of his illiteracy. But the context indicates that Gustave's thought goes beyond the expression he gives it here: Djalioh does not even understand where the *articulations* come from. The connection between letters that compose a vocable is purely conventional. Nevertheless it is a connection; meshing the Other and the self, the subject and the object in a passive syncretism of interpenetration, Gustave has made himself unfit for analytic activity as well as for the task of synthetic recomposition. There are two languages here, which he is told—wrongly, as it happens—are only one. For the little boy, this is an unintelligible assertion; the phonemes enter his ear, slip away as passive syntheses, or come out through his mouth—he *suffers* his own speech. Now he is told that the morphemes must be *made*, that an activity called reading must actualize the signs printed on the paper, one after the other, must activate the last sign without losing sight of all those that have preceded it, and through their systematic unification constitute one of those completed objects called phonemes that pass from mouth to ear, inert buzzings that surround people and are the noise of their life. How is it possible that the speaker should be *spoken* and that the reader should read, and that in both cases the same language is involved? In other words, for little Flaubert the difficulty is one of *principle*—he does not understand what is required of him. Reading presents itself to children as the first rigorous praxis, concerted and conscious of its structures. They have learned of course to walk, to talk, to eat according to the prevailing habits, but this was more or less by imitation. Reading is not only decomposing and recomposing graphemes; it is learning that action, whatever it is, involves decomposing a practical field and recomposing it in view of a given objective. To learn to read is to act. We can well imagine that Gustave, beyond the fact that he does not comprehend the unity of the two languages, finds himself disoriented by the apparition of this unintelligible object—an elementary and abstract theory of action produced by the activity itself and becoming an indispensable light which guides the act in progress. He puts up a passive resistance to this transmutation, which aims at overturning his subjective being. We shall see that all his life he will offer this same involuntary and spontaneous resistance to actions proposed to him in their imperious nakedness. For another child, reading is only a matter of learning; for Gustave it is a question at once of giving himself means he doesn't have and of metamorphosis, of abandoning the uneasy but gentle inertia of experience in order to become the cold and capable subject of an enterprise.

As bad luck would have it, just at the moment others want to make him spell out words, he reaches the awkward age. Certain mothers are irritated by the timid independence they themselves have fostered in their five- or six-year-old offspring; these newcomers stand up and should stand up for themselves, they eat or refuse to eat, manifest all sorts of stubbornness, whims, a personality. As if they were self-sufficient! But they have lost neither their dependence nor their fragility. Now they must be persuaded to accept the cares that used to be administered through authority. "At that age, you have to urge everything on them!" The creature in spite of himself was raised up against the creator; these carefully nurtured children seem to be the negation of maternal effort—which cherished in them this very thing; through the strength of love, they emerge as *others*. Nothing is more infuriating; the mother redoubles her vigilance but lives this contradiction from day to day; she is often offended and distances herself a little. The effects of weaning on the infant are well known; I believe that at this age one can speak of a counterweaning of the mother: quite late she discovers the radical otherness of what she took for her reflection—a son is broken in.

This is not the children's fault. Their body affirms its autonomy, that is all, and its alleged revolt comes simply from the fact that it can walk and run; "will" comes afterward and becomes humanly negative only in order to internalize an animal independence. The little child knows nothing of this; he continues his growth, a clumsy and patient adventure, and more sensitive to identity than to metamorphosis, he feels deeply *the same*; it is his parents who have changed. In short, he no longer understands anything, he lives out his exile in anguish, in the loving expectation of a reconciliation—he was pleasing yesterday, why is he displeasing today? Yesterday his parents laughed at his sulking, why don't they laugh anymore? His only defense is to do it over again; thus he intentionally replays what was accidental two or three years earlier. He only makes matters worse.

What is there to do but get stubborn? Since he is blamed today for what was applauded yesterday, the little boy hasn't made himself understood. So he contrives to exaggerate the effects. All at once spontaneity turns into playacting, and the young actor is openly displeasing: don't play the little beast, don't play the child. He himself, without admitting it, feels *false*. In order to escape from himself, he throws himself into new charades, he shouts, he sings at the top of his voice, he indulges in monkeyshines, wearing himself out and shifting instantaneously from overexcitement to angry tears. Sometimes he may try to get away from playacting by doing something real—but what can he do except destroy? He will break everything and be punished. At other times he may be consumed by anguish— what if everything was a lie, even his filial love? What if his parents didn't love him? He throws himself into their arms to be reassured, mimicking tenderness in order to revive it both in them and in himself. In vain; he is so concerned with putting on a show that he is unable to feel, and as for the adults, his inappropriate moods only irritate them: calm down, they say, let me work. The child is backed into a corner; they reproach him for an autonomy he did not ask for, they keep him at a distance, and when he wants to recover his lost servility, when he wants to shatter the transparent pane that separates him from his family, they quite frankly accuse him of playacting. Then, how he dreams of letting himself slip back! How he longs to relive his former life, the old realm of needs where he was monarch and slave! How he wishes he could retrieve the realities of hunger and nourishment, of appeal and gift, of tenderness! Briefly, he lets himself run on, he "regresses," the only result being that he wets his bed.[39]

Fortunate children are taken in hand by the father at the moment when the mother begins to turn away from them. For Gustave this was not the case. Certainly the paternal regime soon replaced Caroline Flaubert's cold sovereignty. In the small boy's sad life, all love came from Achille-Cléophas. But what a void when the lord too turned away from him. The medical director, as often happens with authoritarian, somber men, loved newborns rather than adults; beside their cradle he felt sufficiently alone to be moved by their innocence. He gave them his favor for a few more years, while he could still be amused by their fragile impotence. But they shouldn't take it into their heads to grow up. After five or six, they fell from grace; skeptical and challenging, dry, slightly cynical, he was horrified by displays and above all by dramas; effusions disgusted him. He silenced good feelings—with a word, but chosen to displease. The little boy blushed in shame, went off to hide under the table, branded. Was Achille familiar with these agonies? Sometimes I tell myself that Dr. Flaubert having been unable to give him brothers, treated him less harshly— the unique hope of the Flaubert family should have the right to consideration in proportion to his fragility. Gustave, on the other hand,

39. We shall come back to all this in the second part of the work.

entered the dangerous zone when his older brother had long since left it. He was less precious and at the same time more annoying. And then, he had bad luck. A sister was born when he was in his fourth year. No doubt she was less valuable to the father since she was only a girl, but after all, she was the daughter Mme Flaubert wanted, and for a few years she was a doll to fondle—she probably aroused the chief surgeon's interest and monopolized his meager store of tenderness. On all sides Gustave found himself frustrated. Was he jealous of Caroline? This is a question we shall have to consider. Let us note for the moment simply that the child did not so much suffer his fall from grace as have a presentiment of it. It was enough to plunge him into anguish. If he surmised that the father's tenderness was addressed to his age, that was reason enough for him to refuse to grow up. To his misfortune, this regressive intention came at the wrong time—the parents had decided he must begin his training, and presented him with the alphabet. The child regarded it as a symbol: he recognized in the primer the path leading to the solitary condition of the adolescent, of the adult. Suddenly it became the means of preserving his age; he challenged the symbol with a symbolic refusal: he would not learn his letters—his whole body resisted. This behavior, as I have said, was neither conscious nor voluntary; that it was intentional was enough, as we shall see, to plunge him into unbearable guilt. Things remained this way for some time; he stumbled and made no progress. In the end, of course, he would have learned. Unfortunately the mother grew alarmed; nervous, and not wishing to take responsibility, she alerted the progenitor—was Gustave a congenital idiot? The philosopher-physician, rightly irritated, took the little dunce in hand. He would not admit that a Flaubert son could be deficient in intelligence; nevertheless this speculator of the Empire was worried, his sperm might be a bad risk; after fathering so many dead children, why not a cretin? He promptly made up his mind: a man who can do great things can do small things; he, Achille-Cléophas, professor of general medicine and surgery, would teach his younger son his letters; guided by an iron will and an incomparable intelligence, the child would recover his ground in a few months. Achille-Cléophas set himself to work and bungled everything: humiliated by his son, he humiliated him for the rest of his life.

Readers may wonder how I know all this. Well, I have read Flaubert; the boy had such lively memories of these lessons that he couldn't help sharing them with us. In *Un Parfum à sentir*, written at the age of fifteen, the acrobat Pedrillo becomes teacher to his sons—he teaches them to dance on the tightrope. The youngest "with a rather brisk step mounted the stairway leading to the tightrope"; he acquits himself very decently. His brother, not very gifted, takes a few leaps, falls on his head, and dies. But now we see the third—namely Flaubert, between Caroline and Achille. Undoubtedly the young author took the precaution of endowing the youngest with the skill that in his other stories marks the eldest; after all, Caroline—as Caroline Commanville tells us—had learned the alphabet easily. And then, the cards must be shuffled. In any event, we have only to read this strange episode, which has no real connection to the plot and seems to have been inserted under the pressure of an obsession, to perceive at once its lyric and subjective meaning.

It was Ernesto's turn.

He trembled in every limb, and his fear increased when he saw his father take a little rod of white wood which until then had been lying on the floor.

The spectators surrounded him, he was on the tightrope and Pedrillo's gaze weighed on him.

He had to go forward.

Poor child, what fear was in his eyes and how intently they followed the outline of the rod, which remained clearly in front of them. . . .

The rod, for its part, followed the dancer's every movement, encouraged him by lowering itself gracefully, threatened him by shaking with fury, showed him the dance by marking the measure on the rope, in a word it was his guardian angel, his safeguard or rather the sword of Damocles suspended over his head by the thought of a false step.[40]

Ernesto's face had for some time been contracting convulsively, something was heard whistling through the air, and the dancer's eyes filled with tears he could scarcely swallow.

However, he soon descended; there was blood on the rope.

All of Flaubert is here; we shall encounter these cunning tricks again. That rod he speaks of so sanctimoniously! A guardian angel no less. But it changes suddenly into the sword of Damocles. The safeguard becomes the risk of death. As for being struck, not a word. A whistling is noted in passing, nothing more. In fact the little acrobat is whipped so hard he leaves traces of blood on the rope. But Gustave has managed it so that what we retain is the single image of the rod supple, agile, fascinating, a symbol of paternal mastery and solicitude.

40. My italics.

This text is an undeniable accusation; the father made the son work, and the son—out of tenacious spite or a sudden access of hatred—denounces his executioner without commentary.

We may wish to relate the testimony to more recent memories—who says the author is not telling us covertly about his unhappiness during the past year or the preceding week? I answer that from the age of ten Gustave no longer had need of tutoring because he understood without any difficulty and succeeded easily. Maybe the father sometimes stuck his nose into the schoolboy's homework or made him recite his lessons; but these isolated interferences—which occur in all families—are whims, irritating the child without permanently affecting him. The son might not even have mentioned them if they hadn't reminded him of the enterprise that devastated his childhood under pretext of reclaiming it. Let us, then, take a better look at the text. The sole pedagogue is Pedrillo; these are daily exercises, and what serious work! It is a matter not of giving a rather accomplished pupil momentary help but of leading a child from nature to culture—he was walking, now he must dance on the tightrope. Briefly, in the face of gravity and vertigo, terror is used to inculcate this elementary but artificial behavior, the ABCs of the profession. The boy is learning to read.

The drama begins. Achille-Cléophas is angry—out of seven children, four are dead and one of the living has no brain. What he loved in Gustave was his own spermatic power; if the pretty little boy is brainless from birth, that success becomes failure—the physician had enough left in him to make one son, no more. When he strikes a paterfamilias in the balls, God announces that he is destitute. Unmanned, the physician-philosopher was no more than a chance father.

Nervous, unstable, undoubtedly paraphrenetic, Achille-Cléophas was not apt to judge himself in the wrong. But there was another solution: a guilty party had to be found, and if it wasn't the father it had to be the younger son. By deciding to open his mind to his son, the physician-philosopher condemned himself to share the common condition of father-professors. Such people are dreadful pedagogues: "If you loved me, if you had the slightest sense of your duty toward me, toward your mother, or even if you maintained the slightest regard for those who created you and cared for you, you would learn your letters in no time, and your geography, and your multiplication tables. Listen, I am asking you just one question: Who won the battle of Poitiers? You don't want to answer? What ingratitude!" The ruse is accomplished, and without hindrance, without changing one term of the discourse, the head of the family substitutes value for fact; scholarly aptitudes are duties—his son will have them all on pain of offending him. A strange sentiment, slippery and confusing; paternal exigence is doubly unreasonable. On the surface it depends upon the idea, which is in itself absurd, that in order to recover lost ground—whatever the underlying motivation—the little pupil must only be willing; at bottom such an idea is based on a theological principle, which remains unformulated, that all creation is a credit given by the creator to the creature—the son must enhance the glory of the progenitor who produced him. Briefly, having legitimized his anger, the paternal pedagogue is no longer embarrassed; he reproaches the pupil severely for his imbecility, but this is no longer a misfortune, a provisional arrest of mental development; it is rather a fault, whose only source is an odious lack of love—and naturally it must be condemned.

The child ought to know the truth his parents hide from themselves, to feel his incapacities as resistances *of fact*, as inert external determinations which have been affected by his birth and brief history; the fact is that he does not understand, that he does not retain. Unfortunately, it is not so simple. Certainly, he feels his limits. But he *is not*, on this empirical level, his own confines, he does not support them passively as wax *supports* a seal, as a prisoner *endures* the walls of his dungeon—he must make them *exist*; in other words, it is by existing that he actualizes their being. This *surpassed past* is preserved and consequently affirmed in the surpassing that negates it. In a word, existence in all innocence creates an unfounded illusion since the existing man appropriates his being at the moment of praxis, which I have called the internalization of the external. The little boy feels his inadequacy as the internal and spontaneous weakness of his project. Incapable of decomposing a word into letters, the child experiences his incomprehension as an enterprise; diluted in his projects, his essence reveals itself to him as a practical decision. Not that he was conscious of ever having made this protean decision; simply, every project demonstrates that it was made within him. Suddenly he is responsible, and his resistances viewed *from the inside* seem closer to laziness, to temptations, than to obstacles; indeed, he almost believes he is resisting *himself* out of ill will. Furthermore, we have seen that basic intuition, in Gustave, engulfs a certain empirical truth, since the young boy bent upon his refusal to grow up is moved by an *intentional resistance* that is confused with the internalized limits of his powers or, if you will, his capacities.

It must be understood that this situation is untenable. For a child to make a mistake is nothing—punishment is purifying; zeal redeems, and provokes the delicious ritual of forgiveness. And to recognize external limits is nothing: "I am little, later I shall be big." But if the limits he cannot go beyond are presented to him and experienced within him as the consequences of an autonomous decision and repeated a hundred times, a thousand times, or, inversely, if he discovers in his freedom a bad *nature* which always *freely* leads him to crime, then he discovers his own slave-will, Luther's demonic invention.

The two Flauberts are implacable toward Gustave; they give *pure privation* simultaneously the status of slave-will and of the inert eternity of matter. The child internalizes *nothingness*—that passive being-there of the No; he changes absence into subjective presence—ungraspable besides—and founds the pure vacuity of his soul on the permanence of a diabolical fiat that never occurred. For the father and for the son—for the son through the mediation of the father—an object is born: inadequacy. Gustave is inadequate; this means that inadequacy is his being and that inadequacy of being is his fundamental choice as well, his original sin. To be sure, the father's criminal madness was to present his son with this relative character as an absolute reality. Gustave was inadequate at around seven years old relative to the father's arrogant aims. One hundred and twenty-five years later, better informed about the nature of childhood, we accuse the medical director of having aimed too high, too quickly, and of having bewildered his unhappy pupil by allowing him to see his exasperation. Today we would determine the young boy's *level*, meaning the interconnected sum of his possibilities and his resistances; starting from this *reality*, the educator would define the method and the objectives, short-term and long-term—tactic and strategy—required *by the object*. If it were necessary to enlarge the field of these possibilities, the psychologist or psychiatrist would try to free the pupil from the fetters and curbs produced by his history, rather than forcing his intelligence without transforming his feelings. Under the Restoration, a physician-philosopher bids a child to experience as his own deficiency the distance that separates him from a model defined by paternal ambition, impatience, and excess.

Scholastically the private lessons were crowned with success. Gustave entered school at the usual age and did rather well. When we recall, moreover, that the earliest letters in his correspondence, which are remarkable for their firmness of tone, date from his ninth year,

we understand that the backward child rapidly made up for lost time
Nor does he tell us anything different in *Un Parfum à sentir*: Ernest
has neither the gifts of the first of his brothers nor the total incapacit
of the second; he goes from one end of the prescribed trajectory t
the other, without any grace but without failing.

Yet he must be beaten in the end; it is the menacing fascination c
the rod that sustains him rather than skill, for Ernesto has no voca
tion—terror has made him an acrobat. Two years of terror? Four years
We shall not know for certain. What remains is only the young au
thor's memory of a horrible constraint—of having *bled*. Indeed, thes
ordeals, barely successful and then only through double violence
maintain a constant tension in the child which is scarcely tolerabl
and in a sense makes success more painful than failure. Failure, eve
if humiliating, has the advantage of being a rupture; you can collec
yourself and sleep off the disaster and shame; defeat can be a respite
Victory too, on condition that you bear it happily, by vocation, an
that ultimately you *find yourself in it*. Gustave never found himself i
victory; however it came to him, it was stamped with his father's face
The father triumphed over his little boy, he conquered his pervers
will to lose, he guided his stubborn intelligence and his hand. For thi
reason the child experienced no lasting relief—whatever the difficult
already surmounted, it only heralded the next, which terrified hir
even more. For the father, intelligence developed by exercising itsel
thus every problem solved was a springboard for jumping off to mor
complex questions. But the child did not sense his progress: if h
found the solution, it always seemed by accident. "This miracle won'
happen again—next time, I'm lost." In short, he lived in fear. Sti
worse, in horror. Was it so terrible, then? Certainly his "inadequacy'
was like a seal and marked him. But it would have been only half a
bad if it had been applied to virgin wax, if some still slumbering min
had suddenly become conscious of itself through this mark. He woul
have defined himself by it, he would have adapted his ambitions an
his projects. Only half as bad, too, if the child, awakened and con
scious, held back by other concerns, pushed toward other ends b
other appetites, had not simply been occupied with learning his let
ters. But this was worse: the little vassal was out of favor.

In any event, as I have said, it is likely that Dr. Flaubert lost interes
in him between his eighth and tenth year. I mistrust fathers who lov
their children *too early*; there is a good chance that later on they wi
make life difficult. What they admire in these children in the earl
years is their helplessness; as soon as the sons are capable, the father

become the most demanding tormentors. What Achille-Cléophas loved when he set Gustave beside him in the carriage was what I shall call *quasi solitude*—he pondered his concerns, considered his next investments, while a mute consciousness on his left adored him. The fact is, as Gustave has told us himself, that he accompanied his father on these famous rounds only in his early childhood, when he was four or five years old. By the time he was seven, it was finished, and no one can believe that Dr. Flaubert refused to take his son anymore because, not knowing his letters, he no longer deserved it. No one but Gustave himself, who learned at the same time—or within six months—that he was out of favor and worthless. The more so since at the same time the Flaubert parents—something of this appears in the memoirs of Caroline Commanville—committed another crime: twisting the knife even deeper, they didn't hesitate in the name of emulation to compare their younger son's meager efforts to the brilliant performances of the older son nine years earlier when he was Gustave's age. But as we have seen, Gustave is only too tempted to overburden himself: he feels his deficiency as a constitutional vice, even as ill will. By instituting the comparison (on the contrary, they should have explained to the child that at his age everyone encounters the same difficulties), the parents confirmed the child's fall from grace; above all, they transformed a vague feeling of maladaptation to reality into that *anomaly* he will hereafter take to be his essence: "I am not like the others." Whatever the meaning of this sentence when Gustave wrote it at the age of twenty, it has an archaic sense: Achille could read at five years old, and I still couldn't at seven.

D. INFERIORITY

At the age of fourteen Gustave makes us party to the shame he felt, that he had always felt, and that had been determined in him by the endless comparisons with his brother. In *Un Parfum à sentir*, Marguerite is abandoned by her husband who loves Isabellada; misery compels the three acrobats to live in daily promiscuity: "What humiliated Marguerite even more was that perpetual comparison to Isabellada she had to bear every day, every moment. Contempt attached itself to her person, to everything she did."

Achille's childhood was one of the most often repeated episodes of the family saga—at six years old he was already exceptional. And of course he knew how to read. "Be like your brother, Gustave!, Be like your brother!" But the fact is, Gustave could not be like his brother, and what is more, for just that reason he was held up as an example. "Ah! Achille would not have answered so foolishly!" Indeed not. But Gustave did say these foolish things and so was different from his brother. Different is an understatement; as long as he was denounced in absolute terms, his *inadequacy* was bearable; but when Achille was brought into the picture, the inadequacy became something relative to the Other, that is, *inferiority*.

The crowning misery was that the inimitable model proposed to Gustave was living, he was even of the same blood; Sundays and Thursdays he had conversations with the father. That was enough; with the best intentions in the world, Achille-Cléophas turned himself into his younger son's executioner. Achille was sixteen; with this young gentleman, a brilliant student who did him honor, Dr. Flaubert took another tone—he spoke man to man, questioned him on his studies, on his teachers, and, above all, told him about the future he was reserving for him as though it were already history. He told him what it means to be a practitioner, that medicine is the finest profession in the world, that it seeks knowledge in order to save lives. Dr. Flaubert took his son with him through the corridors of the hospital, the young man sat in on classes, the students treated him with respectful familiarity—he was the crown prince; as if the medical director were saying: "Here is my realm, it will be yours." Young Achille slowly absorbed his future privileges, which became his nature: he was *born*, and in his person seniority was changed into racism. The younger son saw everything; he overheard his father speaking freely, reminiscing, explaining his projects, and could hardly bear to see his morose, beloved face light up at the sight of his elder son. Gustave was devastated by the interest elicited by Achille, for the big brother pleased his father with his serious, intelligent, and self-confident manner, with the questions he asked, with his attentive, upturned face, his big, open, and unblinking eyes; he was able to charm. In his first years, Gustave recognized Achille's right to be loved—the Flauberts are modes of the familial substance, and the affection the father bears each one is merely a differentiated version of his love for the family. Yet he had to love them equally, so that all members should be united by the same *pneuma* circulating through each of them, which is paternal love. But with a preferential rate for the younger son on the sly. Yet just as Gustave's golden age was coming to an end, he learned at once of his abandonment, his inadequacy, and the true relations between father and brother. As if in discovering Gustave's inferiority Dr. Flaubert had sanctioned it by turning his back on him.

In other words, it was as if Achille's intellectual superiority made him *necessarily* the best loved. By this comparison, Achille-Cléophas transformed inadequacy, a subjective lack, into an objective connection between the younger son and his older brother—inferiority. On the affective level, this inferiority manifests itself in the form of a flat refusal of love. We understand of course that this refusal is not a simple sanction—it finally became the inferiority itself, discovered and experienced by the child as a freezing of his inner substance. A year earlier he was basking in the warmth of paternal love—to be, to be oneself, to be loved, to risk loving, were one and the same thing; now the night is cold; that ego he has such trouble maintaining within him and which came to him from the *outside* is henceforth no more than a word that designates him inside himself, glacial, and I should even say impersonal, with no relation to the immediate givens of his sensibility. One of the structures of the self that has been injected into him is that very inadequacy or, more precisely, inferiority, experienced as a quality which is *other*, meaning defined by the Other (the lord) and determining him in relation to another (the elder son). Put differently, by making an idiotic comparison between an untamed child and a brilliant, already domesticated young man, Achille-Cléophas committed the crime of alienating Gustave from his brother.

Even so, things might have sorted themselves out. Nine years is a long time; the student and the little boy had nothing in common. The serious conversations between Achille and Dr. Flaubert bored Gustave as much as they fascinated him. He simply took their relations *as a whole* for a singular relationship which defined them and publicly displayed their secret intimacy. This *manly friendship* is what made him frustrated with seigneurial tenderness. But without recovering what was lost forever, couldn't he have consoled himself with the thought that nine years later, as a big boy, he would have the *same* conversations, the same intimacy with Achille-Cléophas? After all, the object of these chats was *medicine*. Not that the older son was studying it yet; rather, he was preparing himself by listening to his father talk and, in order to please him, was turning himself into a physician in anticipation. Yet the term "medical science" designated for the younger son a strange, multiple object which belonged to him as much as to his brother; it was the father's profession, the cause of his exhaustion, his nervousness; it was glory, the famous dust raised by the horses' hooves entering villages, the cadavers waiting side by side to be transported to the amphitheater, the House, Flaubert honor, the difficult but certain realities allusively evoked by the father and the elder son in their conversations—the nature of the human body, the maladies affecting it, life, matter. It was Achille-Cléophas's promethean past, it was his future and the future of *both* his sons, a ready-made, almost too easy future in which you could just coast toward eventual celebrity. Medicine, the prefiguration of two young lives, was a setting, a "climate," a style, a human relationship; and Gustave saw in it the elements of his destiny. In this sense he should not have been surprised that Achille discussed his future career with the progenitor—it was his right, as it would be the right of the younger in nine years' time.

The little boy had the misfortune to discover at about the same time that the provisional inequality—which he would have liked to attribute to age—had been transformed by the father's gracious will into a definitive status. Achille was Dr. Flaubert's chosen one, he would replace him, inherit his duties and prerogatives, and would be medical director in his turn. When did Gustave become aware of this? We do not know. But it was not a secret to anyone; everyone at the hospital knew that the physician-philosopher had placed all his hopes in his first son. I have given the doctor's reasons, and from his point of view they were valid; but what could his younger son think? As medical director of the Hôtel Dieu he was the best doctor in all of Normandy; when other doctors came to see him, they assured him of their admiration, of their respect; they were *therefore inferior*, as the child was quick to note. Since Achille was taking the post and the glory, Dr. Gustave Flaubert would be forever inferior. Would he accept this decree with resignation? Would he see in it a humiliating lack of love? A betrayal? Both reactions would have been possible if the child had not been conscious of a primary inferiority for which he alone was responsible: Achille's academic achievements were dazzling and Gustave had not yet learned to read. Wouldn't the judicial and statutory inferiority sanction the real and experienced inferiority? Hadn't Achille-Cléophas made his decision after being disappointed by his younger son? If that were the case, the inequality of destinies would be the deep truth of an inequality of talents; Gustave, being mediocre, would have by paternal decree the suitably mediocre career. But couldn't he have reversed the terms and thought—unreasonably, to be sure—that he had become inferior because it was decided in advance that Achille would be superior to him? We must understand that the little boy fell into a diabolical trap; among these three determinations—inferiority through inadequacy, through frustrated love, through sovereign decree without appeal—each one refers to the other two; they form a synthetic whole of which each element is inseparable from the others and is outlined against the totality which at the same time sustains it and is expressed through it. We must describe the trap in its objective workings before questioning Gustave as to how he *experienced* it.

Far from touching the child's "human nature" and affecting some so-called universal faculty for suffering, this inferiority assaults the *Flaubert* in him; in the younger son's *Flaubert-being* lies his concrete determination, his singularity; as for sufferings, they do exist but they will be Flaubert sufferings. For the excellent reason that a family drama is involved. There is the House of Flaubert and then nothing, and then the crowds—the father knew how to give the children this foolish pride; the mother shared it too, love, pride, the same *pneuma*, the same substance. Taken by itself, inadequacy, which is an inert quality, should eventually be dissolved because it is balanced by the feeling of innate superiority over all men. Better to be an inadequate Flaubert than a statesman; that is what the physician's sons sincerely believe— it is their basic relation to the external world. If this defect of being has substance, it is in the small group and in relation to it; common ambition, internalized, sustains and nourishes it, objective relations of kinship transform it into inferiority. We have seen that *Flaubert-being* is prefabricated, communicated through the family name. Gustave's spontaneity took as its rule the combination of commandments and promises attached to the Flaubert name. This means that he realized his being by surpassing it through the movement of his life, and at the same time that a tacit vow, the counterpart of birth, constituted this being—assigned by the other and by the self—as the unsurpassable limit of his future. Limit, a positive as well as a negative determination: work, medical career, prohibition against losing caste, assurance of success. The father chose for the child, but he felt he made the choice himself—the familial will was particularized in him and became *his* will; inversely, Gustave would have no will other than the one he derived from his family. Before the discovery of inadequacy, when his father used to take him in his carriage and sketch for him in very simple words the common future and his singular one, Gustave learned optimism: persevering and meritorious, his efforts would be crowned with success. His certainty rested on his total confidence in his father, that is, his confidence in human praxis as embodied in the practitioner. Since the paterfamilias offered him his own person as an example, the child grasped his life *in progress* as already lived, summarized, and only to be lived anew. It is not un-

365

important that the little boy should have had a father who was alread
aging and at the height of his provincial glory; Gustave could not se
Achille-Cléophas as a young first son, absorbed in a still risky enter
prise; rather he was a conqueror, a sage, whose existence was alread
wrapped up. This, I believe, is one of the reasons that led him fror
childhood on to consider human lives as finished syntheses whic
integrate the future with the past and death with birth, or, if you wil
as rigorous movements, their speed and direction fixed in advance
which extend from *this* birth to *that* death. In brief, Gustave had
long-standing knowledge of his fundamental passivity. But on th
surface, the Flaubert force bore him upward and he had the feelin
of raising himself.

Good. But this necessary refusal is quite impossible unless he
thrown back on his own incapacities. To become *better* than Achill
by following the same career makes no sense; first of all, Achille
by definition unsurpassable, and furthermore, this perfect being
an ass, a milksop, a bourgeois; he couldn't be overcome without bein
radicalized. A perfect intelligence completely absorbed in makin
diagnoses and prescribing treatments; besides, he has a puny natur
no vigor, an insipid and banal sensibility—he finds release in livin
his life on acquired habits. The prince of science, unlike his fathe
is not a demon—just a shopkeeper. Gustave cannot come to a fir
opinion of this strange animal; he vacillates between two contradictoi
judgments.

1. Achille may be a congenital bourgeois. To put it baldly: bourgeo
stupidity is his vocation because of the vulgarity of his feelings. Tl
father's unjust and foolish generosity alone has made him the gre
man of science he will surely become; the philosopher-practition
has breathed into him his own genius mouth to mouth; he lies c
top of his son, as Julien lies on the leper, and through a slow cementir
process cedes to him his vital forces, his inexhaustible power. In shoi
everything comes from the paterfamilias. This is what Gustave clear
gives Edmond de Goncourt to understand much later in a curiou
confidence which, a quarter of a century after the death of Achill
Cléophas, reeks with bitterness:

> Flaubert exlaimed: "There is no caste I scorn like the caste of
> physicians, and I am from a family of physicians, from father to
> son including the cousins, indeed I am the only Flaubert who is
> not a physician. . . . But when I speak of my scorn for the caste
> I except my papa. I saw him, behind my brother's back when h

received his medical degree, shaking his fist: 'If I had been in his place, at his age, with the money he has, what a man I could have been!' Here you can see his disdain for the rapacious practice of medicine."[41]

We have to admire, if not the lies, at least the string of "countertruths" scattered throughout this paragraph. Until Achille-Cléophas, the Flaubert family had in fact produced only veterinarians. Goncourt cannot be suspected of misunderstanding—there are letters from Gustave in which he plainly states that the Flauberts are physicians from father to son. Is he ashamed to reveal his grandfather's true profession? I don't think so; in other letters he mentions it proudly. Everything depends upon the circumstance. Yet it is clear that Gustave wants to be the only Flaubert who does not practice medicine; thus by benefit of heredity he finds himself eminently possessed of medical qualities; at the same time, unlike Achille, who has submissively, conveniently utilized these same qualities to earn his living like all the men of his race, Gustave establishes himself as the only one who had the audacious genius to say *no* and to utilize the capacity for surgical scrutiny to nobler ends. Suddenly Achille-Cléophas is sanctified in his turn—his disinterestedness is such that he scorns the venal practice of medicine. Certainly the chief surgeon was honest; he sometimes treated poor patients free of charge, and—as Gustave adds in the same conversation—would probably have been happier performing some complex, risky operation that might yield new data but for which he was paid with a dozen herrings, than carrying out the usual humdrum, though lucrative, interventions. But if we took Gustave's words literally, it would be inconceivable that the old man, upon his death, could have left his children such a tidy fortune. In truth, the eulogy of Achille-Cléophas is nothing but a condemnation of Achille. At bottom, Gustave tells us, his father had only disdain for his eldest: you are *my* son, he thought, the son of *my* works, you have benefited from my money, my credit, my knowledge, I have given you everything and *that's all you are*. To my mind, the obscure train of ideas that leads Gustave to conclude, "*Here* you can see his disdain for the rapacious practice of medicine," makes sense only if we consider that Flaubert ranks his brother among those rapacious physicians. I do not know if he is right; the fact is that he believed it. And we know why: Achille doubled the patrimony. But beyond the fact that Gustave condemns in his brother what he found com-

41. Goncourt, *Journal*, vol. 10, 1874–75, p. 160.

mendable in their father—thus distinguishing between covetous and disinterested accumulation of wealth—the reproach, which might have contained some truth in 1874, was certainly not addressed by the chief surgeon to his elder son *before* he was able to practice. As for the rest, what is there to say? We have seen that Achille-Cléophas was absolutely convinced he was a better man than Achille; his difficult youth, his shift in class accomplished by a struggle, had given him a high opinion of himself; at times, out of sheer irritability, he must surely have vented his anger at his favorite son. I can even imagine the terrible progenitor, on a particularly exasperating day, throwing his four truths at his son's face. To mutter them behind his back so that the young man should not hear, shaking a fist he could not see and, what is more, on the very day Achille achieved the title of doctor? I absolutely refuse to believe it. But suddenly Gustave's intention becomes clear: he does not *say* so, but he implies that Dr. Flaubert, inveighing against his elder son, was conscious of his younger son's presence. Can we really believe that Gustave was close enough to the paterfamilias to understand a muttered remark that Achille himself did not catch, and that the progenitor, talking to himself, should not have noticed the child? Yet if he was conscious of his younger son, the medical director was addressing himself to Gustave. More precisely, he was communicating with him in an indirect manner, happy to be overheard. A family of physicians, all contemptible except one, who was a great man. And one other—the rebel son who wanted to devote himself to Art and refused to earn a penny by his pen; these two understand one another, the same strength of character, the same sharpness of mind, the same disinterestedness. This is why, from afar, Dr. Flaubert preferred his prodigal son—who had the courage to displease him by refusing the career he offered—to that mediocrity who had all the advantages, including that of receiving through some mysterious inspiration the paternal intelligence and knowledge, and who did nothing with them, who, with no vocation and through a docility that was suspect because it was too easy, allowed the profession unwanted by Gustave to be thrust upon him and, still worse, profited from his conspicuous advantages in order to commercialize his priesthood. What Flaubert even as a fifty-year-old liked to *make himself believe*—he needed only a listening public—was that his father, at one and the same time and quite contradictorily, had made a gift of all his intellectual endowments to an unworthy son, leaving his younger son purposely without attention, without support, without skill or talent, and then one day, because of this very privation and also, no doubt, disappointed by the usurper, understood that in its earthly history the Flaubert family had produced two eagles: himself and his younger son, who had formerly been cursed. But the pious and deceitful anecdote that Gustave relates to Edmond de Goncourt seems to issue from a calmer soul. At some point in his life, reconciliation with the dead father had taken place. Very late, assuredly. Well after the publication of *Madame Bovary*. In any case, the legend of the paternal curse in 1874 is accompanied by another myth invented later: the progenitor finally understood, the scales fell from his eyes, and he did Gustave the good grace of chasing the usurper away. Now the two men walk side by side, Science for the sake of Science and Art for Art's sake, like Zorro and the son of Zorro.

But in 1835 the adolescent, lost, bewildered, without self-pity, imagines no end or compensation for his torments. The paternal curse is pure, any kind of "happy ending" is out of the question; Achille is mediocre but he is the chosen one, Achille-Cléophas has made him the gift of his unequaled intelligence. What is there to do? Have contempt for his mediocrity? That would be to forget that by the will of his creator he will be the century's greatest man of science. To have contempt through him for science itself—that would be the same as having contempt for his father, an inexplicable and fascinating crime but one he hardly dares imagine. Prove that the abandoned child is capable by himself of surpassing his brother and beating him on his own ground? This cannot be done, for little Gustave still bears traces of the Fall: he was made to understand that he was the family idiot— how could he conceive of challenging such an association of brains?

2. But what if—and Gustave often comes close to believing this— Achille had actually been like *him* in the beginning, merely a vague aspiration, a trans-ascendence, escaping through ecstasy or torpor from the dry truths of science, from the calculations of utilitarianism? And what if the progenitor, with good intentions or—quite to the contrary—out of malice, chose him as his disciple and made him the repository of his diabolical knowledge, and the unhappy boy was utterly tormented? Science, which misfired with Gustave, had succeeded with Achille, nipping faith in the bud without hope of resurrection, effecting a curettage of the heart, replacing love with interest. In this case the usurper was more to be pitied than blamed; exact, desiccating knowledge had made him thoroughly bourgeois. The ambiguity, then, may no longer inhere in the connection between acquired skills and their beneficiary but in awareness itself. Hence

369

the somewhat pitiable element that we find, in spite of everything, in Messieurs Paul, Ernest, etc.

The primitive feeling that compensated for Gustave's consciousness of being a superfluous non-sense was optimism. He believed in himself indirectly, through the Flaubert substance of which he was, after all, a finite mode: the family's merit would always be rewarded, even in him. The sudden discovery of his inadequacy strikes the ambitious young man at the heart of his collective ambition; optimism will be the first impaired structure, for his family name is synonymous with success. Furthermore, nothing is changed: the little boy has the same imperatives, the same love for the lord, the same desire to achieve at school, Achille achieves even more success with the same ease, while the lord's glory is at its height and will not flag; in this sense the Flaubert world preserves its structure of sober optimism—and it is certainly in this unique world that the younger son is prepared to live and die. Gustave perceives himself to be Dr. Flaubert's single error, and an indescribable transformation allows him to bathe in the dynamic hope of the family without being penetrated by it. In him—and on all sides in the Hôtel-Dieu—hope *becomes other*. Gustave has not stopped believing in his miraculous family: a hundred times a day he tries to reanimate in himself the collective trust and pride, and when he manages to do it the child breathes a sigh of relief; but the moment he recovers the great Flaubert confidence, he perceives that this confidence is, in his own person, *the hope of others*. What is this affect, not his own, doing *inside him*? The first answer that comes to mind is that it has no existence separate from what he gives it; he is the one who fans its flame without any right to it. In this case he must disengage from it, rediscover the humility that suits his incapacity, and return the usurped feeling to the community. But he quickly comprehends that this solution is not possible—hope has been set upon him like a seal. Gustave is a product of the enterprise, and it is the first duty of the creature to be unreservedly proud of the creator and his creation; Flaubert honor exists, we know, and each member must affirm and prove that this family is superior to all others. The duty is incumbent upon Gustave as much as upon the others; but the moment he is required to perform an act of faith which is addressed to the entire House—and, through it, to himself as well—a formal condemnation obliges him to exclude himself from the collective portion. To exclude himself? Not entirely; he must praise the father's carnal work in his own person and assume responsibility for the defect in fabrication. That's what Christians do when they give thanks to God for giving them their being, yet hold themselves responsible for their nothingness. It is torture by hope, permitted to the younger son of the Flauberts but forbidden to Gustave. No promotions in this enterprise. The father has decided the possibilities and the merits in advance; his decision cannot be appealed—Gustave is a lesser Achille, forever arrested. Through the efforts of all its members the Flaubert family rises in Rouen society, but no one will rise within the family. There are positions which are assigned forever. At fifteen Gustave is finished; he has found all his literary themes which are the expressions of his anxieties and his violent passions.

We seldom encounter, and I do not recall having ever encountered, such precocity: it is terrifying; not a breath will come from the outside, the future is barred by an iron wall. How can we fail to understand this child who from the earliest years had a "complete presentiment of life," who had discovered his destiny? This strange internal fixity that so struck his contemporaries is the Flauberts' gift to their youngest son. "You will be the family idiot." If the child wants one day to find a way out of this, he must accept the sentence. And whatever his chance of success, he has no hope of altering it. A genius, perhaps; idiots and geniuses, according to the wisdom of the period, have more than one thing in common. A powerful mind, never. Nonetheless, when the younger son affirms the unique excellence of his House, he cannot prevent himself, since he is still part of it, from counting on some miracle, on some passing efficacious grace from the father or from the whole community to its last male offspring. This illusion can be neither dismissed nor preserved—the inferiority is made public, it is the father's judgment renewed each day; how could anyone fail to believe it? In the same way it is engraved in the facts: the child is slow in certain things, sometimes distracted, and then, the mistakes are undeniable, as well as the negative intention that can pass for ill will. If the father has passed judgment, to what God can he appeal? To tell the truth, there was no direct experience of inferiority—the difference in age that separated the brothers condemned the younger to be inferior to the older's past. But the comparison seemed all the truer for being merely retrospective; it discouraged emulation: a young contemporary can be surpassed, but Achille—as a child and a perfect one—might as well have been dead. This was established and imposed by the father; even in solitude the flow of emotions and ideas would be haunted by a model which entailed Gustave's inferiority. That inferiority was never an abstract determination of his being but rather a family relationship and the immediate taste of his inner experience—by which we mean the obscure consciousness of his alienation—and, since he thought he derived constant, bitter pleasure from it, the texture of his person. I was neither a defect nor a vice, it was a constitutional penury for which the little boy held himself responsible and which the presence of the Other inside him continually denounced as his relative-being.

Suddenly all the little advantages of the Flaubert ascendance become alien to him. Only just. He distances himself from them—or they from him. As if they belonged less to him than to the rest of the household. But at the same time he is tortured by rage: *It belongs to me! Everything Flaubert is mine!* This possessive lust characterizes everyone in the Hôtel-Dieu apartment, and they all get it from the father. But there is more: the bonds between things reflect personal relation for these imperfectly bourgeois rustics. *It belongs to me* means: it belongs to my father, to the master to whom I give myself and who gives me all he has. The gloomy rooms, the garden, the carriage are the father himself, as we have seen, the father making himself a material setting for the child. And so? To feel even imperceptibly distanced from the Hôtel-Dieu, from the estate at Trouville, from recently acquired properties, wasn't this the same as being distanced from the father? In his son's eyes, Achille-Cléophas embodied pure generosity; even by devoting himself to him body and soul, the little vassal *did not deserve* the love his lord gave him. And so? Must he now renounce paternal love under the pretext that he doesn't deserve it? Given and refused, near and remote, the things of this world excite and mislead the filial love and avidity of the ambitious boy. The Flaubert force, borrowed from the community and singularized by the age and condition of younger son, tears itself apart by lending its power and its positive qualities to the negation that becomes its obscure and corrosive antithesis. Turned against itself, the force *does violence to itself*—let it increase and the violence will increase as well. Inversely, the accumulated violence will excite ambition; this unique force, now divided, will be pushed little by little to an extreme as a result of its inner dissension and its indissoluable unity. *Inadequacy* is only an abstract moment in the battle that ambition wages against itself, but it is the worst danger. Ineffable in its immanence, this negation of transcendent origin is finally only a fissure of the internalized being; the child suffers it without the power to combat it. Whatever scheme he devises for overcoming it, it has already insinuated itself within him, which is hardly surprising since it is the being he must be; but neither will it be surprising if he exhausts himself in vain efforts—it is the being he must be against what he is. The only result: he is all the more attached to the goods and the career of which he believes himself unworthy; if by some miracle these were recognized as his, it would mark the end of his unworthiness. Indeed, he would not have coveted his father's situation on his own; being passive, a dreamer, quick to sink into states of torpor, he felt no inclination for the difficult profession that demanded constant alertness, a quasi-pathological hyperactivity and quick decisions. He felt frustrated at not having it only when Dr. Flaubert promised it to his brother; it was the image of paternal judgment and of love withdrawn from him, a constitutive privation of his ego and the symbol of his relative-being, that is, of his inferiority. Out of this emerged what Gustave calls Garcia's "dark, jealous ambition."[42] He is now defined in his own eyes as *the one who has not been chosen* and, of course, as one there was no reason to choose. Inferiority here merges with the pure contingency of the weed, which he received from his mother: it is right that I am given only crumbs, I who have come to this banquet uninvited.

But from another point of view inferiority is experienced also as the infernal opposite of contingency, that is, as the strict effect of a prenatal fiat. Set and hardened within him, the familial ambition inhabits him, internalized, as the substantial reality of his ego; it allows him to stand upright, an indeterminate mode of the Flaubert substance. The differential that specifies the mode necessarily becomes inferiority; thus at the moment it appears, the ego is defined in relation to the Other, of which it is only a lesser version. If he wants to know himself, Gustave has only to look at his older brother, of whose ideal perfection he is just a bad copy. This is material for madness; the Flaubert ambition being more violent in Gustave as it is the more contested, the child desperately desires honors, fortune, and success. More ardently than Achille, no doubt. Yet at this very moment, plenitude reveals itself as penury: he knows that he will never have what he desires; moreover, the origin of his desire is the certainty of never satisfying it. The violent demand to contribute to the ascent of the family by beginning his career at the point where his brother left off and the unhappy feeling of not having the required capabilities have been kneaded into his flesh with the progenitor's own hands. For this

---

42. It is also clearly explained in *Quidquid volueris*: before *loving* Adèle, Djalioh must understand that she is *an other*. Previously he could do no more than include her in his general goodwill.

reason they do not reveal themselves to the child as two characteristics closely connected, or as the encounter of two accidents. Were they connected, they would condition each other, the ambitious child's enthusiasm would compensate for his lacks; patience and submission—which are themselves moments of ambition—would pull him out of his inadequacy, at least the little boy would think so. Inversely, if the opposition between the project and the means issued from an autonomous spontaneity, the inadequacies would themselves *make sense*, they would translate inhibitions, resistances deeply connected to Gustave's early history. For this very reason they would have the effect of curbing not only success but ambition—the contradiction would not really contrast desire and capability but, more fundamentally, desire and the lack of it. This is not the case—Gustave's *arrivism* is uncurbed and his inadequacy is non-sense. It is true that the young boy internalizes the contradiction, turning it, as we have seen, into actual *experience*. Yet as the true sense of this attempt remains exterior to him and resides in the father's complex relations to his children and to himself, Gustave submits to it; but inferiority is not *his product*, and it is out of docility that he believes it contains the secret of his being. In consequence, the force that is to him evidence of his *Flaubert authenticity* and the malformation that excludes him from the family group pass through each other, *together* defining his being but without any other bond than this intimate coexistence.

But who would dare suppose that the child takes himself for the fortuitous encounter of these two qualities? Although the significations remain independent, he can see very well that the intensity of his frustration is directly proportional to that of his desire. And then the ego never appears to anyone as an assemblage of parts; it is a sufficiently structured unity, and the most diverse traits in each of us seem, however superficial we may be, to express in different dialects the same totality. The child will soon seek to render through myths the awareness that the relation between excessive ambition and inadequate capabilities, which is neither fortuitous nor logical, is no less internal and synthetic because it was established in advance by a transcendent will. Indeed, it is the father who has given and taken away. Everything contributes to convincing the child that he was put into the world with an imperative mandate; and this is true—no Flaubert without a mandate. Achille had a mandate to be the best physician in town, and Gustave, from birth, had a mandate to be second only to Achille. But paternal condemnation made the child aware that he had been refused the means to fulfill his office. "If I have an ungrateful nature," he can say, "why was I charged with such a difficult mission? If the enterprise is so delicate, why was I made so clumsy?" If the commandments had remained strictly *external*, he would have come to terms with not being able to obey them. But why were they produced within him in the form of such a burning desire? *To succeed*—this was his duty, his passion, to such a degree that he was nothing else, nothing more, a younger son of good family, than this pathos—and the more Flaubert, the stronger the flame. Why? He is thrown from birth into an enterprise he lacks the means to achieve, he is so precisely conditioned that he cannot help either foreseeing his continual failure or beginning again and again. What emerges here is something new, namely rigor in evil. An utterly human inflexibility; a contradiction so perfect that it seems chosen. Can nature manipulate a person like this, inflame his greed, crush him with impotence, and so push him to such extreme unhappiness? No—this marvelous economy leaves no room for chance. One year earlier, a happy Gustave opened his eyes to our world of consequences without premises and found more confusion than necessity. Nothing seemed to him decided in advance, except the happiness of the Flauberts. But constancy of evil narrows the course of things—everything heads straight to the goal, which is the worst. The face of the world is changed, he was tricked; he savors the evidence of his future failure, he derives cruel pleasure from it, and *at the same time* his passion, reheated, exhausted, indefatigable, pushes him to begin a battle lost in advance. Hence the general myth—conceived about the age of seven when the little pampered vassal topples over, when the good, beloved lord becomes an impatient schoolmaster humiliated at having fathered an idiot—that the world is hell.

It might be said that these are the internal but objective structures of a martyred ego as they emerge from our regressive analysis of the earliest works. I have followed step by step a process by which passivity, ambition, inadequacy, and seniority have gradually constituted that ego. The concrete development of Gustave's childhood out of these first structures remains to be shown. It is certain, for example, that his passivity comes from his mother and is the first internalization of the external world; ambition is only the second. How does the little boy experience disappointed ambition *through* the succession of his passive emotions? How can *activity*—for arrivism *is essentially a practice* in the father and older brother—be internalized by the received passivity of the younger son? What of it remains in him? How much of it can the child comprehend when he doesn't even have a firm grasp of verbal signs?

A continued study of the early works will yield the answers to this string of questions, each of which is conditioned by all the others. We shall begin with the simplest myth Gustave invented very early in order to understand himself, the myth of Adam's curse. Marguerite and Garcia have been put into the world expressly to be annihilated; this means that Gustave imagined he was condemned to death by his maker. Let us attempt to understand what this myth of condemnation signifies.

E. SUBMISSION

Of course, it was never taken as truth. It is enough that the myth should have been a subjective certainty that determined the child's fundamental being. Looking closely, we find that it expresses the incessant transformation of a factual necessity into a sovereign option, and vice versa.

1. It is a fact that Achille was the elder son, that being nine years older he continually offered the spectacle of his objective superiority; it is a fact that this superiority was not entirely due to the difference in age, for when he was Gustave's age he had known for some time how to read, write, and count. Moreover, the younger brother himself in early childhood had recognized his older brother's seniority as a right, though without knowing what was involved. But when he learned that it involved recognizing his brother's intolerable privileges, it was already too late—once the principle is admitted, the consequences must necessarily be admitted as well.

2. Achille's primacy was a sovereign and gratuitous choice. Under the Old Regime the eldest had no more than a superiority of rank over his brothers—the institution alone and not his merit or some decision from on high guaranteed his right; everyone was constrained, even the father. Unfortunately the hybrid character of the Flaubert family suggests that the chief surgeon honored the right of primogeniture when it was no longer customary, so that for Gustave the factual necessity was effaced by the option. In one sense he was right, the familial structures reflected the character of Achille-Cléophas; what he did not see was that Dr. Flaubert was a mutant and that his option reflected the values and traditions of his childhood. Wishing to consolidate the Flaubert unit by manipulating the reestablishment of his position as hereditary, he had to choose his firstborn for his

successor in advance, whatever he was. Gustave was not in a position to know that if he and his brother had been only one or two years apart, the choice would have been *revocable*—the better man would have won; he did not understand that it was time and death that made the paternal decision inflexible. For him it was as if the paterfamilias had created Achille by decree exactly as he should be, that is, as he was. And in the younger son the father deliberately produced goods of an inferior quality and with no definite function; it seemed to Gustave that his lord had pulled him out of limbo by a gratuitous act precisely to be what the family did not need. Inessential, useless, *therefore* inferior, the little boy felt afflicted by royal proclamation with a lesser being, and consequently with a lesser fortune.

Worse still, Gustave had the permanent impression, as we have seen, that he had been made according to plan and that each of his characteristics had been conceived as the negative of Achille's. Inferiority—a nonreciprocal relationship with the older brother—was experienced by the younger as the primary qualification of his being. What his instrument Garcia reflects of Gustave is his relative-being, as we have seen. This means that the Other seemed to him to constitute his being as the absolute, uncontested term from which the generating line of comparison was established. Jealousy itself was only Achille's institutionalized superiority as it had to be experienced by Gustave, his inferior. This was what subtly destroyed the young man: he had to live in the world of otherness ordained by an Other for others, where he himself, as Other, was produced as a lesser-being, as a relative being.

This relativity was surely the object of a decree. He was born "with the wish to die." In other words, with the consciousness of being superfluous. But this perfect uselessness does not refer to change, rather he sees it as the father's design. The medical director produced his second son in full knowledge that the child would be a younger brother. Did he create him *in spite* of this or *because* of it? For Flaubert the question has no meaning; his progenitor's will and his understanding cannot contradict each other, for the father is omniscient and projects the consequences of his decisions into infinity; since he is all-powerful, nothing happens that does not precisely reflect his will. In short, for the paterfamilias, "although" is and can only mean "because." He knew about the suffering involved in being a younger sibling; he could have abstained; if he did not, it was because he joyfully assumed responsibility for the inadequacies and inferiority with which little Gustave was tormented. Look at Cosme: making a second son is the same as giving him the demerits that correspond to his status and treating him according to his being and his value— which is precisely calculated—by relegating him to an obscure lieu- tenancy. As if the father, when engendering him, chose both the son's "intelligible character" and his phenomenal life, that is, the temporal reflection of this character. By a predicted fall, Gustave was forced to realize the inferiority Achille-Cléophas deliberately gave him.

The reason the unfortunate boy realizes, in his experience, the servitude of his freedom seems quite clear to him: his father infused him with the Flaubert ambition, a determination of activity which the passive child must have felt as a helpless passion, and *at the same time* this sovereign decreed that the ambitious boy should lack the nec- essary capacities to attain the goals set by familial ambition. Torn by this contradiction, Gustave can only find the truth of the two deter- minations in their conflict: the more violent his desires, the more pitiful the results. In his zeal, in his passion to reach the heights and finally receive his father's approbation, the child sees the direct cause of his resounding failures. This brings him, without even knowing the name, to the world of de Sade, the old friend he would cherish all his life. Gustave is Justine; like her he will see his virtues rigorously punished, and the range of the punishment will be in proportion to his deserts. The minute precision of this law itself demonstrates that it is not natural—there is a preestablished disharmony in Gustave's innermost being.

In the earliest *interpretation* Flaubert gives us of his condition, which is older than he is by a few thousand years, he seems to rediscover more than he invents. When Oedipus fought against Laius, he only meant to give vent to his anger; he was unaware of his lineage and even of the name of the bastard who forced his chariot against the rock. Had he known, and had he remained in Thebes, the appointed parricide might have otherwise conditioned his free spontaneity, but in any case the result would have been the same. *It is destiny*. But what can falsify the meaning of an act and force it, in spite of the agent, to realize an end set in advance and usually contrary to what was intended? Nothing except an adverse enterprise directed by an- other intelligence illuminating another will. A boxer I'm fighting feints and lowers his guard, I take a chance and get caught; this is all arranged to disqualify my movements and make them auxiliary to his so that I may spontaneously and wittingly become a means to serve his end, believing I serve my own. No *fatum* without human intention. Or quasi-human.[43]

Fatum is an obscure wish that furrows our lives and runs from their foreseen ends to their beginnings: the chips are down beforehand. For this reason Flaubert, the prefabricated child, is an authentic fatalist from an early age. He believes in destiny to the precise extent that paternal condemnation seems to him to have provoked the heteronomy of his own spontaneity. In all his early works there is an identical motif, that of alien *intentionality* or *stolen freedom*; in every life a great computer has worked out the *Umwelt* beforehand, as well as its tools and circumstances, so that each desire should be evoked at the very moment when the organization of the surroundings makes it most inopportune. Every behavior is provoked by a deceptive arrangement which, like a boxer's feint, forces it to realize an end that is the very opposite of what was intended. In brief, existence is a succession of carefully laid traps; you get out of one, mutilated, only to be thrown into the next, which is even more mutilating. The outcome is death. Not the *natural* demise that awaits a worn-out organism, but a conclusion contrived from birth by another will, as rigorous and artificial as a contractual agreement. This life inhabited by a stranger is in effect a horizontal fall with a calculated direction and speed. We now understand the meaning of the totalizing tendency we have already noticed in Gustave; taken in isolation the episodes of an existence do not interest him, but each one in its way reflects those preceding and heralds those that follow; each destiny is at once circular and irreversible, all the motifs are simultaneously present in every moment: death in birth and birth in death; everything is known, foreseen, inevitable. Yet to turn back is impossible, the chips are down, no one can take his turn over again; there are repetitions, but even if it should happen every time in the same way the event is always new, its persistent return makes it ever less tolerable. For Flaubert the "nausea of living" comes from the fact that every destiny is predictable for him who must live it, and he must then experience minutely, in detail, what has passed as general knowledge.

For him, destiny is apprehended through a vivid intuition and is not deceptive; it is the same thing, in effect, to say that from childhood he had a "complete presentiment of life" and to say that he "believes

---

43. The forces that steal my praxis and utilize it to other ends will always be found to have an intentional structure. But this intention can remain anonymous. Elsewhere I call it counterfinality, designating that universal category, the authorless act.

in the curse of Adam." But the second statement, which is more precise, rightly refers to an *alien will*. There must be *someone* to pronounce the curse; and it is not an accident if the accursed is Adam, who for a time enjoyed a marvelous childhood in earthly paradise and was chased out for having committed the original sin. In brief, the first man here is Gustave, exiled, guilty, and clairvoyant. Clairvoyance and destiny are one and the same thing. In 1857 all of France would read, totally without understanding (apart from Baudelaire), the story of a *damnation* which is predicted from the first pages and realized in the last. Admirable and lost, like the poisoner Mazza, Emma rushes headlong into hell; she is inexorably thrown in. Hence, far from reducing the excessively weighty words Hell, Satan, Damnation to mere articles of fashion, we must grasp the *sense* in them, beyond *significations*, which they are an attempt to symbolize. What these dense symbols certainly have in common is that they all suggest the dark aspect of the sacred. Let us not forget that the original intuition—the presentiment of life—goes well beyond simple conjecture: it is a *prophecy*, indeed a revelation which supposes the intrusion of the "numinous" in the life of a child. To go still further: the sacred is a fundamental structure of this anticipation; it is, if you will, its guarantee. Let us see what this means.

Gustave at the age of seven or even fourteen could not define his life's trajectory on his own. Foreknowledge—a simple extrapolation—is thus forbidden unless it belongs to the internalized Other. This being the case, the sacred is the mark of his alienation. The child claimed for himself the principles of the father, of the entire family, their parti pris; he was penetrated by them, reconstructing them in his own way as objects at the heart of the subject, objective truths half devoured by subjectivity. What does the familial prophecy have to be to crush a child with its authority on no evidence? Gustave might have questioned an affirmation which had bearing only on the future; thus it had to be based on a judgment concerning the present. They must more or less have declared to him: you are the family idiot. But who can be entirely convinced by the opinion of others if that opinion claims to be merely a statement of fact? Actually Gustave would rank himself among the monsters only if this apparently assertoric proposition—"you are an idiot, a *minus habens*"—disguised a *judgment*. Another monster who was pleased to cite Flaubert and felt an affinity with him, Kafka, showed this clearly in his short story "The Judgment," which discloses the judicial basis of his relation to the Father. The foreknowledge of facts will be a certain and sacred truth for the son only if they are seen as necessary moments of the process involved in executing a sentence handed down by his creator. To live, then, is to draw blood; and the condemned man knows very well if he is subject to ten years of penal servitude or fifteen years of imprisonment. Gustave hears the authorized voice, the paternal voice taking a solemn oath: "Whatever your efforts, you will never be loved, for I have decided in eternity that you were not worthy to be my son" Why shouldn't the child be persuaded that this is so? His father is the admirable man who *keeps his word*; his verdicts cannot be appealed. *Prophecy*, which rests on the notion that the worst is always certain, is but the memory of a condemnation; the horrible progression of sufferings is ineluctable because it is only the development of a sacred order. And why, you will ask, should the sacred present itself to Gustave as punishment? It is because his inadequacy, a received determination that arrests and limits his essence, at the same time appears to be his original sin—he experiences his prefabrication as his own option; this is normal since he cannot *be* his essence but can only make it *exist*, and it is enough to make him infinitely guilty since he has made the criminal and permanent choice of *relative* being. Furthermore, as soon as he suffers, Gustave believes he is tasting the bitter pleasure of his life in total. He sees no end to his present pain— he is cursed; his future pain, sampled in advance, passes for *sacred*. Here we undoubtedly have the basic structure of experience after the Fall: as the present moment is turned toward the past, unhappiness palls since it is the stale realization of what has been foreseen and realized a hundred times over; as it is turned toward the future, on the other hand, it is a prophetic and sacred anguish since every pain contains in itself the promise of an endless and increasingly miserable return—this is living one's guilt. Everything happens, however, as if the child, without losing the feeling that his very existence is an unpardonable sin, attributed to the progenitor the responsibility for his essence and discovered in him the cruel and demonic will to create a Flaubert idiot in order to chastize human stupidity in his person. For Gustave, prophetic knowledge, the presentiment of the Other, and the consciousness of the self are inseparable since he discovers in the sources of his being the same malign intention that presides over his destiny. It was decided to give him capabilities in inverse proportion to ambitions; in the life he lives, the falls which are foreseen will be all the more dizzying the higher his grasping and stupid pride has aimed.

The original fiat comes from the paterfamilias. But *fatum*, the complete presentiment of *his* life, is only the Flaubert family, a living and highly structured organism, as the father governs it and is devoted to it. The second son is totally integrated, meaning that he will live—ambivalently, of course, and we shall return to this at length—only the life of the family, without imagining or even wishing for a way out that would allow escape. But while he experiences the family as the indispensable ambience that nourishes and sustains his being, he foresees that his condition as younger son and his unworthiness will always keep him on the lowest rung. One day the beloved son will be the *father's reincarnation*—Gustave knows this; what then will he, the youngest son, the family idiot, be? Nothing. So the family engulfs him and he slips toward terminal decline. The progress of the Flauberts determines his involution. The first immutable structures are here the relations of kinship which anchor him in his subaltern position; they are expressed by repetitions which permit some foreknowledge; but through these ever more punishing returns, in which the superiority of the older brother is more and more clearly marked, he sees the irreversibility of the process as well, he pessimistically enjoys his being-for-decline, which could also be called his being-for-death. Gustave—between the ages of seven and thirteen—learned to see his life as a temporal totality. That is, it was at once complete within each moment of humiliation, and unfolded like a sad melody toward an awaited end. He saw the world *through* this totality which was himself and his family; he could view it only through his familial adventure. What would later be his "pessimism" must be seen as the generalization of his prophetic intuition: hell, before being *this* world, was his own life.

At this point in our investigation our original question is doubled because intimate experience is characterized ontologically by doubling, or self-consciousness. It is therefore not sufficient to have shown the original structure of this life and its particular kind of alienation, not even to have reconstituted its immediate savor; starting from the facts at our disposal we must determine the way in which this experience is made living. If he is condemned, how does Gustave *realize* his condemnation? Through what actions? What effect do these actions, provoked by his falling into disfavor and in fact only his way of intentionally feeling it, have in their turn on the archetypal event? And how are the inseparably linked affect and attitude made temporal through their reciprocal conditioning? With this problematic we approach what is fittingly called Gustave's *stress*—the unity of his evil that is internalized by suffering and its intentional arrangement, which can manifest itself in certain cases by a reflective manner and a distancing, a tendency to slip into the most immediate suffering by virtue of an *intention* to suffer.[44]

At the age of seven the intention is clear: Gustave suffers *submissively*. For the verdict strikes him in the midst of his love, in the fullness of his vassalage; it takes a while to change. All the more because the little vassal's spirits are sustained by the objective structures of a semipatriarchal milieu. At the Hôtel-Dieu everyone obeyed Dr. Flaubert. How could anyone challenge the divine judgment of a man revered by his family, admired by his students, and respected by all of Rouen? If he loves his judge to this degree, the disfavored child must love him even in his pitiless severity. He despairs at the verdict, but he does not reject it. How could he without ruining the authority of the head of the family, without which the House of Flaubert would crumble? For this child with no visa who—even before the Fall—is never entirely sure of having the right to exist, it is more economical to let himself be destroyed, annihilated, a nonviable mode of the Flaubert substance, and to prefer his creator to himself—as the oath of vassalage requires—even the terrible will that has produced its creature only to pass judgment on it. Everything must be accepted: inadequacy, original sin, inferiority, the objective comparison that affects him with relative being, the merits of the big brother and the prefabricated destiny. "Bless you, my father, for making me a younger son. Bless you for depriving me of all merit and for giving it all to my brother. Bless you for making me unworthy and for punishing me as a consequence. Bless you for depriving me of hope." In this act of submission—I will suffer to the end in accordance with your desires— we easily discern an intention to suffer *less*. Little Gustave, we have seen, was drawn out of his natal contingency not by the warmth of paternal love but by the duty to reflect his lord in his glory. He was created for nothing, or else to display a "fanatic" devotion, to annihilate himself for the sake of the paterfamilias—to choose. To be sure, he lost everything, the glorious rounds in the carriage, Achille-Cléophas's smiles; the little seven-year-old dunce perceives that he irritates his father—the warm light of the golden age was succeeded by a dismal clarity. And coldness. And boredom. This is a privation to which he does not resign himself. But after all, Dr. Flaubert was not so tender, or so present—the gift he had made to this lost child

44. There is still no question of personalization, however.

was obedience. The boy must therefore still obey the father, take the fall from grace as a test. He is asked to hate himself? Very well, he will hate himself, he will live *in order* to hate himself, stripping himself of everything to preserve the *right to exist*.

But that's not the point. If there was some comfort in submission, one can only imagine that in this case it must have been quite intentional. Or rather the intention came from the fact that no other behavior was *possible*. If the family unit had presented a rift of some sort, or if the child had simply revealed its antagonisms, like those that oppose husband and wife in the conjugal family, he could have challenged the authority of the father to the extent that the mother, even loving him, challenges it in her person. He would have had refuge, asylum, even without maternal complicity, even in silence. And if one of the dead sons had survived, they could have joined forces and formed a pair of rebels, each one recognizing the other. But no, he was alone; his sister was too young; his mother, the eternally self-effacing lesser being, was utterly devoted to the father and wanted to be inessential, transparent, so that he might pass through her like light through a window.

And yet if Flaubert during his prehistory had been loved by Caroline Flaubert, if he had profoundly and physically loved his mother, this jealous love might have developed his aggressiveness. But as we have seen, by depriving him of love his mother denied him the means to love. At the same time he lost any chance of being aggressive—we know that the thread of his experience is *passivity*. He would bear the father's condemnation passively; it became his own impairment, an external seal that unified the subjective flow, or more precisely, a *passive synthesis*. The most he could do was attempt to regain, by more frequent stupors, the paradise he had lost. But at this period, when the paterfamilias, alerted by his wife, was seriously asking himsel if his younger son was a congenital idiot, recourse to ecstasies became more and more difficult. Scarcely did Gustave attempt to absent himself, put his thumb in his mouth, than the father, if he was there pierced him with that terrible gaze—the little boy was *under observation* and he *felt* it. *Un Secret de Philippe le Prudent* can serve as testimony Carlos is shut up in his room: "It was large and paneled, with a black ceiling, and in general had the appearance of decay and misery . . . On the walls an enormous quantity of weapons could be seen . . . The door was closed with an iron bar, chains, and bolts; one would take it for the dwelling of a man who feared some sort of betrayal." Nothing so effectively evokes Gustave's effort to shut him self in, to isolate himself in the solitude of the inner life. Even the weapons indicate resentment: the child is fourteen years old, it is long past the Fall. Most striking of all, I think, are the words: "The bed was covered with red curtains, the window had none." A window with no curtains—the only possible escape is cosmic ecstasy.

But Carlos—at twenty, of course, "he is an old man"—barricades himself in his room in vain, he does not escape paternal surveillance. Philippe II—the symbol is transparent—delivers him to the Grand Inquisitor:

"You can see from here, father, what he is doing in his room. . . ."
He removed the crucifix, put his finger on a button, and suddenly a board slid back revealing a little door, from which he again removed two iron plates, and opened it with the aid of a wide pane of glass . . . the room of the Infante of Spain.

Carlos is not unaware of this. He often hears suspicious noises. Flaubert knows they can read his soul:

"He's always there!" he says between his teeth. "Always that man, listening to my words, spying on my actions, trying to divine the feelings struggling in my breast, the thoughts going through my mind, always there, sitting beside me, standing behind me, hidden behind a panel, spying at a door . . . and in my mad, jealous hatred I cannot, I cannot cry and curse, avenge myself! no! It is my father! and it is the king! I must bear all his blows, take all these insults, accept all indignities."

He has gone beyond the stage of submission, as we can see. However, in spite of the bitter indignation that inspired it, this passage allows a glimpse of an ancient alienation. At fourteen—we shall soon have occasion to discuss this at length—Gustave was convinced that his father could read his soul like an open book. We shall see how this feeling would gradually be rationalized. Dr. Mathurin and Dr. Larivière, two incarnations of Achille-Cléophas, will simply be good psychologists, fine connoisseurs of the human heart. But when Gustave wrote Un Secret, the rationalization was not complete; the symbol presents the idea in its antique nakedness. And it must date from an even earlier period; Gustave at the time was a boarder at the collège and saw his father Thursdays and Sundays when the doctor was not occupied with his patients or his duties. Even then, of course, the boy may have felt thwarted, observed with a mixture of surprise and scientific detachment, especially during vacations. But for him to have transformed these brief, rather unpleasant contacts into incessant spying as he does in his story, he must have been in touch with a considerably earlier experience. When humiliated by the little illiterate's resistance and worried by the suspect absenteeism by which his younger son tried to escape him, to escape from himself into himself, Dr. Flaubert silently turned his famous surgical eye on Gustave; the child felt utterly run through, his soul stripped bare, seen by the other; it was impossible to avenge himself, to "cry and curse," for these passions would be visible, his monologue overheard. The child forbids himself any dream of revolt and even negative actions, which would not go beyond to boundaries of subjective life; the father's terrifying eye must find in him only loving submission.

This original attitude will mark him forever, it is at the source of his insincerity; even the rancor and anger he feels later will involve a secret submission. But profound as it might be, it cannot be sustained as it is. First of all, for the child to remain in his own eyes the miserable object of a divine hatred, he would have to *constitute himself* as he was made; passive acceptance is not enough, only an *active* adherence, an implicit and sustained pledge could give this inert aggregate of sufferings the intentional unity of a durable *exis* and thus assume the synthesis of the Other. But at the same time it would be to affirm himself as the subject of an enterprise—the odious *object* of the *alien-enterprise* would vanish. In any event it exists only through the passivity Gustave has constituted, forcing him to suffer his acceptance or, better still, to dream it.

Starting with this, everything unravels; the synthesis is not contested, but since it is *supported* it inhabits him like an alien power, and submission, not being an act, is a nightmare. Thus as we have seen, well before his fall from grace language remained an assemblage of opacities deposited within him by the Other.

F. RESENTMENT

Passive obedience gives rise to resentment and prescribes its limits while preventing it from turning into hatred. Thus the slave, while revolt is impossible—even inconceivable—experiences the master's orders as a rosary of guiding imperatives and as his own life becoming alien to him, yet to be lived as his own. It is submission, a transcendent but immanent duty; yet the secondary results of this zealous accomplishment of obligations—fatigue, illness, pain, humiliation—constrain the toiler to recognize the other's demand within him as an alien evil or, if you will, to grasp his malaise as coming from an Other. A negative character is automatically attached to the order in the course of its execution, and to the person who has given it. This is resentment. The situation marks the boundaries of a sustained process; if resentment happens to arise in a state of servile impotence, it immediately rests on submission, to which it can only add a slight coloration. If on the other hand resistance is conceivable, an oath—generally collective—transforms it into hatred, that is, into praxis. For little Gustave the tyranny is domestic; this slave is the product of the family guild and he is overcome with docility. But this, as we have seen, is both constitutional and impossible; he would have to *realize* in all humility the monster they would have him be and at the same time rid the earth of such a burden. A task which, as it is not assumed by little Gustave, can only appear to him as the negative ascendancy of the Other; the sufferings he endures, since they cannot be assimilated to the profits and losses of an enterprise, must be inflicted by the Other. In this case resentment, without ever raising itself to the level of hatred, becomes the deep *meaning* and *purpose* of submission. Which can be expressed in these terms: when aggressiveness is lacking, when the Other is already established in the subject and deprives him of his sovereignty, namely the autonomous activity that would allow him to assume or reject a constituted character, in short when consent and revolt are equally impossible, resentment appears in the unloved child. It is a complex tactic by which he attempts to recover an impossible subjectivity by exaggerating the alienation that first makes him conscious of himself as object. In the present case the tactic consists of borrowing the force of the other through passive obedience and turning it against him; by turning himself into the pure means of realizing the alien ends imposed on him, the resentful man lets them reveal their own inconsistency and, by their unavoidable consequences, their malignity. In order to understand more completely the nature and meaning of what we shall later term *passive activity*, we can simply contrast two themes which are constantly present in the early works: suicide and "death by thought." In both cases Gustave realizes the father's curse, but suicide, being revolt, remains on the level of fantasy, whereas the other death, being passive activity and resentment, is properly that *experienced death* that will find its realization in the "attack" at Pont-l'Evêque.

When Marguerite hears the shouts of the people coming after her, she has a sudden insight and translates their taunts into *her* language: "*Death!*" This is what they expect of her—very well. She runs laughing to the river. The child, who more clearly understands that these words represent the desires of the father, of the family, of teachers and comrades, reveals the sentence they have pronounced by charging himself with its execution. He informs them at the same time that he subscribes to all the damning evidence: yes, Achille is perfect, yes, I am mediocre; I recognize publicly the nothingness with which my creator has endowed me by publicly committing the act of self-annihilation.

Doesn't this zeal for self-destruction push obedience to an extreme? It probably does, but not *passive* obedience. Marguerite *bursts out laughing* as she strikes her forehead; she laughs at her executioners, at herself, at the human race—by her voluntary death she affirms her independence and takes it upon herself. Claiming as her own the nonbeing which until then was only her determination by the Other, she kills herself when she feels like it and instantly, when her persecutors, or destiny, may have ordained a slow death for her. This is not all: she avenges herself. If Gustave were to kill himself, he would unleash a scandal, denounce the Flauberts for what they are, the creators of monsters. If this physician who passes for a saint were to reduce his son to suicide, all of Rouen would recognize him as the demonic lord of a grim fiefdom.

Gustave's vengeance would be even more far-reaching if he dared to perpetrate it. Naturally the negative aim is passed over in silence, but let us read carefully; for young Gustave—always on the verge of "free association"—reveals more by what he does not say than by what he does. What has become of Pedrillo, for example, that adulterous husband who represents the guilty father? He seems to have been entirely forgotten. Yet he is there, hidden beneath part of a sentence like the Flaubertian negation beneath the affirmation. A grande dame passes by in her tilbury, Marguerite recognizes Isabellada: "She was not mistaken; one day when Isabellada was dancing in the public square, a great lord saw her, and since that day she had become his companion." She must therefore have abandoned the acrobat *on the spot*, unfeelingly. But Pedrillo loved her to distraction—therefore he suffers. Thus Achille's ingratitude will punish the paterfamilias: he will live in Paris, in high society; he will be ashamed of the provincial surgeon who fathered him. At this moment, perhaps, Pedrillo will remember his wife and Achille-Cléophas his other son—they will need their love. But it will be too late, Marguerite and Gustave will have died of that love.

In *La Peste à Florence* we have already shown that the murder of François is an act of self-punishment. But this very real aspect—a self-punishing revolt—masks a more treacherous intention: the younger son assassinates his older brother in order to force Cosme's hand, obliging that inexorable judge to execute the sentence he himself has passed. You were the magistrate! Gustave tells him. Very well, now be the executioner. This is how the head of the family slaughters his own son. In doing so, the poor man falls into the trap Gustave has set for him; he annihilates his House with one thrust of the sword. If François had died of the plague, the progenitor would still have had an heir; pitiful as he might be, Garcia would have carried on. But by this suicidal murder Garcia forces his father to discover his own sin and the ineluctable necessity of its attendant punishment. By making him a younger son and frustrated, Cosme made him monstrous, malicious, and desperately jealous; *therefore* he fathered him purposely in order to realize his essence through fratricide. Garcia's birth decided François's death; and when through the worst kind of crime the younger son finally becomes the monster he was supposed to be, the paterfamilias, who was either stupid or blind, has nothing left to do but finish the job by killing his own son. What a punishment for this awful old man! He will be left alone, meditating on his coming death, in other words, on the extinction of the race he had forged with his own hands.

A curious page from the final version of *Saint Antoine* gives us proof that the dream of suicide, born of negative pride, is Gustave's radical but imaginary revolt against Achille-Cléophas. Antoine, at the edge of the precipice, is tempted to jump:

One movement would have done it, only one.
  Then AN OLD WOMAN *appears*:
  "Go ahead . . . What is stopping you?"
  ANTOINE, *stammering*: "I am afraid of committing a sin. . ."
  THE OLD WOMAN: "To do a thing that makes us God's equal, just imagine! He created you, you are going to destroy his work, you by your courage, freely! The pleasure of Erostratus was not greater. And then, your body is mocked enough by your soul that you should finally take revenge."

The naïveté of this argument reveals its primitive source. No one can imagine—not even the *adult* Flaubert—that the destroyer of the world, even if the whole of creation were smashed to bits, would equal in power the creator who fashioned and ordered it; unless it

389

were admitted that a kick that breaks a clock is equal to the drunken clockmaker who gave the kick. That isn't even the issue; rather, it is the death of a creature who is finite and *mortal as well*, for how could this death alter anything in the creation? The universe will perpetuate itself undiminished, unaffected by it. On the other hand, temptation through pride takes on a fascinating depth when it is traced to its true source and when the confrontation is seen to be not between the infinite creator and his lowly creature but between two finite beings, one of whom has produced the other: Achille-Cléophas and Gustave. Over all of what *is*, over science, money, his sons, and the inheritance, the progenitor's power is uncontested. As for dying by his own hand, the younger son is persuaded that this would effectively arrest his expulsion and the chief surgeon could do nothing to prevent it; over what does not exist, the brilliant lord of being is stripped of all authority. The two men, the old man very much alive and the young man potentially dead, find at last—in Gustave's mind—some sort of reciprocity. "You could create me, I can uncreate myself and at the same time disorder the family, your masterpiece; nonbeing is worth as much as being, and *I* am worth as much as you. Sum: zero."

Still nothingness, of course; this pride is as empty when it clings to suicide as when it attempts to rest on the special quality of the Flauberts. Nevertheless the internal effort is positive; this is the realm of shadows, his realm, in which his father is powerless. Of course nothing will ever be decided—it is enough that the decision could be made. If voluntary death becomes the younger son's intimate possibility, the free meaning he can give to his life from now on, regardless of what he does later, Gustave's essence as the father has forged it remains between parentheses, floating between being and nothingness, between life and death. A monster? Yes, and now. "If I like. As I like. In short, I am a monster by a provisional consent that I can always revoke." In order to be efficacious, the sovereign act of the progenitor needs the approbation of the son. As long as he gives it tentatively and without any guarantee, the *imposed* statute is nothing more than a *proposition*. For the moment, the child does not disclose his definitive intentions; his course has been charted, he answers: we'll see. All at once, through the detour of possible suicide, he takes hold of his own existence; he hasn't the means, true, to change it one iota; it will be what the father made it or it will not be. But the possibility of rejecting it as a whole is already a great deal. Thus by dying his life, living his death, the child recovers himself. By this first movement he constitutes himself negatively as his own cause; the struggle between father and son is situated on the ultimate level of the creation ex nihilo and the annihilation of being. On closer inspection this pride is an option: Gustave recognizes that his father is unsurpassable, but at the same time he abandons knowledge to him, as well as power and virtue; he will equal his father by transporting himself to an entirely unknown terrain, the terrain of nonknowledge, impotence, conflicted and guilty passion. Briefly, the father is a being who sees being from the standpoint of being, everything is full; Gustave decides to consider this same being from his own point of view, which is that of nothingness. Through this change of perspective he sets himself outside the real, an infinite particle suspended in the void. Gustave—at least between the ages of thirteen and twenty-four—never stopped thinking about suicide. Not that he saw it as a concrete, urgent act, something he could carry out or put off from day to day; rather, he recognized in it his freedom-to-die, as much his ultimate and fundamental possibility as his life, the means of becoming, through chosen annihilation, the son of his works.

This means in fact that he never stopped *dreaming* of revolt. But at the same time he knew very well that he would never engage in action and that his rebellion was only an imaginary possibility. Indeed, he writes everywhere: I want to kill myself, and always adds: I shall not kill myself. In a careful reading of the youthful works, we often find the idea that suicide is *impossible*. Not, of course, in general but for the particular protagonists in each work who represent Gustave. Look at Almaroës: "He was bored here on earth, but with the boredom that eats away like a cancer . . . and drives man in the end to suicide. But him! suicide? . . . How many times did he lingeringly contemplate the barrel of a pistol, and then throw it down enraged, unable to use it, for he was condemned to live."

In Djalioh's case it is instinct that restrains him—and ignorance: "Oh! If he had known, as we men know, how quickly life can vanish at the touch of a trigger when you are obsessed. . . . But no! unhappiness is part of the order of nature, which gave us the feeling for existence to preserve as long as possible."

With Mazza, the instinct of self-preservation is deceptive, inspiring unreasonable hopes which distract her temporarily from killing herself: (Ernest has just left France.) "Then she heard a voice that called from the depths, and leaning over the abyss calculated how many minutes and seconds it would take her to draw her last breath and die. . . . However, some sort of miserable feeling for existence told her to live and that there was still happiness and love on earth, that

391

all she had to do was wait and hope and that later she . . . would see [Ernest] again." She will accomplish her own death, nevertheless, but much later, when she has become a criminal and, ultimately, desperate.

Finally, the hero of *Novembre* "thinks for a moment whether he shouldn't end it all; no one would see, no help to hope for, in three minutes he would be dead. But immediately the usual antithesis presented itself as it does at such moments, existence came to him smiling, his life in Paris seemed charming to him and full of the future. . . . Yet the voices from the abyss called to him, the waves opened like a tomb ready to close over him. . . . He was afraid, he went back in, all night long in terror he heard the wind blow."

These passages evidently comment on the same experience that seems to have been repeated a number of times: Gustave fingering a pistol or leaning over a river, the sea. A bullet or drowning. He favors drowning, a feminine form of suicide; Marguerite throws herself into the Seine, Mazza and the hero of *Novembre* would like to let themselves slip into the ocean. Water is *fascinating*, suicide is hardly an act but rather a kind of vertigo; and reciprocally, vertigo is the beginning of suicide: "The voices from the abyss called to him, the waves opened like a tomb, he was afraid." As though the little boy were submitting to his impulse as to an external fascination—*there is only* one thing to be done, says Antoine; and the adolescent in *Novembre*: *there are only* three minutes of suffering. In brief, he chose revolt in its least active form, making it a matter of consent, almost a loss of consciousness. Even then, however, he could not make up his mind to do it. What repeatedly held him back? The "feeling for existence." These three words found in *Quidquid volueris* and in *Passion et Vertu* correspond to those in *Rêve d'enfer*: "condemned to live," and to the "antithesis" in *Novembre*. These words refer us to the appetite for living that Gustave, in spite of everything, believed he had discovered in himself. Was it a genuine appetite? No; he would have had to have a different mother, a different early history. I have said that in order to love life, to wait each minute for the next with confidence, with hope, one has to have been able to internalize the Other's love as a fundamental affirmation of the self. The little exile holds onto existence with all the strength of his negative passions, out of Flaubert pride, that dark and jealous ambition he got from the father; to do away with himself would be to withdraw from the Flaubert plenitude and to let it reshape itself, undiminished, without him. This is precisely what is impossible for him; he wants to participate in the family triumphs even if he is frustrated, and he will not let Achille enjoy them alone; the moment he is about to give in to vertigo, when he feels his hold slipping, he prefers to lull himself with what he knows are false hopes: he too can succeed and be the pride of the paterfamilias. This is enough to pull him away from the cliff, to make him push the pistol aside, to resume his momentary unhappiness in the family he can neither tolerate nor abandon.

And then, voluntary death does not settle anything; far from snatching the victim from the clutches of his executioners, it puts him at their mercy. As we have seen, the cadaver represents a postmortem survival of the persona, which is of course a result of the promiscuity of the living and the dead, the dissecting and the dissected, as Gustave experienced it at the Hôtel-Dieu, but also and above all a result of the child's passive constitution, since his being is a being-other and he is limited to a docile *internalizing*. From this perspective even zealous internalization seems to be a petty, pointless fever, and the plenitude of being will be at last attained when his internalization has disappeared and the being-other remains alone in its perfect passivity as being-for-others—when Marguerite is dissected after her suicide; when the charming Adèle with her "alabaster breasts" is exhumed at Père Lachaise and stinks so bad that a gravedigger feels sick; when Emma, after the revolt that "ends her days," finds a strange survival in a rotting corpse, in memories that decompose and recompose her life in their own way, in chests that burst open, spilling out their most intimate secrets. If Gustave kills himself he will be laid bare, in all senses of the word; the physician-philosopher's surgical scrutiny will dissect his soul. Obscure and defenseless, the child will reveal his secrets; from now on this *passive object* will confirm the contempt of others, no longer having the means to challenge the judgments brought against him. An infinite *freedom of inference* will deliver Gustave to all those who torture him, especially the fools; this is the unforeseen result of the suicide he will commit *against* the person for whom he bears a hopeless love. To die of sickness doesn't wash; one is discovered and then forgotten. But suicide provokes scandal. A highly ambiguous success. In a sense this is just what the younger son wants, he wants his father to be punished; but on the other hand Gustave abhors scandal—we shall see this clearly in 1857—above all (that definitive incongruity) any scandal that might deliver its author to the hands of men. He cannot bear the thought of becoming a monstrous skeleton in his older brother's memory. Nothing better illustrates the "impact" of the family on this unhappy child; for him

393

suicide only results in being saddled with a posthumous but still familial life. Gustave's destiny will not be accomplished with his last sigh but only with the last of the Flauberts; if he throws himself into the Seine, someone yet unborn will one day know him as the obscure, idiot uncle who killed himself out of stupidity, the unique and wanton stain on the honor of the family name.

Furthermore, voluntary death was impossible for this submissive son because it was forbidden. Achille-Cléophas brought a younger son into the world, one of the damned, it is true; the father's inflexible rejection condemned this son to death. But to a *slow death*. The child could not ignore the almost exaggerated attentions with which he was surrounded, evidently intended to prolong his life as far as possible. Here we rediscover the contradiction with which we began: suicide is seductive because it co-opts the Other's condemnation and affirms by destroying; but it is also disobedience, and Gustave, the passive victim of an abusive father, was put together in such a way that he *could not disobey*. He dreamed of *realizing* the autonomy of his spontaneity through a sovereign act. But the possibility of acting is refused him if he does not act *as other*. Besides, precisely because it would be revolt and disobedience, Gustave's suicide would inflict on his master only an exclusively external punishment. Scandal, yes. But remorse? In affirming himself through his voluntary destruction, Gustave would relieve his father of all responsibility—he would become himself by committing against his lord the act that was sovereignly forbidden. The punishment of the revered father would be terrible if, on the other hand, Gustave should die too soon and miserably, out of submission; the contradictions and absurd cruelty of the paternal will would be suddenly unmasked.

This would be *death by thought*. In other words, obedience pushed to a demand for rule—the behavior of resentment. A system of vampire-imperatives, nourished by his subjective life, bind him to the praxis of another, who condemns him and claims to endow him with relative-being; the single result is the ipseity's vampirization of its own occupant. It is fitting to dwell a while on this parasitic form of praxis because it defines Flaubert's essential attitude, one which he must have adopted after the Fall and would preserve until the end of his life.

Beginning with his infancy, Gustave has been constituted as a flow of passive syntheses. Still, he must *exist* for them, meaning that he sustains them by surpassing them in the direction of the self. But the self remains formal because, for lack of a primary affirmation, his constitution relieves him of the practical possibilities of undertaking and leading with any success. Onto this internalized inertia an alien will is grafted, around his seventh year, which compels him to engage in acts he accomplishes uneasily, not recognizing them as his own. He must learn to read, write, and reason; at a more profound level his life must coincide with the intolerable destiny that has been prearranged. It is not enough *to be the younger son*; this relative-being must be made the object of his permanent enterprise, he must make himself what he is—constitute himself—as others made him, assume his incapacities as a backward child through guilt and submission. Actually, submission breaks him, emphasizing his disgrace by proclaiming that he accepts it while he *feels* that it is unacceptable. Here he is provided with an alter ego, since activity, for him, comes from the Other. The ego, by contrast, is refused him; it could be born only through revolt, which he finds impossible. But why couldn't the ipseity secretly lodge itself, like a gnawing worm, in the alter ego that masters it? The acceptance of alienation through perfect, insincere submission is sufficient to allow the enterprise of the Other to develop toward the objectives it has prescribed for itself even as it quietly falsifies their meaning. This is the tactic of gliding: you let yourself be carried by currents that lead to where you thought to go, provided you know how to slip at times from one to the other; in the end you have done nothing and everything is accomplished. The true Gustave, the child without a self, is secretly himself only through the adulteration of the ends imposed on him. His particularization is thus in essence *secondary*. For Gustave there is no real and primary project outside the familial project from which he is alienated; everything that will be specific to him (including his writing, which will absorb him entirely, and the process of *unrealization*, of which we shall soon speak) is posterior to the Flaubert *intent* (accumulation, ascendance), which is the socialization of paternal intent, and to the *alien-activity* which this primitive intent forces on him, with the familiar disastrous results. Through submission the young boy claims to recognize himself in this intent and to specify himself through its results; in fact he only objectifies and recognizes himself here to the extent that the family and the paterfamilias are forced to assume the consequences as the pure and precise expression of their sovereign will (which relieves the child of any responsibility), yet are incapable of recovering the original sense of their enterprise or its intended objectives—in sum to the extent that the Flaubert collectivity sees its image in this docile mirror, is forced to assume it, and *does not recognize itself*. It is obvious

that the falsification of ends as a secondary reaction is not arbitrary—
quite the contrary, it is narrowly conditioned by the primary ends,
or rather because the little boy imagines it is. The father's curse, he
believes, condemns him to death but at the same time he is forbidden
to commit suicide, overprotection consigns him to longevity because
the family is determined to perpetuate itself. Very well, he will docilely
make himself into the younger son, he will destroy himself in the
process, carry submission to an extreme, and so realize the contradiction of the paternal intent by prematurely dying of sorrow. The
father in Gustave courts disaster and will disqualify himself through
the systematic realization of his projects by revealing their absurdity:
he is indeed a fool who refuses his son life while imposing longevity
on him. By taking him literally, Gustave will show him his blunder
and that the duration of an existence is inversely proportional to the
intensity of experienced sufferings: if you wanted me to live a long
time, you should not have made me a younger son. The purpose of
passive activity—and hence of his particularity—is only to demonstrate, through unchallengeable consequences, the injustice of the
destiny imposed on him. Why do anything *unless it brings his* father
grief? This will be the punishment.

Still, it must be understood that a rebel would find other means,
would burn down the house, kill the elder son. But that would be
taking revenge, which is doubly impossible: such misfortunes have no
strict relation to the younger son's unhappiness, and they presuppose
a scale, an external system of equivalences—an eye for an eye, a tooth
for a tooth, etc. Moreover, just to dream of inflicting such pains on
the father would require an open hatred, a real plan of vendetta. But
the child does not hate his executioner; on the contrary, his resentment
is an effort of love. What he passionately desires is that the father
should be punished by the results of his enterprise and by these
alone, as if his orders inflexibly executed had promptly led to Gustave's death. But what about that? someone will ask. Immediate or
deferred, wasn't his death predetermined? Hadn't Achille-Cléophas
sentenced him? And under these conditions, can he be greatly moved
by, or even regret, a premature demise? The judges have decided to
send a guilty man to the guillotine; he is filled with terror, dies of
fear—his heart gives out before the execution. Are they going to turn
this into a permanent malady? Yes, precisely, this is the secret of
resentment conceived as passive activity, a secret hope behind despair. Gustave still hopes that his immediate death will serve to open
the physician-philosopher's eyes. Seeing the boy's demise as the strict

result of his will, wouldn't he suddenly perceive that he loved his younger son? The punishment of the paterfamilias in effect presupposes a reawakened love. What is there for Gustave to do, then, while he is being manipulated? Nothing. Almost nothing; he will suffer by improving upon his pains, by suffering *excessively* and allowing himself to be worn down by the condition of younger son experienced "to the bitter end." Above all there will be no rancor, neither visible nor articulated; an exquisite sensibility exhausts itself doing what it was ordered to do and dies of the effort. In this kind of resentment, passivity and irresponsibility mask a radical accusation, which doesn't present itself as an *act* of accusation but as an incriminating object: Flaubert's corpse killed by his father with no intermediary will accuse him the way the ruins of an incinerated village accuse the regiment that destroyed it. At the same time, death will make him *other* in the eyes of Achille-Cléophas; it will valorize him by revealing the infinite power of his passions and will at once reawaken love, or awaken it, by revealing that this son was the one who deserved it most. "I am dying by thought, I am dead, the impossibility of living, as I experienced it, destroyed my life sooner than you had decreed for the single reason you had not foreseen: the exquisite richness of my sensibility, that is, a power of suffering increased by the passivity with which you endowed me." Passive activity, from the beginning, is a solitary exaggeration of the expression of suffering—a hundred times the original fall, throwing oneself on the ground, gasping, wanting to die; it is a recourse to stupors intentionally conceived as false deaths or as general rehearsals for an imminent death; and growing old, that polyvalent theme whose meaning is this: "I am forever growing old, dying each day; each of these anticipated deaths—which you impose on me—has the dual result of undermining my health and diminishing itself as it squanders my power to feel. You wanted me not to live and, at the same time—in order to affirm the strength of your sperm before the world—to die an octogenarian. You see, I am obedient; I am wearing myself out faster than you could foresee, but this exhaustion is a proper senescence. I shall die an octogenarian of twenty."

Resentment as a passive activity, as the unity of a comprehensive whole, can synthetically reunite aging and death, experience and destiny; nothing is visible except the sufferings of a real love that will perhaps make actual a virtual love—love on all sides. But in reality the child attempts to overlook the fact that paternal love is no longer desired for itself—it must be a dead child's revenge and a father's punishment. The positive element redeems this secret negative or, better, prevents it from forming, from being posed for itself. A child loves, suffers from not being loved, docilely conforms to the familial prescriptions; Gustave sees only this, he *must* pay attention only to this captive praxis and reflexively, for the sake of the alter ego, to the transcendent unity of all his acts of submission. Only on this condition can a clandestine ego, unseen, unapprehended, uncomprehended, be composed as a defect of the Other, as the unity of the workings of resentment which are *passed over in silence*; it is constituted under the self-reflexive eye *so as not to be noticed*, it is at the outer edge of that consuming negativity which, without ever openly presenting itself, vampirizes the alter ego, borrowing its practical efficacy the better to subvert its ends. Everything is perfectly clear: sworn to passivity, bound to pride, Flaubert ambition condemns his inadequacies, and spontaneously experienced subjectivity refuses the *relative-being* imposed on it by others; submission is a sham because it is impossible, but acquired inertia forbids revolt—he hasn't the means to *oppose himself*, to challenge, to display the negative. In this sense his refusal is not flaunted, negativity is never an open break or a visible overcoming. It is hidden and works from below. As a person, Gustave can naturally be just the negation of his received being, but this negation—denied inferiority, denied vassalage, denied relativity—is merely what secretly governs his passivity. I would willingly call his ego the blind spot in his reflexive vision.

These remarks shed a new light on Gustave's precocious fatalism. It is belief that underlies the ideology of resentment; this means that all particular thoughts will take shape by spontaneously surpassing certain schemes—contained and maintained in the act of surpassing which particularizes them—each of which ("the worst is always certain," "the world is hell," "*anangkē* [necessity], that dark and mysterious divinity . . . laughs ferociously when it sees philosophy, and men writhe in their sophisms to deny its existence while it grinds them under its iron heel"[45]) is itself only the expression of this fundamental fatalism. That we know already. But we have taken for granted until now that Gustave, as he repeated it, was *affected* (or infected, if you like) by the primary belief that this was an induced vision of the world imposed by his own experience, a reading—singular, certainly, but adequate—of an almost unbearable life. At the

45. The first formulation is found in a letter to Ernest; the second in *Le Voyage en enfer*, the third in *Un Parfum à sentir*.

very most we imagined that a teleological intention would structure this faith on the level of extrapolation (the child/martyr needing to lessen his shame by thinking: "I am not made to live, but everyone is like this"). But in reexamining the original givens, namely the structures of the Flaubert family, we are forced to conclude that Gustave's fatalism cannot be their mechanical result. The fall from favor around the age of seven was undoubtedly a genuine trauma; that was when the "split"[46] was formed in him which destined him to exile, to "melancholy torpors." But painful as it may have been, this situation could not in itself have determined the possibility or impossibility of being lived. When a bewildered Gustave at the moment of the Fall discovers "a complete presentiment of life," that is, when he makes his first prophecy, it is inconceivable that he should thus hypothesize his life to the very end, unless his conviction is a parti pris, that is, unless it conceals an oath. The child commits himself, like a lover who says, "I will always love you," replacing an impossible certainty with a futile effort in order to fix the future. Gustave swears that the worst will always be certain, which implies a constant acceleration of his life (or early senescence) linked to the constant increase of his sufferings (if the worst must always be certain, what I live through tomorrow will be more unbearable than what I am living through today). Yet the oath cannot be explicit and "brought out," like the kind we swear on the Bible, for this would be rebellion and the beginning of praxis. Besides, what commits the lover is itself highly ambiguous, at once an act mysteriously influencing the future, initiating a cycle (from this point of view it is posed for itself—"Swear to me that you love me, that you will always love me") and the simple statement of something irreversible, an endured institutionalization of temporality. I have spoken of this as well, ranking those objects of pledged reflection on the level of the *probable*. For Gustave the oath is still less visible because it cannot be displayed without being destroyed. The vexed, unhappy boy apparently cannot *say to himself*: "Since my father has rejected me, I intend to *live out the worst*, to push my suffering in every particular instance to an extreme, and to use my past to make my present still more intolerable so that my nerves, frayed by old sorrows, will not be able to bear new ones, and even worse, will be worn out, old, and no longer responsive." To say, this will happen through my constant application, is to admit that without

---

46. In fact the word is Baudelaire's applied to his own malady, quite different from Gustave's; but taken in its general meaning it can serve here.

such application it would not happen. As chance would have it, the child's situation—as he represents it to himself—is difficult and undeniably unpleasant; the fall has traumatized him and it is certainly the Other who provoked it. The first mortgage on the future issues from a father's irritated impatience ("You will never do anything" and other classic stupidities—Achille-Cléophas's fits of rage were famous, and all his students suffered because of them) or from his too obvious concern. Against these the child feels he can do nothing; his passivity forbids him any opposition. What remains, therefore, through submission is that belief which everything evokes and with which he is infused by an invisible parti pris: I shall be the idiot you want me to be, I shall manage always to push failure to an extreme and to suffer from it more than anyone else would do in my place. He is Adam taking his curse upon himself: Adam quietly curses himself and destines himself to misery in order to transform the blame of the Almighty into an inexorable and fatal sentence. Humiliated, deeply wounded by his fall from favor, cursing himself in the name of Achille-Cléophas, Gustave prefers to live out this sentence as a paternal curse, fobbing off the original guilt on his maker. This is all the easier as certainties are forbidden to him—all he has to do is believe; yet all belief implies a teleological intent. Evoked, never imposed, every belief is the result of autosuggestion, a matter we shall describe a little later. Thus Gustave's pessimism is an option of his passive activity; since he lives in a state of malaise and cannot get out of it, he tacitly commits himself to choosing the politics of despair in order to make his progenitor ever more guilty, to make *himself* ever the more innocent victim. The world belongs to Satan, that's how it is, but Satan is himself, he is this frenzied vow of pride and resentment to make himself last in everything since he cannot be first, to let himself sink into the depths under the pretext of submitting to an evil lord who doesn't exist.

In order to understand better the course of such "resentful thinking," let us see how Gustave proceeds when he writes *Un Parfum à sentir*, his first lyric tale; let us look for the narrator's avowed intentions, and between the lines for those he passes over in silence but which are necessarily implicit in the narrative. The young author begins by delineating his plan: *Un Parfum* is expressly directed against "philanthropists," by which we understand him to mean people of property, optimists who still believe that the fate of mankind can be ameliorated. The *reformists*, in sum, partisans of a prudent *evolution*. All right then, the author is going to tell a story that will prove the vanity of their hopes. Man will not be saved, even temporarily, by adjustments; it would take an impossible *revolution* to snatch him once and for all from the clutches of the Devil. He has in mind, he tells us, to bring together the ugly, scorned, toothless [Marguerite] who is beaten by her husband, and the pretty [Isabellada] crowned with flowers, perfumes, and love, and to tear them apart by jealousy to the bizarre and bitter end." Here we have the right-thinking people confronted with the truth they would hide from themselves: that man is unhappy and wicked, that he will not be changed. "What remedies could they bring to the evils I have shown them? Nothing, right? And if they could find the word for this, they would call it *anangkē*."

The theme is clear: against those optimists who are also thought of as "wise men," the option of resentment is that *everything is irreparable*. But as soon as Gustave reports in this inexact way the subject he wants to treat, we are prompted to remark: two rivals? both torn apart by jealousy—in a sense, equals united by an antagonistic reciprocity, by the harm each one does to the other? This is not how it is in the body of the narrative; two women, yes—rivals, no. Marguerite alone is torn apart—her husband is stolen from her under her very eyes. But Isabellada, an invulnerable plenitude, the incarnation of beauty, how could she suffer? Pedrillo is at her feet and she didn't have to lift a finger; besides, she is too ambitious to love this acrobat, and we know that she will drop him in order to sell herself to a great lord. Was the adolescent mistaken about the meaning of his fable or did he change his mind in midstream? Both conjectures are untenable, for in the same sentence Gustave makes the women rivals and lets us see that the pretty acrobat "crowned with love" is nothing but a splendid, glacial instrument of torture for the other, homely woman who is "scorned and beaten"; in short, when he claims to afflict them with the same suffering, he has already conceived the two creatures and the singular bond that unites them. We have here an excellent example of the insincerity that characterizes resentful thinking. If human unhappiness is the object of rigorous planning, then everyone must suffer, Isabellada as much as Marguerite. This is why, being better informed, he will soon choose that executioner and elite victim Mazza, whose superb body will be the direct cause of her misfortunes. In hell, beauty cannot save anyone. But at the time he was writing his first stories, Gustave lacked the means to rationalize his pessimism; universalization was still just a facade, and the true meaning of the story is poorly concealed. By creating Marguerite, Gustave embodies the "unspeakable" decree: hell is for myself alone. Unspeakable, unthinkable, the option can only be parasitic, which im plies that Gustave adjusts and falsifies his discourse *so that* it can be vampirized by this option. He can give the work its true meaning only by *saying something else.*

This is something we shall perceive more clearly still by examining the rest of the narrative. Indeed, the principal theme was first presented to us in its *black* form: humanity since the Fall is hopelessly lost. But here, suddenly, the author is talking about something else, or, rather, he tells us his intention to derive a positive, or "white," consequence from the same theme: he is going to make all the characters innocent. This involves "asking the reader: who is at fault?" He hastens to give us the answer:

> It is certainly not the fault of any of the characters in the drama.
> It is the fault of circumstance, of prejudice, of society, of nature who was a bad mother. . . .
> It is the fault of *anangkē.*

Two conflicting explanations are proposed here. The first, I have already remarked, might be Dr. Flaubert's, and certainly it advanced the view of mechanistic determinism: circumstance prejudice, society, nature—explanation by externals. Is this valid for Gustave? Surely not; prejudice has nothing to do with it. Society can be made responsible for the misery of the acrobats, but while this misery is present on every page, neither this nor even the contempt in which they are held is the source of the drama, which issues from Marguerite's ugliness. And as for the sexual disgust the poor woman provokes in her husband, Gustave is convinced that this is not a matter of prejudice—proof being the horror that ugliness inspired in him. Nature remains. But which one? The nature of Dr. Flaubert? In this case Marguerite's looks are *fortuitous.* Therefore we must not search for a guilty party but declare that the very idea of guilt is a trap. But this would not be Flaubert's position, for he *incriminates* the collection of atoms that is mechanistic society, and personalizes nature in order to reproach it for "being a bad mother" by creating Marguerite. We see how he negotiates his passage from the second paragraph—whose meaning must be that the Christian notion of guilt is a mystification—to the third, which pretends to be only the development of what goes before while openly contradicting it; in this view the inhuman world of mechanism becomes a cosmos ruled internally by an *anthropomorphic culprit,* a dark and mysterious divinity who quite expressly wills evil and suffering on mankind. It is as though he were writing with the same pen, "Men produce their unhappiness by chance encounters, their characters, their passions, their interests conflict by accident and evil is a constant, unpremeditated disorder," and "evil results from a plan stretched over millions of years, a dark and mysterious will has arranged everything so that everyone should be his own and the other's most exquisite executioner." Which again, to my mind, is the mark of resentful thinking; *first* he voices the rationalist thesis in order to assimilate it secretly to his bitter fantasy, and then he quietly transforms it into chance as *fatum*. It will be noted that this does not so much involve making the protagonists innocent as finding a responsible party at the top of the hierarchy, someone who might have committed the crime that is the world. But if this dark divinity is all-powerful, if he is the one who imposes his law, how could he be considered guilty? In the name of what good can men, the docile slaves of his sovereign will, condemn him as *ill*-will? Because he desires their suffering? But if it is the law, they can only worship it. Everything is reversed: evil is the substance, good is only a parasitic accident which is defined by the consciousness of its perfect futility.

Here we have the supreme culprit, fatality—or mechanistic chance—transformed by resentment into a will to the worst. Are the characters in the story acquitted, then? So the young author proclaims. But let us take a closer look. Isambert, we know, is a sadist. He "warmly" depicts for poor Marguerite Pedrillo's love for Isabellada, "their bodies entwined on the marriage bed." He adds: "I know very well you have never done anything to me, perhaps you are better than others, but you displease me, that's all, I wish you ill, it's my whim!" Upon which he departs "with bursts of laughter," satisfied to have hurt her. At this particular moment let us note the line: "For two years . . . everyone lived happily, calmly, without cares, eating in the evening what they had eaten during the day, *Marguerite alone was unhappy*."[47] In short, Isambert is malicious without the excuse of misery. And his malice gives him pleasure—truly the opposite of a damned soul; there are the damned in hell, but there are also tormenting demons. If the world is the realm of Satan, he has men in hand and executioners are never victims. Isambert is one of these. Isabellada, conscious of her beauty, creates Marguerite's unhappiness and later Pedrillo's without ever suffering herself; she will have her recompense—the beautiful demon will become a grande dame. These two belong to the Devil, let us have no doubt about that. On the other side are human beings,

47. My italics.

a pair of the damned. The woman is ugly, but the husband—the incarnation of Achille-Cléophas—is no good. Let us listen to his children:

> "He is always like that . . . opening his mouth only to say things that fester in the soul. Oh! he is really malicious! Our poor mother, at least she loved us. . . . How he beat her," said Auguste, "because he said she was ugly. Poor woman!"

Here we have a truly malicious man: he beats his children, finds words to "fester in their souls"; he beats his wife and insults her. He will do worse, he will take a mistress, force Marguerite to live with them in the same tent, and when she cannot stand it he will throw her into the lion's cage. When Gustave pulls her out, she is still alive, but the beasts have already partly devoured her. Nevertheless, the acrobat is a handsome man, he is strong, he believes himself loved. What is the source of his malice? We are told it is suffering. One winter's night, when everyone's teeth are chattering, the man

> gives his son a shove, and the poor child goes off to bed crying. Pedrillo was suffering as much as he, and convulsive movements made his teeth chatter:
> "How harshly you treated him," said Marguerite.
> "That's true."
> He remained plunged in a deep revery and as though he were asleep in his searing thoughts.

What does he dream about? The unhappiness of man, who is both victim and executioner? Possibly. And Gustave pretends to excuse him. But it will be noted that at this very moment Marguerite is suffering more than he from cold and pain. She has just left the hospital and her wounds are not even healed; more than that, she has endured the most cruel humiliation, and the consciousness of her ugliness never leaves her; yet she worries about her children and cannot bear it when their father brutalizes them. Thus there is a certain disproportion between Pedrillo's troubles and the brutal violence of his reactions; neither the too frequently mentioned treachery of Dupuytren nor constant worries and overwork completely justify Achille-Cléophas's mad rages or his diabolical way of finding words to "wound the soul" of his younger son. Glorious, sovereign, loved, the chief surgeon is partially responsible for his nervousness, for his exasperation, for his harsh words; his malice is not excusable to the extent that it is not purely the product of his destiny. *Fatum* takes the blame, as we see; in the chief surgeon there is a certain autonomy of ill-will.

Thus, when Gustave claims to acquit all the characters, he is actually prepared to condemn them. All except one. Marguerite is not bad from birth: "She had asked heaven only for a life of love, for a husband who loved her, who understood all her tender feelings, and who sensed all the poetry in her acrobat's heart" Unlike the others, she did not make evil her original choice. Gustave will repeat all his life: "I was born so gentle and men have made me malicious." She will undoubtedly grow bitter, but who would reproach her for it? *Fatum* has chosen her to be the *absolute victim*. Precisely because she is good. Or, if you will, it *made her good* according to a plan for making her suffer in the extreme, and for showing virtue punished in this Justine, just as we see vice rewarded in Isabellada, or Juliette. Good, someone will say, but ugly—it is the simultaneous presence of these two characteristics in a single person that drives her to despair. In Sade, on the contrary, Justine is beautiful, or at least desirable; moreover it is a virtuous act that directly and without any mediation provokes her punishment. But can we be certain that the mediation of ugliness does not serve to hide the resentful thinking that Gustave cannot express? Of course, every time the young author speaks in his own name he presents us with Marguerite's physical gracelessness as though it were an inert determination that stepmother nature or *fatum* inflicted upon her a priori and which she must internalize and assume in the course of her calamitous existence. But when he speaks in the name of his character? Don't Marguerite's thoughts about her own ugliness *also* represent Gustave's feeling on the subject? A feeling all the more clearly expressed since the author, declining all responsibility, presents it as his creature's subjective response? What does Marguerite say when she sees "a graceful woman with a sweet smile, tender and languorous eyes, jet black hair?" She envies and hates her and finally cries out: "What would have to be different for her to be like me? Hair of another color, smaller eyes, a less shapely figure and she would be Marguerite! If her husband had not loved her at all, if he had scorned her, beaten her, she would be ugly, scorned like Marguerite." We have read correctly: if her husband had not loved her at all, she would be ugly. Of course Flaubert's thinking is more complex; Marguerite recognizes objectively that the young lady has large eyes, a more shapely figure, beautiful hair; such physical characteristics cannot be changed, and heavy calves, a thick waist, red hair will always be the lot of the poor acrobat. But what about the other woman? It is notable that Gustave scarcely dwells on her charms. Jet black hair, all right. But what Marguerite envies is her grace, the sweetness of her smile, the soft languor of her eyes—in short, gestures, bearing, an attitude, expressions that represent the calm confidence of the loved woman and sometimes substitute for beauty. Marguerite is clumsy, awkward; her face expresses fear, self-loathing; her eyes are red and swollen with tears only because she is not loved. Could she be? Yes; this is what resentment insinuates (without of course departing from the negative mode). She had serious physical defects, to be sure. But Pedrillo could and should have overlooked those details; he ought to have loved her for "the poetry of her acrobat's heart"; it was up to him to give her grace and charm, she would have absorbed his love and shared it with everyone, with Pedrillo himself, through the sweetness of her smile, through the languor of her looks. Here we are close to Sade: Pedrillo gives his wife ugliness in order to punish her for having a soul, for being a "palpable fragrance" rather than a beautiful, visible flower; if he refuses her grace it is because she deserves to have it, if he scorns and beats her it is because she loves him. And her soul, her infinite power of suffering, is also what Isambert hates. This can be readily translated poor Gustave is given as an example a young and brilliant student who carries off all the prizes; he answers: "If his father hadn't loved him at all, if he had continually humiliated him, he would be stupid and scorned like Gustave." To be sure, he recognizes his inadequacies, his giddiness, his torpors, a certain inertia; but what he had in him that was worthy of love, that poetic power which from early childhood ravished him in indescribable ecstasies, was precisely what irritated Achille-Cléophas's surgical precision. The physician loved the beautiful machines that are scientific minds, the way Pedrillo loves beautiful, soulless bodies. "My father hated me from the time he perceived I had a soul; had he loved me, I would have taken the top prize."

This is resentment—shifty, ungraspable, omnipresent. Gustave began with a general pardon, but no sooner has he declared that no one is at fault than he begins a police inquiry into the Flaubert family, at the conclusion of which everyone is guilty except the younger son. The progenitor is guilty three times over in this story: first, in the sovereign form of *fatum*, he produced Gustave as a relative-being, to the child's supreme unhappiness; second, embodied by Pedrillo and reduced to human dimensions, he becomes the accomplice of the supernatural Father, finishing the "job" on Gustave with a clever twist. Indeed, the Creator's work was rather coarse, and the family's

second son—not much gifted for the exact sciences, but a poet—
would have had a chance to pull himself out of the situation if he
had been loved. Achille-Cléophas, an empirical father, transformed
himself into a poor, unhappy, and malicious man in order to hate
close up, moment by moment, his absolute victim and to strip him
of what little means the Demiurge had left him. Third, but episodi-
cally, the dry, brutal father shows himself to be a criminal, no longer
toward Gustave/Marguerite but toward the same Gustave embodied
by the acrobat's "sons"; on this occasion it is the *educator* in him who
is guilty—either he wounds his children to the soul by his corrosive
words or he turns himself into their instructor/executioner. Here is
the "true" subject of this story—a settling of accounts; the younger
son puts his father on trial for having made him badly, loved him
badly, taught him badly. He punishes him, moreover, *without telling
him how he has sinned*; his fault lay in preferring his eldest son and,
by constant "comparison," afflicting his youngest with *relative-being*,
in other words with a fundamental *inferiority*. His punishment will
come from the same preference: he will kill Gustave, certainly, but
Achille will betray him. Thus *fatum* exists in the first place for only
one creature; Achille-Cléophas transforms life into destiny for Gustave alone; but through this inequity the father becomes his own
fatum—in loving Isabellada, Pedrillo has passed judgment on himself
and will suffer like a dog. And quite soon Cosme will do the same.
This Medicis has become destiny for his two sons, as we see by the
double prophecy of the fortune teller. But suddenly, through this Cain
and Abel, he becomes the destiny of his House, that is, his own
destiny. Un Parfum à sentir and *La Peste à Florence* predict the "Fall of
the House of Flaubert"; it will take place through the fault of the
younger son who, tormented by Papa-Fate, will avenge himself by
becoming through his death the *fatum* of his own father: the Flauberts
will die out and paternal ambition will be mocked. This family is a
"feedback" machine. We see that the resentful man aspires to take
revenge on the Other through the very evil that the Other has done
to him. Yet his aspiration must be concealed; if it were openly proclaimed, it would be revolt, that is, *opposition*; there is *nothing to oppose*
to a paternal, sovereign will which is accomplished and by this very
fact reveals its *truth*, which was to run its course by being accomplished. Resentment aspires to be passive—it cultivates docility, absence; Gustave is not, is only, the inert intermediary between the
father and himself. Achille-Cléophas will be more rigorously punished if his unhappiness is not the result of an unforeseen resistance

but comes, on the contrary, from the docility, the flexibility of the world and consequently from the simple realization of his will; thus *fatum* will be interior to this will itself. But such vengeance can be accomplished only if Gustave, without being in on the secret of his own actions, carries everything implacably to its worst conclusion. To hammer away at Marguerite is to torment Pedrillo, or to prepare his torments from a distance. Passive vengeance, passed over in silence; the bitter determination to push to its worst conclusion what was done to him without the least concession; destiny invented by ill-will and the permanent refusal to be consoled—this is resentment, the treacherous, destructive submission of the son to the father in which the son knows yet doesn't want to know that his father doesn't ask so much of him.

If this is the basic intention of the newly discovered, quasi-dream-like realization of a father's punishment through the systematic destruction of a son, what can we preserve from our regressive analysis? Is it still true that Marguerite represents Gustave's hatred of himself? That he made her hideous because ugliness represented what he most despised? Can it still be claimed that he delights in Isambert's sadism and torments Marguerite for pleasure, forgetting that he put all of himself into her? And do those passages in which the author represents her as responsible for her ugliness preserve their meaning when elsewhere it is Pedrillo who is responsible? I answer without hesitation that *everything* must be kept. First of all because Flaubert's thought is complex; it is true that he didn't love himself, that he lived as though he were irrelevant, in a state of malaise; it is true that in many bewildering circumstances he had the ambiguous feeling that he was the innocent victim of inadequacies which had been inflicted upon him, yet that he bore the entire responsibility for them. For this reason he invented the character of Marguerite, a homely creature who must internalize her given ugliness; this is what permitted him at once to see her through the eyes of others, to share their sadism,[48] and to see her through his own eyes as he saw himself. The resentment only appears in the systematic exploitation of her miseries, in the mad enterprise of carrying them to an extreme in order to take revenge on his father by realizing the curse of Adam; and all the while he saved himself from that disaster through the depth of his sufferings, the

48. When Isambert tells the unhappy woman that he wanted to throw mud on her dress, pull her hair, crush her breasts, we can be sure that the reference is to *sexual* desires which certain *excessively* ugly women aroused in Gustave.

negative sign of his magnanimity. This gives us a second reason for preserving all the aspects of this crude yet profound tale, even when they contradict each other. The malaise, the ambiguity of feelings, the shame, the rage, the flight into torpor, Gustave's constant assumption of guilt—this is pathos, a way of suffering the situation, of living experience which is intentional, certainly, but without a definite objective. Resentment is a *passive activity*: intention, means, end, everything is there but everything is hidden, *secondary*; it is a *manipulation of pathos*, a hyperbolic secret which gives meaning and direction by the very exaggeration of a way of life and which temporalizes experience by surpassing it in the direction of the worst, not of course willfully but out of belief and anguish. Thus passive activity needs pathos—or the suffered situation—in order, vampirelike, to sustain itself. I have lingered over this polyvalent tale of which resentment is only one meaning (the most hidden, the only one that is tacitly defined as a project) because it displays the qualities of Gustave's subsequent thought—except when he bursts into empty verbal violence—which can be described as insincere, evasive, and always double-edged. We shall soon see another example of it when we reread in *Madame Bovary* the portrait of Dr. Larivière.

G. The World of Envy

As we have seen, in order to desire one has to have been desired; because he had not internalized—as a primary and subjective affirmation of the self—this original affirmation of objective, maternal love, Gustave never affirmed his desires or imagined they might be satisfied. Having never been valorized, he did not recognize their value. As a creature of chance, he has no right to live, and consequently his desires have no right to be gratified; they burn themselves out, vague transient fancies that haunt his passivity and disappear, usually before he even thinks to satisfy them. You might say that such an austere soul does not covet anything spontaneously. However, he is consumed by the negative of desire, by envy; when he can have them, the things of this world scarcely tempt him—he craves something only if it belongs to someone else. He knows that it's a losing game; what others have, he will never have, and when he is given the equivalent of their possessions, his jealous fury is in no way assuaged. Basically what he demands is not an object but the right to ownership, the *value* that is affirmed through appropriation and possession, in short an *instituted* being-in-the-world of which he feels

congenitally deprived. Whatever belongs to others has a doleful fas
cination for him; whatever belongs to him turns to ashes in his hands
because he never feels *in possession.*

As an adult, Flaubert declared many times in his correspondence
that he detested envious people. But we are getting to know him; it
is in fact envy he detests, because it is devouring him and ruining his
life. Perhaps, too, he feels debased by jealousy and projects onto
others his constantly rejected and endured debasement. Yet between
his fourteenth and his twentieth year, more lucid or more sincere, he
gave this trait to all his fictional incarnations.[49] When, in *Un Parfum
à sentir*, Marguerite "sees a virtuous woman in a hat go by . . . her
heart is seized with envy." She says to herself: "Why am I not like
her?" And if Garcia suffers so much it is because he is tormented by
"a dark and ambitious jealousy." He goes so far as to say: "I envy the
man, I hate him, I am jealous of him." And Djalioh?

> When he thought of himself, poor and despairing, of empty
> arms and the earth and its flowers, and those women, Adèle and
> her naked breasts and her shoulder and her white hand, when
> he thought of all this, savage laughter burst in his mouth and
> rattled his teeth, like a tiger hungry and dying; in his mind he
> saw Monsieur Paul's smile, his wife's kisses, he saw the two of
> them stretched out on a silken bed, their arms entwined, with
> the sighs and cries of lust . . . and when he transferred [these
> images] to his own life . . . he trembled; and he understood the
> gulf that lay between. . . .

Mazza goes "from disgust to bitterness and envy":

> In the public gardens, when she saw mothers playing with their
> children and smiling at their caresses, and saw women with their
> husbands, lovers with their mistresses, and saw that all these
> people were smiling, were happy, and loved life, *she both envied
> and cursed them.*

In each of these narratives, one finds the same crude but penetrating
description of envy *as process*; indeed, for Gustave, envy is not an
inert defect of the soul but a movement that goes from the particular
to the general, passing through three distinct stages. According to
him, this is how an envious person is made. Born of some frustration,
the feeling is first addressed only to the person felt to have usurped

---

49. Envy is one of the rare feelings he describes in the autobiographical works with
as much "openness" as in his first stories.

one's right. With time the feeling is universalized—the unloved person envies everyone and feels frustrated by the happiness of others. In the end, if the unhappiness persists, the envious person becomes a malicious person. At first Marguerite suffers only because of Isabellada, who had stolen her husband; she is jealous of her rival's beauty: "It was the memory of Isabellada's dance that hurt her, all that applause for someone else, all that disdain for her." But by dint of suffering she comes, "when she sees a graceful woman, to mock the crowd that admires her": "she might have been like me!" All she can do is "wish the greatest disasters on the rich," "laugh at the prayers of the poor," and "spit on the doorstep of churches." With Mazza the progression is the same. Of course the usurper is missing— Ernest does not prefer someone else, but he frustrates her because he doesn't reach the same amorous heights. What is more striking is the similarity of reactions. The first stage is skipped over, and we pass immediately to the second—Mazza is unhappy and envies the happiness she scorns: "She both envied and cursed them; she would have liked to be able to crush them all underfoot." Yet this includes— among others—women who play with their children, while Mazza can only dream of the best way to get rid of her own, who prevent her from rejoining Ernest. "She hated women, especially young and beautiful women." But she *is* just that, young and beautiful. What could this mean if not that she envies happiness *wherever* it is? She has known the sweetness of loving her children; and when she sees mothers, her jealousy takes the form of regret. But she would not want to turn back for anything in the world—*indeed, she regrets nothing*. As for those beautiful young women, what can she envy but the calm satisfaction that the consciousness of their beauty gives them, a tepid pleasure that long ago provoked her contempt? In short, she cannot bear the thought that some people are happy whoever they are, whatever they do, even if they find their happiness in the mediocrity of their demands. What exasperates her is their subjective relationship with the possessed object. Now she becomes malicious; like Marguerite, but some twenty months later, "she spits on the doorstep of churches as she goes by."

This progression is so strictly observed and found so often in the adolescent works that the passional movements must surely be attributed to the author himself. From one tale to the next, the deepening of this theme comes not from a lucid and coldly reflective inquiry but from incessant rumination. Between thirteen and seventeen the child made a proud confession: I envy and hate my brother

411

the usurper; my undeserved unhappiness has led me to envy all happiness, to develop an aversion to my species; I am malicious.

He was speaking the truth. He was made envious of one person, he became envious of everyone. Throughout his life the success of others would provoke cries of rage. When Musset presented his acceptance speech to the French Academy, Gustave was only a young man; he had neither the years nor the desire to be an Academician. But Louise—of whom he was hardly jealous—was dazzled and wrote him about it, perhaps to nettle him. That was enough; he grabbed his pen and wrote a twenty-page letter cutting Musset to pieces. Through the effusions of his mistress he had rediscovered the unfair paternal preference he had suffered as a child, the unfair distribution of prizes, in which his classmates had gone up to be rewarded without him.

At the time of writing, what was there to envy? Gustave never stopped repeating: it's a losing game. Much later, in the second *Education*, he wrote:

> Outside the doorkeeper's lodge, Frédéric [who has just failed his second exams] met Martinon, flushed and excited, with a smile in his eyes and a nimbus of triumph round his head. He had just passed his final examination without any trouble. The thesis was all that remained. Within fifteen days he would be a Bachelor of Law.
> His family knew a minister, "a fine career" lay before him. . . . *There is nothing more humiliating than seeing fools* succeed where one had failed oneself.[50] Frédéric [was] vexed.

An odd reflection, one that only an envious person could make. It is humiliating for everyone—to a greater or lesser degree, according to one's character—to fail in a chosen task. But to take things rationally—that is, by making the irrational rational: if the success of others is humiliating, it is because we find out about their superiority; they have capacities I don't have, it's a fact; it is all the more irritating that I underestimated my rivals. If, on the contrary, I recognized long ago the qualities of someone who has been elevated by an examination, by election, or by selection by some organization, if I judge him more able than I am for the office that was conferred upon him, then modesty or humility—reverse pride—spares me jealousy. And if I am convinced, on the other hand, that I have all the requisite abilities

50. My italics.

and he has none—in other words, if a group of friends, my family, or a certain social circle recognizes these abilities in me—I will feel that my interests have been wronged and will hate the intriguer who supplanted me and the examiners who let themselves be taken in, and I will regret—with more or less bad faith—this unsuitable choice for the sake of the enterprise or the country. It will be a virtuous rage, an indignation supported by my friends, a moral condemnation that I will assert with all my pride. *I will not envy* the stolen honor to the extent that I am convinced it is mine by rights.[51]

Besides, we seldom embrace any enterprise wholeheartedly—one would have to accept unreservedly the social order that makes it necessary. The student, for example, although he wants to pass his exams, or write a thesis, more or less resists the cultural context for these projects; he scorns or condemns certain of his professors and is not unaware that favoritism or bad luck can annul a year's efforts. If he fails, and if he really takes for fools those of his comrades who were simply luckier than he was, why should he be *more* humiliated by their success? Will he say, "If this fool has succeeded, it is because I am less than a fool?" No. On the contrary, "This is clear proof that the method of selection is absurd, that the exams as they have been conceived do not allow the candidates to be judged fairly." I have seen students who themselves have failed yet rejoice at the triumph of fools—they cite the name of this or that reputedly idiotic prize-winner in order to disqualify their judges even more effectively.

Either they really weren't envious or else they were concealing their envy beneath a superficial rationalization. For the genuinely envious person, the success of fools is unbearable under any circumstances. Far from challenging the social order, he begins by accepting it, whatever it is. He considers the distinctions denied him and conferred on others valid precisely because his rivals are judged worthy of them. Martinon is a fool, that is a fact. But if Frédéric had drawn the conclusion that therefore Martinon must have answered the examiners stupidly, the system would suddenly have been called into question. Yet the young failure doesn't think so, quite the contrary; he is convinced that his rival gave correct answers to the questions and thus deserved to pass. It is easy to see that Flaubert at the age of forty-five was still thinking about Ernest Chevalier's success. Back when they were both studying law, and Ernest, ahead from the start and in-

---

51. And if envy slips in—as is often the case—it is because no conviction is unqualified and because some uncertainty still remains: what if he merited his position?

creasing his lead every year, was briskly climbing the ladder, it mattered very little that Gustave felt "as vast as the world." The vastness is vacuity—what a paltry consolation in the face of that plenitude, examinations passed brilliantly, a "fine career"! From that moment the letters he wrote to the young deputy prosecutor—soon to be prosecutor—reeked of resentment; he spoke to him quite deliberately in the language of destruction, of anarchy, of the Garçon, in order to contest the value of a career that inspired him with disgust but that he could not help envying. The point is that in order to resent the triumph of a fool, you can't think of him as a complete fool. Better, you must have such respect for honors and distinctions that even someone's social success becomes proof of his intelligence. If Ernest acquired merit through his success, Gustave was also deeply affected by his own failure; he experienced it as a loss of substance. He maintained, however, that Ernest was a fool and spoke to him in a patronizing tone; he felt too embittered to bow before the verdict of the examiners, and his friend had to be a fool not in spite of their verdict but *because of it*. Furthermore, Gustave did not claim that Ernest had no brains; his stupidity lay in taking his position seriously, he believed in the importance of being Ernest. Gustave heaps abuse on this bureaucratic seriousness: "I would like . . . to crash into your office one fine morning and smash everything up, belch behind the door, overturn the inkwells, and shit in front of the bust of S.M.—in short, make an entrance like the Garçon." This passage—there are a hundred others—gives us a clear picture of the situation: Ernest's success cannot be denied, but he attains it in the suffocating world of *being*, of pure positivity; he has a right to it, but at the same time it diminishes him by determining him as a finite mode which is attached to his particularity; that is his stupidity. Flaubert surpasses his friend with all his despair, all his anxiety—in brief, with all the nonbeing that is in him. The envious man, recognizing his original nonvalorization, declares: "I have a right to these honors, these goods, this glory," and at the same time: "I have no right to them," or, more accurately: "I have a right to them *because* I have no right." Taking things to an extreme—and the envious man cannot help doing this—he would have to declare: "I have a right to everything because I have a right to nothing." Property or pleasure when they are manifest *in the other* remind the jealous man of his nonvalorization: others are made to possess, not me. But *precisely* this first movement of envy is followed by a second, which attempts to base a right on nonvalorization.

This teasing disposition is a good example of the attitude described by O. Mannoni in his article "Je sais bien . . . mais quand même" ["I know very well . . . but even so"].[52] Reality imposes a denial on a belief which is itself based on a desire. The subject *repudiates* experience and denies reality—Freud's *Verleugnung*. But the denied reality persists and remains ineffaceable; it is disqualified rather than eliminated, and the subject cannot preserve the original belief except at the price of a radical transformation: "The fetishist, for example, repudiates the experience that has proved to him that women don't have a penis, but he does not retain the belief that they do; he preserves a fetish *because* they don't." The envious man's experience is that society, through the family group, has refused him valorization and the judicial status that follows from it; he discovers his nonvalue as the truth of his being-for-others. It is this pure noninstituted factitiousness that he tries to repudiate in the name of his being-for-the-self. Repudiated, it nevertheless persists; therefore it must be disqualified: "I *know very well*," says Garcia, "that I was made a younger son and therefore ugly, malicious, stupid, and cowardly, *but even so*, I have the right to my father's love, to his goods and favors." Let us reread the curious insults he hurls at his brother when he is about to kill him: "You have had the advantage until now, society protected you, *this is as it should be*; you have tortured me all my life; now I am going to cut your throat. . . . You are a cardinal; I *insult your dignity as cardinal*. You are handsome, strong, and powerful; I *insult your strength, your beauty, your power*; I am holding you under me. . . . You did not know, *you with your vaunted wisdom*, how like a demon a man can be when injustice has turned him into a wild beast."[53]

Where is the injustice? Garcia does not contest the *dignity* of the cardinal's office—after all, he *insults* it. To insult is to recognize, it is pure positivity; by covering the office of cardinal with insults, Garcia does not affect it at all, any more than his spittle would affect the marble of a statue. It is himself he affects with absolute negativity; cursing his unshakable conqueror, *being*, he turns himself into a lacuna, a "double impotence," in order to create a realm of evil in which the insult might be the ineffectual negation of the good; this is a loss of oneself but an escape from being. From *the point of view of being*, in the realm of positive plenitude everything is as it should be. The honor of cardinal has been conferred on the one who deserves it.

52. Mannoni, *Communication à la Société Française de Psychanalyse*, November 1963.
53. My italics.

François is handsome, strong, powerful; he is the elder son. He is *wise* too: he knows how to read the text of the world and to manipulate it; *practically* his knowledge of men allows him to manage them, so he will always prefer negotiations, moderating actions, to violence. As long as he goes no further than this, the younger son is a loser every step of the way.

But the point is that he must go further; the positive creates the negative which is his absolute limit. François's "wisdom" is clairvoyance only when it deciphers mediocre souls who accept themselves; it cannot comprehend nonbeing—any more than the eye of God can decipher the shadows of our inadequacies and our finitude. Confronted with Garcia, who is frustrated from birth and has been transformed by an incomprehensible injustice into a demon—that is, into a madman of the negative—this wisdom is pure stupidity. How could François, who has all the opportunities and merits from birth, understand frustration? But if, against all likelihood, he were able to do so, there would certainly be an explosion, he would be convulsed by pessimism. Wisdom is justified in apprehending the cosmos as the harmonious product of goodwill; but if it could divine that this good, this pure positivity, engenders the infinity of evil and nothingness, it would be horrified and would hate being from the point of view of frustration, privation, rage, which are necessary for the harmony of the world—in short, from the point of view of nonbeing, which is the truth of being. The essence of Garcia, who was turned into a negating demon by respectable people, escapes François.

Injustice does and does not exist; the envious man does not claim any real and practical superiority over the more favored candidate, for he knows that in the society in which he lives and which he *accepts*, no one recognizes his superiority. Considering objectively the other's capabilities or his records of service, one must recognize that he was indeed suited to the position; when Gustave is irritated to learn that some fool has just come into an inheritance, he knows perfectly well that this man was the rightful heir from birth. The injustice is therefore in the fact that François has the merit necessary for obtaining certain distinctions. And, more profoundly, in the idea that only positivity is worthy. In short, the envious man must shift the ground of the argument in order to justify his feeling of being despoiled. The trap of *being* is that as long as we accept it, everything seems just. Crime, which is the rejection of being, at the same time exposes its fragility— the inner weakness of strength, power, and beauty. We find here, apropos a suicidal murder, the definition of suicide that will be given in *Saint Antoine*: the intentional annihilation of the creature, which is equivalent to creation. The text of *La Peste à Florence*—surely the bible of the envious—bases a black authority on the nothingness that engulfs or will engulf all that exists, on the permanent and objective challenge to the heirs by the very existence of the disinherited, an authority that gives the unworthy, the disenfranchised, invisible and nocturnal rights by affirming the supremacy of the negative. The operation is a radical one—and of course it is done in bad faith; Garcia is reproached for his lesser-being, so he radicalizes the sentence and passes himself off for *nonbeing* by taking the negation contained in the idea of inferiority to its conclusion. This is passive activity: his willing submission to the negative principle annuls (in Garcia through loss of consciousness, in François through assassination) the two terms of the comparison. The double elimination (Garcia kills to be killed) reestablishes justice; the second son is saying to his brother: "Everything is as it should be." But it is the justice of the Greek tragedies—the return to zero. Through his futile yet profound desire for universal destruction, the envious man recognizes that he will never obtain the objects of his frustration and that the only possible justice is the suppression of injustice through the elimination of the usurper and his victim.

But this is taking the response of envy to an extreme, to the point where it could conceivably be transformed into revolt, hatred, a real act. The distinctive feature of the envious man is that he bases his rights on nothingness but never goes as far as annihilation (of the self, of the rival or both). This was more evident in the preceding story, in which Flaubert wrote: "As to my choice of title, *Un Parfum à sentir*, I meant by it that Marguerite was a palpable fragrance. I might have added, "une fleur à voir," because for Isabellada beauty was everything." The comparison is made between nothingness and being. Isabellada is the plenitude and the unity of the *visible, we can see her*. Marguerite's appearance too is defined by a perceptible quality, we can sense her. But it is obvious that this fragrance is fugitive, so discreet that no one notices it; the distinctive feature of such delicate odors is that they disturb the sense of smell more than they gratify it, and the nose seeks them out as a definite absence, as a memory more than a pleasure. In sum, the fragrance here is the soul, an invisible lacuna, a mournful demand, boundless, unfounded. The envious person does not recognize in himself any *real* superiority that might justify his claims; what infuriates him is that he is obsessed with a phantom superiority which gives him a conspicuous right to

417

everything precisely because it is *nothing*. This abstract shriveling gets him into incalculable difficulty; he literally cannot express what he feels: everything is *just*, and if he sets such value on nonbeing represented by his soul, it is because he recognizes in advance the superior qualities of the other and his own inferiority. But at the same time the happy rival is *content* with *being*, while the disinherited man goes far beyond him in his total dissatisfaction. Thus he is trapped in the endless circularity of his reasoning. Gustave is worth more than all the others because he is nothing and therefore is content with nothing. In all justice, then, it is appropriate that society should favor him—he deserves to be made the most important of men simply because he considers man to be of no importance. This circular contradiction, of course, comes from the fact that the "I knew very well" corresponds to the world of being, meaning the Other for whom the relation between merits and privileges is supposed to be a strict one, and the "even so" to the subjective world of negativity and privation.

We have seen Garcia recognize the right of primogeniture and François's superiority even as he treats the older brother like a usurper and asserts his own right to honors, wealth, and the father's affection. That right, that keen demand to be valorized, to be first and incomparable, comes from existence itself, from *ipseity*; Gustave/Garcia *feels alive*, he grasps the heart of life like an absolute which in the original nakedness of experience is in itself incomparable; and I have also shown that the source of sovereignty resides in this permanent possibility of *affirming oneself through praxis*. But even if it were a theoretical possibility for the young Flaubert, we have seen that this practical affirmation is half masked by his protohistory because of his constitutional passivity. It is true, inversely, that his passivity is not the passivity of inert matter and must be seen rather as a fettered praxis—passive syntheses are, in spite of everything, intentional. Gustave simply lacked the power to internalize the love of the other as his own value. Thus sovereignty is not absent from his experience—it is abstract and manifest *pathically* as the sovereignty he is denied and which he claims in the name of his unquestionable consciousness of self—in brief, as a *suffered demand*, a pessimistic expectation. He is the pretender par excellence. The misfortune is that he cannot pull this valorization out of himself, it has to come from the Other. Nor can he scorn systems of objective values, for in order to reject such values, whatever they might be, one must have possessed them and—in the name of at least one of them—have occupied an honorable place in the social hierarchy. Here he is, then, forced to claim honors, a standing in the world of objectivity, in the name of a subjective sovereignty which, being the same in everyone, can initiate nothing, belongs to another dimension of the real, and, in his respect, seems to be *desired* rather than truly possessed. At this point in our investigation we discover the depth of Flaubert's descriptions and the convergence of his symbols: the *nothingness* that touches being, the *negativity* that can engulf all positive plenitude, the *suctioning void* that sucks up reality is quite simply pure subjectivity, inchoate and *conscious* insofar as it has become pathos, meaning the desire for valorization. The basis of the *nonexistent* rights which the envious person maintains are his against all odds and which cause him such suffering is *desire in itself*, which knows its impotence and is preserved in spite of everything as a gaping demand, all the stronger because unheeded. The envious man's contradiction is that he knows he is inferior and relative to the extent that he is an other for others, yet he places absolute value in his frustration itself to the extent that he lives it as a negative relationship between inferiority and the things of this world.

Things stay this way for most jealous people. But let a narrow and powerful mind like Gustave's sift his "I know very well . . . but even so" whole years at a time, and it will attempt to suppress the *even so* by setting up an order of absolute values that challenges and disqualifies the order of social values even while preserving the things of this world—indeed, even while finding a conspicuous merit in his disinheritance, which allows him to claim these as his own. In brief, it is a matter of *finding a fetish*, or more precisely of *fetishizing* subjective life. And since the subjective basis of the "even so" is desire, it is *fetishized desire*—lack transformed into plenitude—which will assimilate the "even so" in order to dissolve and replace it.[54] Since the right is based directly on the desire, this right will be all the more unquestionable the stronger the desire.

But first of all, desire itself must be valorized, that is, it must pass from the condition of fact to the condition of demand. This can happen in actuality only if the child gives desire the status of a need. In the work and life of Flaubert, need and desire are opposed and in conflict, each striving to replace the other. We shall soon return to this. For the moment let us note that need, taken in its generality, necessarily becomes demand when its nonsatisfaction involves death. If it is

---

54. "The fetishist *knows very well* that women have no penis, but he cannot add to this any 'but even so' because for him the 'but even so' is the fetish." Mannoni, *Communication*.

419

affirmed, in effect, at the moment the objective situation makes grat-ification impossible, the distant impossibility of assuaging it (as a moral Stoic would have it, one must subdue oneself rather than the world) only makes it more imperious and more urgent. The negation of need by the world results in the total negation of the world—such as it is—by the need. This impossibility of gratification reveals the world as the impossibility of living; on the basis of this *felt* impossi-bility (the discovery is made without words through the failure of attempts at gratification) life is affirmed in the need itself as uncon-ditional demand. The world *must* be such that I find enough to eat and drink. If not, it *must* be possible to change it. And if change becomes clearly impossible when hunger is felt, death is experienced *with horror*, as the triumph of antivalue, of evil.

From the beginning, Flaubert experienced his desire as a need since he recognized the impossibility of satisfying it and managed to in-ternalize that impossibility through experienced *death*. Alone and un-loved, held to be a *minus habens* by his true judges, he was consumed by longing; he desperately desired the status of elder son, the merits and honors attached to that status, his father's love. It was absurd and he knew it; he would have had to break up the Flaubert family, and when he had succeeded in imposing himself, his present desire would evaporate in bitterness, ungratified, like all those that preceded it. Never mind; this desire stands on good grounds, posing its own impossibility, tearing itself apart; its wounds embitter but inflame it. Better, it would be quickly soothed, suppressed, if the thing desired were within reach; because that is impossible, it swells. Impossibility conscious of itself awakens desire and provokes it, adding rigor and violence; but desire finds this impossibility outside itself, in the object, as the fundamental category of the desirable. By its very necessity the absurd demand asserts itself as a right. If Gustave, through the very experience of his own impotence, is plunged into longing, it is because man defines himself as a *right to the impossible*. There is neither mis-understanding nor caprice in this strange determination; for Gustave it is our "human reality" that is thus defined.

In fact, he would not have been wrong if he had substituted desire for need. The needy man is defined by a lack which becomes a fun-damental *right over other men*; a certain humanism would be built on this postulate. But Flaubert does not address himself to his neighbor; with lofty affirmations this drowning man, before going under, in-scribes in heaven a metaphysical law whose first principle is that the desperate love for the impossible is in essence the basis of the *right* to obtain it. And naturally in the Satanic world everything is reversed; rights exist, true, but only in order to be violated. There is no trace of optimism in this judicial and metaphysical claim: a mortgage on the future, his right is a merit which will be negatively recognized by the meticulous cruelty of his future executioners. No matter; he stubbornly affirms it, conscious of the sufferings he is calling down on himself, for this mortgage is only himself—a desire for the impossible. Flaubertian man as legitimate pretender defines himself by the impossibility of living. But we must recall that the origin of this cosmic vision is envy. When Gustave claims that the essence of desire is contained in the lack of gratification, he is far from wrong. Still, this claim must be properly understood. Desire, aside from all the prohibitions that mutilate and curb it, cannot be gratified to the extent that its *demand* is not amenable to a correct statement or has no rapport with articulated language; whatever its current objective, it seeks a certain relation of interiority to the world which cannot be conceived or consequently realized. With the exception that in the present, pleasure exists, even if it is seen as corresponding imperfectly to what was demanded; in order to perceive that by the sexual act one is asking for *something other* that vanishes, one must still "possess" the body of the other and take pleasure from it. In this sense it would be more valuable to say that desire is revealed as ungratifiable the more it is gratified. Gustave sensed this and came to understand it better and better; he was to write about it in *Madame Bovary*. But at the time of his first works he did not base the lack of gratification on the *fact* that the object actually desired is "unutterable"; such a simple declaration would confer neither merit nor the lack of it on the one who desires and consequently would give him no right—even to scoff— over the desirable object but would only indicate *incommensurability*. The *black right* that Flaubert wants to institute must be based, on the other hand, on an original merit; if impossible gratification is the painful mark of election for great souls, it is because they desire nothing less than the *infinite*. In this resides the fetishism of desire, which becomes an inextinguishable lacuna, a suctioning nothingness that gulps down the aged little world of being and still cannot find satisfaction. Look at Mazza, the black saint. Seduced at the age of thirty, "she thought [after giving herself for the first time] about the sensations she felt, and found, thinking them over, nothing but disappointment and bitterness: Oh! this is not what I had dreamed of!" Where does that come from? Ernest is a shabby character but she is unaware of it; Don Juan that he is, he does know how to make love to her. In fact, this woman who makes light of her honor has the impression that she "has fallen quite low," through *love*. She wonders "if behind lust there was not an even greater lust, or after pleasure a greater joy, for she had an unquenchable thirst for infinite love, for boundless passion." As we see, everything comes from her and in the negative. Her flesh was asleep; a cold and devoted wife, she found a certain happiness in the accomplishment of her duties; she sometimes had nocturnal fantasies or temptations, but she triumphed over all of them. She was perfect, but only on the condition that she didn't touch the tree of evil. Scarcely "ruffled" by her new lover, scarcely "fatigued" by their embraces, the unruffled woman—and this is understating it—is ready to burst and open herself: she is gaping, ready to be fertilized by the infinite. Naturally the infinite is made to beg— once again they begin their frolics, she is instructed; and she concludes that "love is only a moment of delight when the lover and his mistress roll about, uttering cries of joy, their bodies entwined . . . and then . . . it is all over . . . ; the man has relief and the woman goes away." After this declaration: "Boredom gripped her soul."

Is she going to collapse? No. At first she goes into a trance— ecstasy—a defensive maneuver as Flaubert shows us quite clearly: "She arrived . . . at that state of languor and heedlessness, that half-sleep that feels like being asleep, drowning, the world far away. . . . She no longer thought of her husband or her children, still less of her reputation, which the other women delighted in tearing to pieces in the salons." This of course is the path to ecstasy. She discovers in it as well—presented in positive terms—only that infinite void of the soul that gave birth to her dreams and then her boredom: "Unknown melody . . . new worlds . . . vast spaces . . . boundless horizons." She gives herself over to optimism: "It seemed to her that everything was born for love, that men were creatures of a higher order . . . and that they ought to live only for the heart." Gustave contemplates this bad faith that was his own without anger; he had searched for God, divine love, he had believed that between men there could be only the loving relationship of vassal and lord.

But underneath, on the level of touch and pleasure, a subterranean and destructive work is being accomplished. There is pleasure *and that is all*; therefore one must renounce it, renounce it for the infinite, or strive deliberately to fuse the two. Is this possible? Yes if the search for pleasure becomes a rage; the revealed soul will put all its vastness into the search for sensual pleasures. Indeed, we learn without transition (Gustave has just described for us Mazza's spiritual flights) that "every day she felt she loved more than the day before, that this was becoming a need . . . that she could not have lived without it, . . . This passion ended by becoming serious and terrifying . . . ; she had such vast desires, such a thirst for sensual pleasures and delights in her blood, in her veins, under her skin, that she had become mad, drunk, distracted, and would have liked to make her love the very limits of nature. . . . Often in the transports of delirium she would cry out that life was only passion, that *love was everything to her.*" It was already everything—at the heights—when she saw love as the supreme purpose of the species; but at that level it was only a softened Platonism. On the level of sensuality it is true madness: what she wants from love is less to feel it than *never to stop making it.* Basically she has made a choice; disappointed by her earlier erotic experiences, she could have challenged them in the name of pure love, but this would be renunciation. She prefers to transform her disappointment into insatiability and to inject the infinite, which she is constantly seeking, into the temporal flow. This will be her forever frustrated project, the quest which defines her as a "not yet," an always future absence, a nest of vipers and misfortunes.

The reader will be struck, I imagine, by the surprising similarity between her behavior and that of some frigid women. The women who are desperate to make love are the frigid ones rather than the passionate. These forever ungratified women, cursed huntresses, nervous, tense, insatiable, are endlessly running after a pleasure they dream of—"vast desires, a thirst for sensual pleasures and delights"— and are always denied it. Is Mazza frigid, then? Yes—like Flaubert— who was inspired to describe her by his first sexual experience,[55] but whose plan was certainly not to reveal to us the disappointment that followed. Mazza's mad desire to love comes from an early frustration. She was tricked, and for this reason she has no desire in its normal sense, only a bitter passional demand: I want to have pleasure, *I have the right to it* since my infinite privation proves that the pleasure, if I had it, would be infinite. Poor Mazza, her frustration will be extreme. Ernest "trembles before the passion of this woman the way a child runs away from the sea, saying that it is too big." One fine day she bites him. Seeing his blood flow he understands "that she was surrounded by a poisonous atmosphere which would suffocate and kill him in the end. Therefore he had to leave her for good." We know the rest; abandoned, this superb creature takes on the resentments

55. Which he had just had—he was, as we shall see, deflowered by a housemaid.

of the hideous Marguerite: "The noise of the world seemed to her a discordant and infernal music and nature a mockery of God; she loved nothing and hated everything."

Flaubert makes her one of the chosen: to love to the point of sexual madness and crime, to terrify the beloved by infinite and *unhealthy* demands,[56] and therefore to suffer to the point of suicide because of the very love one bears the beloved, of which he is unworthy—this is what is required. In order to define it, he finds a word that Gide will take up much later in *Les Nourritures terrestres*: thirst. Thirst, on the condition that it is unquenchable. One sentence, indeed, gives us the key to *Passion et Vertu*: Mazza is "one of those who quench their thirst with the salt water of the sea and whose thirst burns forever." Here we have the *black saint*. The ambiguity of the metaphor, however, will not have gone unnoticed. Why does Mazza drink salt water when she is thirsty? Is it because her thirst is infinite, so that for her, any drink is sea water? Or because the fresh water that would quench her thirst is out of reach? The two explanations overlap. How can this be? Well, first of all, Mazza is shipwrecked—she is floating on a raft, the ocean is everywhere. In other words, Ernest is all she has to drink; if he withholds himself, her thirst will never stop burning. In Flaubert, envy is structured too early and too deeply for him ever to lose the feeing that pleasure, possible for men *by divine right*, is forbidden him by the will of others: it is he himself who is shipwrecked. But at the same time he is careful to warn us: if Ernest had loved Mazza, if he had remained, if he could have "thrown himself with her into the vortex that sucks you, dizzied, into the vast course of passion, which begins with a smile and ends only in a tomb," still nothing essential would have been altered. Everything happens, in short, as if he were saying to us: black souls are made of such delicate stuff, their perceptions of resonances are so profound and so vast that they transform into infinite torture what for insensitive natures might be pleasure. But the worst occurs when they focus all their desires on a certain finite and therefore unworthy object. What is more, he says as much in *Quidquid volueris*: "We are all born with a certain amount of tenderness and love which we gaily toss to the first objects that come along . . . to the four winds. . . . But gather this up and we will have an immense treasure. . . . And so he would soon concentrate all his soul on a single thought, and he lived for this

56. Later, in the letters to Louise, Flaubert applies the epithet to his adolescent reveries.

thought." *Power* and *concentration*, then. A *single* concern: for Gustave, what disappears is the father's love; for Mazza, Ernest's. The result: "A world apart that turns in tears and despair and is finally lost in the abyss of crime." *The depths of the infinite*—everything is there. And Gustave, after Mazza has sent her lover fleeing and massacred her whole family, says dreamily, seriously, "What a treasure, the love of such a woman."[57] A treasure for whom? For no one but God, who does not exist. Mazza's passion remains egocentric, she wants *her* pleasure, and she claims it. This is not very surprising since—as Gustave's father taught him—hedonism or interest can be found at the base of all emotions. But there are great souls, black and frustrated, for whom the indefinite deepening of demand has the effect of sublimating the ego. Injustice is therefore solidly established, for in the case of universal unhappiness the finest souls are those who suffer most. Put differently, the intensity of their suffering is the single mark of their distinction. Mazza is all eagerness; she loves Ernest for herself, not for him. But that aside, the soul that infinitely desires a finite object must be recognized as infinite. Given this premise, the coveted object which is not comparable to the vast and primal desire it has awakened ought to revert *by right* to the infinite soul that covets it and whose thirst it could not possibly slake.

Such is the ideology of envy as Flaubert construed it for his own use. This negative de-ontology can be justified only if one affirms, as he does, the primacy of nothingness over being. We have already understood how he manages this conjuring trick: *right*, to the extent that it is guaranteed by institutions or a social group, a family, a father recognizing this or that person as a function fulfilling a position, is a *fact* that characterizes a society defined in the eyes of the historian, the ethnographer, or the sociologist; in this sense it appears as a finite determination of being. But within the society or group, to the extent that its content is normative, the law prescribes actions rather than *describing* them, and presents itself—at least for those who do not challenge the regime—as a *duty-being*, meaning an imperative which is not exhausted in actual behavior but is intended to structure *possible* behavior as well. Seen from this perspective—which, I repeat, is *internal*—it often appears as the contrary of being. *What must be done* is precisely *what is not done*; right is never invoked more preemptorily

---

57. Underlying the story is a meditation on crimes of passion. Flaubert found his subject in the judicial archives. In other words, he built his narrative on a crime envisaged as the proof of love. The *fetishistic* intention (to present evil and make it look like the only possible good) is therefore original.

than when it has been violated or is in danger of being violated. The existence of repressive agents indicates in every society that the legislator foresees that the law will not be spontaneously respected. Gustave plays it both ways: he considers the right of others from the outside as a pure determination of being; on the other hand, he assimilates *his right*, since he is bitterly conscious of not having *the divine right* to be man, to *duty-being*, that is, the challenge to what exists by what does not. Through this he confuses nonbeing with an imperative and makes a virtue of privation.

The primary source of this ideology lies in the very structure of envy. When Gustave declares that the essence of desire implies insatiability, it is not (as we have seen) that he considers it "unutterable," in fact he presents it to us as the infinite aspiration of nothingness necessarily frustrated by the finitude of being. But—beyond the fact that it is inspired by certain Romantic themes—this construction is self-defensive; for Flaubert it's a matter not of saying what he feels but of asserting, come what may, his right to have rights. On the other hand, what is fundamental and defines not only Gustave but all envious people is *insatiability of the first degree*; for anyone tormented by envy, pleasure—even immediate pleasure—is impossible. Desire *comes afterward*. If dissatisfaction characterizes desire, it is because it is never awakened except by the acknowledged impossibility of being satisfied. In other words, the envious person can covet only what the other already possesses. Look at Djalioh. The poor anthropoid, as the author himself admits, at first feels only a vague tenderness for Adèle; another must enjoy her before he can feel desire; better still, such exclusive enjoyment must reflect the apeman's inferiority. For this reason the envious person *has no hope of winning*. Look at Gustave himself. From adolescence he toyed with the dream of being fabulously rich, already coveting what was refused to him in principle and wishing to be someone else, a rajah loaded with gold and precious jewels *as his birthright*. Still, this is only half bad since those oriental millionaires are not much more to him than creatures of his imagination; they exist so little that they *steal* nothing from him, and through a directed oneirism he succeeds in slipping into their skin. He is consumed with envy, on the other hand, when he learns that an uncle or the mother of one of his friends died leaving a fortune; modest as it might be—compared to the fantasied treasures of the orient—this legacy provokes cries of rage and torments him unmercifully. This is because Gustave knows the heir, a being of flesh and blood who *dispossesses* him, not by usurping the position of legatee but, quite to the contrary, by asserting his legitimate rights. Gustave was not concerned with the money or properties before the will was made public; they belonged to others, of course, but the owners were old people who scarcely bothered him. *From the moment of transmission,* these meager riches become the object of his futile and anguished desire, not for themselves but because they refer to the *right* of a young man his own age. The fetishization of desire is merely a process which masks in Flaubert the impossibility of spontaneously desiring anything. Envy is not desire, it is *passion* in all senses of the term; Gustave is not jealous of the possessions of others, it is *their being,* their *divine right* of possession and the mysterious quality (of which he will be deprived all his life) that allows them *approbation,* that fascinating pleasure which, provided it belongs to them, makes the most mediocre things of this world sparkle in their hands.

The primacy of nothingness over being, Gustave's only claim to possession of the world, does not involve a theoretical affirmation; the child is too young to construct a theory around it, too passive to pass judgments; he must *believe* it, *live* it; and, since his sole activity is resentment, he must *turn himself* into an implacable, supreme, and empty nonbeing by experiencing it as if he were simply *submitting* to his totalitarian intention to disqualify what exists in the name of what does not. We shall soon see that this disqualification of all reality (I know very well . . . but even so) is at the source of his option of unrealization—Gustave seems to be devoured by the imaginary. But it is still too soon to envisage this dimension of his existence. What must be shown here is that the child, by *submitting himself* as a disqualification of the real, has exposed himself as malicious. Later on, indeed, he announced that he was a misanthrope; between his tenth and his fifteenth year he spoke more simply of his malice. But far from seeing this as a precise activity, intended to do harm, he took it for a kind of pathos with which he had been infected. Let us recall Garcia: "Indeed, Garcia was a malicious, deceitful, and hateful man, but who could say that the malice, the dark and ambitious jealousy which plagued his days, was not born of all the vexations he had endured?" Malicious because they had "done him wrong," because he was created to submit to this basic wrong, to internalize it as jealous hatred and externalize it again as crime, Garcia submits to evil as his subjective determination, his substance, his lot—he inhales and exhales it with every breath, it is his oxygen and thus his sustaining atmosphere, his environment. As Gustave describes it, malice is endured as a kind of suffering; it never goes beyond the level of passive activity—we have seen that the murder of François, the dream of a dream, is not convincing. Besides, Gustave himself, more indolent than Garcia, never dreamed of killing; it was enough for him to imagine a character who accomplishes a self-punishing and vengeful murder in a dream. As for him, he satisfied his hatreds by engaging in prophecies. The principle is simple: he was cursed and injected with the sacred belief that *for him* the worst was always certain; that was sufficient to motivate his oracular pronouncements on his own destiny. Malice externalizes and generalizes this principle—it is the cunning work of resentment. For every man, in any case, the worst is always certain. This induction claims to be based on experience, but in fact it is a malign intention with the aim not *of doing* evil but of predicting that it will be done.[58] But the disqualification of being can work in two different ways. First, every man has a destiny and everyone's future is furnished in some sense with misfortunes increasing from birth to death; this is the pure and simple universalization of the inflexible law which, according to him, regulates his own existence. Second, the human species is a fraud so that one must expect the worst of everyone, meaning the worst conduct based on the worst motives. These two interpretations do not offer the *same* notion of the *worst*. In the first it is suffering, man's only dignity. In the second it is baseness, the vice Gustave hates most of all—the stubbornness or stupidity, the narrowness of ambition, thick-skinned materialism, cowardice, the reign of belly and balls, the ferocity of indifference.

Gustave is obliged to bet on both scenarios for the simple reason that universalization, which is the bedrock of malicious thinking, cannot be accomplished in either case without stripping him of his unique privilege. Indeed, in the first, all men become Justine, and the *black saint*, younger son of the Flauberts, is no longer the only one to suffer. And this is just what he wants: since I am roasting in hell, let the others roast too; the whole of creation is implicated. But if all men are cursed Adams, Gustave reenters the ranks; negative right, based on suffering, becomes the most common thing in the world. And in the second universalization, if all men are base and their baseness

---

58. Gustave lives out this formal principle of malicious thinking more than he expresses it in his early works, yet it is implicitly contained from his first *known* writing in the assimilation of our world to hell. But it is referred to quite clearly a little later, chiefly in his correspondence with Ernest. In particular on 20 October 1839 (he was seventeen years old): "*The Turk* took a baccalaureate exam yesterday and passed. This was perhaps the sixth time [he sat for it], he said it was the second, but *he who thinks worst often thinks right*." My italics.

brings them happiness—Gustave often repeated that stupidity and health are all you need—the young man similarly loses his privileged position. This time it is baseness that is most common; he can expect only the worst from himself as well as from anyone else, and this sort of universalization is only too easy for him—we know that he doesn't like himself. Gustave manages to jump from one version to the other the moment the universal is about to close in on him.

Gustave's intention in the second version has nothing metaphysical about it. It is a disqualification of the *being* of the human race insofar as men claim to have rights that Gustave is lacking, not only the right to possession and pleasure but others less material; *dignity* is one such right, *respectability* is another; both are based on services rendered to society and presuppose the right to be good, or rather, according to Gustave, to believe oneself good. Optimism is a right over oneself and over others: I have the right to believe that *I* am good, that *you* are good until proven otherwise; you have the right to believe in my goodness, in the goodness of the species. There is a conspiracy among all the members of society: man is possible only if everyone tacitly promises everyone else not to go beyond appearances. Gustave's determination is to do harm; his passive activity makes his objective the *destruction* of man by refusing to conspire with the vital lies of this animal split open to reveal, behind the inconsistency of the actor, the human beast, the swine. To do harm, in this case, is to *unmask*; when he has dismantled all our poor defenses and has revealed our carrion stench, he is delighted; not that he likes those gamey odors for themselves, he is simply pleased that our species smells bad. *Knowledge*, as he conceives it—as it *is* for many people—represents malicious thinking in that it destroys humanity, that illusion willfully maintained by everyone. The destructive intent of his prospecting is clearly explained to us in a letter to Ernest dated 26 December 1838 (Gustave had just turned seventeen): "Since you and Alfred have been away from me, I have been analyzing myself more, myself and others. I dissect endlessly, which amuses me, and when I have finally discovered the corruption in something believed to be pure and the gangrene in places of beauty, I throw back my head and laugh." We note that in this passage Gustave does not claim to be different from others. We are dealing here not with scientific objectivity but, as the two words "when finally" indicate, with animosity. He seems to be telling us that one must dig deep in certain cases to discover the gangrene; sometimes the adolescent is tempted to abandon his enterprise—a desperate one—for everything seems to be healthy. Happily, his initial

429

parti pris compels him to continue the search—and, indeed, corruption of the soul does exist; despite appearances, he *must* find it, in himself and in his neighbor. At first the malice is unconditional, the malicious man must desire his own evil. Moreover, as a good culprit he is only improving upon the judgment others have brought against him: condemned, he condemns himself, this is the masochistic moment in his malignity. But the conduct of others is particularly difficult to decipher—consequences without premises, opaque events that "jump him from behind" or unfold under his very nose. The sole object of analysis which he can thoroughly dissect is himself; in this sense, when his relentless search yields the swamps of his own soul, he is not only seeking to inflame his wounds—the essential purpose is to unmask in himself, to himself and by himself, the universal defects of the species. Whether he accuses himself or others, he has only one purpose: to desecrate man, that "marvel of civilization" which Achille-Cléophas so well embodies with his science, his glory, and his natural virtues, and in so doing to show that this dignified and respectable being is only the odious dream of doorkeepers.[59] That his intention is to destroy and not to know is clear from his "satanic" laugh when he finally discovers the underlying putrefaction. Why laugh rather than cry unless he *wanted to discover evil*, which is a passive way of doing it? A sado-masochistic laugh: he jeers at the derisory contrast between his illusions, his false consciousness of himself, and his reality; he is sadistically enchanted at having caught the others out—he himself was a dupe but a sincere one, the others are frauds. Later on we shall see that this enterprise is still excessively passive; *unmasking* will be transformed, thanks to literary tools, into that other thing he repeatedly proclaimed: *demoralizing*. The silent discovery of abjectness is itself a punishment; even if that hypocrite, man, appeared entirely naked—and ignorant—to a single "analyst," he would stand chastened by his imposture; in the second round, literature would do the job by unveiling to readers their inhumanity. Gustave bases his taste for the "telling little fact" on this malicious postulate; the self-analyst also demands reports of clearly ignoble conduct, this time on the part of others, on which he might exercise his scalpel. The correspondence swarms with claimed "observations" which all have the same meaning: stupidity, baseness, cowardice, vileness. And much later, one evening when Flaubert was simply a

59. This was, we know, the title he was at one point tempted to give his last "Mirror of the World," which was called *Bouvard et Pécuchet*.

famous old man, the young Sully-Prudhomme, who had just left him and hardly knew him, was dumbfounded and disturbed by the great man's observations: When someone tells me of a base act, Gustave had said, "it gives me as much pleasure as if they had given me money." Not only does the occurrence confirm his views, it is reported and therefore known to everyone—the punishment is in the publicity. Caught out! Besides, he hopes that this public exposure will have even graver consequences for the guilty party, that he will be beaten, mocked, tossed into the street; when his prayers are answered, what a windfall! At fifteen Gustave learned that his school proctor had been surprised at a brothel and was going to be arraigned before the academic council; he exalted: "This is what makes me rejoice, revives me, delights me, warms my heart, my chest, my stomach, my intestines, my innards, my diaphragm. . . . *Adieu*, for I have gone mad over this news."[60]

What particularly delighted him in the proctor's misadventure was the unhappy man's suffering: "When I think of the expression on the proctor's face, surprised in the act and finished, I write again, I laugh, I drink, I sing, ha! ha! ha! ha! ha!" More precisely it was the visible expression of that suffering, the culprit's demeanor, his pitiful air. This is true passive malice. Yet it sometimes happens—this is usually the case—that the sanction is not so brutal and is not even noticed, except by the young "observer"; it lies in the act itself, which is ridiculous, in the phrase uttered with the pretense of nobility that only reveals its ignominiousness. Not to all witnesses, too busy lying to themselves, but to the singular clairvoyance of the malicious little boy. Gustave is satisfied that the sentence is passed by the act itself, which destroys humanity while claiming to create it—as if baseness were its own punishment.

This malice is limited to a malevolent look and is never translated into action. For Gustave, to observe is to charge the course of things with executing in his place the sentences he passes secretly; better still, with informing him of them by their execution. Not that passive and hidden hatred is the universal basis of observation and hence of knowledge. It involves a particular kind of observant expectation which I shall call *feminine* because it corresponds to the particular situation of woman in societies in which she still remains a relative being, living in connivance with her oppressors, sanctioning the status that reduces her to a level below theirs, and sharing their interests

60. Letter to Ernest Chevalier, 24 June 1837.

in such a way that it is nearly impossible to break away through revolt. This is how our "wives" live, to our blame, poisoned by the other world of the Other, the world of the "first sex," with an inevitable future which they cannot help foretelling. They are all bitter, only the bitterness is hidden; they are too afraid to pronounce the sentence themselves, but resentment accumulates, and when it reaches its full measure, men's relations to the world are expected to yield a natural sanction against their vices. This is observation: observing in a salon that polite, assiduous husband whose wife knows his low tricks, observing the way he flirts discreetly thinking she doesn't see, hearing him repeat for the hundredth time the phrases he thinks he is inventing for the occasion, listening when his superiors approach him, and rejoicing in his slightly servile manner or his awkwardness; to others he may be reserved, but she is delighted that to her he is as naked as a worm. This knowledge is based on details from his attitude, his clothing, every perceptible particular she expects the objective exposure of her oppressors, who are condemned in her eyes as ridiculous. Objects are part of the game as well. An armchair that is too large or too small can make a person seem ridiculous as much as a hat that is too loose or too tight. Once the threshhold is crossed, the resentful woman looks for the signs of future sanction and marks them in detail with bitter anticipation. The chairs are too high, the desk is, conveniently, too small; he will make a poor impression. Having foreseen all this, the wife feels a spasm of joy at seeing her predictions realized so soon. And the process is not exclusively reserved for the torturer-in-chief—if he is one—but is extended to the assistant judges, to the criminals who betray their sex, and finally to the whole world. Naturally, these punishments pass unnoticed; at least the guilty party is not conscious of his punishment. So much the better; it is crucial that the integrity of his person should be preserved. Indeed, the condemnation will be more profound, the degradation more complete if the condemned is not even informed. This is the secret of a certain wild feminine laughter. As well as of Emma's black delight when Charles botches the operation on the clubfoot. Gustave is a woman—why? his bitter perspective is the source of his powers of observation; his directed passivity is an overture to evil. He looks, notes details, selects, sure that a sudden, discordant, but inevitable combination of things and individuals is suddenly going to crown his hopes and denounce the inanity of the species in the person of one or the other of its particular representatives. A double coup: the internal relation of man to the environment

objectively reveals our irremediable baseness; inversely, the mute verdict of things indicates that the cosmos is hostile to mankind and
passes judgment against us.

But how, someone will ask, does Gustave hope to escape the trap
of the universal—will it not close in on him as well? The answer is
given by the young man himself on three distinct but dialectically
related levels. First, *he does not escape* the snare he himself has set, the
less so since most of his inductions are made on the basis of his
intimate experience; he thinks this is sufficient proof that the "curse
of Adam" weighs on all members of the species, and the accusing
witness is all the more convincing as he begins by accusing himself.
Second, *he escapes it nevertheless.* For the simple reason that he is
conscious of his baseness and *suffers from it.* This notion of the use-
fulness and necessity of pain is Gustave's salvation in the nick of
time—that sadistic laugh of relief when he discovers his own gangrene
is also a laugh of despair. When he *refuses* the universal, then, he has
lost in advance, and he knows it, but for this very reason his impotent
horror of the human reality *within him* gives him another dimension:
by his reflexive disgust he escapes his condition as man. But if the
world belongs to the devil, someone will say, and if all men are
damned, are they not by definition plunged in torment from birth to
death? Will they not fall from Charybdis to Scylla, that is, from the
second generalization to the first? If suffering is virtue, isn't it enough
simply to be a man to become virtuous? Gustave gives various answers to this question. First of all, every being with a human appearance is not necessarily human; there are demons—Isabellada,
Monsieur Paul—who torment and are never tormented. Then, a distinction must be made between good and bad suffering; there are
sorrows—the most common sorrows, in fact—that do not bring salvation because they are the result not of reflecting on the human
condition and vainly rejecting it but, quite to the contrary, of accepting
it. The "shopkeeper" who fails in his business is truly tormented,
anguish keeps him awake nights; but that doesn't make him any less
base, for misfortune strikes him in his shopkeeper's soul, caring as
he does only for his interests and his stomach and respecting *himself*
in the respect he has for magistrates, important people, and the authorities. Quite frankly it is not enough to hate one's neighbor; one
must hate him as man and with the same hatred one has for oneself.
Finally, among those who are afflicted for good reasons, a hierarchy
must be established on the basis of these two qualities: the depth,
amplitude, intensity of one's "sudden consciousness" and the deli-

cacy of the nervous system. Gustave places himself at the top of the scale; he is perfectly lucid and suffers infinitely. Third, more hidden and already virulent, is the belief which he will soon make explicit: *for me* there is no trap *since I am not part of mankind*. An odd conviction, which has its source in a real and experienced situation but which passes necessarily over into the imaginary. Its origin is his "anomaly": I am not like the others. But the others are men, all of them, who have been appointed from birth by a divine right. We have seen Gustave, in rage, shame, and pride, embody himself in an anthropoid. Since he is refused the status of the species, he escapes the infamous human condition—who would be in a better position than he to comprehend that man is a mirage, a hypocritical dream? Gustave profits from his subhumanity in order to challenge the aims of those mad beasts who take themselves for human beings. He feels close to idiots, to children and dogs—he will not bear responsibility for the vices and false virtues he discovers in *others*. Because he is *beneath them*? Certainly, at first. But high and low are frequently inverted for him, as we shall see. If he isn't fooled—though this is because he is an anthropoid—by the universal illusion which Achille-Cléophas and Achille share, isn't he therefore *above* mankind? Undoubtedly he has his swampy spots of humanity, as does Djalioh, who has the misfortune of being not entirely an ape; but this is precisely what allows him to˙ understand *the others* and to suffer—without ever becoming their equal or, more important, their fellow creature. From the age of thirteen and a half, in *Le Voyage en enfer*, we find Gustave perched on Mount Atlas meditating on the vices and virtues of a Lilliputian race which he contemplates from above; afterward he would only rarely and with poor grace leave his imaginary heights. In any event, we must point out here that his withdrawal from the species somehow inaugurates the choice of the unreal, a passive option that is quite conscious; which amounts to saying that he escapes the trap of the universal by taking refuge in imagination. We shall return to all this at leisure. Let us note only that, for him, the imaginary solution to a problem is not a *false* solution but the only valid one for a quietist who has, *against the real*, made himself the incarnation of that vitriol which is nothingness.

Here we have passive malice: the subhuman vision that passively does harm to man by constituting the visual field as the territory where this usurper is destroyed, or the falsely candid vision of the child who, by rejecting the general conspiracy, disqualifies the whole society when he sees that the emperor is naked. But this malicious

turn of mind takes another direction when it predicts the worst suffering for everyone. The worst suffering, which is every bit as violent
as the virtuous kind, far from elevating the sufferer above his condition, degrades him even more by defeating him. This prospective
malice lays the groundwork for prophecy. The *other, endured,* and
sacred character of every oracle masks the heinous wish at its source;
indeed, as I have said, seeing the life of other men is all Gustave
needs to proceed from the numinous principle that "the worst is
always certain." Submitting to his life as to a sacred ceremony—
because it is manipulated by the all-powerful will of the Other—Gustave sees every other life *through* the unfolding of his own and, in
consequence, gives it the *time of destiny.* Not always; when he pleases,
when he thinks that the predicted event will make things difficult for
someone whom he dislikes. The correspondence contains the blackest
wishes, which this Cassandra offers us as visionary intuitions. Gustave tells us, for example, that he was tormented very early by the
idea that his father was going to die prematurely. This did happen.
But when as a young man he was anguished at the thought of his
future orphaning, nothing seemed to him to justify this anguish.
Nothing except the religious principle that the worst is always certain.
And what could be worse than losing your father? Especially when
you adored him. Therefore Dr. Flaubert would die in the prime of
life, in full glory. This is a satanic certainty. A conviction that is scarcely
tolerable, he tells us, but that you eventually get used to. Proof being
that when Achille-Cléophas actually did die, Gustave grieved very
little, since, as he explains, he had so often deplored this misfortune
in advance. How, then, did he accept the prophecy that so often returned to plague him? As a stabbing anxiety? As a forbidden pleasure
quickly repressed by terror and disguised as sorrow? And had there
been nothing but dread, what was its nature? Was it the real fear of
seeing a beloved parent die or merely the correct guise in which a
parricidal wish might enter consciousness? Didn't it ever occur to
him—in anguish, of course—that the physician-philosopher's death
would deprive the whole House and especially the elder son of the
most precious support? If the father should die very soon, he would
have to be replaced by another chief surgeon; Achille, who was too
young, would not be a candidate and would end up as a local doctor,
neither more nor less than Gustave. And then, he knew very well
that the *Flaubert worth* was based chiefly on the worth of Achille-
Cléophas; without this eminent man, the family would disappear.

435

From his adolescence, the younger son desired and foresaw the worst: death for the paterfamilias; for the older brother a miserable career, which would be public proof of his nothingness; disgrace for the household and a return to the lower classes from which it came. At other times, of course, he did not hesitate to pronounce another oracle—*La Peste à Florence* is testimony to this. Achille would die at the age of twenty-five; his death would not be so deplorable, the worst thing would be the father's grief. Gustave dreaded this because it would demolish the good, magnanimous lord, who would never recover from it; and also, of course, because the practitioner-philosopher, cut to the quick by the death of the usurper, would have no more tears to shed for the approaching death of his younger son. Perhaps Gustave himself would die of sorrow in the face of his father's grief, Achille's last usurpation, and the father would feel nothing in the face of this second death, which was provoked by his unjust preference. But hidden beneath these fatal fears, *La Peste à Florence* reveals a vicious desire: let him croak, that imbecile, so that the "comparison" will stop and my father will finally submit to the punishment for his crimes. We shall find him again, after the Flauberts' double bereavement, this time prophesying the death of his mother—the poor old woman hasn't much time left, surely. Besides, Gustave curiously adds, he loves this unhappy woman so much that if she wanted to throw herself out the window he wouldn't have the heart to stop her. In brief, the young Pythias dreams of completing the massacre: let them all croak, father, mother, daughter, and let him finally be left alone. For once the oracle is mistaken—Mme Flaubert survives. But he was not mistaken at the age of fifteen when, in *La Dernière Heure*, an unfinished narrative that inaugurates the autobiographical cycle by mixing oracular fictions with reality, he prophesied the death of his sister Caroline. Was he so set on the demise of the family? Yes, to the precise extent that he knew his own dependence and was exasperated by feeling his irreparable need of the familial setting. Thus this ravaged soul confused desire and prophecy; he *believed* in what he augured, meaning he was persuaded that the postulates of his rancor revealed the future to him and at the same time, through a kind of black magic, created it. Easy; this is a question not of a waking nightmare—always a little suspect, after all, since one *produces* one's dreams—but of *unfamiliar* evidence which he acquired only by operating in the shadows and which, as a strange spectacle, caused him anguish—a beautiful example of passive activity. He was never completely fooled, however, since these dreams become crimes in his fictions and he proudly proclaimed that he was malicious.

His characters, moreover, pass from the vision to the curse, which under the impact of a strong emotion is only a sudden consciousness of vision. Marguerite mocks the poor, happy that they are already suffering, and wishes the worst misfortunes on the rich; Mazza does the same, and so does Garcia. The author himself at twenty was not ashamed to curse his native town: "I despise it, I hate it, I call down upon it all the curses of heaven because it witnessed my birth."

Yet these wishes, whether disguised or unmasked, were inert demands, and Gustave did not lift a finger to satisfy them. The very fact of such an *oath* seemed to him an absolute and black reality that plunged him into internal evil and magically elicited external catastrophe. He who curses charges the *Other* through words with acting in his place; a sacred power—God, perhaps—will do what is necessary. In certain social systems, however, social indictments have the power to unleash divine vengeance on someone's head—the priest can hurl anathema, the father of the family can curse the prodigal son. But when Gustave curses his neighbor, he knows quite well that he has no magic power and that providence will do as it likes; indeed, he is already convinced that the rewards are going to Isambert, to Isabellada, to Ernest, to Paul and their like, and that the worst troubles lie in wait for people like him, they are the accursed. Not being an exercise in power, his curses are no more than the inert and verbal images of acts. Gustave takes revenge through words all the more easily as he is conscious of his impotence. As if absolute evil were not so much, in his eyes, the effect of the curse as its simple appearance in the soul of a desperate child. In truth, it is the externalization and projection onto others of his condemnation by the father. For Marguerite, for example, it is her *ugliness*—the original sentence pronounced against the unfortunate woman—that she turns into the curse of beauty; so, as the general basis of envy, the negative is meant to dissolve the positive.

Flaubert's "malice" would evolve in the course of his life, and we shall have occasion to come back to it when the "conclusion" of Pont-l'Evêque has definitely structured as character what was only a singular history. But at this point we can observe that the young boy is *harmlessly malicious.* He knows it too; when his malice ceases to be contemplative and prospective, it can then be lodged in language and is simply verbal. When the Flaubert group was complete, what was Gustave doing with his prophesying and cursing except to render his

magical power in language? It is the words and sentences that ar
evil, nothing more. Gustave was malicious to have written or pon
dered. At this point it seems that his true vengeance, pondered b
resentment, unlike the *vendetta* which is negative praxis, could pro
ceed only by passive activity, meaning that it had to be a secret actio
of the self against the self which the victim managed by utilizing th
praxis of the other (the force the other exercised over him and whicl
he internalized as his own determination) in such a way as to mak
his executioners even guiltier, testifying openly: see how maliciou
I am; their greatest crime is to have made me like this. Indeed, i
Gustave is to be believed, everyone does evil except the malicious
They are merely victims of mankind. They sweat evil through ever
pore, but bound as they are, how could they commit it? And then
the evil that devours them, after all, has made them. Starting fron
this, everything is turned around: blackness and greatness of soul ar
the same thing; malice does not arise just any place, it presuppose
first that the chosen have suffered a profound injustice—which in th
universe of the other would be the most inflexible justice—and the
that they endure this injustice like the most agonizing passion; henc
their exquisite sensibilities and lucid consciousness. This is still no
enough; the martyr, the disinherited man must become *on oath* th
Lord of Nonbeing; he must assume his frustration and reexternaliz
it in an impotent and conscious dream of being that lord who abolishe
being through a universal conflagration. The malicious man, in short
must make himself the Prince of the Imaginary against the *real whicl
is crushing him*, and he must have enough constancy and strength tc
preserve this title until death, enough imaginative power to builc
nothingness into a fabulous opera by vowing every moment of hi:
life to use fantasmagoria to disqualify reality. In brief, in Gustave':
world, he is not malicious who wants to be—only the best and the
most unhappy can have this honor. The young boy knew only one
candidate who fulfilled these strict conditions: himself. So he desig
nated himself, or was co-opted if you prefer, without any increase ir
self-love or self-esteem. This is as it should be; continually passing
from humiliation to an impotent bitter pride, the malicious man suf
fers because he cannot suffer himself.

SEVEN

Two Ideologies

Gustave was not content just to live his unhappy condition as younger son; he had to ponder it. By this I do not mean either that he understood it objectively or that he made a theory out of it; I mean simply that he believed he was clarifying it by discourse—when on the contrary he was obscuring and mythifying it. In other words, he undertook—as we all do at first—to approach experience through the ideologies of his time. He had two at his disposal: one, faith, came from his mother; the other, scientism, from his father. This last is the one we shall discuss first—we shall soon see why. The paterfamilias, in effect, was not only the *black lord* who had created his vassal in order to cast him into the worst possible world, or even the chief instructor embodied by Pedrillo, who revealed to Gustave his inadequacy by forcing him to learn his alphabet. He was also a great man of the provinces, a *capacité*, a philosopher; on the outside his statements were respectfully received, within his family they had the force of law, which conferred on him still another function, that of educator and model. In short, when he had the time or the inclination, he spoke; by his intermittent statements, his allusions, his judgments, more rarely his conversations, he infused his sons with his convictions, which instantly became gospel. His authority was so great that even when he evoked a personal memory his conduct in those circumstances unintentionally assumed an exemplary, sacred cast. Hence the ethic of duty and mechanistic thought, although radically contradictory, were simultaneously accepted by the children, issuing as they did from the same hero, from the founder; and both expressed him completely. What did Gustave gain from this teaching? How was he penetrated by bourgeois ideology? How was it structured in this

439

dark soul who rejected it with all his might, in vain? How could Gustave use it to "illuminate" himself and the world? We shall not answer these questions decisively until we have studied the two portraits Gustave drew of his father, one long after Achille-Cléophas's death, which depicts him as Larivière, the other drawn from life in August 1839, which describes him in the guise of Mathurin.

A. Regressive Analysis

The study of these two incarnations seems indispensable since the single valid connection between morality and mechanism, for Gustave as much as for Achille, was the celebrated man who managed to produce sacred words as well as exemplary behavior. Both words and behavior were worth only as much as he was. Here the very person of Dr. Flaubert is thrown into question. For Achille, time would have no effect on the matter; his father would last until the incontestable end, as we have seen. And for Gustave? Let us return to Dr. Larivière, what makes the pages relating to him in *Madame Bovary* so valuable is that they allow us to see the deceased father the way Gustave at thirty-five remembered him. The testimony is irrefutable. Not on Achille-Cléophas but on his son's opinion of him. Unfortunately, the cult of the great man has become so virulent in our century that the most lucid critics have seen this character as an "admirable figure" drawn "with love." Isn't the enterprise even more noble and pious since this effort by the scion of a distinguished practitioner to reconstruct him for sentimental readers softened the features of his deceased father? So the portrait is flattering, flattered perhaps. What an allegory: genius immortalizing talent!

But let us take a closer look. Flaubert's work is relentless. Everything about Larivière is positive. And what does he amount to? A nothing, worse, a negation.

So he is one of the greats of this world, a prince of science, a true physician, admired, dreaded, powerful, who is announced with fanfare and makes his entrance amid a round of applause. But when? at what moment in the book? When Charles Bovary is studying in Rouen? Not at all; rather when death has won, the very moment we are saying: "Science can do no more." I know, it was too late in any case; but for this very reason, if Flaubert had wanted to fill us with admiration, he would have had to summon his deus ex machina on any page but this one. He looks good, old Larivière—after all, prestigious physicians are in the business of curing people. But when he is called in for a consultation, what does he do? Makes a diagnosis. Impeccable, of course. And then he lambastes his colleague; the superior makes his appearance, proceeds to judge his inferior and condemn him without appeal, and the unhappy man is crushed. And immediately afterward the medical bigwig has only one concern—to make a quick getaway. There is, indeed, that little line full of innuendo which seems to have escaped the commentators: "Canivet, who did not care to have Mme Bovary die on his hands *either*." *Either*: someone else wanted to slip quietly away? The published text adds nothing. But in one of the manuscripts published by Pommier we find an indication which leaves no further doubt: "[Dr. Larivière] went out *on the pretext* of giving an order . . . *in reality* to return home." I know, the most conscientious physicians do this—if there is nothing left to try, why be saddled with the responsibilities of an inevitable death? And I recognize that these precautions are reasonable. Except that they are a bit shabby. It would be wrong, you say, to judge all practitioners on this basis? I don't say anything different—I know some who are able to devote themselves night and day to a terminally ill patient and save him in spite of the medical establishment. Flaubert, portraying his father, chose to show the doctor's boredom at this moment of precaution, not his devotion or effectiveness. An odd business: a great man makes a stunning entrance, blasts his colleague, and collapses in impotence and spiritual mediocrity. And then, did he have to take such a hearty lunch at Homais's immediately after his visit? What I mean is that physicians do not have to burden themselves with all their patients' miseries; their business is to cure, nothing more. For Larivière, death is a familiar occurrence—is a suicide going to make him lose his appetite? But if Flaubert wanted only to emphasize the *acquired* indifference with which physicians have to arm themselves in order to survive, did he have to do it at his father's *expense* and, moreover, without showing the other side? And why let us hear the rumors of the crowd who judge him "not very obliging"? Naturally, people who talk like that are greedy peasants and profiteers who would like a free consultation and feel slighted at not getting one. Still, from the beginning of the chapter, the physician from town has done nothing but refuse, shatter, disengage himself, and flee. We are *told* he is a luminary, but we do not feel it; and if we did, how absurd this Apollonian clarity would seem in a desperate work whose meaning is still, despite everything, that the only true world is darkness.

441

CONSTITUTION

Dr. Larivière is anything but a nocturnal being. He possesses that debonair majesty that comes with consciousness of great talent, fortune, and forty years of a hardworking and irreproachable life." Isn't he something of a pharisee? And certainly we feel that for Flaubert the calm consciousness of having great talent can only be the acceptance of mediocrity. As for genius, which is all that counts, it remains unaware of itself and dies despairing. The celebrated practitioner does not know that one must seek through suffering; so he cannot see past his nose. His is borrowed majesty, and the word "debonair" is not conclusive. From the beginning of the nineteenth century it had taken on a slightly ironic meaning, and Stendhal wrote in *Le Rouge et le noir*: "[they] are going to laugh at me for being debonair." For it to apply to Larivière, however, the word must be given a rather special meaning. His debonairness is not benevolence and is not defined in terms of the doctor's relations with other men. Otherwise, why wouldn't Gustave, who weighs his words carefully, speak of "generosity"? Rather, what is involved is confidence in his own powers and reasonable optimism about the course of events. Pleasantness of demeanor is there only to modify *majesty*; it disappears as soon as circumstances work against it. Furious at being called in too late, he crushes his colleague. Naked majesty passes judgment—Larivière is a man with *divine right*. Besides, his self-assurance is *also* based on wealth. Gustave, as we have already seen and shall see even more clearly, is hardly scornful of money. But the smugness of the well-heeled—see Dambreuse in *L'Education sentimentale*—he flatly condemns.

A hardworking and irreproachable life—perfect. In whose eyes? The word "irreproachable" does not come from Gustave's pen by accident; a pseudopositivity barely masks its real negativity: Achille-Cléophas was irreproachable, meaning that the people of Rouen had nothing to reproach him with. No faults, no vices, no scandals. But how could the younger son of the Flauberts cherish all these characters *at once*: the ridiculed husband who is lost, ruined, but transfigured by an infinite love; the woman spewing black vomit, with a black heart, who dies one of the damned; and the clever practitioner so easily content with his success, so proud of his virtues? Confronted by Emma, who is in agony and already one of the damned, the doctor embodies success and knowledge. But he is the one who is damaged by this comparison; he reveals himself as Flaubert's sworn adversary, the enemy who in the most varied forms appears in his work a hundred times. And in his life: Ernest passed his exams and Flaubert

442

failed his; Maxine DuCamp made a career in Paris; Musset, a facile poet, tasted the vulgar pleasure of being accepted by the Académie; and Achille, above all Achille the older brother, made money, gave dinners. Each of these men in turn had achieved professional success compared with Gustave, impotent, unknown, cloistered; and the chief of them all in terms of priority, Achille-Cléophas, whose death brought grief to his fellow citizens, was yanked from the grave and thrown into Emma's room so that the vanity of his triumphs should be revealed in the face of our infinite wreckage.

We have yet to discover why the younger Flaubert son turned his lord into an old buffoon. Why does he hold a grudge against his father? For cursing him, for preferring Achille? No doubt. But this is not what is in question here, at least not directly. Let us go back to the portrait of Larivière, which is both black and white. We have just seen his white garb, which clothes a rather insignificant man. Now we have his black one: the physician, we are told, knows "all" of life. For Gustave, to know *all* of life, to have a "complete presentiment" of it, is to know its fundamental horror. Emma too has discovered everything—her suicide is the conclusion and summation of her experience. This world belongs to the Devil, and no doubt Larivière is in his confidence. The proof: "He might have passed for a saint if the keenness of his intellect had not caused him to be feared as a demon." But how can you be convinced of the horror of living if you don't die of it? How can the majestic practitioner be in possessin of that knowlege and still be "debonair"? The answer is obvious: he *knows* the horror scientifically but does not *feel* it. The expression "keenness of intellect" alerts us simply because it first seems off the mark—what is it doing here? Is it really through "keenness" that we discover radical evil? Are demons "keen intellects"? Particularly if we want to understand Gustave's intentions in the works of his maturity, what he publishes is less important than what he deletes from his text before publication. Pommier offers us this variant: ". . . if the Voltairean keenness of his intellect . . ." etc. It is striking that the adjective has disappeared in the definitive version. Because it *said too much*. In fact Flaubert delighted in repeating that he loved Voltaire and detested Voltaireans. Did he really love Voltaire himself? In numerous passages in the correspondence he implies that he has mixed feelings about that writer. He is annoyed when people speak ill of him and equally annoyed when they praise him. The Romantics, to the extent that they were horrified by the revolutionary and dechristianized bourgeoisie, willingly took its ideologue Voltaire for a demon—let us

443

not forget the "hideous smile" Musset attributes to him. Hideous because, according to that child of the century, it epresses subversive "contentment" before the despair of the godless. It is a bad shepherd who causes suffering and does not suffer himself. When Flaubert wrote *Madame Bovary*, Romanticism was dead. However, its influence persisted for those who had felt it first in adolescence. And Gustave would always think of *Candide* as a masterpiece, just because of a certain pessimism which he himself radicalized. "Let us cultivate our gardens" becomes for him the very expression of his devotion to a reclusive life—the world is bad, flee from the real, take refuge in religion—that is, in literature. In this sense he loves Voltaire for the very reasons which impelled the Romantics to despise him. Gustave is not unaware, however, that the bitter philosophy expressed in *Candide* with such "keenness" and playfulness was not *lived* by its illustrious author, and that Voltaire did everything in this world *but* cultivate his garden. The cold-blooded, contagious despair one inspires in others with a sinister and sadistic gaiety without feeling it oneself—this is what he recognizes in Voltaire and the Voltaireans. They are demons, like Isambert, Monsieur Paul, Ernest, etc., because of the suffering they provoke but do not experience. Such a monster is Larivière, who takes pride in honors received, in wealth acquired, in his irreproachable habits, when he knows full well their frightful futility.

Now I ask, *in whose eyes* did Dr. Flaubert pass for a demon? His students—whom Gustave calls "disciples"—seem to have loved him; they respected his knowledge, and if they feared him it was rather for his sudden moods than for any diabolical penetration of their souls. He terrorized by his shouting, by his famous bursts of temper, and perhaps, on occasion, by those venomous words common to high-strung people when they are exasperated. As for his clientele, far from dreading his "keenness of intellect" they were enchanted by it. In liberal circles Voltaire was held in high esteem, he was their thinker; in his name the liberals condemned Romanticism, which celebrated the past and collaborated with the regime; they even went so far as to defend *Zaïre* against the new theater. Thus Achille-Cléophas reflected for the provincial bourgeoisie their own ideology, clearer and better elaborated; this sealed the understanding between the practitioner and his patients—they referred to the same bible and back to the same sacred texts behind it, to the same vision of the world. The chief surgeon could never have appeared a Satan to his rich clientele.

Nevertheless, Flaubert insists. It might be noted that Dr. Larivière seems rather incapable of inspiring love or friendship, but in any event the novelist is silent on this subject. On the other hand, he provides information liberally, obligingly, about the fears this demonic saint inspires: "His glance . . . dismembered every lie beneath all assertions and reticences." An earlier version added: "and let the fragments fall at your feet."

This might be Freud. But what need had Larivière for such penetration? I know that in 1830, even more than today, the physician had to fight with his patients; women refused auscultation, called constipation "the vapors"; there were even some doctors who, on the English model, would designate the site of illness by pointing to a doll. A doctor had to put up with this, make an intuitive diagnosis on the basis of external symptoms, press the client with questions, and make her give up her lies. I know that very well. Still, it doesn't take us very far. Besides, the men were cooperative and did not lie. And when the truth was falsified, it was neither so profound nor so hidden; people lied a little about organs, habits; drank more often, made love more often than they admitted. But the chief surgeon lacked the tools necessary to push the inquiry further. In short, he fathomed kidneys, not hearts. Except one: the heart of the little vassal who adored him. A demon: this word, dating back to childhood, betrays the bitterness and fears of the early years. This time it is not a question of the inadequacy, the inferiority, the relative-being that the admirable, unjustly just father granted him at the age of seven; now Gustave reproached his father for reading his son's soul like an open book. The dreams, wishes, and lies his scrutiny violated and dismembered belonged to Gustave. More than once he saw his inner life "fall in fragments at his feet." In an unpublished passage collected by Pommier we find this detail: "He is the man who makes more people blush than you can find in five districts." One meaning is obvious: women blushed when speaking to the physician about their bodies. But this is not worth mentioning; such modesty was peculiar to the period. The words will be more striking if we remember that long after the doctor's death, Gustave would blush to the roots of his hair under his mother's glacial eye—for she was the repository of paternal authority. But the great man's look sliced like a lancet, plunging into his son's eyes to dissect them. It was the *father's look*, sublimated, generalized, that Flaubert would later try to appropriate under the name of a "clinical" or "surgical eye."

445

We see the source of this bitterness. At table or in the evenings after supper, the medical director attended to his sons; and he seemed to know them much better than they knew themselves. But his nervousness, his sudden attacks of malice wounded Gustave all the more. Achille was spared or else bowed his head and quietly accepted the attacks; furthermore, as a boarder at school he was at the Hôtel-Dieu only twice a week. And then, he wasn't irritating; Gustave irritated his father and worried him (we have seen that Achille-Cléophas spied on his son); the conversation would go from understanding to irony, and from irony to sarcasm. The very word "sarcasm" figured for a moment in the portrait of Dr. Larivière and was then suppressed because it was too revealing; it is found, in fact, in *La Peste à Florence*—Cosme's "sarcasms" have made Garcia malicious. "I have provoked such outcries," Gustave would write to Louise; the father's bitter mockeries confirmed the little boy in the shameful feeling of his anomaly and marked him with a red-hot iron. *What* mockeries? The text is clear: Achille-Cléophas accused Gustave of *lying*. This is what we must try to interpret.

In the beginning, as we know, he did not fear the great man in his lord. From the moment he was capable of doing it, the child devoted himself to the cult of the progenitor; he was its priest and vestal. Let the reverend God be hard, exigent, dark, and often mute, so much the better. Gustave is a man of the Old Testament: the father's inexhaustible generosity lies in providing his younger son with a certain status by making himself a perpetual source of obligations. In a word, the family structure and Achille-Cléophas's imperious severity produced a child vassal. Yet he had to be accepted in his fundamental vassalage and given the means to ponder it; he had to be given a synthetic ideology which would justify the inferior's enthusiasm for his superior by revealing the experienced relationship of interiority that linked the part to the whole. During his first years, little Gustave believed that Achille-Cléophas shared Caroline's views, the religious faith that was so well adapted to the hierarchical structure of the Flaubert family, when in fact the philosophical practitioner merely tolerated it. When Gustave reached the age of seven, the veil was torn away: the progenitor had little to do with feudal antics; he made this known and the child was crushed—he imagined that his love was no longer wanted because he had lost favor. This wasn't at all the case. Certainly Dr. Flaubert laid his cards on the table at the moment of the Fall, just when Gustave understood his inadequacies. And I can allow that he was rather brutal, partly through irritation, with this offspring who did him no honor. In any event, this Moses was not fond of demonstrative behavior; we have seen that he was tender only with very young children. He must have found the little boy too obsequious. In the evening, when he hurried to the paternal armchair, Gustave must have had to endure certain Voltairean glances that made him lose face; he must have been ashamed of the kisses he wanted to give his father. We shall return to this later.

But what Achille-Cléophas rejected was *above all* an ideology. He had proceeded no differently with Achille nine years earlier; he may have been more polite with his older son, of whom he was already proud, but in any case, from the moment he thought the time was right he wanted to introduce his sons to bourgeois thought. When he was in an amiable mood and had the time, he did not hesitate, of that we can be sure, to express what he took for his ideas—on man, on nature, on religion—and what were, in fact, only part of the ideology of his time; if not, how could Gustave have admired the practitioner's "philosophy"? Overwhelming admiration: he saw in his father's rebuffs the practical applications of a true and frightful doctrine in whose name his progenitor refused him the right of vassalage and at the same time made his very essence his deepest lie. In order to understand the reception the younger of the Flaubert sons reserved for Achille-Cléophas's theories—according to him, the *truth*—we must temporarily take leave of Larivière and examine the chief surgeon's other incarnation. Gustave was seventeen years old in August 1839, when he finished *Les Funérailles du docteur Mathurin*. The great disillusionment that put an end to the golden age was still festering in his wounded heart and manifests itself almost in spite of the author.

The short narrative interrupts the autobiographical cycle. It is a philosophical tale in the style of those he was writing two years earlier. Mathurin is in his seventies, "solid in spite of his white hair and his bent back." "In a word," Gustave writes abruptly, "a hero." In spite of his age, the old man curiously resembles Dr. Larivière:

> He knew life . . . ; he plumbed the heart of man and there was no escaping the measure of his sagacious and penetrating eye. When he raised his head, lowered his eyelids, and looked at you out of the corner of his eye, smiling, you felt that a magnetic probe was entering your soul and prying into all its corners . . . ; through the clothing he saw the skin, the flesh beneath the epidermis, the marrow in the bone, and from this he exhumed all

447

those bloody fragments, the heart's corruption, and often discovered in healthy bodies a horrible gangrene.[1]

Other features contrast with these. We are told that he lived an "indolent life of the senses," which hardly corresponds to our idea of Dr. Flaubert. The author adds that his life was spent "without happiness or unhappiness, without effort, without passion, without virtue, those two millstones with double-edged blades." And this reminds us that Dr. Larivière practices virtue without believing in it, and Achille-Cléophas was virtuous by nature.

Yet in other respects this character must be recognized as an embodiment of Gustave himself. The synopsis alone, exhibited to us at the outset, in "close-up," is adequate proof: "Feeling he had grown old, Mathurin wanted to die, thinking rightly that an overripe grape has no flavor . . . ; the true motive of his resolution was that he was ill and that sooner or later he would have to leave the world here below. He preferred to anticipate death rather than to feel taken by it."

It will be noticed that Gustave offers two motives for Mathurin's decision; I shall not say that they are altogether mutually exclusive; but the second—which is particular and concrete—relegates the first to a level of superficial generality. Rather, the first is only a transplanting of stoic wisdom, whereas the second betrays Gustave's anguish. The fact is that since he had entered his seventeenth year, the family was once again on the alert; Dr. Flaubert was worried, and the young man himself, eight months after *Les Funérailles*, confides his anguish: he is afraid of dying. Yet we shall see in the present chapter the reasons why death—which inspired him with constant horror—never really frightened him. Let us say that he had the feeling of having arrived at a point of no return and of irresistibly approaching *something* which in his eyes could be only death. Gustave is not Gribouille—he never dreamed of killing himself to avoid death; what he sometimes considered in this period was a suicide arresting in time the irreversible process that was leading him toward the *unnamable*,[2] which he sensed as his most intimate possibility. But in 1839, and even in *Novembre*, he could scarcely formulate this threat for himself—

1. We shall also note that the author gives Mathurin his "disciples" and that he designates Achille-Cléophas's students by the same name.
2. This process is the acceleration of the preneurotic state which was completed by the neurotic explosion at Pont-l'Evêque. We shall discuss this at length in a later section of this work.

the simple indication that his life in itself would change through a calamitous attack—other than as a conviction of premature demise. In fact, his Mathurin is not only an *old man* (old age was a way of surviving his life which was not displeasing to Flaubert, at least at this time, since in *Mémoires d'un fou* the child imagines being at the age of retirement when he can withdraw from the world and all its passions); he is also ill. Having contracted a lingering pleurisy the week before, and knowing his state, he decides to hasten his destiny and rid himself of life through indigestion. Is this a kind of suicide? Hardly—where is the act? And where is his weapon? He kills himself without pistol or poison—no hemlock for this Socrates; he will hasten his last moment by overindulging in the things of this world. Alcohol is toxic, true, but until now Mathurin "knew how" to eat and drink. He stuffs himself and gets drunk on this particular night in order to demonstrate by his grotesque end that the good can be murderous. In other words, a choice must be made between abject temperance, the necessary condition for longevity, and the infinite desire for all, which is killing. This theme is found again in *Novembre*: an adolescent who dies the victim of ungratified passions. An old man who succumbs to the weight of years is no better and no worse, a cowardly mean-spirited scatterbrain. Mathurin's death is certainly no accident—he took suspicious liberties with his health. At the last moment, however, he is transported; suddenly "in death he had a certain grandeur." We recognize Gustave in this: to act, for him, is to suffer willingly. And then, in a sense this suicide is a summation; by abandoning himself to pleurisy, he might live three days more, but who knows? In the midst of fever he could fall from coma into nothingness. In one night of drunkenness this Socrates without his hemlock reviews his entire life and experience—the "disciples" are there to receive his knowledge and transmit it. His jesting interrogation—"since I am going to die, am I going to kill myself?"—will find its definitive form in *Novembre*: since I shall not escape the destiny I hate without a humiliating metamorphosis, isn't it better to "call it quits" with a bullet? It's not as clear a this, of course, but the outline is visible: Mathurin must follow to the end a strict development, every moment of which is foreseen, or make a clean break by killing himself. The specific aim of annihilation through suicide is a *recuperation in extremis*.

What is Achille-Cléophas doing here in this guise? How did he slip in? I answer, first of all, that Gustave links him directly to evil: the father began by giving his younger son's troubles an objective existence, if only by letting him see in his anxiety that he verified them.

From this point of view, religious fear and resentment ensure that the black lord becomes for his son the synthetic unity of his objectified troubles, in short, the malady itself. Gustave can internalize its symptoms—which he does not know but believes he knows about, quite wrongly—only if these are known by Achille-Cléophas yet do not attract the scrutiny that diagnoses and gives meaning to what the young man confusedly feels. The father will be present in his experienced dislocation as the will that has discovered and perhaps invented it, as the *other* face and hidden name of the evil which has no name.

Suddenly the physician is transformed into the patient; the alien subject becomes the intimate object, the occupant is imprisoned. Dreaming of his own suicide, Flaubert freely sets about recounting the last future moments of Dr. Flaubert; he is only following his inclinations, since *the death of the father* is one of the fantasies he most willingly embraces. Let us note that this ritual murder is also, from a certain angle, an attempt at identification: father and son, sewn into the same skin, die together. An aborted attempt; the identification is barely sketched out when it breaks apart and produces a doubling. The character successively realizes its contradictory components, first the father then the son. Mathurin, to begin with, shares that equilibrium that comes both from reason and from mediocrity. He is one of those "wise men who linger over their food and who in the end, at dessert, when some are sleeping and others are already drunk . . . finally drink the most exquisite wines, taste the ripest fruits, slowly savor the last bouts of the orgy . . . and then die." In sum, he has economized his whole life in order to enjoy existence in his last moments. This calculated temperance, this calm epicureanism does not even disappear at the onset of drunkenness: "At first it was a calm, logical drunkenness, a drunkenness which was affable and leisurely."

After the first few bottles, Mathurin's soul is still described as "a goatskin full of liquor and happiness." Affable yet serious statements suit this intoxication: "After all, I have lived, why not die? Life is a river, mine has run through fields full of flowers . . . *adieu*, evening breezes . . . life is a banquet," etc. Considered and banal comparisons which are meant to express the commonplace, an old man's acceptance of death after a fulfilling life. Is he going to die, then? We would say so. At this point in the narrative, in fact, Flaubert writes—still the "close-up"—these lines, which could pass for the conclusion: "Before dying he plunged into a bath of fine wine, bathed his heart in a beatitude which has no name, and his soul went straight to the Lord like a goatskin full of liquor and happiness."

What then? Life might be good? In this well-made world, should he suffer to avoid perils, rein in his passions in order to gather the golden fruits of autumn? This hardly resembles what Gustave thought and felt at the time, and what he would think and feel all his life, or even what he wrote at the beginning of the narrative; let us recall that Mathurin "saw . . . the heart's corruption and often discovered in healthy bodies a horrible gangrene." The ambiguity of the last phrase reeks of bitterness. Do the bodies in question only *seem healthy*? In that case, everything is rotten despite appearances. Were they truly healthy? In that case the "sagacious eye" of the good doctor *infects* them with the gangrene he claims to discover. One thing indeed is indisputable: the gangrene *exists*. Gustave is telling his father: "I know, my soul seemed pure, but you, reverend lord, discovered the radical evil that was hidden inside," and at the same time: "I was pure, and it was your demonic look that made me wicked by assuming in advance and on principle that I was." In any event, for Mathurin the universe is rotten—how could he take pleasure in it, even at the moment of death? The author adds in the same passage, moreover, that he lived "without happiness or unhappiness, without effort, without passion, and without virtue." This is all one could wish for in the realm of Satan. In sum, Mathurin uses his knowledge of the heart in order to impose a scientific self-control. The result has certainly not been to make the river of life run "through fields full of flowers" as he claims after his first libations. At the most, he has managed in the course of his long existence to maintain in himself that pure emptiness, the *ataraxia* of the ancients. This doesn't sound like Achille-Cléophas, who was gloomy, irritable, and recriminatory; however, he must certainly have thought and told his children that inner detachment represents the sole possible perfection. Not that he desired it for himself, passionate researcher that he was. But utilitarianism—his only ethic—was based on sensationalism, which always came back to Epicurus, like a horse to its stable. Above all, we find here once more one of Gustave's dreams, the dream of no more suffering. Suffering, according to him, being the very flavor of life, he seriously imagined only two ways of avoiding it: the first, which is contemptible, is to stay on the surface of the self; the second, or precocious aging, is to suffer so much that one can suffer no more. He adds a third solution: knowledge of causes and the scientific regulation of the self. This conception seems to me a vestige of his early childhood. For a long time the little boy trusted in his father, convinced that the eye so quick to dissect souls knew how to scrutinize the self as well. At the time of *Funérailles* the idea disturbed him, he toyed with it without seriously believing in it. Or rather, it is a sign of his astonishment: how is it conceivable that in spite of his diabolical powers of penetration, which discover evil everywhere and even in himself, Achille-Cléophas was not unhappier? Of course he had his moods, he shouted and sometimes went so far as to shed tears. But these surface disturbances did not prevent him from leading a most pleasant life. And the father's truth, in his younger son's eyes, is the debonair majesty of Dr. Larivière. In *Les Funérailles*, Gustave is assuredly describing one of Achille-Cléophas's usual attitudes, which shocks him deeply: when the paterfamilias raises his head and looks at his son obliquely (and up and down) through half-shut eyes, Gustave feels that a magnetic probe is entering his soul *necessarily* to find its rottenness, or to put it there if none is present. Yet, while this demon sees the evil at the bottom of his son's heart, he *smiles*, the monster—this is the shocking thing. Does the philosophical practitioner enjoy inhaling the stench of corpses? Does he enjoy discovering in this son he has cursed the rigorous effects of his curse? Or else, as an insensitive father, is he pleased to find in the child's tortured heart confirmation of a hypothesis, or more generally of his philosophy? Gustave feels something of all this. But when he wrote *Les Funérailles*, he seemed chiefly struck by his father's insensibility. We shall note, indeed, that Mathurin lives "without passion"—he thus lacks the passion for knowledge which to a certain extent could serve him as an excuse. This strange character is a devil in spirit; in life, he is a small-minded, timorous man who always spares himself. The young man avenges the child martyr and takes credit for scorning his executioner. Could Monsieur Paul be concealed behind Mathurin? Along with the shock there is an insoluble epistemological problem: Where does Mathurin's knowledge come from? How did he acquire it? Gustave promises to inform us in a lengthy book of which *Les Funérailles* can only be the conclusion. But this is concealing his difficulty. He takes as his premise that experience is the basis of knowledge. But if this is the case, how can anyone become wise without having been foolish? He *will give* the answer in *Madame Bovary:* "[Larivière] was like an old priest entrusted with domestic secrets." But he knew this answer already when he depicted Dr. Mathurin. And he found it pitiful; his father knew the repertoire of follies, passions, and pains by heart, having studied them *in others*. To which Gustave implicitly objects that one can never understand madmen without having been mad oneself; without the personal experience that can only lead to despair, one can grasp only the outlines, and while one can attempt a classification from the outside, the "lived reality" will escape.

This then is Mathurin: the *knowledge* of evil but not the evil of living. A skeptic, in sum; he believes neither in God nor in the Devil nor, above all, in fine sentiments. And here he is, grown old, dulled, an overripe grape that has lost its flavor—a sad end for a Voltairean. And yet what if, before dying, he were to internalize and recapitulate the experiences of others? If he were suddenly to make them his own? The powder keg would explode, the skeptic would burst and become a "hero" in Gustave's heart.

Abruptly, everything is transformed in effect by the doctor's unforeseen mutation:

The smoke from their pipes[3] rose to the ceiling and spread in rising blue clouds; one could hear the clinking of their glasses and their words; the wine fell to the ground, they swore, they snickered; something horrible was about to happen, they were going to attack each other. But there was nothing to fear, instead they attacked a fat chicken and truffles, which escaped from their red lips and rolled onto the floor.

Mathurin's discourse changes—he laughs; he becomes vociferous. Gustave wants to terrify us by the irreverence of the dying old man; if he does not succeed it is because his cynicism is reduced to commonplaces, just like the elegant stoicism of the previous pages. In any case, the intention is clear. Listen to this:

That last night something monstrous and magnificent happened between the three men. If you could have seen them exhaust everything, tarnish everything . . . ; everything passed before them and was greeted with grotesque laughter and a fearful grimace. Metaphysics was treated in depth in the space of a quarter of an hour, and morality by getting drunk on a dozen glasses of wine. And why not? If I shock you, don't run away, I am only reporting the facts.

This story—like *Mémoires d'un fou*—is dedicated to Alfred; it was with Alfred that he engaged every Thursday in these exhaustive and pitiless reviews in which nothing was spared. As for the wine, Gus-

3. This Socrates dies amid his disciples.

tave scarcely indulged, but Alfred got dead drunk, literally—he drank in order to destroy himself, as we shall see. These two indications are enough for us; until this point, the role of Mathurin was played by the father; now the son interprets it. "Having become a cynic, he would embrace cynicism with all his might, he plunged into it and died in the last spasm of his sublime orgy." By the words "Having become a cynic," Gustave is telling us that the metamorphosis has a certain decision as its object: Mathurin's diabolical knowledge, bearing its final fruits, saves him from an ignobly modest death. It is not as though the approach of his last moments has taught him nothing— it is *totalizing*; but for Gustave, totalization cannot be realized without a willful cynicism, exposing the man's damnation and his nothingness. Pleurisy determines that the modest doctor shall become what he was—a devil:

> The priest entered, Mathurin threw [a decanter] at his head, dirtied his white surplice, overturned the chalice, frightened the choirboy, took another, and emptied it into his mouth, howling like a wild beast; he twisted his body like a snake, he turned, cried out, chewed his sheets, digging his nails into the wooden bedstead.

After this paroxysm, of course, he calms down—we are told he dies quietly. Still, what has just been described is Satan under a shower of holy water. In other words, Dr. Flaubert, having become a cynic, passes from scientism to baseness, and resuming at last his vaunted experience, he becomes while dying a "statue of derision." What satisfaction for Gustave's bitter soul: not only does he murder his father but he forces him in the bargain to die in the guise of the Garçon. Mathurin sacrifices himself at Yuk, stronger than death. But this is going too far—a moment before, the father was eclipsed, and the son, the sacrificer, took the place of the victim. Achille-Cléophas's Voltairean skepticism did not prevent him from enjoying universal esteem; the son, by assuming this skepticism in suffering and hatred, transforms it into a shocking cynicism. The slightly suspect austerity of the skeptic finds its truth in the cynic's mocking despair. Intoxicate Achille-Cléophas and you will find Gustave.

The unsuccessful identification (there are unquestionably two Mathurins) is therefore transformed into *filiation*. Yet one cannot say whether the father has become the son or has engendered him. The only certainty is that the son, in Gustave's eyes, *is* the father, but radicalized. This strange metamorphosis clearly marks the young man's attitude toward his father's scientism. For the younger son, the power to dissect bodies and souls is an object of horror and respect—Gustave covets the medical director's experience.[4] At the same time he perceives it as a viral infection, the very cause of his anomaly, the origin of his "complete presentiment of life"; his father *makes* knowledge, Gustave *suffers* it, which is a way of being frustrated by it—he is marked by it unwittingly, like the condemned in Kafka's *Penal Colony*. All at once, while admiring this murderous knowledge, he perceives at the height of his unhappiness that his father is not worth it: how can he remain temperate, seriously fulfill his professional obligations, practice virtue without believing in it, and make such considered investments? With Gustave, at least, experience is all-consuming—suffering, universal mockery, and death. We can ascertain, at the end of this analysis, Gustave's singular situation. The paterfamilias does not consider mechanism a *pessimistic* ideology; it is the thinking of his class, a way of conceiving of the world and society, a means to success; scientism is not a kind of skepticism, quite the contrary, it is a theory of truth—this is how Achille looks at it. But the frustrated younger son sees in it a desperate cynicism, the rejection of all value, all religious consolation; far from rejecting the paternal knowledge which has disabused him too soon of his illusions, Gustave wants to realize that knowledge, push it to its logical conclusion, radicalize it. The theory of truth becomes the theory of despair. Atheistic mechanism, which was *felt*—rather than considered—by a young prophet haunted by his destiny, loses its essential character, which is to describe the world from the outside, and becomes Satan's latest trick. For Gustave it was the theory of his destiny: the Devil purposely created a religious soul who aspires to the infinite, to ecstasies, to spiritual heights, in order to cast him into a universe without values, without God. According to this scheme, internalized mechanism—contradicted by instinct, by the need for belief, that is, for escape from exteriority through an internal bond with the infinite—seemed to him at once his fundamental frustration and the scientific explanation of all frustration. Once more he had lost in advance, since he passionately unified an ideology which through the atomization of man and the cosmos claimed to expose our illusions and free us from our passions. We shall see the role played by resentment and negative intention in this business; it is hardly in all

---

4. This, we shall see, is the meaning of an adolescent story, *L'Anneau du prieur*. The word *experience* (taken in the sense of empirical knowledge) appears in *Novembre*.

innocence that Gustave deflects mechanism from its official path in order to turn it into the gospel of the Devil. But we know enough about it now to attempt to reconstruct the evolution of this falsified thought and its impact on the experience which borrowed and modified it in order to produce an ideological justification for it.

B. Progressive Synthesis

Scientism

Experience, experience alone—everything flows from it, everything returns to it. This was Dr. Flaubert's act of faith, which he imposed on his sons. Gustave did not doubt for a moment that his father was a *man of experience*. Very early he envied him his knowledge. Hence a new misunderstanding arose which the father would never perceive but which would always weigh heavily on the son.

Achille-Cléophas *observes*. He dissects zealously, but dissection is often only a way of taking inventory: one establishes the geographical map of the human body; after death one constructs the verbal process of modifications that the illness contributes. Dr. Flaubert also gathers information from accidents which happen in the course of certain surgical interventions—he classifies facts, risks certain interpretations which remain untested for lack of being verified by experimentation. From this point of view, his "Memoir on Accidents Caused by the Reduction of Dislocations" fully merits its title, provided we change "memoir" to "memories" or "recollections." This is explained first of all by the rudimentary state of techniques and instruments, but also and more particularly by the impossibility of working on living bodies. The time for "experimental medicine" had not yet come; it was necessary to rely on illness to bring about on its own the experimental systems to which the physician could only be a passive witness. But, as we have seen, empiricism's humble "submission to facts" concealed the most arrogant intellectualism. Leaning on a collection of symptoms, the man of science had to pursue his analysis to the point at which he could base universal knowledge on a finite and rigorous system of analytic truths. Thus an ambitious *logic* is discovered as the reverse of submission to apprehendable givens—mental passivity is the principle posed to justify the activity of the intelligence. Achille-Cléophas is eminently active; in other words, analytic decomposition or, if you will, the work of the lancet cannot be done unless the various moments in the process are sustained and linked by the unity of a project, of a piece of research, and even of an idea to be verified—analysis is in itself a synthetic enterprise. But at the time, this aspect of the maneuver was not recognized, the object alone was of interest, the need to reduce it to its basic elements. For the chief surgeon, of course, decomposition had to be followed sooner or later by "recomposition." But this practitioner, heir to the eighteenth century, went no further than Condillac, who wrote:[5] "In effect, should I wish to know a machine, I would decompose it in order to know each part separately. When I had an exact idea of each and the knowledge that I might put all the parts back in the same order, then I could perfectly conceptualize this machine because I would have decomposed it and recomposed it again." Everything depends, of course, on what is meant by "order." It is worth noting, however, that a recomposed machine is not a machine in *running order*—energy is required to set it in motion. It took Lavoisier, beginning with the elements, to succeed in recomposing water. But the good abbé foresaw everything: in the absence of things themselves, we shall recompose the order of signs in the conventional language that we shall have invented for the purpose. The consequence of an ideology that makes movement and energy disappear is that *as far as knowledge is concerned*, there is no difference between a machine at rest and the same machine at work. More accurately, the truth of the second lies in the first. A conception which, applied to life, is the equivalent of making death the truth of life. Achille-Cléophas saw nothing untoward in this. He dissected a cadaver, and the recomposition was done on the anatomy charts; after being cut open, the body was stitched up again, or rather the replacement of organs was represented by images "in the same order" in which they had been found; this was knowledge, exact knowledge of the human machine. It is clear today that this kind of putting back in order cannot account for functioning organs, namely for their role in the structural unity of a living organism. But Achille-Cléophas was among those who fought, quite rightly, against organicism and who held this doctrine to be a bastardized perpetuation of religious thought. The physician knew very well that life differed from nonlife and that the difference had to be taken into account. But since the truth of phenomena, whatever they might be, resided in *mechanism* anyway, the opposition between the living and the inanimate did not seem to him fundamental; the *synthetic* truth of our life, in his eyes, was that the synthesis is only illusory or verbal. Following Condillac

---

5. *Logique et langue des calculs.*

and La Mettrie, he extended to the human race the Cartesian idea of the animal-machine.

Gustave knew very early that his father dissected human bodies; when the young boy played with his sister in a small garden behind the left wing of the hospital, all he had to do was hoist himself up on the grillwork of the windows to see the cadavers. If the young son of a surgeon today should witness his father's work, he would place these procedures—directly or indirectly—in a therapeutic perspective. The dead save the living—the cadaver on the marble table has an immediately utilitarian aspect. A child can be made to understand this; death is in the hands of men because men are in the hands of death. And it is becoming—without ceasing to be the absolute limit and hence a given of nature—less *natural* every day. In this perspective, it can preserve its subjective horror in a young boy's eyes (from the earliest years he can feel anguish at the idea of his future annihilation), but objectively it is less frightening; repulsive as it is, the cadaver is a means of the living. The younger son of a surgeon in the middle of our century would be enthusiastic about heart transplants.

In the fragmented France of 1830, when the recruitment of physicians had slackened, the corpses little Gustave saw were already objects of scientific knowledge. But it was a passive knowledge, which analyzed but did not recompose, an impotent science which wanted to know but did not know how to cure. It claimed, of course, to know in order to cure. But it knew that it knew nothing, and that it would have to observe corpses for a long time to come without learning the means to prolong life. And since this knowledge could only rarely be practical, the Flaubert children vaguely sensed the almost disinterested character of the paternal investigations. The country was dozing and took traditional attitudes toward the great problems of the human condition, and it was precisely these attitudes—in particular the attitude of laissez-faire—that the medical director's family assumed, thanks to him. Thus for the two children playing in the garden, death, unbearable yet familiar, seemed above all *natural*. It comes when it comes and will not give an inch. Gustave thought that his father studied death the way a botanist studies a species. Later, when we read his letters, his works, we never see him conceive of medicine as a *fight for life*; he considers it a science rather than an art. It is the surgeon's eye he admires, not his hands. He vaunts his father's and Larivière's theoretical knowledge, their virtues, but not the cures they have worked. Charles Bovary, who fails so miserably when he operates on the club foot, could certainly be called an ignoramus. The same goes for Canivet, who makes a mistaken diagnosis. But the pharmacist Homais, whose intelligence Thibaudet emphasizes, is scarcely more brilliant—unable to cure the blind man, he drives him away. Larivière, Canivet, Bovary, Homais—this is the "medical establishment" of 1830; some kill, others let their patients die, the biggest ones take off to avoid being compromised. Referring back in the correspondence to Flaubert's imprecations against physicians, we understand his deep conviction that medicine does not cure; he believed this is in part because medicine was still in its infancy, but also, and more important, because it tackled the natural limit of man, his unsurpassable destiny. And this feeling—which he would preserve all his life—simply reflects the attitude of the still peasant bourgeoisie from which he came. Death is *suffered*; it is—partially—an object of knowledge; it offers itself as an analysis in the etymological sense of the word since it suppresses the living connections between organs and facilitates analytic—namely *anatomical*—knowledge of the human body. Dr. Flaubert, at least, thought that life, such as it is, must one day be the object of a body of knowledge which would reveal—behind an illusory organic unity—the complex of moving mechanical systems which are all governed from without. The child does not go so far— he believes what he sees. If death seems to him the truth of life, this is not only a conviction of the abstract necessity that makes all men mortals; for him, the cadaver represents the permanent and concrete reality of the living body. He very early became familiar with drawings and anatomy charts that reproduced the organs more dead than in nature—*bathed in their own blood*. That is what people are like too— unsuspecting cadavers. Not future cadavers; *today, this minute*; he is sure he carries his own inside his skin. Of course this is more a feeling than an idea—magical thinking, if you will, which he would never discard. The primary reason for it was his discovery of the autopsy, the shock of seeing his father bent over a corpse, determined to wrest from it the fundamental secret of man. But the child is his accomplice; submitting to analytic rationalism without understanding it, he does not realize that the paternal scalpel is seeking to lay bare the subtlest movements of a precise and complex machine, or that Achille-Cléophas considers exteriority the basic status of matter, whether animate or inanimate. Passively constituted, Gustave is sensitive only to the obscene resignation of the cadavers which seems to reflect his own passivity. He acts, when he is obliged to, he knows the proper way to use a fork, a spoon, he dresses himself; but beneath these commanded activities he has long sensed his inertia, his indifference to everything that is not a bitter contemplation, his profound absenteeism; this is the skull beneath the skin. Fascinated by the stinking matter made in his image, he discovers in it a *lesser-being* which has the double, contradictory character of being the mockery of beauty, youth, human dignity, and at the same time the repository of *truth*. The cadaver horrifies him when it crawls with *posthumous* life, when decomposition manifests itself as an inner power of *self*-decomposition. But what does the negative unity of its putrescence reflect if not the "anthumous" life Gustave is enduring now? Isn't this too a kind of decomposition? Not only in the abstract and because it seems an irreversible process of involution, but directly, concretely, because he is assimilating the feverish enchantment of matter at this moment—and which is producing *him himself*—to the *alien activity* which from the moment of burial pursues the dead. In the base chemistries of his digestion, in the stench of his excrement, in his fetid breath and perspiration, in the blood that flows under his skin, in his juices, in the pus which for no apparent reason gathers in reddened swellings, yellow abcesses, carbuncles, phlegm, the spurting liquefaction of his flesh, isn't he in his lifetime the corpse he will be *post mortem*? There are two lives, and Gustave will submit to them one after the other; though separated by a break, they are both directed toward his annihilation: one took him in his mother's belly and torments him through the irresistible process of aging; the other will take him on his deathbed and corrode him until he returns at last to the pure inertia of inorganic matter.

We find here for the first time the irrational but indissoluble connection between Gustave's *fatum* and his father's mechanism. If truth lies in the second, then the curse of Adam is *the organic*. The eternal Father and the paterfamilias have mysteriously produced a combination of molecules and infused it with a specious interiority expressly so that it should decompose itself, so that once again, through the worst sufferings, it should become that mechanical system of atoms—governed by the law of exteriority—which it never ceased to be *underneath*. Achille-Cléophas explained to his son that life is a complex machine and that analysis sooner or later will reduce it to its elements; and the child understood that he is a piece of cursed matter, an artificial assemblage of atoms which only the ill-will of a black lord keeps bound together, just enough so that its dispersal will be progressive. The alter ego, the miserable unity of diverse elements, cannot desire or know organic life. It endures it. Mysterious metabolisms continually remind it of the shadow side of its existence by indicating through pains or needs other demands which, gently at first but irresistibly, it is obliged to gratify, though the gratification, far from restoring the integrity of the organism, only hastens its decline. This is the source—in part—of Flaubert's horror of natural needs; for him, eating is feeding his corpse in conformity with the *alien-will* and against his own. This strange alteration of scientistic mechanism suits his constitution to perfection; the dynamic and practical aspect of biological organization escapes him—he lives his experience as a flow of passive syntheses, rustlings, slidings, gradually diminishing repetitions, senescence. But it must be recognized too that this doctrine, which is never made explicit—it will come to light quite suddenly— is quietly wrought by his resentment. Somehow or other Gustave has given an ideological structure to his belief in the curse of Adam. At the same time he curses his father as both creator (of the enchanted dead) and analyst—the action of the scalpel and the process of natural decomposition are one and the same thing; hadn't the paterfamilias created Gustave in order to observe his decay in life and in death and to dissect him at his ease? Analysis does not kill since we are all the unconscious stillborns of being, but before reducing the organism to the purity of its inorganic components it makes putrefying juices squirt out everywhere. This would become a general rule for Gustave: the object of knowledge stinks.

The consequence of this, curiously, is that he never had a great fear of dying. What should he fear since it is *already done*? There is the fever that takes hold of the dead, that *danse macabre* that is life; and then the fever subsides, the imposture is unmasked, lunatic matter casts off its illusions and recovers its natural inertia. What secured Gustave against the immediate anguish of mortality was what I shall call his ideological alienation. The chief surgeon's authority was such that his younger son became accustomed to considering experience, his own consciousness of himself, the cogito, nothing but inessential appearance, and to placing his essence in his status as a clinical object. Science, rooted in him at an early age, was necessarily right and not his inner experience, just as the philosopher-practitioner was right and he was not. It is evident why I speak here of alienation—he alienates or gives up his obscure feeling for existence in favor of the absolute Other's, the paterfamilias's objective knowledge of other cadavers; it follows that he is, for himself and immediately, dead as other. Or, if you like, his alter ego presents itself to him as the late Gustave Flaubert, which is a mythic way of experiencing his occupation by the black lord who is turning him to stone.

But if he claims the myth as his own and radicalizes it—by the tactic earlier described as gliding—it is because this serves his purpose. He grabs hold of death and takes it for supreme knowledge. This is the name he would give it in the *Saint Antoine* of 1849. Not that he believes in the immortality of the soul; on the contrary, he is convinced for good or ill that he is going to return to nothingness. The illogic here is strikingly apparent: if nothingness awaits us, absolute knowledge will be achieved by no one. But in the first instance this sophism is concealed, in the same *Saint Antoine*, by an alternative which can be summarized as follows: "Either there is *something* after you and you must annihilate yourself to know absolute truth, or there is nothing and therefore death is absolute all the same; by choosing self-destruction you are adopting the point of view of nothingness." But we must go beyond appearances; the father's ideology, misunderstood, entirely justifies Gustave's resentment, and he exploits it thoroughly—the point of view of nothingness is his bitterness and frustration which have made him adopt it. Beneath this purely philosophical form is an abstract perspective; *the point of view of death* is much better: first, it is guaranteed by the visible remains on the marble slab; and second, it allows the human race to be killed off at the wink of an eye, or an enchanted cadaver to be discovered in every single person. We shall see later how this point of view, which at first seems to Gustave that of the scientist, gradually becomes that of the artist. For the moment, death's superiority over nothingness, of which it is only a particular expression, dictates for Flaubert that as long as the human body it has just struck continues to exist, even putrefied, nothingness remains within it like a residue, a mournful consciousness of nonbeing. It is in this way, finally, that nonknowledge becomes knowledge—due to those vacant and festering eyes that know their own absence and embrace the whole of being with their still living nonregard. Cadavers suffer. This isn't of course a *speakable* thought—still, Gustave believes it.

What obsesses him about cadavers is that they place things at issue. They denounce our foolish species, which has the insanity to undertake what it is incapable of accomplishing. As a schoolboy, he and his comrades would amuse themselves by dressing up stolen skeletons, putting lights inside the skulls, and parading with them through the streets. As an adolescent, he would examine his body-object in mirrors until he was stupefied. He claims he was unable to shave without laughing—we shall have occasion to return to the question of Flaubert's relation to his own image. For the moment I want simply to point out that he delighted in the stupidity of his enterprise: his hair would survive him, it would still grow in his coffin when he was already stinking; what good was it to be rid of it now? Sadistic laughter: by mocking himself, Gustave takes his revenge on all men, at any rate on all of them who shave and through them on all those who dare to *undertake*, whatever their proposed objective. But the fascination of the morgue[6] or the dissecting table must also be seen as an expression of his masochism. We have shown in a preceding chapter that the young man felt dominated by others, incapable of tearing himself away from their powerful grasp, and that death appeared to him a radicalization of his impotence—the cadaver is the Other's thing; we have seen him bent over the remains of his heroes, delivering them defenseless to their executioners—hell goes on *post mortem*. Medical students get hold of Marguerite's body, they strip it and cut it into little pieces; isn't this obscene flesh, cut open and carved up so carefully, a reminder of his early history? Isn't it like the passive consent of the infant fashioned by his mother's severe, exacting hands? Of course this doesn't involve an actual memory; however, the students *unmake* passivity with as much solicitude and indifference as Caroline mustered to *make* her younger son. And this fable's primary meaning is: my father will dissect me, he dissects me in other bodies every day. So what? Lucretius would say, you will no longer be there. But Gustave's magical thinking resists this somewhat limited rationalization. Suffering and mockery must be internalized—death is a horrible birth that must be *lived*. We have seen how by a strange osmosis his *living* body is penetrated by the death of others; inversely, it lends a larval life to bodies that life has abandoned, and first of all to his own future remains. In order for his damnation to succeed, the damned soul must retain some kind of sensibility in that heap of shadows he will one day be and which his survivors are going to handle. The sadism and masochism of resentment, horror and fascination, malice—all these themes are brought together in a passage from *Agonies*, a work finished on 20 April 1838—Gustave was sixteen—and dedicated to Alfred.

They exhumed a cadaver, they transported the pieces of an illustrious man to another place. . . . This spectacle sickened us, a young man fainted. . . . Where had this illustrious man gone? Where were his glory, his virtues, his name? The illustrious man

6. As a student Gustave spent many hours there.

463

was something foul, *undefined*,[7] hideous, something that spread a stench, something sickening to behold. . . . His glory? You see, he was treated like a worthless dog, for all these men had come there out of curiosity . . . impelled by the feeling that makes one man laugh at another's torment.

The illustrious man is not Gustave. Not at first, in any event. The words the young author employs to describe him indicate a hostility on principle; the man is "illustrious" *for the crowd*, he is a benefactor, a *philanthropist*, an "optimistic man of science"—the enemy. We might be inclined to doubt it, but the single word "virtue" ought to convince us, knowing what the malicious boy thinks of people who are virtuous "without believing in it" or "by nature"—these are the "Larivières," the provincial surgeons who sometimes deign to treat the poor for nothing. Flaubert does not expressly intend to portray his father but, rather, the category of which Achille-Cléophas was merely one representative; by a trick frequently found in Gustave's work, the parricidal intention is concealed from itself by the movement of universalization. On this level it is clear that Gustave is *sadistic*—the Other is the victim of his resentment. But a single word is all it takes for the father to become the son as well, by an abridgment of the process of filiation which would be developed in *Les Funérailles*. The younger son aspires only to the *glory* that would compensate for his family's contempt and would condemn them retroactively; we shall soon see that for him there is all the difference in the world between the *illustrious*, who are legion; the mediocre, the "haves," who die as they have lived, tranquilized; and the great and superior damned, who will become *glorious* only through their capacity to suffer. So the son, at first a witness "impelled by the feeling that makes one man laugh at another's torment," is suddenly incarnate in the cadaver himself, and the laughter is abruptly turned against him; he hears it from the bottom of his violated grave. He used to say to his progenitor: What good is your reputation, you are carrion; now he says to himself: Even glory is no salvation; after my death I shall be prey to vultures. He passes from the body of the Other to his own body-for-others.

But what is most striking in this curious text is the survival of death precisely in the process of decomposition. He is not saying, "The illustrious man *had become* something foul," which would presuppose an irreversible passage from one state to another but would also allow—which Gustave plainly rejects—that the putrefying cadaver no

7. Flaubert's italics.

longer has anything in common with the magnificent doctor who *no longer exists*. Let us read: "The illustrious man *was* something foul, *undefined* . . . sickening to behold." Certainly Gustave says "something" and not "someone." But the use of this form of the predicate marks the identification of the living with the dead. This *someone* has always been *something*, and for this reason that *something* still remains *someone*. Observe, too, how the young author catches his quarry; he pretends to be looking for the great man, as if he were playing hide and seek: "Where is he? Where is he?—there he is!" He is the one we were looking for, and we have found him. In fact he is living—his cadaver is swarming with life in the liquefying flesh. More curious still, in this decomposing organism there is a kind of "slave-will" which assumes its own stench, since we are told: "It was something *sickening* to behold." Here again we find Marguerite guilty of her ugliness. And this poor man on the way to reification preserves enough sensibility to suffer: "He was treated like a worthless dog," and the curious have come to laugh at his "torment." When, after death, the decay hidden beneath our often pleasing envelope (recall Adèle—a gravedigger faints when she is unearthed) bursts to light and reveals what we are, we submit to this objective misfortune supine, powerless, probed by the surgical scrutiny of others like a kind of *torture*. The probing of the worms, the running flesh, the fetid syrups that hollow the eyes, the internal organs now visible and putrefying—such are the tortures inflicted on the illustrious dead. And the sadistic contempt, the laughter of the crowd are also part of the ill treatment. But would they be if no one were to suffer? It seems that objective evil is internalized in these poor leavings in the form of an impersonal power of suffering, their last unity before the final dispersal.

At this juncture we perceive that the mechanistic materialism of Achille-Cléophas is doubled in Gustave by a fetishism which tries to correct it. The process of fetishization resembles what Marx calls "the fetishization of the commodity" and is a specific instance of it; in a market economy, which is the work of men, the seal affixed to inert material appears as the *alien power* of the finished product, as its unity of interiority. In the same way, the *meaning* of human objects—a social event, a cadaver, "Charbovari's" cap—seems to Gustave not a result—of work, of antagonism, of usage—but the menacing and static objectification of suffering and thinking which resides in them and on them as the externalization of their inner unity. This is perfectly *logical* if we recall that beneath the ideology of mechanism Gustave's pro-

465

found and ravaged soul is filled with a belief in destiny. If *fatum* exists, events and things are intersigns, they designate us, turn us into sign; inhabited by an alien will which has put them in our path to be transcended, in order to show us that the worst—*our* worst—is always certain, they are thought and even consciousness, but *alien* thought, *alien* consciousness. In each of its prophetic projects, the will of the Other is particularized; the result is this impenetrable enigma: a piece of inanimate matter enchanted by a soul so that its life is only an enchantment of cadavers.

We can thus understand how, at the end of the process of decomposition, when the body is reduced to its inorganic elements through natural analysis, Gustave can perceive death as a peaceful survival; rid of impurity, one can finally dream, like the last Saint Antoine, of "being matter." But this too is still haunted by a soul. The young hero of *Novembre* likes to dream in front of effigies on tombs: he envies them—they have been given human shape *without life*. Fashioned in the image of a particular deceased who, whether prince or cardinal, suffered until death, the stone absorbs that restless memory and endows it with the eternal calm of minerality. Between inert matter and thought there is no more need for intervention: incorruptible, the tomb effigy retains the fixed consciousness of having been, of no longer being, of escaping unhappiness forever. Nothing could be clearer: Flaubert gives things a soul because under the authoritarian eye of the paterfamilias he transferred his intimate experience to the object he was for others, to that system of mechanistic systems which he considers both his *truth* and his cadaver. Furthermore, these haunted statues offer resentment its best observation post. By envying their *ataraxia*, their calm mineral challenge to everything, Gustave decides his destiny for himself: one day he too will certainly be a tomb effigy. We shall see how he goes about it. In any event, from the age of thirteen, well before the option of neurosis, the adolescent gave himself the means, while living, of taking the point of view of nothingness—it was enough for him to look at the world with the dead eyes of the cadaver within him. But this cadaver, someone will say, existed only in his imagination. True. That's the basis of the whole business; to die, in this case, is to become unreal. But it is still too soon for us to study Gustave's imaginary aspect. It is sufficient to note here the use he makes of material *analysis*, in other words, the work of the scalpel. The misunderstanding arises on just this level. Gustave and his father both make *experience* the foundation of all worthwhile knowledge. But they are not talking about the same thing. When Gustave declares that as a young child he had a complete presentiment of life, he is referring to an *existential* experience which might be reconciled, for example, with what was customarily called, using William James's term, religious experience. Obviously this involves neither a sum of experiences in the sense intended by empiricism, nor experimentation in the modern sense of the word. Flaubert's experience, as he reports it to us, is at once singular and complete: it is an experienced event that says everything there is to say about itself and instantly overflows the present in order to predict the future or—which amounts here to the same thing—in order to reveal it. This is related at once to *discovery*—in the sense precisely that religious experience, mystical experience, and neurotic experience discover an area of existence that is qualitatively irreducible and new—and to *totalization*—in the sense that *conversion* is totalizing as a sudden consciousness of the implications contained in one's limited day-to-day existence. For this very reason, the unveiling is experienced in its singularity as something that will never again be questioned. Of course, grasped from the outside and as an objective determination, this claim seems extravagant; religious experience, for example, can be followed later by a radical loss of faith—I know some people, and even a few priests, who have followed this path; the conversion itself can be succeeded by a demobilization of the soul. But what is important to us here is that the existential experience is felt in itself to be irreversible; it can certainly be repeated endlessly and even enriched, but it cannot fundamentally be modified by other experiences. At least it is not deceptive. In this sense, as long as the subject remains faithful to this first involvement, the succession of his *Erlebnisse* refers only to an archetypal event which is felt inside to be a fundamental and invariable intuition. In other words, this archetype is presented as a unique and fundamental experience, to which subsequent experience can add nothing.

In order to demystify the revelation-experience I have just described, one should mention first of all that the experience is rarely genuine; the subject refers to it constantly; he *believes* it has taken place, but there is nothing to prove it has. Take Gustave. In *Le Voyage en enfer* he clearly marks the passage from rumination to illumination. Perched on Mount Atlas, he meditates, he dreams of the human race and its passions; yet he derives no knowledge from these vague marvels—which are already syncretic, of course, since the human condition is what is in question. Then comes the Devil, who carries him off, like Lesage's Asmodeus, on a tour of the world and transforms

467

his revery into an inevitable conclusion: the world is hell. Clearly this totalization of our species is the equivalent of existential experience; meditation is transformed—stiffened, hardened, it becomes a conviction, a conclusion. But who can swear that the metamorphosis has taken place at a particular, precise moment? As often happens—and in quite different areas—the child was able to live a long time *before* the totalizing intuition and to continue his life *after* it without ever having to live *during* the moment of illumination. In other words, there was probably no sudden actualization of the archetype; in the continuity of experience, Gustave referred to it as though it were something that had *already* happened, and from this point of view the experience itself never had the thrilling freshness of novelty.

We can be certain, moreover, that this hypothesis of the future issues from the single immediate experience and necessarily carries a promise. When Flaubert summarizes experience as a presentiment of life—or *fatum*—he is extrapolating; starting from the past temporalization, which he realizes is involutional in character, he engages in prophecy: out of resentment he lives the future as an accelerated degradation. This amounts to swearing that the worst is always certain, as we know. But promise, for him, cannot present itself in the form of a *decision*—that would be acting; it becomes *belief*. And this belief claims to refer to a possibly fictive illumination.

What is true is that the young boy has passed from the realm of the immediate to the realm of reflection. This passage and the extrapolation, even as they claim to reconstitute the unembellished savor of experience, change its *quality*: each moment of experience, instead of being lived for itself, separately, or being assembled in blocks—aggregates without true unity and without synthetic connection to the other moments of life[8]—now appears as part of a totalization in progress which will be accomplished with Gustave's death. And as the part is the particularized expression of the whole, each moment presents itself to Gustave as a condensation of his entire life. *It is all there*; he revels in it outrageously and at the same time he is reminded of all past temporalization which was directed toward this present, of all future temporalization which leads toward annihilation. In the present, the unity of his experience comes from the fact that every perception confirms an archetypal proof which may be imaginary but which one retrospective intention seeks in the past

8. Gustave is alluding to these false and quickly disintegrated totalities when he tells us that Djalioh as a child had lived many lives.

without attaining, while another—an oath that is kept—seeks in the most distant future by swearing (belief) that it will always conform to the original prediction.

Such is the first contradiction which, in the realm of knowledge, sets Gustave against his father without either of them perceiving it. Gustave *knows everything*, a unique experience has given him a complete presentiment of life; Achille-Cléophas, on the other hand, as a good empiricist, holds that experience is the sum—never completed—of all the particular experiences that are produced not only in the course of a human life but since the birth of humanity. Gustave understands; he believes his father, who is the principle of authority. He therefore adopts the ideology of his time, which bases knowledge on the passive registering of perceptions, a summation made from itself—death shoots an arrow, the addition is complete. This conception could only please Flaubert; as a passive agent who has the greatest difficulties affirming or denying, who prefers associations of words and images to "logical connections," he willingly accepts that knowledge is an automatic accumulation—of the passive syntheses that cross his path. But that was to fall into a trap from which he could not escape. At the time, conventional wisdom held that knowledge was proportional to longevity; let us recall the English philosopher and his sages, sailors, merchants, statesmen retired from political life, all persons of property, bourgeois, who had seen the world and were chosen in the evening of their life, having seen and remembered a great deal, to counsel young people, businessmen, and governments, and hold the post of intimate adviser. If Flaubert at thirteen had declared, "I am unhappy," such a person would have believed him, *perhaps*. But if he had extrapolated and claimed that the world was completely rotten, they would have laughed in his face and said he knew nothing about it. In short, he had to keep quiet. To adopt bourgeois empiricism was to deny a priori the meaning of his existential experience.

He perceived this from the age of thirteen—and probably much earlier. I have shown how, in *Le Voyage en enfer*, his vague meditation is transformed into a horrifying certainty thanks to the concurrence of the Devil—an abstract allegory which undoubtedly was inspired by Dr. Flaubert, that "demon." But the young boy arrives at the totalization which concludes this tale only after a long journey around the earth. Satan shows him *everything* in succession, after which the child only has to draw a conclusion from what he has seen; or, rather, the conclusion is self-evident since it is Satan who whispers it to him.

469

As we see, existential experience is displayed—it is transformed into a general enumeration of the misfortunes and misdeeds of the species. But, since we are dealing here not with a life—a slow process of degradation—but with a general survey which, with the help of the Devil, is made perhaps at the speed of light, the young author is forced to find a solution to his problem: experience, he seems to tell us, can be resumed in an instant or stretched out over a whole life. The result is the same.

This is what he expresses still more clearly in an undated story probably written prior to September 1835, *L'Anneau du prieur*. A young monk descends into a crypt to open the coffin of a prior who has just died and steal his signet ring; he succeeds, but the coffin closes on the young man's habit, and, unable to escape, he dies next to the corpse he sought to rob. Bruneau has found the source of this story, a work published somewhat earlier and intended for students, which contained subjects for composition and suitable "models." The child took this subject, followed the development to the letter, and gave the story a title. Done. But it is regrettable that Bruneau sees this story only as a stylistic exercise and scoffs at a German critic who claims it contains a parricidal intention. Bruneau in effect fails to answer three essential questions: First, why did Gustave choose this subject among all the others? Second, why did he keep this copyist's work in his drawer all his life? Third, what is the meaning of the modifications he made to the original sketch (and Bruneau himself acknowledges that he made them)? In point of fact, while the author of the book made some concession to the Romantic mode, the proposed theme was edifying: this monk is a petty thief who is punished by the site of his sin. Therefore the students ought to have displayed their horror at this pillager of corpses and depicted him from the outside. The little copyist, on the contrary, puts himself inside the monk's skin; the character is no more sympathetic, but he becomes a victim, the predecessor of Marguerite and Garcia, destiny's dupe. Are we to believe, however, that by writing *L'Anneau* Gustave accomplished the ritual murder of the father and punished himself for it by dying with the corpse? I am not convinced we are. Certainly, as we have seen, the child does not hesitate to slay Achille-Cléophas in his thoughts; a little later he was to assassinate him under the name of Mathurin. There is nothing to prevent this murderous intention a priori from being at the origin of his choice. But it is enough to read the copy of the model attentively to understand that Gustave's purpose is something different; if his parricidal impulse figures among the motives that prompted him to choose this subject, it may be only a very secondary element.

The prior is burdened by years. He has lived a great deal and suffered, he knows all the secrets of life. The old man has one foot in the grave, and yet a young monk envies him violently. It is not the signet ring he covets at first but the prior's memory, which is coming to an end and is about to slip into nothingness. In other words, little Gustave, embodied by the envious young monk, craves to possess his father's integral experience, that omniscience which can be summed up only at the end of a long life. Here is where the ring comes in, the brilliant jewel that the prior has worn on his finger for half a century, almost embedded in his flesh, its fascinating sparkle representing the knowledge which, by a kind of cementing, it now contains. Let us say that—as the tomb effigies will be later—it is a *fetish*, the mineralized survival of a memory. The monk wants to get hold of it; scarcely will it slip onto his ring finger than the prior's experience will revert to him by an inverse cementing. Is this to say that Gustave desires his father's death? Perhaps, but I see the myth of the signet ring rather as a first and futile attempt at identification with the progenitor: Gustave, omniscient, becomes Achille-Cléophas's equal; better, he *is* Achille-Cléophas himself.

What led the little boy to pick this subject from among all the others was that it *spoke* to him; he glimpsed in it the mythic solution to a problem that disturbed him: how can one obtain the findings of an existence endured to the bitter end without having to live it out? The signet ring is the solution: if it has absorbed the prior's hopes and disappointments, it becomes their *condensation*; the time he has lived is coiled within it, it is the sum of separate moments reduced to a *pure quality* which is immediately accessible, to a metaphysical virtue that can be acquired on the spot through a kind of *participation*. The fiction borrows its framework from Genesis: the ring is the apple; it gives the thief knowledge the moment it is stolen, so the monk will know good and evil. Nevertheless, in Flaubert's tale as in the biblical narrative, this wrongly acquired knowledge is an indiscretion followed by prompt punishment. Adam gathers the *forbidden* fruit. Why forbidden? We do not know. Gustave is more explicit: his grave robber is a parasite, he vampirizes a dead man in order to take his life's experience; his knowledge will therefore be *borrowed*, grafted to *an alien existence*. If we set aside the embellishments, hell and the gnashing of teeth, we see that the adolescent author presents the signet ring as the site of his contradictory demands and not as their solution.

471

The old have knowledge, the dead have even more; but when a child plunders knowledge from a corpse, he gets only the recipe for it since he hasn't distilled that knowledge in suffering himself.

We can now understand Gustave's predicament: radical evil is his experience; he sees it everywhere and feels it every moment, coming up against it in himself at the very sources of life. In short, his pessimism is not a *conclusion*; it is an intuition and a promise, a profound intention which is recognized in its affirmation. Why the need to find a basis for it in truth? It *exists*. But when he has to communicate his certainties to others, that is, to transpose them into the universe of discourse, the child encounters the words and ideas of his time, which are his only instruments. His basic intention is diverted; no unvalidated intuition or evidence—admissible in more spiritual centuries—has any currency in bourgeois ideology. Gustave submits to that ideology; or, we should say, it makes him submit, for he is launched before he knows what he is doing. But by a predicted reversal, he in his turn diverts language by bending it to his personal needs. His thought was stolen, he steals the vocabulary; and hence the monstrous compromise. Flaubert agrees to base total truth on the totality of existence, but scarcely has he admitted this principle than he declares that the experienced "All" can manifest itself to men in two equivalent ways: either by decompression, through the progressive development of a life, or under infinite pressure as a flash of inspiration. When such a visitation occurs at a very early age, it makes a youngster the equal of his grandfather. The equal—what am I saying? The superior. An octogenarian has frittered away eighty years; a child like this can save seventy. In terms of good bourgeois economy, hats should be doffed to the child. All the more since a leisurely experience, stretched over time, owes its useless length to its inauthenticity; its brutality, grounded on its victim, stirs up unfathomable filth and can stop a heart; why survive? But that is what makes it great. Gustave always comes back to this contrast between surface and depth, convincing us of his stubborn intention to run an existential structure through the mold of empiricism. Yet in this short narrative he asks himself only on what conditions integral experience is possible for an adolescent. The symbol of the signet ring has a problematic meaning. *if* this experience is possible, it will fulfill the aforesaid conditions. The author is pulled up short at these words, he cannot decide. And he deliberately leaves us in the midst of uncertainty—we shall never know if the ring had a magical power or if the monk was tricked by his imagination.

472

In any event, the discussion has bearing on the kind of knowledge that Lachelier would later dub the basis of induction. Naturally, such intellectual scruples can hardly distress an anti-intellectual of thirteen—he knows what he knows and will not give an inch the rest of his life. Besides, he wants to establish his right to impose his notions on others. The principles and the method, which theoretically ought to be discovered and forged through research, Gustave researches *after* the moment of inspiration in order to prove his belief and not to evaluate it. But that's beside the point; by accepting the equivalence of existential and acquired experience, he is lost. Because, as we have seen, the principles of empiricist ideology conceal an analytic intellectualism which issued from the positivist methods then in scientific use. This is how analysis as an operative scheme was artfully introduced to Gustave and, substituting itself for acquired experience, became by paternal authority a methodological imperative that passed for the equivalent of existential experience. In other words, on the superstructural level of empirical *knowledge*, Gustave found himself obliged to affirm the identity of opposites—a syncretistic and prospective intuition and an *active* method organized to reduce a so-called whole to its parts. Meaning to its indivisible elements. He declares that the law of his being is destiny (a relation which is *other* but experienced in interiority) and at the same time that he is, in fact, exterior to himself.

Dr. Flaubert was not content to ransack cadavers, he was "like an old priest privy to domestic secrets." Anecdotes, in sum—which Achille-Cléophas took for an "experience of the human heart," given his expertise in the art of *analyzing* lies. In fact, the components of the anecdote were invariable, found because they were put there: blood, pus, sperm, gold. One could go all the way back to self-interest and reduce it to a calculus of pleasure. Gustave was dazzled—all those bodies, all those hearts "reduced to fragments"! In those false moments of domestic abandon when the head of the family sat in front of his wife and children, the father must have let it be understood that "souls too can be dissected." This naïveté would not be worth noting if it had not done his son so much damage.

The little boy took it all for gospel. He saw his lord leaning over putrefying bodies, and here was the same lord assuring him with his divine voice that souls are more putrid still, that the surgical method must be applied to them as well. He believed it immediately, passionately, like a good vassal; all his life he would assimilate truth to physical purulence and mental hideousness. Toward the age of fifteen he wrote to Ernest, explicitly reproaching the psychologist's analysis and the physician's dissection: "The most beautiful woman in the world is hardly beautiful on the table in an amphitheater with guts on her nose. . . . Oh no! It is a sad thing to analyze the human heart and to find nothing but selfishness in it!"

This comparison must be taken literally and is to be found again almost everywhere in the first volumes of his correspondence. He is persuaded—as he will always be—emotionally and through images, that the application of the analytic method to the "human heart" has material results neither more nor less than a surgical intervention; for him the dismemberment of the psychic object is not an operation of the imagination done with signs, but a real action, modeled after the glacial look of the medical director entering his son's soul and working it over with the scalpel.

The result: analysis was soon declared in rage and pain to be "antitruth"—which doesn't surprise us since, according to Gustave, truth is the unmasking of being and he has taken the part of nothingness. And soon, to be worthy of his father and to get rid of his older brother, he claimed to analyze souls—beginning with his own: he would later declare, after the crisis at Pont-l'Evêque, that he had fallen ill from so much self-analysis. In fact, though it is true that he most often took a reflexive attitude in contemplating his own case, he did not dissect it. Precisely because the analysis was *already done* and he already knew what it would tell him; better, since the principle was given to him at this period and according to this ideology, all the results were given too. Psychology for Gustave is an autopsy which shows us the cadaverous state of the soul. From his very first letters we ascertain that he was conversant with the method and knew how to reduce instantaneously all so-called "generous" impulses to the movements of self-love. This would *never go further*; happily, his works are not analyses followed by synthetic recomposition. Gustave, the inverse of his father, who practiced virtue without believing in it, believed in analysis *without ever practicing it*. Analytic intellectualism was like a wound in him, like a complete body of knowledge that was devoid of life, like a curse, like the rationalization of his pessimism and of his misanthropy, but it was never an operative plan, a method of investigation. It was a bleak belief, to which he referred when he wanted to be convinced that the world was an absence, but he never derived anything from it that he did not know from childhood. We must recognize all the same that it never stopped inhibiting him; he lacked curiosity, was not interested in other people's thinking and still less in their personalities; he would turn endlessly in the infernal circle of death, analysis, impossible totality, pulverized by science and the sole object of art.

His hagiographer, René Dumesnil, piously affirms that Gustave "controls analysis by synthesis." Where did he take that from? Flaubert regrets that psychological analysis shows him selfishness everywhere. But not for an instant does he think to compensate for this sad discovery by a synthetic recomposition of our feelings and our thoughts. No, the job is done: when analysis discovers the indivisible, science has had its last word. He is still affirming this at the age of thirty-five when he shows Larivière dismembering our poor lies, which fall in fragments at his feet. One would like to say to this prince of science: "Well cut; now you must sew it up." But the good doctor never restitches. The original synthesis was false: bad faith, lie, illusion, self-deception, mythmaking; the doctor finds truth and dissipates fantasies by reducing the whole to its elements, after which he can go away, his work accomplished.

Synthesis in the sense of the systematic reconstruction of a whole from its elements is totally alien to Flaubert. His letters are emanations, escapes; the order and succession of sentences seem uniquely governed by affective and rhetorical linkings—the argument is lost, strange *lapsus calami* manage to shatter or deviate all argumentation. All his life he would be the man least capable of "making a sketch," of painting a picture of the whole, of gathering in a single perception or rendering in a single description the principal features of an object, a scene, a character. This does not mean that his novels have no unity, quite the contrary, but it is a mysterious and fascinating unity which is anchored in the perpetual flow of men and things, passive, distant like an idea in the Platonic heaven.

It would be more accurate to say that he dreams of analysis and of synthesis without practicing either one. If he deals with synthesis, particularly in the first *Tentation*, it is in order to set the limits of knowledge. Look at the way such knowledge appears in the eyes of Saint Antoine as a child who is an old woman at the same time, "a child with white hair, an enormous head, and spindly legs"; she is "always crying" and has more than one feature in common with Almaroës. ("Let me run a little in the country and roll in the grass," she asks Pride; "I want to sleep, I want to play." Of course, this will not be allowed.) No soul, the sad desire to desire. Here knowledge and its object are confused. At the same time Gustave indicates quite clearly that the mechanistic moment (which corresponds to observation) is only an instant—perhaps unsurpassable but surely insufficient—in scientific research:

> I have found nothing. I am always searching, I accumulate, I read. Why then, oh mother, do you make me gather all these plants, learn the names of all these stars, spell out all these lines, collect all these shells? . . . If I could penetrate matter, embrace the idea, follow life in its metamorphoses, understand being in all its forms, and discover causes one after the other like a flight of stairs, if I could reunite in myself these scattered phenomena and set them again in motion in the synthesis which my scalpel has pried apart . . . perhaps then I could make worlds . . . alas!

In sum, we are at the stage of analysis and dissection—this is unhappiness. One can leave it behind only by arriving at a synthesis that seems impossible. But curiously, the purpose of this synthesis is not so much the recomposition of the cosmos in which we live as the creation of other worlds—which, according to Flaubert, can be accomplished only by art and in the realm of the imaginary.

Haunted by a radical and ready-made analysis and by an impossible synthesis, Gustave remains fixed in his original syncretism. At fifteen he charges the writer with reconstituting as a syncretistic totality the *cosmos* which the man of science has pulverized, not *after* the process of analysis, as a recomposition, but before it: "You do not know what a pleasure it is to compose! To write, oh, to write is to get hold of the world, its prejudices, its virtues, and to sum it up in a book; it is to feel your thought being born, growing, living, standing on a pedestal, and staying there always." Progress in art, not in knowledge. How did he come to be fixed from such an early age in this syncretistic totalization? We must look for the origin of the fixation that forbade him knowledge and at the same time infused him with the contradiction of the Flaubert family, a semipatriarchal structure with liberal opinions and a clodhopper parvenu at its head, a peasant from childhood, an intellectual by advancement. Little Gustave internalized this contradiction—described above—on all levels, and we have seen it is the key to the golden age, to the frustration and the Fall that accompanied it. Here we see it on the level of attainments. In the first years he felt his dependence as happiness. It was his raison d'être; in short, he revived in himself as his true nature the peasant traditions which even in Achille-Cléophas seemed to be disappearing. And immediately afterward he prematurely received the maxims of liberalism, the irrefutable negation of this first nature. If only he could have sustained the disenchantment, resigned himself to it, found his truth in liberal individualism. But no, the "physician-philosopher" was a paterfamilias; he demanded an absolute submission based solely on religious adoration. He continued to maintain with his demands the feudalism he had abolished with his arguments. So Gustave was forced to oscillate endlessly between two contradictory ideologies, each of which contained in itself the key to all problems, the answer to all questions. At times the family seemed a social unit, at times a juxtaposition of solitary persons; sometimes Gustave had the feeling that the divine generosity of the master gave him a social status in order to save him from nature, and sometimes he once more found himself to be *natural*, a simple determination of space without right or privilege, a general assemblage of elementary particles. This was not enough; they weren't satisfied with pointing out his insignificance, they showed him his crimes. And these would not have existed if he had had only one ideology; but he possessed two, and each condemned the other. How could he fail to believe in virtue when he revered the most admirable of fathers, the very model of probity, of generous disinterestedness; how could he believe in it when this infallible father explained that the finest actions were motivated by self-interest? The vicious circle always closed in on him: this first nature which Achille-Cléophas's admirable authority had implanted in him was precisely what the father dismantled. Flaubert passed from dream to disenchantment, from innocence to sin, and continually returned to innocence only to lose it again. In a way, this victim of analysis had internalized the method only too well—he decomposed and recomposed himself indefinitely. But, as we have seen, the analysis remained purely verbal, and the real truth of his condition was the vassalage he had to live out and was determined to destroy. The pretended dissection—presented as the dismemberment of the lie—was itself the true illusion; it was confined to repeating principles and applying them formally to present circumstance: everyone follows his own interests, therefore I follow mine, and this burst of filial love is only an effect of my selfishness. Yet to Gustave's unhappiness, his love was based on the real structure of the Flaubert family and indeed expressed it; but the father had condemned the system of signs and symbols that would have reflected it to the child as the truth of his condition. This condemnation came from the outside, from the physician-philosopher; but the child took it into himself as a perpetual imperative, a sentence to be suffered endlessly as the somber illumination of his acts, as his point of view on himself and

477

others. *His* point of view? No, it was the point of view of the Other; Gustave's most intimate and personal will could only be his father's will experienced as an alien power: the father, in him as Other, revealed him to his own eyes as other than himself, forced him to treat his immediate affections as ruses to be frustrated, and to treat *himself* as an eternal liar and at the same time an eternal dupe. Gustave believed that the wounding remarks of a father exasperated by the inadequacies of his younger son emanated from a mechanistic knowledge which was itself based on a sacred experience. Analysis was his condemnation through humiliations and frustrations. After a few distressing experiences, knowledge and paternal scrutiny became the same thing: the eye of Achille-Cléophas entered his son's soul like the eye of God in Cain's tomb. Even in solitude the little boy could not decide if he was deciphering himself or if he was being deciphered; analysis, personified and made sacred, became his permanent superego. Not a corner to hide a hope in—the paternal truth is within him, living on his death. For this hyperconsciousness, which extended itself through his consciousness, he was an object before being a subject, universal before being singular; or rather his singularity and his subjectivity were denounced in this objective setting as pure living appearances; his need to feel his affections personally, like everyone else, to experience them as they are, seemed to him a criminal insistence upon living in error rather than truth. We shall find proof that Gustave at times felt hatred and fury at the omnipresence of such a judge in a text I have cited above, *Un Secret de Philippe le Prudent*. Here Gustave internalizes the analysis: a look from the "grand inquisitor" penetrates the most intimate recesses of his person, "trying to divine the feelings that beat in my heart, the thoughts that lie behind my brow, always there . . . like a bad genie, opposing my happiness, robbing me of my wife,[9] depriving me of my freedom . . . and I could not cry and curse, avenge myself! No! He is my father

9. Although it is reported as a historical fact, we shall surely be struck by the oedipal resonance of this portion of the sentence. We shall return to this point when we discuss Gustave's sexuality. But it is also a question of the maternal ideology. The father abandons his son to the Grand Inquisitor—who is none other than himself. What shuffles the cards here—not unintentionally—is that Philippe II is prompted by his Catholic faith. Yet it is not religion that is at stake in this case but a narrow, mean, sectarian ideology that disparages everything in Carlos/Gustave by the basest instincts, when in fact the young man possesses "the kind of soul . . . so full of passion, so charged with feeling that it expands, bursts, and collapses, unable to contain all it possesses."

478

and the king! I must bear all his blows, take all his insults, accept all these outrages."

The last lines show us clearly that this passive agent is incapable of revolt; and then these furies do not last, they are replaced by despondency, and the wheel turns once again: the wicked inquisitor is actually the best of men, devoted to his sons, to his fellow citizens, to his students, "paternal to the poor," in short, a saint. But surreptitiously, the frustrated, humiliated, exiled child bitterly dreads the spirit that possesses him and pushes him to despair *as though it were a demon.* Thus Dr. Flaubert, inside his son, is primarily experienced in the unity of a perpetual tension as the insurmountable contradiction of good and evil, the subject of a love he provokes and demands only to force its repudiation and denunciation as a hypocritical cover for selfish impulses; he is a sacred power that devastates holy places and whose blasphemy must be believed in the name of the religious respect borne him; he is the superior light that illuminates the depths and crevices of a soul devoted to light and shade, dissipating the half-light which always threatens to return. As the lord of a black feudalism, he sometimes drives his vassal inflexibly to the point of abjectness by sadistically abusing his sworn faith; at other times he is a virtuous man of science who considers the truth a universal remedy, even when it is bitter, and who teaches it to his children in order to protect them against the absurdities of religion. Is that all? No, this is only the revolving ambivalence of the sacred. Gustave is touched at times by a suspicion: and what if analysis too were only a farce? In this case the crushing intelligence of the father could only represent an irremediable form of stupidity.

Although the little boy dares not approach it, he perceives one path of escape from the cyclical return of the demonic and the holy: why not apply the analytic method to the father himself? And since it amounts to the same thing, why not turn it against science as well? One could have a good laugh dismembering the best established truths and throwing the pieces at the feet of these men of science. Indeed, we have just seen a text from the first *Saint Antoine* in which science, represented as a rather weak figure impelled by pride, simply collects facts. At the age of twenty, in his *Souvenirs*, Gustave criticized his father for the same things: collecting, classifying, analyzing—yes, but the royal road of progressive synthesis was closed to him. *Bouvard et Pécuchet*, that colossal and grotesque work, would plunge its roots into the soil of an alienated childhood; and close to fifty, Gustave would undertake the murder of the father in earnest and quite deliberately. For the moment, he once again represses his revolt; to do otherwise he would have to observe Dr. Flaubert, detach himself, take his distance, and consider his father as an object. Impossible— the terrible superego forbids it since detachment would break the ties that bind him to his lord, in spite of everything, in a reassuring identification; he would have to live in exile in the heart of this reverential family, alone and in secret, naked—this father who is killing him is after all his best defense against the barbaric world he is allowed to glimpse through mechanistic materialism. Gustave is an object for the doctor, by whose will he even becomes an object for himself; but despite the highly equivocal portrait of Mathurin, Achille-Cléophas would never, *before* his death, become an object for his younger son. We have seen the meaning that must be given to the appearance of Larivière at Emma's deathbed. This is the single reincarnation of the paterfamilias that Flaubert published in his father's lifetime.[10] As to the correspondence, the father is rarely mentioned, and always in very official terms: he is going to heaven, he is the eponymous hero of the family; there is nothing to suggest that he should be identified as that monstrous adversary of the "two woodlice," Science. One sentence and one alone informs us of the evolution of Gustave's feelings toward his father. It too is highly ambiguous. We know that at the end of 1838, Flaubert had put together several sheets of copybook paper to make a notebook in which he jotted down—until 1842— impressions, maxims, reflections on himself, sometimes memories. The notebook, which will be very valuable to us later in this study, was published only in 1965 through the efforts of Mme Chevalley-Sabatier. In it we find the following remark, which is undated but obviously goes back to the autumn of 1838, or somewhat later, the winter of '39: "I have loved only one man as a friend and only one other, that is my father." We are struck first of all by the incorrectness of the sentence—quite apparent—which corresponds to a leap in thought, a deviation of the statement: "I have loved only one man, that is Alfred." This is what he wanted to write down in the first place. But—was it in order to correct the vaguely homosexual aspect of the sentence? Perhaps, since we know that Alfred called him "my dear pederast"—he adds, to make his statement precise: "as a friend," which immediately prompts the idea: "There is one man I have loved not as a friend but as a son, that is my father." Nevertheless, Achille-Cléophas comes second; moreover, it would not be surprising if Gus-

10. Except in *La Légende de Saint Julien*, which we shall discuss later.

tave had written: "I have loved only two men: my father and Alfred."
"I have loved," meaning "I no longer love." Is this how we should
understand the statement? If we attend to the grammar, yes.

> Car je t'ai bien aimée, Fanny,
> De Noël à l'Epiphanie.*

But things are not so simple. First of all, the cycle of autobiographies
had begun; the previous summer, Gustave had put the final touches
on *Mémoires d'un fou*, and for several years he would have a habit of
telling himself stories about the past as if he no longer existed, as if
a dead man were speaking. This would be clearer still in *Novembre*:
"I have deeply savored my lost life. . . . Have I loved? Have I hated?
. . . I doubt it still." The purpose is clear: to sum things up *from the
point of view of nothingness*. In this case, it isn't love that is over, but
life: it is the deceased who says, "I loved Alfred," and he might have
added, "while I lived" or "until my last breath." An old man too,
knowing that in his last years his advanced age, his isolation, mental
lethargy, and withered feelings—which often accompany physical
deterioration—are so many barriers that deny him any change, any
new affection; he will surely—at least this is Gustave's idea—be able
to say at the conclusion of a now fixed life that he will no longer love
anyone and that for this reason his father *will have been* the only person
he has truly loved. This is because for young Gustave, old age is at
once the totalization of experience and death experienced in anticipation. If a passion, whatever it might be, should warm these old
bones again, the totalization would not be exhaustive since this final
feeling would escape it; such a passion would not even be possible
since it could exist only from the point of view of this last ardor, and
therefore of life.

And then, who would dare to claim that in 1839 Gustave had
stopped loving Alfred? Any attempt to support such a conjecture
would be instantly given the lie by subsequent letters. If Flaubert's
father is mentioned in the same sentence—even in second place—
and if he is the object of the same verb, it is because he is still loved
as well.

All this is true. But—as always when it comes to Gustave—the
opposite is also true. First of all, a bloodless young old man, conceived
on the Flaubertian model, faithful to his childhood affections and
certain he will conceive no new ones, was to write: "I *will have had*

* [For I have loved you well, Fanny, / From Christmas to Epiphany.]

only two loves in my life." This sentence is correct only because the verb contains a precise reference to the future: When I am dead, I will have had . . . ," etc. Let us not suppose that Gustave is ignorant of this—his pen is precise; the ambiguities manifest in a statement always correspond to an ambivalence in his experience and to intentional structures. If he preferred to use the future perfect rather than the perfect tense, there must have been a reason. Furthermore, the text of *Novembre* already cited, written less than two years later, shows an uncertainty which in retrospect clarifies the sentence from the notebook: "Have I loved? Have I hated? . . . I doubt it still." Reflecting on his past between the ages of nineteen and twenty, he is not sure of having felt the two passions he speaks of at eighteen. And the word "still" indicates that his perplexity dates back to the last years of his adolescence. Did he doubt in 1839 that he had loved Alfred? No, but he doubted that he still loved him.

Always fascinated by Alfred, ready to open his arms to him but disheartened by his friend's coldness and disloyalty, Gustave *believes* he no longer loves him. That is Alfred's punishment. Achille-Cléophas instantly appears—for his younger son this is the great moment of liquidations: his first lord, just like the second and well before, disappointed him, here's a chance to send them both packing. The philosopher-practitioner *has been* loved, like Alfred; he is still fascinating but no longer loved; and liberated, Gustave remains alone. Is it true, however, that the paterfamilias has stopped hurting him? Certainly since Alfred's appearance he has moved—as the construction of the sentence indicates—to second place. And indeed I think that his younger son, after so many pangs of love, so much jealous suffering, permanently detaches himself; he begins to dream of his death, recognizing the father as his judge and oppressor. And if he speaks here of the affection he formerly bore the paterfamilias, it is because he is reproaching him with being unworthy of that affection and ultimately responsible for the fact that it no longer exists. What remains, nevertheless, is the paternal power—did we notice the strange contrast between the perfect, "I have loved [only] one other . . . ," and the present, "That *is* my father," which is synonymous with eternity? Whether he loves him or not, Gustave remains in Achille-Cléophas's power, fascinated by the progenitor as he is by Alfred. The proof lies in a contemporaneous text which I have cited above: "Since you have been away from me, I have been analyzing myself more, myself and others. I never stop dissecting; it amuses me."[11] Nothing could be clearer: since Alfred has turned away from me, my father has come back to *inhabit me*: analysis, dissection. The chief surgeon has won. A year earlier, Gustave was writing to Ernest: "Oh no, it is a sad thing only to criticize, to study, to descend to the depths of knowledge and find only vanity, to analyze the human heart and find only selfishness in it, and to understand the world and see only unhappiness. There are days when I would give up all of science . . . for two lines from Lamartine and Victor Hugo. Here I am, becoming anti-prose, anti-reason, anti-truth." Defeated in advance, he is still protesting. Now *analysis amuses him*—when he discovers gangrene, he lifts up his head and laughs. The laughter "of the damned," obviously. Nonetheless, mechanistic ideology has carried him off. The enemy father, established inside him as an alien force, dominates him and bends him to his will, all the more powerful as he is no longer loved; the father's surgical eye, internalized in Gustave, reveals to him—we shall return to this—that "what is called consciousness is nothing but inner vanity."[12] He believes it; not completely however, since it is alien thought. He adds, in fact: "This theory seems cruel to you, and as for myself, it disturbs me. At first it seems false, but as I pay more attention I feel that it is true." This result of method—an a priori of psychological analysis which he takes for an a posteriori—plunges him into "discomfort" and malaise. Its effect is to devalue everything he feels. Furthermore, his first impulse, continually repeated, is to consider it false; let us say that it does not take account of the immediate, of what he feels in being himself. But he *applies himself*; he pays "attention," meaning he is set upon substituting the paternal schema for his spontaneous understanding of experience until he has reconciled everything to his model, namely to analytic atomism. When everything is reconstructed (fictively) and universalized, when he has thought *against himself*, measuring the credibility of the alien "theory" against the intensity of the displeasure it causes him, he ends by "feeling" that it is true. No evidence for Gustave; what takes its place is the acknowledged power of his alienation.

Why allow oneself to be alienated by the *patria potestas*? Why be made accessory to a degrading look and see oneself through it, at the same time knowing that one is other? Could Gustave have saved himself by identification with the father as Achille did nine years

11. To Ernest, 24 June 1837, *Correspondance*, 1:27.
12. 26 December 1838.

earlier? To do so, he would have had to place his reality in the impassive light that illuminates the universe and not in the sordid, crawling mass it searches out. The answer is simple: Gustave attempted the identification repeatedly and, as we have shown, always failed—he could not identify with his progenitor *because Achille had already done it*. Achille prevented the younger son from finding in Achille-Cléophas his own future reality as observer just because the paterfamilias had chosen his elder son as his future replacement. The sovereign authority of the chief surgeon left only one exit, and Achille found it—after him the way was barred. Gustave would always be the one observed, his truth remaining on the level of what is dissected, analyzed, and he would never reach the level of the analytic act; even though he would subject himself—and he often made this attempt, as we have just seen—to "surgical scrutiny," he would succeed only in borrowing his father's eye. Having drawn his first son inside himself as *the Same*, the medical director could only inhabit the younger son as *the Other*, universal and singular. In the first son, identification saves—at least on the surface—the autonomy of spontaneity; in the second, alienation implies its heteronomy. Except in early childhood, Gustave never had the chance to dissolve himself in his father—he carried him inside him like a wound. This helps us to understand Mathurin's metamorphosis: internalized by his son, the father's mechanism becomes a hopeless cynicism, for the very reason that it remains transcendent in immanence while the son, called upon to make it his own, succeeds only by forcing himself. This alien system then takes on a pessimistic hue it never had for Achille-Cléophas.

There is more: the pessimism comes from resentment. And then it is radicalized, since the father's mechanism is the only theory the son has at his disposal to evaluate his existential experience. Passive activity is quick to realize the alien imperative and by pushing it to an extreme out of zealousness gives rise to results which contradict it. Mechanism, for Achille-Cléophas, implied no value judgment of the world; besides, empiricism, which is entirely dependent on facts, cannot allow for the deduction of norms, and the very notion of cosmos is alien to it—analysis suppresses unity, resolving the universe into infinite movements of innumerable corpuscles. In the process of internalizing this method, Gustave omits the plan to suppress the world and preserves its synthetic unity even as the principles he adopts make this impossible; the cosmic totality and the relation of the microcosm to the macrocosm, the bond of interiority which unites the parts among themselves and the whole to the parts, are preserved even as mechanism rids them of all content by admitting no link between molecules but a relation of exteriority. Through this process he gives himself the right to judge mechanical successions as a satanic dissolution of the universe, or to consider the cosmic totality as a "dream of hell" endlessly reborn and endlessly dissipated. In any event there is deception, therefore man is on earth to suffer; he is brought into the world with the idea of an All and then thrown into an endless agitation of molecules. Destiny reappears: Gustave, an enchanted cadaver, believes he is alive but sees no further than to allow exterior forces to lead his dead body in a dance of death; born to be integrated with the synthetic unity of the world, he sees everything decompose outside him and within him, and this contradiction makes sense only if it was calculated. In short, Gustave appeals from one alienation to the other, the "curse of Adam" protecting him in part from "Voltairean irony." If earthly unity is scattered in rounds of atoms, the very fact of his deception reveals the temporal unity of his fate. Ravaged by an alien look, he protects himself against it only by evoking the cohesion of an act which is *other*, that is, the premeditated unity of his creation and his damnation. Hence the ambiguity of Mathurin and Larivière, debonair and demonic Voltaireans. Hence the strange portrait of science in the first *Tentation*: the daughter of Pride, that other incarnation of Achille-Cléophas, supported by Logic—the logic of which Gustave/Djalioh some years earlier swore he understood nothing—seems to have no other purpose than to crush faith, which is always reborn. Gustave, constrained to express his existential experience in terms of analytic intellectualism, falls into a trap since he cannot believe in the first without denying the second; but he in his turn falsifies the discourse of analysis by charging it not only with accounting for the original experience but with *betraying* it, without destroying its prestige or its authenticity as an archetypal event.

It is within the unified frame of the primitive experience of involvement, a totalizing presentiment, the apprehension of destiny, that mechanistic decomposition takes place; it is as the *denial of interiority* that the cosmos crumbles into indivisible particles governed by the laws of exteriority. Thus mechanism—pure affirmation a priori of a universal rationality—appears at the heart of primitive irrationality, and all at once the rigorous interplay of concepts retains a sort of satanic unity. It becomes the instrument of damnation. Certainly existential experience had nothing pleasing about it; this child with one night in Edom felt the fire and brimstone, had a prophetic intuition

485

that an *alien will* had given the success of experience a vectoral unity: the worst was always certain because it had been *organized*. This complex construction of unhappiness, passivity, and resentment did, at least, have a positive counterpart: since Gustave, being cursed, had the unity of a destiny, he defined himself through inwardness. The very future, reflected in the present, made this temporality, at once finite and marked by moments interlinked at a distance, into a continuing totalization, and therefore *a person*. On the level of the archetypal experience, *greatness* was possible since the person existed; the child tried to save himself by an ethic based on the experience of pain. Mechanism was introduced into this unitary system, and the person was pulverized; what remained were pathetic molecules, colliding, rebounding, gathering just to scatter again more than ever. The ego was only an illusion, consciousness an epiphenomenon. But suddenly psychological atomism itself became the *prophesied deception*; the worst, its content unpredictable but formally certain, was mechanism, a fall into exteriority, a denunciation of the futility of the pain ethic, and the disappearance of values. In short, on the level of knowledge it was the accomplishment of the curse; it couldn't have been plainer to the doomed young man, for the demonic creator who had assigned him a fate and the cruel demon of knowledge who had made him despair of revealing the *truth* were one and the same, and in both cases what was affirmed was the priority of the Other over the Same: destiny was the will of the Other, mechanism was the science of this same Other, utilized as other against the ipseity of the victim. Gustave's destiny after the Fall and his dispossession by a usurper must have mocked his very anguish by revealing its inanity to him through the lens of mechanism. We see the ironic twist: for Gustave to accept the infinite dispersal of matter and the principle of exteriority, an alien will is necessary, meaning a unity of interiority; for Gustave to suffer like the damned from the dissemination of his being, he must preserve in himself, pulverized as he is, the secret unity of an *interior totalization*. In this sense the emphasis must at times be put on the unity of the person—in this case mechanism is a kind of nightmare *provoked and directed* within Gustave by the Other—and at other times everything is reversed, and it is the person who becomes the nightmare of matter, a pretence, and nothing is true but the immense *unfelt* solitude of the archipelagoes of being. Neither of the two positions stands up under scrutiny, and Gustave is forced to shift endlessly from one to the other. In the end this merry-go-round is so familiar to him that there is no longer any need to go on turning—each position contains the other, and he is aware of it. A strange vision of the world in which succinct analytic reason is placed at the service of unreason, in which mechanism, while remaining *truth* based on experience, is merely a trick that Satan plays on the flock of the damned and in particular on Gustave, in which this *truth* itself or discourse on being is an absolute but in which a system of protesting atoms can be declared "antitruth." In the name of what? Of nothingness or of another principle? We shall see. If this is *thinkable* it is because the young boy is not accessible to *knowledge*, meaning to the affirmative or negative certainties which are based on evidence or reasoning—as we have seen, he can only *believe*. Also, he *believes* in science as he *would believe* in God if he could—neither more nor less. The truth, for him, is only a belief imposed from the outside by a principle of authority; he submits to it, of course, but it is only hearsay, it doesn't mobilize the forces of the soul. A little later, in his *Souvenirs*, believing that he is offering a theory of knowledge, he succeeds in defining himself: "Ideas are neither true nor false. At first one adopts things very eagerly, then one reflects, then one doubts and stays with that."[13]

The Other Ideology

As we have just seen, the supreme lord, Achille-Cléophas, only had to demand tacitly the adoring submission of his wife and sons for Gustave to dream of a great feudal thought that consecrated both the unity of the person and the relation of interiority between vassal and master; it was enough for the paterfamilias, in the name of his sovereign authority, to impose belief in liberal ideology as a categorical imperative for Gustave to turn away in spite of himself from his theocratic ideal. At first, then, the contradiction is not in him but rather in the family structures. There is a collective Flaubert pride but also a Flaubert anxiety, which translates the objective conflicts of the period; during the first ten years of Gustave's gloomy childhood, agrarians and bourgeois, Romantics and Voltaireans, liberals and ultras continually crossed swords. And these superficial grand battles expressed in their way the breaking up, the deep rending, the anguish even, of a society on the way to industrialization. This meant economic and social transformations demanding a complete overhaul of institutions, the rapid growth of a new class tied to the development of technology, a transformation and a provisional complication of the

13. *Souvenirs*, p. 96, sec. xxvii. The note is a little later than 25 January 1841.

class conflict, and from our present point of view the necessity for a still rural society to absorb the experimental science which was being developed and to adapt to it. This relationship with science, which had to be both forged and directed, would be the great intellectual adventure of the nineteenth century; we shall see the role Gustave would play in the drama. If the Flaubert family was conditioned by this climate of civil war, it is clear *in any case* that the war did not provoke the least dissension. In other words, Gustave did not have the slightest *family* conflict to internalize. The antagonistic forces that were tearing France apart and tearing him apart were not embodied, at the Hôtel-Dieu, by people. If they had been, he might have felt less crushed—when lords do battle, the emancipation of the vassals is hastened. But the Flauberts would have had to be a conjugal family; under the father's staff they were, on the contrary, implacably united. The contradictions lay in the group structures which each member of the group internalized all at once, giving these structures the unity of his person, and if he noticed them, he considered them merely his own character traits. Thus Gustave, to his amazement, discovered in himself the violence of his time without finding any part of it at the heart of the Flaubert enterprise. Was he a monster, with his tempestuous despair? We cannot doubt that with his uniquely ambivalent relations to an excessively loved, unloving father, he incarnates the drama of French society. To understand Flaubert it must never be forgotten that he was forged by the fundamental contradictions of the period, but at a certain social level—the family—in which they are masked in the form of ambivalences and ironic twists. This product of civil war never had a chance to experience combat—he experienced the world through a unit so highly integrated that the relations between persons, even when deteriorating, *never* reached the point of conflict. A Flaubert, even if he were furious at another Flaubert, remained—since they were both Flauberts—his alter ego. The *real* relations between Achille and Gustave have nothing in common with fierce antagonism of usurper and victim that we have discovered in the early works of the younger brother; on both sides we find, rather, a veiled contempt. For Achille, Gustave is the family idiot, and when he gives a dinner party for the bigwigs of Rouen, he is careful not to invite his brother. Gustave scorns Achille as a mediocre caricature of his father, the bourgeois; a burning resentment lies beneath but it is never recognized, never expressed by actions. And when danger threatens the family honor, the two brothers present a united front: in 1857 when Gustave was threatened with a lawsuit, he immediately appealed to Achille, implicitly recognized as head of the Flauberts, and Achille gave of himself unsparingly; in 1871, when the Prussians occupied Rouen, the two Flauberts rediscovered solidarity in their despair. Still later, when the Commanvilles were dragging Gustave to financial ruin, Achille, who was much richer than Achille-Cléophas had ever been, offered to pay his brother an allowance; according to the letters it seems that Gustave had not the slightest difficulty accepting it, although in his heart he no doubt felt the offer to be a supreme humiliation—the triumphant usurper has the last word and the younger son must submit, humbly recognizing the authority of the new paterfamilias. I have given this example to show that the younger son's contradictions could never be overcome *in the real world*[14] because they did not of themselves, except on a level highly abstract for the little boy, pose any great social conflicts. It is characteristic of a child to singularize the man he will be by living the universal and the objective in the particularity of concrete and subjective relations; in this way he somehow determines himself as a particularized mode of intersubjective experience, that is, of the familial substance. And Flaubert finds the strict unity of the family simultaneously within him and outside him, but on this foundation of bourgeois integration his situation as younger son obliges him to *actualize* the virtual discord which exists, masked, in every Flaubert as a potential passed over in silence. For this very reason, unable to discover such discord in his father, in his mother, in some opposition between father and mother, he takes on the burden himself and learns to experience it as his personal unity.

It is certain—and this is what concerns us at the moment—that the mother was a deist and that she was the first to speak to him about God. But it must be understood that in doing so she did not set herself against Achille-Cléophas's disbelief. At first, as we have just seen, his feudal authority—even if he used it subsequently to impose his mechanism on his younger son—had fostered a hierarchy in which God had to be at the highest level, just above the progenitor; in this sense, if God's name had never been pronounced in Gustave's presence, he would have had to be invented or at least presented as an essential gap—the revered authority of the paterfamilias had to be solidly anchored. Faith was not brought to the child from the outside, as would have been the case if he had only received religious instruction from

14. The overcoming did occur, but through unrealization and in the world of the imaginary.

his mother; faith was his innermost self—and for this reason he would always speak of the *instinct* that prompts us to believe—because during the first years the paterfamilias—that feudal old man estranged from feudalism—gave him license to live by pulling him out of his natal contingency and making him enter a universe of devotion in which the "fanaticism of man for man" is accomplished naturally through the fanaticism of man for God.

But there is more. This intersubjective relation of a certain son to a certain father was inscribed in an objective ideology that the father condemned in spirit but subscribed to in practice. The aristocrats, returned to power, had their theologians, Maistre and Bonald, and above all they had their watchdogs—the Congrégation had spies everywhere; thus the Restoration, without making it obvious, set itself up as a police state. The stoolpigeons and the cops imposed a system which was simple and coherent, childish even, and hence perfectly adapted to the needs of children.

God had created the world; a monarch chosen by God governed France in His name, dependent on a hereditary aristocracy. The only possible relation of the Almighty to the king, of the king to the aristocrats, of the aristocracy to the people, was one of generosity. From the people to the nobility, to the king, to the Almighty, the only worthy relation was one of loving obedience. This is precisely the ideology the Bourbons tried to restore. The landowners, a good part of the peasantry, especially the poorest, those who had acquired no national benefits, were not opposed to it. The workers themselves were uncertain; the Revolution had disappointed them, they were not yet conscious of their true interests; frequently—and even after 1830—it was in the name of God that they beseeched their employers not to throw them out, to stop lowering salaries. The first proletarian newspaper, *L'Atelier*, disapproved of dechristianization, for which it held the bourgeoisie responsible. If the bourgeoisie was lacking in *charity*—the editors vacillated between placing blame and appealing to generosity, in other words, between justice (recognize our rights) and the Christian ideal (we have no rights, but beyond justice there is love—love us in God because, like you, we are divine creatures)—it was because they had lost *faith*. It is common knowledge, furthermore, that it was not the people but the Jacobin bourgeoisie that was the impetus in 1794 for the great movement of dechristianization.[15]

15. Working-class atheism—which would arise a bit later out of a sudden awareness of the real structures of the society and the class struggle, the driving force of history—owed nothing to bourgeois agnosticism; positive and concrete, it was created by the machine that was not only a practical imperative and an instrument of exploitation but

But what did this agnostic bourgeoisie do between 1815 and 1828?[16] It bent its back. Prudence is the governing concept of liberals. As a consequence, for those who were living history from day to day and did not worry about knowing the actual and hidden connection between social forces, for those whom the withering of France had deceived and who believed it had fallen back once again into agricultural somnolence, the outcome of this doubtful battle remained uncertain. These fence-sitters took no part. When thought was favorable to the progress of science and technology and it was desirable to preserve the conquests of the Revolution, vagueness was a good thing. On the other hand, reactionary ideology was all the more arrogant the less the regime was sure of itself. Propaganda which for the time seems remarkably effective was extended to all the classes and penetrated the bourgeoisie through a hundred different channels, slipping into intimate family circles and finding collaborators even under the roofs of libertines. By forcing fathers to participate in religious ceremonies, the cops and the defenders of the faith put them in a precarious position in the eyes of their sons; it was difficult to call these rituals rigamarole in private while subscribing to them in public.

To a certain extent this was the case with Achille-Cléophas. Although he was a free thinker, his family, which was related to peasants and to country gentry, was nevertheless among those who offered the least resistance to the penetration of religious and monarchist ideas. It is quite natural that Gustave should have been baptized; in 1821 the Congrégation was well established, no one cared to challenge it, and his paternal grandmother would have required it in any case. Furthermore, Achille-Cléophas was a functionary. He depended upon the government and on a partly Catholic clientele. It seems that under the Restoration he was extremely prudent. A police report which has come down to us charges the doctor with liberalism but acknowledges his "wisdom" and his "moderation." These words take on their full meaning when we recall who was in power and from which police the report came. The chief surgeon must have declared himself a Royalist out of precaution or political indifference. As for religion, he rejected its dogma *in private*, in front of a few intimate friends including Le Poittevin, but he submitted to its rites in public. The children made their first communion. Caroline was married in the

---

also an organ of perception. Through it, paid labor became aware at once of its own reality and of the world of the practico-inert.

16. After 1828, the rising class visibly resumed its ascent. Suddenly the government was worried—this was open war, which would end in "les Trois Glorieuses."

church during her father's lifetime; he was evidently unable to act differently at a time when the reign of the Congrégation was long over. A little later on, when the young woman died—shortly after the death of the progenitor—the family welcomed the attendance of a priest. Had they called one to the deathbed of Achille-Cléophas? Shattered by these two deaths, Mme Flaubert, we know, lost faith; nevertheless she agreed to the baptism and later to the first communion of her granddaughter, thinking to conform to her husband's wishes. Is this inconsequential? Indeed not; the disbelief of the previous century was timid. Those very people who had established a certain libertinism of speech would have been shocked if such agnosticism had been manifested publicly in actions. Everyone, I suppose, sensed Achille-Cléophas's disbelief, and later Achille's. They would have lost their clientele if they had refused the holy sacraments for themselves or for their children. One could be an atheist but within the Christian religion. For the agnostics themselves, these practices were only signs of one's bourgeois status, like clothing, living quarters, furniture, food, and the adoption of a certain way of speech in which words chosen for their nobility became passwords because they allowed conversation to be permanently maintained on the level of what English-speaking people call "understatement"; through the elegances of this attenuated faith the bourgeoisie affirmed its spirituality and acknowledged its distinction.

The result? We can guess: by his relative observance of rites, Achille-Cléophas made religion enter into the family enterprise as an objective structure of Flaubert intersubjectivity; both present and rejected, it was the world of the Other, inaccessible and obsessive in the heart of the family and each of its members, Christianity not as it is revealed to faith but as it is imposed by works. By baptizing Gustave, Dr. Flaubert committed a crime that would have been unforgivable if it had been deliberate: he threw his son on his knees before God while preparing to show him, when the time was right, the proper use of analytic reason and as a consequence to censure his belief. Having been baptized, having made his communion, Gustave was *instituted a Christian*—which he discovered from the moment he knew how to talk; this means that a high law granted him the perpetual possibility of grace and faith; by permitting him access to the sacraments, the paterfamilias introduced his younger son to Catholicism and made him, if not one of the elect, at least eligible. If Dr. Flaubert had had less authority, he would have had to be on the defensive; hearing him profess a scientistic agnosticism, the child could have accused him of illogic or pusillanimity. But the progenitor of the Flauberts reigned as an absolute monarch, inspiring his son with too much respect for this trait of prudence—linked, perhaps, to the vague remnants of his distant rural past—to have directly influenced their relations. When it was time, he went on the offensive and made the little boy swallow the antidote to faith, the healthy principles of analytic atomism. Achille-Cléophas thought he would have no great difficulty in demolishing the feeble religiosity in his son that he tolerated in his wife. In fact she was barely a deist. But as the daughter of a Cambremer de Croixmare and distant relative of the counselor de Crémanville—a character she had introduced into the family mythology and who had a permanent place—she had retained from her frivolous and aristocratic education, as well as from her convent years, a sentimental and comfortable faith, all effusion, ruled only by the heart; and we know today how widespread that kind of faith was in the second half of the century of Enlightenment. Her religion without the Church, her God without obligations or sanctions who was manifest only to justify and envelop her with a tenderness her husband hardly lavished—she could not have *imposed* these on her sons; she respected everything about the chief surgeon, and whatever belonged to him was sacred, even his atheism. But it is certain that she *proposed* these beliefs; one of the novelist Flaubert's characters remembers the time when as a small child his mother took him on her knees to make him say his prayers. What prayers? The prayer of the Savoyard vicar or the *pater noster*? Mme Flaubert hardly knew the difference. I am inclined to think, however, that she believed it her duty to teach the Catholic orations to her son—even if she did not use them personally; the child was a Christian, he had to be given the means to be integrated into the community of the faithful; later, he could choose.

Be that as it may, Achille-Cléophas had tolerated this uncertain deism during Achille's early childhood; then, when his elder son was old enough to leave the nursery, he liquidated the superstitions from the child's naïve soul effortlessly but cautiously—the return of the priests in full force, the new obscurantism, the white Terror and persecutions constrained him to proceed gently, and he must have demolished the fables of sacred history painlessly, by a smile, by a note of Voltairean irony. Out of conjugal courtesy he did not directly attack the private religion of his wife, but her abstract faith disappeared by itself: if Cain did not kill Abel, if Jonah was not swallowed by a whale, if Abraham was not stopped by an angel when he was about to sacrifice his son, what was left? And what is left of God for a Catholic

493

child without monumental churches, without the embellishments of priests, without the organ, the cantatas, the incense? The stirrings of faith must be nurtured by these things. This is what Achille-Cléophas was dead set against—liberal anticlericalism was growing with the number of processions. The Flaubert father defined early on the limits of his tolerance: the sacraments, yes; the daily practice, no. This social exercise necessitated qualified monitors and could not be conceived without the integration of the catechism—a believing child meant a priest in the house. Achille-Cléophas probably did not forbid any-thing—that would have been dangerous; he ridiculed rites, dogmas, and especially parish priests. A child could draw his own conclusions. With Achille, he hit his mark for the simple reason that he gave more than he took away. Father and son spoke about the rigamarole man to man; by laughing at Jonah, the elder son of the Flauberts identified with his revered progenitor and out of love he adopted the master's skepticism, seeing in his father his own future image.

Nine years later the good lord wished to begin again: Gustave was seven years old, it was time to take him out of the hands of women and teach him sound principles without being too obvious about it. The results were less fortunate, mainly because identification with the father was forbidden to the younger son. The chief surgeon must have undertaken his work of undermining at the very moment his second son experienced the shame of discovering his own inadequacy. Poor Gustave confused the agnostic's skeptical irony with the wound-ing jests of a hypersensitive and overburdened father; suddenly it seemed to the child that the irony had the same source as the sarcastic comments; it seemed black, profoundly discouraging, tinged with malice: in order to punish his stupidity, they would deprive him of God. Furthermore, we have seen that the maternal deism—which was plucked from Achille like a dead leaf because it seemed rather abstract—was something Gustave *needed*. As an adolescent, when he writes of the long dazes he used to lose himself in, he describes them sometimes as free falls, sometimes as a decompression of his being which was diluted in his surroundings; indeed the chief surgeon had, at the time, partially succeeded in his enterprise of demystification. But *before* his seventh year and no doubt for some time afterward, God gave a meaning, both literal and figurative, to these ecstasies— thanks to Him, they became elevations. When the child felt so pure, so vast, so calm that he believed he was on the verge of vanishing, the Almighty did not disdain to be mirrored in his vacuity. All at once Gustave was *transported*. At the age of thirty-five, Flaubert still remembered his ecstasies, alluding to them in an unpublished passage from *Madame Bovary*: "The happy time of his youth when his heart was as pure as holy water and reflected only the arabesques of the stained glass windows with the calm elevation of celestial hopes." Note the double movement so characteristic of Flaubert: there is the *visitation*, the generosity of the Lord who fulfills his vassal by allowing himself to be mirrored in his heart, just as the stained glass windows deign to entrust their image to the holy water; and simultaneously we are given the suggestion of a burst of hope, a "calm elevation" of this metalloid element in reverse. The image is curious in that the objects brought together to evoke movement suggest, on the contrary, perfect immobility. Indeed, these mystic elevations occur for Gustave instantaneously—the way man, according to Malebranche, sees the truth in God. This shallow, still water—anyone taking from it must protect it from the slightest vibration—is Gustave lying on his back, visited, carried away by a nontemporal and vertical ascension; in a word, it is the very symbol of quietism. The reflection of the infinite in the finite—with the reverse and complementary ecstasy of the finite beyond itself in the infinite—is what gives the creature his dignity. "Simplicity" becomes the ontological dream of the frustrated child: the created being, limited but undivided, is by his complete nothingness made host to an infinite power which suddenly deigns to be contained in this narrow vessel and sanctifies it, valorizes it, floods it, suppressing its limits and reabsorbing it into itself.

All right, but this mysticism makes no sense unless God exists. And this is precisely what his father throws into question. How can he resist his lord? And wouldn't his resentment inspire his fascination with mechanism, that deicidal machinery which is bound to plunge the entire world into despair, beginning with Gustave himself? Between childhood and adolescence, the younger son of the family lets his God fly away. We must understand that he is seduced but not convinced. He cannot defend himself against the discourse of analytic reason through any argument, and so he *accounts himself wrong*. Let us not say that at this moment of slipping he no longer believes in the Almighty, but rather that he *accounts himself wrong to believe*. Moreover, God has no place in the discourse of analysis, meaning, for the little boy subordinated by his father, in the only possible discourse. To speak is to deny the Supreme Being. At once, this Being takes refuge in the "unspeakable"; Gustave at ten has not yet chased Him away—he is ashamed of his belief and inwardly *passes over it in silence*. When he speaks *for himself*, he must admit that devotion is an inferior attitude, an inferior act; Mme Flaubert believes, and she is allowed to believe because she is a woman; but his master, man—*homo faber, homo sapiens*—cannot abase himself, even if he would like to, with an unthinkable, unspeakable thought: reason has no way of knowing the reasons of the heart.

Beyond discourse, against discourse, religion nevertheless remains his permanent *temptation*, thanks to him who was determined to take away his faith. At first, as we have seen, he searched for God because the philosopher-practitioner who imposed mechanist egalitarianism was first constituted as the father by divine right, implying a feudal ideology which, though incomplete, tended to complete itself in Gustave. But especially since the Fall, the lord had rejected his vassal; cursed, Gustave confused the principles of liberalism with the contemptuous hatred he believed his creator bore him; the master no longer paid attention to him except to dissect his feelings; in his exile the disappointed child felt deep inside him the scalpel's horrible and painful work. Destroyed by analysis, religion was still dazzling because it would combat, if he could believe in it, the father's analytic eye with the absolute and encompassing eye of God. No doubt he searched for some years for a way to go beyond selfishness—which had been inflicted on him through terror—toward Christian faith. Had he managed to find it, the feudal system would have been doubly reinforced. First, hierarchy would have replaced egalitarianism, devotion would have become once more the basic attitude, the only truly human relationship. Second, rejected by the Flaubert hierarchy, the little boy would have been the vassal of the Supreme Being, from whom the paterfamilias himself derived his authority. Let us imagine in sequence the two benefits Gustave thought to reap from regained religion; such an investigation will allow us to advance our understanding of this torn soul.

1. The child accepts selfishness, hedonism, and utilitarianism on the principle of authority, but he is horrified by them. He is, precisely, *not* selfish—he doesn't love himself enough. And as for his desires, they fade on this hostile terrain of a soul that does not even recognize its own right to exist. His respectful heart has only one vocation to begin with: veneration; only an *accepted* veneration would justify his being born. Stupefied by the psychological atomism that is drummed into him, he is forced to find his truth in it, but it never completely sticks; he is estranged by the false consciousness of self imposed on him. If he could regain his faith, he would find *himself*: the unmediated relation of the creature to his creator revives feelings which, through

their simple existence, defy the analytic psychology that decomposes them. One can always deny that human relations in general are governed by love, by "altruistic" feelings, because these are established between individuals of the same kind, which, being homogeneous, are none of them qualified to pull others to themselves, that is to humankind. On the other hand, to declare that the believer is following his particular interests, his profit motive when he prays, one must place oneself deliberately outside the system, declare that God doesn't exist, see him as an imaginary representation which masks the true movements of the heart rather than their source. In effect the believer does not attribute his elevations to his *nature* as man but rather to the action of the Almighty. He makes us break out of our essence through his dizzying and fascinating existence: how should we not feel inessential before God? And the reason for selfishness is finitude, that negative determination which prescribes limits in the face of what is unlimited. But when God calls his creature, shouldn't he go beyond his limits toward God? Shouldn't he want to be the All, that is, to prefer the All to the self? In his finitude itself the believer finds his reasons for surpassing it toward the infinite—for him, his determination—or the negation of the All—is to live *before God* as the abstract moment of a dialectical movement which poses the negation in order to deny it. In moments of inspiration, the infinite would be his visitation by an infinite power, a crushing yet sweet burden; but when the host has retired, it can be only the internalization of his infinite incompleteness, and this would be the infinity of absence, the appeal for love. The precise, limited, egocentric desires of liberal psychology can arise, on the other hand, only in those who take their determination for the positive source of their reality; meaning that selfishness is only a consequence of atheism, of blindness to God, and of a malign aberration that makes one see nonbeing as being and infinite being as nothingness. If only Gustave could have believed, the absolute Eye substituted for the surgical eye would have reduced hedonism and utilitarianism to pure appearances; dissatisfaction, suffering, infinite desire, the synthetic bond of interiority uniting the creature to the Creator would have been revealed under the eye of God as our truth. Gustave expected not that faith would guide his actions but that it would transform his soul or, better, rid it of the grids and scrapings of analysis in order to let him see it in its native transcendence. Against scientism—which he takes for science—he asks religion to justify his hierarchical and medieval *Weltanschauung*, the pure ideological expression of the character that was molded by the cruel lord who now thinks of nothing but destroying his work. I would say that *he was made to believe* and that at the last moment he was deprived of the means. It is his *constitution* that craves God, and the reason of an Other, inside him, that rejects Him. In his maturity, he said it clearly to Mlle Leroyer de Chantepie: "I do not like the Philosophes who have seen [in religion] only trickery and foolishness, I myself have seen it as necessity and instinct." *Necessity*: unjustified, unjustifiable, passive, disgusted with himself, given to fanaticism, Flaubert feels hemmed in by his finitude, he will not stop trying to break out of it in order to discover himself, paltry as he is, as a mode of the divine substance. *Instinct*: it is a subterranean need—organic like Félicité's devotion, and "brutish"—the very need that makes him akin to animals, to idiots, a silent postulate and at the same time an "unspeakable" perception which presents itself and disappears when he wants to grasp it, an "aperture of being" which immediately closes again. All the while, on the surface, the psychic atoms which are the products of reason follow their course untroubled. All the characters who will later preoccupy him will be visited in this way. Frédéric, Emma, all ask—unknowingly—to be delivered to atomism. Frédéric "felt something unfailing rise from the depths of his being. . . . A church clock struck the hour . . . like a voice calling to him." Bouvard and Pécuchet will be implacable against God and seek in a hundred ways to demonstrate that he doesn't exist. Nothing helps: they open the door of a church and immediately feel that they are seeing the sunrise. It doesn't last, it never lasts; the awakenings are bitter—one more failure. Still, even if ecstasy in Flaubert is a brief moment, it provides some respite from cares, from paltry and pitiless misfortunes; one is saved during prayer because one forgets oneself. And indeed, the end result is positive. "Any devotion," he writes, "provided it absorbed his soul and allowed the whole of existence to disappear."

2. This need to burst the matrix of the individual allows us to understand why Flaubert's particular religiosity could have taken the form of a rather vague Spinozist outlook: "To be matter!" Antoine will say. This saint is matter already, that's all he is, in fact—the son of Achille-Cléophas has no doubt about it. But what he would like is to be *all* of matter, infinitely infinite in its unity. From the beginning, therefore, the little vassal's battle against analytic erosion includes possible recourse to that religion of exchange, pantheism, in which he could satisfy all his postulations. Except one, the very aspiration to vassalage. He is really not thinking of the kind of impersonal Absolute that he could dissolve into rather than rise up toward. In

the eyes of his family, Gustave is *truly* inessential—he is gratuitous. Under the eye of the Almighty, he is the lowly object of an infinite generosity who wants to feel essential in his inessentiality. A servant of God, born for his Glory, nothing more than a means. But the means chosen by the absolute Being to become the supreme Creator and make himself adored. It will be noted that the mysterious and infrequent elevations of his characters are always tied to the sacred calm of holy places. For Gustave himself, it is always *in church* and mostly during a ceremony that he is overcome by religious emotion. If he wants to believe, it is not in Christ but rather in a paternal, harsh God who burdens him with incessant demands. He is waiting for a sign from on high to come and give value, not to his individuality, oh no— he wants to escape from that—but to his simple existence, which will be *charged with a mission!* To Frédéric, as we have seen, a bell sounds like a call, and this is what little Gustave wants, a murmur from on high: "You were not born for nothing. You were awaited." In this sense, Flaubert's God has nothing in common with the God of the bourgeois faithful; for them, the Almighty guarantees order, meaning real property; for Gustave, God guarantees only existence, and the sole justification he gives for it is a mandate—this is the God of the Crusaders, of the Spanish mystics, of the poor, the God of the Middle Ages. This is not surprising, for the Bourbons and the Church, skipping over the centuries, made medieval feudalism a model and the chief theme of their propaganda.

Above all, as I have said, by baptizing his son Dr. Flaubert *pledged* him. This means that he gave him at the outset and marked in his flesh the right to be integrated into the most totalitarian of feudal hierarchies. We are no longer dealing with thoughts or ecstasies but with an objective and strict order in which he has a place. In this sense he searches for God in order to find the Church. Gustave has little liking for the religions of individuals, by which I mean private arrangements with heaven. And whatever the value he attaches to ecstasy—to the direct communication of the creature with the Creator—the imperatives he was given through exquisite torture, the right to live that Achille-Cléophas bestowed and then took away, must pursue him and overtake him, supernatural as they are, through *human* superiors. Nothing would suit him better than a religion practiced in common with others; what he goes to look for in temples, even more than the sacred silence of the stones or the holy light filtering through the stained glass windows, is the spectacle of the kneeling crowds raising and lowering their thousand heads at the imperious signal of a bell, obedient to the orders of the ministers of the cult who repeat the archetypal event in front of them each day, the supreme and distant gift: a Creator who makes himself mortal and dies in agony to save his creatures. Not that Gustave loved the common herd; quite to the contrary, he detested them; their numberless multitude reflected the status of molecular solitude that Achille-Cléophas had imposed on him; but when they prayed in the churches they became an organized *people*. The flock under the staff of the good shepherd. The *faithful*—no word could have had more attraction for the little vassal. Baptized, he was conscious that his place was among them, he belongs to this humanity encompassed by God through the priests, to Catholicism. For this reason he gives Pascal's words their true meaning: kneel down and you will believe, he says to the libertine. All right, one can always try. On the condition one has received the first sacraments and is a virtual member of the Church. The most hardened libertine of the seventeenth century met these conditions out of necessity, for who would have dared to refuse to baptize his children? And Gustave Flaubert, around 1830, a son of the most cautious of libertines, met these conditions as well. Should a Hindu or a Chinese fall on his knees, what would he see, what would he feel? Nothing. Genuflection itself will not have the symbolic meaning for him that we attribute to it. But for Gustave, who has made his first communion, the symbol is part of him, it is the signification of a habit, the structuring of a posture. He falls on his knees and revives his trans-ascendence, an empty but decipherable intention that aims at heaven. Afterward, faith either comes or it does not; the Christian *form* either does or does not receive its contents. What matters is that Gustave from the beginning is *signified* Catholic by the permanent possibility of genuflection, of murmuring the *pater noster*, by what the things surrounding him *say*—the walls, the rose window, the altar, the odor of incense, the organ. *He is a potential believer*: to believe is to become what he is. Hasn't he tried countless times? He writes in *Novembre*: "Two or three times he went to church in time for the service; he tried to pray; how his friends would have laughed if they had seen him dip his fingers into the holy water and make the sign of the cross." His friends? I doubt it. Naturally, those around him—primarily Alfred—affected a preference for black masses as opposed to church masses. They defied God, putting themselves defiantly—and under the influence of Byron—on the side of Cain, of Satan. But as we shall see later, these blasphemies were only vain efforts to transcend a contradictory situation common to an entire generation tormented by the need to believe and dechristianized by their parents' agnosticism. More than one of them, I imagine, could have been found secretly kneeling at prayer in a distant church, ready for a quick getaway, making his escape by scaling the walls like some town notable leaving a brothel. Indeed, the only "friend" who might snigger behind Gustave's back, or whose "hideous Voltairean smile" and analytic scrutiny he might have feared to encounter by looking behind him, was his father. This means that the laughter came from Gustave himself: the laughter and the prayer are one and the same. This can be seen still more clearly in an earlier text, *La Main de fer*, a story begun in February 1837 and left unfinished:

> Now and then a young and pure heart is found that comes to be nourished by faith, and still more often some surfeited and withered soul comes to be rejuvenated by heavenly love, to be revived by belief, to be sanctified by prayer. This latter soul takes God for a young love and faith for a passion, while the former gives himself entirely, kneels with delight, prays with ardor, believes out of instinct; the mass for the dead is no longer a grotesque sing-song for him, the chanting of the priests ceases to be venal, the church is something holy, and hope becomes palpable and positive, he is happy because he believes.

We shall note—all the themes of Flaubert's work and life are expressed by the time he is fifteen years old—that he makes faith an *instinct*; this is the word that will come to his pen nearly thirty-five years later in his letter to Mlle de Chantepie. To be sure, the pure soul and the withered soul both belong to Gustave; what is essential is not their differences but their common attitude: to love God religiously with a profane passion. His hero, in effect, seduced by the ceremonies of Catholicism, lets himself slip into "a sweet revery of faith and love"; "this revery was his youth, he took God for another passion—it would pass like the others." Is this a condemnation of Christianity? It is a confession, rather, a self-reproach; this sensuous deism—he takes God like a woman, and this carnal love will exhaust itself like all loves—is not Gustave's style. It belongs to that epicureanism he affects to criticize in himself, wrongly. We have just seen that in fact he is not seeking in faith the pleasures that Mme Guyon found there. The passage just cited is completely dictated by resentment: I could not believe, he says, full of rancor, or not long enough; I could not adapt the wild raptures of my deism to strict ritual discipline. This seems to be a circular argument: in order for the sacred to manifest itself in holy places, the faithful must be sacred himself, must enter infused with the sacred in advance. It is not enough to cross the threshold of a church to pass from nature to the supernatural—the supernatural is a grace that must never leave the believer; only on this condition will it be manifest to him in the temple as the numinous and terrible condensation of the supernatural of everyday. In other words, in order to become a believer, you must be one already. Otherwise, the best you can hope for is to be charmed by the incense, the light, the music, and to be lost in a *mundane* ecstasy. This is Gustave's conclusion. Faith, for him, is the torment of Tantalus, though he has all the prerequisites and the sacraments have structured him as a believer. He thinks that all he has to do is imitate the ritual gestures of others— the holy water, the sign of the cross, the prayer. But no—go down on your knees and you will not believe. It is impossible to make actual the virtual faith that haunts him. Hence frustration; baptized, given communion, Gustave *owns* a seat amid the other seats in the nave of the cathedral, along with all the attendant privileges, in particular the privilege of possessing God. He takes part in the mass, he takes the posture of a believer in order to receive the joy of His goodness. And the deception angers him every time. He will have his place, he will make the gestures and say the words, the mystery of the Passion will be played before him; at best he will feel inside the beginnings of something like a "dawning," he will have the feeling, "this is it!" He is about to find faith, he does, and the next moment everything crumbles, he finds the void once more, and a withered heart.

Resentment was growing during this time; demonic thought was gaining ground. This does not mean that the religiosity of the adolescent gave way to positivism but that he reversed the signs and gave himself to Satan. Now, continuing to be passive, he feels an iron hand lift him into the air, and it often seems to be the Devil's—the elevation persists, but what awaits him on the summit is radical evil. What becomes of God in this reverse mysticism? That depends. He can be the evil principle itself, more wicked than a demon, as in *Rêve d'enfer*; sometimes, as in *La Danse des morts*, he appears in the form of Jesus Christ, watching the tortures the Evil One inflicts on men and weeping in silence, overcome. Flaubert's Manichaeanism conforms to his pessimism of resentment: the battle between good and evil will not end—any more than that between science and faith. But is it really a battle? Evil is quite real, tangible: Ahriman is the uncontested master of the earth; as for Ormuzd, we are told he is in heaven, he must be; otherwise the dissatisfaction, the infinite desire that torments the souls of men would be a mere trick. But he keeps quiet—not a sign from on high; all the admonitions we receive, all the warnings that pave our way are authored by Ahriman. The issue, as we see, is not agnosticism—Flaubert does not complain, like so many disappointed believers, of not having found God; of course he doesn't deem the proofs of God's existence convincing, but at bottom that does not worry him; indeed, if the Eternal could be felt in the heart, Gustave would only have to make scholastic proofs. Nor is he very concerned about bumping into facts—those ubiquitous, sudden, and silent walls of rock; as a religious soul, he sees the world from a religious point of view, feeling at his own expense the ambivalence of the sacred; what he complains about is having found the Devil. The meaning is clear: if the Church doesn't accept me, if I am not saved by faith, I fall back into the clutches of the Other who conceived me, bore me, cursed me, who inhabits and alienates me with his consuming atomism. God thus becomes the Counter-Father; the father, being Counter-God, a black lord, seems like a henchman of the Devil if not the Devil himself. Gustave's resentment finds what it expects to find: the worst is certain, the younger son will forever be a martyr to his progenitor. He does not go so far as to deny the existence of the Almighty, but irritated by His intolerable silence, Flaubert makes him impotent: God allows the world to be stolen from *under his nose* by the spirit that always denies; now vanquished, he shuts himself up in sullen indifference.

That Gustave considers divine silence the original scandal is clear from a story written at the age of fifteen, *Rage et Impuissance*, a tale about a man buried alive. The unfortunate man hears approaching steps and knocks on the wood of his coffin, but the steps die away and he dies blaspheming. There is no doubt that it is Gustave suffocating in the coffin. The steps of the gravedigger indicate the presence, above, beyond the sleeping dead, of *Someone*. If he is heard, the child will be saved, like a Lazarus he will *be raised up*. The gravedigger departs. Could God be simply a trap? This isn't openly stated, just that he is a little hard of hearing and cannot or does not want to help anyone. It is easy enough now to interpret the symbol. A few key words we have seen take on greater meaning in the course of this study will help us. In particular the word *impotence*, which so aptly characterizes Gustave's passivity and so poorly describes—*in appearance*—what one generally thinks of as the "search for God." In fact, what ordinarily takes place—or at least what is claimed to take place—is, for the arrogant, a hunt, for the humble, begging; in any

503

event it is an act. The arrogant, at full speed and accompanied by huntsmen and valets, aim to track God down and corner him like a deer; there are no tracks, they get lost in the forest. Indeed, they think God is the one who has defaulted—would he make a man run like this and fail to keep the appointed meeting without even an excuse? Perhaps he doesn't exist at all. This is what the others wonder too, the beggars; they themselves have not run, they have acted on themselves; they have fasted, humiliated themselves, transformed themselves, killing their pride, tearing apart their persona in order to *make themselves* into that chasm, that opening to all being which Gustave sometimes, for a moment, *becomes*. And then? Nothing; their hollowed souls are traversed only by the night wind. Some people think *today* that this is not really so bad. In Flaubert's time, most were vexed— all that work *for nothing*! These poor people had the choice of being struck by their unworthiness or by the suspicion that God might be only a joke. In any case, they did not remain passive; some thought they had acted wrongly and that each step they took only brought them further from God when they believed they were approaching him, whereas others thought they had done their best, that their soul was a great, empty reception hall stripped of its furnishings and perfectly suitable for receiving a divine guest; if the guest did not answer the invitation, it was likely that he had lost his way or was long since dead, or had never existed. No one, in any case, either among the cursed hunters or among the beggars, would have charged himself with impotence. Flaubert, however, does just this. And look how he presents himself to us: lying on his back like a corpse on a marble table, with the blind eyes of a cadaver; but a cadaver's eyes are as hard as pebbles, or running, or worm-eaten, whereas his are penetrated by darkness. Yet after all, perhaps this is how the perpetual life he attributes to the dead experiences the joint disappearance of the visual organs and vision. In any event, Gustave is deceased, *socially*. Let us understand that the others consider him departed and immediately subject him to the rules of the dead. He is dead for the Other and therefore soon eliminated by the Other; all he has to do is resign himself to becoming what he already is for everyone else. He has one last chance: deprived of sight, of movement, half suffocated, consumed by anguish, this recumbent figure can still clench his fist and knock on the coffin wall. Let us note, however, that he has very little hope of making himself heard—his position prevents him from knocking with all his strength, he can barely move his elbow. It is certainly true that he has been *reduced to impotence*. Let us translate: the young man, in spite of his ecstasies, has been manipulated in such a way that he no longer has the means to appeal to his Savior.

He nevertheless has great need of him. Let us reread Musset, his elder, who had become only a half believer. When he wrote *Rage et Impuissance*, Gustave had not yet read *La Confession d'un enfant du siècle*, which had appeared a few months earlier. What is the sickness Musset claims has infected his entire generation? The withering of feeling, skepticism, the lack of specific objectives, a nihilistic nonchalance, a boredom that is taken for despair—these are the symptoms. It is maddening—unquestioned faith would have given these young people a purpose, assured satisfactions, an ethic, and would have spared them debauchery, the flight into alcohol and opium. But after all, you can live without it—cheerlessly, badly, with the intermittent scintillation of love, which always ends in sadness but begins again a little later. Besides, it's fun to moan of a despair you don't entirely feel. In short, for the sons of the imperial warriors, the absence of God or his barely perceptible presence seemed a profitable lack. It was quite a different matter for Gustave, threatened by a horrible death imposed on him inadvertently by others; faith offered itself as his only recourse and was a matter of extreme urgency. If we delve further into the symbol, the meaning is clear: the Other made me such that I need God (the earthly creation of the false cadaver puts him *in need* of appealing for help to those on high; if he does not make himself heard, then he will be a cadaver *for real*). Which means that if God does not exist, then I am *already* that enchanted cadaver created by the paternal curse; then mechanism, the infernal trap in which I cannot believe, becomes my *alien truth*. I am dying every moment since at every moment I pass from the belief that a cosmos exists encompassed by a supreme will that created me in it by a particular decree, to the conviction—which is foreign to me by nature—that this cosmos, like myself, is only an illusion and nothing exists but chance, exteriority, disintegration. Thus I was made in such a way that faith is my urgent and singular need. But the very reasons that force me to believe deprive me of the possibility of believing; the man buried alive *must* attract the attention of the gravediggers or die, but precisely because I was put into a coffin and thrown into a grave, there isn't a chance of being heard. If he had used a different image, Flaubert might have written Villon's marvelous line: "Je meurs de soif auprès de la fontaine." The one he chose, however, suits him still better. Pinioned, reduced to impotence, lying on his back, he is looking upward. But between him and heaven there is that low, oppressing ceiling, the creator of shadows which is the lid of the coffin. In other words, he has been plunged into the abject universe of things: below him, the earth, the mud where the worms are already crawling; above him this lid and soon the engulfing earth—*we cannot leave the earth*. Which means, all told, that the real is a horrible plenitude from which one cannot *find a way out*; direct communication with the supernatural *is not possible*. In this story Gustave disavows his religious raptures. To be raised up we need steps, a stairway that begins on earth and is lost in the heavens, an objective hierarchy. Who is the gravedigger whose footsteps he hears? God, certainly, but perhaps also his representative on earth, a minister of the cult who walks away, like Larivière, so as not to be compromised. God's silence, we see, is in itself evil, the negative sacred: He refuses to aid the pitiful martyr and buries him. Accomplice of the Devil, who has reduced his victim to impotence, God abandons him just when he ought to be sending his angels to tear him away from the Devil. What is worse, this sacred (since it is divine) abandonment is what consecrates the woeful human executioners and their sad task; Achille-Cléophas is a layman, a secular person; he becomes the Devil because God consecrates him by his very indifference; by watching coldly as the chief surgeon performs an autopsy on his son, God lends him a little of his own numinous power. When the adolescent, buried alive by his father with the blessing of the Creator, becomes conscious of his situation, his impotence is turned to *rage*, another key word in the story. Here's another of those masculine rages that impel Marguerite and Mazza to spit on the doorsteps of churches and are in fact only the other side of impotence or, if you like, passion overturning the whole body to give it the illusion of being totally mobilized in action. Gustave feels it and says it clearly here: his impotence is constituted, it is the consequence of his primitive passivity. There is perhaps something he ought *to do* to attract divine attention to himself; but his passive activity does not allow him to do anything but offer himself, immobile and mute, to the forces of the cosmos. Invisibly, by the imperceptible expression of his submission, he makes a tacit offer—an intention winding through experience between flesh and skin—of his permanent submission to the Supreme Being, if absolutely necessary calling out feebly and in vain, the way an infant in its cradle, bound in its wrappings, calls out in anguish for its mother when she has just left the room. This is not at all sufficient, of course, to justify a lasting visitation. But the moment he has recognized it, he adds in rage: *they made me this way*, inadequate in my father's eyes, inadequate in the eyes of the Almighty. On this ideological level, he could, if he wanted to, justify the principle of his pessimism by stating: the paternal curse made me into this monster who can live neither with God nor without Him.

Afterward he deepened the meaning of this conflict, which arose from the fact that he was marked by the two dominant ideologies of his time and whose primary characteristic was that the terms of the contradiction, far from repelling each other, interpenetrated. In the notes he took in Jerusalem, 11 August 1850, we find these curious remarks: "This is the third day we are in Jerusalem, I have felt none of the emotions I expected in advance, neither religious enthusiasm, nor stimulation of the imagination, nor *hatred of the priests*. . . ."[17] In the face of all I see I feel emptier than a hollow barrel. This morning, in the Holy Sepulcher, the truth is that a dog would have been more moved than I was. Whose fault is it, God of mercy? Theirs? Mine? or Yours? Theirs, I believe, then mine, Yours."[18]

In leaving Egypt for Palestine, Gustave *expected* a revelation from Jerusalem; he foresaw a gamut of possible emotions. This is no longer quite the same young man we are describing here, for ever since his "nervous attack" he has been consumed by the imaginary; he permanently retains what he calls the "aesthetic attitude," which signifies that he is continually trying to unrealize the real, to grasp what he sees as a painted spectacle, what he hears as an impersonal and stupefying exchange of dramatic dialogue spoken by no one, accompanied by noise from the wings, and to view what he does as a sequence of savage rites of ancient and unknown origin. So it is normal that in the Holy Sepulcher, a place with a formidable and more than half mythic past, he should expect Christ's tomb, if only by its site, to communicate an aesthetic emotion to him—that is, with the help of sacred history to let itself blossom forth from the surrounding reality. This is not to desire faith, quite the contrary, but to aspire to the moment when the highest place in the Christian religion should appear to him as a beautiful, nontemporal image, neither true nor false. Here we find that aesthete's religion that had Chateaubriand, an agnostic, as its prophet and Barrès, an unbeliever, as its last priest. What is more surprising is that Gustave, after so many professions of nihilist faith and so many affirmations of his "belief in noth-

17. Flaubert's italics.
18. Edition du Centenaire 4:147.

ing," gives highest place to the emotion "expected in advance," *religious enthusiasm*. It is clear that beauty is certainly not what he is primarily seeking in Jerusalem; of course it is the *artist* who anticipates the pleasures of imagination, but they come second. Religious enthusiasm is the act of the *believer*. But if Gustave believes in nothing? That's just it—he does not believe *enough*; this is not unbelief but rather a faith that must suffer from a kind of inner weakness, some sort of inconsistency that prevents it from moving from religiosity to religion. The young man hopes that *something* will pass, like a discharge of the sacred, from the most numinous object in the world— potential infinite—to his own sad flesh—potential nearly zero. On this point he has not changed since the story denouncing his impotence; he can only open himself and wait—it is up to the Almighty to make the first step. If He is willing, Gustave will be struck by faith; he will not die of it, he will keep it like an incurable burn and the game will be over; unless it stays in the tomb, ready to strike the next pilgrim, in which case even in his unfeeling moments Gustave will be able to refer, as to another archetypal event, to the sudden false lightning flash that seared him to the bone and was lost.

On the nature of the expected emotion, a letter written to Louis Bouilhet the following week gives us details. Gustave returned to the Holy Sepulcher. Another disappointment. He adds: "I did not cry over my lack of feeling or have any regrets, but I experienced that strange feeling that two men 'like us' experience when they are alone in front of the fire and digging with all the powers of their souls that old pit represented by the word 'love,' try to imagine what it might be—if it were possible."[19] Sacred love was the object of his expectation. Which kind of love? Was he hoping to feel the weight of the love God bears toward men, or to feel as a rush of fire the love the creature ought to feel for the Creator? We shall know by recalling the circumstance that gave rise to this "tender bitterness": "I was looking at the holy stone; the priest took a rose and gave it to me . . . , then took it back from me, placed it on the stone in order to bless the flower." In the beginning, there was the Gift. A gift from heaven—Gustave acknowledges it explicitly since he calls it, two lines below, a "gift." All at once the feudal hierarchy is resurrected in its entirety; the Church is there as mediator, for it is through the priest that the supreme Lord offers the rose, a drop of his son's living blood. The

19. To Louis Bouilhet, 20 August 1850, *Correspondance* 2:231.

blessed flower is a sign and an invitation: the Lord gave his body and his life for everyone; he is giving them again, to Gustave in particular; in exchange, he demands that the young man pledge himself unreservedly, that he recognize through an act of love the sacrifice of love that has just been renewed. What is being proposed here, on the initiative of an authorized representative, is the feudal ceremony of homage. This is what Gustave came to look for in Jerusalem: the resurrection of the golden age, the rebirth—a hundredfold—of the faithful passion he had borne toward the paterfamilias and the demanding generosity the father had deigned to show him. Love, that "old pit," Flaubert wrote after his two visits to the Sepulcher, is impossible; he had said it again and again to Alfred, to Bouilhet, "in front of the fire." But during the night of 7–8 August in Ramla, when he couldn't sleep "because of the mosquitos, the horses, and the idea that I must see Jerusalem the next day,"[20] he was convinced of the possibility of love, even its imminence: "I was not asking for more than to be moved, you know me,"[21] he wrote to Bouilhet. And in his travel notes, when he mentions the useless gift of the rose, he adds: "It was one of the bitterest moments of my life."[22] A man of twenty-eight who runs after divine love, not so much for the feeling of being loved as for the devotion that the rite of homage will kindle in his heart, is quite unlikely to change and more than likely to languish all his life, dreaming of a radical and qualitative metamorphosis of experience that would give him access to *felt* holiness.

Gustave will never believe, and he knows it. Because it is impossible for him to believe. The emotion "expected in advance," religiously awaited, he also senses "in advance" will not happen. Is it really true that he "was not asking for more than to be moved"? Here he is, at any rate, before the Sepulcher, dry as an empty barrel. Whose fault is it? He says: "Theirs, mine, Yours." Let us not suppose that he discovered the guilty parties only when religious enthusiasm eluded him in Jerusalem. He knew them long before. Only one is not mentioned: Achille-Cléophas. We shall see why shortly. Let us examine the briefs of the accused in order.

Theirs . . . How false it all is! What liars they are! How it is whitewashed, disguised, varnished, made for exploitation, propaganda

---

20. *Voyage en Orient*, Edition du Centenaire 4:147.
21. 20 August 1850, *Correspondance* 2:230.
22. *Voyage en Orient*, Edition du Centenaire 4:156.

and profit!"[23] And in a letter to Bouilhet: "Everything possible has been done to make the holy places ridiculous. It is all whorish to the last degree: hypocrisy, cupidity, falsification and impudence, yes; but as for holiness, not a trace. I resent this foolishness because I was left unmoved."[24] The same day, he writes to his mother: "The turpitude, baseness, simony, ignoble things of all sorts that one sees here surpass the usual bounds. The holy places do nothing for you. Falsehood is everywhere and too obvious. As for the artistic side of things, the Breton churches are Renaissance museums by comparison."[25] We should add to this the fanaticism and hatred: "The Holy Sepulcher is the agglomeration of all possible execrations. Within such a tiny space there are four churches: Armenian, Greek, Latin and Coptic, all heartily insulting and cursing each other and quarreling over candlesticks, rugs, pictures—and what pictures!"

Fine. But none of this is really new for him. Let us recall that in *La Main de fer* he ridiculed the last rites as a grotesque comedy and criticized priests for their venality. Flaubert evinced quite early a fierce anticlericalism. And throughout his correspondence he attacks priests with great relish. Later, under the liberal Empire and after the Commune, he urged his friends to fight against the "Priest's Party"; and the Catholic church, which triumphed under Thiers and MacMahon, worried him much more than those "mad dogs" the communards.

It goes without saying that parish priests were hardly appreciated in the family of Achille-Cléophas. The Congrégation with its tyranny, its spies, its processions, had done everything possible to make itself despised by the bourgeoisie. After 1830, when one could speak out, Dr. Flaubert had not hidden from his younger son what he thought of that organization. The paternal influence is not in doubt, but it does not explain everything. In fact, Gustave's anticlericalism is suspect. At first it is passionate—a convinced atheist would have been more decorous and above all more moderate; the priest would be an enemy to combat but not the infamous object of lewd and futile vituperation. And then, Gustave is not content to feel this burning hatred of the "cross," or even to broadcast it—he projects it in Homais, the odious, absurd pharmacist, in order to *make fun of it*. These two observations allow us to conclude that behind the sarcasm of an unbeliever who reproaches priests with wanting to impose their mum-

23. Ibid., p. 145.
24. *Correspondance* 2:230.
25. Ibid., p. 233.

510

meries, there is the very personal rancor of a man who *wants to believe* but is continually discouraged by priests. We shall see later on, Homais is right to rail against the stupidity and materialism of the Abbé Bournisien; he is wrong *to be untroubled by it.* This makes all the difference. This ambiguity is Gustave's style: agnostic and scientist through his father, he jeers at religious "rigamarole" from the height of his rationalist knowledge and at the same time criticizes the parish priests for not coming to his rescue; they don't have the strength of mind necessary to refute the Voltaireanism and serious objections of scientism, and at the very least they fail to prove their virtue sufficiently to convince him by example. In a word, they show themselves to be incapable of snatching him from his father's hands.

In her distraught state, Mme Bovary goes to ask for help from the Abbé Bournisien; his foolishness and triviality seal her damnation, and she becomes melancholy. Yet someone has correctly noticed that this episode nearly reproduces a story written at seventeen,[26] the same year he slandered the Abbé Eudes in front of the "poor faithful" of the religious institution. A desperate young man wants to meet with a priest so that he can "be persuaded of the immortality of his soul." He goes to the priest's house, sits down in the kitchen in front of a great fire on which a pot with "a huge quantity of potatoes is boiling." The priest soon joins him. "He was an old man with white hair, his bearing full of gentleness and good will. . . . But scarcely had I begun than, hearing the sound of the cooking, he cried: 'Rose, be careful with the potatoes.' And turning around, I saw . . . that the connoisseur of potatoes had a crooked nose covered with pimples. I left with a burst of laughter and the door closed immediately after me." Curiously, Gustave follows his story, twelve years before his trip to the Orient, with the same question he asks at the Holy Sepulcher: "Tell me now, whose fault is it? . . . Is it *my* fault, if this man has a crooked nose covered with bumps? Is it my fault if his eager voice struck me as gluttonous and brutish? Certainly not, for I had gone in with devout feelings." We recognize here the precaution Flaubert will take in 1850: "I was not asking for more than to be moved"; hence the trinity of the guilty: them, me, you. He adds, in fact: "Yet it isn't this poor man's fault, either, if his nose is ill-formed and he likes potatoes. Not at all; it is the fault of the one who made crooked noses and potatoes." This time everyone is acquitted except God. But the acquittal of the priest is not very convincing: the Creator made him this way, that is

26. *Agonies*, written in April 1838. IX.

all Gustave can say in his defense. He was given the mission of guiding souls and only shocks them by his ugliness, his materialism, and his gluttony; a troubled adolescent appealed for his help and he was more concerned with his potatoes. It is futile for Thibaudet to remark that all priests are not like that. For God's sake! And if taken literally, the story would have to remain inconclusive. Did Flaubert think that *all* priests were gourmands like this one or insensitive, materialistic fools like Bournisien? I don't think so, although I admit there is a rule well known to novelists and offering few exceptions: when there is only *one* black person in a novel and this person commits a crime, the author is suggesting to us that *all* blacks are potential criminals; when only *one* Jew is found in a story and he is clearly treacherous and avaricious, the author is a militant anti-Semite who condemns *all* Jews and invites us to share his opinions. But Flaubert "hasn't any ideas," and he "doesn't reach any conclusions"—he himself says so. He *feels*, and his rancorous memory broods endlessly on the same odious recollections. If he takes an episode seriously enough to reproduce it in two such different works fifteen years apart, it must be linked to profound delight or displeasure. Between the ages of thirteen and fifteen, Flaubert seems more concerned with displaying his Manichaeanism (the worst is always certain, the world belongs to Satan) than with regaining the faith of the golden age; the arrogant technique of ecstasies without God yielded appreciable results, and he was learning other spiritual exercises, in particular the exercise of unrealization which we shall shortly take up; the friendship with Alfred bore fruit, and then, intoxicated by writing, the creature allowed himself the joys of the Creator. But, and we shall see why, this calm exterior did not prevent the growth of unhappiness or ennui or anguish. The great nihilist orgies on Thursdays—when he and Le Poittevin "exhausted everything, made everything pass before them, greeted it all with a grotesque laugh and a fearful grimace"—left him worn out, anxious; school overwhelmed him, and the chief surgeon did not disguise his preference for Achille. For Gustave's wounded heart, everything was unhappiness and spleen. The raptures, at first nonreligious or pantheistic, now end in a collapse; the void is infinite, the contemplation of the All becomes the perception of nothing. The world, if it is not created, is nothingness for Gustave. He is convinced he will suffer more every day until his death; if there is no other life, his miseries will have been grotesquely useless. He proclaims it, of course, since it is the result of his demonology, of the paternal mechanism reviewed and corrected by his resentment—he has visions of

512

horror which do not entirely displease him. But between the ages of fifteen and sixteen, he panics and takes fright in the face of the nihilism he himself has forged. Not for long; only a few months are needed for him to return to absolute pessimism. In *Mémoires d'un fou*, however, which dates from the summer of 1838, he gives evidence that what had become unbearable anguish obliged him to take time out. "I came to doubt everything, I laughed bitterly at myself, so young, so disillusioned by life, by love, by glory, by God, by all that is, by all that can be. I had nonetheless a natural horror of embracing that faith in nothingness; at the edge of the abyss I closed my eyes and fell in." There are, in fact, three periods: bitter cynicism, ironic skepticism is the first. In the second, Gustave perceives the consequences of his attitude: if he continues what he will later call his "unhealthy reveries," if he is too complacent with the black boastings to which he is prompted by resentment, he will end by "believing in nothing." In the beginning he toyed with this belief; now it floods him, he is afraid of losing control—on the edge of the abyss he is seized by a "natural horror." Another passage in the same book indicates that Gustave was not content to "close his eyes"; indeed, he wanted to prevent the fall: "Man . . . poor weak-legged insect who wants to cling to all the branches on the edge of the abyss, who is attached to virtue, love, selfishness, ambition, and who makes all these into virtues so as to cling the better, who holds fast to God and who continually weakens, lets go, and falls." At the age of fifteen, Gustave saw the abyss and, dizzy with vertigo, held fast to God. What is he, then, this God of Mercy? Blind, deaf, insensitive? A nonentity. He doesn't make a move to catch the desperate boy. But it isn't that a rotten branch breaks and spins off into the void with him clinging onto it; it is that Gustave's hands are too weak. He is the one who *lets go*.

It was most likely between 1837 and 1838 that he wanted to consult a priest. Against his father, against that part of himself that proscribed this faith he so badly needed. For a long time now he had secretly been entering churches; for a long time afterward, no doubt, he continued to visit them intermittently. But the decisive meeting—perhaps there were several—happened during his fifteenth or sixteenth year. I am willing to believe that he was less disappointed than humiliated. When an adolescent wants to tell his troubles to a strange adult, he is at a loss to make himself understood, and nine times out of ten the adult cannot listen because he is feeling the approach of death and is losing the keys to his own life one by one—what is there to say to a child when you have such a poor understanding of your own past? The youngster feels offended; his malaise, formulated badly, perhaps, but nonetheless profound and unique, has been reduced to the generality of an adolescent crisis. The priest's primary advice must have been dull and cautious; he was certainly familiar, if only by hearsay, with the terrible Dr. Flaubert, and after the harsh defeat of the Church Militant in 1830 and the triumph of the bourgeoisie, such a priest was not interested in heedlessly converting the younger son of this family of freethinkers—the priests had discovered their unpopularity and were keeping very quiet. This wary attitude—which showed greater consideration for the political situation than for the vital needs of a soul—rather than pure and simple gluttony is what the potatoes symbolize. The parish priest has interests other than those arising from his office; he is an adult pickled in the juices of adulthood, in his adult problems which essentially concern his relations with his superiors and the laity in the great freemasonry of grown-ups from which Gustave is excluded on principle. The child holds it against him that he is closer, at bottom, to Achille-Cléophas than to his young visitor, more concerned with respecting a tacit agreement with the liberals—powerful in the cities—than with slaking a soul's inextinguishable thirst for God. In this sense, Flaubert's anticlericalism was *specific to his era*. The Church had taken the victory of the allies in 1815 for its own victory; it was inclined to react with terror to the bourgeois current of dechristianization, to stick to its dogmas, to impose them by formal and already outmoded arguments, and above all to depend on the "secular arm." Rejected in 1830, wounded but still powerful, it retreated and entrenched itself. The clerics did not yet know the true dangers threatening them; they hadn't time to mount a defensive strategy against the scientific spirit, which was quite different from scientism. Their sole response to the slow erosion of Christian ideology was tactical: they fought to preserve their monopoly on primary education.

But what Flaubert was demanding of the ministers of the cult was to defend him against science. Behind the mechanism and scientism that characterized the ideology of the liberals was a new conception of the truth perceived as the unity of the new methods employed to attain it—methods forbidden to his "weak hands." But this passive and submissive child did not dare ask the priests to combat science head-on; he *believed* in it because his black lord practiced it daily: he believed that a rigorous and anatomical knowledge of organs could be based on dissection; he believed in the propositions of the natural sciences. And during his lifetime he would have nothing but sarcasm for ignorant priests who had the audacity to attack scientific laws in the name of dogma. Between Galileo and the pope he certainly chose Galileo. What he was asking of the Church is more subtle; it was not to hurl itself against Newtonian mechanics like Don Quixote tilting at windmills, and still less to multiply false miracles to make us see God on earth, for He is not there and the laws of nature are never suspended. No, Flaubert's problem goes deeper, it was the problem of an entire generation that wanted to react against the Jacobinism of its fathers but found itself in new difficulties because of the expansion of knowledge: how could one keep or rediscover faith and at the same time absorb experimental science? The question would soon be posed to the Church itself and was a vital one to this great body, which remained medieval in the early years of the industrial revolution. At this time the Church was not aware of the danger. Certain young laymen were agonizing over it, but no one else. Between 1835 and 1840 Gustave was looking for a young priest who could prove the existence of the Creator by the eternal silence of created worlds, his ubiquity by his universal absence, his omnipotence by his radical and acquiescent impotence, the inflexibility of his law by its mutability and the anarchy of human societies; his goodness and love by our sufferings, his inexorable justice by the virtue of the miserable and the happiness of the wicked. If, radicalizing the bourgeois and Jansenist conception of the hidden world, such a priest had said to Gustave: "God is nowhere, neither in space nor time, nor in your heart; and what is this infinite void, this cold, our eternal hopelessness, if not him? You search outside yourself to discover a mandate; there is nothing, of course. The sign and the mandate is this absurd and futile quest that you pursue against all evidence, and against your father's arguments. No, you would not search for God if you had not already found him; and for that very reason you must never hope to see him or touch him: He is found, I tell you, therefore you will seek him to the end in ignorance and anguish." In short, if this precursor could have invented just for him the religious dialectic of the negative, which today is developed and practiced everywhere by specialists, he would have worked the permanent conversion of the Voltairean philosopher's son. This is what Gustave was asking for, nothing more: that his religious impotence should be transformed into "God's gaping wound." We have seen him in this same period pronounce himself to be antitruth, which amounts to saying: "Truth exists, I know it, I believe in it and I am *against* it." If he is alone, if

515

Catholicism has abandoned him to himself, this rejection can have only one meaning: I prefer error, the unreal, the dream. In one sense, this is a way of disqualifying himself: truth surrounds me, encloses me, penetrates me, inhabits me, but I haven't the strength to stand it, therefore I evade it by dreaming or by going into an ecstatic trance. But this dissatisfaction is a profound challenge: there must be something rotten in man or the world for *homo sapiens* to be unable to bear the knowledge he himself has produced. If Catholicism, through one of its functionaries, should deign to institutionalize, to sanctify this dissatisfaction, it would become the ultimate case in point for Gustave; recognized by the Other and at the same time resented as an Other, it would manifest itself to him as his most profound instinct, the brute postulation of God, that is to say, his *creatural* being. Nothing more. Unhappiness and frustration are not thereby eliminated because of course the postulation remains futile, the instinct can manifest itself only through malaise since there are no words, no reasons to explain this need for belief in the rational universe of discourse. However, with a negative theology Gustave might have kept his distance and imagined science with distaste, from the point of view of the non-knowledge that enveloped him and that would have been consecrated by the priests. The little boy would not have challenged the brilliant system of imposed truths—that is the sun, it is daytime—but he would simply have identified with the night surrounding them. Nothing could have been better suited to his passive soul consumed by resentment. If one is firmly anchored at the heart of knowledge, truth is what it is. Neither good nor bad. If one can perch on the outer edge of knowledge and summarize *what is* from the point of view of what is not but what might be, truth is horrifying. On one condition: that this syncretic scrutiny of the creation be socialized, that is, guaranteed by a community. From this moment, then, nonknowledge ceases to be a matter of subjective ignorance, a simple defect, an inadequacy; it is nothingness, certainly, but a calculated nothingness, an appeal of being, a suffered impossibility (much more than a refusal) of reducing the infinite Being to the sum of "beings" that human knowledge illuminates. The nothingness *of knowing* is then imposed as the nothingness of *knowledge*: the Absolute is elsewhere. Never revealed except by that devastating power that finally reduces the humble system of our truths to nothing, and by the infinite suffering of the soul infinitely frustrated and therefore chosen—unknowingly, of course, yet with some presentiment—this is the fundamental hypocrisy.

We see how little would have sufficed to transform Flaubert's vision of the world. Resentment, passivity, misanthropy, pessimism might all have been preserved, but he would have been saved by his belief in the ethic of pain: *belief in nothing*, then, becomes the negative sign of belief in God. This void into which the author of *Mémoires d'un fou* falls, terror-stricken, would have been the first level of a spiritual ascent he might never have completed but whose goal he could have surmised. In fact, we know that this first level is a point of departure for mystics—the "dark night" of Saint John of the Cross. But the Church in France around 1840 was far from favoring mysticism; we know what it cost Lacordaire to present such a negative theology. Gustave was defeated from childhood by the ideology of his own class, and his questions would be answered only at the end of the century by a church itself defeated and made bourgeois, when the clerics finally invented a religious escape that would be compatible with the ideology of the dominant class. The Church accepted everything in the end, even Darwin, only contriving a safety valve of ignorance which allowed a leak of faith.

Since this had not yet happened in the middle of the last century, the child martyr, the Flaubert family idiot, was forced—like Baudelaire, his twin—to invent the questions and the answers himself; and like Baudelaire, he would be a lay promoter of negative theology. But since it was not sanctioned by an institution, this negative theology that dared not speak its name, that he would create by "gliding," would be at once his Calvary, his neurosis, and his genius. Waiting for 1844 and the neurotic option, Flaubert—as an adolescent and later as a young man—criticized priests for their materialism, which he willingly called stupidity; as far as he was concerned, they were wrong to oppose being to being and dogma to knowledge, as if "revealed" truths constituted for the Christian a knowledge of the same order as scientific knowledge. Certainly they spoke of faith, which is belief; they did not conceal the fact that these revelations were mysterious and the impenetrable designs of God; but their ultimate reference, Flaubert thought, was a system of obviously untrue fables resting on the principle of authority, which were imposed through the catechism with all the material weight of *alien* pseudo knowledge, of practico-inert determination. For Gustave, the materiality of dogmatism was all the more painfully felt as science and scientism were imposed on him *in the same way*. He did not *do* science, unlike Achille-Cléophas; incapable of affirming or denying, he accepted it because a constituted body—the world's men of science, of which the paterfamilias, director

517

of the Hôtel-Dieu and acclaimed throughout the province, seemed to him the symbolic head—used the principle of authority to enforce its acceptance. He *believed* in mechanism, we have seen, but never completely; he would have liked to challenge it in the name of a beyond in which he fully believed, which could have happened only if he had had the audacity to affirm himself within against what was external; this is what he craved from religion, lacking the means himself. The young narrator of *Agonies* seeks out the "connoisseur of potatoes" in order to be persuaded, not by proofs but by his prestige, of the immortality of the soul. But in fact he isn't asking so much; if his soul is immortal, it is mainly because it exists, a nest of interiority escaping the laws of mechanism and even the paternal discourse. From Flaubert's point of view, this is what religion ought to be: a lordly bounty that would endow him with a certain relation to himself, invisible but indestructible, which would challenge the surgeon's scrutiny as spurious. And what does the priest give him, or, rather, what does he claim to give him? An enormous, and cumbersome piece of machinery that must be swallowed whole—all or nothing. If you claim to have a soul, Jonah's whale and Balaam's ass are fobbed off on you as well, take 'em or leave 'em; but at the same time the longed-for soul is changed into an ass, a whale, and you believe in it as much as—not more than—you believe in the crossing of the Red Sea. If Gustave could have let himself, he would have been informed by two equally weighty orders of belief, both exterior to him at the very core of his interiority, both destructive of that subjectivity which seeks itself and escapes itself endlessly for lack of having first been grasped through the original affirmation of maternal love. And of these two systems, one would unceasingly challenge the stupidity of the other without crushing it completely; when the father's eagle eye had reduced these fairy tales to "fragments," instinct would remain, the empty postulation. Gustave rebukes the priests for failing to confirm him in nonknowledge, in nonbelief, for failing to consecrate his malaise. They did not do it because nothing seemed clearer to them than the world as mirror of God, than God as present to the world and men's souls. Their little universe presented this puerile discourse to their flock, and it was repeated among the faithful. In a word, the battle was being fought *on the same level*, whereas the child would have liked both cases presented, the higher of which would have engulfed and disqualified the other without denying it. For Gustave, the wise dog and the pious dog are fighting over the same bone. Consequently, the diabolical intelligence of the former is permanent witness to the stupidity of the latter. We shall find them again at the bedside of Madame Bovary, who dies damned.

"Mine . . ." The priests are not the only guilty ones, then? No, the young pilgrim does not hesitate to admit his complicity. For true faith—he knew from the age of fifteen—cannot be refuted by their all-too-human weakness. Let us reread the passage from *La Main de fer* cited above: "He . . . who takes faith like a passion, gives himself to it entirely, he kneels down with pleasure, believes out of instinct; the mass for the dead is no longer a grotesque sing-song, the priests' chanting ceases to be venal, the church is something holy for him." We have noted above that Flaubert had already marshaled the serious accusations he would hurl at priests all his life: venality, the cold repetition of the same ritual nonsense in the name of—this is not said but it is obvious—the same idiotic fables. But on closer reading we notice that for a believer these "charades," transfigured by the religious "instinct," become the steps of faith, the objective supports of his "enthusiasm." Because he is an integral part of them, these collective ceremonies have *another meaning*: the mass for the dead reflects both our mortal condition and the immortality of the soul; the chants are acts of grace from which he draws his optimism, and in spite of the terrible necessity of dying, he thanks God for having created him; the place itself returns him to an ancient time when all the acts of life were bathed in a holy light. The Church never said anything different; the organist may play badly, the sexton may have "a bulbous and crooked nose," the choirboy a foolish laugh. Aren't the Latin words recited in haste, "garbled" as we say in the theater—are they even understood by the tonsured clods who pronounce them? But he who persists in seeing only their weakness, who is sensitive only to the contingency of the celebrated rite, cannot or does not want to understand that a transcendent mystery is incarnate through these miserable errors; that God has chosen to make it shine there, ungraspable, like the surpassing of our inadequacies, even as he, being all-powerful, wanted to descend into a woman's belly and be born into our helplessness in order to take our original sin upon himself and die for it. In this sense the mass has two aspects: it is a particular meeting of men and women between four walls, and it is mystically the death of Christ, the archetypal event, our salvation. Hence our defects, our sins, our errors—those of the faithful and their pastors—are *necessary*; the walls must enclose this enormous mass of degradation for the Passion, begun once again and played by bad actors who are no less guilty than the spectators, to be manifest, unattainable yet accessible

519

to all, the redemption of all our crimes and the ineffable revelation of our participation in the divine.

Indeed, Gustave recognizes that faith is the transfiguration of the everyday. It is true that he treats it a bit cavalierly and prefers to see it only as a profane passion, as a youthful love. But this doesn't much matter *since he is young*; he writes like a disillusioned old man who has seen his feelings die, one after the other, but this casual drama hardly fools us; each of his characters still preserves the potential for deciphering the rites and myths *differently*, for seeing the *sacred* in them as a manifestation of the supernatural, not despite their inadequacy but because of it, just as the numinous, being negative, bursts forth when the real collapses. The test case of *La Main de fer* proves that Gustave is quite conscious of the circularity of faith: in order to believe, he tells us, one must believe already. Thus he recognizes here that bulbous noses, dreadful looks, the pitiful mugs of God's ministers cannot be invoked to excuse agnosticism. He is not always so sincere. In *Agonies* we have seen him exclaim in his haste to free himself of blame: "It is not my fault if the parish priest is too ugly, too gluttonous." In *La Main de fer*, and later in his meditation on the Holy Sepulcher, he pleads guilty; the devout man has no eye for such pathetic details, his gaze cuts across the human comedy, seeing only the sacred tragedy. Suddenly it is Gustave himself who is being challenged. Directly. His cruel lucidity is not what prevents him from believing; quite the contrary, it is this void in his soul, this dryness, this absence of fervor that allows him to undermine the ceremonies and those who perform them through "analysis." Religion is an *instinct*. By which is meant an impulse that is found in all the members of an animal species, immediate and "brutish" like life itself. If it happens to be missing in someone, he must be a monster; what is more, he is sure to suffer the worst torments and a premature death for lack of that protective *equipment* which permits survival.[27] Is Gustave, then, a freak of nature? Is he lacking in the religious instinct? No, this is not what he means. On the contrary, he finds in himself the need to believe, the trans-ascendence which pulls him out of himself; yet this fundamental demand becomes his perpetual torment because it is never *fulfilled*—his religious instinct never results in faith. His inquest must begin on this level: Why can't he believe? Isn't he worthy of it? Is it some imperfection in his nature that prevents him? Or his ill-will? We are going to see that as Flaubert acquired greater

27. Obviously I am presenting Flaubert's thought here, not mine.

depth, he would give two successive answers: "I am made this way" and "I make myself this way."

To begin with, of course, he was angry. He had been frustrated. In the guise of Marguerite he prowls around churches and spits on their doorsteps. At the end of the year 1837, disguised as Mazza, he would begin again. He simply loathes those God-owners peacefully kneeling in the pious shadows—what do they have that I don't? But above all he spies on them. He enters places of worship, hides behind a pillar, and *watches them believe*. See what happened at the Holy Sepulcher: he went "in good faith . . . very simple, no Voltairean, Mephistophelian, or sadist." However, he remains unmoved; by his own account this is one of the bitterest moments of his life. Why? Because the gift of the rose has unleashed a crisis: "I thought of the devout souls whom such a gift and in such a place would have delighted, and how much it was lost on me." This should not be viewed as some obscure regret at stealing from poor Christians a place that belongs more to them than to him; on the contrary, the useless gift has awakened his envy, he is consumed by jealousey. Everything in this place speaks of Christ and of the infinite love he bears all men and each one in particular, but it speaks of this *to the others*. An unparalleled election, a recruitment by the absolute is a permanent offer, but not to Gustave. The Savior hides himself from Gustave, giving himself to the wretched who will never go to Palestine and refusing to give Himself to the traveler who has taken the trouble to visit His house, who has been kept awake all night by his fervor, and who that very morning has been overwhelmed by the sight of Jerusalem's ramparts. Once more Achille is preferred to him. While the eternal Father maintains a stubborn silence in this soul who was nonetheless promised to him by the first sacraments, he babbles on in others who are quite mediocre. Why does he reward those simpering idiots? After all, they are only Rouen shopkeepers. How is it that they are granted vivid, burning, happy certainties when the future Saint Polycarp is refused them? He was still incensed at this injustice when he addressed himself to the third guilty party: "Especially Yours."

But envy plays a losing game. Gustave proclaimed his contempt for those bigoted shopkeepers in vain, for he could not help seeing them as *beneficiaries*. They are the ones who throw him back on his congenital contingency and denounce his anomaly which is by now enriched, expanded, extended to all the nerves of his being. When the host melts on their tongues and they return, moved, to their benches, certain of having eaten the Christ, they are men of divine

521

right: their half-closed eyelids, their meditative attitude bear witness to a crushing presence whose weight he is the only one not to feel. This is the fall and the shame; inaccessible outside their gathering, religion invests *all these men together* with a majestic plenitude, while in Gustave faith retains the consistency of a mayonnaise that is about to blend but never does.

Curiously, shamefully, he needs others; when he is on the brink of belief it is always through an intermediary. He was so conscious of this that he described the process admirably in a celebrated passage from *Un Coeur simple* that is illuminated by the notes written in Jerusalem. Alone at the Holy Sepulcher, he lacks the means to capture the sacred. On the contrary, there is a crowd present when Félicité witnesses Virginie's first communion: "And with the imagination that true tenderness bestows, it seemed to her that she herself was this child . . . ; by closing her eyes she escaped fainting at the moment the girl had to open her mouth. The next day . . . she devoutly received [communion] but did not taste the same pleasure." The allusion is obviously to his niece Caroline, who believed, who made communion, and whom he used to ask whether her priest had found her strong in catechism. This is what makes these lines so precious: for once, he does not hate the devout person who frustrates his need for God—indeed, she is a child he loves. Suddenly, free of envy, he manages—almost to the point of fainting—an incredible identification with his niece. Imagine this jovial man, nearly forty years old, trying for a moment *to become* a ten-year-old communicant—"the child's face became hers, her dress clothed her, the girl's heart beat in her breast"—in order to vampirize her sacred emotion and resurrect through her the difficulty he felt thirty years earlier when he had made his own first communion. Neither love nor real tenderness prompted this pithiatic metamorphosis, or he would have tried it many times before and after the ceremony, every time his niece experienced great joy or even violent suffering.[28] The real tenderness he felt for Caroline functions here only to suppress envy and open the way to hysteria. What Gustave wants to capture, what he does capture for a moment, is God as Other, God-in-a-loved-being. In order to obtain this extraordinary presence from absence, this acceptance/rejection, a single means—which is not given to everyone—remains to Gustave, that adroit technician of autosuggestion: he must become

28. In other words, he would have shown us Félicité making many attempts at identification.

522

unreal as his niece, *make* himself into Caroline in imagination. In the end, directing his spiritual exercise by the movements and attitude of this familiar child, he takes on the other's ecstasy, he enjoys it in an unreal way, and everything ends—as usual—with the beginning of a fainting spell. Unlike Félicité, he certainly did not return to the holy altar; his comment that she made her communion with "less pleasure," though devoutly, implies that he could enjoy God only through an intermediary. From 1884 on, his relations to religion would undergo a profound change. But he would continue to vampirize the faith of others. His jealous obsession would lead him so far that he would "seriously" dream toward the end of his life—him, the unbeliever—of having a mass said for Mme Tardif, who had believed.[29] As if her soul, which Gustave was convinced did not survive the destruction of the body, could, if raised from nothingness by its informing faith, benefit magically from a ceremony its organizer took to be a futile sham. As if this faithless organizer could, in spite of everthing, derive some benefit from a piece of "mimicry" whose unique meaning rests on a dead woman's faith. Couldn't it be said that part of this vanished piety would revert, almost without his knowledge, to the sorrowful libertine who contributes to the salvation of a Christian soul out of pure human devotion? To tell the truth, the mass would never be said—Flaubert only dreamed about it. To dream, for him, is of course *not to act*. But as we shall see, this man chose to be a visionary; he dreamed, told his dreams to his friends, fixed these dreams, and therefore determined himself in what he took for his essential truth and what we shall call his *unreality*. In this perspective, it is quite accurate to say that he dreamed *seriously* of having the mass said, and that this dreaming *characterizes* him in his own eyes more than our dreams ever would. For Gustave the dream is an ersatz act, and the dreamer engages his responsibility in the dream as though in a real enterprise. Gustave delights in imagining the mass in order to tell us: I am the man who is capable of dreaming this. And then, at the same time and at a deeper level, he is moved, without betraying it, by a sublime humility. Rejected by the Lord who has denied him grace, without hope or jealousy, the wretched man contributes through a commissioned ceremony to helping a chosen soul ascend to Paradise.

29. To Caroline, 16 January 1879, *Correspondance* 8:188: "I recall with tenderness the moments I spent with her, and I would like to have a mass said for her, seriously."

Does God exist, then? Well, yes. But not for Gustave. Everyone can believe in him except the younger son of the Flauberts, who explains his strange position clearly in *Rage et Impuissance*: "Do not believe the people who call themselves atheists, they are only skeptics and deny out of vanity." Some pages earlier, however, closed in his tomb and without hope of getting out, the poor man buried alive, Monsieur Ohlmin, has diverted himself by invoking hell: "since heaven had not wished to save him, he appealed to hell; hell came to his aid and gave him atheism, despair, and blasphemy." But this atheism is a gift of Satan, the trick of an illusionist who misleads us one moment and disappears the next. In brief, an untenable position. Gustave/Ohlmin is himself a "skeptic," that is, an agnostic. Does this mean that he wavers between two conclusions—the negative and the positive—without being able to settle on either of the two? This is what he seems to be saying: "Ah well, when you doubt and suffer, you want to eliminate all probability, to have reality empty and naked; but doubt grows and devours your soul." The attitude of the poor man buried alive hardly corresponds to this description. How can there be blasphemy if God does not exist? He throws himself into it, however, in earnest: "I will not go on begging you, I despise you." And when he seems to be professing disbelief, he is in fact only cursing the Creator: "I deny you, a word invented by the fortunate, you are nothing but a fatal and mindless power, like lightning that strikes and burns." What is he denying? The existence of God? Not at all. Certainly he begins by declaring that God is a word. But the following proposition is limited to denying intelligence and goodness to a "fatal power" which the young man, enraged, continues to inveigh against in the second person. It is an attempt to reduce the Catholic divinity to *fatum*—that archaic religion which the adolescent harbors within him—and at the same time, by speaking familiarly to it, to personalize destiny. Above all, he is *denigrating*, insulting by diminishment, as if in a moment of anger he were addressing himself to Rousseau, Voltaire, the great names of classical literature, in order to tell them: "I deny you, fake geniuses, usurped glories, you are mere scribblers, and the rare beauties of your prose are the result of chance." When he writes, "a word invented by the fortunate," Gustave is not really claiming that the fortunate of this world invented the discourse of religion. That would be absurd and, furthermore, in contradiction with the general context; let us compare this apposition with a few lines that describe his agnosticism, and the meaning will emerge by itself: "When you doubt and *suffer* . . . , the doubt grows and devours your soul." "God, a word invented by the fortunate." It is all there: God is not a vain word, but he is on the side of the fortunate in order to make them more fortunate still—he lends himself only to the rich. This is the supreme reward of the usurpers. But he withholds himself from those who "suffer" and seek his mercy, and his absence "devours their soul." In this sadistic universe, the God of goodness reserves his favors for the "contented," for the pigs who roll in the dirt and have no need of him; the unfortunate, on the contrary, are condemned by his silence, and in depriving them he multiplies their unhappiness infinitely. Beneath the invective we rediscover the old shame, the guilt of the disappointed child: my father is good, he is just, the whole world sings his praises; if he has cursed me, it is because I am wrong—you cannot be right against the whole universe. Moreover, Ohlmin goes from reproaches to supplications: "If you exist, why have you made me unhappy? What pleasure does it give you to see me suffer? *Why don't you want me to believe in you? Give me faith!*" I have emphasized the last lines because they shed a surprising light on Flaubert's agnosticism: God exists, the young author tells us, but he does not want me to believe in him. How, you might ask, can he affirm and deny the same thing in the same sentence? I answer that he does not affirm or deny anything. The others are the ones, through their religious enthusiasm, who affirm God and impose him on Gustave like the unknown lodestar of all his frustrations; as for him, without doubting for a moment this doubly transcendent God, he finds nothing in himself resembling faith. A desire to believe, yes, but one that results in nothing. Gustave's true grief is that God is an Other—perceived by all the others; He does not manifest himself in this religious and consecrated soul and shines only by his absence. The young man's desires are modest, however; he doesn't ask the Almighty to visit him and doesn't even demand that proofs or revelations should inspire his belief; what characterizes his doubt, as he understands it, is not even an impulse to dispute but simple powerlessness. What he wants is a simple, intimate transmutation of experience, a leavening that would make the flat dough of his existence rise and give him the strength he lacks, the faith to move mountains. In other words, he complains of not having *grace*. But perhaps, after all, he didn't deserve it? Here we have come back to our starting point.

"The fault is mine." He is alone in the Holy Sepulcher, the business with the rose has awakened his envy, and for a moment he hates everyone, the pilgrims and the stay-at-homes, all the believers on earth. But since no one is there to serve as a target, he sets to musing about himself. Troubled, doubtful, a stranger to himself, one might say that he discovers in himself an inadequacy of being, for which, this time, he holds no one responsible. He is no longer Djalioh, made monstrous by human caprice, nor Almaroës, the pure soulless product of paternal mechanism; he is a man of chance who says to himself sadly: I am punished for my constitutional inadequacy, consequently for the few efforts I have made. Did he recall his earliest raptures and discover something tepid in the undefined, indefinable *animula vagula* which felt them, or which they produced in him in order that it feel them, that *animula vagula* so well adapted to the languors of quietism and to certain incommunicable perceptions? Did he tell himself that he had never played for high stakes or given anything of himself, and that he might have been more audacious in tempting God with his forcefulness? Did he understand that faith—any faith, even profane— requires great patience, an invincible obstinacy, blinkers, a blind confidence in the responsible officials charged with dispensing and renewing it, and that ecstasy is nothing without doctrine? Did he tell himself that he never undertook the lengthy and disappointing job of breaking one set of values in order to erect another on the ruins of the first? Did he dream about his constituted passivity, did he make it the warp and woof of his being? Did he consider that the *belief in nothing* was its consequence and that, hardly capable of embracing an idea wholeheartedly and sticking to it, he preferred—for the comfort of his soul—the soft pillow of doubt, even hopeless doubt, lacking a power of decision that would have allowed him to choose once and for all between dogma and science? Did he admit to himself that it was easy for him to curse the paternal scientism, considering that it had ravaged his soul, only because he had abandoned his soul to scientism without a struggle? No doubt he reexamined all this in a strict but affective order. More than once he pondered these wrongs *against the self*, and all the more easily since he did not like himself. He looks backward: properly speaking, everything began at the age of seven. He did not believe in God for the same reason it took him so long to learn his letters, out of a torpor affecting his faculties, out of that quasi-pathological inadequacy of being that the good Dr. Flaubert detected in him, isolated, and punished by expelling him from paradise. But at this moment he holds no grudge against his father; he has the good grace to blame only himself. Does he believe he is guilty? Yes, deeply, since the "bitter tenderness" that has flooded him is nothing but his reawakened childhood. He rediscovers himself after the Fall, disarmed, ashamed, miserable; he adores his judge, he kisses the hand that has cast him into the hell of disgrace, he *thinks his father is right*—the sentence was just, I am unworthy. This tone surprises us by its modernity. What is Gustave doing when he is dreaming in his study, or kneeling in a church, a barren dreamer in Jerusalem endlessly haunted by an impossible fervor? He is waiting for Godot. This kind of waiting was rare in the first half of the nineteenth century—men were better integrated. Waiting for Godot—what for? He had *already* come; he could be received every morning on the tip of the tongue. But in 1850 Flaubert was set on crossing the Christian world. Plagued by the memory of an ancient curse, still smarting from the failure of *Saint Antoine*, bewildered, pushing "skepticism" to the point of doubting he would ever become a writer, hating the journey he had undertaken and quite close to hating Maxime as well, he was very near to Beckett's heroes: he waits, knowing it is to no purpose and yet not growing tired of waiting; this is living. Why doesn't the Other come? Perhaps it is because Gustave has been misinformed and no one by that name exists—perhaps he ought to be looking for Godin, for Godard; or perhaps he is being held up. An urgent appeal might be made, except that he is probably downing a glass at the bar or has lost Flaubert's address or has simply lost his way. But chiefly Beckett has made us understand that we are too weak, too flabby to have real need of him; we do not wait for him enough, and we lack that literally mad obstinacy which *alone* could give us a sense of urgency. Godot says to himself: there's no hurry, I will take a turn down there when I have put my affairs in order; unless our appeals are so weak that in good faith he hasn't heard them at all. Gustave reflects on the rose: he has no genius, Maxime and Bouilhet have given him proof of that; perhaps faith might take the place of this failed vocation? But no, faith—like genius—is a gift and requires great patience. Perhaps it is one and the same thing. Flaubert thinks bitterly: Godot didn't come because it wasn't worth the effort.

I have said that Gustave's head was turned by the harsh, sad blast of childhood and that he *believed* in his inadequacy. I have not said that he believed in it *sincerely*. Not that he only acted out the drama or that he secretly contested what he pretended to feel; but we must understand that this deep humility was structured by an intention of self-defense which he could not escape. In fact he overburdened himself so as to be more effectively exonerated: I am made this way, God of mercy, so that I cannot believe in you; as you are my witness, however, I am not resigned, and I increase my efforts, though I know they will be in vain. Pledged by the sacraments but unworthy—through a defect of being for which I alone am guilty because it is nothing but myself—I submit to this unworthiness in rage and impotence, being too weak ever to find you and too religious to stop waiting for you.

This is certainly a sad story. Do we have a martyr here, who has not been given the benefit of divine light in a created world and aspires with all his soul to a Creator who hasn't given him the means to reach him? Wouldn't this make him a saint? Wouldn't his God-given disbelief, far from being a mark of contempt, be the supreme proof and sign of his election? No. Not yet. Certainly after Pont-l'Evêque Gustave would not refuse the halo. And the visit to the Holy Sepulcher comes after the crisis of 1844; we shall deal with this meaning of the visit later, and the notes taken in Jerusalem will then merit a supplementary *reading*. But *in their form* they are a new version of Gustave's religious disappointments between the ages of ten and twenty-two. After the "nervous attack" he would discover the rules of the game, of *his* game: loser takes all. We shall return to this at length in the second volume of this work. But for the moment it is the angry young man of the 1830s who interests us, and this Gustave does not make a gift of himself: he who loses, loses all the way. Since the world belongs to Satan at this point, the unbeliever is made to roast in eternal hell or sink into nothingness. Look at poor Monsieur Ohlmin: in his miserable position he allows himself to doubt. Not blasphemy, but a painful sigh: "Doubt grows and devours your soul." Suddenly he is transformed into a demon: "He gnashed his teeth like the Devil being vanquished by Christ." Doubting on the threshold of death, he is on the point of committing the sin of despair. In fact, hell comes instantly to his aid and makes him the tainted gifts of "atheism, despair, blasphemy." At fifteen, at twenty, Flaubert's mind was made up: he would be unmercifully damned. He would simply have the bitter satisfaction of knowing himself to be the Devil's chosen—the greatest souls are those most severely punished. This is obvious since the *quality* of a man is nothing more than his power to suffer. Ohlmin/Gustave will have a choice place; the last circle of hell is reserved for him *alone*—Satan is fond of this infinitely guilty soul who dares to despair of the infinite.

Transformation is in sight. We were feeling sorry for the miseries of a half-baked creature consumed by religious feeling and severed from all religion. A poor guy, in short, whose sole value came from the fact that he continued to wait for the One he knew would never come. Suddenly everything is turned around and the emphasis is put on the futile guest, displaced here onto negative certainty: God has abandoned me. Suddenly the poor guy becomes immensely and supernaturally guilty—he is the hero of despair. Is this the same man? Not entirely. The one who was waiting for Godot could hardly do anything but *endure what he was*. A monster of privation. But a monster is not guilty. He is what he was made. The other man is a prince of evil; when the Church teaches us that the supreme crime against God is despair, it does not mean to condemn some constitutional inability to believe but, on the contrary, that *negative action* which is the refusal of hope and faith. It seems, then, that Gustave realized himself in two different ways: on one level as simple suffering passivity, and on a deeper level as demonic activity. Is this possible? Yes; *in any case* it is possible for Gustave. We shall see why he can simultaneously answer, as I have formulated above: "I am made this way" and "I make myself this way." But first we must give a more precise account of Flaubert's notion of despair.

We have to move fast. Isn't total despair the supreme purpose of resentment? Let us understand that the rejection of God could have been foreseen from the time of the Fall, from the first moment of the pitiless battle opposing son to father. In fact, only the son is pitiless because he believes he is the object of a merciless curse; he will punish the guilty father by rigid obedience, always opting for the worst, as prescribed, and consequently for the soul-rending contradictions that finally bring about his death at the feet of the paterfamilias; there he lies, the accuser/object, silently pointing to the father as his murderer. Under these conditions, how could he fail to choose the basic contradiction, which is that he *needs* God—indeed, how could this religious and subject soul bear to live if the sacred did not exist?—*therefore* God is refused to him. Refused by whom? Well, first by the father, then by the Eternal Being, who becomes the father's accomplice. But on the deepest level by the martyr himself, that is, by an intentional choice always to make himself become what he believes he is, namely *the unhappiest man alive*. Is it possible that this passive agent should live this inner determination as a negation, since we know that he cannot affirm or deny anything? No, it is not possible. Furthermore, if he thought clearly, God exists and I reject him, the ruse of resentment once unmasked would instantly collapse; this is what he expresses indirectly by saying that atheism, that perfidious relief from hell, is only a mirage. In other words, he is not responsible for his disbelief, which is offered by the Devil. And yet he is guilty because this disbelief derives its provisional substance from him alone—who at this moment is at once the victim, the executioner, and hell itself. We shall see him a little later dumbfounded by the warnings that sometimes come to him from his gaping, terrifying, and dismal depths, glimpsed through the sudden yawning of a chasm and instantly lost from sight. This is his inner hell, himself and not himself; these anonymous quagmires escape him—there, no one says "I." He recognizes those quagmires, however, and knows that they condemn him; the intentions belong to him, not to the ego but to that perpetual return of all to all that we have named the ipseity; atheism and despair originate here, not as a deliberate negation nor as a criminal decision but simply as a belief. As we have seen, the only way an inert soul can *choose* is to commit itself to a belief, to slip into a tacit vow. Such is Flaubert's pessimism, his misanthropy. Yet he cannot appropriate just any opinion ex nihilo, he must suffer it by borrowing his sovereignty from the Other within him. Achille-Cléophas is this occupant, and Gustave is persuaded that the paternal skepticism has convinced him. In other words, through criticism and close analysis, the paternal ideology of pure reason with its train of demonstrations and empirical proofs soon made the child turn away from his dogmas requiring blind faith. Is this true? No. Certainly it was not easy to *believe* under Dr. Larivière's surgical scrutiny; but when Achille-Cléophas revealed his conception of the world or amused himself by refuting the proofs of God's existence, Gustave easily understood the linkage of ideas and yet was not in the least convinced, having neither the desire nor the practical possibility of acquiring a *body of knowledge*, that is, a system of objective truths based subjectively on intuitive evidence or deduction. In this sense he is wrong in *Quidquid volueris* when he refuses to give his incarnation, Djalioh, the capacity to make "logical connections"; it is not these connections that he lacks but the determined, practical intention of using them to say yes or no. The most serious mistake, he would write later on, is to draw conclusions; this is not an axiom, as he pretends, but a trait of his constituted character: any conclusion logically imposed can be internalized only by the subject's decision to do so and by an act of appropriation, all areas in which Gustave is defective. If the paterfamilias's arguments fascinate him, it is primarily because of his lord's unquestioned authority, and also because Gustave cannot contest those arguments. In order to refute the philosophical practitioner he would have to fight on his father's turf and use reason. Gustave understands that the progenitor's ideas are proven truths *for him*—in other words,

Gustave sees in them the ordering of an *alien thought*, luminous and convincing *for another* but as far as he is concerned just an imperative belief. Thus, he believes *out of submission*. This means that he is obliged to believe that he does not believe in dogmas. Indeed, if the products of reason can be only objects of belief, there is no qualitative difference in his eyes between demonstrated truths and revealed truths, which are in effect revealed only to others. Religion attempts to impose itself on village scribblers through the great, majestic images found on every street corner; the *appearance* of Catholicism penetrated the streets of Rouen, surrounded Gustave, penetrated and tempted him, but was revealed in its captious vanity the moment the little boy tried to appropriate it. For others raised in religious families, the ceremonial canopies, the mitres and chasubles and gildings had a hidden meaning; but mythic thought, accessible only to the faithful, removes an option, for like the discourse of reason held up to him by his father, such thought *imposes itself*, and in order for the little exile to enjoy it he would have to commit himself to believing in it by a secret vow. The child has already taken such a vow: God exists, thousands of kneeling believers bear witness to that; God exists, and his envy whispers in his ear that God exists *because* Gustave is deprived of him. His obedience to paternal preference is what deprives him of God; the imperative belief that the philosophical practitioner put into him cannot stand up against the existence of the Almighty—for it does not depend on certainty, reasons have not convinced him—it is simply the sacred command of a certain lord addressed to a certain vassal and to him alone, the command not to believe. Thus when a child overcome with loneliness and boredom goes to the window and looks with envy at the kids playing in the street, he discovers the internalized parents who tell him: "I forbid you to play with those little ragamuffins."

Gustave goes further: he makes himself into the only unbeliever in the realm in order *to pay homage* to his father. The son of the celebrated Dr. Flaubert can do no less. The deception is perfect; the little boy "would like nothing better" than to believe, but the vassal of an atheist must at least be agnostic. The younger son gives his black lord a useless gift of love, the thing he holds most dear—to please him he renounces his most fundamental needs; he concedes that for him alone life might have no meaning, when he can see with his own eyes that it has meaning for others. The Creator would be a comforting refuge from the despair into which his father has plunged him; God is there at hand, but out of feudal loyalty the poor child refuses double allegiance. He preserves the infinite handle of nonknowledge—this is the vital minimum—but he refuses to personalize it. In short, he falls into the void and stays there, spinning for all eternity, having made his progenitor a gift of his Christian vocation. Let us listen to the whisperings of resentment: your will is what prevents me from believing; by taking this to its conclusion, I unmask your true aim, which is to make me despair. Now turning toward God, the good apostle whispers: naturally, everything would have been very different if you had given me your grace; you should have ravished me, pushed me onto my knees before your terrifying power and then taken me in your strong hands and raised me up so that I couldn't resist; that way, no one could have accused me of betraying my father—when you make up your mind, the most hardened atheist cannot resist you. You did not—so be it. I remain alone, rejected by a capricious lord and with no other view of the world than that cruel atomism in which I do not entirely believe.

In *La Tentation* of 1849 there are many vestiges of this first conception of science as a passion, the monstrous child of pride, *its mother*. But "this white-haired child with an enormous head and spindly legs" can also be seen as the image of little Gustave, lashed by the vanity of his progenitor from the age of seven. In the dialogue that follows, isn't the curious "mother" who bears a masculine name reminiscent of Pedrillo, the terrible father, the merciless educator?

PRIDE [l'orgueil, m.]

Oh! It's you! What do you want?

SCIENCE [la science, f.]

What do I want? (*Looking at Pride and starting to cry*): Oh, you want to beat me! You are already raising your fists.

PRIDE

No, speak, tell me everything.

SCIENCE, pouting.

Well, I'm hungry, then! I'm thirsty, do you hear me? I want to sleep, I want to play.

PRIDE, smiling and shrugging her shoulders.

Ba! Ba! Ba!

SCIENCE

If you only knew how sick I am, how my eyelids are burning, how my head is buzzing! Oh! Pride, my mother, why do you force me into this slavish position? *Sometimes when I doze a little, I suddenly hear the whistling of your whip that strikes me on the ears and slashes my face*[30]. . . . You always cry: Again, again! Go on! Aren't you afraid of killing me?

PRIDE

I don't hear what you're saying, you're always pestering me with your moaning and groaning.

This aging gnome, we know, nursed the dream of escaping from empiricism, of "reconciling [diverse phenomena] in the synthesis from which [his] scalpel detached them." "You promised me that . . . I would find something." Flaubert's testimony is explicit, science is in a period of simple accumulation: "I seek, *I hoard*, I read." This involves knowledge based on sensory evidence; we should understand that such knowledge is characterized by the contingency of the very facts it collects and of the assertorical judgments that constitute it. *Problematic* evidence; even when the object is accessible to perception, it does not lead to total adherence, all the more so if it appears with an index of probability that increases as a function of the frequency of appearances. In short, the scientist's relation to the proposition he is advancing does not go beyond the level of *belief*. Collections, enumerations and general reviews, classifications—nothing more. But the feminine son [*Science*, f.] of this masculine mother [*Orgueil*, m.] is *pushed* by his mother onto the path of ambition. He wants to know *through reasons*: "Where does life come from? Where does death come from?" He is interested only in the ignorant "whys" that an inferior Polytechnic student, dismissed from school, tries to replace by "hows." Suddenly his mind wanders, he is "lost in thought" or "turns around it" like a "horse harnessed to a wine press." The result is that he falls into "unceasing amazement" or takes fright. Ignorance and anguish are the issues of science; nonknowledge, in which knowledge is lost, becomes prophetic and demonic. "I see [it] pass on the wall like vague shadows that terrify me." There is nothing surprising about this: Pride, a mortal sin and apparently the Devil's favorite whore, can only lie; it promised its offspring an articulated body of knowledge, but this is a mirage—the more one knows, the greater one's ignorance and terror. Science, caught in the

---

30. My italics. This is the same as in *Un Parfum à sentir*, when Gustave describes the humiliating lessons given by Dr. Flaubert.

trap, perceives too late that it is only a name for ignorance and suddenly senses that it is the ghastly dream of one of the damned.[31]

At least, we might say, in certain areas precise pieces of information exist which are strictly linked to one another. No; Gustave *deliberately* separates *logic*—that other tempting allegory—from knowledge. Demoness or demon, it is little enough to say that this creature of the Devil remains strictly *formal*. It is pre-Socratic in the sense that it utilizes the principle of the third person in order to refute any synthetic judgment, that is, any proposition whose attribute would not already be contained in the subject.

> LOGIC
>
> If it was not displeasing to God, Antoine, you could sin. (*Silence.*) Does God hear prayer?

> THE VIRTUES
>
> Yes.

> LOGIC
>
> Pray to Him, then, to permit and bless sin, for since He is all-powerful . . .

> ANTOINE, *softly.*
>
> What is the answer?

The backbone of the argument is a tautology: He who is all-powerful can do everything. By this Megarian purity Gustave intends to refute all the synthetic (or syncretistic) constructions of those who try to limit the power of God for the accomplishment of the good—whether they want to bind him by his perfection, whether in the name of his goodness they proscribe his wanting to fool us, or whether they define him by the *plenitude of being* and at once refuse him any dealings with nothingness.

31. This is what Gustave was saying literally in *Smarh*.

> SATAN
>
> Ah! You are lost in your ignorance and the gloom terrifies you? You wanted it.

> SMARH
>
> What did I want?

> SATAN
>
> Science. Well, science is doubt, nothingness, the lie, vanity.

> SMARH
>
> Nothingness would be worth more.

> SATAN
>
> Nothingness exists, but science does not.

534

The same purity will intervene from time to time in the dialogue through reflections which are all of the same order. For example, on the subject of Christ: "He was certainly not the son of David since Joseph was not his father." A statement which is all the more curious since Jesus descended from David on his mother's side and Gustave knows this very well. Or again: "Why did he curse the fig tree since it wasn't the season for figs?" Moreover, Gustave is close to considering this miserable Megarism to be a mirage—which is natural since it comes from hell. In any case, he sometimes rules against it—as the following dialogue shows:

SCIENCE

Let me in! Open the door!

FAITH

No!

LOGIC

Then let the hermit out so he can come to her![32]

FAITH

He would be lost with her.

LOGIC

But Science is not sin since she is the enemy of sins.

FAITH

Worse than all of them.

LOGIC

But she fights them!

FAITH

She helps them too.

LOGIC

How is that?

FAITH, *softly, to Antoine.*

Look here, Science is the one who has made these holes I'm covering with my feet.

Indeed, a moment before, Science has sent all the seductive Sins about their business—Avarice (why give me your riches, they were my doing), Gluttony (eating is always the same, I am going to grow vineyards and hunt), etc. And it is certainly true—in this mythology—that the vices cannot tempt the son of Pride, who is miserable today but whose visionary ambition aims at nothing less than conquering the world. But he is the son of a sin and his ambition is sinful; and

32. Note the abrupt transition to the feminine: the "little boy" becomes a woman.

knowledge, to the extent that it is developed against religion, deprives others of protection and abandons them to all the temptations—in particular, as in Gustave's case, to the temptation of despair. Although scarcely anyone knows how to answer him, it is clear that the author disapproves of the crude formal identity (an enemy of sin cannot be a sin) which is given here as an argument against dogma, the strict application of which would lead straight to a substantiation of the concepts and famous *aporia* of the ancients. The deep meaning of the dialogue is something quite different; at issue is Flaubert pride, to which the son submitted when the father forced him to read and which he then judged to be demonic. Gustave thought the progenitor had no vice but was evil personified until he himself internalized this very pride *in the negative* and it became the vulture endlessly tearing at his liver; yet in his assumed destitution it seemed to him—though still demonic—the unique source of his value. The objections of the concept's formal logic are only superficial sparks—the young man is settling his account with those "logical connections" of which poor Djalioh was so maliciously deprived. Flaubert is cunning enough to make contemporary science into an accumulation of "consequences without premises," and to rob it of any possibility of linking together its empirical findings by making logic a *separate* function exercised in a vacuum; across the infinite variety of analytic judgments, logic is limited to repeating indefinitely the principle of identity and is incapable of producing and combining synthetic judgments in a rigorous way. At this moment, that arrogant and painful desire to equal the Creator by knowing the creation as well as he does ought to be stifled in anguish—we should rediscover the sentence pronounced by the other Satan, the Satan of *Smarh* whose statements I reported in a footnote; science should be "doubt, nothingness, the lie," and stripped naked. This means that scientific doubt is as unbearable as religious doubt and that both have the same origin. Moreover, we see the beginnings of this sudden consciousness—all at once, the son of Pride is afraid. But the moment he begins to despair, the Devil beckons to him and shows him Faith; the child's sobs subside, his voice becomes "clear and vibrant," the monstrous gnome shows poor Antoine "a face with a sweet pallor and eyes that shone like the dawn." What has made him so cheerful? Hatred. He claimed, when envy tempted him, that this emotion was unknown to him. He was lying. Men, of course, one at a time, only inspire him with indifference. But he hates their faith. "Ah!" he says, "Faith! I searched for it everywhere—and I didn't find it. Ah! You were here!" The Devil reminds him of his mission, not to refresh his memory but simply to cheer him up: "Wherever it is, you will go, you will pursue it, and when you have seized it you must roll it in the mud so that even if it gets up again, it will never be able to wash its face clean of the ignominy of its fall." This is what is so pleasing to the little abortion; so much so that he forgets his misery. However, it is revealed to him that he has only a relative existence. Satan, furthermore, puts great emphasis on this: "Although you will not be killed, you will have neither happiness nor rest." And the young "Science" cries out *"n anger, and spite*: 'Oh, I know that very well, I know that very well.'" In other words, faith is primary; one could say it is the belief in the plenitude of being and it determines the nature of Science, who with the help of the Devil will revive it and define it as its negation. No happiness or repose for the hoary-headed brat who would destroy the believer's calm certainties in order to replace them with that other faith—disbelief, doubting, ignorance, and despair. Briefly, aggression is all on the side of science while faith remains on the defensive, and its adversary's aim in this dialogue seems less to acquire knowledge than to replace one kind of nonknowledge with another. One might almost say that Flaubert, when he recalls his golden age, is tempted to consider faith as the immediate, natural state of man before the advent of culture, his animality; divine grace would be required only later on, after the Fall. Stimulated by pride and hatred inspired by the Devil, little father "Science" believes in the mirage of empirical knowledge. This is simply a trick of hell, manipulating its product in order to fuel his rage against faith; if he succeeded by some miracle in destroying it completely, he would suddenly perceive that the Devil's weapons are only dead leaves and that rational knowledge is by definition contradictory. Through his anguish and his blundering sorrow he would witness his disillusionment—God's work remains unknown—and his profound frustration, that is, the infinite absence of God, who has not ceased to surround him but whom he is hysterically determined to doubt and will doubt forever. He would have found nothing to replace God and would conceive of his own doubt, his blasphemous despair and anguish, as generated by God's unquestionable existence. In other words, Gustave sees science and faith as a pair. As long as faith remains, the search for knowledge will preserve its freshness, the man of science will be able to dream of a total knowledge of the world—faith gives his quest meaning; total and cosmic, it is faith that he must destroy in order to substitute a rational totalitarianism. But what its furious detractors do not understand is that the synthetic idea comes from faith and vanishes with it, leaving them holding only the irrational crumbs of micro-findings which can never be reassembled and so denounce the irrationality of reason.

In relation to science, faith is therefore prior, and science undermines itself by undermining faith. Taken by itself, on the contrary, faith is only a deception. Listen to it speaking to Antoine:

> Believe what you do not see, believe what you do not know, and do not ask to see what you hope or to know what you worship. . . . How could certainty be acquired by one who is mortal and transitory? Through the fog, can you see the sun? . . . What do the revolts of reason or the negations of science matter? Science is ignorance of God, and reason is mere spinning in the void. Nothing is true except the eternity of the eternal, and grace alone has an understanding of this. Hope for it. . . . If you should obtain it, you will then possess that incomprehensible comprehension and your inspired soul, burning ever stronger to climb higher, will leave itself like the rising flame of the fire.

An exact but disturbing description of religious belief as it might appear to someone who "does not have grace," who can only hope, and who without this providential gift may easily get lost in irrationality; surrounded by the incomprehensible, he loses his way and is distressed by an incomprehensible comprehension. Shall we say that he believes? No doubt, but as Logic so aptly puts it: "Faith, faith, unquenchable, are you sure of being what you say? Split in two, you bless with one part, you curse with the other, you hope through the first, you tremble through the second. But if you trust in God, why do you fear evil?" Logic then adds for the sake of hope: "To hope is to doubt with love, to desire something to happen and not know if it will. . . . Do you doubt? Do you believe? Do you delight in God or do you yearn for Him? But if you desire him, don't you have him? If you have him, you no longer desire him. And . . . you go enclosing him in formulas, in conventional gestures, in . . . little saintly banalities." These arguments were already old; indeed, by Flaubert's time they were threadbare. They are reproduced here largely because they clarify Gustave's position: to believe is to doubt—or at least, *perhaps* to have grace; in fact, the objects of belief are defined by their radical absence; to doubt is to believe, since the objects one doubts are precisely the same as those to which faith is attached. Thus the doubter *believes* he has the right to doubt, just as the believer *believes* he has the right to believe. He who believes without grace is a fool. He who doubts without even knowing whether or not "science is ignorance of God" and reason a senseless spinning in the void *believes* in the infinite power of human understanding. And going from deception to deception, the moment he begins to doubt that understanding, his universal doubt—extending itself to the tools of skepticism— attempts an underhanded recourse to the Supreme Being and perceives itself hysterically as an incomprehensible shutting out of God.

Hence Gustave sets the two ideologies of his time against each other; neither is presented as the truth or even as the quest for truth. Forcing things just a little, one could say that the young man, having been antitruth, has come to the conclusion that truth does not exist or is not accessible to us because we haven't the means to establish it conclusively. What is especially striking is that the two adversaries are made to tear each other apart. Faith surrenders, breaks down, swoons, falls, and gets up muddied, out of breath; it has nothing to confront the arguments of science with. But science, which often reduces faith to silence, never entirely prevails. Indeed, it hardly begins its work; it merely collects, and knows nothing—later, it tells itself, the battle will be serious; but after the most violent scuffles, it perceives it has barely torn the hem of Infamy's dress—rather like the gnawings of a rat, Flaubert explains.

In one sense, Gustave is right, the ideologies are not demonstrable, scientism any more than religion; each of them is the expression of a class, the false consciousness it has of itself, the mythified ensemble of its options, the symbolic gratification of its desires, and its essential combat maneuver to demoralize the enemy classes. This complex, theoretical, and practical ensemble, weapon and imago, cannot in any way be offered as a truth—it can only be believed in. The Flauberts' younger son, out of respectful resentment against his father, made the unique mistake of assimilating science, the production of exact knowledge, as well as scientism, the thought of the wishful bourgeoisie; and we shall see that it weighed on him all his life.

What is certain about his adolescence is that he was by no means forced into atheism by one of those luminous proofs that, after Descartes, command our instant adherence. He obeyed the will of the Other and even superseded it, he affected disbelief in order to please; thus the father was doubly guilty since he deprived his son of the lights of faith without giving him those of science, which do not exist. The blame being thus shifted onto others, Gustave—he does not *know* himself, but no one *understands* himself better than he does—still cannot help but feel that the guilt is entirely his own. We should not imagine, however, that he discovers in himself, even obscurely, the *refusal* to believe—we know already that he has no means of accepting or refusing anything. In the process of self-examination he perceives, and must perceive, only a manipulated impotence. But the manipulator is not always the Other, it is sometimes—as in this particular case—himself passing for another. God was long ago inscribed in his flesh, another name for the verdant paradise of childish loves, and then the Christian religion offered him those admirable fables, sometimes puerile, sometimes profound, but always accessible to children. He was therefore made this way from the beginning, having a greater inclination for the Catholicism that humbly offered itself to faith than for the authoritarian reasonings of liberalism that claimed to carry a conviction he did not have. If he let himself slide toward disbelief while preserving nostalgia for a God he was losing without truly doubting his existence, if he renounced childhood and paradise forever, the principle of authority cannot suffice to explain this voluntary exile—from which Gustave would never return. The Other is there to mask a choice he could not impose, and the adolescent is conscious of this: something negligible, a bit too much zeal perhaps, a certain docility—this is all it takes for the whole operation, shadowed by an experienced grief, to seem like the result of his own vow.

And why make a vow to be unhappy? He doesn't ask himself the question in these terms, but this is the meaning of his estrangement, and the answer is promptly given. If he chose unhappiness, it is because he was made this way by the Fall, by inadequacy, by resentment and pride, so that unhappiness became his natural setting. Under the barrage of "jibes" and frustrations, the adolescent erected for himself an arrogant ethics, the ethics of pain, a scaffolding of bitterness on a foundation of absolute emptiness; he made himself into the unhappiest man alive in order to condemn the universe that could generate an infinite unhappiness. Let us recall that powerful line he would later borrow from Rachel, giving it a new depth: "I do not want to be consoled." Do we believe he could break his vow to be a permanent loser, to be the only loser of the human race? Impossible—he lives by it, it is his only support. If there were a paradise, he would refuse to enter it so that he could envy and scorn the elect from the outside, or, if he were dragged in by force, he would arrange to transform it into hell. What does this wretch have to do with God? If he were to admit the presence of God, everything would be compromised, he would remain the frustrated, inadequate child, inferior to his brother, cursed by his father, the family idiot, but he would no longer be permitted to seek his salvation in pride; the signs would have been changed. The rebuffs and aversions would not be trials, his sufferings would become the chastisements through which God confirmed his Christian vocation; and Achille-Cléophas's curse, reduced to its true proportions by the supreme Lord, would lose its satanic power and become the progenitor's sin to be lovingly punished, the surest means for the cursed child to reach heaven. In short, despair would be forbidden. Gustave is chosen; Achille-Cléophas and Achille may not be if they persist in their scientistic incredulity and if he who sees into souls finds no dissatisfaction or even anxiety in theirs. Here we find the executioners becoming the damned, those who arrogantly put their hand in the stone hand of the Commander. This is not admissible; lost through their intelligence, these wretches, these "marvels of civilization," would end by becoming interesting. The adolescent trembles with horror at the thought. What? The worst would cease to be certain? Would Gustave become a believer, one of those good little souls, narrow and fulfilled, to which God gives himself parsimoniously because they are not made to contain the sacred in its terrible immensity? Impossible! This means that he is constituted in such a way now that he *can no longer* change the blind furies of resentment through love, or through hope. But the "I cannot" is all the more easily transformed into a pathic assumption of the endured "No," which, through the mute but never entirely disregarded enterprise of resentment, makes it seem to him that *he is making himself just as he has been made*. Moreover, since his inner prophet of doom cannot accept divine grace without bursting, he understands quite well that his disbelief is *his*, not as an active refusal but insofar as it is inseparable from a certain horrified but haughty adherence to what he has done with what they have made him. In his eyes this means that his very essence—the victim making himself into his own executioner in order to realize himself through his executioners and against them by radicalizing their work—can only be despair, and this incriminates him by becoming an unpardonable sin when God is offered to him in vain. If you like, Gustave is conversant with the operation by which he has made God—who exists for everyone except him—the infinite frustration. "Docile disciple of my father, I am eager to believe that the world is a vast desert and that nothing has any meaning, not even my suffering; I am not unaware, however, that the Almighty exists, but I am made in such a way that I deprive myself of him." Perfect: God exists and withholds himself, which is an infinite crime; but at the same time Gustave is guilty and sets against him that other infinite, the sin of despair. Thus building on a childhood unhappiness, the vast and demonic adolescent turns himself into hell's only chosen. The presence of God in his heart would have disqualified his unjust sufferings; God's absence, on the other hand, consolidates and burnishes those sufferings like premonitions of the supreme injustice—infinite privation or, if you like, the creation of Gustave as he is, searching for the Father and having found him, tearing faith from his heart with his own hands.

As we see, as *he* saw *himself*, far from denying God the adolescent exploited him to the full; imagined through the fatalism of resentment, faith becomes the most radical instrument of torture for this indelibly blackened soul. Made to believe, pledged to God but his faith destroyed by the father's scalpel, endlessly tempted by a constitutional need for the absolute, he would feel an obscure call from above, some kind of summons whenever a bell rang, whenever he opened the door of a church, or simply whenever he was too unhappy. And these incomprehensible and doubtful messages troubled him, provoked a timid hope in his soul, a "dawning," purposely so that it would vanish, leaving him more alone and wretched than before. The essential reason for these false illuminations, whose only purpose is to increase his misery, is mentioned in passing in *Rage et Impuissance*: "God, a word invented *by the fortunate*." He returns to this in 1849:

ANTOINE

I beseeched God in my weakness, I sought to come closer to him.

FAITH

It is not in your moments of distress that you must beseech God.

This much is clear: God is not made for those who have need of him. The reason is that the pious soul takes pleasure in God's existence and in happiness; even if one "beseeches" the Creator, there always is something suspect, a hidden despair: if he is there, my miseries must disappear. Who are these dark souls, then, who suffer as though he were not there? Flaubert presents his theory as if it were an article of faith; in fact—whatever might have been the attitude of the priests—the New Testament and the Church have always said the opposite, and it was through *consolation* that Catholic missionaries made the greatest number of converts. Gustave knows this too, and suddenly he understands very well that his idea—unhappiness falling by its own weight into despair—is a parti pris inspired by his pessimistic vow and that it might be translated this way: he who suffers is damned by his suffering, which will never stop growing until it results in the unpardonable sin of despair. For this partisan of pain, suffering is election because it bears witness that God has turned away from him forever; yet how could Gustave be unaware of the way he tips the balance of doctrine?

He is all the more aware of it because its inner barrenness serves his purpose. God withholds himself and the system is perfect. Everything is preserved: anguish, the believer's call for help, the religious instinct, resentment. Heaven has only to keep quiet, and God can remain absent except as one man's infinite frustration. More aptly, Gustave has given himself the means of accepting paternal mechanism and disarming it gently without losing his pride or disarming his own resentment. Achille-Cléophas says to Gustave: "The All does not exist, there are only composite masses." Gustave answers: "That may be, but it exists at least in my desire; and he whom an instinct carries beyond himself toward the infinite totality is something quite different from the sum of indivisible fragments to which your scalpel would reduce him." The father explains to the son that there is no such thing as nature; the name "nature" is given to an infinite scattering of atoms whose movements are governed by the principle of inertia or, rather, of exteriority. The son responds: "Feeling unifies what your science pulverizes." Why shouldn't there be something like the synthetic unity of the world when the unitary impulse of a composite mass reveals the world beyond the diversity of its molecules as the undeniable unity of a trans-ascendence, and the cosmos beyond the dispersal of composite masses as the transcendent unity which alone could produce this nostalgia for the All in one of its parts? Gustave raises himself above mankind by a magnificent flight; his surpassing of the self is offered as a direct linking of the finite to the infinite, of the part to the whole. During this operation, it is best that he encounter *no one*. Especially not the Creator, who would return him, fulfilled, to his particularity. Indeed, if it is God who transports him, all the credit reverts to God, and sublime frustration gives way to the banal happiness of the elect. If Gustave is irremediably alone in his interstellar journeys, if he perceives nothing but assemblages of atoms separated by vacant space, if he descends once again mortified, stiff, and bruised, having retained from his voyages of discovery only the naked memory of the "eternal silence of infinite space"; in brief, if he is forced to proclaim that *everything which exists* supports the claims of the paternal science, of the arguments of libertines, if he despises the ignorance and stupidity of priests who speak so duplicitously of the creation and make its creatures regard it with horror, if he understands in his despair that everything is and can be only matter and that God gives himself only to fools, then Gustave alone deserves the credit for this exhausting and futile quest. Trapped like a rat, squeezed between the babblings of science and the silence of the world, deeply disappointed because everything conspires to confirm Achille-Cléophas's atheism, he is nonetheless enormous, a little martyr rejected by everyone, who agonizes but does not resign himself and in his heart never accepts the convictions with which others have filled his mind. The point is not that he might have other convictions, only that he is dissatisfied with them, that he is determined to believe, if he likes, in the mechanistic universe, provided he raises himself above this tumultuous non-sense by the purely negative and inarticulable feeling *of privation*: "Having a superior nature, a more elevated heart, he asked only for passions to nourish, and searching for them on earth, following his instinct, found only men. . . . Our poor lusts, our shabby poetry, our incense, all the earth with its joys and its delights, what did all this mean to him who had something angelic about him? All that nature, the sea, the woods, the sky, all that was small and miserable." Almaroës's angelic qualities are manifest only in his maladaption, which is immediately linked to the condemnation of all reality: "Poor body, how you suffered, thwarted, displaced from your proper sphere and confined to a world as the soul is confined to the body." Zeal fueled by resentment has already set to work to condemn the cosmos; Gustave, the prisoner of his finitude, is at the same time beyond men and things, the infinite is his torment—or rather the transfinite, meaning in this case the summation of the infinite. He must therefore be defined by privation of the infinite. And if he is so deprived, isn't it just because he has a soul powerful enough to conceive of the infinite, big enough to contain it? This unhappy consciousness of finitude is pierced by a need for the infinite which can only be an infinite need; Gustave represents it for himself as a void which expands outward indefinitely. What arrogant intoxication: the infinite, present in the finite as a negation and painful refusal, is *his nature*, which he didn't get from anyone else, either from his father, who wants to tempt him with the nonsense of scientism and who only believes in what he sees, or from God, who is importuned by Gustave's desire and prefers the fortunate of this world, gratifying only coarse-souled shopkeepers. If by some miracle their soul gets punctured, they seal up the sizable gap at once, screening the holes and cracks with tape, and go to mass on Sundays to fill up with God just as they would go a century later, at the same time and on the same Sundays, to fill up with gas. These are the people to whom he gives himself, allowing the priests to break him into pieces so that everyone might have his portion. The Lord does not want the openness of being that belongs to the cursed little boy; quite the contrary, irritated by the child's superhuman demand, he reveals himself only to punish this soul for its magnitude. No, Gustave *has opened himself*—he has opened his heart the way others open their veins, not by some violent action but by his haughty distaste for compromise; he has turned himself—against the little white-bearded Gods and pretty Christs sold around the churches—into the witness of the terrible hidden God whose absence is eating him alive. We see that he is on the brink of a negative theology. But he would not invent it before 1844. Far from proving God by his *universal* absence and his goodness by our common abandonment, he thinks that the Almighty has deserted him forever or is punishing him in proportion to his virtues. Flaubert's abandonment is the effect of a particular decree of Providence; there will be no compensation either in this world or in the next, which he will not reach since he doesn't believe in it. This certainty, he knows, is in itself the sin of despair—the greatest and finest sin: the creature rising up against the silence of the Creator and cursing it, which automatically leads to his damnation. Damned on earth, then carrion, Gustave is the sole inhabitant of hell.

Let us understand that Flaubert *deeply believed* this at the time. Yet the enormous advantage of this miserable situation is that it *does him honor*. For this pessimist who sees the good being punished and the wicked rewarded,[33] the value of a soul is measured by the torments inflicted upon it; thus since his misfortune is to be frustrated by the All, he is superior to everyone. He will be rigidly punished, but the very meaning of his pain will be in revealing to him his incomparable grandeur. He will have no opportunity or license for pleasure—only the meaning of his sufferings. That is enough for him, for pride finds justification in it; Pride, who in the first *Tentation*, "tall, pale with reddened eyes, hides her wounds, her teeth chattering, kisses the mouth of a snake that is gnawing at her breast, and staggers on her feet." Flaubert takes this pride that he ferrets out in himself for radical negativity, making the Devil summon it in these terms: "Oh Pride,

---

33. In his maturity he would modify the formula: "The wicked are always punished, and the good as well."

you will annihilate yourself with the pressure of your feelings; *because you suffer immeasurable pain, don't believe you are a god."* I have emphasized the last part of the sentence because it defines precisely the basic falsification and its limitations: pride is hardly immeasurable since it is defined as a privation of the infinite; these are its limits—the absence of the infinite separates him as such from ordinary humanity, but he is not permitted to consider this absence the sign of his own infinity. Did he want to live out his pain, then, as the mark of his divinity? Absolutely. *In any case*, these lines relate to the years of his adolescence and his young manhood before 1844. We shall see later that he considered himself at the time to be the anti-Christ, Satan, not simply in the free play of his imagination but more concretely as author and as "demoralizer"; we shall see that his sadistic dream—to stand up to the human race and laugh in its face—had its source in his feeling of *sacred* privation. Moreover, the idea of equaling his progenitor through suicide had tormented him for a long time; Satan, here, only carries it to its absolute conclusion—the algebraic sum of positive infinity and negative infinity is zero,[34] *therefore* total privation is equal to total plenitude provided it is self-conscious. But in 1849 Gustave is on the far side of his youth; if the desire to be the God of the pain ethic sometimes seizes him, he rejects it as a *temptation*. Doesn't he conceive of pride as an *enterprise*? He assigns it certain limits: save me, go that far but no further. And for proof we have the answer Pride gives to the Devil in which Gustave, recalling his own fall, lays bare the entire strategem: "Do you remember . . . how frenzied your soul was to possess me when you fell from the heavens? . . . I raised your head, oh accursed one, and your breath went up to Jehovah, who closed his door in horror." When Pride speaks, Gustave, who listens and approves, has *become Satan*; he is the one, humiliated by his inadequacies, who is moved by Pride to push those inadequacies to the point of absolute penury and claim them, not by an act but by sanctified suffering. Here, then, we have the primal drama, the Fall, and demonic pride—his only salvation. Pride is a nurse, she acts, plays the whore, relieves the poor devil; but this action is presented to us in relation to Gustave/Satan as *suffered*, therefore as *other*. However, no one but Gustave could think that he was saved; for Jehovah, the curse is definitive. Here we have the secret unveiled: Pride relieves the wretch, but structuring his action in the interest of constituted passivity, he makes himself submit

34. At least this is what Gustave thinks.

as though to the action of another, as though to the loving enterprise of a mother he never had. The text is perfectly clear: Gustave is not unaware that the pride is his, that it is in truth *his* action—the hyperbolic assumption of infinite evil; against God the Father he becomes the absolute, terror-stricken witness. If he made pride the Devil's whore—she is quick to answer back but in the end she obeys him—it is because a profound intention—conforming to his constituted character—compels him *to suffer* his actions in the form of passions. Still, he understands himself. If we could translate what is implicit in the discourse and what he would have us understand by this dialogue between allegorical figures, we would state it as follows: I know; because I am cursed, I must burn with shame or else internalize the curse, making it the very stuff of my soul, evil, which means the radical absence of God and the heinous, scornful challenge of everything in the name of that All from which I wanted him to expel me. I have pushed this folly to the point of believing that I am a counter-God, I have had unbelievable temptations, I have known the arrogance of damning myself by a despair that I manipulated even while believing it was given to me. Today I know my limits, and that knowledge is a wound to the pride that I am: I float on air, rootless, above men, damned alone because I am the only creature who was put together in such a way that the infinite would be *his* need and *his* impossibility. But I am not a god, I am the harbinger of silence, the All-powerful's *mortal* enemy, in every sense of the word, an enemy who always loses and is proud of losing because his defeats always make him endure his all-powerlessness. If I cannot believe in you who exist, our Father who art in heaven, it is because through incredible hyperbole I have made myself the most disgraced being in the universe; and consecrated to you, feeling in myself the humble and persistent instinct to believe, that is, to become integrated with the creation, I left my infernal father to dismember your work in order to deepen my rancor and define myself against all possibilities by my impossibility. Thus, while "every faith attracts me, and the Catholic faith more than any other,"[35] I have nothing to do with churches or priests, those intermediaries who offer a watered-down God to those who could not take his wine straight.

Mine. He knows whose fault it is; he says so. On the surface, this means: it's because of my all-too-human weakness; but underneath:

35. Although these lines date from 1856, he might have written them as early as 1830.

it's because of my resentment and my foolish pride. For this reason Gustave's false agnosticism oscillates between love lost but empty and unresented, which is the fault of the respondent, and blasphemy. But it is blasphemy to tempt God and then to claim, when prearranged conditions have made it inevitable, that God is the one responsible for failing to keep the appointed meeting. The folly of pride leads Gustave to put himself in the position of being able to say, "Me and God." Moreover, this is only a matter of amplifying the paternal curse: he has projected it onto heaven but it is the same thing, and *he knows it*. Achille-Cléophas engendered him purposely to deny him his love and the position that was his by right; Jehovah, crueler still, pulled him out of the mud purposely to deny him his presence, and gave him an unquenchable thirst for infinity, ensuring that the poor creature would have the horrible perception of his privation and at the same time would condemn himself by despair. Achille-Cléophas produced only one usurper, his elder son. God, however, made Achilles by the thousands—*all* the faithful, in other words, numberless humanity. When Gustave furtively enters a church, is it true that he is humbly searching for faith? Only on rare occasions, as he very well knòws; otherwise, why would he set *everything* against himself? Why, just when he ought to be asking for help from the mediations of Christianity—from the incense, the candles, the chanting of the priests—does he take it into his head to think about his atheist friends, about how they would roar with laughter if they could see him on his knees? What he really goes to look for in the temple during the ceremonies is the confirmation of his exile, the deception, the hatred, the envy and bitterness rediscovered in his vain superiority over those usurpers who will always triumph over him in the sheepfolds of being, and whom he might vanquish only on his own turf, which is nothingness. And when he pretends to consult a priest, he knows in advance that the man of God will have a crooked nose, dull eyes, and that the banality of his statements will be discouraging. Why make these attempts? Because a confirmed despair ends by resembling torpor; Gustave does not hesitate to sustain his own despair by frequenting holy places from time to time in order to revive in himself, as he hastens toward such sanctuaries, the vital hopes that will die the moment he has crossed the threshold.

This is what he resents, and also the fact that he is guilty in the eyes of all men and first of all before God, who is good. But also that he is right to be wrong and that God is wrong to be right. Now here is the basic question: since he catches himself red-handed when he closes up like an oyster while vainly pretending to be open to being, can he truly believe that God is withholding himself and that he is enduring immeasurable suffering? Doesn't he *have to live* these great movements of the soul as they are, as he makes them, that is, as dramas with an intention that cannot escape him? Gustave dreams of being the Accursed; the singular proof of his demonic aristocracy is his suffering, and this—which is the experience of being deprived of the infinite—must itself be infinite. Everything rests on this sophism: if the positive infinite is hidden from me, I become a negative infinite, which is expressed subjectively by an unsurpassed and constant despair. But is Gustave convinced of this? After all, even to those whom God overwhelms with small favors he refuses to show himself in fullness; are they then consumed by an infinite gap? Are they not, on the contrary, rather tightly knit within themselves and quite snug? They may seem infinitely stunted compared to the Almighty, who gives them only as much of himself as they can bear without bursting; but this is an observation of those who examine them from the outside and compare—as Flaubert himself does—their infinite smallness to the infinite greatness of the Almighty. Certainly there are those among them who sense that God's essence is not given and that, devout as they might be, what they possess of God is nothing compared to what is still hidden. They will call this frustration by all the names that please them—their human weakness, their inadequacy, an appeal for love that is lost in the night, or, on the other hand, the agonies of doubt, the fragility of their faith, the portion of nonbeing that resides in every creature and makes him incapable of receiving his Maker. In any case, their anxiety, their malaise, their sufferings will never equal in depth or intensity the infinite Being of which they feel deprived; first of all, every finite being is in each of his manifestations, whatever these may be, determined by his finitude—this far, no further; and this is as true for mens pains as for their pleasures.

Thus being deprived of the infinite can only inspire finite feelings, however painful. Is Gustave any different? Besides, this hidden God, who parcels himself out so parsimoniously to the faithful, conceals himself so well that no one, even in the wildest hypotheses, can even conceive of what he conceals. The sorrow we feel on leaving a town we have loved, or at the death of a wife, is based on memories, but—except in the case of some mystics—the attributes of the Almighty are merely abstract concepts: we can be sorry for being ignorant, but how can we grieve for what we do not know, especially if the narrowness of our minds prevents us from imagining it? Of course there is reminiscence. Lamartine did a great deal for theology when he described man as a fallen god who remembers heaven. But Gustave, despite a certain platonism which we shall examine further on, never attempted to base faith on memory. And he would have been even less inclined to do so had he preserved a certain memory of heaven, less comfortable railing against his abandonment had God not left him entirely in the dark. The only passage to my knowledge in which the young man alludes to vague recollections that seem to pertain to a previous life is found—and it has already been cited—in *Rêve d'enfer*: Almaroës sometimes recalls that he has not always lived on this earth, which keeps him prisoner; *elsewhere* he knew blessings but can no longer retrieve their meaning and nature. Yet the context proves that the magnificent robot, wholly matter, kneaded out of the slime of our world and deprived of a soul, can have lived only in the material universe, and the young author's nostalgia is related to his own childhood, to the golden age. Flaubert is no fallen god; his thought would be rendered better by saying that because he is a fallen man, he is not far from being a god. Besides, the sophism is the same in Gustave and Lamartine, except that it is negative in the former and positive in the latter. We have just seen that being deprived of the infinite is not an infinite privation; in the same way, the man who desires the infinite and does not know exactly what he wants, since he cannot truly and concretely comprehend the immortality of the soul, eternity, etc., is not really infinite in his desires. Trans-ascendence is, of course, a surpassing; the believer will say that he is going beyond himself toward the infinite, and we will not dispute it; but he himself will recognize that without the grace of God, this surpassing is finite.

How can Gustave, without sophistry, believe that he is the empty receptacle of the infinite? How can he believe, whatever his "bitter passions," that he has a soul large enough to contain immeasurable suffering? And if he truly suffers, how can he experience this suffering as a horror vaster and deeper than the universe? To these questions— which he never asks himself but which he endures as the interrogative nuance of experience—Gustave can give only two contradictory answers. Either the immeasurability is a real determination of his interiority, in which case he must have grace—the infinite can be revealed in the finite, even as infinite penury, without the concurrence of God; in this case the whole system collapses, and the infernal and vain pursuit, the unheard appeal, the desertion, the frustration *is faith itself*, a gift and proof of the Lord. Indeed, blasphemy was predicted in the program, as well as fake damnation, and on his deathbed Gustave will see all the devils who are actually angels come to cure the soul that well before his birth was the chosen of God. Or else, as he persists in repeating, the Almighty created him in order to abandon him, so that nothing in him should bear witness to God's existence; hence God took care that Gustave's cursed heart should remain cold and unfeeling, containing the infinite void, and in this case Flaubert's true curse is that he cannot even feel the extent of his unhappiness: human, all too human, he is obliged to play out his forever disappointed fervor and despair.

He cannot accept either of the two answers. He is not ready for the first, which will reappear after 1844 in expanded form; he has not yet found the secret places of his soul and the double drawers that will allow him to keep all the despair along with an inarticulate hope, and both in secret. He is still too close to hatred and resentment to want to be pardoned, that is, to accept a single chance to be less unhappy; he wants to go on pitilessly punishing himself so as to punish his executioners. And he does not want the alternative for anything in the world, at least not in this form. How could his passionate pride accept mediocrity? And how could he unashamedly confess that the "Accursed" is only one role in his repertoire and that Gustave is only *playing* a man in despair?

The second answer, however, is the one he is going to choose, with some modifications. Let us say that he adopts it between the end of his adolescence and the "closure" of his youth, and that he sticks to it—at least on a certain level—even after 1844, although by then he would have opted for the first answer.

One of the principal themes of his work—which runs from his first stories up to and including *Madame Bovary*, where it is exhausted, and which reappears sporadically in the subsequent novels—might be formulated as follows: "I am too small for myself." We shall return at length to this theme apropos of *Novembre*, and we shall see that it is not only a literary motif but a permanent subject of anguish kept alive by self-loathing. The unloved man has little self-esteem and never takes the risk of trusting himself; he is constantly enraged at the contrast between his immense ambitions and his derisory mediocrity. We already know the origin of this obsession—which will be one of the principal factors in his neurosis: a surgical eye was turned on the child; a magisterial voice said, "He is not gifted." This, at any rate, is the way Gustave thinks it was. Fleeing the condemnation and entering other domains, such as religion and art, he carries with him a prefabricated blueprint: Flaubert pride and ambition incarnate in this finite mode of the august substance as the family idiot. At a deeper level, it seems to him that his magnificent projects are the *familial* truth of his being, his fundamental and, as a last resort, collective being; from this point of view his immediate truth, experienced in its passive flow, in its powerlessness and its everyday banality, seems to him a *congenital* failure; to exist is a sin since it expresses only in vague sentiments never fully felt, in meaningless attitudes, in muddled and inadequate works, that transcendental and hidden being, the Flaubert patrimony, the burning bush of imperative Faustian demands which constitute his honor and his intelligible ego.

Yes, the expression of intelligible character would be rather fitting for the being-for-duty that is specified in a hidden "Me," provided one adds that Gustave's *empirical character* is not the pure transcription of intelligible choice in a human experience, let alone choice itself being deciphered through the spatial-temporal forms and unitary structures of that experience. His empirical character is a deviation, a weakening, a de-substantiation, in a word, a betrayal of that superb and demanding ego the Flauberts have given him; the empirical "Me" is too little and too inconsistent for the "I" it represents, which Gustave takes for his own and which is never touched, never lived, and manifest only through the scope of the projects that it imposes but are never undertaken. This is how Flaubert, in *Novembre*, would explain his quite self-conscious instability, and even at the age of fifteen he attributed it to Djalioh. The idea of work to do is greeted with enthusiasm—the hidden ego thinks big; but the empirical ego knows its limits, beginning the job without hope and soon abandoning it. The theory of the two egos was never articulated; but Gustave must have believed in it since he presented himself to Louise sometimes as the Accursed (transcendental ego) and sometimes as an amorphous and malleable substance (later he would call it "a malleabelly"), incapable of knowing and judging himself because, first, he was too close to the subject; second, his faculties were limited and his sight blurred; and third, he had nothing characteristic or definite about him. A hard-hearted Numidian, splendidly stoic, or a mushroom swollen with boredom? An adventurer of the mind, conquistador of art, or a bourgeois living in the country, busying himself with literature? He is all these things. What I want to emphasize here is that unlike most people, when he is in despair his ambitions are not like subjective aspirations consisting only of what solidity he gives them according to his mood, but rather like features specific to the arrivism of the Flauberts made manifest in a child cast aside by a strong-minded family; indeed, these ambitions are marshaled in his eyes as his objective reality. This means that even when they are internalized they preserve their acquired objectivity because they define the direction of his little enterprise and seem to him at once what he ought to be—ironclad orders given to an amoeba futilely pushing his indecisive protoplasm around—and eminently *what he is*, everyday experience being a confused mirage unless it is the incarceration of proud strength in the naked, unprotected body of a soft animal, which would be the foulest curse of all. What applies to his vast enterprises, always present as remorse but never pursued, holds also for his affective nature. Gustave is the *Accursed*; he *is* Satan or at least that bold Cain who slew his brother under the very eye of the eternal Father; and he resents the abominable state of abandonment in which God has left him; his regret for the infinite is surely infinite regret, and his pride, answering the Creator blow for blow, chose hell out of despair. This is what he *is* but it appears to him only in the form of a being-for-duty: somewhere in the abyss of the infinite, the magnificent damned creature writhes with pain, and his gasp "terrifies Jehovah." The news is communicated to Gustave daily, that big boy with the handsome stubborn face who laughs when he looks at himself in a mirror, in the form of perfectly ordinary imperatives which are nonetheless based on a diabolocal inversion of the Kantian principle: *You must, therefore you cannot.* We shall find this ethic of the Devil again, quite often; we shall even see Gustave turn it against his readers. For the moment, it means: *in order to be what you are,* you would have to gnash your teeth, curse, despair, suffer especially, suffer like one of the damned; but a special curse which was added to the first has made it impossible for you to realize your being—you are incapable of cursing and you can experience only moderate sufferings; at the same time, moreover, this appeal is directly addressed to you by yourself, by the matchless Accursed, and you must force yourself to respond to it knowing that you will not succeed. This second interpretation of the diabolical imperatives allows Gustave to play the drama of the damned as well as to understand and justify himself by it; he does what he can, poor soul, he throws himself on his knees in order to believe, and doesn't manage to reject in advance the one who rejects him; he shakes his fist at heaven and, blaspheming properly, throws himself moaning on his bed, looking for fear and suffering. God the Father and Achille-Cléophas are to blame if each of these *actions*, once undertaken, is transformed into a gesture—meaning into a *representation of an action*—and if, though duly called forth by certain attitudes, the requisite feelings, refusing to be tested, constrain him to act. He is in good faith, good will, but lo and behold, the classic transmutation: pure gold is transformed into vile dross, Gustave's empirical nature being to his essential ego as dross is to gold. Of course he feels nothing, or nearly nothing, with regard to his absolute demands—rage, a tender and bitter sadness, melancholy; what he does feel is that the infinite is doubly eluding him, first as plenitude, then as privation. Never mind; things being what they are, you are better off falling back into native apathy; you must play what you are because you cannot be it, and for this reason alone the young man will seem, in the contingency of experience, to be one with his intelligible being. These official blasphemies will show that he accepts in full consciousness being the blasphemer he must be, to some extent, for real. Or perhaps this drama of damnation makes him exist as infinite and damned; after all, if he acts out despair, the sublime and inexpiable sin, it is *on command* and beneath the invisible eye of an Absolute who is hidden—isn't this enough to transform the relative into the absolute? He moans, cries out, tears at his hair, says, "I am in despair," and the *animula vagula* hasn't the strength to despair—or to hope—but the intention was there and God cannot have failed to take note: to play the role of Satan consciously ought to be enough to get yourself damned. And then, if more is required, there is something in writing—*scripta manent*. It is perfectly possible to write the "Discourse on Despair," and in fact Gustave began it again and again between his fifteenth and twentieth years; it is better than playing a role, for that unattainable ego which must be his reality inspires him, describing itself, and whispers to him the damning words. Author of *Agonies*, or *La Danse des Morts*, Gustave is closer to the *Accursed* than when he turns himself into his own actor: he makes himself the intermediary between the terrible infinite and this little aging world. He is not quite infinite suffering, but he reveals suffering and serves it, introducing it into our nature only to be farted out—you can count on that. We shall see, in effect, that he believes the writer must be a demoralizer.

He is suffering, moreover, and he is bent on suffering. One of the functions, as we have seen, of that polyvalent myth of old age is to justify him in his own eyes when he suffers less than he would like. There is consequently something "of the respondent" in this falsified soul. And the falsification begins only with hyperbole when Gustave, in the face of an absolute plenitude—which he does not conceptualize because it is inconceivable—wishes for an absolute emptiness. After this long journey, then, we have simply come back to our point of departure. *The fault is mine* means, first of all: Godot will not come because I am unworthy, I haven't enough strength or fervor to draw him to me; my tepid soul can only wait: I am fireproof, I shall never know the delights of conflagration. And then, beneath this protoplasmic indolence we have found an arrogant myth: God has cursed me in particular; without his help I am in agony and my pride pushes me to finish the work; empty, infinite, I am gaping, inferior to all, superior to mankind; anti-God, I am equal to the Almighty by choosing to despair of him. But on a closer look, this wild option seemed to us *unrealizable*: Gustave can only believe in unrealizing himself— soon we shall see the techniques used to become an imaginary man. However, this strange drama is imposed on him by the Flaubert substance, in other words, by honor; in order to combat his all-too-human nature he forces himself to represent an empty heaven. Clearly, the *animula vagula* we found at the outset is also what we find at our return. We never really left—except to examine superficially and in depth the representation Flaubert gives of himself, so as to try *on the whole* to show its eminent value (by a systematic reversal of the commonly accepted set of values) beneath its excessively weak nature; and to give a superficial interpretation of the vacuousness of his religious soul, viewing it as a result of the subversive influence of his father's wretched truths. In a way he exploits the situation (I need faith, I cannot believe) and at the same time defends himself against it. Furthermore, we find *two* devils in him, one of which is Achille-Cléophas and the eternal Father beyond him, complicit in his silence— these being only one, like the Father and Son in Catholicism; the other is the Accursed soul himself, becoming a devil by the internalization of his curse as an intentional despair, the younger son of the Flauberts in his person but out of reach. Openness and closure of being correspond. The first, which he calls the religious instinct, is constitutive and fundamental—life must have an absolute meaning, this superfluous little boy must know what he is doing in the world. But the dyad *diabolical father/creator* forbids this knowledge; in the face of such privation reserved for him alone, the little boy closes himself to God, right in the depths of his being. Deprivation of the infinite will remain, allowing him to embrace the universe with its millions of stars; but *knowing* that God exists and withholds himself, Gustave in his turn closes up and chooses to summarize the *mechanistic universe*: absolute nothingness—this is what he names his sin of despair, or his decision *to believe in nothing* in the presence of the hidden Creator and against him.

It is impossible to playact without being conscious of playacting. Even in a psychodrama—where one is often acting out what one is—an obscure ludic consciousness is indispensable for freeing hidden violence. Gustave knows that he is playacting. At the very moment he is justifying himself by a Promethean drama opposing heaven and earth, and which he claims is unfolding in eternity and can be evoked only by a *representation,*[36] he is conscious of creating the drama in order to hold the sacred torch to a fundamentally mediocre soul, a damp wick that will never catch. At the same time, this disgorging of boredom, this misery, is absolute reality, it is living. Once again, Gustave himself is *called into question*; once again he repeats to himself beneath the Byronic drama he is playing: "I am not big enough to have." For God too, he is the family idiot. To tell the truth, he does sometimes stop playing Cain, but he *never* stops being conscious of his essential poverty, because the very drama that is justified by the man Flaubert cannot take place without exposing his ludic character. The inadequacy is there, the old inadequacy, first suffered when he was faced with the alphabet and later, until the end of his life, when he was faced with the blank page. At times the inadequacy is experienced as evidence for the prosecution: my God, my Father, why have you made me so mediocre? At other times—at the Holy Sepulcher, for example—it is posed for its own sake, humbly, without any reference to its creators. At this moment, all that remains is a poor contingent existence penetrated by a need to believe—that is, to feel necessary to the world—which he does not have the means to satisfy precisely because of that contingency which is experienced as disgrace but which cannot be transformed into necessity. It is at these moments of self-loathing, of bitter sadness, that he begs the God of mercy to give him his grace, that is, the means to love God and to be loved in him. My God, be the father I would have wanted, the father I didn't have; my weakness cannot repel you because you know the sincerity of my expectation and because the others, the Lord's annointed, are no more worthy than I. Nothing. Silence. And the wheel turns again: the resentment and negative pride that were lulled to sleep for a few minutes awaken with a start and throw him into the drama: and why

36. It is the same thing, after all, since he is refused the illuminations of faith, just as the ceremony of the mass is merely a bad representation of an archetypal event that must be placed, if one believes, in a millennial past and in a living eternity.

did you make me unworthy of your visitation? The carousel doesn't stop until one particularly dark night when the younger son, dropping the reins of the carriage, is crushed under the feet of his elder brother the usurper. And this is precisely how, after he has been accused, in the face of that rose given and lost a bitter sadness tears from him the name of the primary culprit. *Theirs, Mine. . .*

Especially Yours. We have hit bedrock, at least apparently: *Yours,* who turned *me* away from faith in You by acting through *them.* But rather than start up the carousel once again, let us note the new gentleness, the respect in this invocation. The intimate "you" which was so often used during his youth, and whose brutality was calculated to mark the cursed vassal's proud independence in the face of his Lord, has given way to a "You" beginning, as it should, with a capital Y. Although grace has not touched him, Gustave is using the language of faith; he speaks of God like one of the faithful. Except that the bitter tenderness marking his relations with the hidden God belongs to him in his own right. He invokes the language of faith in due form in order to state clearly that he has no faith. At the time, he had been suffering for five years from a nervous illness, and we shall see that the route from Deauville to Rouen was in a sense his road to Damascus: he thought he had been chosen to lose God irrevocably, and deep down he believed that this supreme loss accompanied by despair might, after all, be a way of regaining God. This metamorphosis need not detain us now—Gustave would never admit to it, and to bring it to light would take a lengthy effort. This is what is important here: the fact that he has dropped Ohlmin's tone and addresses himself to the Almighty as one of the faithful (all the while maintaining the conviction that he is not), endows the question in *Rage et Impuissance,* "Why don't you want me to believe?" with a breadth and even a universality that it could not have when the adolescent considered himself the sole outcast of creation. He is speaking now for himself, certainly, but in the name of many others whom he has never known. He no longer asks, "Why have you dealt me this blow?" but, in a more general way: "Why have You chosen to elect us, who are the best, by depriving us of You? Why, O Almighty, when it was so easy to dazzle us by Your revered and unbearable presence or by the majesty and the sanctity of Your representatives, have You chosen Your ministers from among the vulgar herd of those wretched and ignorant creatures? I understand very well that priests are men and that as such they must be sinful, and I even understand that You have not necessarily elected the best of us for the priesthood.

557

But was it really necessary to choose only the worst? Are the stupidest really the best qualified to teach Your doctrine? Are the most licentious best suited to free us from our faults? Is it by following their example that we will most surely achieve chastity? Are those vulgar heaps of sluggish and sated matter best equipped to persuade us of our spiritual existence and our immortality?" To which the reply, too facile we know, would be that priests are neither the first nor the last of men. What matters is that Gustave considered them abominable, and in fact they were—between 1815 and 1830; you did not grow up with impunity in an authoritarian police state under the double surveillance of the cops of the cloth and the lay spies of the Congrégation. It was as though the Sacred had mysteriously chosen to be in rags, to be reflected in dross, to be the ineffable meaning of some intolerable buffoonery. In this astonishment at the baseness of those who are nonetheless charged with an essential mission but who seem chosen *precisely* because they are not qualified to fulfill it, I find something similar to the uncertainties of K. the land surveyor in his relations to the messengers who are or claim to be sent by the Castle. They too are little insignificant people, often ridiculous, sometimes vicious, always incongruous, who exist at the lowest echelon of an invisible and cumbersome bureaucracy and communicate with their superiors only with difficulty by means of telephones that are out of order, etc., transmitting to the villagers—when there is something to transmit— obscure news they themselves do not understand. The central issue in all this intrigue—at least as it concerns the land surveyor—seems of secondary, or at least secular, importance: will he or will he not receive authorization to stay in the village? However, the paltry intrigue, not despite its paltriness but because of it, gradually takes on primary importance: the Sacred, absent, unintelligible, refracted through the absurdity of the bureaucrats, skewed, even secularized, appears to be the single admissible meaning of this buffoonery. The sacred drama, for Kafka, can be represented to men only in the form of a farce, no doubt because of the impoverished human condition, but unquestionably too because of the privative essence of the Sacred and of the possibly insurmountable difficulties that prevent a religious message from reaching its human destinations and remaining religious. The result is that K. is surrounded by signs which—being neither altogether natural nor completely supernatural—seem grotesque and often scandalous and in a way mean nothing on the level of connotation; only the contrast between these persistent indicators and the comic and sinister absence of any indicated subject allow us to infer that an elusive or impossible denotation might be the sole worthwhile explanation of these absurd signposts marking the wilderness.[37]

In this area, Gustave does not have Kafka's rigor; he does not pursue the challenge to the Sacred—not in itself but in its powers of communication—with such stubborn, inflexible humility. However, he poses the question in a *radical* way by passionately exaggerating the human weakness of priests. But at the point where Kafka concedes that the Sacred has a certain impotence and mystically experiences his own abandonment as being at once his own basic culpability and God's distress and incapacity to reach men, Gustave pulls up short and in the last analysis reverts to making us the only *immediate* culprits; God's only fault is to have created us as we are, or indeed to have created us at all. When we leave his hands, finite and contingent, we can *live* this status only by trying to surpass it: contingency, becoming conscious of itself as pure original non-sense, must be only an appearance, and unable to anchor our existence ourselves, we discover that a Great Clockmaker put us into the world because we were necessary to the optimal functioning of his clock. Our finitude conceived as a limiting determination, that is, as affected in its being by a profound nonbeing, can tear itself away from the horror of this inner nothingness only by devoting itself faithfully, fanatically, to infinite being. In other words, the only way we can escape nothingness *in this life* is by making ourselves God's instruments. In this surpassing of the self toward infinite and necessary being, Flaubert sees the very meaning of our nature. There is no difference between the horrified awareness of our inconstancy, our gratuitousness, and that trans-ascendence which is our effort to escape, retrospectively to change the meaning of our birth. Here we have the *religious instinct.* We see that the son of the rationalist surgeon cannot prevent himself from rationalizing his problem: faith is nothing more than the basic need of every creature to live his status as animal; the relation to the self, according to Gustave, being always one of loathing, comprises *at the same time* the unsavory disclosure of facticity and its refusal *in the name of its opposite.* But if everything seems simple on the level of what is *lacking*, everything is complicated the moment we try to know the supreme Lord who justifies our existence. The finite can negatively grasp the infinite but merely as a certain illumination of its finitude;

---

37. For Kafka one might say that the Sacred, being *cruelly* uncommunicable, is affirmed as such through the fact that a whole communications system is out of order.

how should it be possible, in effect, to make the one support the other as Gustave *represents* it when he plays out his "autosacramentales" as infinite privation? And where would the sad product of a fortuitous coupling gain his knowledge of absolute necessity? Only through the self-loathing that is ours from birth. It will have already been understood that this loathing—which is the religious instinct itself, according to Flaubert—is an intimate relation directly linked to the anomaly of the unloved younger son, an overprotected infant deprived of smiling faces; in the same way, the proclaimed ignorance of absolute necessity is founded on the idiosyncrasy of this passive agent, who is resistant, *out of passivity*, to logical connections. Being a mathematician, however, does not automatically confer a knowledge of necessity as it would appear to the divine understanding; one would at least have to have a sense of what Milhaud calls *logical certainty* in order to pose the question correctly and to show at the outset the interior dialectic of irreducible contingency and necessity which *practical* agents continually forge as an indispensable tool for producing bodies of knowledge and organizing these into systems. There is no question of this as far as Gustave is concerned—necessity can be only the futile and *pathic* revolt of contingency against itself.

The religious instinct, according to Flaubert, excluding on principle the possibility of knowledge, is conceived as a *need to believe*, but the objects of its faith cannot be defined. The consequence is that without conceptualizing the objects of faith, we will either remain mired in anxiety and malaise, and our frustrated need will not even be proof that something exists somewhere that might satisfy it, or else we will invent the divine object. Religions are nothing but *socialized imaginary constructs*. But—here we find again the generalization of the formula "I am too small for myself"—the finite's imagining of the infinite can only result in childish and clumsy fables. On this level of superstructure the curse of Adam originates because his power to form images is not in proportion to the need that prompts them. Man cannot try to quench his thirst by creating a fantasy that might satisfy it, at least symbolically, without inevitably sinking into foolishness. If he gives in to the temptation to believe at any price (like those who say: "You must believe in something"), he will become increasingly stupid. To our misfortune, the religious need draws us away from this shabby and faded earth, yet the myths it generates imprison us even more in the dungeon from which we wanted to escape. Imagination— unless functioning by itself and for its own sake—can only give us images which are singular, human, terrestrial; by attempting with the guidance of instinct to represent the supernatural as an *object* of faith, it mixes natural and supernatural together in anthropomorphic myths, and the infinite is engulfed and lost in a black stone or an old man with a white beard. There is no perceptible difference between the two. Nor between fetishistic rites and Catholic rituals. God created man in such a way that man cannot live without God but only believes in idols and dies deprived of his light.

In the three versions of *Saint Antoine*, the Devil tempts the hermit with the *history* of religions: all are *transient*; the religious instinct fastens itself onto a barbaric object, people believe in it for a few centuries, and then the god of wood or gold falls apart and another is made. Nonetheless, these grotesque and ephemeral fables have a positive aspect; to the very extent that the materialization of the Almighty is deceptive and puerile, it allows the religious instinct to be transformed: it was a malaise, an endured absence, a disgust with finitude, and it becomes faith. Flaubert has expressed himself with the greatest clarity on this subject. And frequently. Never more clearly, I think, than in his first letter to Mlle Leroyer de Chantepie:

> The hypothesis of absolute nothingness doesn't . . . terrify me. I am prepared to throw myself into the great black hole with equanimity. And nevertheless, what attracts me above all is religion. I mean all religions, one no more than another.[38] Every dogma in particular is repulsive to me, but I consider the feeling that invented dogma to be humanity's most natural and poetic. . . . In it I find necessity and instinct; I respect the negro kissing his fetish as much as I do the Catholic at the feet of the Sacred Heart.[39]

In another letter, criticizing the philosophes, who condemned religious fanaticism, he declares that for him, on the contrary, tepidness or tolerance make no sense in religion and that a true believer can only be a fanatic. This praise of fanaticism is astonishing from the pen of a man consumed by the "belief in nothing." But Gustave is being

38. He is not being entirely sincere; he would write in another letter to her that he has his preferences, foremost "for the Catholic faith." Because of the myth of Christ, naturally—this god who became man in order to suffer must appeal to a man who suffers from not being God. And then, he has to admit that while fetishism puts man in touch with the Sacred, the dimension of the infinite is missing. One can imagine, then, that from his point of view the Christian religion marks an advance in the religious imagination. To tell the truth, he sometimes thinks that all religions are equally valid and sometimes that Christianity, without escaping the inalienable law of finitude, is closer to the "modern soul."

39. 30 March 1857, *Correspondance* 4:170.

perfectly consistent: what he loved in the first Empire was the fanatical devotion of Napoleon's old guard, that rigorous "homage," that un- qualified commitment to take the life of another and to give up their own at the emperor's command. The personality of the leader was not at issue; what mattered was feudalism regained, the inferior jus- tified by total allegiance to the superior, whoever he was. This is also what he admired in *constituted* religion: devotion, perfect allegiance, oblivious of any negative determination; whether an amulet, a voodoo charm, or the figure of Christ on the cross, the idol concentrates in its vulgar effigy all the love of which the faithful soul is capable. The vast soul of Djalioh is concentrated entirely in his limitless love for the pretty little thing that Monsieur Paul is going to marry. A profane affection, no doubt. But what Gustave means to demonstrate is that the value of the chosen object is of no importance. In the same way, when it comes to sacred love it is quite true that the adored object is in reality only a piece of wood or cut stone, but what does it matter if circumstances make it attract to itself, like a thunderbolt, all the believer's violent desires gathered in a single sheaf?

Gustave's prudence is noteworthy; there are numerous Christians today who think that devout love expressed through the finite, what- ever it might be, aims at and attains the infinite, sometimes unknow- ingly. Such people go so far as to conclude or to imply, like Mauriac in *Le Fleuve de feu*, that carnal love, through the body of the other, is blindly addressed to God as testimony, it seems, to their perpetual lack of satisfaction and their desire, at the heart of desire, for some- thing beyond possession. Gustave himself. is quite cautious. The sacred object summons up all the forces of the soul, which once assembled build on it to secure the infinite; but if it is true that fa- naticism aims at the infinite through an idol, it is also true that nothing is achieved. Quite the contrary; the cult object creates the most absurd passion because it concentrates in itself what is dispersed, but *precisely for that reason* it diminishes its scope by narrowing its field of appli- cation. The infinite, for Gustave, is more easily glimpsed in those vague cosmic ecstasies in which the soul is dilated to such an extreme that it darkens into unconsciousness or into "melancholy lethargies." Hence we see that Djalioh "loves Adèle at first like the whole of nature, with a tender and universal sympathy," and that *"this love grew to the extent that his tenderness for other beings diminished."* In sum, the passion for the infinite has to be infinite; by attracting it entirely onto itself, the sacred object touches it with finitude. The Moslem's fanaticism does not come exclusively from his love for Allah but from the stubborn violence that makes him love *his* God in his negative determination, that is, in the pitiful difference that separates Allah from the God of the Jews or the God of the Christians. The mobilization of all one's powers—including fierceness for killing Infidel dogs and the courage to endure torture and death rather than renounce one's faith—can be effected only by the nonbeing of the pseudo-infinite, meaning by that differential which in the system of gods and their opposites makes one particular Infinite among others, hence a finite Infinite. The violence of faith being inversely proportional to the breadth of religious perception, the result, according to Flaubert, is that fanaticism, born of the need for the Infinite, is a finite and exclusive passion for the finitude of an object which finite beings present as the Infinite deigning to appear at the heart of the finite. The fanatic is actually someone who in the face of everything loves *one* Infinite for its finitude. From this point of view, the world is made in such a way—through God's doing—that any belief is a deflection of the religious instinct. Gustave knows that faith can move mountains, he admires that incredible power which, in conjunction with self-forgetting, accomplishes both the full realization and the total destruction of human nature; he admires nothing so much as *religious man*, provided he is called Saint Polycarp or Torquemada rather than César Birotteau. But at the same time, he unmasks the diabolical trick: born of the need for the Infinite, religions are *particularities*, and these alone give birth to faith, which must be attached to precise dogmas; suddenly, however, the dogmas become the miasma in which the original instinct is engulfed and lost. Religion kills the religious instinct.

It is not the Devil who is responsible for this demonic cunning but God, who created us *finite*. Those conscious of the trap will no longer fall into it and no longer agree to particularize their need, even in a spacious theism like the Vicar of Savoy's, which, once professed, is singularized within the system as a variant of the dogma that denies dogmas and, in order to make its specialness universal, dissolves the obscure power of mysterious and perfectly irrational rites which are perhaps, unknown to us, our true communication with the Sacred. In short, since faith deflects instinct, to preserve the appeal in its purity the initiated will refuse to believe, although they realize that they are thus depriving themselves of any satisfaction. This is what Gustave, in the same letter, explains to his correspondent. At the time, Mlle de Chantepie was suffering from a strange neurosis; as a Catholic, she considered confession obligatory—deservedly—but could not confess that she believed she was "burdened with all the faults of humanity"; in the confessional, however, she suddenly thought of "the most unthinkable, the strangest and most ridiculous sins." At first she did not believe in them but eventually she believed she was guilty. She added: "Being no longer able to fulfill a duty which has become impossible for me, I am a lost being, without God, without hope." Flaubert answers her:

> This is what I think: you must try to be more Catholic or more philosophical. You have read too widely to believe sincerely. Don't protest! You would certainly like to believe. That's all. The meager pittance they serve up to others cannot satisfy you, you have drunk too deeply and with too much pleasure. The priests have not answered you, which is not hard to believe. Modern life has gone beyond them, our souls are a closed book to them. Make a supreme effort, an effort that will save you. You must take the whole of one or the whole of the other. In the name of Christ, do not remain sacrilegious for fear of being irreligious! In the name of philosophy, don't degrade yourself in the name of that cowardice called custom. Throw it all overboard since the ship is sinking.

We might think that Gustave's answer hardly applies to the case at hand. But this would be a mistake. He recognized in Mlle de Chantepie a pithiatic nature like his own. He well knows how to describe the malaise that torments her as an autosuggestion obviously sexual in origin;[40] it begins with the desire *to have sinned* accompanied by a "troubling and fearful pleasure," and is satisfied oneirically: the dream of sin begins—and passes. Then comes the hallucination, and with it conviction, certainty, remorse—along with the need to cry out: "I have sinned!"

But he does not limit himself to this sexual interpretation. Mlle de Chantepie is of course an old maid, probably an aging virgin assailed in her menopause by troubling and perverse regrets; she is also a Catholic, and Gustave has understood that these neurotic spells—always experienced at church, in the confessional or upon entering it—have another intentional function, which is to make it impossible for the poor lady to live any religious life in strict obedience. If it isn't Mephistopheles whispering these incongruous desires into her ear to prevent her from reaching the Holy Altar, it must be she herself. Gustave—an expert in the matter, as we shall see—judges that she

---

40. Gustave does not say this openly but he implies it.

has lost faith but dares not admit it, and that the base aspects of the soul, reveling in their work, are trying to separate her from the sacraments by allowing a few of her hideous desires to filter through, a shocking and incongruous attempt that terrifies her without giving her the courage to break with Catholic custom. Gustave has understood the basic intention of this neurosis: I don't know anything about it. What is certain is that he judges correctly the opportune moment for the surgical intervention; this woman *would like* to believe but does not *want to*, therefore faith must be removed. Gustave performs his intervention with great delicacy; he does not say: no longer believe, but: be Catholic completely, blindly, or be entirely philosophical.

All this is well and good. The diagnosis is more than plausible, the treatment plan worthwhile; except that Flaubert, in describing the course of treatment, offers his own. In other words, he *is talking about himself*. He is the one who has drunk too deeply and with too much pleasure to be content with the meager pittance of common wine; meaning that he scorns the vulgar fables served up by shopkeepers. Why? He says so very clearly, almost naïvely: he has read too widely to believe with sincerity. Is faith for illiterates, then? Let us say that in them alone—or nearly—faith can be fanaticism, fervor, wonder; they do not have the means to compare the god they are shown with others, nor to make their religion into a particular Western version of monotheism. Blind to the nothingness that undermines myths and ceremonies, they throw themselves into faith, give it their allegiance, and are hence confined unknowingly in their indelible finitude. Gustave himself does not believe, not only because the Catholic religion seems to his erudite mind a particular confession localized in space and time, its current meaning the function of a long history, but also because he has drunk strong wine, by which we must understand that certain poems and even certain prose works have given more substantial nourishment to his religious instinct. Even when there was no question of God? *Especially* when he was not at issue. Any dogma, then, contracts his immensity; the Sacred, unnamable, unnamed, glimmered between the words, between the lines, in the great silence that closed upon the work with the last page turned. In the preceding paragraph, moreover, he had declared: "It is a great pleasure to learn, to assimilate the True through the mediation of the Beautiful. The *ideal state* resulting from this joy seems to be a kind of holiness which is perhaps higher than the other because it is more disinterested." The highest form of holiness, to which Flaubert aspires, can be born only in him who renounces faith in order to preserve the religious instinct, and who nourishes this instinct—without altering it—with that radiant and ineffable truth that dazzles without determining when it filters through beauty. The beautiful, no doubt, is formed of a particular determination; but it is not the face of truth, which is only sensed through it as an infinite presence. Truth is not *given*—as the priests claim to give it through a relic—but the object testifies to its existence. Is this testimony a *proof*? No. It is evidence only that trans-ascendence is possible, that man can be devoted to the work, which surpasses him, that the *aesthetic demand* is objective and addresses itself to the reader as it does to the artist, asking him to forget his finitude. On this level we find Gustave's anticlericalism once again. More firmly grounded this time: the priests are not condemned for their baseness and their vice; the Christian myth has simply had its day. Those who preserve it are outstripped by modern life; Gustave's soul is a closed book to them precisely because he renounces faith—whose object, whatever it is, is finite since it is the product of our finitude—in order to preserve malaise and dissatisfaction in their purity as conscious and, unhappily, finite privation. Now Gustave knows very well that being deprived of the infinite is nothing but the finite determination of the infinite, infinitely necessary. When he enjoins his correspondent to choose between Christ and philosophy—that is, he claims, between faith and disbelief—we should not assume that he is using philosophy to mean the libertinism or atheism of the eighteenth century, which, indeed, he condemns over and over again. No; philosophy is equivalent here to "conscious grasp." Gustave renounces belief because he has understood his own contradiction: a finite particle, he is through his own existence the negation of his own negation, therefore a reference to the infinite; but all the products of finitude are finite, including the religions that could raise him above himself by falsifying his religious instinct. All confessions are temptations; he *would like to believe* because the fanaticism of believers fascinates him. But fanaticism, the highest degree of human passion, the triumph of devotion, is at the same time a trick of the Creator, forcing the creature to choose finitude while believing he is giving himself to the infinite. Gustave would therefore refuse any sort of faith, any happy adherence to some human figuration of the divinity, and would live in absolute destitution; bereft of God because he understood only too well that he could not be filled with him, he would painfully live an impossible devotion, letting his finitude cry out to an inconceivable and necessary infinite. He has understood that Being—if it is not already saying too much to name it in

566

this way—created us in such a way that we can neither find it nor give up the search; that the creature can live neither without God nor with him, bearing witness to man by the acceptance of original dissatisfaction, painfully living his false acceptance of the nihilism in which nothing prevents him from believing. He bears witness to man in the face of God and *against him*. Especially *Yours*: why have You failed us, God of mercy? And if the products of Your Will had to be "limited in their nature" and ignorant of their purpose, why did You create us? Why decide that something like a world should exist rather than nothing? Flaubert would exclaim, well before Valéry:

> *Soleil, soleil! . . . Faute éclatante*
> *Toi qui masques la mort, Soleil . . .*
> *Tu gardes le cœur de connaître*
> *Que l'Univers n'est qu'un défaut*
> *Dans la pureté du Non-Etre.*
> [Sun, Sun! . . . dazzling blunder
> You who mask death, Sun . . .
> You keep the heart from knowing
> That the Universe is only a blemish
> In the purity of Nonbeing.]

The creation is God's sin or his glaring error; if he believed he was making man in his image, so much the worse for us and for him—the fragments of the mirror are microscopic and cannot reflect the immensity that claims to be mirrored there. If being is suffering, one is better off with nothingness.

Such is the young Flaubert's philosophical conclusion; if he drew any other after 1842, he says nothing about it. But we can easily see that the system as it was formulated is enlarged and completed: in the first round, the priests turn people away from believing; in the second, Gustave, the only one of the damned, deprives himself of the infinite by refusing what he is refused; in the third, the world is hell and God alone is guilty because he could not produce creatures without at the same time depriving them of him. Their finitude makes them mad for an unattainable infinite.

God exists, his ministers and my father turned me away from him; God exists, but not for me: he withholds himself from my weakness, he withholds himself by way of a curse and renders me infinite by the infinite privation he engenders. A strolling player, I act out my refusal of him and my negative infinity. God exists but withholds himself from his creatures; only the most limited have the illusion of possessing him; God exists and has chosen me by giving me despair, and if I want to win, I must push the resulting disbelief and desolation to an extreme. Here is the twist in his wholeness—only it must be specified that Gustave's last position is subsequent to the others. I have detailed all the stops on the carousel in order to clarify the way we live our opinions. In Gustave, we see "what you all are, a certain man who lives, who sleeps, who eats . . . firmly closed in on himself, and, wherever he is transported, finding the same continual destruction of hope, beaten down as soon as it is raised, the same dust of things crushed, the same paths trodden a thousand times."[41] And it is one such hope "beaten down as soon as it is raised" but endlessly revived, one of these circular paths, trodden a thousand times and leading back each time—at least so it seems—to the point of departure, that I have attempted to describe: Flaubert's interior movement, passing the same places again and again, endlessly, *our* movement in relation to God, perhaps, or for the atheists, of which I am one, in relation to any other thing. The circular structure of this "pondering" is perfectly clear: the fixed landmarks, the contradictory interpretations that pass into each other without ever advancing toward a synthesis. I see two fixed points here: God exists, I cannot believe; there is no escape from this illogical and profound thought: I cannot believe in the god in which I believe. The interpretations turn around, confront each other, and often interpenetrate; although contradictory, none of them is substantially distinct from the others because they all aim to account for a fixed and experienced illogicality. This is what the notes taken in Jerusalem show clearly, for Flaubert jumbles together the reasons for his nostalgic disbelief—theirs, mine, Yours—which, when developed, refer to incompatible conceptions of the nature of religious belief. It will no doubt have been remarked that he gives two contradictory interpretations of the finite in its relation to the infinite; in one, the finite internalizing the deprivation of the infinite can be a negative infinite; and in the other, which is more rigorous, the deprivation of the infinite produces precisely finitude in its radical destitution and gives it simply a *finite* impetus toward the infinite. In any event, whatever he does, the two ideologies of his time would remain within him, implacably locked in that doubtful combat between science and faith which is waged before the eyes of poor Antoine. These are not ideas but the matrices of ideas, not

41. *Novembre.*

feelings but affective schemes; he uses everything he can—contemporary doctrines, personal inventions, accommodations that come from the outside or are born inside him, hyperbolic writings mythifying the contradiction—in order to live his religiosity and the paternal scientism, in other words, feudal hierarchism and bourgeois liberalism, as economically as possible. Neither of these two systems originated with him; rather, he internalized them one after the other; what do properly belong to him are the attempts at compromise, futile as they are. He makes himself the unwanted mediator between these mortal enemies, and we have just described the mediations; whether they are done out of rage and resentment or out of the humble desire to believe, they inevitably fail, and we shall come a little closer to the concrete experience if we see his double allegiance—rejected, certainly, but suffered—as a constant determination of his inner experience which can be compared either to a kind of humus on which everything he sees and feels is stamped and which gives every *Erlebnis* its particular savor, or to a double and permanent illumination of his affective life, or rather to a rigorous structuring of his internal space.

Three-dimensional space. High and low, first of all. "Hope beaten down as soon as it is raised." The path "trodden a thousand times" is a mountain path. It leads to the peaks, and when Gustave gets there he falls into the void and finds himself once more at the lowest point. Where? Underground, like Ohlmin, with the whole world weighing on him? Spinning in the void, like Smarh? Or simply, like Jules in the first *Education* before his conversion to art, the victim of longer and longer falls into some unknown abyss? Actually, these determinations of internal space are very general. What is particular is the use Flaubert makes of them. First of all, they enter into the very definition of the concepts he uses. I could cite a hundred examples. The best known will suffice: "The ignoble is the sublime debased." Any description of the ignoble must of course begin with the feelings, attitudes, and behavior it inspires. However, the determination would not be complete, according to Flaubert, if the ignoble were not related in its essence to absolute verticality and given a vectorial orientation. The comparison enlightens us; in one respect, the sublime is the highest peak—the "high point"—and the place from which the whole universe can be viewed. On the other hand, *it must be reached*, which supposes a *conatus* and perhaps an *ascesis*, in any case a basic intention. The peaks themselves are pure inert expectations; what is sublime is the man who has got up to the top, pulling himself with a single effort (or at the price of painful and repeated exercises) out of the human condition. Thus ignominiousness is the pathetic courage—still admirable, nonetheless—to extirpate the human by plunging into filth; the ignoble is *oriented* and in a way involves the same *conatus*, that is, the same contempt for our species and the basic intention *to cease being man*. The astonishment lies, therefore, in the infinite acceleration of the fall, in making oneself into a diver or speleologist and, as a self-declared subman, contemplating the human race *from below*, that is, from the truth of resentment. That is not all; for a Flaubert son, ignominiousness demands courage. Cursed by an illustrious father, he is prey to all the others, to that crowd that asks only to confirm the father's judgment; plunging into the ignoble like Marguerite into the Seine, he thwarts them by giving them *more than enough reason*, by making himself *beneath* contempt. Might there not be an invisible point—like parallel lines joined at infinity—where the highest peak and the bottom of the abyss are joined? Gustave is not far from thinking so. There is a hidden circularity of high and low. But in order to be entirely convinced, he needed the fall of 1844. What is certain, in any case, is that the arrogant choice of falling into subhumanity comes, according to Gustave, only *after* one has recognized the impossibility of raising oneself above mankind. We shall have occasion to return to this at length. Let us note, at any rate, that he reserves all his sympathy for the ignominious plungers, even when they are other than himself. What merits his contempt, on the contrary, is the complaisant stability found among the lowest ranks of humanity: "I call bourgeois anyone who thinks basely." The low, here, is not sought out of despair, we are already there—and besides, there is something lower still; the bourgeois is human and gives himself the right to scorn those who are sublimely ignoble—this puts him at his ease. The ignoble is an innate dissatisfaction with the infinite absence of the Master; the bourgeois is satisfied, therefore blind to the vast scale of the creation which crushes him, its "high point"—in spite of the bench provided for admiring the panorama—remaining indefinitely deserted. When he acts the Garçon or engages in the antics of the Idiot in front of the Goncourts, the most reserved of his colleagues, Gustave *is playing* the ignoble man. But we shall see that his drama has a deeper meaning. Perhaps, indeed, he can only play baseness, perhaps the unfathomable underworlds are more accessible than the summits. We shall have to decide about that later.

For the moment, let us recall that the young man's first coherent work is *Le Voyage en enfer*, and that in it he depicts himself as a colossus meditating on the world from the height of Mount Atlas. The journey on which he is taken by Satan can lead only downward; certainly he will fly, but below, in order to get a closer look at man. In Flaubert's last published work, the *Trois Contes*, Julien l'Hospitalier is angry with himself and, though he does not fall into ignominiousness, seeks physical abjection. After he has touched bottom—the point at which he shares his bed with a leper and warms him by pressing his body against the rotten flesh—Jesus will bear him up to heaven. Between the two extremes we frequently find rises which are falls in reverse: it is Satan who bears Smarh and Antoine, terrified, up to interstellar space; in this case, the sublime is transformed not into the ignoble, of course, but into horror or despair. *There is nothing on high* except heaps of molecules; therefore mechanism is right, there is neither high nor low. Rare are the people—Nietzsche among them, but for quite other reasons—who attribute such importance to verticality. Still, it must be noted that certain of them—like the author of *Zara-thustra*—try to make the structures of the objective space in which they live conform to the structures of their internal space; it is not an accident that Nietzsche had—or thought he had—his fundamental illumination at *Sils-Maria*. But Flaubert spent nearly all his life at his desk; furthermore, he was a man of the plains, a Norman for whom actual changes in location were almost always made at sea level, whether he was following the course of the Nile or looking for the traces of Punic Carthage. Once in his life he spent a few days in the mountains for his health, at Kaltbod-Rigi. He was "bored to death." Irritated by the hotel guests—Germans, whom he had despised since 1870—he says without much warmth: "The landscape is very beau-tiful, certainly, but I don't feel inclined to admire it."[42] Nevertheless, this man of low places, this stay-at-home, spent his life going up and down, flying like an eagle only to plummet headfirst; perching, soar-ing, sinking, he becomes by turns a mole scratching under the earth in search of the "telling little fact," and an airborne consciousness turning in space around the earth; humiliation hurls him down but, as he says in all the letters, pride helps him to bounce back; or else, running after art, his nose in the air, he falls into pits, like the as-tronomer in the fable. His works and his correspondence contain an incredible number of metaphors and images aimed at reducing his behavior and that of others, or his relations to those who, according to him, claim to be like him, to positive or negative translations along

42. To Princess Mathilde, July 1874, *Correspondance* 7:166.

the absolute vertical, or to stable relations defined by the only verticality: above, below.

In this system of symbols, one thing is striking: the two absolute terms, the highest and the lowest, even if he does not manage to reach them, do not exist outside of Gustave but within him—his personal space is closed, The space of the believer extends above his head to the infinite and below him to the last circle of hell; in brief, the vertical impales him and travels through him. In the guest book of a hotel built on one of the highest peaks in France, I read this significant bit of nonsense written and initialed by a Catholic couple on their honeymoon: "Nearer, my God, to thee!" It is repugnant to imagine these young marrieds and their nights, certainly. And all the more so, I imagine, if one is oneself a believer. Still, this white lie clearly indicates that faith has structured what the gestaltists call their "hodological space." God is *on high* above the stars, and after death the soul will go up to him. While waiting, the body approaches heaven by scaling mountains. Here we have the structured extension: an absolute term is perpetually aimed upward, if only by the upright position that becomes an impetus, the cranial cap pushing toward God. Among atheists there are also people who—out of pride or for quite another reason—feel crushed by overhanging structures, hence verticality is structured as a *fall*, as an avalanche of debris; they do not stop until they are at the highest point. Flaubert is not concerned with this symbolic arrangement of space, the lines of force crossing it in accordance with our infantile options and reflecting to us our *imago*;[43] for Gustave the exterior extension is only the inert place of our residence. We have seen, however, that he is defined in his own eyes by trans-ascendence; yet this does not seem to pull him out of himself, though it is by definition an impulse toward the Supreme Being, a surpassing of the self from above. This is because the Creator and the paterfamilias both shirked their duty. If God had done him the favor of existing and his father had allowed himself to be loved, Flaubert might have placed them well above himself, at the zenith. But since all things were refused him, since he was locked into his

---

43. These structurings are particularly marked when people in mountainous country are asked how they *view* the rise of mountains—from bottom to top or from top to bottom. Is this enormous mass of stone and earth a heap of rubble (to the perception, I mean, not to the understanding) or a monstrous construction? Are the pines clinging there halfway up mounting to the summit or descending toward the valley? The answers have value as projective tests. And it often happens—which is equally significant—that the ascendent reading and the descendent reading coexist and merge, giving the object its natural ambiguity.

social class, he views that class as base, low, the abode reserved for "all those who think basely." In one sense he is rooted there; in another sense it dwells inside him as his bourgeois nature, and we shall see that he is conscious of it. It is meanness, pettiness, but he has to admit that it is reality; sometimes he says to himself, it is *my* reality. Therefore we will say that in spite of everything, there is a structuring of hodological space—toward the low point. The fall *beneath man* toward the subhuman is permanently inscribed in his body. Obviously; we have seen that his passive constitution makes him permanently disposed to swoon in the event of contradiction. But for Gustave this is not only a loss of the senses, it is a renunciation of the status of human being and the intentional adoption of the status of thing: Garcia, having fainted, is swept out like garbage, *he is* garbage. Since for Gustave then, the contradiction is continually renewed, the temptation to escape the human condition through reification is permanently inscribed in his physical being. The desire to die, to be an effigy of stone, to transform the living matter in him into inanimate matter, and the desire to escape men by choosing subhumanity out of resentment, are one and the same vertigo, a felt attraction to the ground. Certainly this is an internal determination, but it is experienced as an internal-external rapport with an exterior extension: in his impossible revolt, passivity is lived as an always impending and provisionally deferred fall. The upright position, understood by the young Catholic couple as a glorious push toward heaven, is on the contrary experienced by Gustave as a permanent threat of *falling*. He does fall, moreover, he falls endlessly; he is crushed, he drops onto the couch at Croisset a hundred times a day and we shall see that the primary meaning of the "nervous attack" that felled him in 1844 is a radical and voluntary fall beneath the human. In a word, the *ground* represents *for his body* a perpetual invitation to drop into baseness. The symbolic character of this attraction is curiously manifest in the fact that Gustave, *falling on his nose*, as we say, finds himself in his dreams stretched out, by some miracle, *on his back*. Ignominousness, for him, is the fall, but it is not experienced as accommodation to the base—he never looks at the cracked earth overrun by insects; stretched out, his shoulders touching the ground, his eyes turned toward the empty sky, he is condemned to contemplate the cosmic hierarchy above him, from which he is excluded. It is useful to note that in this quietistic ecstasy he can reverse the signs; let us recall the holy water lying at rest in its stoop, reflecting the vaults of heaven. Let us say simply that most of the time the sign is negative: his eyes are open but see only the horrible world of men, the triumph of the wicked.

In one sense, therefore, low is a determination of interior space; in this subjective extension, when you are below, lying on a bed of garbage, you are looking upward. But on the other hand, it is a surpassing of the self toward an exterior place, a certain way Gustave has of feeling his body as if at any moment he were going to drop, to stop living. Those who have read the beginning of this book will not be surprised; I have shown that from childhood he felt like a wounded, exhausted soldier, dragged along by the others, constantly tempted to let them continue on their way without him and to lie down and wait for the enemy. On the level of superstructure, the fall becomes a plunge—better hell than liberalism. Meaning: better blasphemy than disbelief. The reason this interior determination is found both as an assemblage of the body (the disposition to drop) and as a transcendent structuring of the environment is to be found in the first place in the fact that the plunge into hell can be experienced in a passive agent only in the form of a sudden loss of muscular power— whereas it could be an inner determination of a practical agent who has decided out of rebellion to rejoin the unfathomable depths of the self. In the same way, Gustave never assumes responsibility for his changes of condition; his parents constituted him in such a way that he necessarily attributes these changes to an external force. He will necessarily experience his impulse to fall as a vertigo resulting from the fascination exercised by an alien reality, or, if you will, from an earthly pull that is felt as a call to the worst—and at the same time as his material truth, inert and haunted by life. It must be added that according to another scheme, the *posture* that attracts him—to be stretched out on his back, crushed, reduced to impotence—symbolizes, though he cannot state it explicitly, the return to his earliest infancy, to the cradle, the futile appeal to strong maternal hands to resume that diligent work that was supposed to have made a man of him but failed. We shall have occasion to return subsequently to this point. Let us note only that this desire in itself surpasses all of Gustave's interior determinations since it is connected to a past time, to a vanished place, to a posture that was real but cannot be reproduced. Finally, the symbolic system we have just described, "low" is an obvious perception—it is visible and tangible. Thus the inferior limit of subjective space is found to be at once an immanent determination of experience and a symbolic bond with the transcendent world. We shall see that he would fall, that he would never stop falling after 1844, or fearing it—to the point of no longer wanting to go anywhere except in a carriage—and that he would continually cultivate the ignoble—to the point of alienating the Goncourts by his statements—as if his taste for filth (which of course masks a profound disgust) represented the Devil's despair and his desperate eagerness to challenge God by showing Him the horrors of His creation.

"Low" is where one can fall to: this is why the symbolic space is subtended by a structuring of the surrounding space. There is no "high." Or, if you like, there is a "high," but it is inaccessible; you can make the *gesture* of climbing a hill or a mountain, but to Gustave these are only molehills; you ought to be able to rise up to heaven, yet no act is at man's disposal that could even symbolize such an ascent. Gustave speaks readily of *flight*; in his fantastic stories, his creatures readily spread their wings; but this language itself betrays him: he pretends to describe a human movement when in fact he is only lending us the powers of birds. "High," therefore, can exist only as a determination of interior space, and if it does exist, Flaubert will have a chance to escape from himself without leaving his own skin. It is a mad hope, a conscious illusion, unreality lived as the subjective movement that carries him toward beings who would be superior to himself *inside him* and who are not manifest. In other words, vertical ascencion, at first an impossible fervor, becomes at length the imaginary movement by which Gustave unrealizes himself in the direction of the unreal. In particular toward that unreal being which he is himself as the subject of pride. But as we shall see, unreality for Flaubert is not the absence of all reality, it is the challenge to it. From this point of view, a new light illuminates for him the radical impossibility of grasping God except as the unknown lodestar of the imagination, aimed in the abstract toward the end of a systematic and ascendent derealization of the self. Might it not be a message that can no longer be decoded? Gustave would never explicitly decide whether the place of honor in his inferior firmanent should be reserved for a surly absentee host who nevertheless exists, or whether, assuming that he does not exist, it is up to Gustave to hoist himself up to the throne and sit there because the ascensional movement in itself has a sacred value. But in fact, no decision is required and the two hypotheses are merely different ways of explaining the same thing: for Gustave, if God exists it is as if he did not, because he will never come to fill the place that awaits him; thus the movement of faith, always followed by a great tumble and always begun anew, is in the eyes of the spectator a credit to the young Sisyphus, for although he is desperate he has never given in to despair.

And if, in spite of everything, the young man allows himself to go so far as to believe that God does not exist, this abandonment must be secretly contradicted by an invisible faith or otherwise the ascent, far from seeming a credit to him, would not be worth the trouble even once. In other words, sometimes Gustave takes flight toward the upper regions of his soul in the hope of at last encountering fervor and faith, all the while conscious that he will find nothing but himself. And sometimes, under the proddings of shame, he perches on the summit of this barren soul in order to encounter himself in his arrogant truth, that is, such as he ought to be. God is not even named; but then, who would make this flight an absolute credit except One who has distinguished for all time the pure fire of the heights from the obscure rumblings below? Gustave's trans-ascendence does not at all prompt him to go out of himself, it will never become that true leap toward the transcendent which is faith. And when he uses it to raise himself above shameful failure and biting sarcasm, he knows that he can do it only by tearing himself away from reality and sitting on his throne like an imaginary prince. But although this internal vertical, far from being part of an infinite vector, is a tiny segment of a perpendicular broken at both ends and separated from any other line above or below by a *break in continuity*—although the ascendent movement, like its opposite, the plunge, can lead Gustave only from appearance to being, but leaving the real, leads him by a progressive derealization to pure appearance—the fact remains that this small interior scale never seems to Gustave to be relative to his person. On the contrary, it has "high" and "low" as its absolute determinations. Sometimes, we know, the young man at the end of his ascent finds the Devil, who is manifestly lord of the underworld; this makes no difference—if the Evil One is in heaven, it is because he has entered by some kind of ruse and will soon be thrown out, or, better still, because he is the Almighty himself. In any event, whoever is above, good or evil, is revered as the norm, the principle of all values; whoever is below, whatever his nature, is base, formidable vermin lost and saved by his despair. At infinity it may be that the two terms are united; here and now, in Flaubert's consciousness, an invincible power distinguishes between them and contrasts them one with the other, but far from defining them by this contrast it gives each one an independent signification—as if "low" could exist even if "high" were abolished—and extends the sovereignty of each one to every sector of being. For Flaubert it is as though this fragment of the vertical, decayed, fallen into a human head, were being held upright by itself and, though unable to break out, continued to designate the two cardinal directions of being. Or rather as though the Creator, with his all-powerful right hand poised, were pointing rigidly toward heaven and hell. For Gustave, the inflexibility of this double indicator is thus a silent proof of God's existence. *On condition that it is never mentioned*; it is of little importance that there is no one on the peaks— *there are peaks*, that's all, for at the antipodes, as at Rouen, the peaks are *absolutely* above the plains and valleys, and the sky is *absolutely* above the Alps and the Andes. For this reason, to go up and to descend are sacred activities; and "high" and "low" for Gustave are forces of attraction and principles of classification, like yin and yang for the ancient Chinese. We shall return to this later; let us note simply that Gustave's soul is in perpetual movement, and that he is carried endlessly above himself in his stoic, sacred contempt for the human race or below himself in an anguished quest for a principle of origin, punishing his progenitor by damning himself through despair or by falling into subhumanity.

Does he therefore refuse to be *himself*? Yes indeed! Because the *self*, for the young man, is not a "particular and positive essence"; it is his depth dimension or, if you prefer, his class-being experienced as a destiny. On this level, an archaic religion subsists—the belief in *fatum*. He continually doubts the Eternal Father, but he has never doubted that fierce, sneering divinity. The worst is certain because the paterfamilias has cursed his offspring. But also—and curse apart—because this offspring is constituted in such a way that the future can be for him only an object of terror. If this seems doubtful, the following letter ought to convince us. Gustave had just turned seventeen when he wrote to Ernest Chevalier:

> What are you going to do? What do you expect to become? Do you ask yourself that, sometimes? No: why should you? And you are right. *The future is the worst thing about the present.* The question, "What are you going to be?" thrown into a man's face is like an open pit in front of him that keeps moving forward with every step he takes. Quite apart from the metaphysical future (which I don't give a damn about because I can't believe that our body, composed as it is of slime . . . and equipped with instincts lower than a pig's . . . contains anything pure and immaterial when everything around it is so impure and ignoble), quite apart from that future, there is still the future of one's

life. . . . *I am one of those people who is always disgusted from one day to the next but is always thinking of the future.* . . . The most beautiful things in the world, quite modestly, I have imagined in advance. But you, like the others, will have only boredom in your life and a grave after death, and you will rot for eternity.[44]

For a passive agent, the future is never thought of as *doing* but only as *submitting*. If he is active, a young man tends to exaggerate his powers—his life will be strictly *his* undertaking. He is unaware that if, as Hegel says, in the course of action contingency is transformed into necessity and necessity becomes contingent, all at once the undertaking itself in the process of realization will deceive the one who undertakes it, for what seemed to him most necessary, what ought to have been his fundamental objectification, becomes in the long run the entirely contingent origin of praxis. Instead, certain conditions which he took for contingent or disregarded will little by little take on the unrecognized face of necessity. Gustave, by contrast, reckons that he has no power over his own life; it will happen to him as necessarily *other*, and its necessity will change at every moment into simple negligible contingencies or better, into the occasion for realizing himself negatively by destroying or ridiculing those contingencies which are his most fundamental desires. He must live his life, nevertheless; in other words, even in "rage and impotence" he must make it his own, let himself be defined by it and progressively swerve away from what he wanted to be in order to die definitively *other*, a traitor to his dreams, to his ambitions, to his youthful vows, and, what is worse, holding them in contempt. In this sense, it is himself he fears, that disgusting cockroach he will become. This abject metamorphosis is sacred to the extent that for Flaubert it is neither accident nor simply the course of things that will effect it—yet these will be the malleable means of his transformation—but the sovereign will of the father, that fierce idol who demands the immolation of his younger son. On this level, as we see, Gustave's *self* cannot be conceived or lived as an articulated and permanent set of distinctive characteristics; these characteristics, if indeed they exist (the desire for glory is one of them, in any case), are there only to be ridiculed and replaced by others. This is an interminable process that remains in great part in the future but which he can see as a whole, thanks to that blessed certainty that reveals his life to him from beginning to end: "I'll get my law degree, be admitted to the bar, and end up

44. 24 February 1839. My italics.

as a respectable assistant district attorney in a small provincial town, like Yvetot or Dieppe. Poor fool who dreamed of glory."[45] There is no *logical* contradiction in the idea that a district attorney might write a good book. The contradiction exists, nevertheless. Let us say that it is not in the form but in the content of these two ideas: public prosecutor, masterpiece. What Gustave means is that he knows he will never write the work he wants to write now. Not that the profession of attorney is so absorbing or that talent—he knows nothing about that, he would never know anything about it—is necessarily lacking. He will not write because *he will become a district attorney*, because he will think, speak, act as an attorney, and because attorneys have contempt for books and sometimes go so far as to imprison those who have written them; an attorney would not want to write books for anything in the world, even if he were to recall with a smile that in his naïve youth he dreamed of being a writer. Gustave's death and transfiguration is the sacred event of this barbaric religion: what I burn, I will worship; what I worship, I will burn. The *self* does not simply exist, it becomes the opposite of himself; he must always be spying, lying in wait for the immediate future in order to flush out the imperceptible transformation which the distant future is preparing. Everything that does not yet exist is suspect, even the next turn of the carriage wheel—the future cockroach penetrates the unhappy boy with each breath. This self-directed espionage is surely beneficent for a boy who does not much like himself as it is. In brief, *fatum*, the self, is Gustave's temporal depth, that "horizontal fall" I mentioned above. It will be remarked that, apart from this, it is the realization of his *class being*; born into the middle classes, with a father exercising a liberal profession, a child infused in spite of himself with liberalism is destined in his turn to a liberal profession. And in a way this realization can easily pass, *even objectively*, for *fatum*: man is the son of man, and by engendering him in the class into which he himself is born, the father obliges the son before birth to make himself into what he is.

Gustave rejected this class—we shall see why—but the times were such that he was not given the means to escape it. There was only one way: loss of class status. Yet this had to be a real possibility. France in 1830, however, witnessed the death throes of the social reality that would have made his ascensions and even his plunges effective; religion—at least as Gustave knew it—maladapted to the

45. To Ernest Chevalier, 24 February 1839.

new men, belonged to a system which was definitively outmoded, though people were still unaware of it. Little Flaubert found in religion the image of a half-discredited, still fascinating recruitment which his parents told him had been reestablished since the return of the Bourbons. Slowly, obliquely, the bourgeoisie made progress only toward itself: you were born into it or else you entered automatically from whatever class you had come, provided you fulfilled certain conditions of an essentially economic nature. In principle you had to be born into the aristocracy. There were exceptions, true, but these were severely controlled. Intruders were not recognized, base bourgeois promiscuity was rejected; the highest dignitaries of this powerfully hierarchical class sometimes leaned in the direction of the elite of the lower classes and recruited them *from above* by pointing them out to the supreme head, to the prince of divine right who *ennobled* them in God's name. The little boy was in fact no enemy to this recruitment, to this call from above. His mother claimed to be *born* into the aristocracy; Dr. Flaubert let her say so—this peasant embraced free thought with passion, but nothing could have convinced him that he was a republican; on the contrary, he had along with his father a long-standing fund of royalism, and if he had a political demand—which is quite certain—it was for a lowering of the property qualification for the franchise, which would have allowed him to speak his mind from time to time in the context of a monarchical society. This was enough to make the child a legitimist. We have indications of this in his correspondence.

Of course, he never had a soft spot for the Bourbons. Here, nonetheless, is the happiest memory of his childhood as he proudly and wistfully recalled it for Louise:

> One day the duchess de Berry was passing through Rouen and was out for a drive along the quays, when she noticed me in the crowd, held up in my father's arms so that I could see the procession. Her coach pulled alongside; she had it stop, and was pleased to fondle and kiss me. My poor father went home delirious over this triumph. It was the only one I ever brought him. I still tremble at the proud joy that must have moved that great and good heart, now dead.[46]

He was still thinking of it in 1859; in the comic autobiography mocking the genre which he gave to Feydeau, he again recalled that the "duch-

46. 4 October 1846, *Correspondance* 1:355.

ess de Berry had her coach stop so she could kiss me (historical)."[47] It is obvious that everything about this incident made it unforgettable: the father was there, first of all, the golden age was not yet over; this libertine—who, as we see, did not despise the monarchy—took care to stand along her Highness's route and brought his younger son with him to participate in this sacred joy. Even better, he raised his son toward this pretty, numinous woman: Gustave's good lord lifts him up, bears him passive toward heaven, and the little boy has the joy of feeling that virile force penetrate his torpid body. And what is the progenitor doing here if not presenting him to God or—since the future adventuress who would know Louis-Philippe's dungeons is here playing her role—to the Virgin Mary? Presentation followed by election. The duchess de Berry leans down and singles him out from all the children offered to her; she orders the coachman to stop, she takes the little boy from the father's arms and holds him in hers; representative of a power of divine right, she accepts homage and seals it with two kisses on the cheeks of the vassal, a symbolic accolade. That is not all; the child gained in an instant what he had always wanted, what he would soon lose forever: he became his father's pride. That glory which Achille-Cléophas allowed him to share when he entered a village full of reverential admirers Gustave gives back to him intact in one dazzling moment: it was, he says, a triumph. That is what he would look for in vain after the Fall, and he immediately adds that it was the only triumph he ever brought his father. False modesty? No; naturally, in front of Louise he cannot help posing, and for obvious reasons he chose that evening to play great tragedies, but he is only *utilizing* his deep conviction that the worst is certain, which indicates how much he valued this first triumph. At the time, Gustave was dazzled and felt his elevation to be a contact with the supernatural, but he was not astonished; this was the golden age, his father loved him, and that love which pulled him out of natural contingency was the true supernatural, the permanent miracle that made all miracles possible. Later, after the Fall, he returned to this episode and rethought it *in bitterness*, evoking it out of resentment, out of despair; the Fall seemed to him the central event that could not be effaced except by the return of this triumph and that made such a return definitively impossible. The impossibility refers both to his "anomaly" and to the disappearance of the two conditions indispensable to the manifestation of the supernatural: the

47. *Correspondance* 4:327.

divine monarchy and the sacred power of the progenitor, which reflected each other, the king of divine right confirming in the person of his son the divine omnipotence of the paterfamilias.

Even more convincing is the fact that Gustave evokes this memory to explain to Louise a sentence he wrote to Eulalie Foucault:[48] "You will ask me what it means," he says to his mistress, "when I say that I have grown ugly." He adds: "You should have known me ten years ago. I had a distinction I have now lost; my nose was not so big and there were no wrinkles on my forehead." Ten years ago—in 1836, then, at the age of fifteen.[49] In spite of his wiles, he has the decency not to write: it was in 1840 that you should have known me, in Marseilles, when Eulalie seduced me. What is certain is that Mme Foucault admired him wholeheartedly, otherwise why would he have taken the false precaution of warning her that he had grown ugly? And the Muse? She must have repeated to him a hundred times a day—when she saw him—that she thought him handsome, since he took the trouble kindly and gently—sadism again—to explain the meaning of a sentence that might naturally have puzzled her. Some years earlier at the theater, as he was returning to his seat after the intermission, accompanied by his sister Caroline, the audience had burst into applause, struck by the splendid appearance of the young Flauberts. What is remarkable is that Gustave did not pick it up; this plebiscite smacked of something republican that sickened him. He often looked at himself in the mirror, we know—sometimes with great astonishment, sometimes laughing out of pity, very rarely with satisfaction, never out of narcissism. However, he imagines narcissism; there is no doubt that he unrealized himself in Mazza at times and masturbated by caressing her in his own skin. But without this mediation of the imaginary, he seems to have had little real communication with his reflection or with his own person. Perhaps he acquired some cold vanity when as a student in Paris he saw that he was better looking than his comrades; but his problems lay elsewhere. And he would have infinitely preferred a crooked nose and an inheritance that would have permitted him to dine at Tortoni's. We must read these surprising declarations, then, keeping in mind that for Gustave there was no other temporality after the golden age than that of involution and decline; therefore, the duchess's blessing preserved him from naturally growing ugly for more than ten years. At fifteen

48. In a letter he was sadistic enough to send through the Muse.
49. The age at which he "lost" his imagination.

he had preserved intact the benefits of the accolade. And then, beginning in 1836, the decline began, the flesh showed stress and slowly began to rot. Did the homage and innoblement come to an end with the fall of the Bourbons? Without forcing the texts, and especially without imagining in Flaubert a belief articulated as a miracle, we will yet be struck by this sentence in which he tries to explain his decline: "There are still moments when I look at myself and think I am attractive; but there are many when I strike myself as perfectly bourgeois. Do you know that during my childhood, princesses stopped their carriages to take me in their arms?" In fact, this "triumph" took place only once. But the generalization is significant. Ugliness, for Gustave, is the externalization of his *class being*; what he sees in his mirror is that the bourgeoisie within him is gaining ground, seated in his flesh, and that his body's slow aging coincides with the despised victory of vulgarity. Here we find *fatum* once more, this time in its physiological aspect; it is the assistant district attorney of Yvetot who is announced by this enlargement of the nose, by these wrinkles. And immediately a leap of pride and rage: "Do you know that princesses . . ." The memory is not reawakened logically by the explanation Gustave claims to give Louise: he has wrinkles, a big nose, less distinction; that is quite enough. But the affective movement of thought beneath the writing passes artlessly *from distinction to bourgeois*: he is becoming bourgeois because he is not more distinguished. The royal idea is raised from the depths of his memory. One is distinguished only by a superior: I have fallen into decline, but in my childhood *royal princesses* ennobled me. This child in his father's arms who religiously witnessed the passage of the sacred coaches of royalty has nothing but ridicule some years later for the ninnies who run off to gape at Louis-Philippe: "Men are so stupid and the people so hidebound! To run after a king . . . to go to such lengths, for whom? For a king? . . . Ah, the world is stupid. As for me, I didn't see any of it, no review, no arrival of the king, no princesses, no princes. I only went out last night to see the fireworks, just because the others were plaguing me."[50] He isn't even twelve years old; Louis-Philippe came to the throne three years earlier. Has he discovered the vanity of the monarchical principle? We might believe this to be the case since he had been calling himself a republican for several months. But we know that he religiously preserved one festive memory: not so long ago he himself had been gaping, along with his father, awaiting

50. To Ernest, 11 September 1833, *Correspondance* 1:11.

the arrival of the duchess de Berry. Decidedly, then, he was not a republican in his guts. If he welcomed the Republic it was chiefly out of spite: the bourgeoisie had stolen *his* king, the one who had made him his vassal one evening on the quays of Rouen. They banished him, put a bourgeois king, a false king, in his place. Just as they had the courage to declare what they were, to display the vulgarity of their egalitarianism by proclaiming the second Republic. He sulks at the masquerade, shuts himself away. His parents, above all supporters of the government, exhort him to go out; the father no doubt out of some malicious reflex, would have "plagued" him—perhaps by questioning the sincerity of his new attitude. If this was the case, the philosophical practitioner was wrong: Gustave's contempt for the citizen-king conceals what we might well call his legitimism.

We know him—it is hardly worth the trouble to say that this frustrated legitimism will be lived in resentment. Not only against the bourgeois regicides but also against the Bourbons. Nobility existed, crude and brutal but sanctified by its fanatic devotion to the royal house; it was lost through its own fault and the stupidity of kings. The bourgeoisie did not gain power by its merits but by the progressive decline of the aristocracy. After 1830, the noblemen sulked on their lands or became bourgeois—they no longer even had the right to *distinguish* and *co-opt*. Unlike the ruling bourgeois, who were, Gustave knew, prepared to create aristocrats by the batch. But this institutionally based right does not come from God, and suddenly the act of ennoblement seems only a masquerade, a shopkeepers' Mardi Gras.

Does Gustave regret not being nobly *born*? Would he have wanted a qualified aristocracy to give him lands and a title? It may have been an occasional dream—the young bourgeois of his time, born twenty years earlier or ten years after, had such dreams—Hugo, for example, and Baudelaire; alas, even Mallarmé.[51] But if Gustave was sometimes secretly amused to think of himself as "Monsieur de Flaubert," he never took great pleasure in it. His father was a prince of science, and in spite of his resentment, his Flaubert pride came from the progenitor and returned to him, and through him to this family of brains that misunderstood its youngest son. The episode he reports to Louise shows in fact that he would have liked a legitimately hierarchical society, one that would have *imposed* him on his father by consecrating Gustave's peerless qualities through a public elevation. But even so,

51. At fourteen years old, true, and because of his grandmother.

he did not want any titles; to be sure, he had taste only for aristocratic societies, but he had too much contempt for the aristocrats of his time to want to become one of them. The consecration he dreams of would be a marginal knighting: when the duchess de Berry held him in her arms, she placed him above the rest and pulled him away from the bourgeoisie that loitered around her coach without integrating him into the upper classes. Gustave asks no more than this, a strong fist descending from heaven to lift him up and place him on the highest level, *beside* the great titled vassals but not among them. We shall see later that from the time he first heard of them, he was madly jealous of Diderot and Voltaire, who had mixed familiarly with monarchs; superior to kings by virtue of their bourgeois intelligence, they were superior to the bourgeois because they had merited royal favor. By themselves. Apart. Aristocrats without title. What could be better?

It was this particular kind of *supernatural* that Gustave must have coveted *at first* after the Fall, against the paternal curse and the religion of *fatum*. Even while he was persuaded that access to such a supernatural would be refused him. In other words, for a while he was able to maintain in peaceful coexistence a tepid deism and the passionate aspiration for a sacred without God—better, for the ceremony of consecration. The fall of the Bourbons destroyed his dream of a social supernatural, determining in him—as in many of his contemporaries—that myth born of resentment, the invisible aristocracy. It was at this time that the Catholic religion offered him its ostentatious images and he felt drawn to internalize an impossible objective elevation; the Church, that great hierarchical body, was made in the image of a secular and sacred society that was, as he was bitterly aware, bankrupt. What he now demanded was the repetition *on the subjective level* of his recruitment by the duchess de Berry. As we have seen, he wanted to ascend to God: he wanted the priests to bear him toward the Almighty, who, leaning from his carriage, would take him in his arms and *distinguish* him by his grace.

This passive soul needs an ascensional force to penetrate it from the outside and carry it toward God; only then could the Creator, leaning down from the heavenly heights, take him in his arms. And what would this half-earthly, half-celestial force be if not the Church, which he cannot help condemning for its stupidity? Isn't he still turning to the Church when he asks the holy places of Jerusalem to awaken his enthusiasm? Fervor ought to come to him, then, from the *outside*, from the very contemplation of the tomb of the Man-God. "I resent them," he says, "because I was not moved." It's their fault, of course, with their excessive hatreds and disputes; they are a bunch of temple merchants. But he is simply forgetting that *these* are the people who retail and guarantee that a certain Christ, God made man, was buried in this hole. In this sense, Gustave's reproach to the Church is that it is unworthy of itself. Even if *he* is worthy of the Church, its arms are not strong enough to raise him toward the Almighty. Never mind, God will recruit him himself. Here is the note he jotted down in his notebook at the age of sixteen:

> I would love to be a mystic; what exquisite pleasures—to believe in paradise, to be drowned in waves of incense, to be annihilated at the foot of the Cross, to take refuge on the wings of the dove. There is something naïve about First Communion; we shouldn't laugh at people who weep on that occasion—an altar covered with sweet-smelling flowers is a beautiful thing. The life of a saint is a beautiful thing, I should have liked to die a martyr; and if there is a God, a good God, a God the father of Jesus, let him send me his grace, his spirit, I will receive it and prostrate myself.[52]

He is no longer asking just for faith but for mysticism. For two reasons. First of all, if the Church, degraded and debased, is no longer in the position to guarantee its dogmas, how can faith be preserved without God interceding in person to ensure it? But if he comes, there is no longer any need *to believe*: he is there. In the face of this unbearable evidence, the creature bursts his limits and swoons in adoration; without the Church, there is no middle ground: either the "belief in nothing" or ecstasy.

All at once—this is the other reason—the blessed soul itself becomes numinous. The worshiper without grace may be worthy, but he is not consecrated by his arid obstinacy. The one whom God has chosen and entered, however, is a sacred vessel, and even if God should subsequently withdraw, he has been marked forever as God's man. This would be ideal—no more priests; grace drops like Jupiter's eagle on certain Ganymedes, seeking them out to the edges of the earth and carrying them off, divine darlings, in its claws. Spiritual feudalism has disappeared, but deeper than bourgeois egalitarianism Gustave still dreams of a change of class status—*a royal act* coming from above to pull him out of his milieu. Gustave craves martyrdom because a painful trial, once surmounted, would allow him to enter the knighthood of Saints. This *marginal* elite—like that of the untitled "philos-

---

52. *Souvenirs*, pp. 60–61.

586

opher" aristocrats on the margins of the aristocracy—is closer to God, though the majority of its members were not recruited from among the high dignitaries of the Church and might have been ordered to show blind obedience to the prelates. Does the Church still exist, then? Didn't Gustave abolish it? Precisely; but the saints and martyrs have quickly reestablished it. By giving himself to them, God has raised it from its ruins. The Church is rotten, perhaps, and a little senile, but since the saints and martyrs have received God, it must be admitted that on the whole the Church is right. It speaks the truth. If God deigned to visit him, Gustave could take unique revenge on its ministers by *testifying* in their favor. In fact, in the note cited above, the Church is not explicitly mentioned but it is still present—the waves of incense could be spread only by the priests. Who in all of France could organize that moving ceremony of first communion, if not the priests?

Such is the new turn in his thinking, his direct and solitary rapport with God—which is drawn from the spontaneous Protestantism of the "liberal" classes; but he can conceive of it only in the framework of the Catholic confession, and his conception of the Almighty is itself hierarchical. If God is *all*, he is in himself an ascendent order: "Oh! the infinite, the infinite—an immense gulf, a spiral that mounts from the depths to the highest regions of the infinite," he would write in *Mémoires d'un fou*. The repetition of the word "infinite"—probably involuntary—should not be taken for redundance; what is involved, in effect, is an "unspeakable" thought. The infinite is found in the highest regions of being; it is a personal and all-powerful God; but this God is also the ascension of matter toward himself, since his strength produces this graduated aspiration. He is at once at the *top* of the feudal pyramid, as the calm attraction of the All, and at the bottom, as an intimate impulse born in the dark abysmal depths. He is the prince as well as the spiral that goes from the humblest sub-vassals to the great liege lords. This text shows that even when Gustave seems to be in line with Spinoza his pantheism is suspect: the forms of matter are hierarchical.[53]

But let us return to the note in which the young man informs us of his vow to be a martyr and mystic. He clearly seems to be conscious of its emptiness. God is hidden, Gustave would like to believe, but this desire itself does not seem to be a sign of his election. Nothing

---

53. It is true that certain historians of philosophy have been able to ask themselves if the Spinozistic substance was not *subject*.

could be more secular: he is ready to receive God if God exists, but he is still filled with doubt. We will note, furthermore, that this uncertainty has bearing not so much on the existence of the Almighty as on his bounty. Gustave is quite precise, indeed, so as not to be misunderstood: if the God who exists is really the father of Jesus,[54] let him give me a sign. But we know that as far as Gustave is concerned the creator or simply the administrator of this world could as easily be the Great Illusionist. In this case, the hierarchy exists but in reverse. Quite simply, Gustave is asking Satan, if he is the one managing our affairs, to do him the favor of staying home—no visitations, please. In fact, it is the Evil One who is going to reveal himself to Smarh, to Antoine; the old fatalistic belief remains, the worst is certain, the world is nothing but hell. What a fine demonic farce it would be if the noblest soul opening itself to God were on that account to raise up the apparition of the Devil. In any event, Gustave knows that no one is coming or will come. This despairing invocation is tossed out, besides, amid other regrets—more secular at least in appearance. The unloved younger son would have liked to know earthly and carnal love, a woman's profound attachment might have given him value; and he craved genius in vain. He is nothing: "I cannot even depend on myself—I might yet turn out to be vile. . . . And yet I think I shall have more virtue than others because I have more pride." He adds ironically, "Therefore, praise me." Because he is convinced, we know, that virtue based on pride is in essence infernal. Around this time he jotted down the following thoughts in his notebook, perhaps inspired by a poorly understood Kantianism: "Never will man know the Cause, for the Cause is God; he knows only a succession of phantom Forms; being a phantom himself, he runs after them, tries to catch them, they elude him . . . ; he stops only when he falls into the absolute void, then he is at rest." The belief in nothing and the belief in God are one and the same in this text; the Cause exists but by definition can produce only effects, and these are by nature unable to return to it; thus the very existence of God is the reason why we—vain phan-

---

54. He wrote in the same notebook a few months earlier: "I want Jesus Christ to have lived, I am sure of it—why? Because I find the mystery of the Passion the most beautiful thing in the world" (*Souvenirs*, p. 49). The Passion is the infinite generosity of the Lord who made himself man in order to save his vassal. Inversely, it is the principle—glimpsed by Gustave at this moment and which will later impose itself on the sly—of "loser takes all": this ignominious and voluntary death, the awful failure of the prophet *on earth*, is somewhere in the heavens a mysterious victory. Gustave never took himself for Christ, but the Christian scheme would soon help him to organize his neurosis, to give it a deep meaning and its temporal orientation.

toms ourselves—will never know anything but phantoms before falling into absolute nothingness. Which amounts to saying that without the Church, mysticism doesn't exist or is merely a comedy, a drama, pleasurable but meaningless, that is, a phantom. Nevertheless, "I want Jesus Christ to have lived, I am sure of it." There is no Christ without apostles: "You are Peter and on this rock . . ." No Christ without a Church. Well yes, in other times, in the first years of Christianity and probably until the Middle Ages, there was a Holy Church expressly charged with ensuring the communications between the village and the Castle by a hierarchical route. But it failed in its task, just like the secular aristocracy, at the same time and for the same reasons; since then, communications have been cut. Mysticism is a trap—it had meaning only in a religious universe ruled by the popes, when certain persons were granted a white telephone with a direct line to the Lord of the Castle. But unlike the pietism of the bourgeoisie, this privilege, far from destroying the hierarchy, *presupposes* it; certainly the Church order felt challenged and reacted poorly at first; but the Church quickly understood that the direct presence of God in certain chosen souls could only confirm for all others the necessity of an intercession. A few exceptional people were allowed to take a shortcut while the majority of the faithful took the monumental staircase, but the end of the ascent was the same; and these special privileges, allowing a quicker and higher ascent, bore witness to the whole of Catholicism. Gustave would dream of the mystical experience all his life. But he understood very early that this experience, far from compensating for the disappearance of the Holy Church, had vanished with her. We would say today that spiritual feudalism, losing its charismatic power, was transformed for Gustave into a bureaucracy. Flaubert would never leave his class—not this way, in any case. All he could do was never consent, never resign himself to the accomplished fact, eat his heart out with regret, and transform himself, a bourgeois liberal, into a martyr of the impossible ascension.

What this loyal heart deplores is the failure of the Old Regime: a pope, representing God on earth, a church; a monarch ruling by divine right, his nobility; and the rabble, lowly but illuminated by the fidelity and faith of the two great sacred bodies. Their *holiness* derives from the fact that, whether priests or soldiers, their instituted members at each echelon are characterized by their fanaticism—a radical selflessness, unqualified devotion to their superiors, to the entire body, to the transcendent principle that is summed up in each person and constitutes their unity. In that society, though bound to his plebeian condition, Gustave might have escaped the bourgeoisie through a martyrdom or a masterpiece; in that society a *triumph* might have changed his class status.

Unhappily, this regret itself is falsified. First of all, by resentment—in one sense. Gustave despises the lovely world of feudalism; he fervently wants it past. Most of the time, the strength of his nostalgia in his letters and statements can be measured only by the violence of his invectives against the vanished regime or against those who still claim to represent it. And in the very fact that that society did not persist he finds proof that it was nothing but a human arrangement—if God established it, how could he have allowed its decline? If he had sustained it by his providential favor throughout more than a millennium and against human nature, is it conceivable that one fine day he would wash his hands of it? Thus, Gustave's nostalgia is destroyed by itself—he cannot wear mourning except as a beautiful lie: if I had lived in the golden century of Christianity, the thirteenth century, it would have been impossible for me not to believe in these naïve phantasmagorias. In other words: I was born too late to be the happy victim of the lie that is so vital to my needs. What is left, then? A religion so well constructed that it could answer to the demands of the religious instinct for many centuries, but which, that aside, is as much a fabric of absurdities as fetishism is. The Gods are dead—that is what Gustave means. But this very thought—which if rationalized would mean that religious illusions hold sway only for a certain time and that one faith replaces another—is often given a *magical* significance: the Gods are dead, therefore they have lived; they were not entirely the inventions of men, unless they took on a kind of supernatural virulence before they withered. Just as the young bourgeois is dissolving all religions in history, he confers on history a sacred dimension. As if religious ideology, just as it was being crushed by liberal ideology, had infiltrated and bewitched it unseen. In this sense, for him, the Old Regime—triumphant error and the only *possible* gratification of the religious instinct—never was and never would be, and yet would never cease being, a normative system; rigid and unrealizable, denouncing the pettiness of our values and our institutions and in feudal societies unmasking the stupidity and egotism of the aristocrats, it is the sole valuable objective of our species' transcendence. But it is also unattainable; in this sense it must be conceived as a mysterious light illuminating history and investing this heap of incongruous accidents and stupid contracts with the obscure and troubling meaning of a formidable failure which began with the fall of Adam and has been indefinitely repeated ever since. We are not surprised; Gustave is not the first and will not be the last to consider his own life a summation of the human adventure.

As an adolescent, Gustave had already discovered the three-dimensional structure of his internal space. Rises and falls are the repetitive determinations of the vertical absolute, that is to say, his relations to the Eternal; depth, by contrast, is an irreversible movement toward that other absolute, death, the orientation toward the worst. Thus, whatever the occasion, experience is deployed on a triple register. A religious and primitive allegiance to the family, or *fatum*; an allegiance apparently rational and secular—but underneath irrational and sacred—to the ideology of the paterfamilias; an allegiance to the monarchical and theocratic hierarchy which excludes and yet enslaves him—three systems, three types of interpretation that come to mind simultaneously for every experience and tear it apart. Let us understand clearly that even if the great religious, ethical, or social themes are not in question, even if what is involved is the most banal perception, the simplest reflection, it will have a tendency to be broken off and twisted by these divergent forces. For this reason, everything he thinks, everything he feels, everything he writes will always appear to us triply based; his statements or his reactions will also seem forced to us, or, as he says, "strained," because of the extreme tension to which a perception is subjected, being penetrated as soon as it is born by three constitutive and divergent intentions. We should remember that a single glance in a mirror while shaving awakens in him at once a powerful desire to laugh and analytic reason in its primitive form—a terrifying superstition—Gustave is seeing his skeleton. But simultaneously his resentment condemns these stupid bourgeois customs (in the name of death and nothingness)—what folly to shave his future cadaver! All of which does not prevent the young man from attentively surveying his image in order to decide if his nose has grown larger, if bourgeois vulgarity is on the way to conquering transcendent grace, that beauty which a princess's kiss had fixed on his face for a few years. As we see, all the fundamental and divergent intentions work on him at the same time: first, the cold satisfaction of finding he is not so bad as all that and then, with a burst of rage, the bitter intention of making everything as bad as possible and making himself horrible not only as a species but in his contingency as a creature without a creator.

I have spoken of tearing apart; in the example chosen, indeed, every dimensional force is like a bent tree springing back up, tearing out the stakes that were pinning it down toward the ground. But we have also seen that these lines of force, instead of diverging from each other, often coexist like the structures of a curved—sometimes even spherical—space, forcing the perception to bend according to the curvature. In this case the extreme terms are joined, and the plethora of meanings, far from bursting under the unbearable tension, yield to each other in a closed circuit as the contradictions intersect. This is the jungle of vicious circles; in these moving labyrinths violence gives way to torpor, but Gustave's malaise is just as great since the very movement of his thought leads to the idea of its opposite without his being able to deny or acknowledge the rigor of the transitions. We have shown in passing a certain number of vicious circles in which *fatum*, scientism, faith, God, nothingness, feudal hierarchy, and the egalitarian bourgeoisie are organized as carousels, compelling the exhausted young man to "turn around his thought," as he says in the first *Tentation*.

C. GUSTAVE'S "STUPIDITY"

> *The fool does not always have*
> *the oppressed look that suits him.*
> Marcel Jouhandeau

The result of this battle between the two ideologies is not that one wins or loses but, surprisingly and at the same time quite logically, that Gustave *is stupid*.

All the bourgeois intellectuals of the nineteenth century were in agreement on one point: to be bourgeois was to be a philistine. Beginning in 1830—the publication date of *Scènes populaires*—Joseph Prudhomme haunted their conversations and correspondence; for all of them—for Flaubert himself—Prudhomme hovered between the singular universality of myth and the abstract precision of a concept. Sometimes they said, "He speaks like Joseph Prudhomme," and sometimes, "He's a regular Prudhomme." And everyone, of course, invested this legendary figure with his own meaning. But the denunciation of bourgeois foolishness was accompanied in the writers, who were constituted into more or less organized bodies and *recognized* each other in the literary salons, by an agreeable feeling of superiority. Whether they were young noblemen, "bohemians," or bourgeois idealists and completely unconscious of their class, it seemed to them that their irony or their spiteful declarations proved clearly that they were not of the same species as the subhumanity they stigmatized. Their indignation was tonic and even briskly cheerful. To be sure, stupidity was everywhere in evidence, "its name is legion," but in their eyes it remained a privation, an absence; those afflicted by it were considered harmful, but chiefly to themselves. For Flaubert, and for him alone, stupidity was a positive force and the fool became an oppresser. This abject plenitude was triumphant, it was *already* triumphant, and the artist was on the defensive. But the struggle was too unequal; in relation to this opaque, universal presence he was the one who felt like an impotent and shriveled negation, a defective being. We must take a closer look. In fact, Flaubert yokes together under the same name two contradictory kinds of stupidity, one of which is the fundamental substance and the other the acid eating it away. Between the two, the struggle is continual and always a stalemate. One thing is certain: under one or the other of these aspects, stupidity always triumphs. This is deliberately suggested by the hideous spectacle of the abbé Bournisien and Monsieur Homais, overcome by the same sleepiness and snoring at each other, at the bedside of a dead woman they could neither cure nor save from hell.

1. On Stupidity as Substance.

At the age of nine, Flaubert discovered the two complementary faces of stupidity: ceremony and language. He wrote to Ernest on 31 December 1830, "You are right to say that New Year's Day is stupid," and at the end of the same letter, "There is a lady who comes to see papa and always says stupid things; I'll write them down too."

a. Ceremony. New Year's Day: gifts and compliments, visits, embraces, good wishes. Children are the victims and accomplices—they are dressed in their best clothes, shake hands, and say the right thing. Gustave *discovers* the stupidity of these solemnities. Actually, Ernest—though better integrated—is the one who first made the discovery. Gustave only *realizes* the situation. But forever. Guided by his friend's possibly casual remark, he takes the smallest retreat that the invisible fissure of his frustration will allow him. It must be noted too that this is more a question of foresight than of experience, since the stupidity of January 1st comes to him on December 31st. But worried or irritated by something, he knows in advance what will happen the following day—Achille will be present perhaps, and the object of particular attentions. The fact is that Gustave, exiled at the heart of ceremony, tears himself away from the immediate, stops taking it seriously by discovering its conventional character. Yet it isn't dissolved; far from being reabsorbed into individuals, the objective relation becomes dense, charged with mystery. This ceremony is absurd because it is not based on religious belief. Christmas and the midnight mass certainly did not provoke the child's scorn and suspicion; New Year's Day, however, a secular holiday, seems to Gustave, who is already misanthropic, like a series of senseless congratulations that brings together for a few hours people who can hardly stand each other or even despise each other. Worse still, the sentiments expressed are learned for the occasion; we are trained to disguise our hatred. There is an affective banality which momentarily masks the true color of feelings for the subjects themselves. Flaubert would not forget this; it has often been shown that his characters receive "emotional abstracts" from the outside—and especially from literature—that are supposed to anticipate real emotions. The *Dictionnaire*, which during the course of thirty years he was bent upon publishing, makes no distinction between ready-made ideas, of which we shall soon speak, and accepted sentiments. For example:

> *Gibberish*. The way foreigners talk. *Always* laugh at the foreigner who speaks French badly.
> *Whitewash* (on church walls). Thunder against.
> This *aesthetic anger* is highly attractive.

Shall we say that the required laughter is forced, that the anger is only acted? Not at all. These are affective ceremonies, celebrated inside but on the surface. And people believe in them—this is emotional stupidity.

But at the same time, learned gestures and sentiments constitute the rites of integration. The child feels that if he could seriously observe the custom of New Year's Day, he would truly participate in the gathering. He cannot decide if his discerning eye has discovered the stupidity of the ceremonial or if his discernment exists because of the discovery. In any event, Gustave at the age of nine is neither the ingénue nor Micromégas—he makes the New Year's Day visits with his family. The first letter to Ernest dates from 31 December, and the same evening he had written to his grandmother, in a note surely dictated and corrected:[55] "I am eager to do my duty and wish you a good year." Even better, in the same letter to Ernest denouncing the

---

55. Not one error in spelling.

stupidity of this etiquette, he bows to it quite willingly and spontaneously: "I wish you a happy 1831, and give my affectionate greetings
to your family." Are the New Year's wishes meaningful when they
are addressed to real friends? The child, of course, cannot and does
not see the contradiction in his behavior. He is indeed more than half
seduced by the custom; only a rebellious adolescent could claim to see
a certain practice in all objectivity, from the outside, and refuse to
conform to it. Gustave hesitates; he senses the strangeness of these
mores which are his own only because he is not entirely able to share
their communal ends. We can identify here a kind of diffuse objectivity, a dulling of actions: persons become abstract, inessential, and
what is essential is the drama they play out *while believing in it*. The
collective attitude absorbs individuals, uses them, and is affirmed in
its absurdity like the material reality that suppresses individuals to
its advantage. The ballet is staged for its own sake, and no longer
ruled by anyone; on the contrary, it is itself thought of as the rule.
This is a complete inversion of the classic relationship, *mens agitat
molem*: here it is matter that activates the spirit. Every year, in effect,
the ceremony emerges from the dark of the ages, always denser,
thicker, more inert, more absurd, and it is this ceremony that animates
the community of living men. Until the end of his life Gustave held
the same opinions about collective attitudes; he never imagined that
they might have ends other than those of provisionally uniting beings
whose essence is impenetrability, or that they might reflect a defensive
or offensive movement of his class, of the governing circles. In 1866,
speaking of chic, "that modern religion," he uses the same tones as
in his letter to Chevalier:

> Chic (or *chiques*) opinions: to be for Catholicism (without believ-
> ing a word of it), to be in favor of slavery, to be for the Austrian
> ruling house, to wear mourning for Queen Amélie, to admire
> "Orphée aux Enfers," to be involved in agricultural shows, to
> talk about sports, to act reserved, to be such an idiot as to regret
> the treaties of 1815. This is the latest thing![56]

For him, "chic" was not a matter of propaganda or a reactionary
practice trying to oppose the rising forces of liberalism; it was a lot
of shoddy nonsense imposed on the new generation because it was
imposed on preceding generations ("the latest thing!"), animated by
a movement originating in the past and governed externally, like the

56. To George Sand, 29 September 1866.

bodies in Newtonian mechanics. Thus stupidity is infinite because it always comes from elsewhere—from another time, another place; it is inert and opaque, imposed by its weight, and its laws cannot be modified; it is a *thing*, finally, because it possesses the impassability and impenetrability of natural facts. The mechanical flattens the living, generality suppresses the originality of singular experience, the prefabricated reaction is substituted for adapted praxis. This is the impersonal reign of the "One": I pay a visit to my uncle because *one* pays visits to uncles on New Year's Day. But from another perspective it is the *reification* proper to bourgeois society, lived in complicity and refusal by a bourgeois who does not know himself. To the extent, in effect, that certain "distinguished" ceremonies had lost their Christian meaning and were revealed as simple conventions, to the extent that the bourgeoisie seemed to the young Flaubert incapable of inventing its own notion of the sacred and establishing truly human relationships, this reification only served to denounce its enterprise of atomization in the very same way in which it tried to fight it on the surface, or at the very least to mask it.

If stupidity is a thing, things can be stupid. Gustave would despise all clothes, all tools intended for *any kind* of usage—his tirades against boots, the train, "omnibuses," are well known. "What could be sadder than a hotel room with its formerly new furnishings that everyone uses?" Here the material thing is affirmed and the hotel guests denounced as interchangeable, inessential.

> It is art alone that gives you all your charms. . . . A man is in love with the dress and not the woman, with the little boot and not the foot; and if you do not have silk, lace and velvet, patchouli and kidskin, brilliant gems and a palette to paint your face, the savages themselves wouldn't want you, since they have tattooed wives. . . . Besides, clothing being a manifest sign of chastity is part of virtue and is a virtue itself. . . . Therefore, the more your outfit is a costume, that is, antinatural, uncomfortable, and ugly, the more beautiful it is . . . and distinguished, especially![57]

Here we have woman reduced to her toilette. All at once the skirt, the bodice, the gloves, or the makeup are in themselves the whole woman.

57. *Le Château des Coeurs*, in *Théâtre*, ed. Conard, pp. 242-43. We shall see when examine Flaubert's sexuality that this reduction to materiality both is caused by and *has as its effect* sexual fetishism, and that it also reveals sadomasochistic tendencies.

Inversely, Gustave would contemplate, entranced, every material object that in its singular spirit reflected the materiality of its owner. We know the importance Louise Colet's "little brown slippers" had for Flaubert ("the sight [of them] makes me imagine the movements of your feet inside them when they were still warm from being worn"), or after his mother's death the clothes she wore. But particularly memorable is "Charbovari's" cap, which bespeaks the stupidity of its owner to such a degree that truly Charles himself is tranformed into a cap. The double movement that makes a coquette into a thing and raises a piece of headgear to the level of human dignity can be considered here a certain aspect of what I have called the practico-inert; in this realm, men absorbed by materiality and things bewitched by the act that confirms them are interchangeable. The inert unity of the *seal* that is imposed on persons from the outside is identified with the active unification of wrought matter, which is degraded by its very triumph and subsists only through inertia. Still, the practico-inert is a generic term, of which stupidity, as Flaubert conceives it, is only a species. Indeed, there is no question here of the avatars of production but only those of usage; in the complex movement of appropriation and enjoyment and in the accompanying ceremonies, the inanimate thing and the human being perpetually exchange their functions and their status, though the human being never produces the thing.

Everyone has his way of incorporating objective inertia. With the abbé Bournisien, the principles of Catholicism have taken on the weight and mass of lead and sunk inside him. His stupid and complacent faith is reduced to the level of his material needs; whereas this faith ought to deny the body, it has become corporal. The priest's sectarian intransigence is his livelihood and no longer distinguishable from his gross carnal appetites. By contrast, "distinguished" women are transformed into delicate mechanisms. In "Le Château des Coeurs," the fairy queen explains by what diabolical operation the "Gnomes" have put the *exterior* inside us in place of interiority:

> The Gnomes steal [the heart] of men to feed on and put in its place some sort of mechanism of their own invention which perfectly imitates the movements of nature. . . . And the poor humans let this happen without revulsion. Some even find it pleasurable. . . . Men . . . abandon themselves to the exigencies of nature. The Gnomes' spirit [materiality] has penetrated to the marrow of their bones, envelops them . . . and, like a fog, hides from them the splendor of truth, the sun of the ideal.

Carrying this metamorphosis to its conclusion, the same play shows us a young girl trying to reproduce the gestures and speech of two robots so as to be able, "wherever she might be, to chatter away about nature, literature, fair-haired children, the ideal, horse-racing, and other things." The scene reproduces the double movement previously indicated: with a turn of the key the mannikins are animated, *turned into men*, and the young girl, terrified, fascinated, tries to turn herself into a mannequin. But the materiality of the pair of robots is reduced to *spatiality*. When the "Lady and Gentleman" begin to dance, the accepted gesture possesses the couple and unites them while mechanizing them; what is left is a spatial form animated by external movement, the rotation of a polyhedron: "He, chin raised and elbow in the air, she, straight as an arrow and nose lowered—the two of them jut their hard angles into space, a true geometric figure with a cheerful air."[58]

b. Language. In any event, stupidity in the first instance is the idea become matter or matter aping the idea. This leads us to envisage stupidity in its other aspect, which is perhaps the most important. For sometimes thought is transformed by itself into a mechanical system, and sometimes the mind is invaded by autonomous mechanisms. New Year's Day is stupid, but there is also "a lady who *says* stupid things." Saying stupid things: the sentences inside her that come out of her mouth, which are so mechanically rigid as to exclude any living relation to situation, to truth, or quite simply to preceding sentences. Do inert and isolated systems therefore exist in the consciousness? A moment ago, the thing was still *outside*—it was Charles's cap, Bournisien's breviary, the coquette's dress and gloves. Now it is inside us and buzzes in our heads; the external has intruded into our interior life, provoking the explosion of thought. *Things in the mind*—the child would call them "stupid things people say" and the man "accepted ideas." We are given a glimpse here of naked language, that sonorous matter that goes in the ear and takes hold in the brain. Every moment, everywhere, in total anonymity, a system of speech is fabricated, transmitted from mouth to ear, and ends up inside me. The meaning of each word is the inert unity of its matter, the inert assemblage of words determines a passive contamination of every meaning by others, and a pseudo-thought is perpetuated in my

58. *Théâtre*, ed. Conard, pp. 253–54.

head, its apparent signification not concealing its profound absurdity. Indeed, it has no other end than to unite men and reassure them by allowing them to make a *gesture of agreement*; what could these impenetrable beings with such diverse interests agree upon except *nothing*? The thick materiality of the "intelligible mouthful" is accompanied by an absence, by a nothingness which is something other than signification. And more seriously, if the accepted idea is a pseudo-thought, it produces in us a pseudo-consciousness; what we call reflection is only a return of language to itself, a pleat in the system of words. The robots in *Château des Coeurs* present a semblance of interior life; this means that accepted ideas are fabricated for the purpose of stealing souls: they are similar to other ideas, moreover, except that they resonate in the brain cavity instead of filling the air outside.

The Gentleman:
At your service.
(*Aside*) What imagination! . . . She sparkles!
(*Aloud*) But allow me to advise you: I will take charge of your
    investments.

As we see, the "Gentleman's" internal monologue is loaded with platitudes that betray his origins, for only a "bourgeois" could say or *say to himself* (which is all the same, since the exterior is the interior) that a woman sparkles with imagination.

Flaubert would spend his life sifting the commonplaces we retail to others or to ourselves. At the end of his life he would write in *Bouvard et Pécuchet*: "Trivial things depressed them: newspaper advertisements, a bourgeois profile, a foolish incidental remark; thinking of what was being said in their village and that to the ends of the earth there were nothing but more Coulons and more Marescots, they felt oppressed by the weight of the world."

Many questions come instantly to mind: Where did he get what Monsieur Dumesnil nicely calls "his surprising aptitude for seizing stupidities"? Why did he pursue them so furiously? And why did the stupidity of others become such an unbearable burden?

We shall begin to answer these questions if we give up that other commonplace, that it takes intelligence to spy out stupidity. I say at once that in such operations, intelligence is useless; indeed, it often gets in the way. Every writer knows this; when you correct proofs, the printing errors elude you if you consider the text from the point of view of sense or style; in order to perceive that a word is one or two letters short or has one letter too many, you must put yourself on the level of the writing itself, empty yourself of anything else, and passively let the printed characters take form and disappear before your eyes. In other words, in order to discover a commonplace, you must submit to it and not surpass it through its usage. If Flaubert was crushed by ready-made ideas, it was because he was conditioned in such a way that he grasped language on their level.

An example will help us to understand his particular conviction. Let us open his *Dictionnaire*; under the entry "Railroads," we read: ". . . Talk about them ecstatically, saying: 'I, sir, who am speaking to you now—I was this morning at X; I left by train from X, where I had taken care of my business, and in X hours I was back here.'" It is true that all travelers were making such statements at the time. They made them, slightly modified, when the automobile made its appearance; they make them still today in nearly the same words when speaking of their plane travels. At every appearance of a new form of transportation there is a certain discourse which is always the same and related to the speed of the vehicle, and found in everyone's mouth. Is this "stupid"? Is it an accepted idea? The answer depends on your point of view. Certainly such statements involve truisms: if you know beforehand that the speed of an airplane is five hundred miles an hour, there is nothing surprising about being transported a thousand miles within two hours of takeoff. But to make such statements into self-evident truths you must first shut yourself inside the concepts. If, on the other hand, you adopt the affective point of view, everything is different. The marvel of finding yourself in Moscow four hours after leaving Paris is certainly not a profound emotion; nevertheless, it is naïve and spontaneous. Those four hours were spent above the clouds in a sort of limbo of undifferentiated space; they do not seem to matter in our lives, as though we were passing without transition from one world to another. At every new step in perfecting the machine, when for example jet aircraft replaced four-engined planes, our joyful stupefaction is reborn—it seems as though the whole world is within reach; the contrast between Paris and the Soviet capital is more shocking, we indulge in logically absurd notions which are nevertheless emotionally sincere, saying, for example, that Moscow is closer to Paris than Lyon. This is "stupid" because the means of transport is not the same in both cases; the logically correct sentence, "Moscow is closer to Paris *if you go by plane* than Lyon *if you travel by train*," is, from the point of view of the understanding, quite trivial. It takes on its whole meaning, however, if we consider that the same traveler goes regularly to Lyon by train and to Moscow by plane; our astonishment comes, therefore, from the practical comparison of two *absolute* speeds: for the same time "lost" (four hours), our disorientation is more or less radical, etc.

If, therefore, the same phrases come to everyone's lips, it is not because everyone hears them spoken but because they awkwardly express a common but spontaneous and appropriate, if not logical, reaction to a situation which is identical for everyone. For everyone except Flaubert, for whom train trips were a dreadful trial[59] and the railroad a symbol of the industrial civilization he despised and the social progress in which he did not believe. Since he did not share the aims and values of other travelers, he did not recognize in the words they all pronounced an expression of their sensibility. From the outset, their infatuation seemed suspect to him—they "were ecstatic"; we shall not find it astonishing, then, that the set of proffered words, severed from the affective state they express, appeared to be a mechanical product of conditioned reflexes. From childhood Flaubert had a "surprising aptitude" for catching commonplaces and stupidity because he lay in wait for them and listened to speech without grasping the synthetic activity and real intentions of the speaker. We must still ask why he was this way, but we already know the answer: he was what they made him. We know that from his earliest days he was locked into passivity. This means, effectively, that in his early childhood he was incapable of an act of affirmation. I have shown above that he was quite unaware of the possibilities of reciprocity—which is the measure of truth—and that the indifference of a morose mother had condemned him without reprieve to the terrain of simple belief. For this reason he received language, not as a structured collection of instruments to be assembled or disassembled in order to produce meaning, but as an interminable commonplace that was never based on the intention to express something or on the object being designated; and keeping a kind of consistency of its own, language inhabited him and was spoken inside him and even designated him, without his being able to use it. Of course, Gustave took great pains to change—he had to learn to *make judgments*. But too late. He was already deeply enmeshed in a world in which the truth is the Other. When he made judgments he stopped *believing*, but he failed to create reciprocity: the Other lost his authority, that's all. In other

59. He suffered from what might be called "railwayphobia."

words, he never completely believed what he said, or what was said to him.

But he doesn't believe the opposite of what is said either; he is insincere where he is concerned, and skeptical where it concerns his interlocutor. Lacking intuition—that is, a practical insight—he plays at judging. The judicial act is in part a gesture for him; he doesn't choose the words, but from among accepted ideas he chooses those that suit the situation; they are prefabricated, that is, the vocables and their very order are givens. The sentence is ready-made: he surprises himself by stating it, feeling the gap between the sad, vague sounds of his life and those noisy little pebbles that are words. At the same time, he receives the sentences of others as prefabricated determinations of discourse; for it to be otherwise, he would have to view them as judgments (true or false), that is, he would have to vote for or against. Thought is a common and revealing praxis which has only words as its tools but which, when engaged in the work of reciprocity, pilfers those words to the profit of the thing spoken. When this signifying activity—which reaches beyond its instrument toward the world—ceases to be manifest, the world reappears in its material density as the pure negation of the signified. In effect, the word "cattle" is a means of access to the real herd when it is part of a complex signal relating to a practical fact or an action (the cattle are sick; the herd of cattle must be moved). But at the same time, no one perceives that it was pronounced. When it rejoins the passive flow of experience, on the other hand, it is posed for itself and seems to be the negation of cattle, namely an audio or visual determination that refers only to other determinations of the same kind. Flaubert never *thinks*: the defender of "objectivism" has no objectivity; this means that he does not take any *real* steps toward himself and the world, so that language reappears within him and outside him as an obsessive materiality. Even so, he does not lose his essence, which is to signify, but the significations remain in the words, referring only to themselves. This is a kind of *alien thought*—materiality aping thought or, if you like, thought haunting matter without being able to leave it behind. Language, being organized inside him according to connections that are proper to itself, steals his thought (which is not explicit enough to govern words) and affects him with pseudo-thoughts, which are "accepted ideas" and belong to no one since they are always other, according to Gustave. On this level, Flaubert does not believe that *people speak—people are spoken*. Language, as a practico-inert and structured whole, has its own organization of sealed materiality; thus resonating all alone inside us, according to its laws—that is, precisely according to the imposed seal of its inertia—it infects us with a thought that is inside out (produced by words instead of ruling them) and is only the consequence of the semantic work or, if you like, its counterfinality. Language for Flaubert is nothing but stupidity, since verbal materiality left to itself is organized semiexternally and produces a kind of *thought-matter*.

In one sense he is not wrong, and we are all stupid to the extent that every pronounced speech contains within it the counterfinality that consumes it. And, if you like, we all express ourselves all the time through commonplaces. The word by itself is a ready-made idea since it is defined outside us by its differences from other words in the verbal spectrum. But in another way we are all intelligent: commonplaces are words in the sense that, by using them, we move toward a thought that is always fresh. Is this to say that such commonplaces do not steal our thought from us? On the contrary, they never stop absorbing and diverting it. I have shown elsewhere that the word "Nature," an eighteenth-century commonplace, limits and diverts de Sade's thought and that sadism is an antiphysis which can be conceived only as a kind of naturalism. But intelligence is a dialectic relationship between verbal intention and words. Always diverted, always reclaimed and governed, then diverted once more—and so on to infinity—thought is caught in the trap of commonplaces when it believes it is using them; and, inversely, when we believe it is trapped, it goes beyond those commonplaces and bends them to its original intention. The results of this doubtful combat are variable; in any case, it is a continuing operation. So as not to carry on this combat in full rigor, Flaubert is constantly in a state of *estrangement* in the face of words: they represent the outside transferred to the inside, the interior grasped as exterior. He writes and discovers with horror that he has penned a commonplace unwittingly. This is what explains his oratorical precautions. He adds to his sentence at least a hundred times: "as the concierge says," "speaking like a shopkeeper." Or again: "I am like Monsieur Prudhomme who . . . ,"[60] "as Monsieur Prudhomme would say,"[61] "I declare . . . (like Monsieur Prudhomme)".[62] This comparison comes spontaneously to mind; scarcely is the word spoken when Flaubert sees it and no longer recognizes it; some bour-

60. *Correspondance* 5:2.
61. Ibid. 5:153, 6:288.
62. Ibid. 4:450.

geois must have stolen his pen. In fact, it is his own bourgeois leanings that come to him like a stranger and that he hastens to deny. He wants to make us believe that he is amused, that he is imitating salesmen and shopkeepers. But why would he do this? And why *precisely in this place*? Most of the time, indeed, the part of the sentence added in haste, "as . . . would say . . . speaking like. . . ," seems perfectly preposterous; the letter is serious, violent, eloquent, and the movement of the thought is abruptly interrupted by this unhappy addition. In fact Flaubert does not express himself *like* a bourgeois; he speaks *in* bourgeois terms *because he is bourgeois*. He did not write the incriminating phrase *to mock his class*, it came to him spontaneously, he saw it suddenly and wanted to save himself by lucidity: oh yes, I know, I am talking like a shopkeeper—and at the same time to prevent his correspondent from making fun of him: you are talking like Joseph Prudhomme—come on! don't you see I did it on purpose?

But the stupidity explodes—in the sense he intends—especially when this tardy lucidity is lacking and he has allowed a sentence to pass without comment; his correspondence is crawling with commonplaces and Prudhommeries.

Socialism, Prudhomme would say, is a dangerous illusion. And Flaubert: "These deplorable utopias that agitate our society and threaten to destroy it." For Henri Monnier's heroes, travels form their youth. Gustave agrees with him: "You rub up against such different kinds of men that you end up knowing a little about the world (from having traveled through it)." "There are no roses without thorns," says Monnier. And Flaubert: "Beneath most loving tenderness is there not a bitter kernel?" Joseph is famous for saying, "The carriage of State is rolling over a volcano" and "This sword is the light of my life." Now listen to Gustave: "Pride is a wild beast that lives in caves and deserts. Vanity, on the other hand, hops like a parrot from branch to branch and chatters in full daylight"; and "Genius like a strong horse pulls humanity along the roads of ideas"; or again: "Humanity, a perpetual old man, periodically takes blood transfusions for its agonies."[63] It is he, not the shopkeeper, who writes: "That gallant

63. It will be remarked that this last sentence is, strictly speaking, devoid of sense. In revolutions and wars, humanity loses blood and is given none.

Here we see a passage from a letter to the Muse that shows us Flaubert falling into the shabbiest commonplaces just as he is trying to escape them.

Having written that "success with women is generally a sign of mediocrity, and yet this is what [all men] envy and what drowns others," he tries to describe the "fair sex" in its true colors; this is what he comes up with:

"'Selected Maxims:' They are not frank with themselves, they do not admit to having

genital organ is at the source of all human tenderness," or drunkenly declares: "This is where an excessive love for alcohol leads." It figures even in his *Dictionnaire*: "*Greece*: Admire the miracle of Greece. *Statues*. When a statue is beautiful, say that it could walk away (or be alive)." Yet he writes from Athens: "Here is the eternal dazed and admiring monologue I recited to myself, looking at this little patch of earth amid the high mountains surrounding it. 'All the same, this earth produced bold fellows and bold things'"; and (apropos a broken statue): "[the breast] seems about to swell; you feel that the lungs beneath it are about to expand and breathe."[64]

We can be sure that he was more or less conscious of all this. He doesn't have a clear knowledge of all the banalities that escape him, but he has no doubts that language is, in him as in others, a "moving sidewalk" of banalities. And this indeed is what it is if it isn't appropriated for one's own use. We can therefore understand Gustave's double attitude toward stupidity. Sometimes it fascinates him and sometimes it repels him; it is both an abyss that makes him dizzy and the weight of the whole earth oppressing him.

First of all, the fascination. Stupidity, a passive synthesis, is plenitude, being. And order, as well. Or at least it is *one* order, the one that is imposed from without, imprisoning every person in a corset of ceremonies. Flaubert wrote ironically that the *Dictionnaire* would connect the public once again to "tradition, to order, to general convention." But beneath this irony J.-P. Richard was right to discern seriousness and envy. Is there such a big difference between integration through rite and the social success of fools? In order to succeed, you must play the game to the end, that's all. To make communion, you must take it seriously. So the group or the individual is mineralized; mystified, dazed, Flaubert contemplates this compact mass cast from a single mold that is formed against him yet still retains in its inert cohesion human significations in the process of petrification. Stupidity is a passive operation in which man is affected by inertia so as to internalize insensibility, infinite depth, permanence, the total and instantaneous presence of matter. Every time Flaubert witnesses

---

any sense, they take their ass for their heart and think that the moon exists to light up their boudoir.

"Cynicism, which is the irony of vice, is not part of their makeup.

"Their heart is a piano on which man, the egotistical artist, takes pleasure in playing tunes that make him shine. . ." etc.

To Louise Colet, 15 April 1852, *Correspondance* 2:391.

64. To Louis Bouihet, 9 December 1850 and 10 February 1851, *Correspondance* 2:273, 298.

the operation, he feels tricked and frustrated at the same time. His uncle Parain, on 6 October 1850, received a very curious letter from "quarantine at Rhodes":

> Have you sometimes thought, dear fellow, about the serenity of fools? Stupidity is something unshakable; nothing can attack it without being broken. It has the quality of granite, hard and resistant. In Alexandria, a certain Thompson, from Sunderland, wrote his name in letters six feet high on Pompeii's column. It can be read a quarter of a mile off. There is no way of seeing the column without seeing the name of Thompson. This imbecile has become part of the monument and is perpetuated with it. What can I say? He crushes it by the splendor of his gigantic letters. Isn't it very clever to force future travelers to think of you and remember you? All fools are more or less Thompsons from Sunderland. How many times in life do we not encounter them in the most beautiful places, at the purest moments? And then, they always get the better of us; there are so many of them, they return so often, they are in such good health! On a trip you meet a lot of them . . . but they soon go away; you are amused by them. It's not like in ordinary life, when they manage to drive you crazy.[65]

To travelers' eyes, Thompson is continually transformed into a column; all they have to do is read his name to reanimate the initial operation, otherwise called *writing*, the perfect crime, the pure act of stupidity, inert and virulent. Flaubert doesn't know whether in the end this act will transform Thompson into a monument or the column at Pompeii into Thompson. Shall we say that this Englishman proved there is invention in such foolishness? Not at all—all the monuments on earth are covered with inscriptions. Thompson's conduct in itself is entirely conventional. It designates him, moreover, as a traveler and a bourgeois; for this businessman, the Roman column has lost all meaning, he is from a century and a world for which ancient civilization no longer represents anything and which therefore—according to Flaubert—has fallen below that civilization. But his behavior also gives us information about his morality and character; he is a utilitarian: instead of admiring the work of art as an absolute end, he makes beauty into a means of serving his personal publicity. What serenity of soul it must take to pull this off! To be sure, it also takes ignorance, lack of taste, insensitivity, blind conceit, and "vulgarity."

65. *Correspondance* 2:243–44.

These vices appear to be merely negative: in fact, they represent the other side of plenitude. Thompson has conquered matter because matter triumphed in his soul long ago. If he were conscious, he would be an iconoclast, a sadist, a madman, a neurotic, and the neurotic character of his enterprise would probably have doomed him to failure. His success is based on his unconsciousness (which for Flaubert has no connection with the unconscious), and this unconsciousness is already materiality. Is it therefore a triumph to defile a work of art by writing your name on it? Flaubert honestly believes it is. The "tirade" against Thompson is introduced in the letter by an obscure allusion to the Hôtel-Dieu's relations with a young couple. The Hôtel-Dieu is then "the Achilles." Achille and Thompson resemble each other in that both are usurpers. The first has confiscated the father's glory for his own profit; the other has made himself the parasite of an eternal work, usurping the glory that ought to belong to the artists whose names have unhappily been lost. Glory, that is the point. Gustave long dreamed of perpetuating himself until the end of time by becoming part of the raw materiality of a work of art. And in 1850, during the journey to the Orient, he was just recovering from an almost devastating fall: the first *Saint Antoine* had left Maxime and Bouilhet decidedly unimpressed. Gustave was miserable, anxious, doubted himself: maybe he would never be a writer, maybe his name would vanish with him from the earth. With Louise Colet he had long played the braggart: to be annihilated, to vanish like a bad dream, that is what he wants—and for humanity to be left unmarked by his brief existence, as though he had never lived. But we are beginning to know him, and we know that his declarations must often be read differently; behind the one just cited is a horrible anguish. Not that he fears death, quite the contrary. But life, for him, is an all too brief delay conceded for the preparation of one's burial. When he played the tragic figure for his mistress, at least he had his work *before* him; *Saint Antoine* was going to be his parting shot. In 1850 the work is set aside, it is *behind* him, life and death are equally absurd: chance provokes purulence, and when decomposition has taken place and the bones are picked clean, nothing is left. And this is exactly why the column was set up and carries a name: Thompson has stolen someone else's work, and stolen the glory, living as a parasite of an alien eternity. *He has won.* Is this winning? Do we have to deal with fools *in saecula saeculorum*? Yes, since fools are legion, since they are capable of committing such a repugnant act again and again for their own benefit. Since humanity is stupid, Thompson imposes himself on humanity. As Achille does on the people of Rouen. What appalls Flaubert, what overwhelms him is not the act of stupidity but the fact that it is immediately accepted by man and nature. External matter obligingly lends him its *eternal* permanence, its *present* plenitude; internal matter, which is cast in the hearts of men, confers upon him immortality. We now understand that stupidity is dizzying for Flaubert: it is a free fall to the depths of material and social eternity. We understand that to him it seems infinite; in fact, the fool's action is a paltry mechanical gesture, but the general complicity gives it an incredible substance; Thompson is infinite because the young traveler discovers that this Englishman has succeeded in pulling off something the adolescent from Rouen hardly dared to dream of: the possibility of man becoming mineral.[66] The fool and the artist have the same ambition. Naturally, Flaubert had tried to realize his by other methods: glory is a superior form of mineralization—we raise up glory to support significations instead of weighing down significations until they are changed into matter. Genet once said: "A statue by Giacometti is a victory of the bronze over itself." And this is just how Flaubert imagines his work: a victory of language over its materiality. Except, however, for the book's inertia, handed down from generation to generation like a torch, the inertia of the name on the cover. Glory is only a small stone, or—what amounts to the same thing—my cadaver in the hands of others. If Flaubert is like this, how can he condemn Thompson? Is the man a barbarian? Yes. A usurper? Of course. But what has he done except take a short cut?

Saint Antoine, in a later version of the work, would make quite another vow: "To be matter." This is reclaiming the radical excision of the human determination in favor of the totality. The anchorite condemns man's limits, his discomfort, his consciousness, and even his life; but he does not dream of debasing him; if particularity bursts, the being remains in his impassable virginity. These two opposed desires—a material victory of matter in its materiality, matter realizing its plenitude by the abolition of life and thought—allow us to understand both what Flaubert detests in stupidity and why it makes him dizzy.

In fact, between the two extremes stupidity provides an ignoble "golden mean." Far from de-realizing matter by making it into art,

---

66. We shall see, moreover, that Flaubert *admired* Byron for writing his name on a column of the Swiss castle. And Gustave dreamed of writing his own name there as well.

stupidity casts a spell on it by permeating matter with degraded meanings; it does not abolish that which is human but it makes man into an inert meaning that can still be deciphered on the basis of the mechanisms that have replaced his mind. Nevertheless, Flaubert's double postulation is related to the project of fools: one wants to leave a name on a column, the other on the back of a book; there is not much difference. Flaubert knows this, all the more as he discovered stupidity first and his dreams of the artist and the monk are defensive. Above all, if the fool has missed pantheistic fusion with the universe, at least he is rooted in the material unity of a materialist society. In the real world this fraudulent victory is the only one possible, and at the bottom of his heart Flaubert is never certain that he doesn't want it for himself.

Even on this level, we can discover and understand the ambivalence of his feelings. He condemns the fool unconditionally, with the "fierceness" of despair. But stupidity itself, that impersonal substance, fascinates him. From his adolescence until his death he would maniacally and obstinately collect *accepted ideas*. This is pursuing two contradictory ends. The first—the only one he could have clearly expressed—is, if you will, cathartic. No one *sees* commonplaces; they are used to unite us, to please, they are the means to success. But when they are being passed off to a neighbor, their familiar aspect allows them to go unnoticed—neither seen nor acknowledged nor scrutinized, they remain hidden in full daylight. We would only have to *point them out* to horrify everyone—no one would dare speak anymore. And this purifying exposé could be accomplished only by an outsider. But in order to expose commonplaces he would have to track them, catch them on the wing, and *write them down*. And even as they are written down, their substance is once again confirmed, they are engraved on matter; and the writer is participating—though in order to destroy it—in ceremony. Hidden in the hatred Flaubert feels for the commonplace is an indirect pleasure—he is penetrated by the commonplace as he writes it down; if he is the only one not to benefit from social unification, he has his revenge in discovering, all by himself, and noting—for himself first—the instrument of that unification. Through it he catches a glimpse of what again eludes him, the infinity of matter and the mineralization of society. But the dizziness he feels when he is fascinated by the written sentence includes *in itself* and as its fundamental structure the blueprint for a free fall into the heart of matter; Flaubert dreams of crushing his thought on words, in short, of making himself stupid. The ambiguity of his attitude stands out clearly in the following lines:

> I would attack everything [in the *Dictionnaire des idées reçues*]. It would be the historic glorification of everything generally approved. I would demonstrate that majorities have always been right, minorities always wrong. I would immolate great men on the altar of fools, and do it in an outrageous style. . . . This apologia for human vulgarity in all its aspects, ironic and riotous from start to finish, full of quotations, proofs (which would prove the opposite), and ghastly texts (that would be easy), would be aimed at putting an end, once and for all, to eccentricities, whatever they may be. This would lead me back to the modern democratic idea of equality, Fourier's remark that great men will become superfluous, and it is for this purpose, I would say, that the book is written.[67]

Of course, the intention is ironic. But the method is still surprising: combating stupidity in others without ever attacking it but, quite to the contrary, *by realizing it*, by making himself its *medium* and martyr— in order to *make it manifest* in his person. In short, Flaubert dreams of taking upon himself all the stupidity of the world, of making himself its scapegoat in order to free others from it, of losing himself in it for a moment in order to denounce it, and of carrying it to an extreme, to the point of ignominiousness, the "sublime below." As to the method itself—so manifestly conceived to be extreme that no reader would be fooled by it—it speaks eloquently of Flaubert's submission to the family, to the social order. What then? He begins his letter by declaring that he "has a furious itch to lash out at other human beings" and that he will do it some day, "ten years from now." Then he adds that he has come back, "meanwhile," to his old idea for a *Dictionary of Accepted Ideas*. This young man of thirty-one, dying to lash out at the bourgeoisie, still hasn't got the courage to do it. What is he waiting for? Fame? Fortune? Power? And why does he hasten to explain: "*No law could touch me* although I would attack everything [in the *Dictionnaire*]." What precautions! And what an odd *attack* that takes on the appearance of submission. All of Flaubert is here, cunning and docile: he prefers to show the foolish cruelty of social conventions through the absurd, through a hypocritical eagerness, through conforming strictly to the rules. Apparently conceding, gently exaggerating, pushing to the limit and at the same time *showing himself*, the pure passive

67. To Louise Colet, 17 December 1852, *Correspondance* 3:66.

result of the will of others, making himself into an object in order to give others a horror of themselves—this he will do; but fight openly, directly—*never*. However, in the case at hand, it is a question of stripping the materiality away from other men in order to be penetrated by it himself. On this level, essential stupidity *is his temptation*. And let us make no mistake, in stupidity he is seeking both materiality and social integration. It is as though he were repeating to himself, horrified and full of hatred: "What if the Good Lord were stupid?" If he were, there would be nothing left but to imitate Achille and Thompson. Better to be a satisfied pig than a discontented Socrates. For Socrates does not know that he is Socrates—and those who surround him and condemn him to death don't know it either. Whereas the pig, quite comfortable in its sty among its own kind, enjoys being a pig.

Maybe Flaubert himself is merely a dissatisfied pig? The thought terrifies him; temptation becomes disgust when he discovers *in himself* the accepted ideas that fascinate him in others, that is, language as a passive synthesis experienced in submission. If that were the case, his particularity would not be in soaring above stupidity but in being devoured by it; the exile would not be to the heights but to the depths; he would discover the stupidity of others only to be infected by it himself. Better still, perhaps there is no stupidity except *in him*, and he is the one, with his narrow point of view, who seeks to confine the thoughts of others within limits that are not really there. Here the role of the parents cannot be overestimated. His passivity was developed by Mme Flaubert's tepid ministrations; Achille-Cléophas's impatience made him think he was the "family idiot"; and Achille's acknowledged excellence consigned him to an inferior status which his mediocre scholarship only confirmed.[68] For a long time he had internalized the judgment of others. Proof is that Djalioh does not know how to reason. How could Gustave be unaware, after this, that stupidity not only is a permanent dizziness but also constitutes his *own heaviness*, and that his pride is only a defense? Once again we find him on the rack, caught in the vicious circle mentioned above: stupidity is outside and inside. Only a slight fissure, a tiny fault, prevents Flaubert's integration into bourgeois stupidity. But this "distancing" through resentment, far from saving him, puts him in hell: he recognizes his own stupidity in that of others, although he cannot dissolve his in theirs. As for him, he cannot even declare that

68. Mediocre *in the head surgeon's eyes*. We shall come back to this.

he *is not stupid*—the "moving sidewalk" passes through him and he feels *absent at his own stupidity*; it inhabits him, it uses his mouth or his pen to express itself, and yet he opposes to it a kind of passive denial. Or perhaps this eternal outcast simply hasn't the luck to make it stick.

His recoil is not sufficient, however. Let us judge by comparing his grand design—of seizing catchphrases in their natural habitat and showing them to us—with what he actually accomplished. What he wanted to do, a writer of our own time, Georges Michel, has succeeded in doing marvelously in his play *Les Jouets* ("The toys"): the characters express themselves only through commonplaces. But these "accepted ideas" are still kicking, they have been captured alive—they seem strange to us and at the same time our own. This is because, conventional as they are, the characters' statements are located. First of all, in time: they are still current, for the most part, and if they were current yesterday or the day before yesterday, they still have some bite. And then, in social space: the couple who follow what might be called a double monologue from one scene to the other belong to a defined milieu—the husband is a clerical worker, they live in low-cost housing. Finally, the author strives to show us the origin of these commonplaces. The radio, which is in great part responsible for them, is constantly blaring. We witness the entire operation: the phrases come over the air, enter the characters' ears, are recorded, and come out of their mouths scarcely modified by what might be called, in spite of everything, their individuality. It is all quite clear: this middle-class couple is being manipulated, their desires and thoughts are being directed to make them into good consumers and good citizens. Other members of the middle classes can more or less recognize themselves—there is common ground between one level and the other, between one milieu and the next. Intellectuals, for example, are *perhaps* more resistant but are equally beseiged. The rigorous localization of the characters does not prevent the public's fascination.

Flaubert would have been pleased by this farce. He certainly could not have written it; in the mid-nineteenth century, the mass media was represented only by the press with its limited circulation; the origin and itinerary of a prefabricated idea were difficult to pinpoint. "Word of mouth" did exist; commonplaces circulated from one milieu to the other, but they varied: some crossed boundaries, passing from one social stratum to another, while others defined a particular group.

612

We might have expected Gustave to situate the commonplaces he proposed to us, but he made no effort to do so. To begin with, he gives his *Dictionnaire* a subtitle that marks the irresolution of his thought.[69] "Chic opinions" are only a subdivision of accepted ideas; the second are found everywhere and only the speaker varies, whereas the first are *well-bred* notions properly held *in the upper levels* of the bourgeoisie and are often inspired, or claim to be inspired, by opinions attributed to the aristocracy. And what is he doing? Is he impugning only the attitudes and words passed around in "good society"? Not at all; commonplaces of every kind are found in the *Catalogue*, some coming from shopkeepers, as far as he is concerned, and others circulating in his own class. He is not concerned with categorizing them; indeed, he simply presents them alphabetically. Everyone knows that we use alphabetical order as a last resort when we want, as Descartes says, "to presume the same order between [objects] which do not naturally follow one another" or, if you like, when the material contents have no internal relation to each other. This external juxtaposition translates a refusal or inability to rearrange the opinions. The *Dictionnaire* is therefore and ought to be by nature a catch-all.

"*Impiety*. Thunder against." This was not often done at Dr. Flaubert's. Doubtless that bourgeois pietism which was hardly compatible with his Voltaireanism was not "chic," nor was it regarded as a reflection of upper-class piety. For the same reason, the condemnation of the "hideous smile" of "*Voltaire*: famous for his frightful *rictus*. Superficial learning," reflects aristocratic romanticism much more than it does the opinion of the liberal bourgeoisie. See also: "*Philippe d'Orléans-Egalité*. Thunder against. . . . Committed all the crimes of that disastrous epoch." Who is saying this? A republican? A defender of the July monarchy? Certainly not. But a legitimist, that is, a nobleman or a bourgeois "snob." *Religion, Republicans, Girondins*, etc.

On the other hand, we have "*The Judiciary*. An excellent career for a young man." This was a commonplace of the liberal bourgeoisie, and Dr. Flaubert was no doubt of the same opinion. A little later, the same bourgeoisie would declare: "*Engineer*. The finest career for a

---

69. *Catalogue des opinions chic.*

young man." But in Gustave's anomalous nomenclature, nothing *dates* commonplaces.[70]

Our Voltairean bourgeois also says of priests: "Sleep with their housekeepers and have children whom they pass off as their nephews." Gustave likes to set commonplaces against each other; not being critical of them, he wants them to neutralize each other. Thus the anticlericalism that is betrayed in his reflection on priests is in contradiction to the "proper thought" expressed in the entry on *Religion*. Actually the contradiction would lose its force if Gustave, as he ought to have done, had shown that these opinions come from different groups whose interests are opposed. Of course, this is what he does not do; everything is on the same level so that we never know *who* is speaking.

Or about *what*. When he writes: "*Invalid*. Raise his spirits by belittling his ailment and discounting the tale of his sufferings." Is this a "chic" opinion? Isn't it rather an oddity encountered in every milieu, which he complains about because he has suffered from it?[71] And this: "*Memory*. Complain of your own and even boast of having none. But bellow if someone says you haven't any judgment." In the *Dictionnaire*, infinitives function as hypothetical imperatives:* "If you want to be integrated in your milieu, *do* or *say* . . . etc." But certainly it is obvious that the second imperative in this case is out of line. If it is well bred to complain of one's memory and if, consequently, this verbal conduct can be ironically commanded, to "bellow" out of vexation is a spontaneous reaction. Flaubert is using *the same grammatical form* to designate a voluntary and a psychological trait, that is, an obligation and a fact. Finally the fact prevails, and we ought rather to read: "People willingly declare that they have no memory, but they bellow when someone tells them they have no judgment." Again, we find ourselves at the beginnings of an accepted behavior. But what shall we say to "*Lacustrine* (cities). Deny their existence because man cannot live under water"? Is this an accepted idea or simply a bit of gross stupidity born of ignorance that hasn't enough substance to

70. When Flaubert, between the ages of eighteen and twenty, imagines all the "bourgeois careers" only to reject them heartily, he *never* pronounces the word engineer. Industrial progress would have to take place, the development of Saint-Simonism and positivism, for the liberal bourgeoisie to begin to respect technicians more than magistrates.

71. And isn't this one of Achille-Cléophas's attitudes, which we find in his thesis?

* [In the original French, for example, we find: "*Mémoire*. Se plaindre . . ." (lit. "To complain . . ."); "*Mais rugir* . . ." (lit. "But to bellow . . .") The infinitive in French is often used to express a directive, as in public notices.—Trans.]

perpetuate itself? I would say the same of *"Crayfish*. Female of the lobster" *"Frog*. Female of the toad," etc. It may be, indeed, that certain people *believe* these statements. But even if the belief is widespread, it has nothing to do with a commonplace and still less with a "chic opinion," but is simply a mistake. Gustave goes further still, however, and does not flinch from trivial wordplays: *"Affairs*. . . . A woman must avoid speaking of hers." How do we recognize anything in all this? Accepted ideas, locutions, puns and wordplays, "gems" are all jumbled together. Certain citations—rare—correspond to living habits of thought that have been passed down to us: *"Mistake*. 'It's worse than a crime, it's a mistake' (Tallyrand). 'You have no more mistakes left to make' (Thiers). These two remarks must be uttered with an air of profundity." But most of the others are hackneyed phrases already outmoded in Flaubert's time. For example: *"Agriculture*. Short of hands," was already being said with irony. A strange work: more than a thousand entries, and who feels stung? No one.

Yet one man does: the author himself. The most curious thing is that he *is* stung and does not seem to be aware of it. For often the accepted ideas he discovers in others are quite simply *his* ideas, those he amply exhibits in his correspondence. First, he ironically advocates *tirades*—but his letters are full of them. And who has *thundered against* institutions, social practices, parties, etc., more than he? *"Doctor*," he writes, "Always to be preceded by 'the good.'" Yet this is *his* mania. Moreover, he doesn't stop at saying "the good doctor," but "that good fellow, Gautier," "nice Béranger," "young Maxime du Camp," "good old Parain," etc., etc.; in short, he too has contracted the mania for preceding proper nouns with a qualifier. It is true that his intention is to denigrate: "good, worthy, young," etc. indicate a condescending familiarity. But the origin of this tic is bourgeois, and in the case of "the good doctor," if the adjective is taken in its positive sense as a mark of confidence and esteem [72] it also frequently takes on a slightly pejorative sense among the upper classes when the superior uses it to designate his inferiors. But there is something even more serious. We find some curious citations: *"Time* (our own). Thunder against. Complain that it is not poetic. Call it a time of transition." What else did he do from the time he was fifteen until his death? And *"Glory*. A mere puff of smoke." Let us recall *Agonies*: "Even the glory I pursue

72. And chiefly he intends to give a personal tour of relations between doctor and patient. The doctor is good because he loves us. Today we say that he is "very concerned," etc. The economic tie is masked by the human relationship.

is but a lie." And above all: "*Education*. The common people don't need it to earn their livelihood." We read this sentence—taken from a letter to George Sand: "Free and mandatory education will only increase the number of fools." And this: "What does it matter if so many peasants know how to read?" Men don't need to know how to read to be laborers and reapers. Many more citations could be added but the conclusion would be the same: Flaubert caught as accepted ideas in others, *outside him*, what he experienced *inside* as real products of his reflections.

Is it possible he didn't recognize this? Dumesnil has noted that in the collection of foolish remarks Flaubert amassed in the margins of the *Dictionnaire*, where he copied down the "gems" of his most il-lustrious contemporaries, he was not afraid to enter passages from his own works, which indicates that he didn't claim exemption from the common law. Nevertheless, the project of collecting foolish remarks—the greatest men have their moments of stupidity—is not the project of the *Dictionnaire*; it is coyness on Flaubert's part. He is telling us: I am just like the others; like the greatest men, I have my failings. (In the same way, the *Canard enchaîné* awards itself the "Noix d'honneur.") This is different, however, from recognizing the ready-made idea in what is being proffered as the expression of pure spon-taneity. All we can say for certain is that Gustave was not altogether clear-minded in his attempts to represent his thoughts in the diction-ary of nonthought. But it is equally certain that these attempts were not made without discomfort. Let us recall those incidents abounding in his correspondence: "As Monsieur Prudhomme would say," etc. The truth is that he "does not have any ideas," and he knows it. In other words, he doesn't have the means to distinguish thought as a synthetic and constructive activity from language, either in himself or in others. A letter from 15 July 1839 enlightens us in a curious way about his manner of conceiving the act of judgment: "I would love to see it begin to abandon . . . revery for action, the dawn it finds so beautiful for the day it imagines to be misty. Here I go again, indulging in empty talk, in words; when I inadvertently start making stylistic flourishes, scold me severely." "Style" here is only empty talk—Gus-tave abandons himself to metaphors, to what he would later call "hyperbole," in short, to words. Language floods and diverts his thought from its original course; he feels that it is being stolen from him and happily allows this to happen. But at the same time, he puts his trust in this hyperbolic speech, which speaks in him without being spoken. "The master is in Hades" and the "knickknacks of sonorous emptiness," far from being banished, jostle each other at the gate. This involuntary assemblage of words prefigures automatic writing. For the Surrealists, however, it is the unconscious that is being expressed; for Flaubert, the obscure product of language has only a verbal depth. He does not trust in it any the less, for all that; if he jots down on paper the sentences that come to mind, the idea will come as well, he *waits* for it: "Thoughts would come to me." In fact, they may or may not come. But Gustave's attitude is typical: passive but attentive, he lets a semantic order grow out of his pen, he even helps it along with rhetoric—his only activity; and in this sonorous void where meanings are created by the words attracted to them, he watches for the moment when the monster will gush out—a phrase, a determination of discourse that is in itself an *idea*, and in order to understand it he will have to observe it patiently, as if it were a thing. The letters on *Smarh* and the prefaces and commentaries he attached to his early works prove that this intellectual procedure was familiar to him. And above all there is a relevant letter to Caroline,[73] to which we shall return. After describing metaphorically but with real depth the difficulties of knowing himself, he adds: "If I knew why this comparison occurred to me, may the Devil take me. It has been a very long time since I have written, and from time to time I need to indulge in a little style." Style is the comparison. But the comparison is made by playing on the meanings (literal or figurative) of words. Here the process is reversed; Flaubert produces an idea that is surely not clear or pure and is drowned in the verbal material expressing it; he does *not look at it* the way he would make a judgment in full knowledge, but he *senses* it, as if it were *behind him*, inseparable from the jumbled up play of metaphor. Precisely for this reason he misapprehends it, or pretends to misapprehend it, and claims to see it only as an exercise in style. But whether he starts the process from one end or from the other, he hopes that the idea will come to him, opaque and profound, if he abandons himself to words—what would later be called free association. Indeed, we see how the sentences are linked together in the letter to Ernest: there is not a single logical connection—it is not a controlled discourse.

Yet if liberated language sometimes happens to produce profound maxims—for Flaubert, the maxim and the aphorism were the most evolved forms of thought—the vocables more often group together according to habit, that is, according to social customs, and reproduce

73. To his sister, 10 July 1845, *Correspondance*, Suppl. 1, p. 50.

commonplaces by themselves. How is Gustave to distinguish new ideas from accepted ideas, since both seem to emerge from the same depths and intrude on him during the same state of abandon? By the contents, one might say. But he would then have to shake off his torpor and compare them, judge them. Most of the time he simply watches them surge and flow, both sorts of ideas, with the same *estrangement*. But the commonplaces provoke in passing some kind of vague, nagging reminiscence. He has hardly begun to examine them when they vanish. And this impression of *déjà vu* is all the more frequent because he has a singular aptitude for secreting his own trivia—his ideas are leaden. At fifteen he had formed all his opinions (we shall see this better later on), and when they were repeated in the course of his life, they became ready-made ideas; he expressed himself ten years later on the same subjects in the same words— nothing had budged, not one part of the maxim had been altered. Thus he was frequently unaware of whether he was remembering something that came from himself or from common sense. On the other hand, where did the impression of recognition come from that he sometimes got when listening to a conversation? What did the other person just say? Was it an idea that Flaubert accepted from the outside? An idea that came to him and was mineralized inside him? He doesn't have the vaguest notion, it all happened too quickly. He nevertheless retains the impression that it has been falsified, like other ideas. In *Mémoires d'un fou*, he addresses himself to man—the context proves it, as well as to himself—and writes:

> You, free! From birth you were subjected to all the paternal mala-
> dies; with your first breath you were given the germ of all vices,
> even of stupidity, of everything that will make you judge the
> world, yourself, and everything that surrounds you according to
> the term of comparison, the measure that you have in yourself.
> You were born with a small mind, with ideas about good and
> evil that are ready-made or will be made for you.

Several Pascalian lines follow: Truth on this side of the Pyrenees, error on the other; Nature is only a first custom, etc. And the adolescent concludes: "Are you already free from the principles by which you would govern your conduct? Are you the one who supervises your education?" In short—although in this text he still distinguishes original ideas from accepted ideas—he is perfectly conscious of the fact that others, through education, have composed for him a "ready-made nature" that is no different from their own. And at the same time, this text—more valuable for what it implies than for what it says—reveals to us that the adolescent, at least at that period, never even thought of reacting to commonplaces with critical activity. All he could do was set them against one another and let them expose their own contradictions in the hope that they would destroy one another; this is the very essence of passive activity. The examples, however, were too general, borrowed, and bookish (here incest is forbidden, there customary), demonstrating once more that his consciousness of the commonplace was diffuse and muddled—commonplaces were everywhere but constantly elusive. And the *Dictionnaire des idées reçues* is pitiful because the bourgeois Flaubert no more succeeds in defining the real ideology of his class than in clearly recognizing the essential qualities of that class itself. The intention remains, which is worthwhile though poorly served by the citations. Bourgeois ideology in 1840 was not entirely determined; after all, the bourgeoisie felt comfortable only with a monarchical regime. Thus its own ideas were found in every consciousness alongside the survivals of aristocratic notions—two contradictory forms of stupidity that adjusted to each other very well except in the case of a few representatives of the new generation who were chagrined by their contradictions, of which Flaubert is a typical example. The young man was smothered under the weight of others' stupidity and of his own, which were inseparable. He tried in vain to heave off these crushing boulders; but he was conditioned *from within*, not only by his education but by his passivity, so that he could not take an objective view of himself or of the other. The trap was cunningly contrived—Gustave would never be able to avoid it.

2. On Stupidity as Negativity

The only way to transcend a commonplace is to make it serve your own purposes, to make it an instrument, a means of thought. This is what Poulhan has shown in *Les Fleurs de Tarbes*. Flaubert never succeeded in doing it. I have said that he limited himself to discrediting accepted opinions by setting them against one another; it is this procedure—and this alone—that he uses again at the end of his life in the vast and monotonous *Bouvard et Pécuchet*. But he knew the temptation of dissolving the matter heaped at the bottom of his mind by throwing a corrosive on it—through analysis, as the philosophical practitioner had taught him. Still, distinctions must be made: the stupidity of "the shopkeeper" resists the acid; it can corrode only reactionary stupidity, that collection of false syntheses, of idealist illusions that claimed to inspire aristocratic ideology. If at least these lies were dissipated, if the fine sentiments and elevated ideas corresponding to them could be reduced to their constituent elements—needs, selfish impulses, vanity—one could be quite comfortable in the bosom of a monolithic stupidity without any internal conflict. From time to time, Flaubert dreams of attempting such a coup; and what would it be, finally, if not the act of stripping bourgeois ideology of the feudal survivals that haunt it and tear it apart?

On the subject of *Graziella*, he "thunders against" Lamartine: this writer created "the conventional, the false," so that the "ladies should read [it]. . . . Oh, what a stupid lie!" Someone could "make a fine book out of this," but "that would require an independence of mind that Lamartine does not have, [a] surgical scrutiny of life, a vision of the truth."[74] And what would this surgical scrutiny have revealed? Flaubert takes pleasure in telling us: the son of a good family might have slept "by chance" with a fisherman's daughter and "sent her packing"; the girl would not have died but would have been consoled, "which is even more banal and bitter." Here we have come back to liberal thought: small people, small passions, small interests. And Flaubert leans *on Voltaire* to attack Lamartine: "The end of *Candide* is . . . proof of a genius of the first order. In this calm conclusion, stupid like life itself, the lion's claw is evident." Gustave calls his father's eye to aid him against the stupidity of others and especially against his own. Surgical scrutiny will reduce the "poeticization of reality" to dust.

It is unfortunate, as we have seen, that Flaubert hated analysis. We know that he writhed with shame and rage beneath Achille-Cléophas's "surgical scrutiny," that he tried a hundred times to tear himself away from the universe of contemporary science. It is true that Dr. Flaubert was a Voltairean and that he "made lies fall to pieces" at the liar's feet. But where does this refusal to be stupid take us? Chased out of thought, stupidity takes refuge "in life"; when reality is "depoeticized," the shoddiness of the bourgeoisie is revealed. For this invitation to cultivate our garden is profoundly bourgeois. When it is a matter of crushing Lamartine, Flaubert thinks it splendid. But if he had to follow it in his own life, it would seem appalling. In *Le Château des Coeurs*, for instance, he denounces this morality:

74. *Correspondance* 2:398.

The High Priest:

Citizens, bourgeois, drudges! On this solemn occasion . . . we are gathered together to worship the thrice-holy Saint Beef-stew, *emblem of material interests, in other words, our dearest!* . . . In your duties, O bourgeois, none among you . . . has transgressed. You have stayed philosophically at home, *thinking only of your own business, only of yourselves*. . . . Continue to trot quietly along and you will find *tranquillity, wealth, respect.* Don't forget to hate *whatever is extravagant or heroic*—no enthusiasm, above all!—and do not change anything whatsoever . . . for private, like public, happiness is found only in spiritual temperance, the immutability of customs, and the bubbling of the Beef-stew. . . . Gentlemen of science . . . commit yourselves. . . , as in the past, to making only little, innocent investigations that cause no trouble.[75]

He knows this morality very well because it is his own, the bourgeois morality of straitened circumstances that one is forced to reinvent for oneself when one cultivates one's garden at Croisset or has it cultivated by a dishonest gardener, the morality that rejects the changes brought about by universal suffrage or socialism. Calling such reforms utopian and asserting the "impenetrability of beings," this is the morality that replaces the bonds of generosity ("a friend would give his life for me") with negative relationships (honesty: to touch nothing; friendship: never to irritate, interfere, or disturb), that buttressed by individual interest prescribes *living social atomization as a common solitude.* Who else but an aristocrat could so vigorously defend a *heroism* in which Gustave does not believe against utilitarian baseness? In his abstract effort to rise above his class, Flaubert once more slips into the organicist and aristocratic thought of disillusioned poets—he makes use of Voltaire against Lamartine, but he delivers up Voltaire to Musset and Vigny. First of all, theological thought is crushed by the father's science—this is what Flaubert denounces above all as first-class stupidity manifest in the form of meaningless traditions (New Year's Day), poetic ecstasies ("they take their ass for their heart"), Catholic ceremonies (processions especially infuriate him), or superstitions. But when free thought believes it has triumphed, it finds itself suddenly enveloped by the ideology it has just defeated; this ideology in its negative form as anxiety, dissatisfaction, the scornful rejection of finitude, a desperate leap toward the empty heavens, makes itself in its turn the negation of negation; liberalism as the

75. Flaubert, *Théâtre*, p. 263. Sixth tableau: "Le Royaume du Pot-au-feu." My italics.

systematic destruction of the accepted idea is denounced as *second-class stupidity*. The freethinker is penetrated by the opaque beatitude of fools to the precise extent that he accepts the mediocrity he has discovered. This is not the stupidity of the shopkeeper or the bureaucrat; rather, it is what characterizes bourgeois intellectuals, and Gustave finds it *in his own milieu*, in the Voltaireans who surround him; it is nothing other than intelligence. In *Madame Bovary* he succeeds in showing us analytic reason as mental baseness and supreme foolishness, even while accepting its principles and conclusions as truths—the stroke of genius was to embody it in Monsieur Homais.

For a long time Homais was considered a fool. Flaubert probably enjoyed this. But Thibaudet smelled a rat, observing that the pharmacist was unquestionably *intelligent*. Furthermore, in this lugubrious novel, which ends in wreckage, Homais alone is triumphant. Superior even to the medical practitioners, he rules the province. Fragmentary as it is, the scientific knowledge he displays bears witness to a certain education; Homais's ascent resembles the rise of the Flauberts, in fact: the son will be a doctor and the grandson will say, "We are *a family*." No doubt Flaubert wanted to make this freethinker look ridiculous; but at the same time he wanted to *make him right*. Isn't it obvious that Bournisien is conceived expressly to justify Homais's diatribes? What might have prevented the author from showing us a parish priest less repulsive than this materialistic, ignorant cleric who eats and drinks enough for four, understands nothing about the soul, and whose stupidity pushes him to the point of intolerance? What a strange attempt at mystification: in the same book Flaubert shows us the odious stupidity of an anticlerical pharmacist and the odious stupidity of a priest who fully justifies this anticlericalism. In fact, he ridicules his own thoughts in Homais. For in the last analysis, he is the one who writes to Michelet, 6 June 1861, a line that the pharmacist certainly would have countersigned: "The great Voltaire signed his smallest notes E.L.I.[76] Let us shake hands on the hatred of Antiphysis." On the other hand, what is it that repels Flaubert in the famous profession of faith he gives to the pharmacist? Let us reread it:

> "I have a religion," said Homais. . . . "I believe in the Supreme Being . . . who has put us here below to fulfill our duties as citizens and heads of families . . . but I have no need to go to church. . . . I do not accept Christian beliefs which are absurd in themselves and completely opposed to all physical laws, which

76. *Ecrasez l'Infame* (crush the infamous).

demonstrates . . . that priests have always wallowed in shameful ignorance."[77]

The ignorance of priests? Flaubert is convinced of it. Dogmas? Indeed, in *all* religions he considers them perfectly stupid. The superiority of scientific to religious thought? He maintained it all his life. What is more, Homais concedes more than Gustave ever would: he has a religion, he believes in the Supreme Being. We have seen that Flaubert, for his part, searched in vain for belief. What could be so ridiculous about it, then? The pharmacist's sanctimonious satisfaction. Flaubert does not blame him for using science to destroy Christian beliefs; he reproaches him with placing *unconditional trust in science.* His stupidity resounds in the words "opposed to all physical laws, which demonstrates . . ." This is enormously fatuous, an equally stupid faith; the Absolute has merely been displaced, religion lodging it in heaven, liberal scientism placing it in human reason. And that Supreme Being in which the pharmacist claims to believe reminds Flaubert of the revolutionary cult founded by the "despicable" Robespierre. Abstraction has no other purpose than to guarantee the rationality of the universe and the bourgeois ethic: the God of Homais does not challenge man but, on the contrary, is invented by man and is at his disposal. There is all the difference in the world in these positions: Flaubert, fated to be an unbeliever, desperately disputes the absence of God, the foolishness of myths, the shameful ignorance and materialism of the priests; Homais, the heir to revolutionary deism, makes the same statements quite serenely; moreover, he even bases his tranquillity of soul on them. When the pharmacist confronts Catholic dogma with physics Flaubert has nothing to say, having so often written: "I hate antiphysis." But the author does not despise his creature any the less for that; in fact he criticizes Homais for taking delight in crushing humanity's greatest concerns under the accumulation of precise and cutting little truths. In order to discover the hideousness, the abject inadequacy, the shortsighted materialism of this invincible and victorious stupidity, which always succeeds in its adroitly managed undertakings and ultimately includes all of *reality,* all that we are, we must adopt the point of view of what might have been and was not, the point of view of absence, of nothingness, of the void, of our vain desire and our helplessness. And finally, what is the caricatured thought with which Flaubert endows Homais? Well,

77. *Madame Bovary,* ed. Conard, pp. 106–7.

it is quite simply the experimental rationalism of Dr. Flaubert; it is science as a whole, disparaged to the point of imbecility. When Gustave makes this semiscientist ridiculous, a vulgar pedant who makes antireligious propaganda out of the laws of physics, he knows perfectly well that the scientific movement taken as a whole is in contradiction to Christian ideology. This is why he hates it. At the age of nineteen he writes in his *Souvenirs*: "One day it may happen that all of modern science will collapse and we shall be derided for it—I hope so"[78] And in the following years he often condemned the century of enlightenment in the name of an irrationalism that dared not speak its name:

> Fanaticism is religion; and by decrying the one, the philosophes of the eighteenth century overturned the other. Fanaticism is faith, faith itself, ardent faith which makes works and acts. Religion is a variable conception, a human invention, an idea in fact, whereas fanaticism is an emotion. What has changed on earth are the dogmas . . . what has not changed are the amulets, the sacred waters, the ex-voto. . . , the Brahmins, the Santons, and the hermits, the belief, finally, in something superior to life and the need to place oneself under the protection of that force.[79]

Be that as it may; the moment he condemns the analytic thought of the philosophes, the analytic spirit haunts him, for this dissolving principle has been part of his mind since childhood—an idea merely touches him and it is instantly decomposed. How could he renounce surgical scrutiny, his father's legacy? That would be to yield the entire patrimony to Achille. On the contrary, Gustave has to lay claim to the scalpel-eye that dissects hearts. He does not hesitate in his correspondence to affirm his merits as a psychologist; indeed, he is the prince of analysis. Yet analysis is so repulsive to him that he never does it himself. He always presents it as *already accomplished*, that is, he recites the results of his experience in maxims which are intended to be the passive registering of his impressions and their surgical dismemberment. But Flaubert has *no* experience—whose analysis is it, then? What he has hidden under this name is the pure principle of analysis which, when posed for itself and separated from scientific practices, ceases to be a method for making theory and instead con-

78. *Souvenirs*, p. 109.
79. *Correspondance*,3:148n49. Cf. also, much earlier, around 1838–39, this thought in the *Souvenirs*: "The eighteenth century understood nothing about poetry, about the human heart, it understood everything about intelligence."

tains, a priori, utilitarianism, associationism, empiricism, etc. Starting from this position, observation is no longer necessary, there is no more need to experiment and no real analysis to do; we know in advance that the most generous act *must* be decomposed into selfish impulses, that female idealism is a matter of "ass," etc. This assumed knowledge is a priori nothing but an abstract postulate masked by rhetorical effects, which comes down simply to this: *analysis is always possible*. Therefore everything is already thought, already known; Flaubert's experience is behind him, his principles are already posed, the search for and discovery of the truth have already taken place. But in what past? Flaubert's? The past of his class or humanity's? Gustave does not tell us. And through his very passivity he allows this a priori to be present in him as an *alien knowledge*. The battle between science and faith develops inside Gustave without his taking part in it. Between the two stupidities there is a reciprocal envelopment, hence mutual denunciation. Flaubert doesn't lift a finger; he claims and rejects each of the two equally. The ideal would be for the two adversaries to annihilate each other at the same time. Analytic stupidity, in sum, is a parasite, it is quite simply the negation of basic stupidity which alone possesses the positive thickness of matter; there is nothing to prevent Flaubert from hoping that in the process of dissolving basic stupidity, analysis will destroy its own support and be lost in nonbeing.

A vain hope. The accepted idea is scarcely abolished when it is reborn from its ashes and revives the analysis that devours it. Ravaged by this doubtful and continually renewed combat, Flaubert takes refuge in skepticism: "Ineptitude is drawing conclusions." He is careful not to form any ideas on his own: "There is no true or false idea. At first we adopt things enthusiastically, then we reflect, then doubt, and there we remain."[80] All the same, skepticism plays against analysis just when it is triumphantly affirmed as knowledge and truth. But the challenge remains passive. Read the *Correspondance* from start to finish, never will you catch Flaubert judging, reasoning, making a critical examination; never will you find the birth of an idea, a new perception, an original point of view. In Flaubert, thought is never an *act*; it invents nothing, it *never establishes* connections; it is not distinguishable from the movement of life itself. Passive activity, swept along by the current of experience, is only the verbal form of pathos; the linking together of sentences sometimes recalls the linking

80. *Souvenirs*, p. 96. Written after the end of January 1841.

of images in dreams and sometimes the verbal associations a patient produces on the analyst's couch. In this interminable monologue in which rhetorical connections are continually substituted for rational ones, the same bitterness, the same rancor, recur endlessly in the most diverse disguises; the great eloquent passages hide his constant flight from the idea or, more accurately, his flight *before the idea*. This bourgeois who demands his integration bitterly resents his exile and can neither *see* his class nor forget it, since it is—like a family setting—as much the object of his desire as of his contempt. He accepts himself insofar as he is rejected, and rejects himself insofar as he demands to be accepted; he arrogantly condemns the foolishness of others, that shortsighted conformity which despises his particularity, and he despises that particularity which prevents him from being dissolved in the bourgeois community. In brief, he is a martyr to stupidity; he has taken it into himself with all its conflicts: it turns and, devouring itself, devours him as well. The wounds make him bleed, but he is constrained to immobility; since every idea inside him can only reflect the materiality of commonplaces or the materialism of analysis, he improves upon his painful passivity and rejects all forms of thought. Beginning in 1841, indeed, he writes: "I am neither a materialist nor a spiritualist. If I were something, it would be rather a materialist-*spettatore*-spectator." Upright, silent, stoic, he casts a disdainful eye on the universal moving sidewalk, he listens distractedly to the conventional chatter which is nothing more than his interior monologue. Truly a witness.

He lives, however; he cannot prevent himself from living nor can he prevent obscure, almost animal thoughts from forming in him all the time. These profound significations, which are scarcely disengaged from perception, from emotion, from dream, are untouched by analytic rigor: they are syntheses—hesitant, timid, irreducible. But they are not like accepted ideas either, for they are formed without the concurrence of language—"soft" and fluid thoughts that run close to life and matter and are often merged in dreams. In them we might see nature without man, for man is absent from them, contracted in his negation, in his willful absence; in any case, they express the deepest solitude, the solitude *of the beast*; such thoughts are what give *Madame Bovary* its incomparable richness. We shall have to describe them. For the moment we must note their double character. They are rigorously *motivated* by negativism and by Flaubert's abstention, that is to say, by his complex relations to his class; in this sense he produces such thoughts by his very way of being bourgeois while refusing to be, and this entire system blocked by passivity serves to frame their lawless proliferation. If Gustave had gone beyond the commonplace and beyond analytic decomposition by means of an intellectual act, these thoughts would have disappeared or would have lost their softness; their contingency would have given way to order, a systematic exploitation would have risked distorting them by regularizing their course. But contemporary ideology did not provide Flaubert with the instrument he required—it all comes down to this. He sensed that he was lacking the practical notion of synthesis;[81] he found and rejected it in superstitions, and he sought it in vain in scientific rationalism. In effect, stupidity is decapitated reason, it is the intellectual operation deprived of its unity, in other words, of its power of unification. Thus Flaubert's absenteeism was merely the expression of his class consciousness, and this is what made possible the swarming of untamed thought inside him. But on the other hand, this untamed thought, *through its contents*, escaped social determinations; not that it was *above* social particularities and on the level of a universal humanism—such humanism does not exist and Flaubert did not care to invent it; on the contrary, these obscure significations touch us profoundly to the extent that they express man's universal animality. Again, we must be precise: this is not a reflection of need or physical violence; rather it is the expression of that "pure boredom with living" which seems especially to be the lot of domestic animals. Such as it is, this cunning proliferation, born of an absence, represented for Flaubert the only possible form of spontaneity. And let us be careful not to read into it some kind of immediate and irreducible subjectivity—the object is present at all levels; I would call it, rather, the animal consciousness of the world.

We have come to the end of part one. We have tried to establish the larger outlines of Gustave's *constitution*. But as yet we have only uncovered an abstract conditioning, and no one can be alive without creating himself, that is, without going beyond what others have made of him in the direction of the concrete. We are now going to explore what I have called his *personalization*.

81. Cf. *Souvenirs*, p. 107.